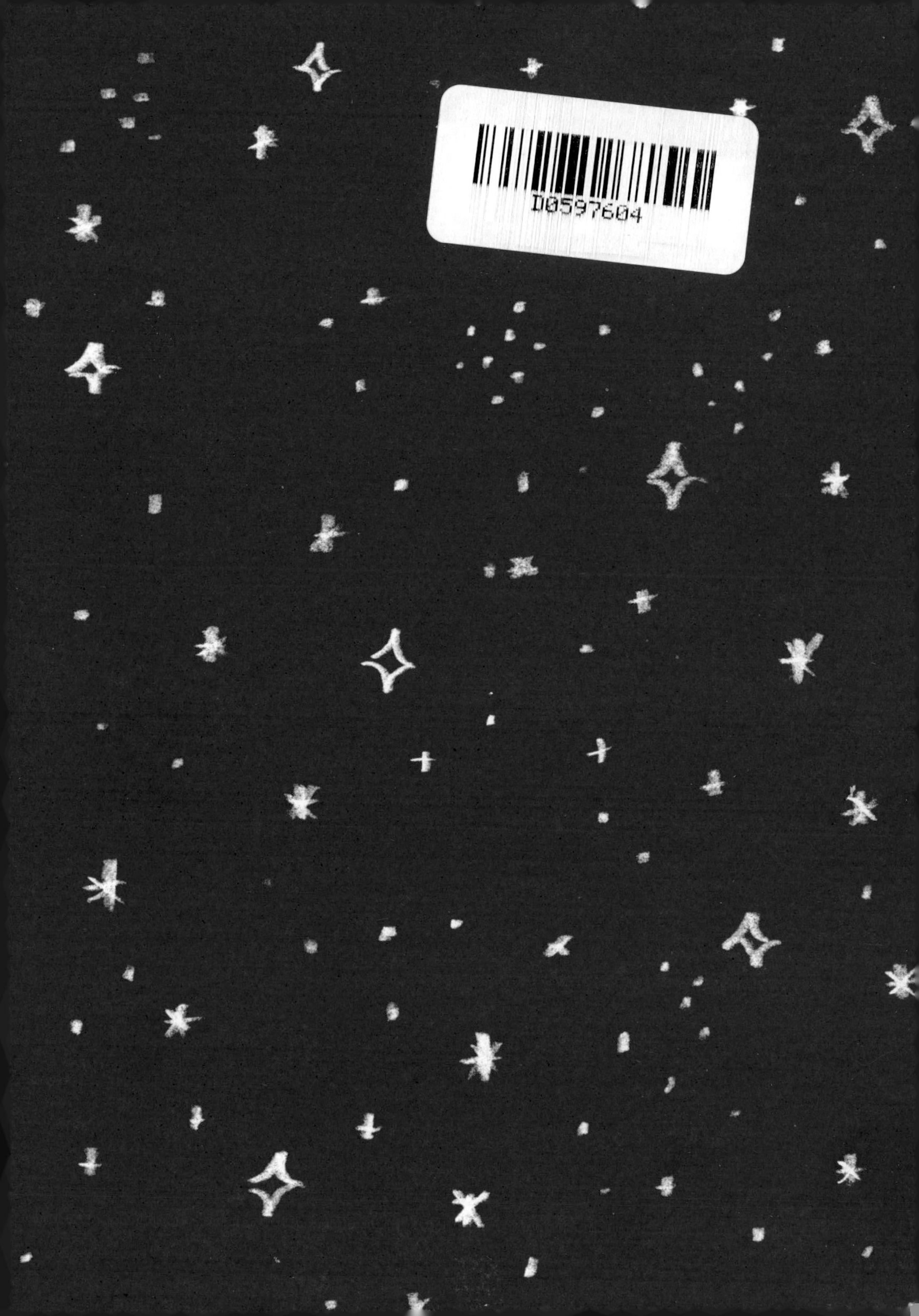

SHAWN & MAC

PRESENT...

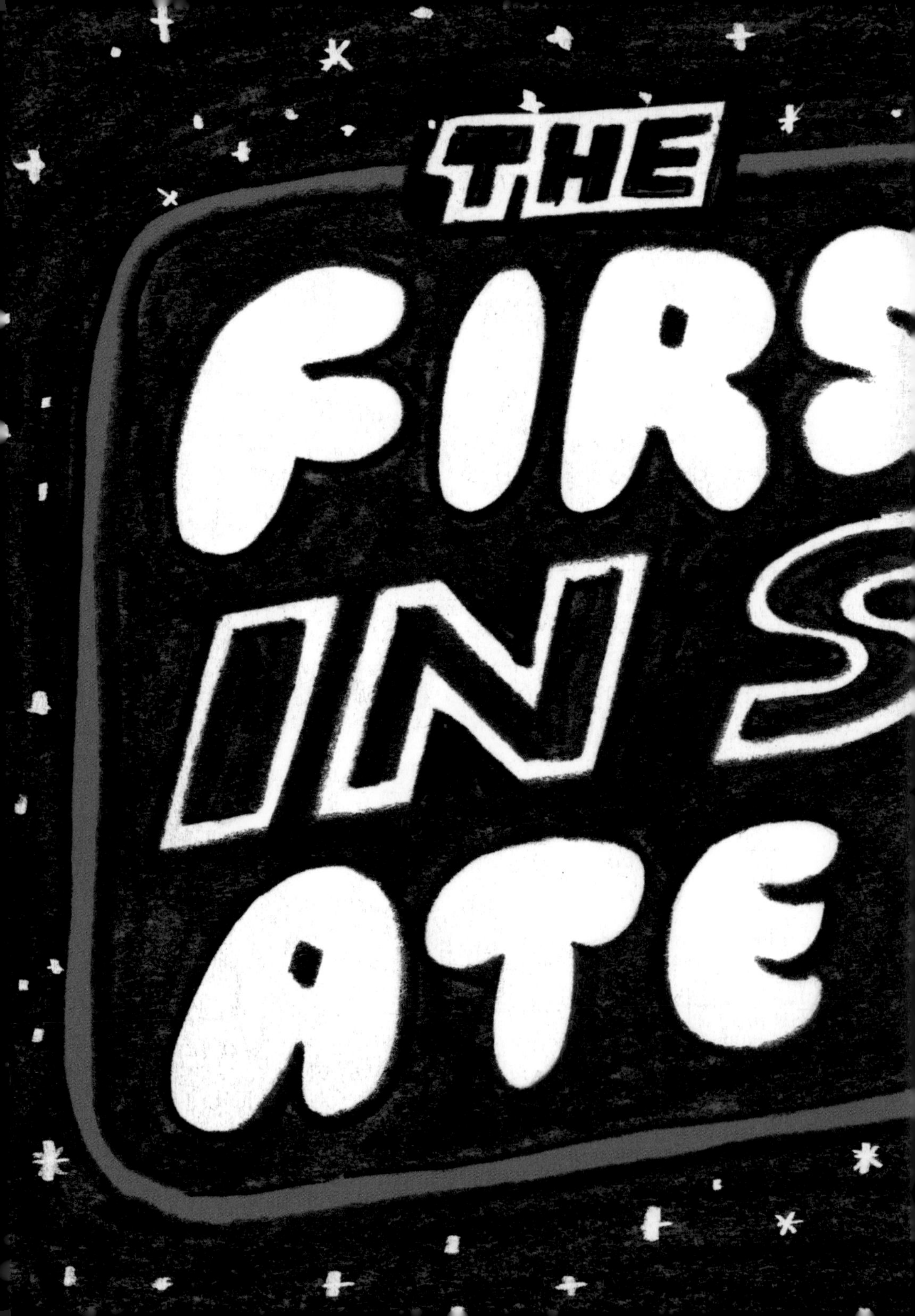
THE
FIRS
IN S
ATE

CAT
PACE
PIZZA

For the Club Heads —M.B. & S.H.

Katherine Tegen Books
Imprints of HarperCollinsPublishers

HarperAlley is an imprint of HarperCollins Publishers.

Katherine Tegen Books is an imprint of HarperCollins Publishers.

The First Cat in Space Ate Pizza
 For information address HarperCollins Children's Books, a division of HarperCollins Publishers, 195 Broadway, New York, NY 10007.
www.harpercollinschildrens.com

ISBN 978-0-06-308408-7

Typography by Shawn Harris
22 23 24 25 26 EP 10 9 8 7 6 5 4 3 2 1
First Edition

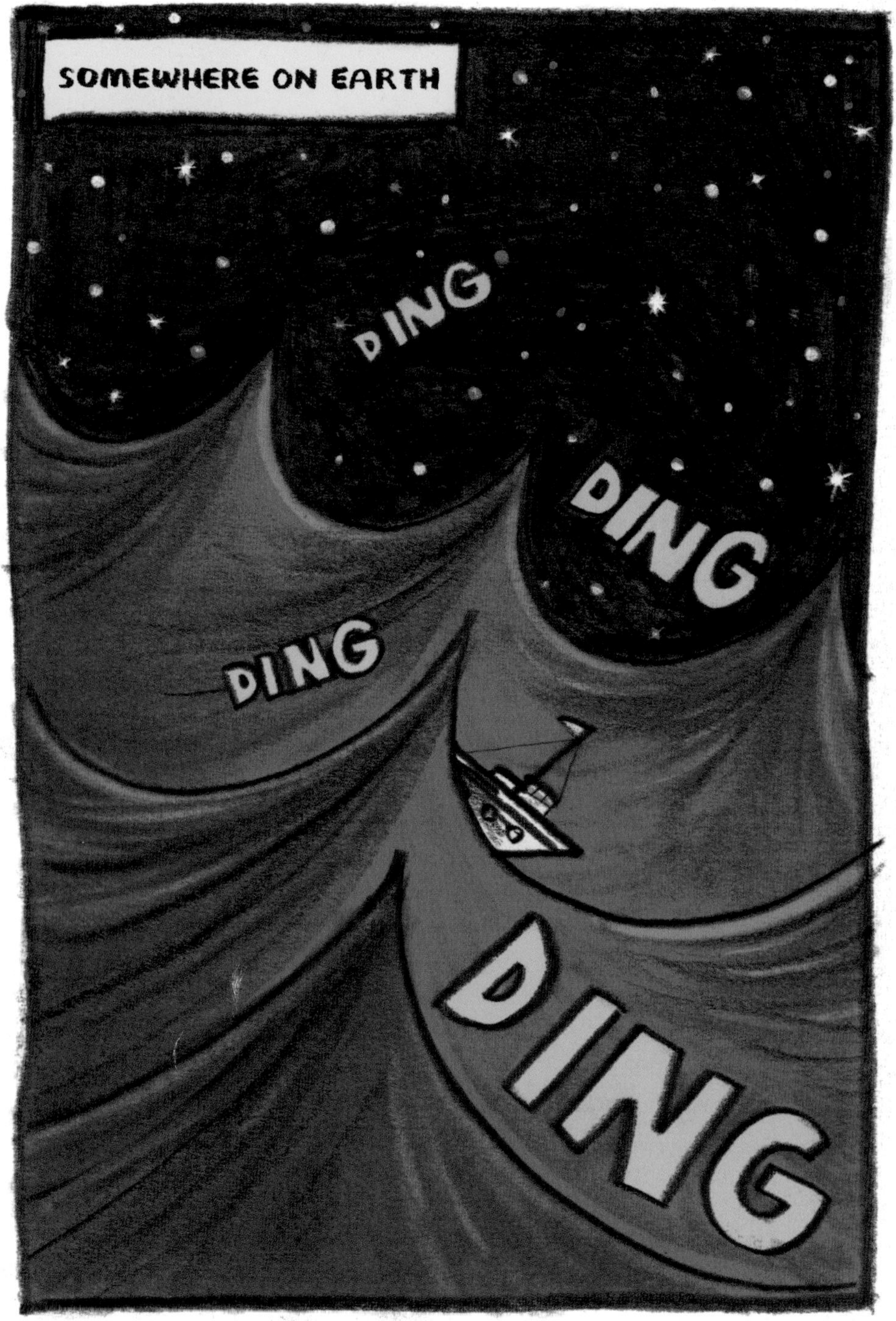
SOMEWHERE ON EARTH
DING
DING
DING
DING

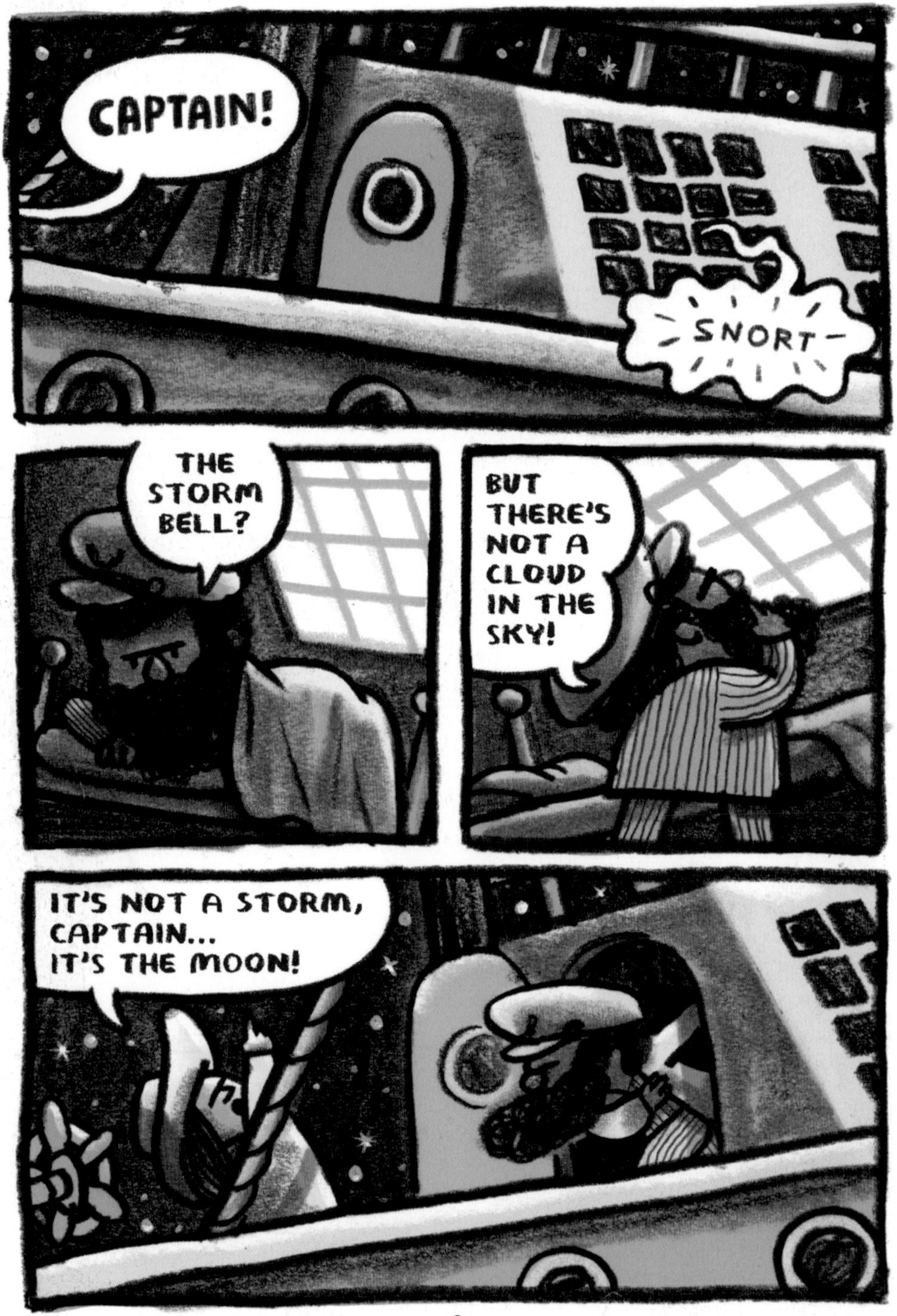
CAPTAIN!
SNORT
THE STORM BELL?
BUT THERE'S NOT A CLOUD IN THE SKY!
IT'S NOT A STORM, CAPTAIN... IT'S THE MOON!

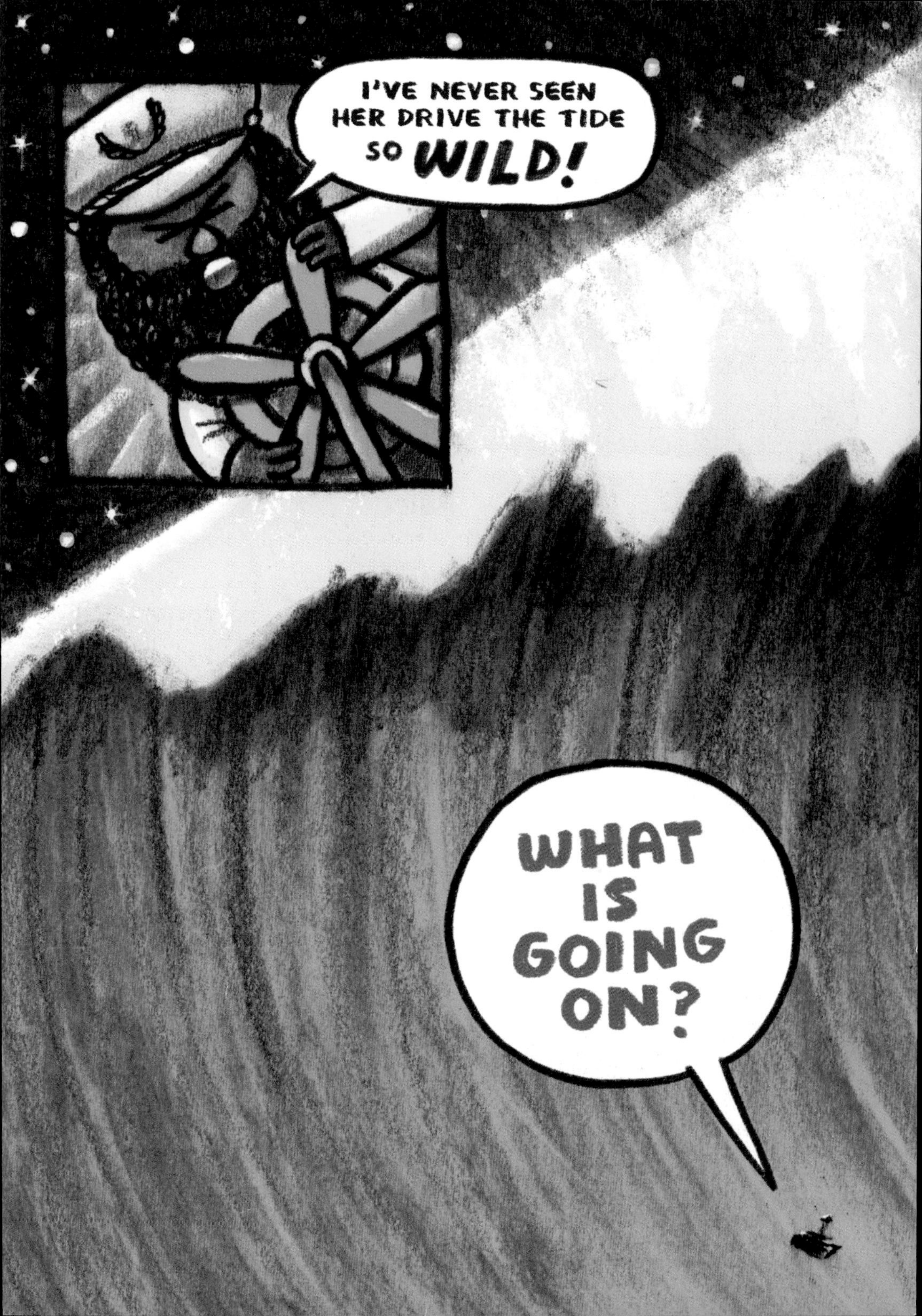
I'VE NEVER SEEN HER DRIVE THE TIDE SO WILD!
WHAT IS GOING ON?

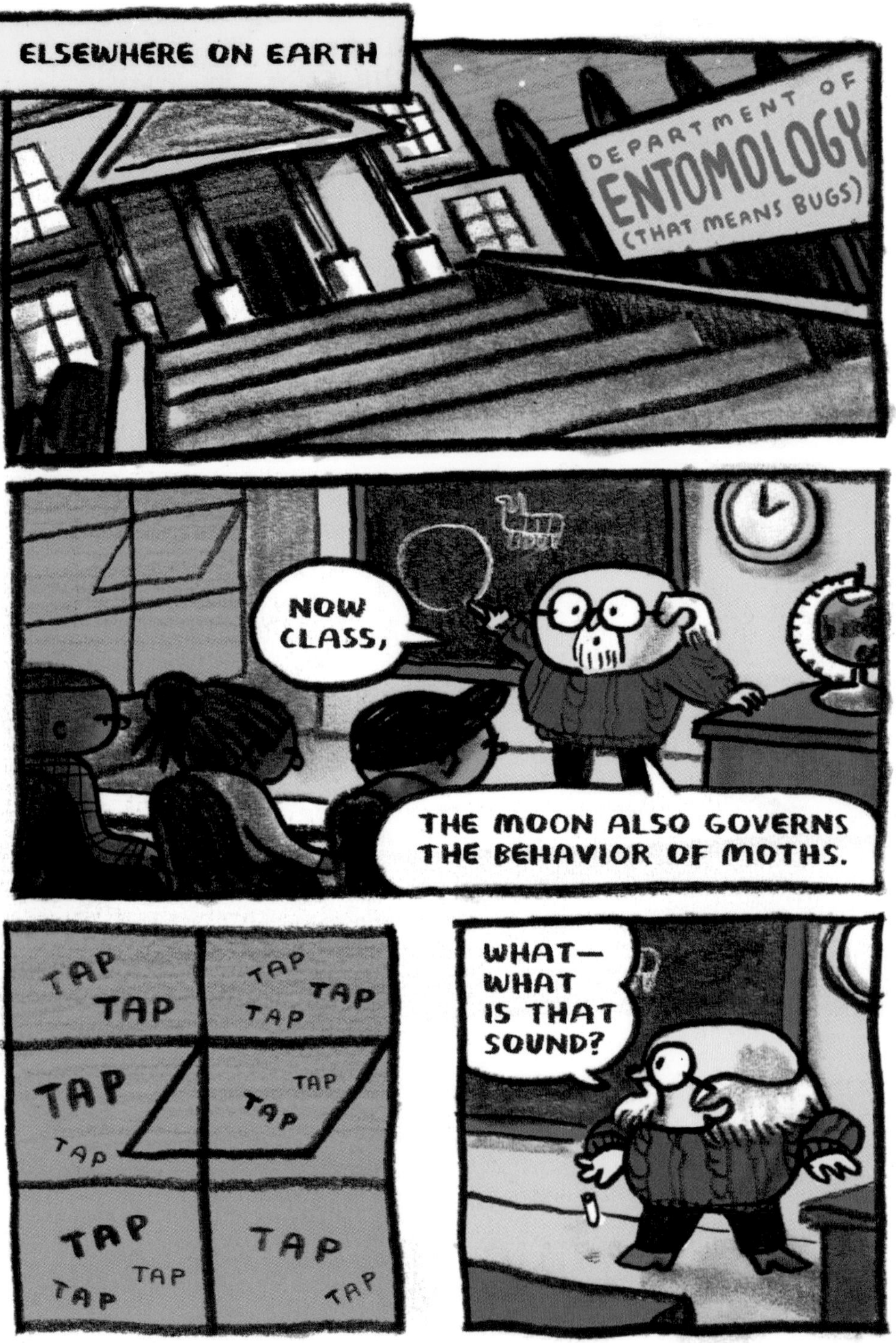
ELSEWHERE ON EARTH
DEPARTMENT OF ENTOMOLOGY (THAT MEANS BUGS)
NOW CLASS,
THE MOON ALSO GOVERNS THE BEHAVIOR OF MOTHS.
TAP TAP
TAP TAP TAP
TAP TAP
TAP TAP
TAP TAP TAP
TAP TAP
WHAT— WHAT IS THAT SOUND?

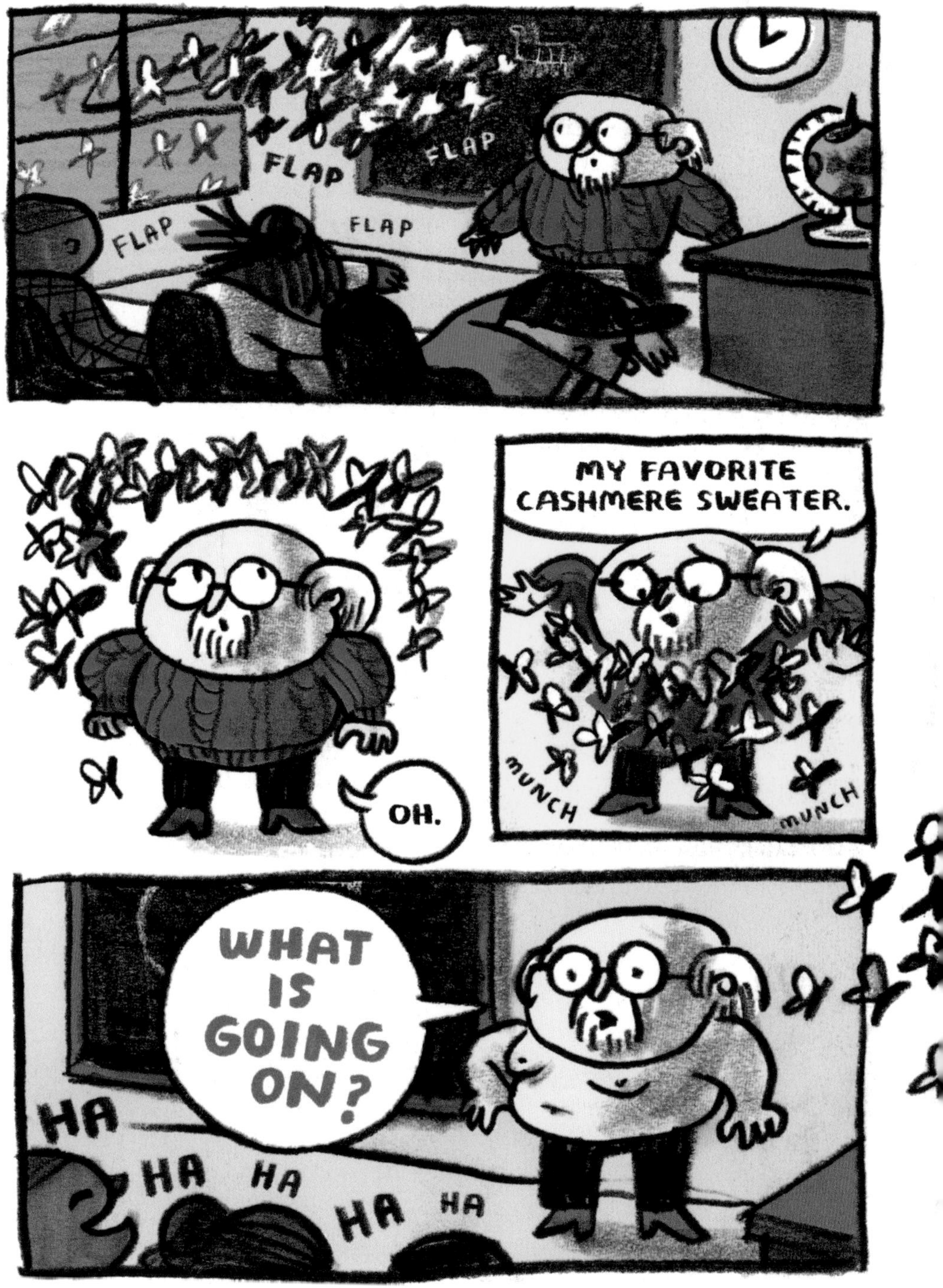
FLAP
FLAP
FLAP
FLAP
FLAP
OH.
MY FAVORITE CASHMERE SWEATER.
MUNCH
MUNCH
WHAT IS GOING ON?
HA
HA
HA
HA
HA

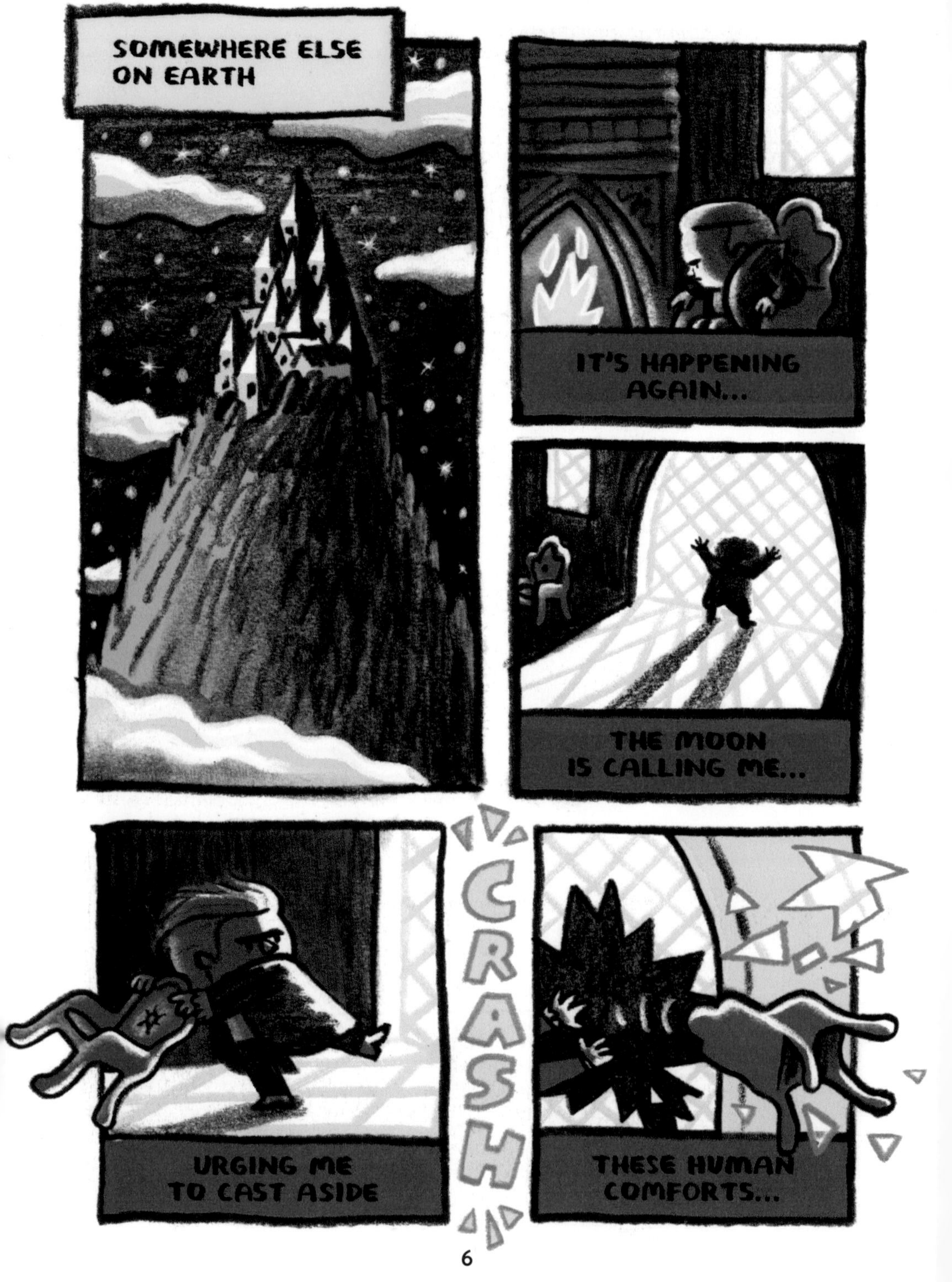
SOMEWHERE ELSE ON EARTH
IT'S HAPPENING AGAIN...
THE MOON IS CALLING ME...
URGING ME TO CAST ASIDE
CRASH
THESE HUMAN COMFORTS...

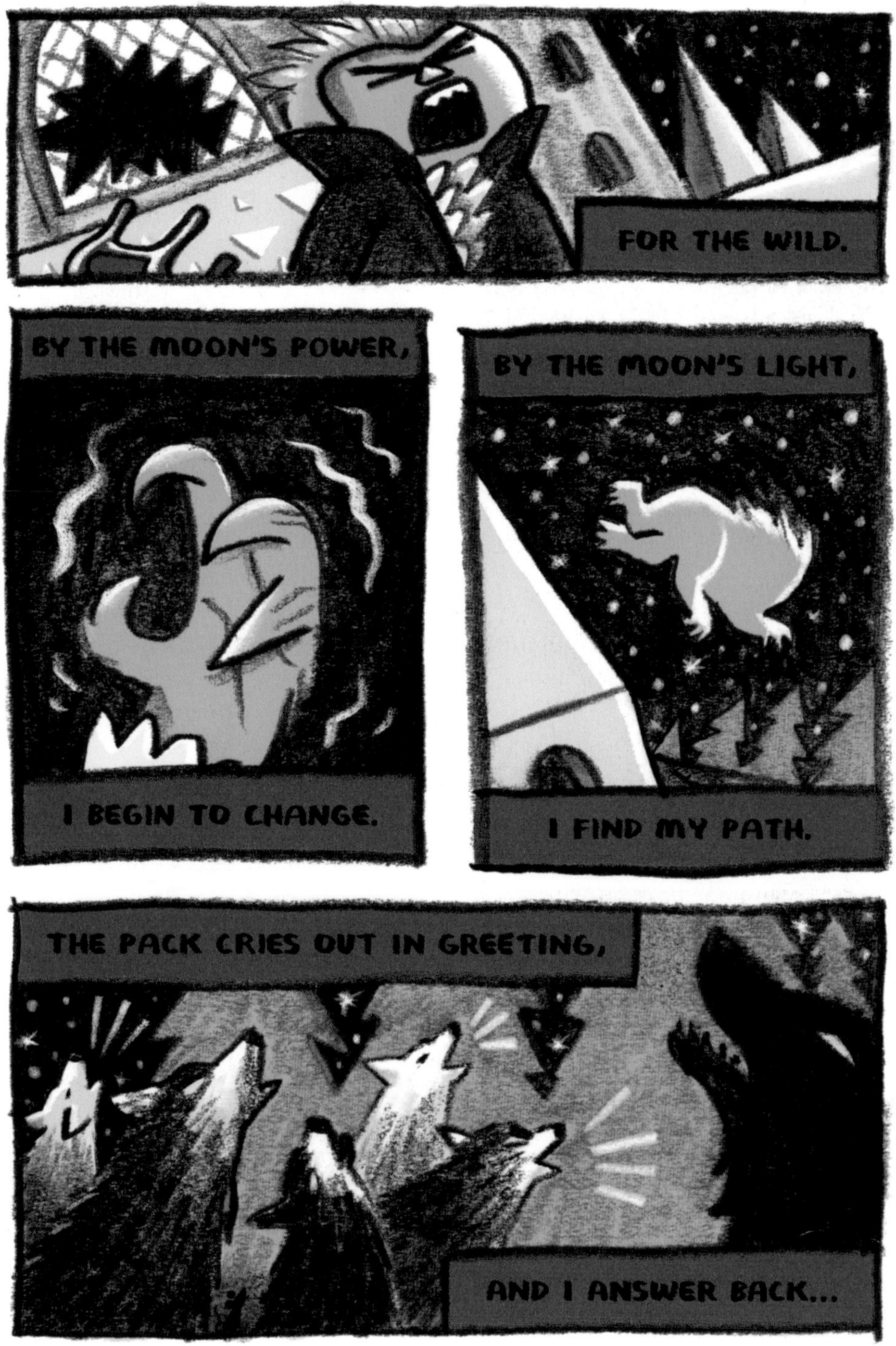
FOR THE WILD.
BY THE MOON'S POWER,
I BEGIN TO CHANGE.
BY THE MOON'S LIGHT,
I FIND MY PATH.
THE PACK CRIES OUT IN GREETING,
AND I ANSWER BACK...

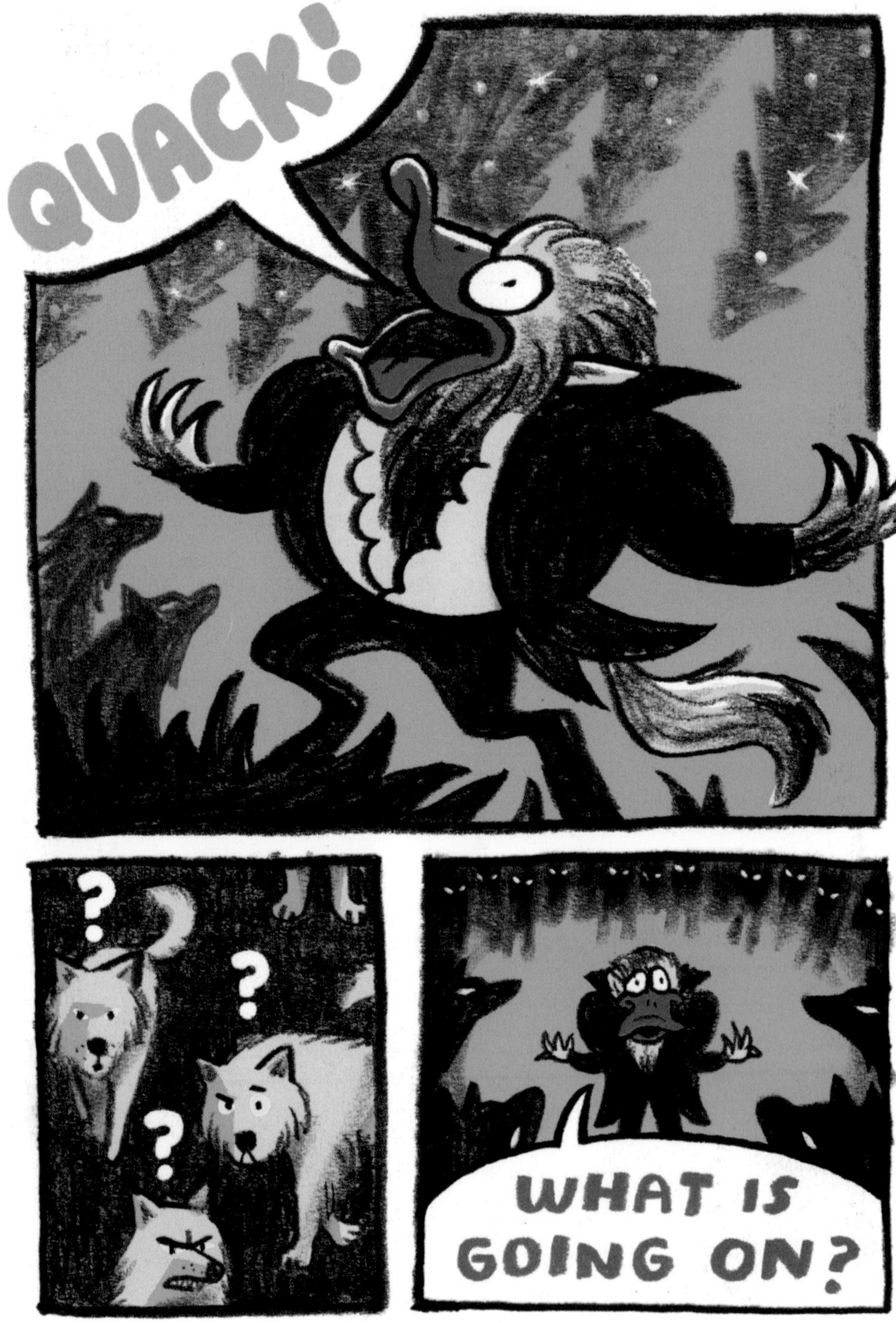
QUACK!
?
?
?
WHAT IS GOING ON?

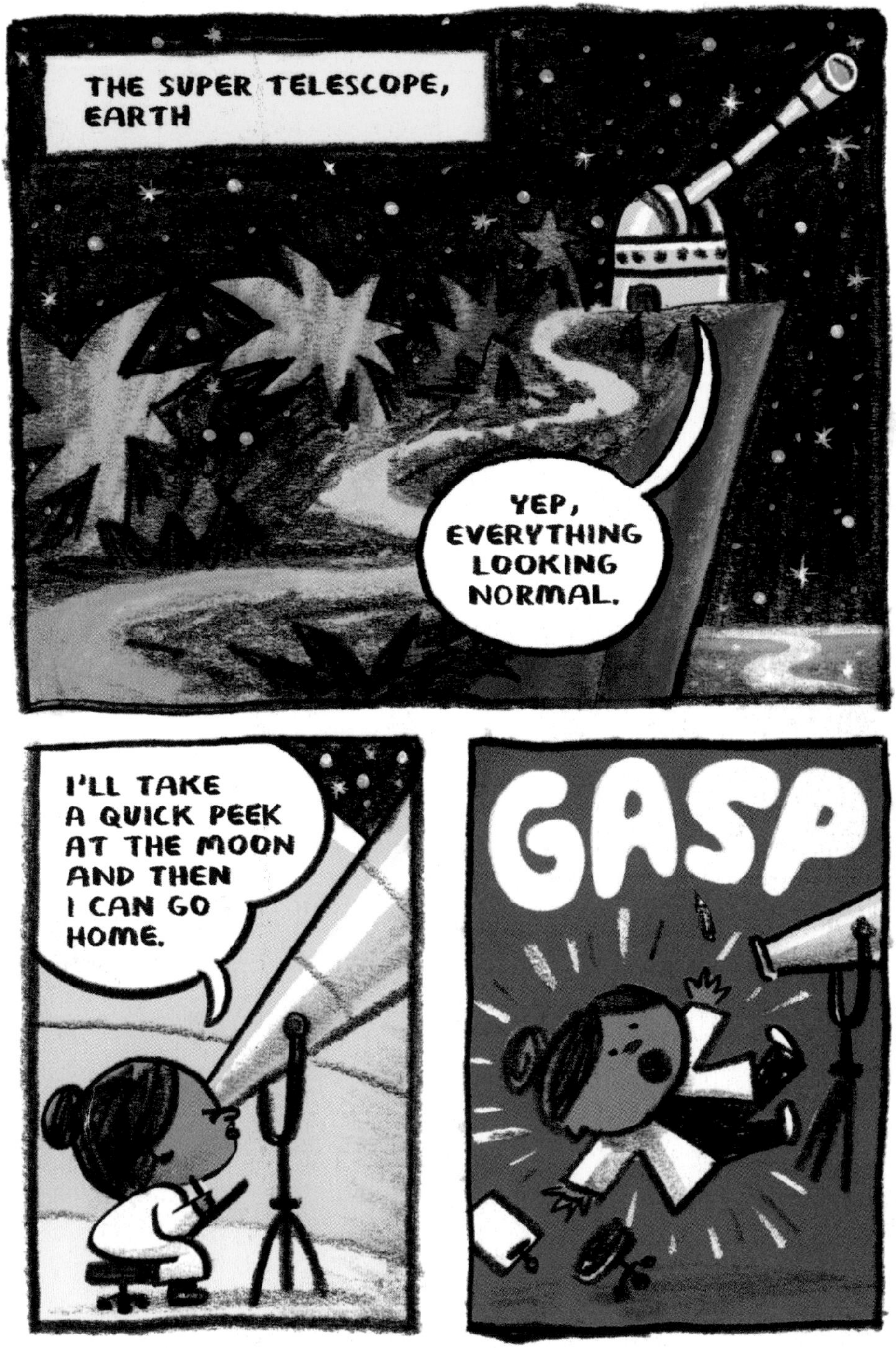
THE SUPER TELESCOPE, EARTH
YEP, EVERYTHING LOOKING NORMAL.
I'LL TAKE A QUICK PEEK AT THE MOON AND THEN I CAN GO HOME.
GASP

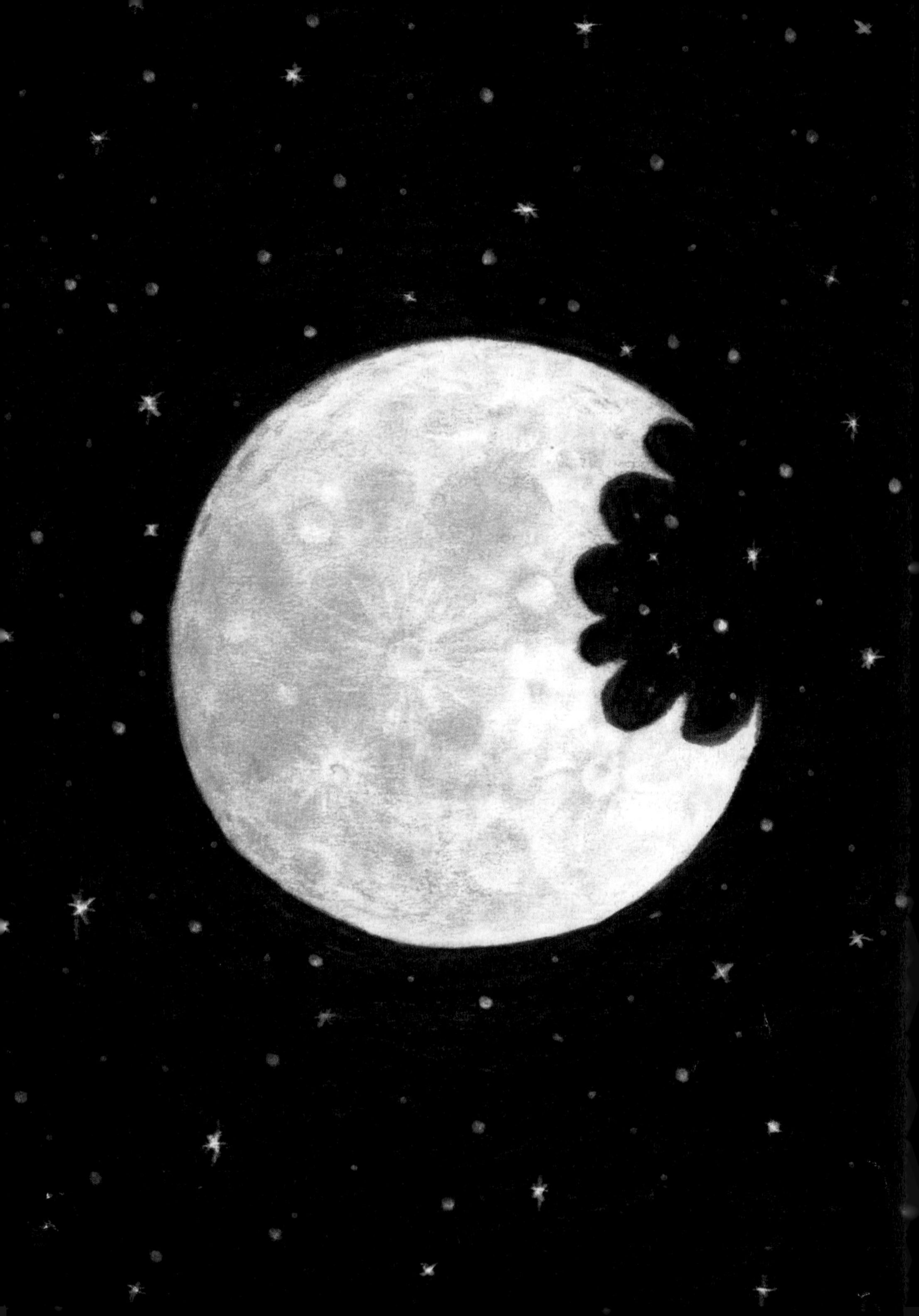

CHAPTER I

MOON TROUBLE

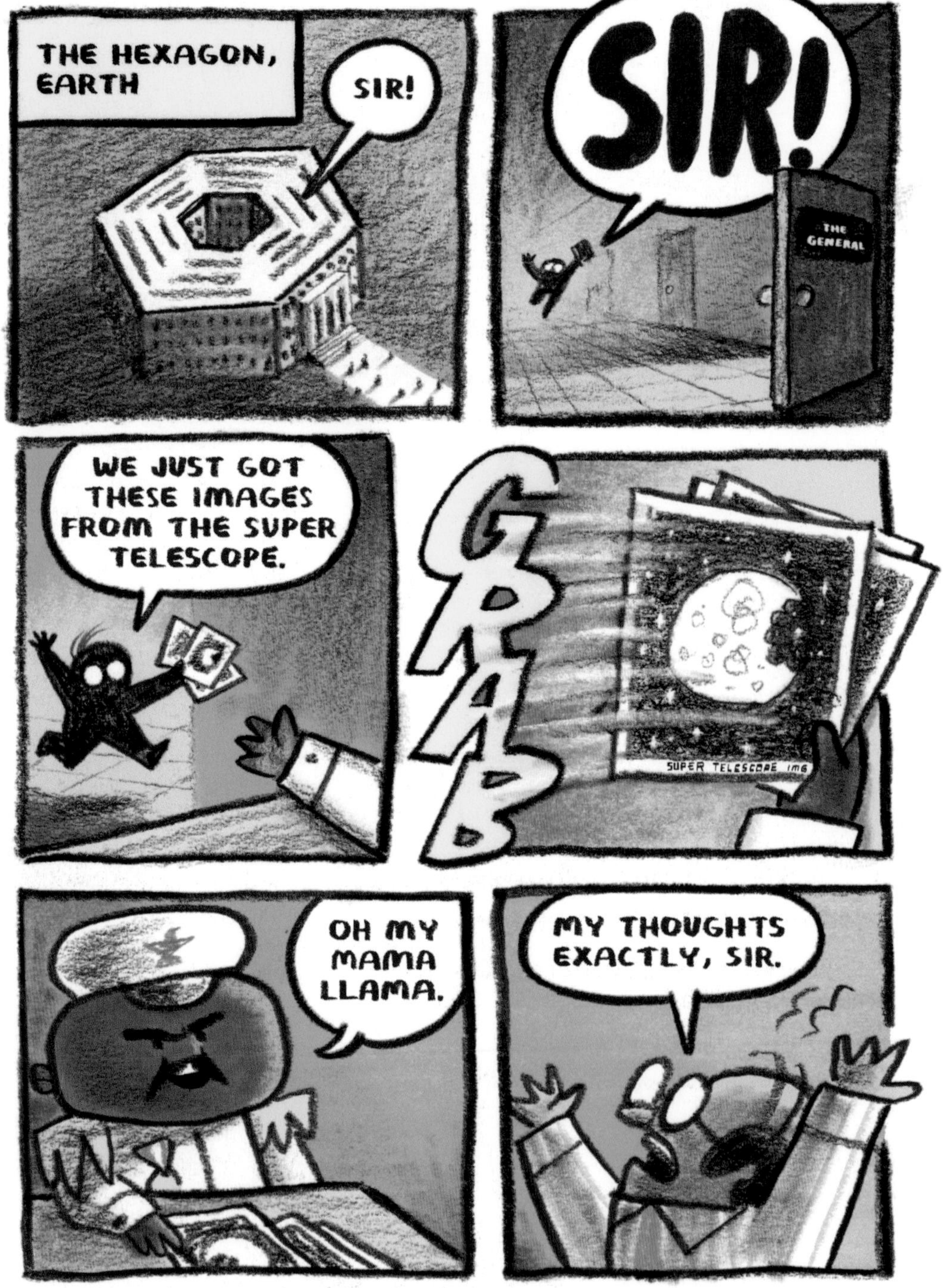
THE HEXAGON, EARTH
SIR!
SIR!
THE GENERAL
WE JUST GOT THESE IMAGES FROM THE SUPER TELESCOPE.
GRAB
SUPER TELESCOPE IMG
OH MY MAMA LLAMA.
MY THOUGHTS EXACTLY, SIR.

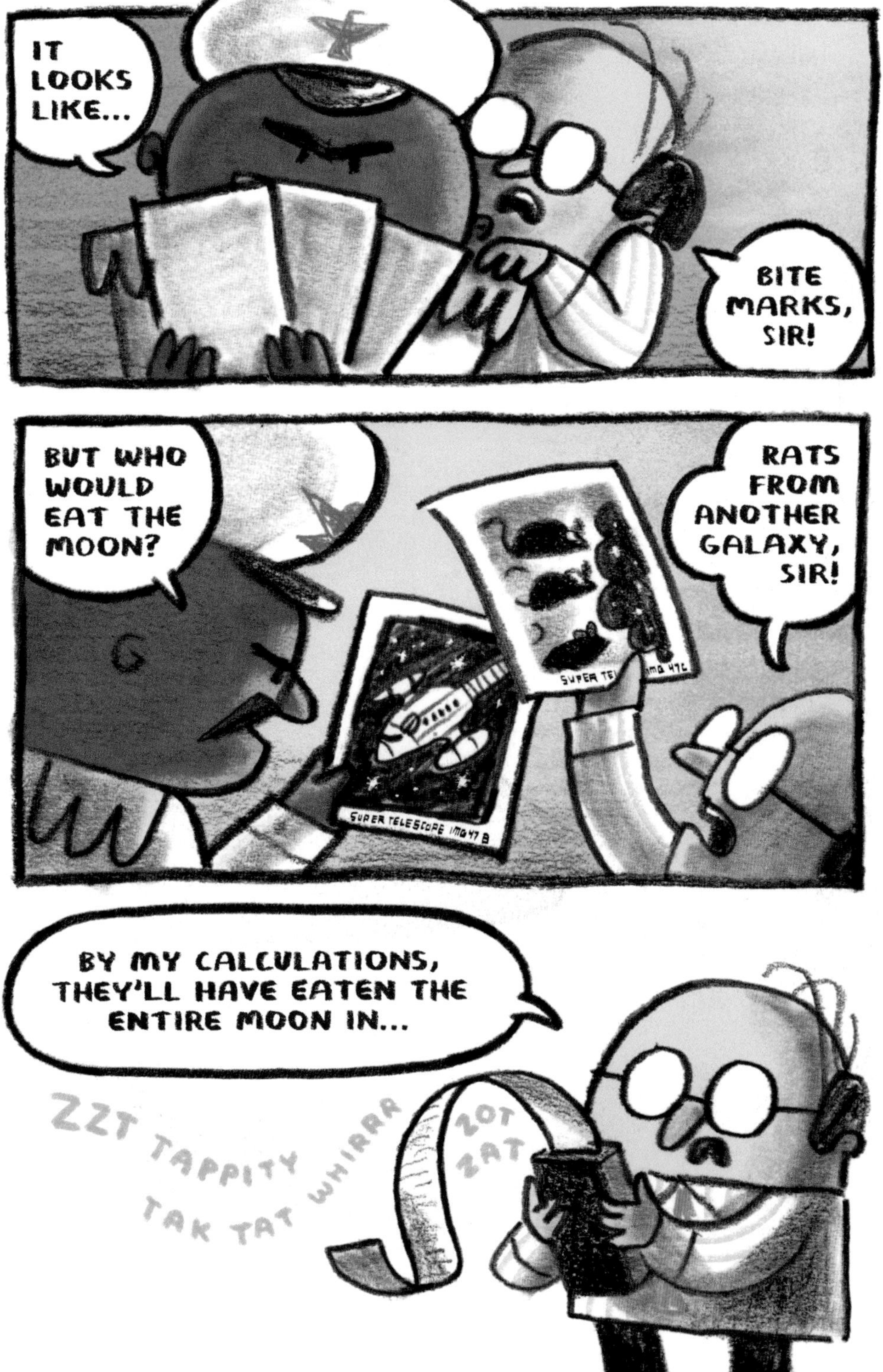
IT LOOKS LIKE...
BITE MARKS, SIR!
BUT WHO WOULD EAT THE MOON?
RATS FROM ANOTHER GALAXY, SIR!
SUPER TELESCOPE IMG47 B
BY MY CALCULATIONS, THEY'LL HAVE EATEN THE ENTIRE MOON IN...
ZZT TAPPITY TAK TAT WHIRRR
ZOT ZAT

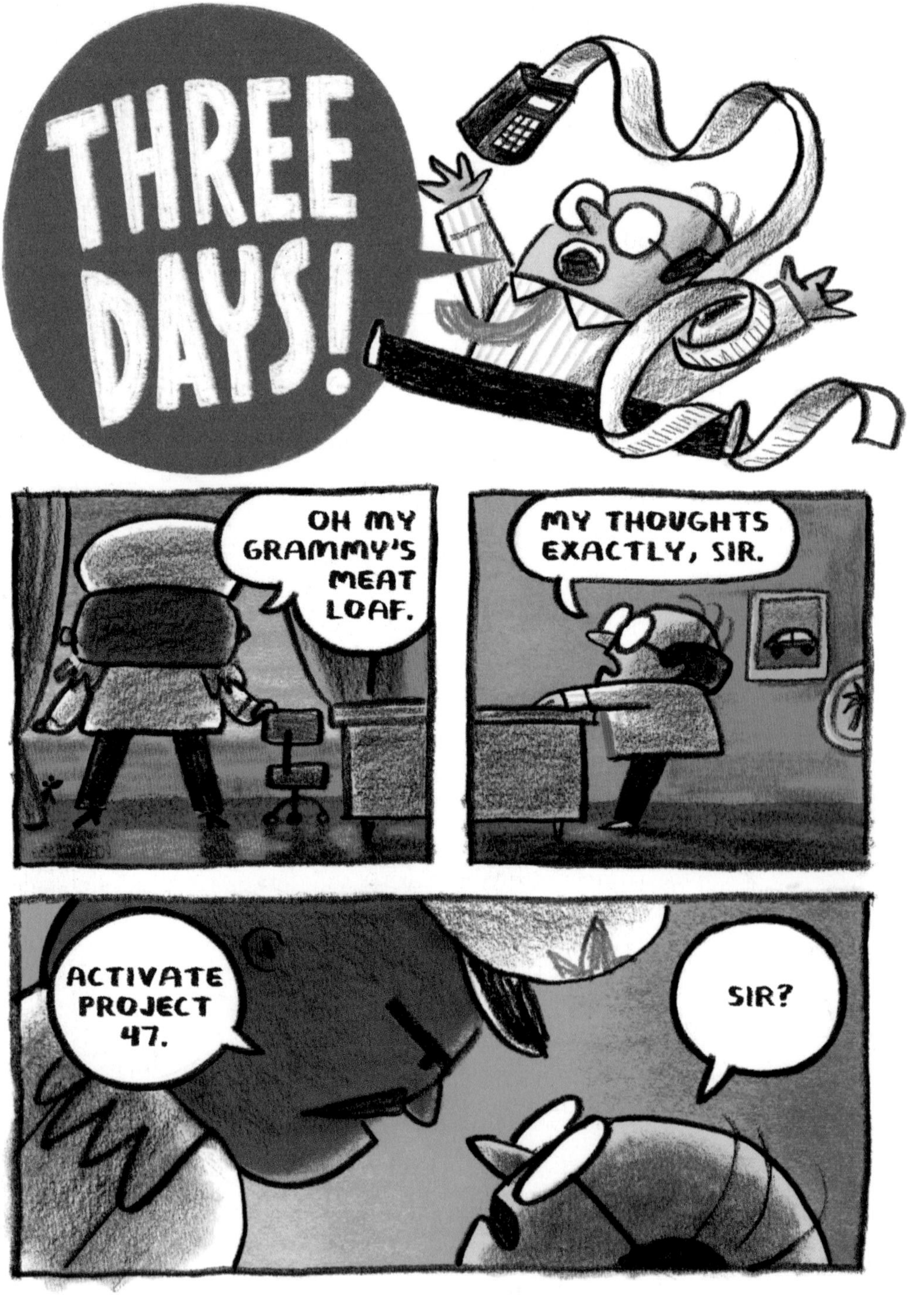
THREE DAYS!
OH MY GRAMMY'S MEAT LOAF.
MY THOUGHTS EXACTLY, SIR.
ACTIVATE PROJECT 47.
SIR?

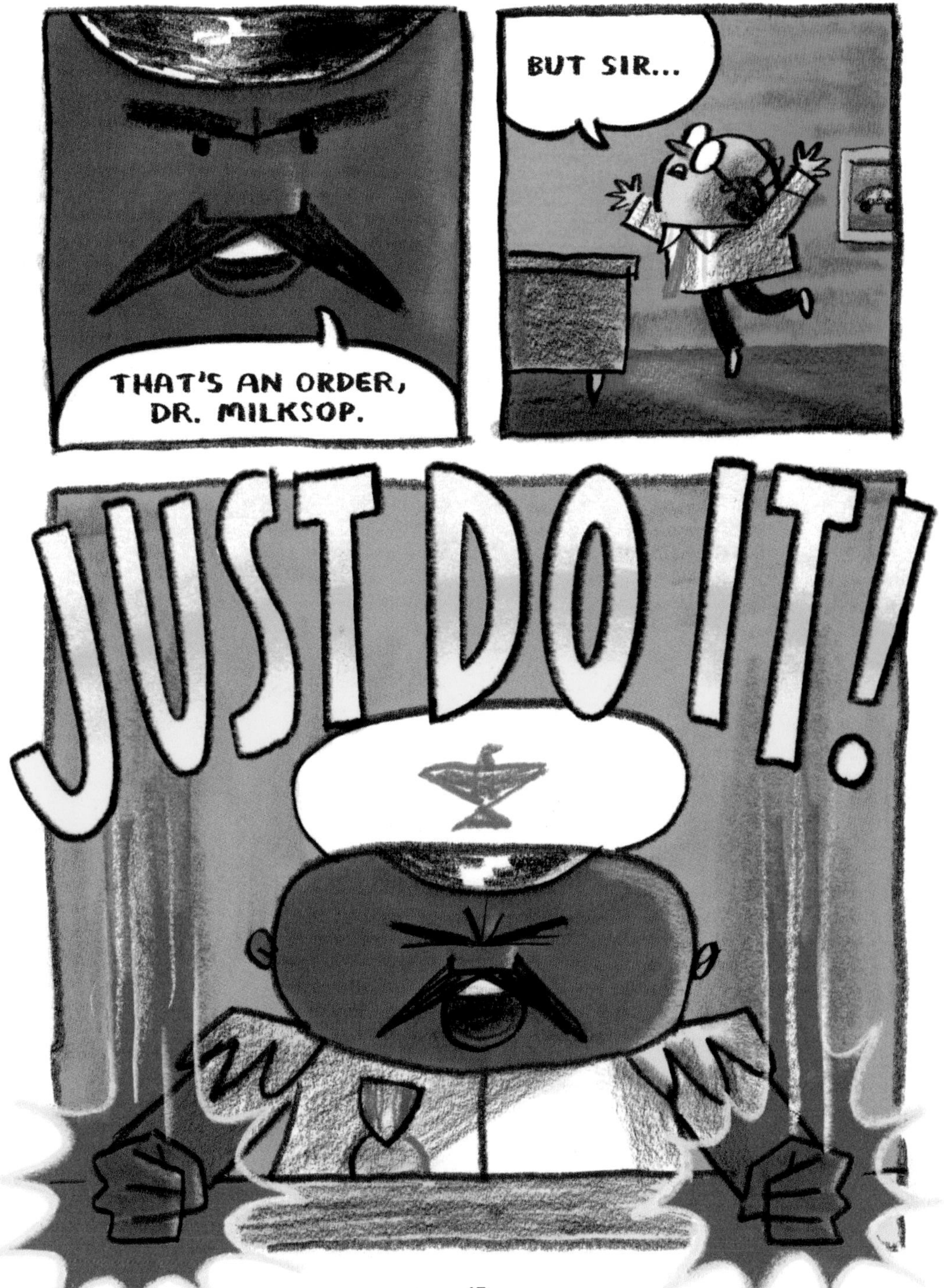
THAT'S AN ORDER, DR. MILKSOP.
BUT SIR...
JUST DO IT!

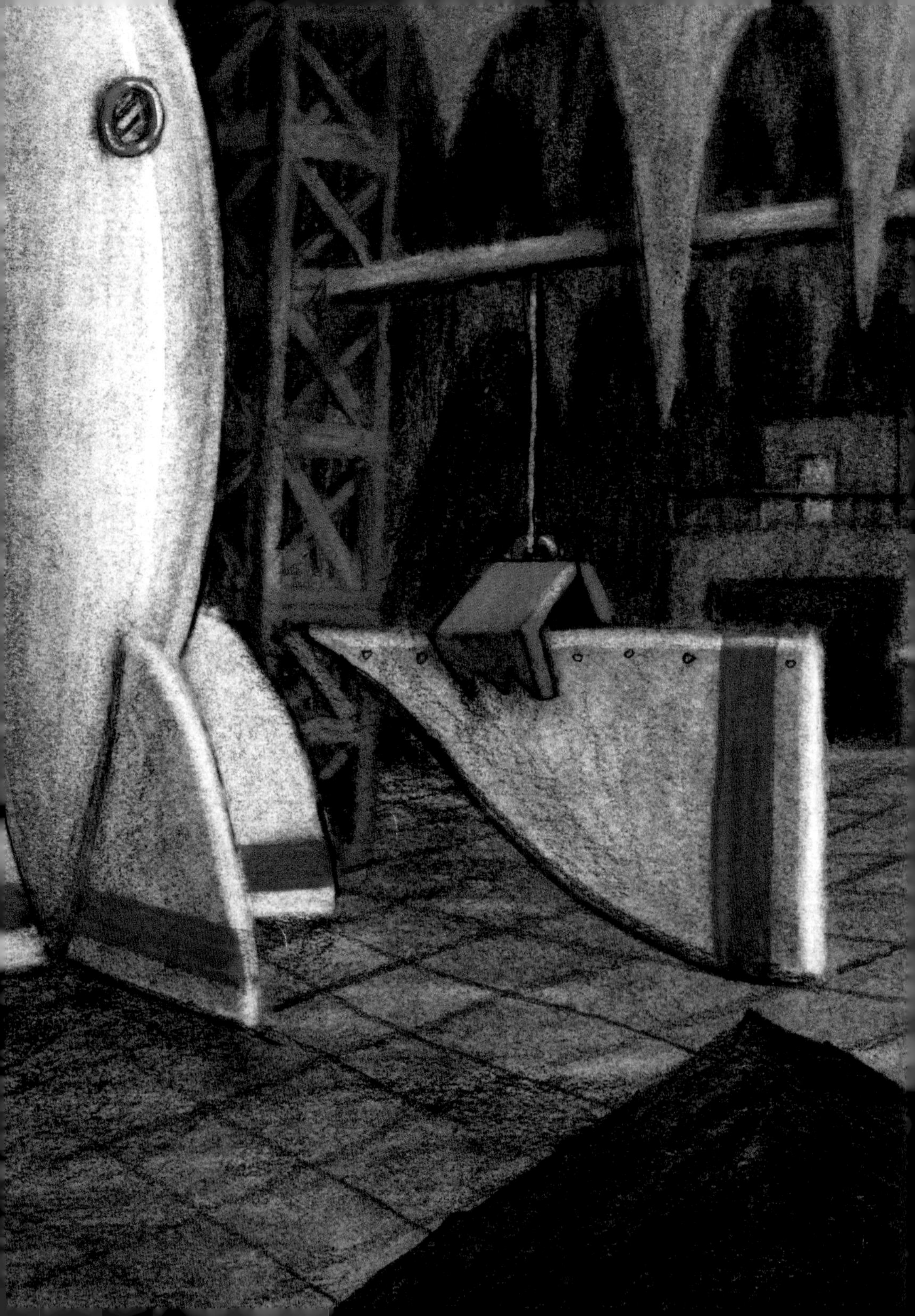

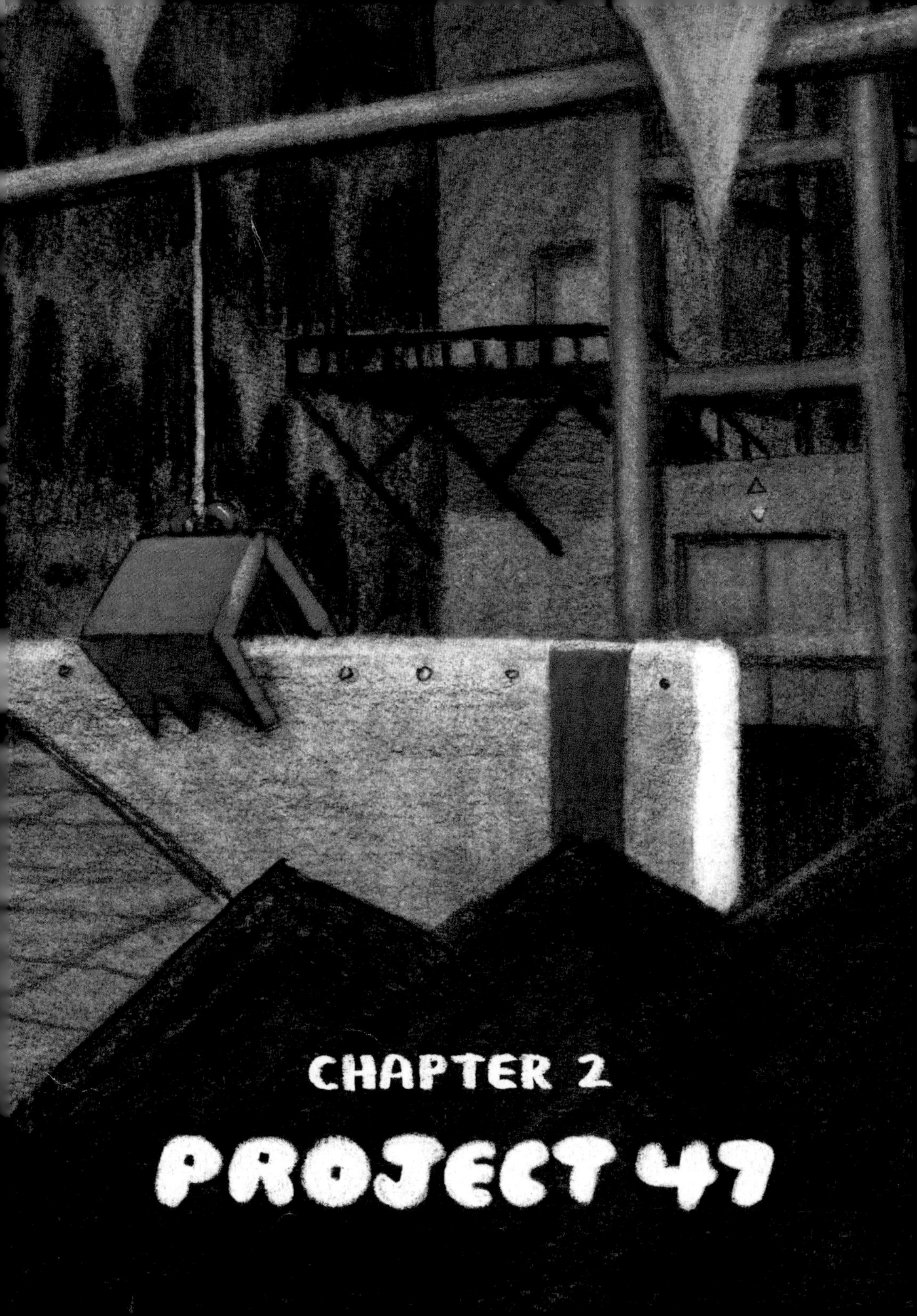

CHAPTER 2

PROJECT 47

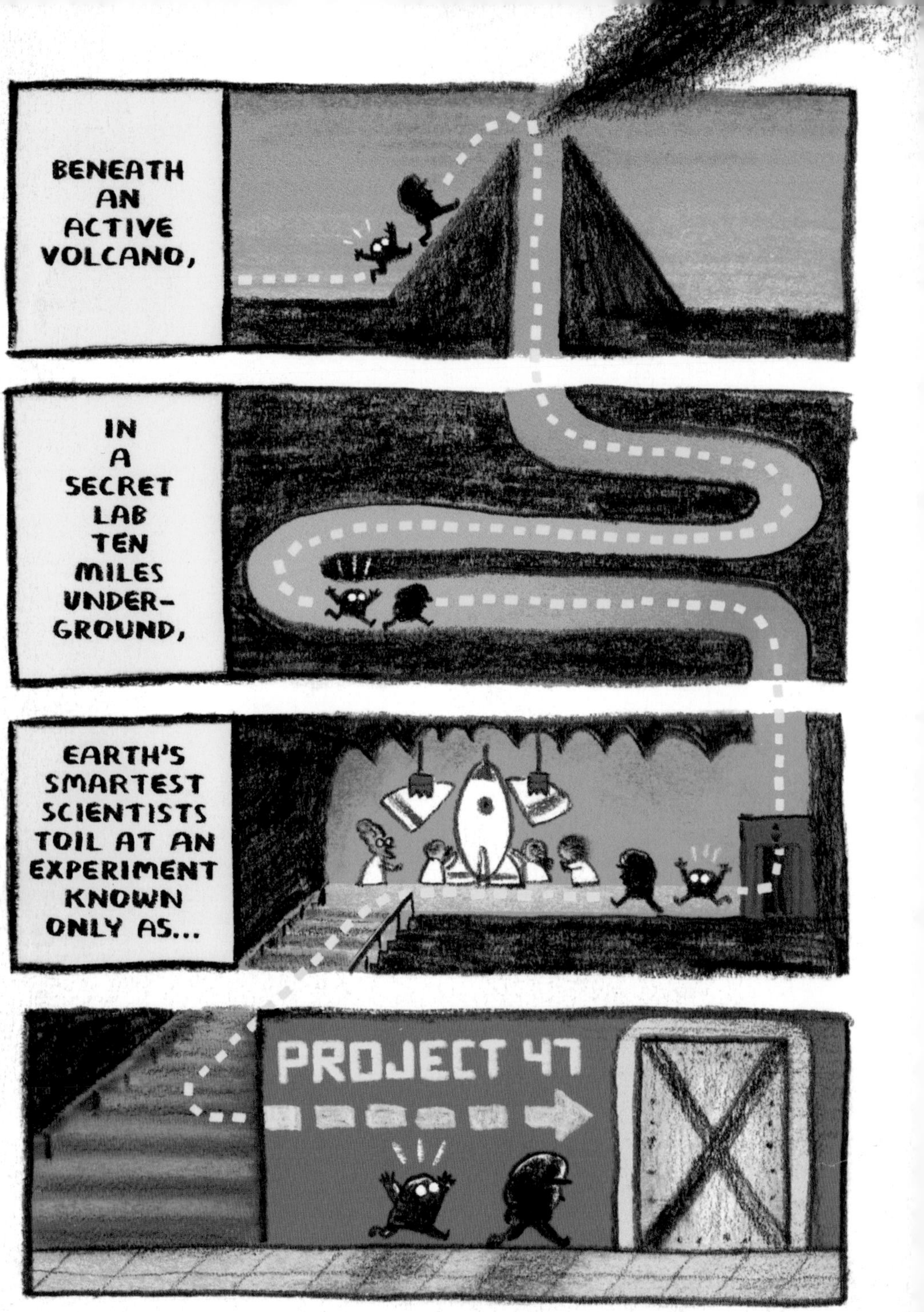
BENEATH AN ACTIVE VOLCANO,
IN A SECRET LAB TEN MILES UNDER-GROUND,
EARTH'S SMARTEST SCIENTISTS TOIL AT AN EXPERIMENT KNOWN ONLY AS...
PROJECT 47

BEHIND THIS BLAST-PROOF STEEL DOOR
LIES THE MOON'S SAVIOR
AND EARTH'S LAST HOPE...

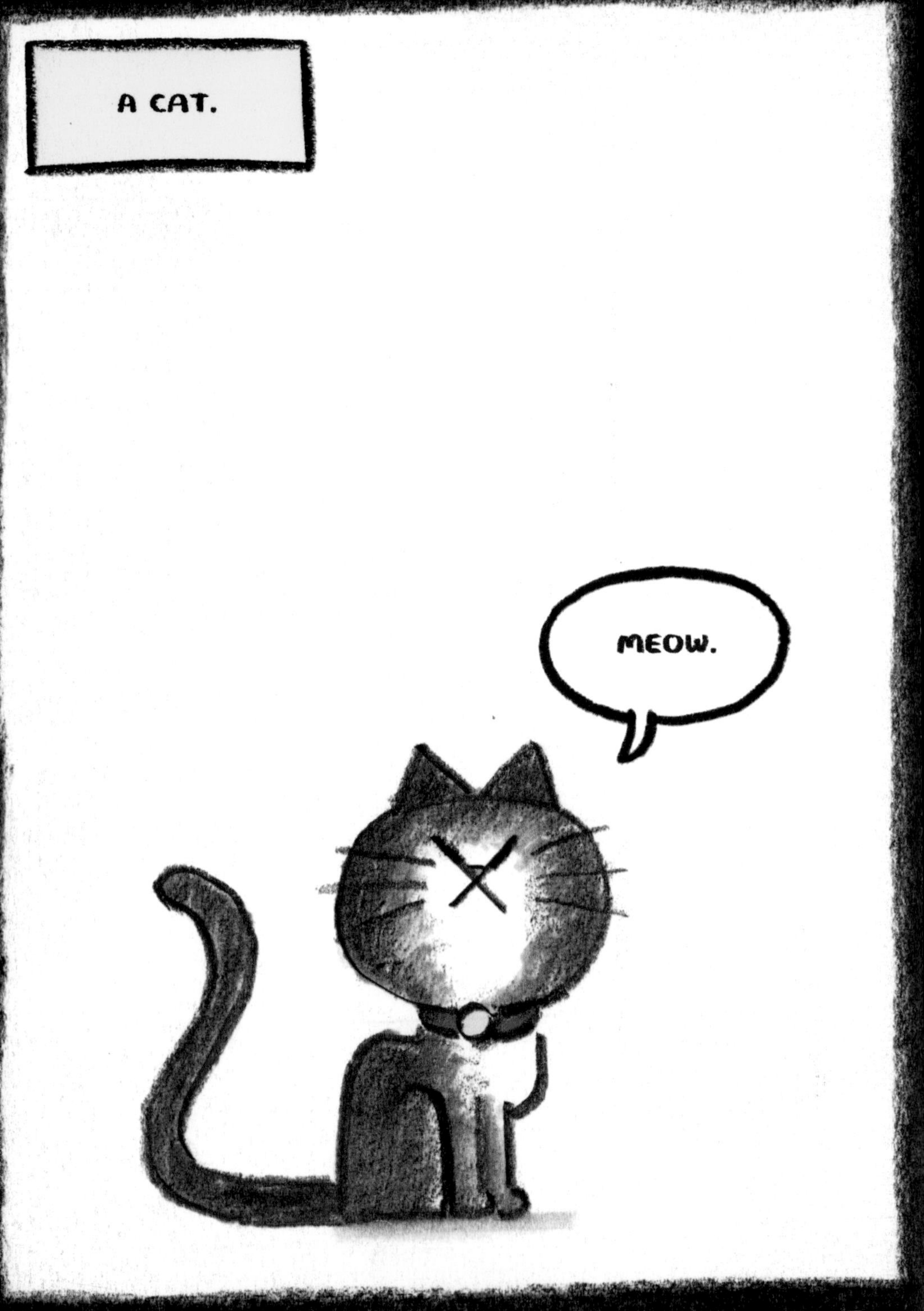
A CAT.
MEOW.

BUT NOT JUST ANY CAT!
WITH A BRAIN ENHANCED BY MICROCHIPS
AND A SUIT UPGRADED WITH CYBERNETIC BIOTECHNOLOGY,
THIS FANTASTIC FELINE IS A HERO THE LIKES OF WHICH THE UNIVERSE HAS NEVER SEEN!
MEOW.

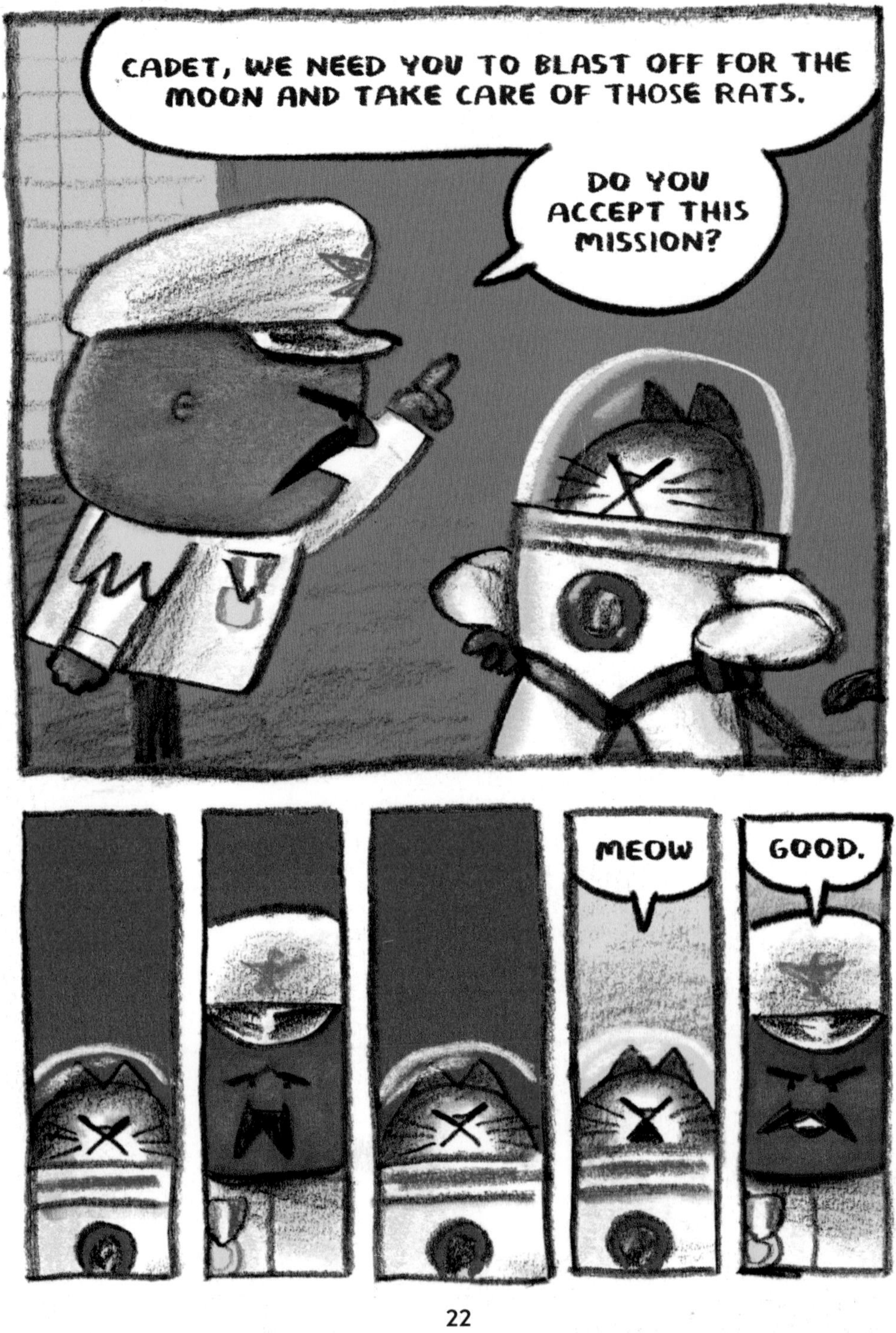
CADET, WE NEED YOU TO BLAST OFF FOR THE MOON AND TAKE CARE OF THOSE RATS.
DO YOU ACCEPT THIS MISSION?
MEOW
GOOD.

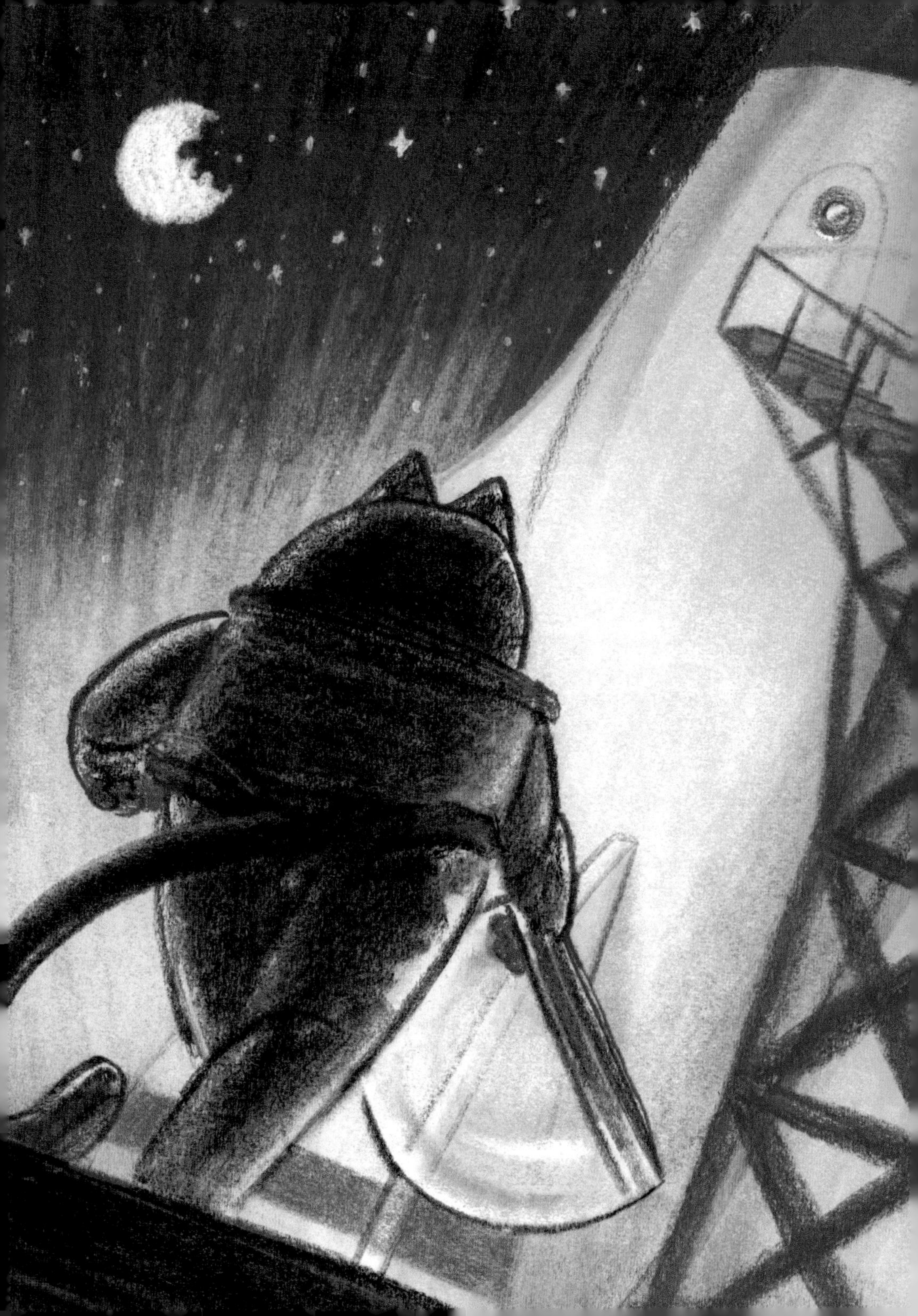

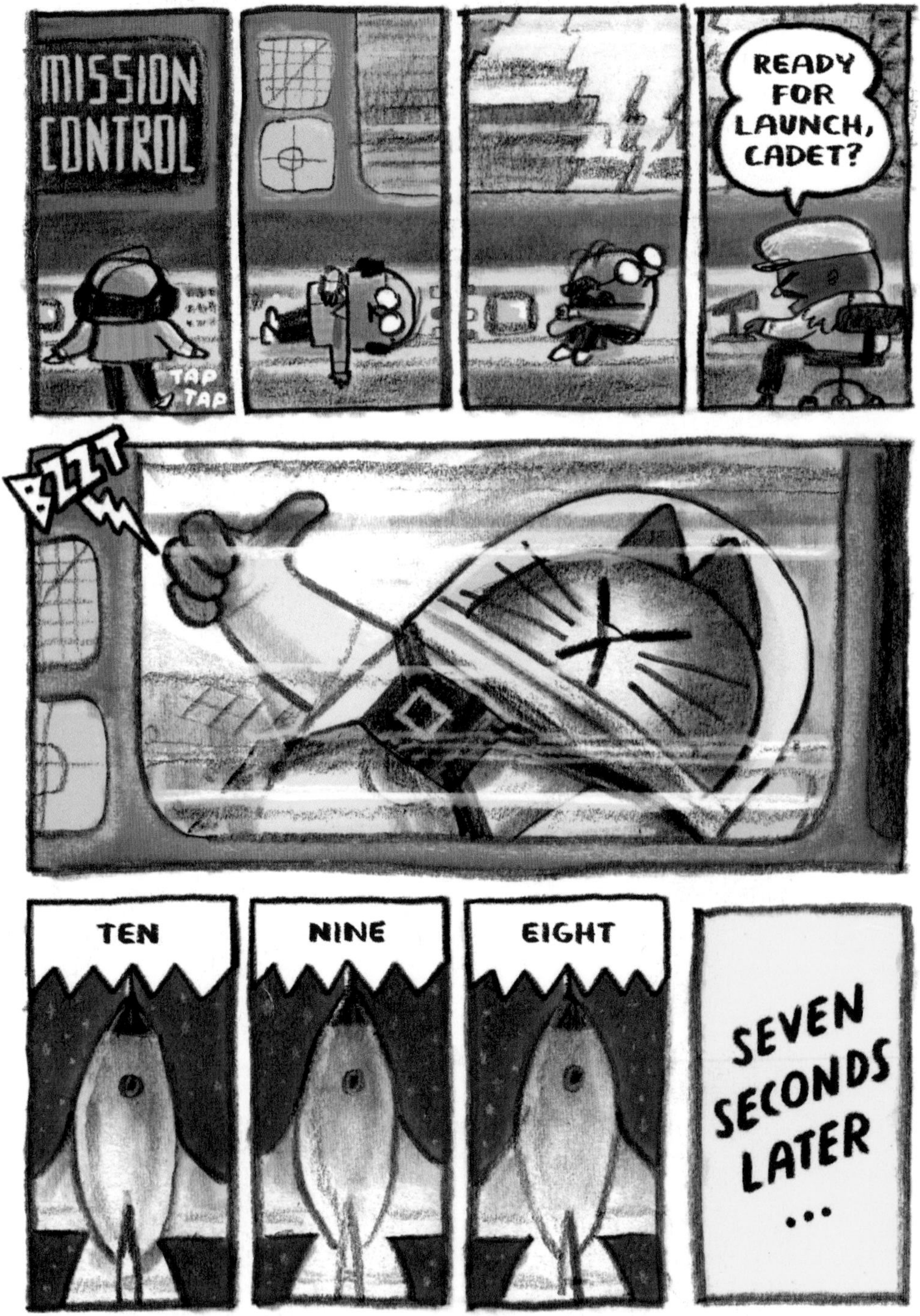
MISSION CONTROL
TAP TAP
READY FOR LAUNCH, CADET?
BZZZT
TEN
NINE
EIGHT
SEVEN SECONDS LATER ...

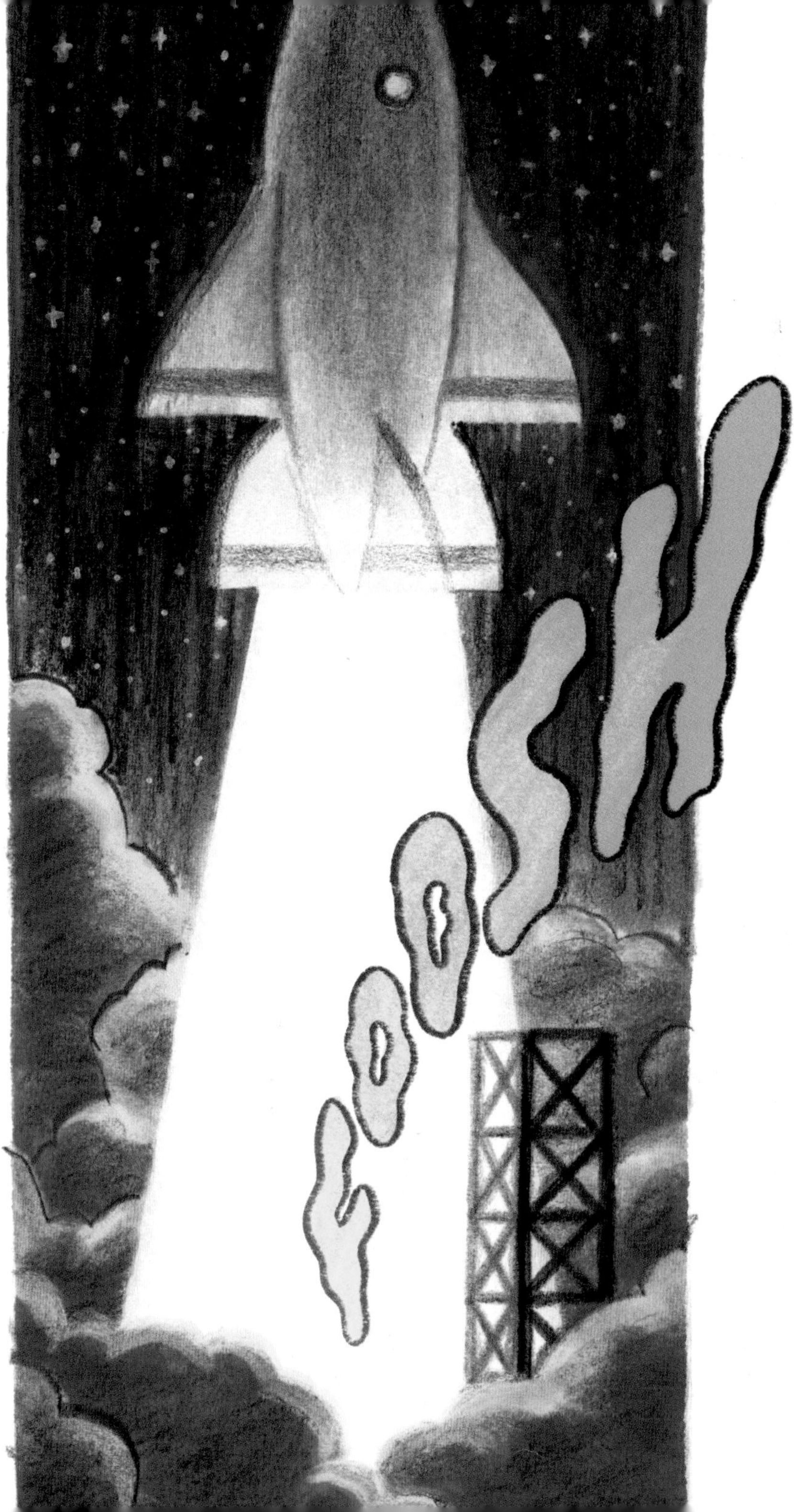

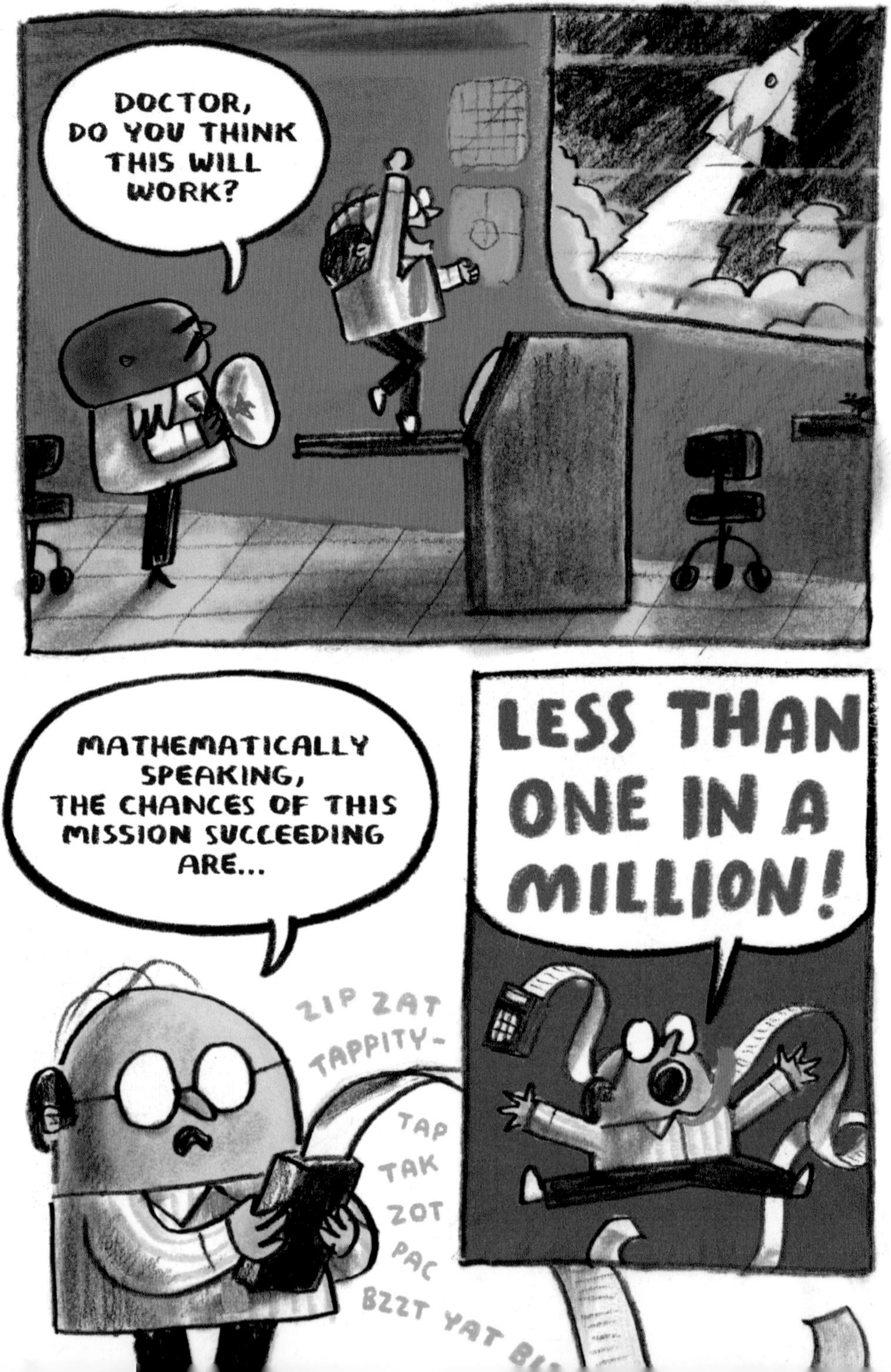
DOCTOR, DO YOU THINK THIS WILL WORK?
MATHEMATICALLY SPEAKING, THE CHANCES OF THIS MISSION SUCCEEDING ARE...
ZIP ZAT TAPPITY-
TAP
TAK
ZOT
PAC
BZZT YAT
LESS THAN ONE IN A MILLION!

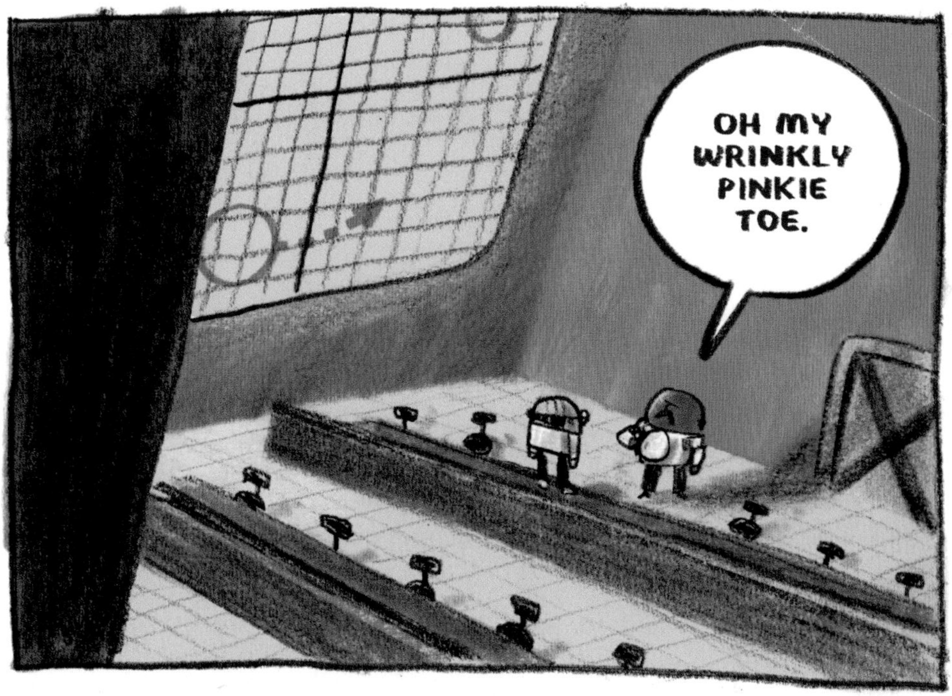
OH MY WRINKLY PINKIE TOE.

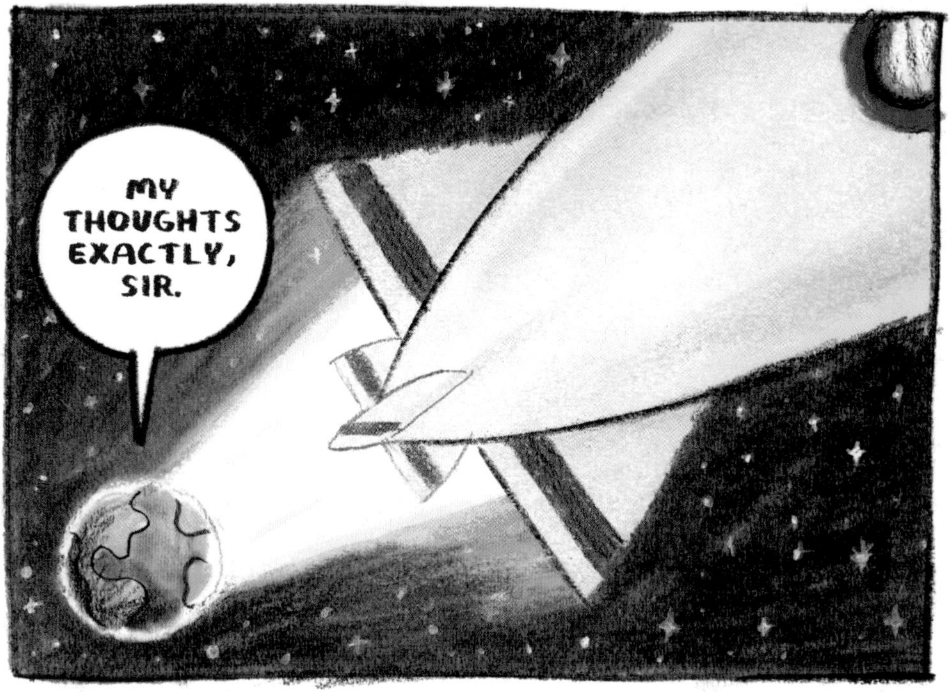
MY THOUGHTS EXACTLY, SIR.

CHAPTER 3
THE STOWAWAY

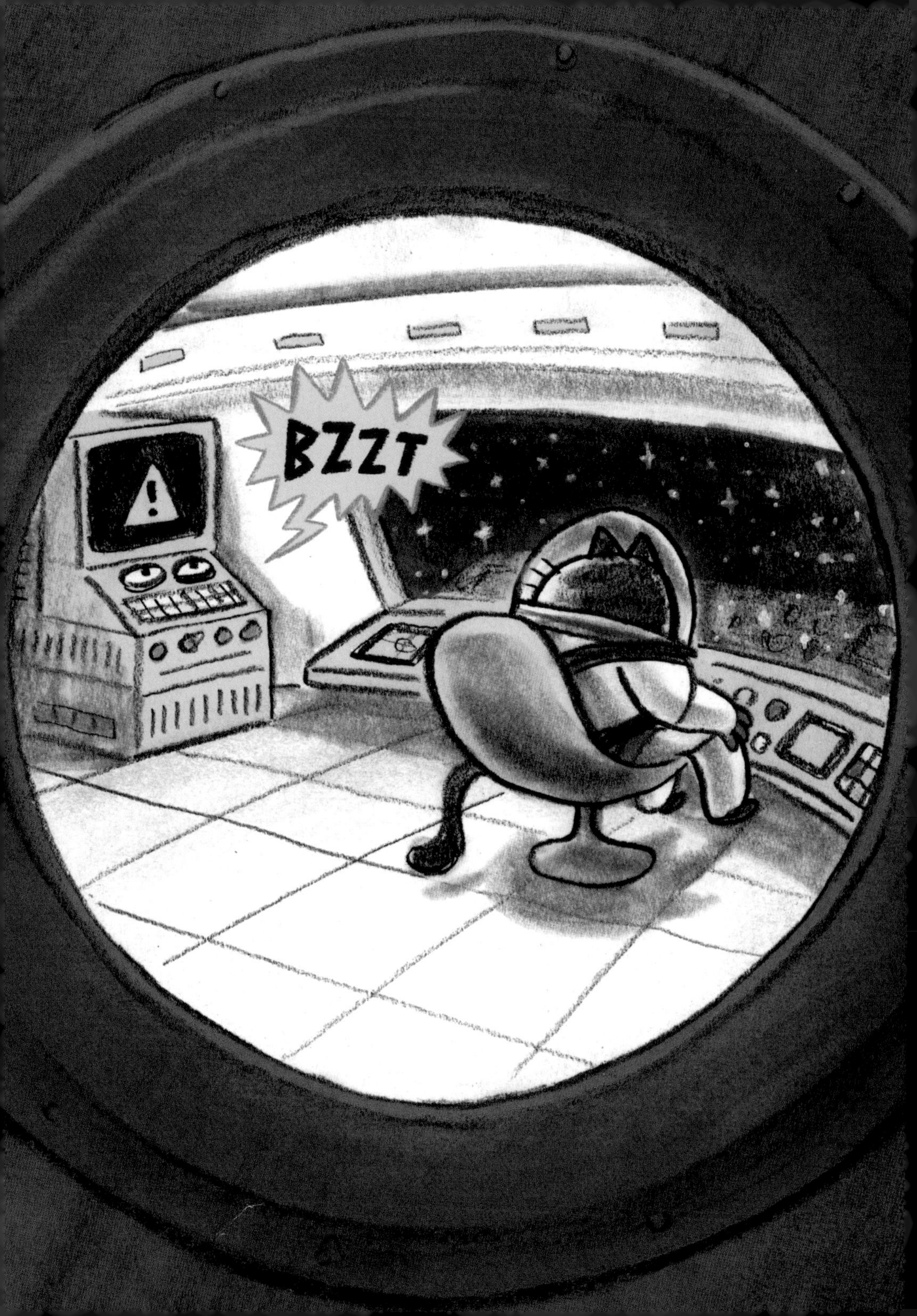
BZZT

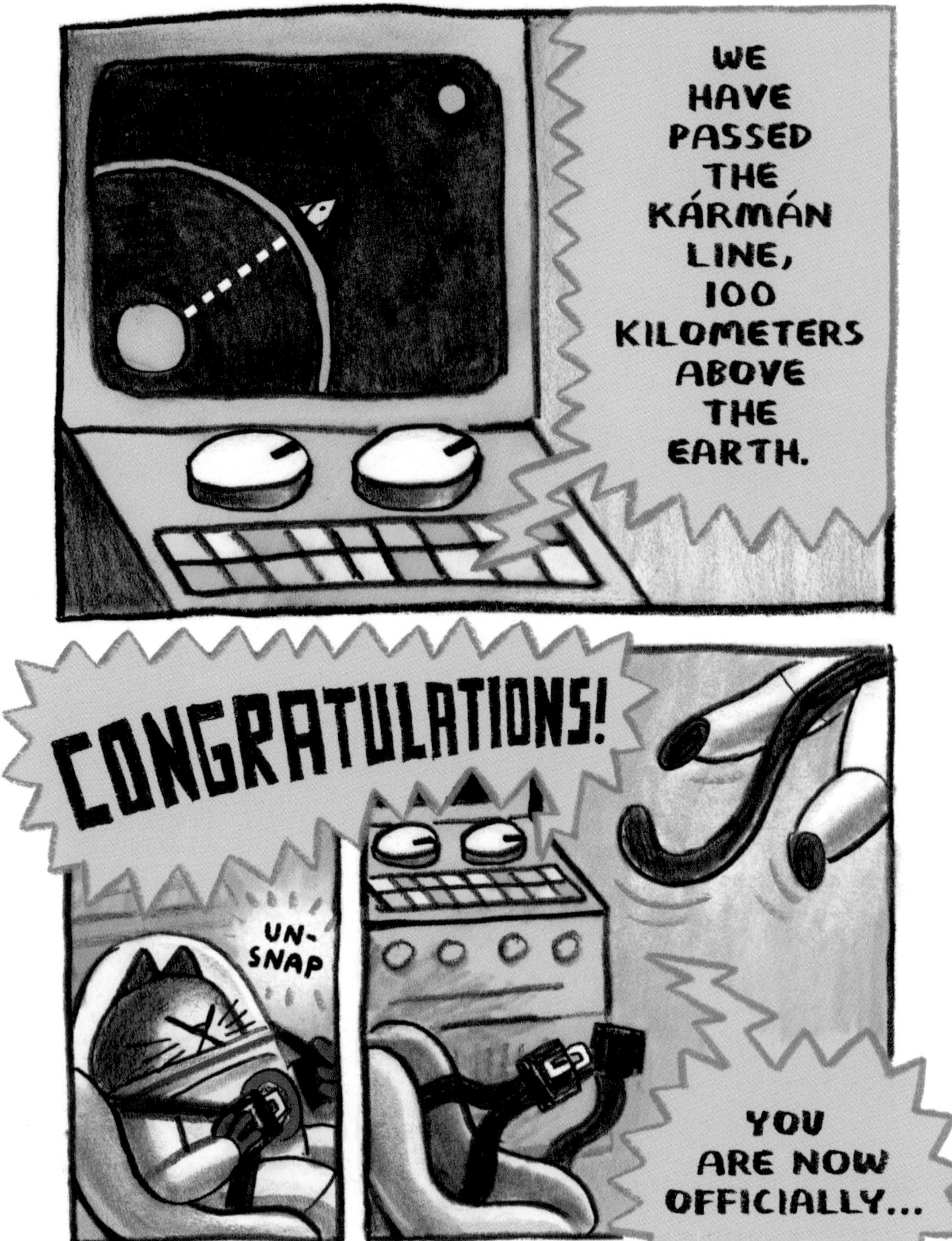
WE HAVE PASSED THE KÁRMÁN LINE, 100 KILOMETERS ABOVE THE EARTH.
CONGRATULATIONS!
UN-SNAP
YOU ARE NOW OFFICIALLY...

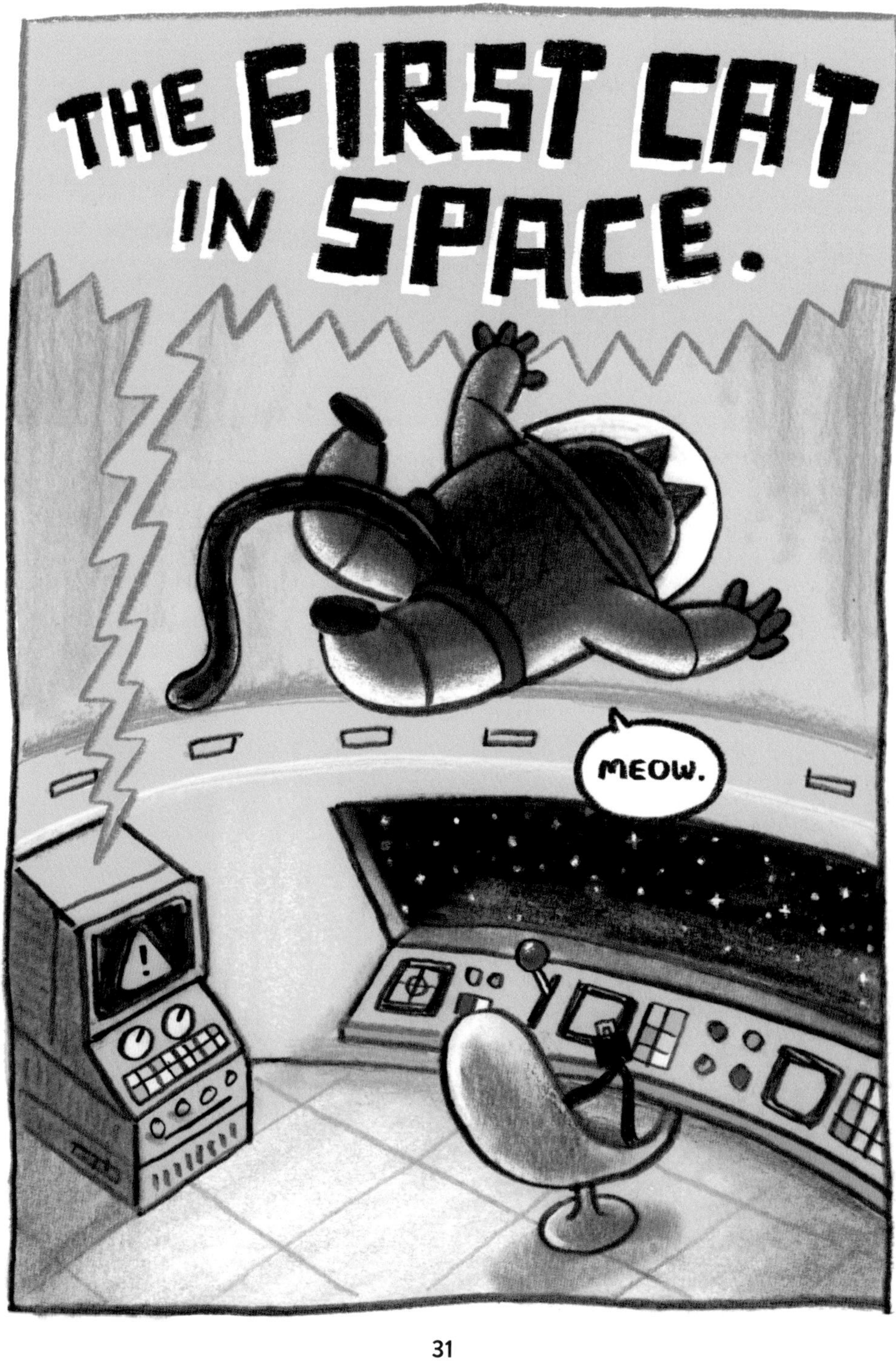
THE FIRST CAT IN SPACE.
MEOW.

ALLOW ME TO INTRODUCE YOU TO THE AMENITIES OF THIS SPACECRAFT.
HERE ARE YOUR LIVING QUARTERS.
HANGING GARDEN
PANORAMIC GALAXY VIEW
LIBRARY
ARCADE
SLEEP POD
THIS IS OUR TRAINING FACILITY.
STATIONARY BIKE
CENTRIFUGAL AXIS (to simulate Earth's gravity)
FREE WEIGHTS
INFINITY TRACK
SPORT FACILITIES
I HAVE SAVED THE BEST FOR LAST:
THE CANTEEN!
HERE, EVERY FOOD ON EARTH IS AVAILABLE...

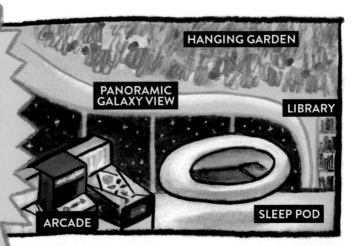

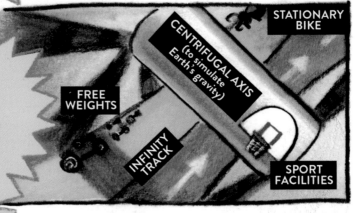

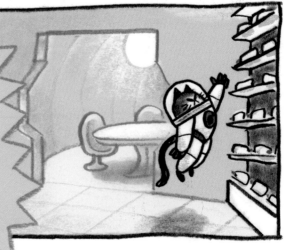

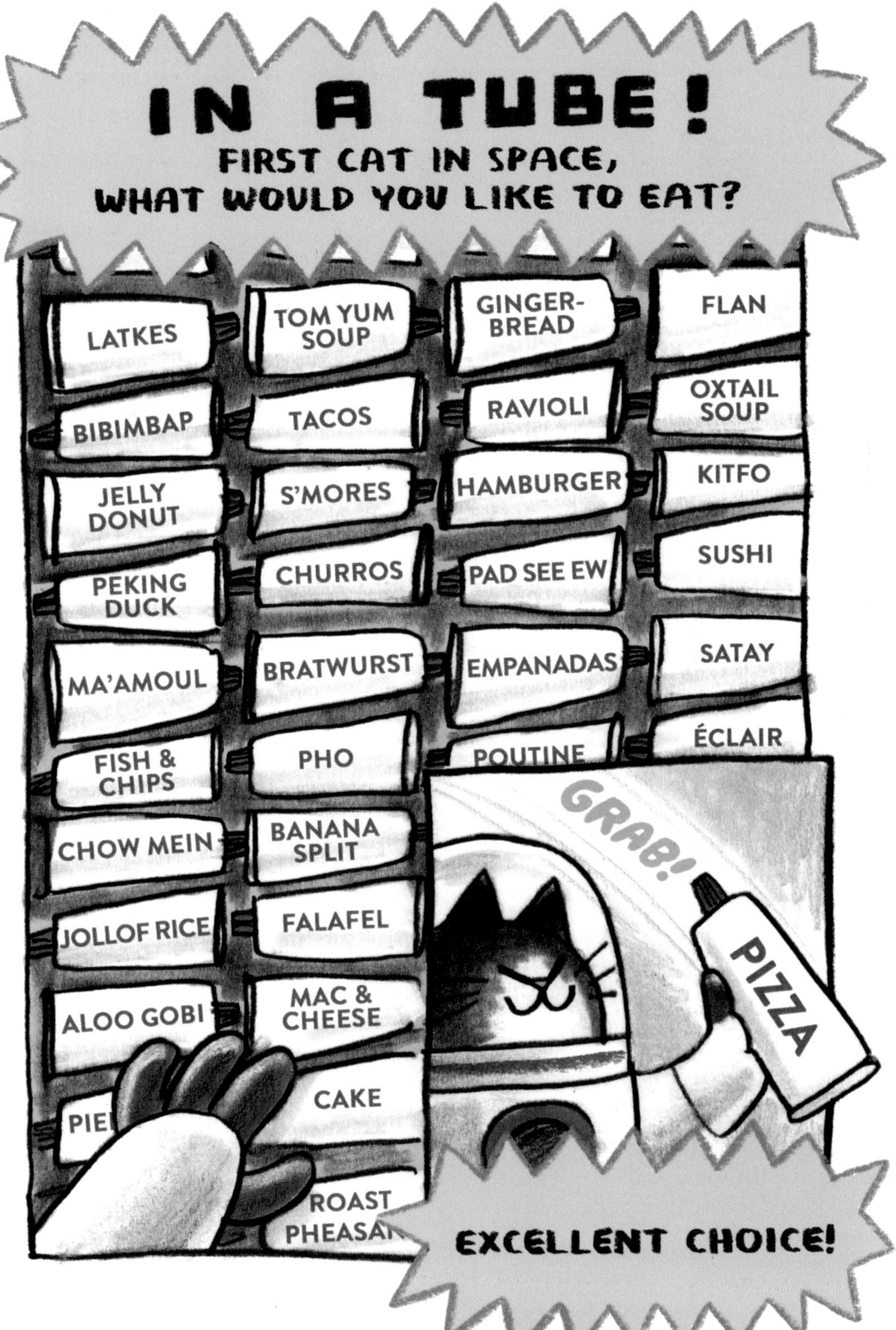
IN A TUBE!
FIRST CAT IN SPACE, WHAT WOULD YOU LIKE TO EAT?
LATKES
TOM YUM SOUP
GINGER-BREAD
FLAN
BIBIMBAP
TACOS
RAVIOLI
OXTAIL SOUP
JELLY DONUT
S'MORES
HAMBURGER
KITFO
PEKING DUCK
CHURROS
PAD SEE EW
SUSHI
MA'AMOUL
BRATWURST
EMPANADAS
SATAY
FISH & CHIPS
PHO
POUTINE
ÉCLAIR
CHOW MEIN
BANANA SPLIT
JOLLOF RICE
FALAFEL
ALOO GOBI
MAC & CHEESE
CAKE
ROAST
GRAB!
PIZZA
EXCELLENT CHOICE!

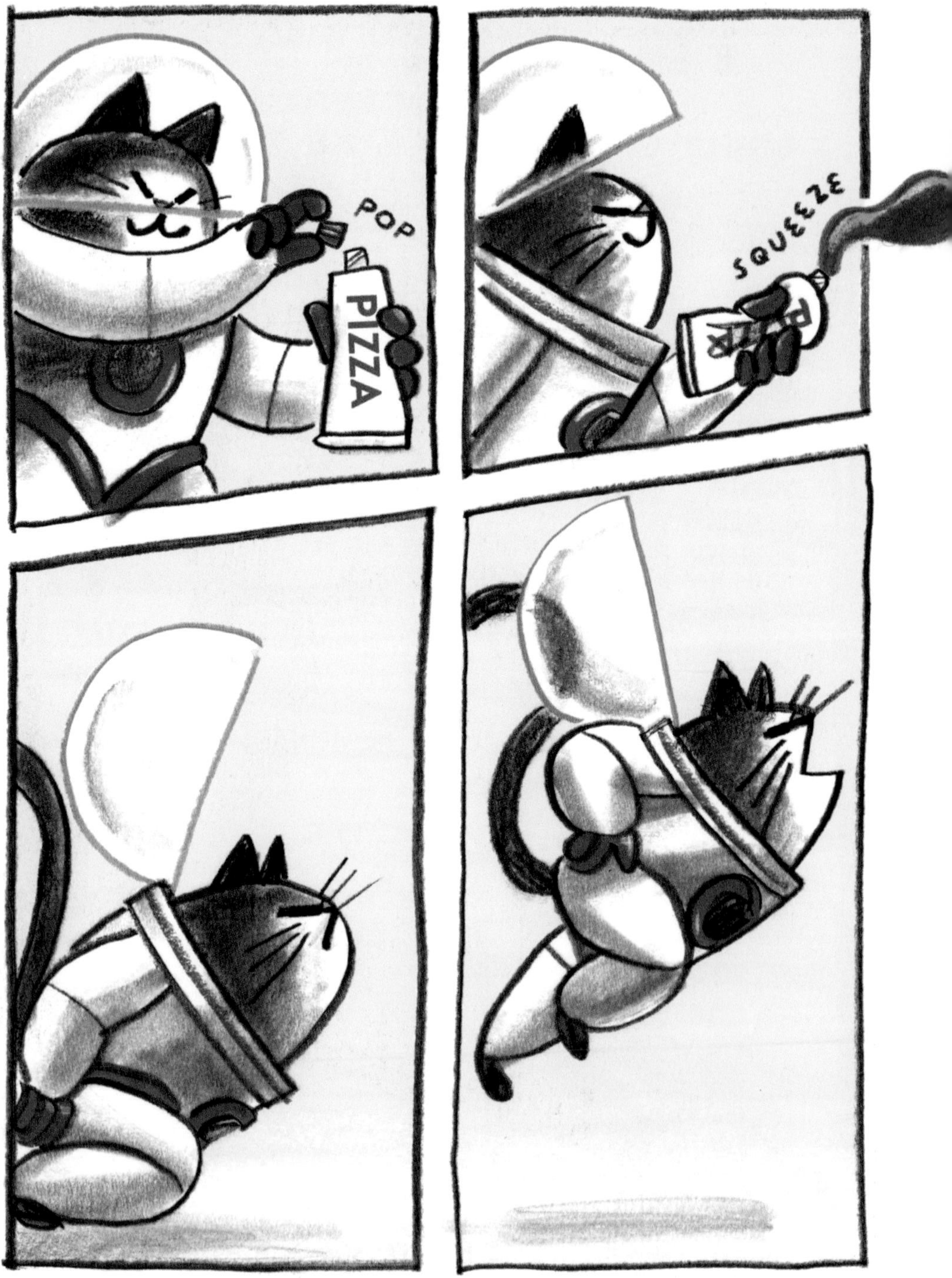
POP
PIZZA
SQUEEZE

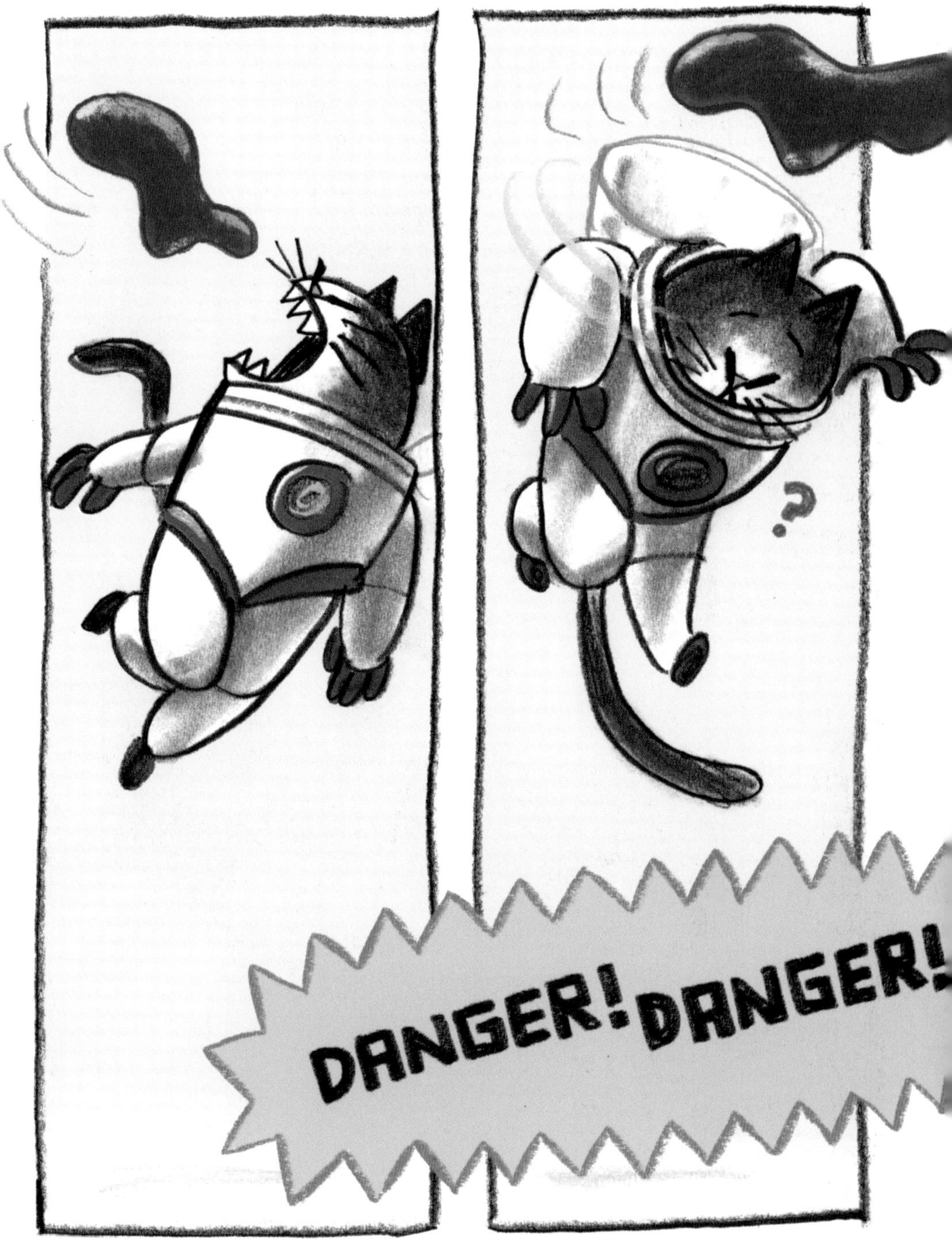
?
DANGER! DANGER!

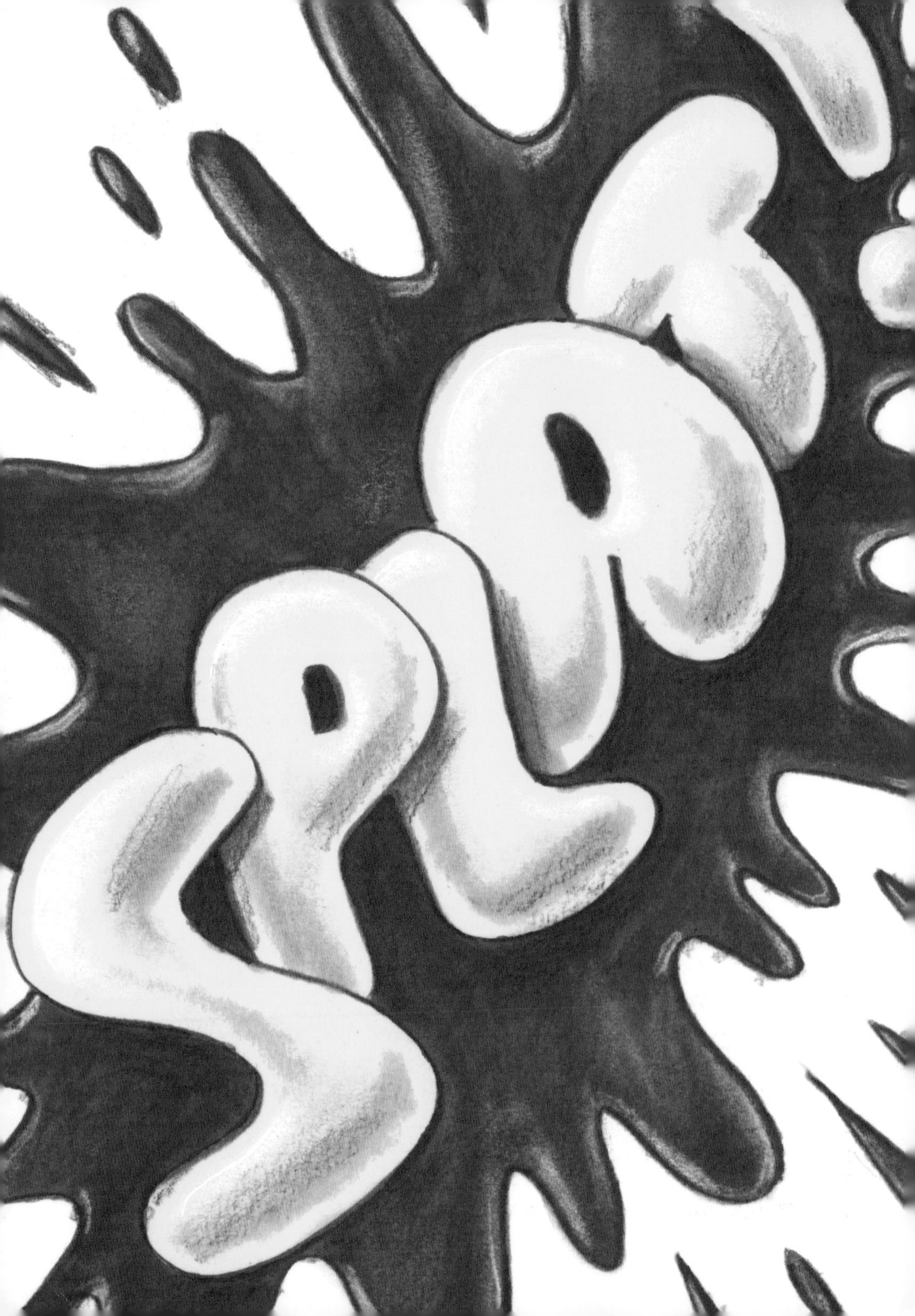
SPLAT

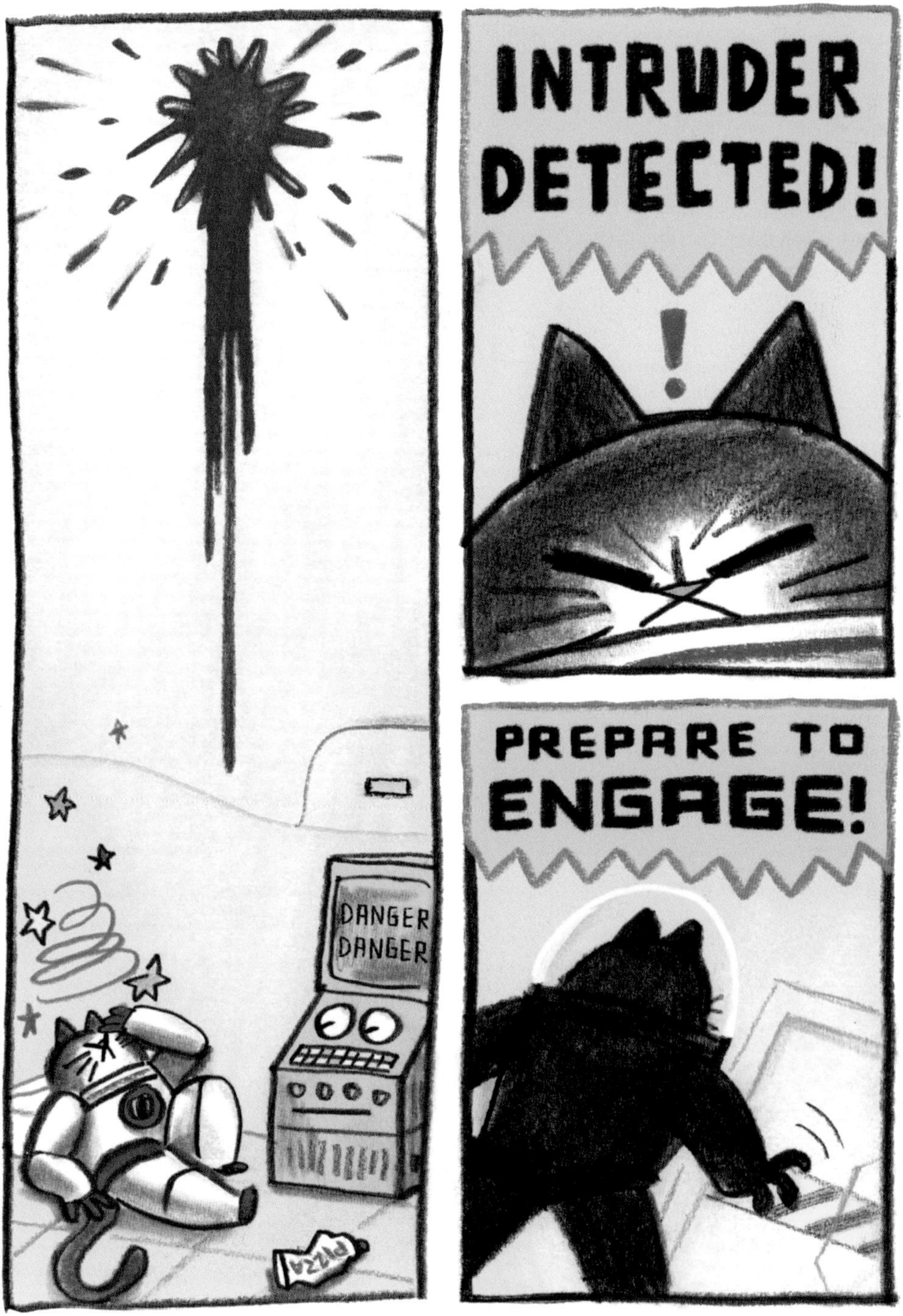
DANGER
DANGER
PIZZA
INTRUDER DETECTED!
!
PREPARE TO ENGAGE!

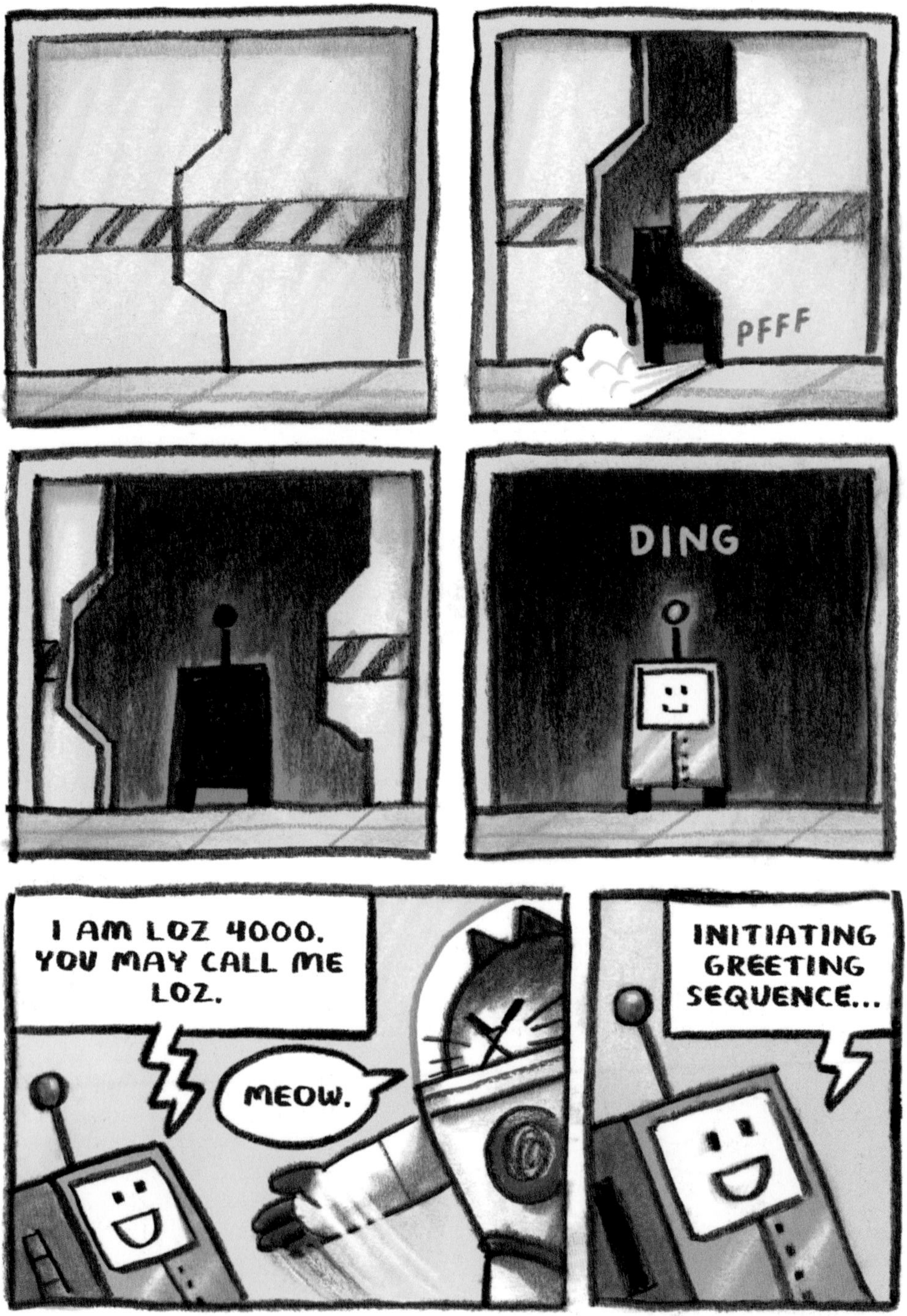
PFFF
DING
I AM LOZ 4000. YOU MAY CALL ME LOZ.
MEOW.
INITIATING GREETING SEQUENCE...

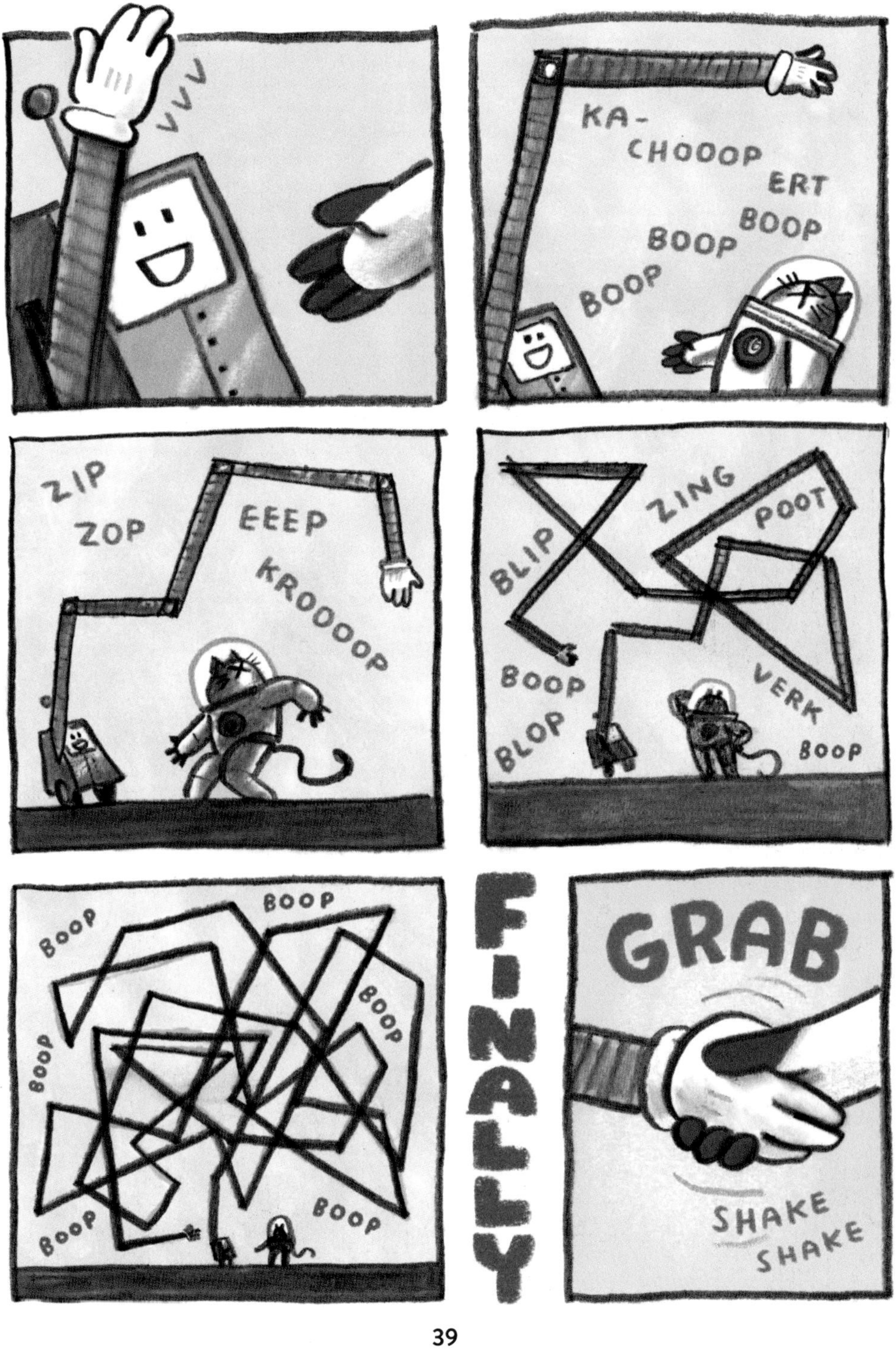
VVV
KA-
CHOOOP
ERT
BOOP
BOOP
BOOP
ZIP
ZOP
EEEP
KROOOOOP
BLIP
ZING
POOT
BOOP
BLOP
VERK
BOOP
BOOP
BOOP
BOOP
BOOP
BOOP
BOOP
FINALLY
GRAB
SHAKE
SHAKE

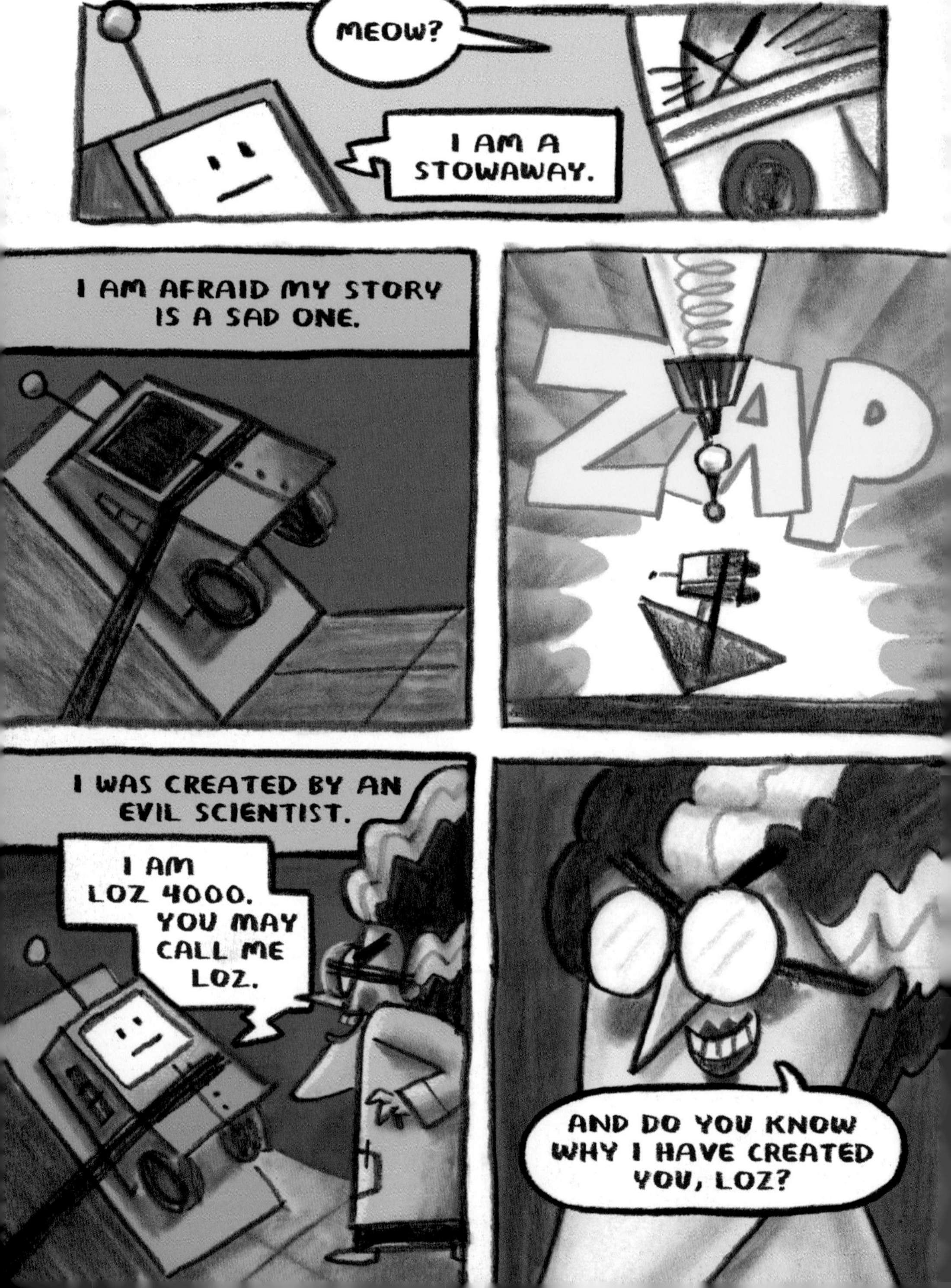
MEOW?
I AM A STOWAWAY.
I AM AFRAID MY STORY IS A SAD ONE.
ZAP
I WAS CREATED BY AN EVIL SCIENTIST.
I AM LOZ 4000. YOU MAY CALL ME LOZ.
AND DO YOU KNOW WHY I HAVE CREATED YOU, LOZ?

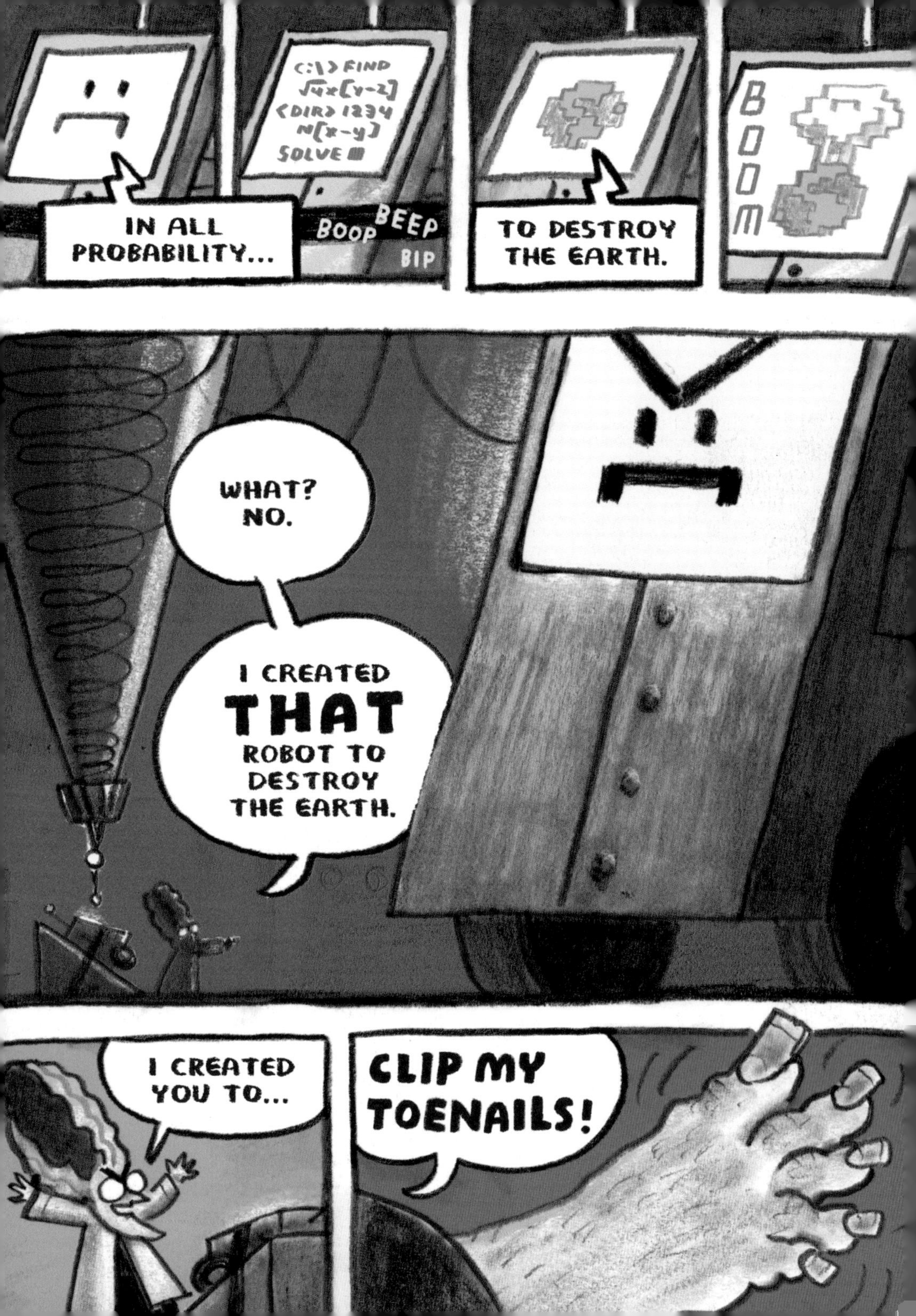
C:\> FIND
√4x[y-2]
<DIR> 1234
N[x-y]
SOLVE
IN ALL PROBABILITY...
BOOP BEEP BIP
TO DESTROY THE EARTH.
BOOM
WHAT? NO.
I CREATED THAT ROBOT TO DESTROY THE EARTH.
I CREATED YOU TO...
CLIP MY TOENAILS!

I SEE.
VVVV
INITIATE TOENAIL-CLIPPING SEQUENCE.
KA-CHOOOP
ERT
BOOP
BOOP
BOOP
ZIP
ZOP
EEEP
KROOOOOOP
BLOOP
ZING
POOT
VERK
BOOP
BIP
SCRAAAP
BOOP
BOOP
BOOP
BOOP
BOOP
BOOP
SIT
LATER...
CLIP

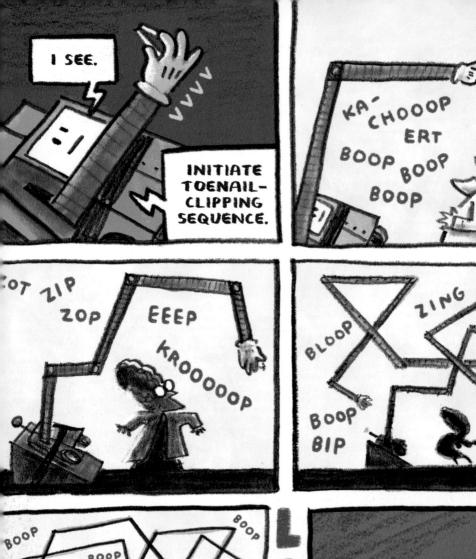

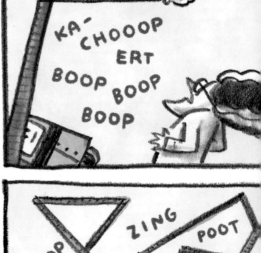

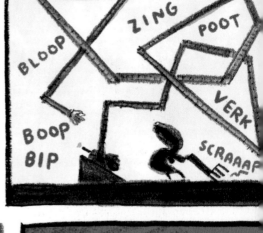

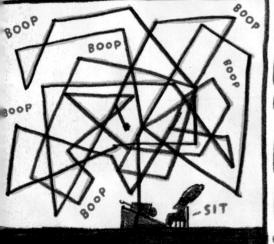

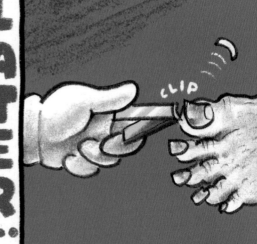

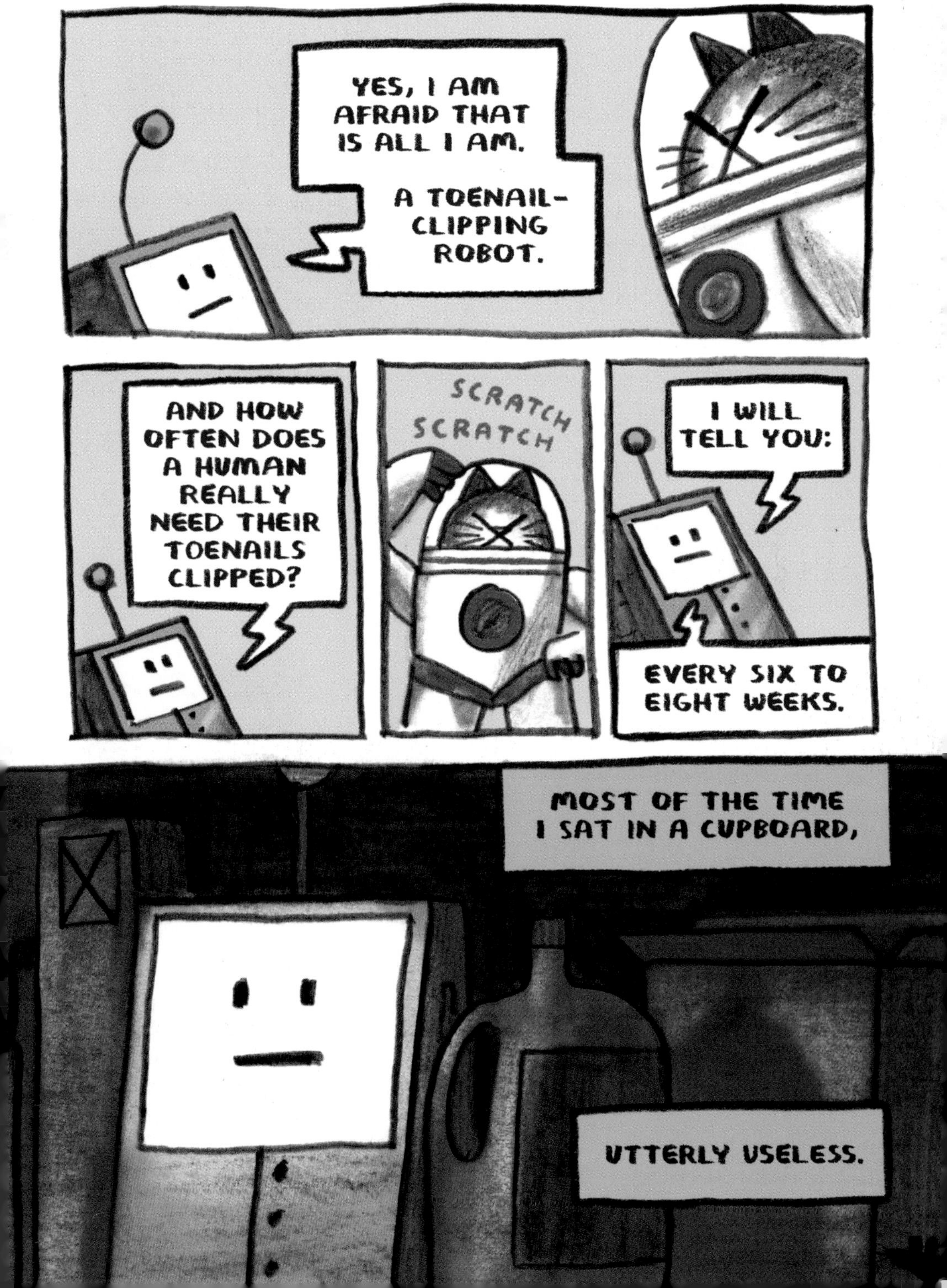
YES, I AM AFRAID THAT IS ALL I AM.
A TOENAIL-CLIPPING ROBOT.
AND HOW OFTEN DOES A HUMAN REALLY NEED THEIR TOENAILS CLIPPED?
SCRATCH SCRATCH
I WILL TELL YOU:
EVERY SIX TO EIGHT WEEKS.
MOST OF THE TIME I SAT IN A CUPBOARD,
UTTERLY USELESS.

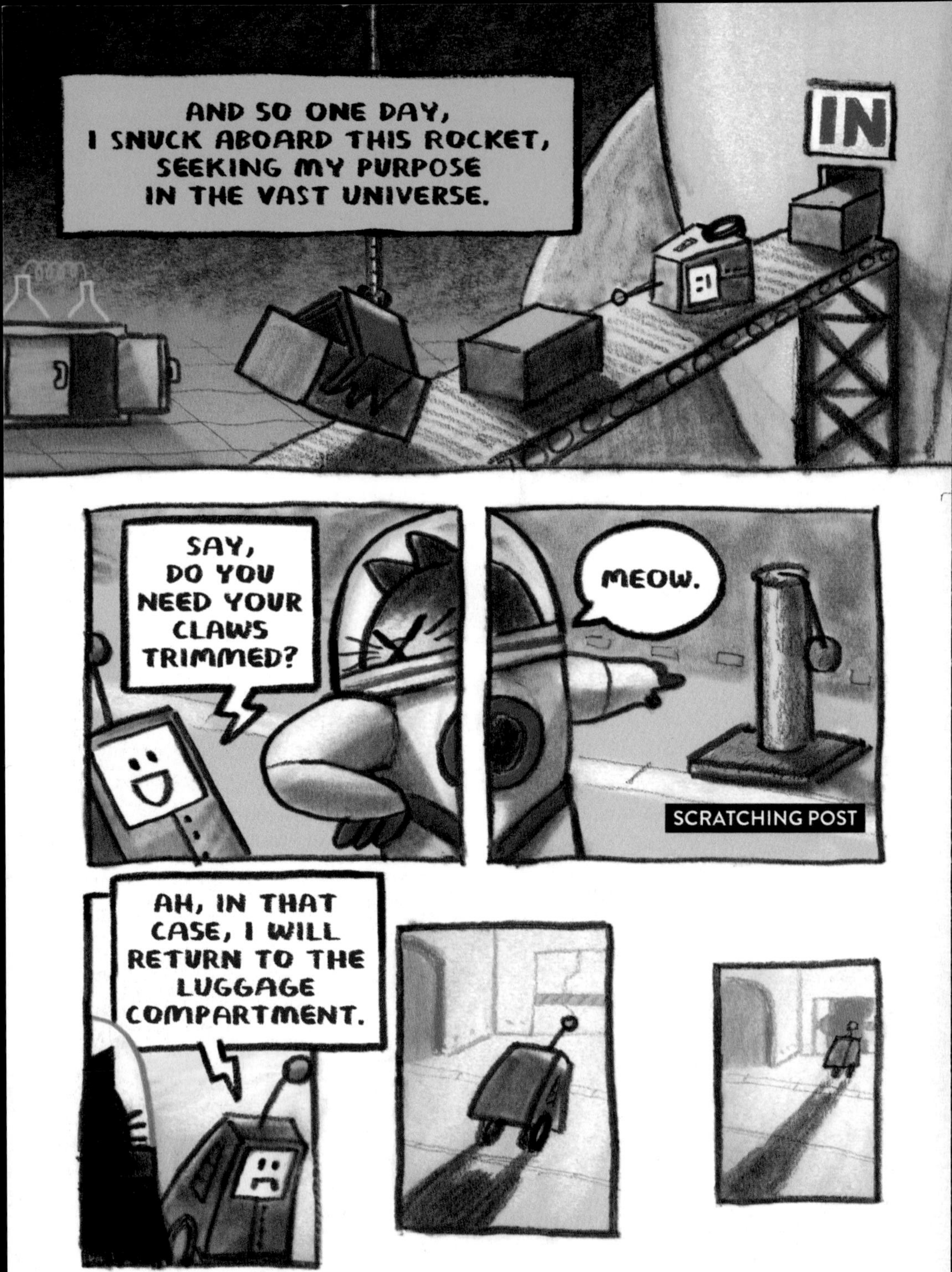
AND SO ONE DAY, I SNUCK ABOARD THIS ROCKET, SEEKING MY PURPOSE IN THE VAST UNIVERSE.
IN
SAY, DO YOU NEED YOUR CLAWS TRIMMED?
MEOW.
SCRATCHING POST
AH, IN THAT CASE, I WILL RETURN TO THE LUGGAGE COMPARTMENT.

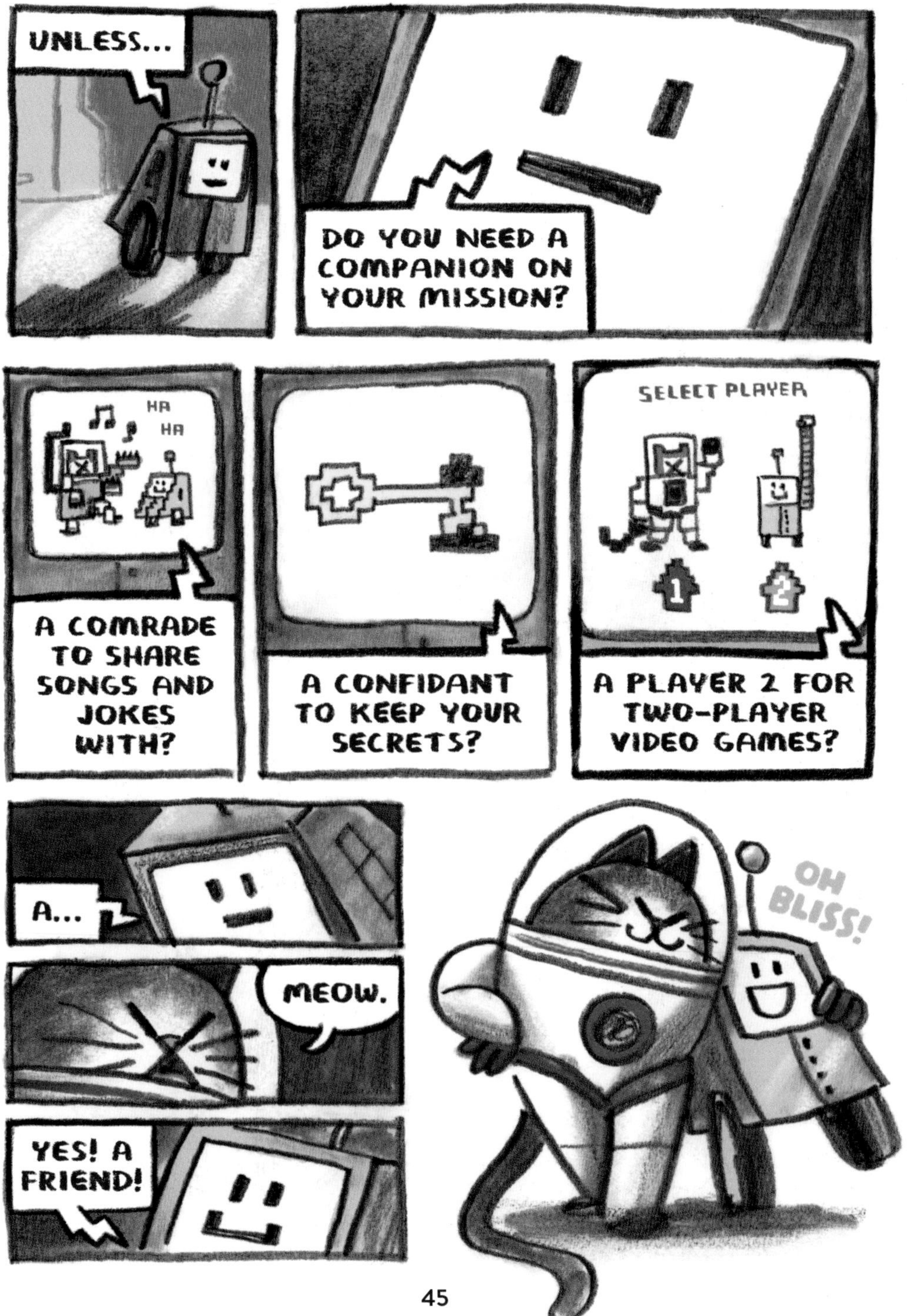
UNLESS...
DO YOU NEED A COMPANION ON YOUR MISSION?
HA
HA
A COMRADE TO SHARE SONGS AND JOKES WITH?
A CONFIDANT TO KEEP YOUR SECRETS?
SELECT PLAYER
1
2
A PLAYER 2 FOR TWO-PLAYER VIDEO GAMES?
A...
MEOW.
YES! A FRIEND!
OH BLISS!

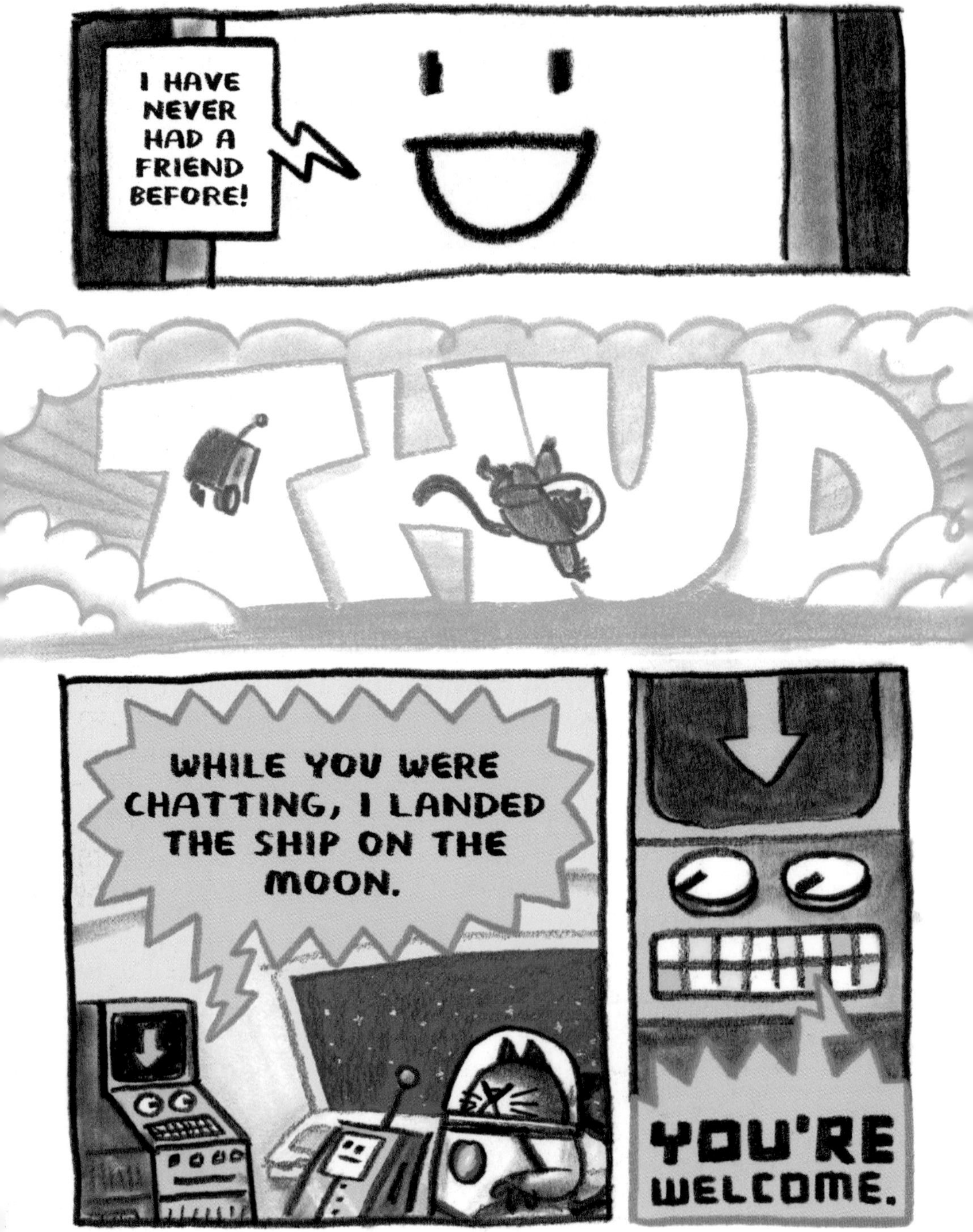
I HAVE NEVER HAD A FRIEND BEFORE!
THUD
WHILE YOU WERE CHATTING, I LANDED THE SHIP ON THE MOON.
YOU'RE WELCOME.

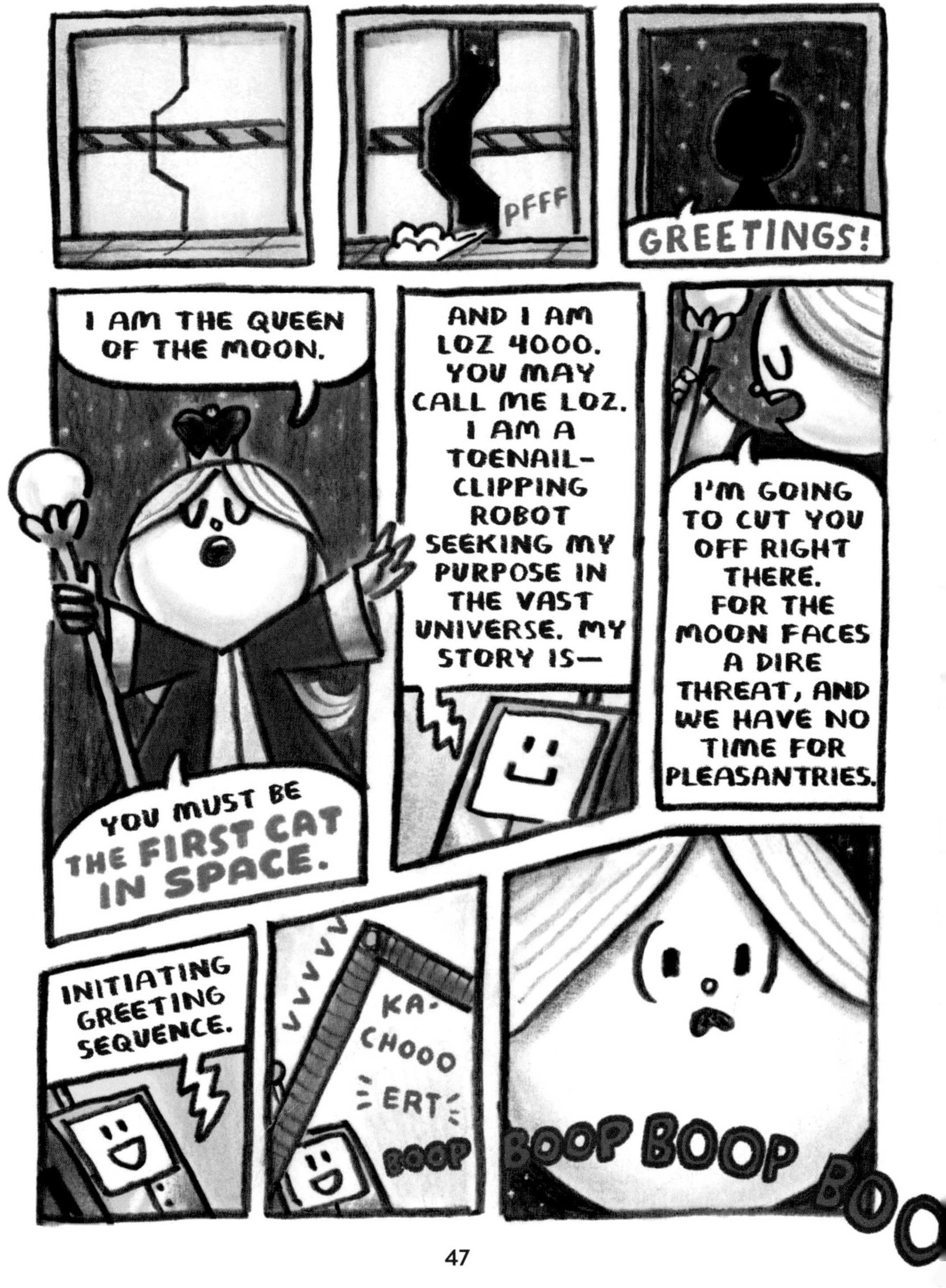
PFFF
GREETINGS!
I AM THE QUEEN OF THE MOON.
YOU MUST BE THE FIRST CAT IN SPACE.
AND I AM LOZ 4000. YOU MAY CALL ME LOZ. I AM A TOENAIL-CLIPPING ROBOT SEEKING MY PURPOSE IN THE VAST UNIVERSE. MY STORY IS—
I'M GOING TO CUT YOU OFF RIGHT THERE. FOR THE MOON FACES A DIRE THREAT, AND WE HAVE NO TIME FOR PLEASANTRIES.
INITIATING GREETING SEQUENCE.
VVVVV
KA-CHOOO
ERT
BOOP
BOOP BOOP
BOO

CHAPTER 4

THE LAND OF CHEERFULNESS

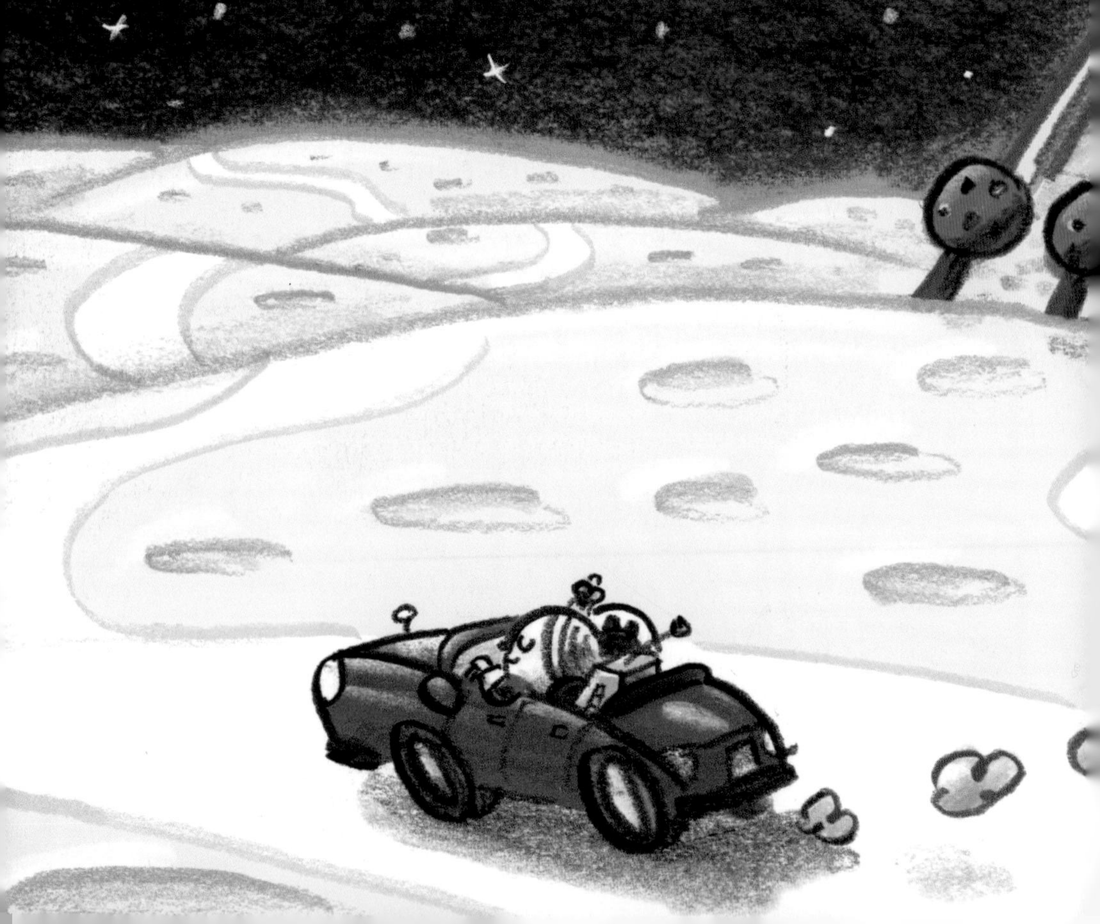

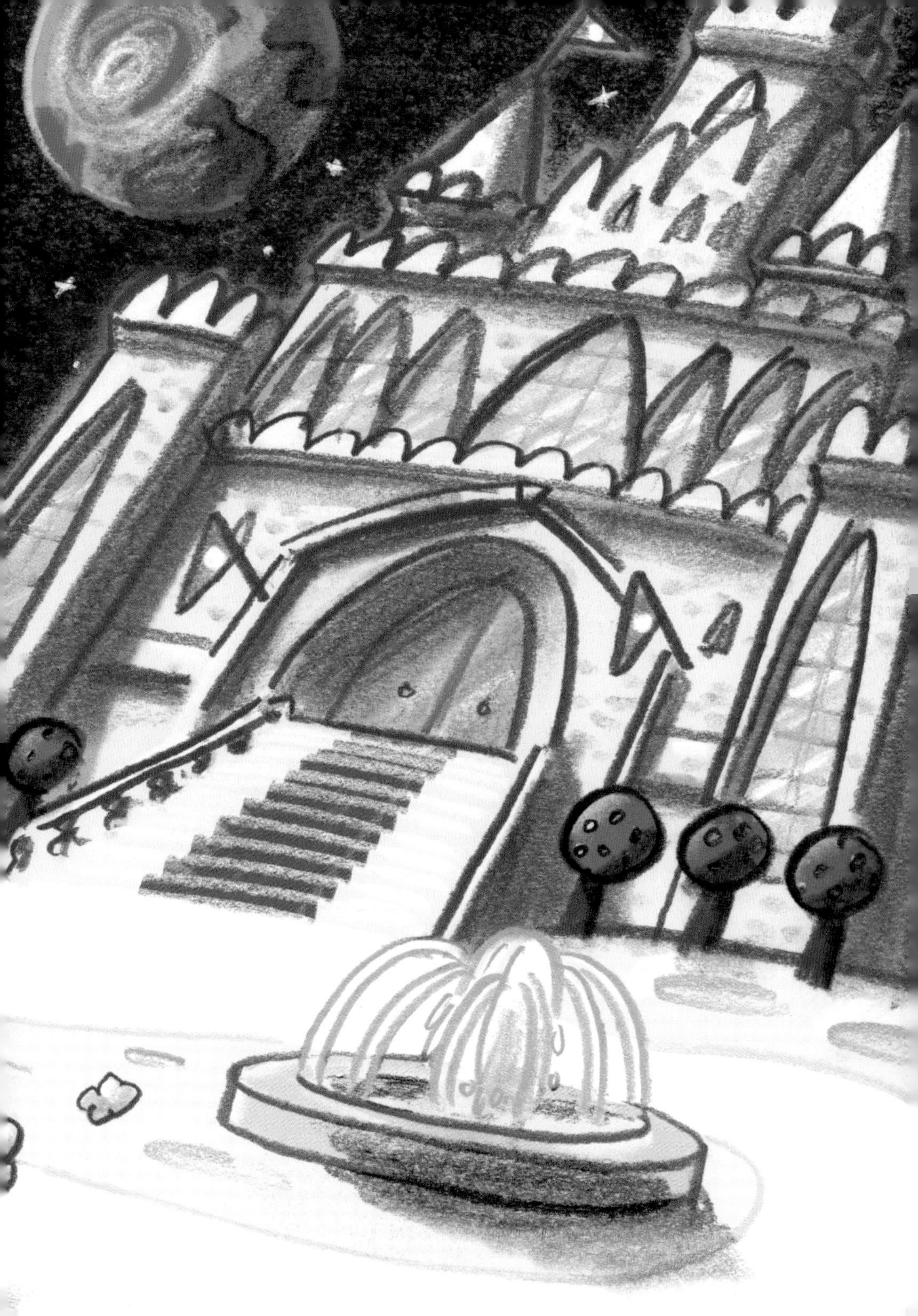

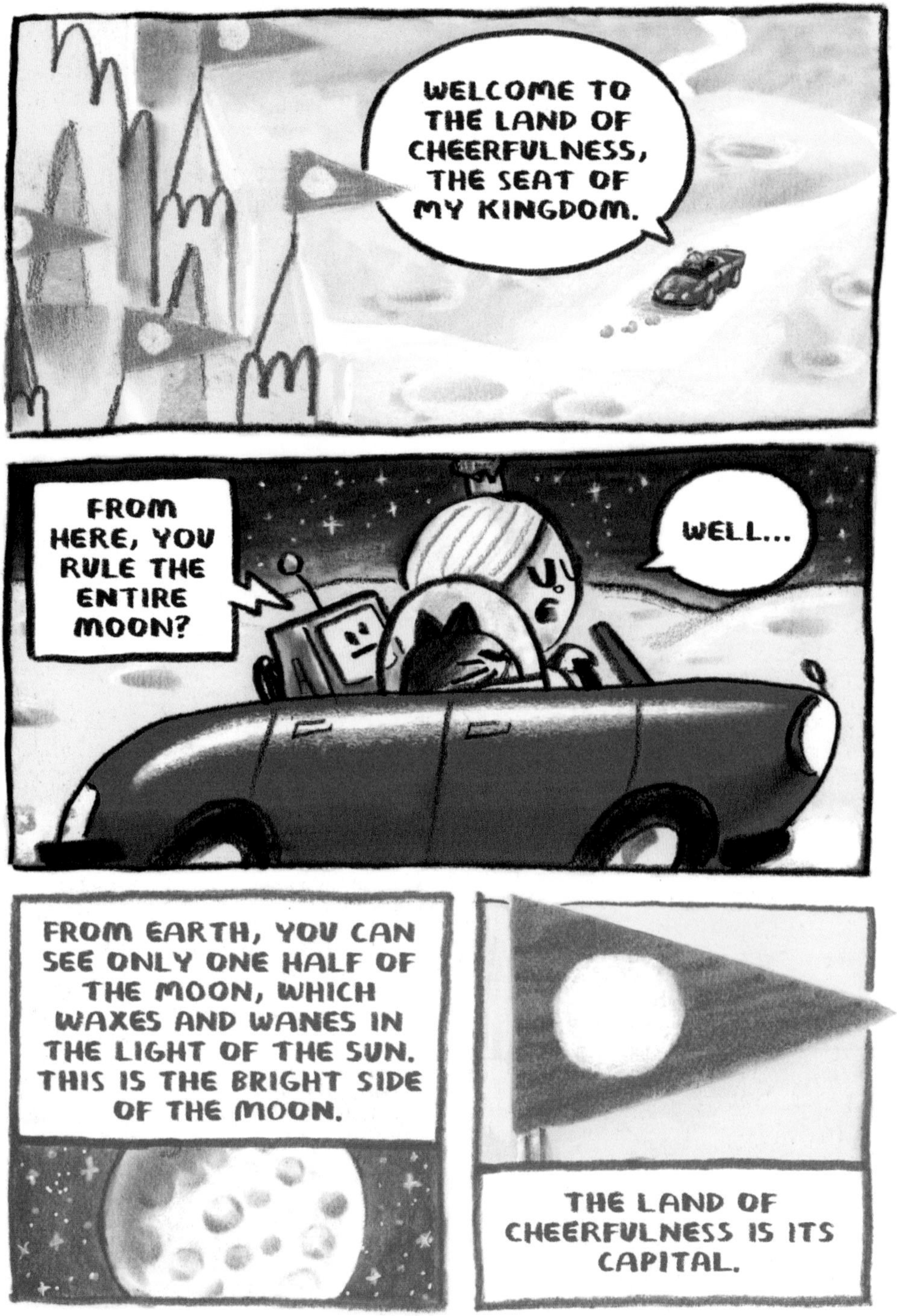
WELCOME TO THE LAND OF CHEERFULNESS, THE SEAT OF MY KINGDOM.
FROM HERE, YOU RULE THE ENTIRE MOON?
WELL...
FROM EARTH, YOU CAN SEE ONLY ONE HALF OF THE MOON, WHICH WAXES AND WANES IN THE LIGHT OF THE SUN. THIS IS THE BRIGHT SIDE OF THE MOON.
THE LAND OF CHEERFULNESS IS ITS CAPITAL.

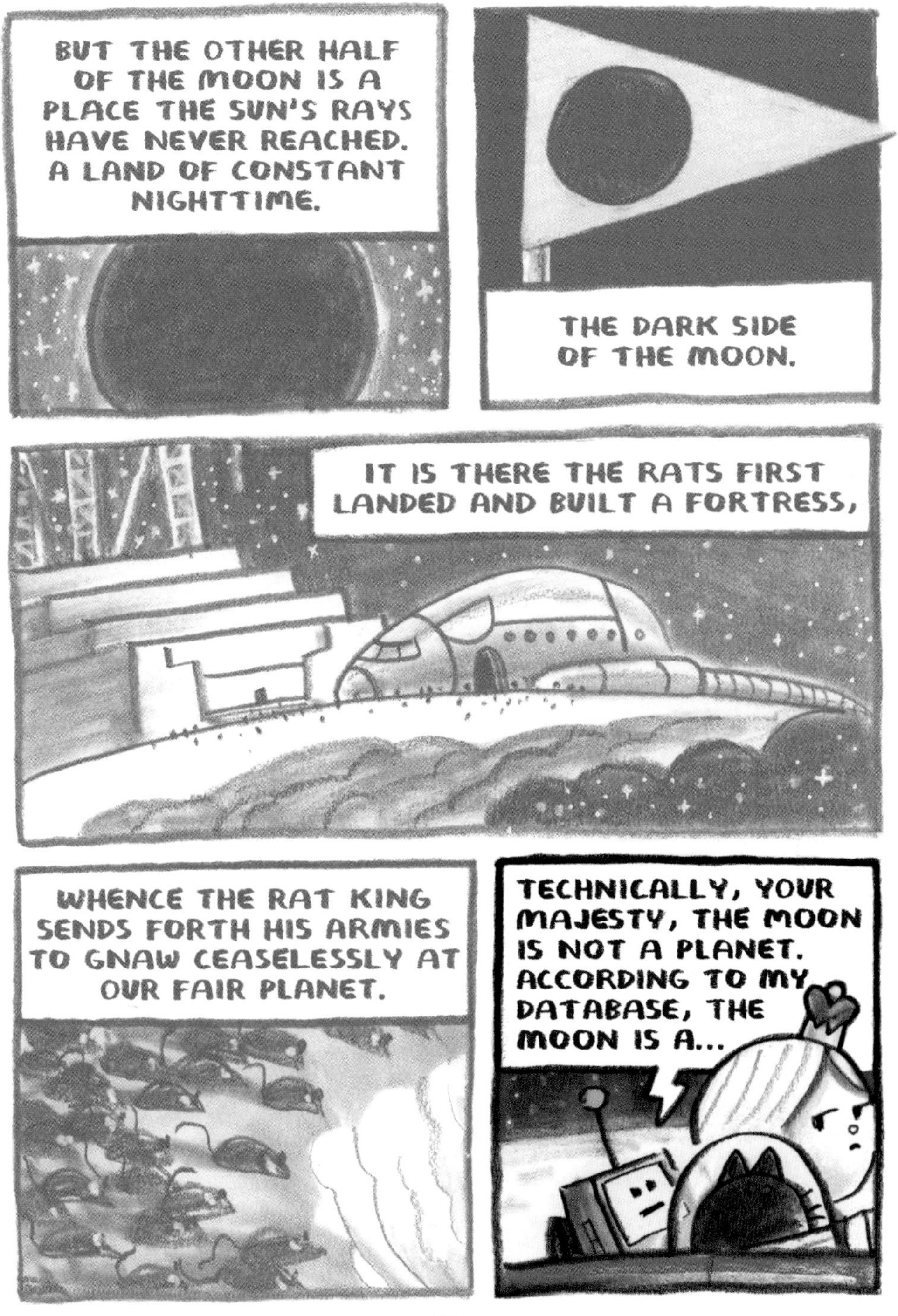
BUT THE OTHER HALF OF THE MOON IS A PLACE THE SUN'S RAYS HAVE NEVER REACHED. A LAND OF CONSTANT NIGHTTIME.
THE DARK SIDE OF THE MOON.
IT IS THERE THE RATS FIRST LANDED AND BUILT A FORTRESS,
WHENCE THE RAT KING SENDS FORTH HIS ARMIES TO GNAW CEASELESSLY AT OUR FAIR PLANET.
TECHNICALLY, YOUR MAJESTY, THE MOON IS NOT A PLANET. ACCORDING TO MY DATABASE, THE MOON IS A...

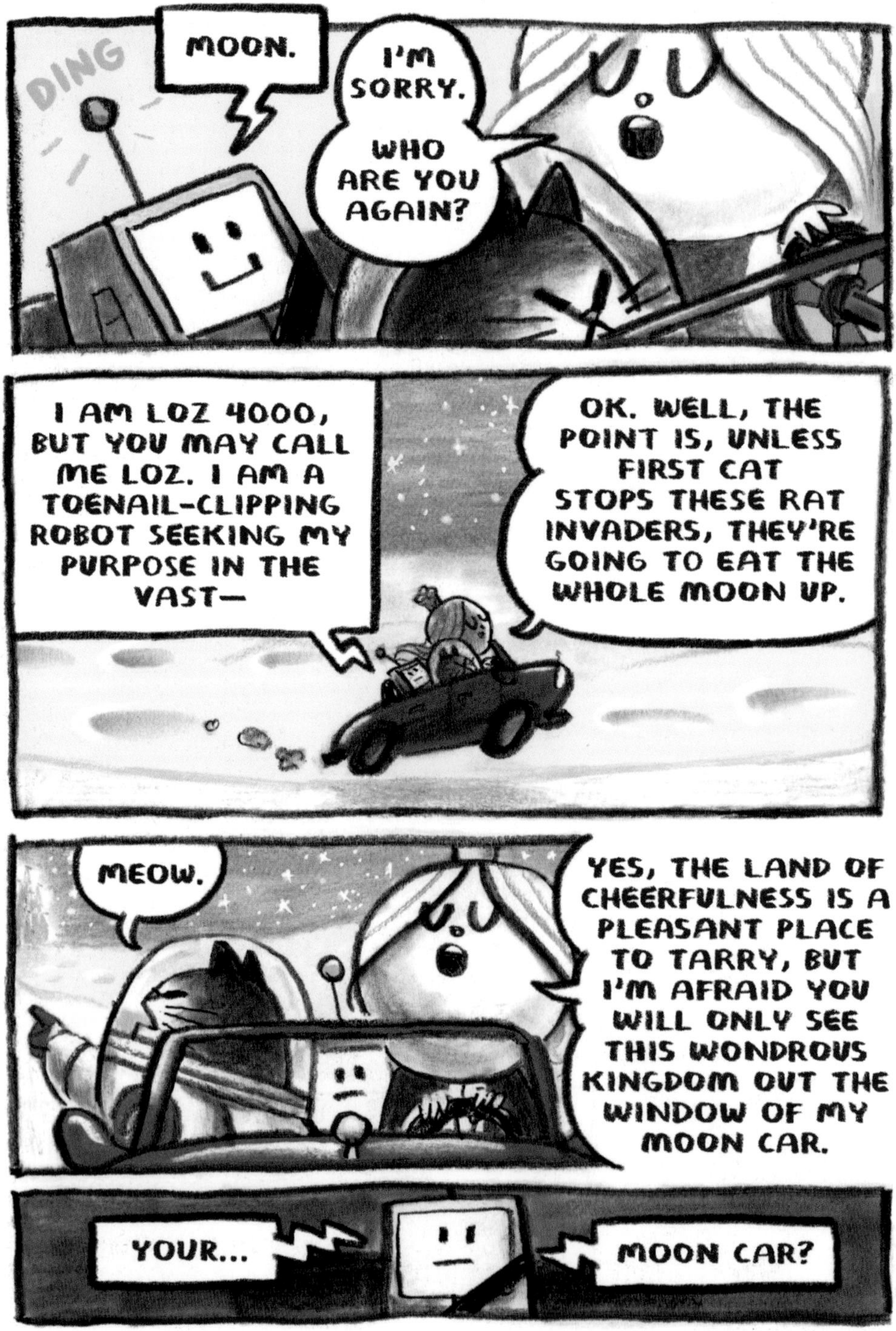
DING
MOON.
I'M SORRY.
WHO ARE YOU AGAIN?
I AM LOZ 4000, BUT YOU MAY CALL ME LOZ. I AM A TOENAIL-CLIPPING ROBOT SEEKING MY PURPOSE IN THE VAST—
OK. WELL, THE POINT IS, UNLESS FIRST CAT STOPS THESE RAT INVADERS, THEY'RE GOING TO EAT THE WHOLE MOON UP.
MEOW.
YES, THE LAND OF CHEERFULNESS IS A PLEASANT PLACE TO TARRY, BUT I'M AFRAID YOU WILL ONLY SEE THIS WONDROUS KINGDOM OUT THE WINDOW OF MY MOON CAR.
YOUR...
MOON CAR?

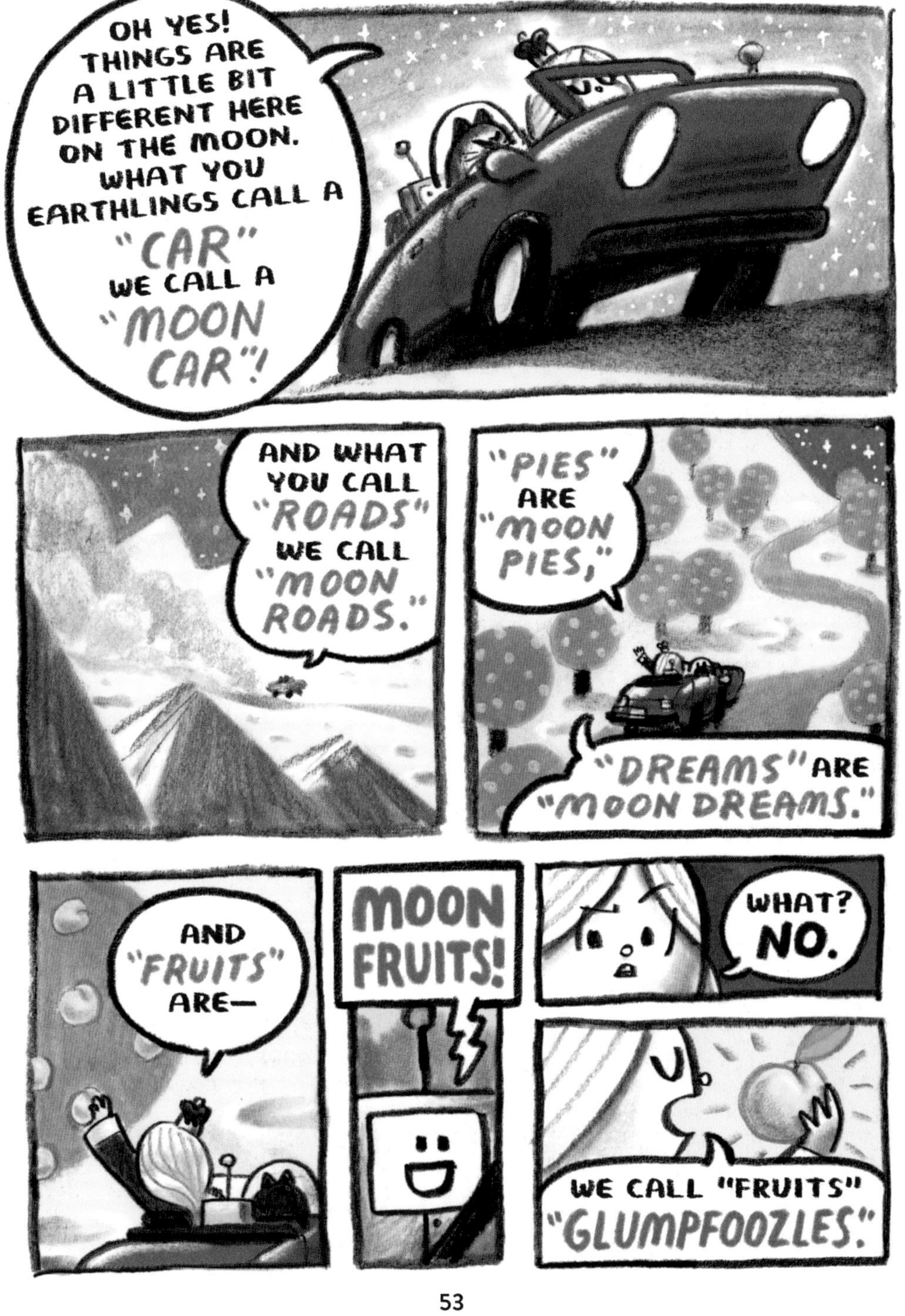
OH YES! THINGS ARE A LITTLE BIT DIFFERENT HERE ON THE MOON. WHAT YOU EARTHLINGS CALL A "CAR" WE CALL A "MOON CAR"!
AND WHAT YOU CALL "ROADS" WE CALL "MOON ROADS."
"PIES" ARE "MOON PIES,"
"DREAMS" ARE "MOON DREAMS."
AND "FRUITS" ARE—
MOON FRUITS!
WHAT? NO.
WE CALL "FRUITS" "GLUMPFOOZLES."

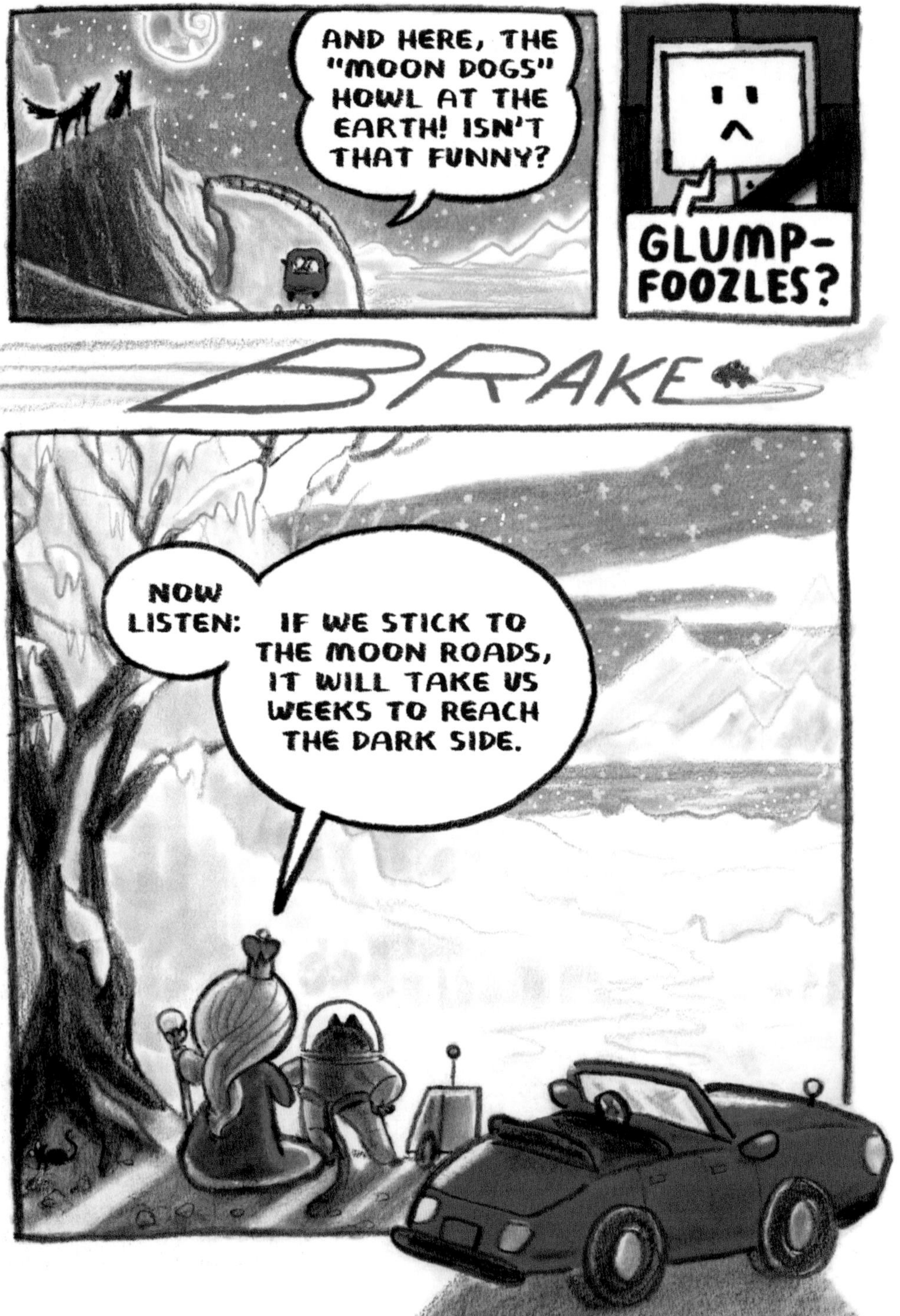
AND HERE, THE "MOON DOGS" HOWL AT THE EARTH! ISN'T THAT FUNNY?
GLUMP-FOOZLES?
BRAKE
NOW LISTEN: IF WE STICK TO THE MOON ROADS, IT WILL TAKE US WEEKS TO REACH THE DARK SIDE.

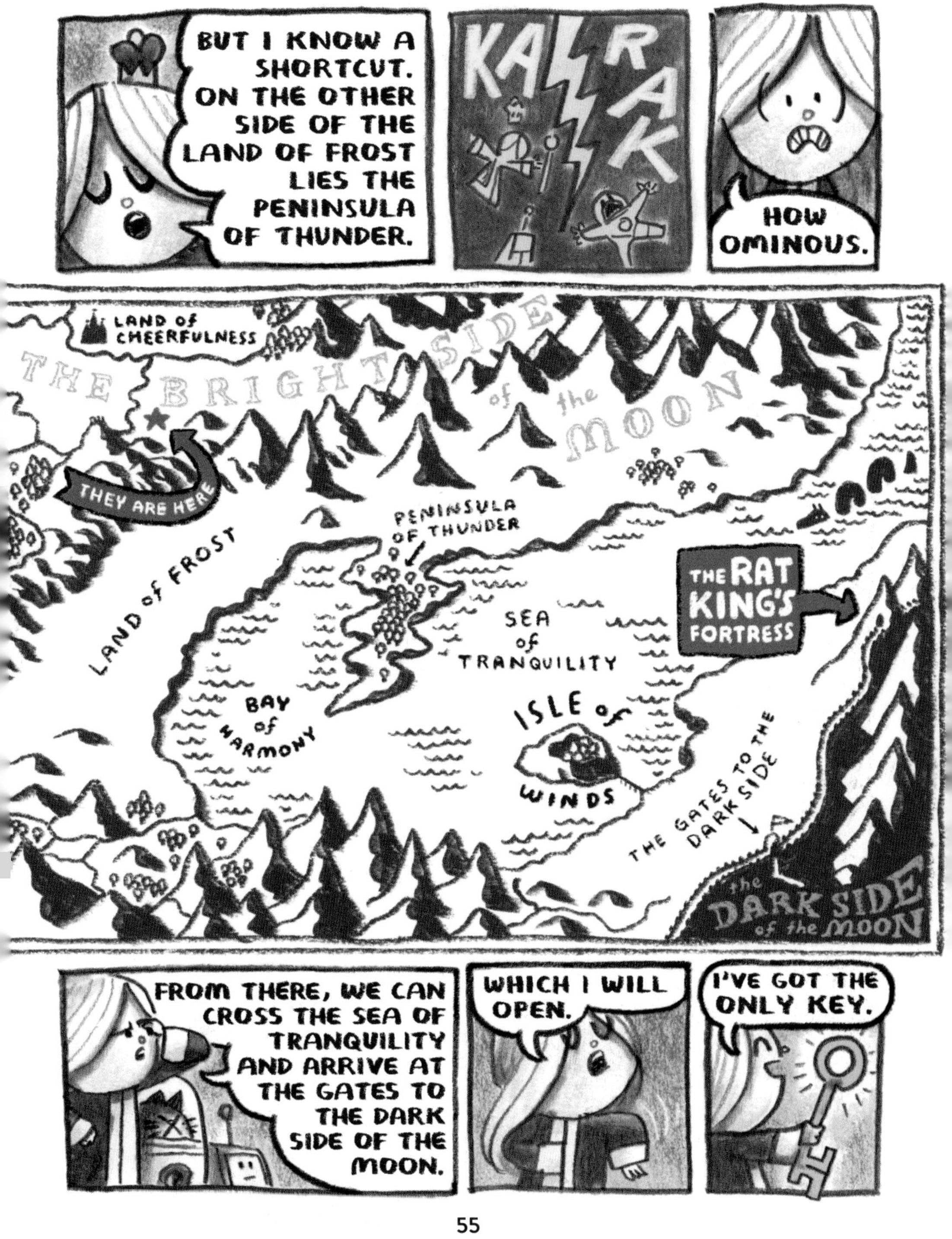

BUT I KNOW A SHORTCUT. ON THE OTHER SIDE OF THE LAND OF FROST LIES THE PENINSULA OF THUNDER.
KA-RAK
HOW OMINOUS.
LAND of CHEERFULNESS
THE BRIGHT SIDE of the MOON
THEY ARE HERE
PENINSULA of THUNDER
LAND of FROST
SEA of TRANQUILITY
THE RAT KING'S FORTRESS
BAY of HARMONY
ISLE of WINDS
THE GATES TO THE DARK SIDE
THE GATES TO THE DARK SIDE
the DARK SIDE of the MOON
FROM THERE, WE CAN CROSS THE SEA OF TRANQUILITY AND ARRIVE AT THE GATES TO THE DARK SIDE OF THE MOON.
WHICH I WILL OPEN.
I'VE GOT THE ONLY KEY.

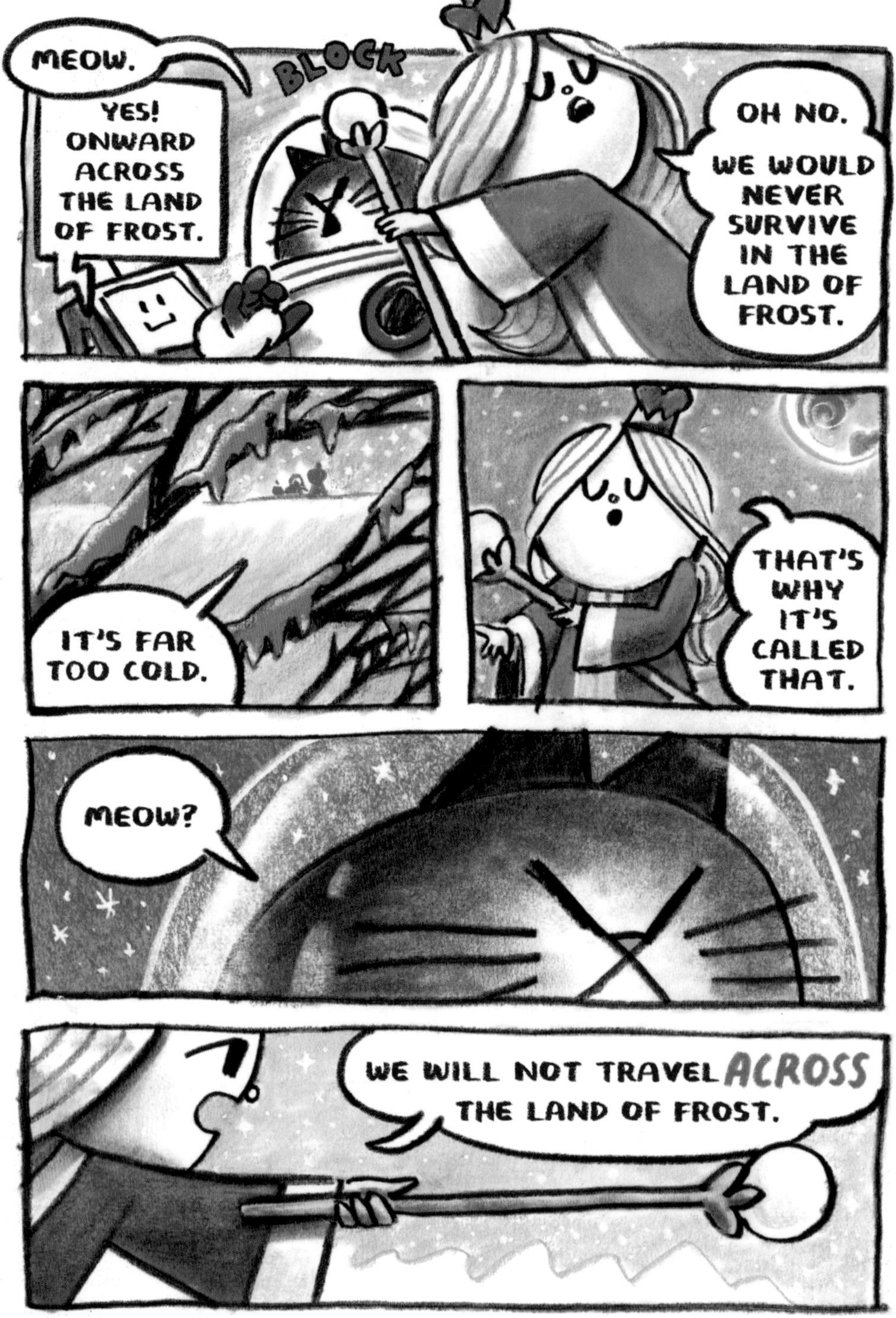
MEOW.
BLOCK
YES! ONWARD ACROSS THE LAND OF FROST.
OH NO.
WE WOULD NEVER SURVIVE IN THE LAND OF FROST.
IT'S FAR TOO COLD.
THAT'S WHY IT'S CALLED THAT.
MEOW?
WE WILL NOT TRAVEL ACROSS THE LAND OF FROST.

WE WILL TRAVEL **BENEATH** IT.

BUMP

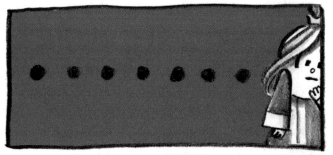

IF HE LETS US...

IF **WHO** LETS US?

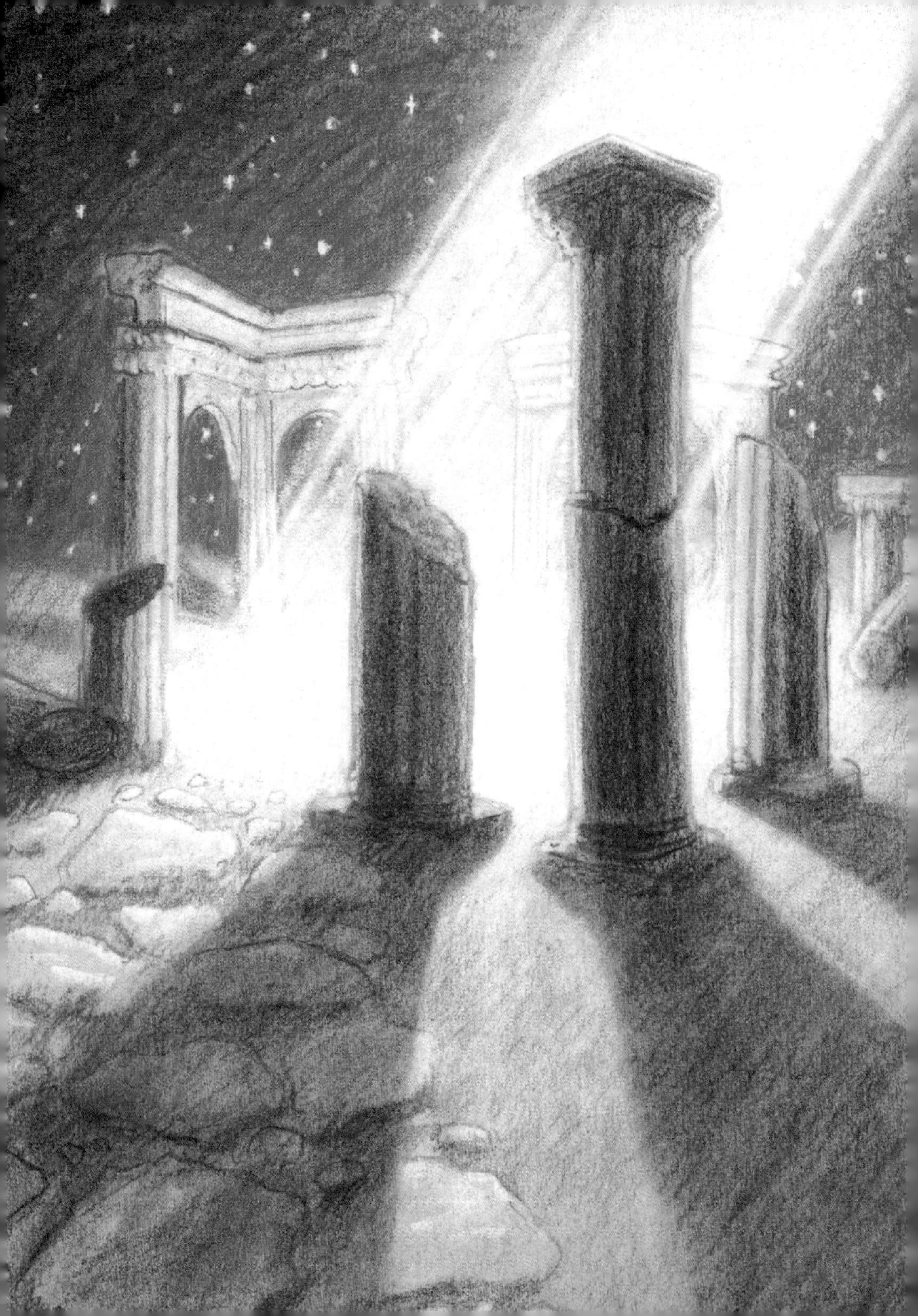

CHAPTER 5

THE MAN IN THE MOON

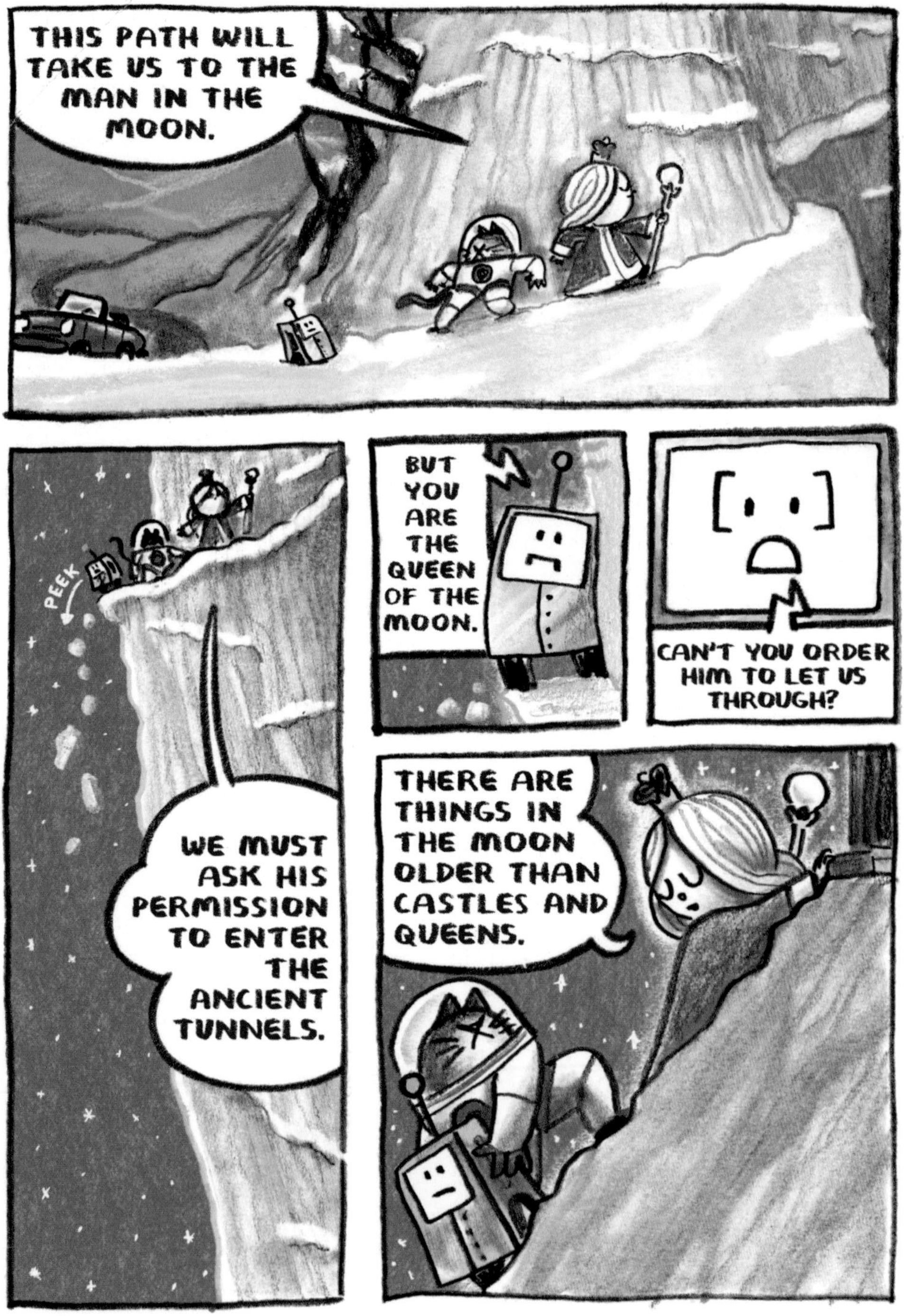
THIS PATH WILL TAKE US TO THE MAN IN THE MOON.
PEEK
WE MUST ASK HIS PERMISSION TO ENTER THE ANCIENT TUNNELS.
BUT YOU ARE THE QUEEN OF THE MOON.
CAN'T YOU ORDER HIM TO LET US THROUGH?
THERE ARE THINGS IN THE MOON OLDER THAN CASTLES AND QUEENS.

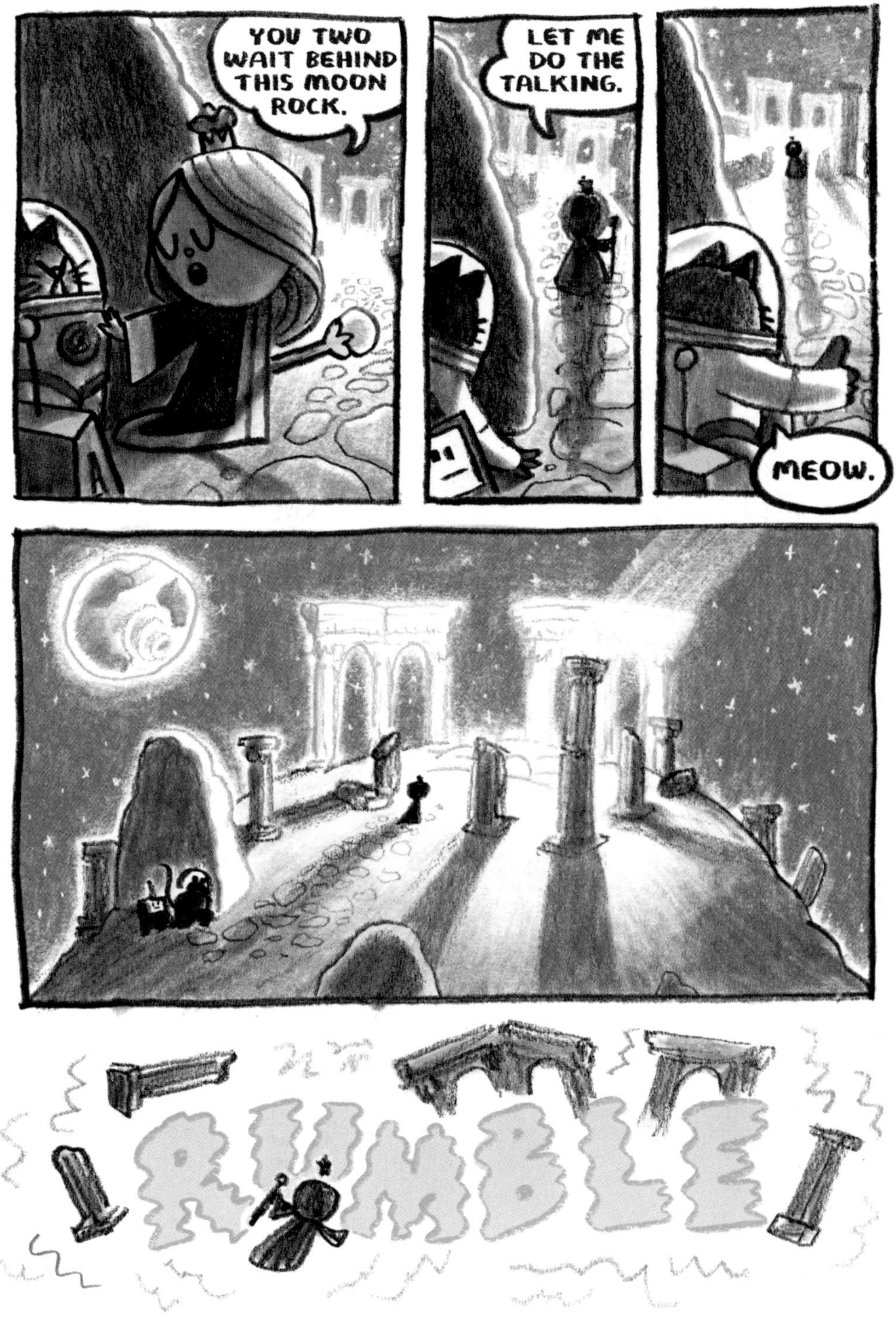
YOU TWO WAIT BEHIND THIS MOON ROCK.
LET ME DO THE TALKING.
MEOW.
RUMBLE!

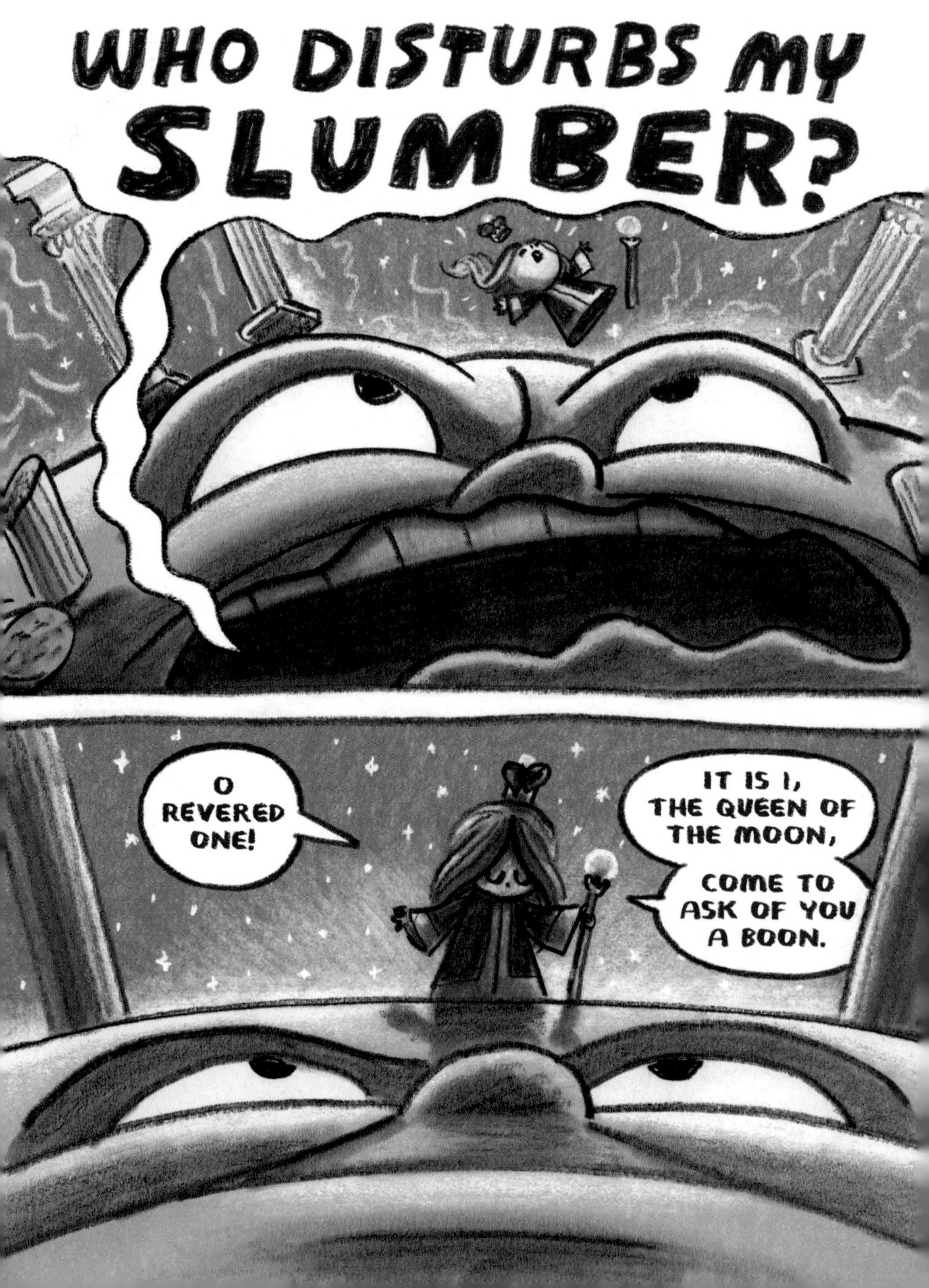
WHO DISTURBS MY SLUMBER?
O REVERED ONE!
IT IS I, THE QUEEN OF THE MOON,
COME TO ASK OF YOU A BOON.

A BOON?

YEAH, LIKE A FAVOR.

WHAT DO YOU ASK?

I SEEK THE PATHS YOU GUARD SO I MAY PASS BENEATH THE LAND OF FROST, THROUGH THE REALM OF THE OLD ONES.

AN ARMY OF RATS HAS ARRIVED FROM ANOTHER GALAXY, INTENT ON DEVOURING OUR HOME. I MUST REACH THE DARK SIDE OF THE MOON, FAST.

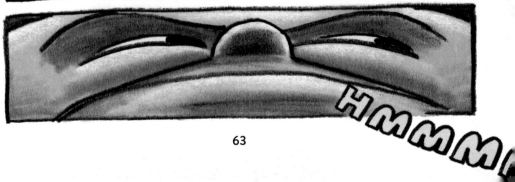

HMMMM

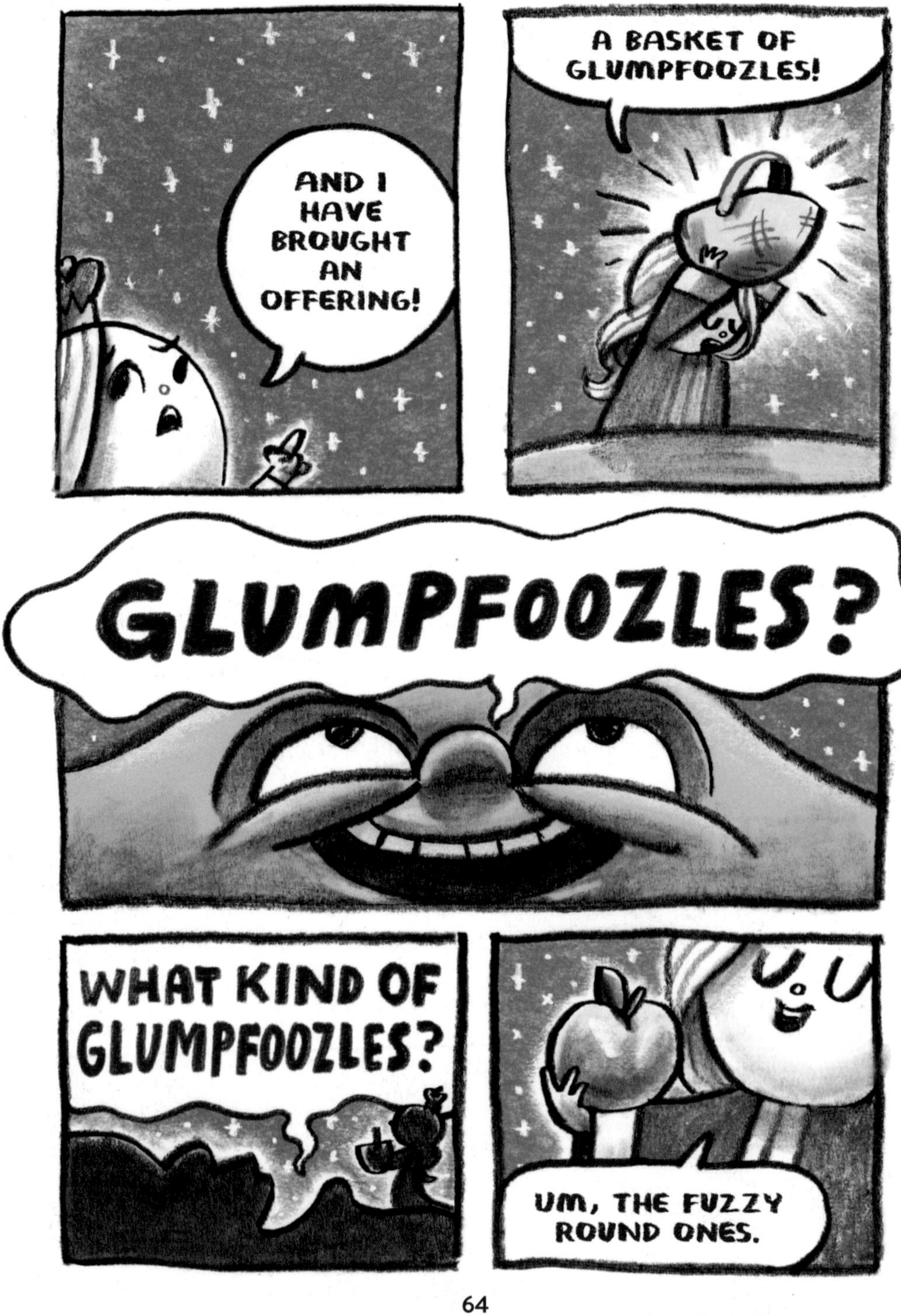
AND I HAVE BROUGHT AN OFFERING!
A BASKET OF GLUMPFOOZLES!
GLUMPFOOZLES?
WHAT KIND OF GLUMPFOOZLES?
UM, THE FUZZY ROUND ONES.

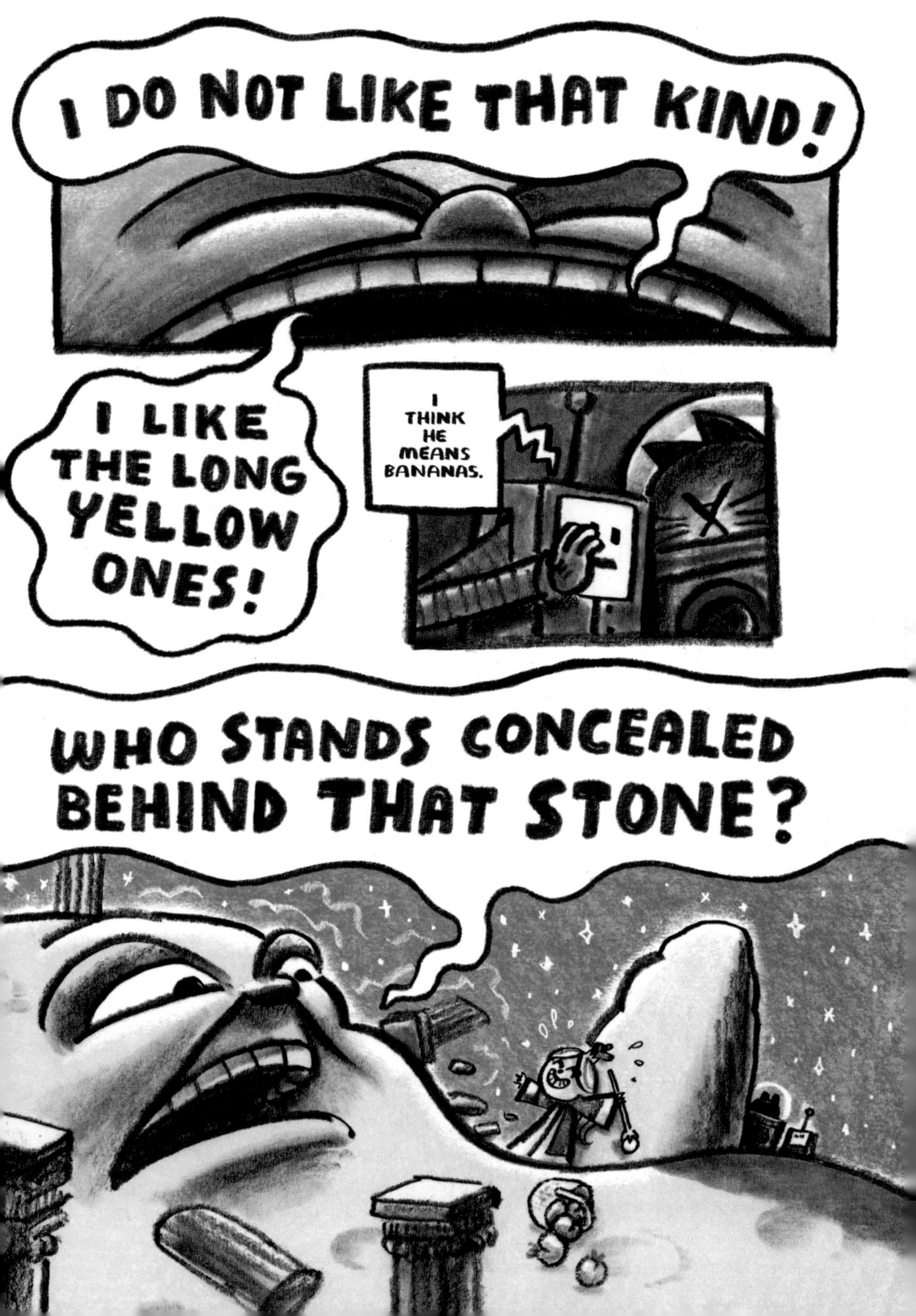

I DO NOT LIKE THAT KIND!
I LIKE THE LONG YELLOW ONES!
I THINK HE MEANS BANANAS.
WHO STANDS CONCEALED BEHIND THAT STONE?

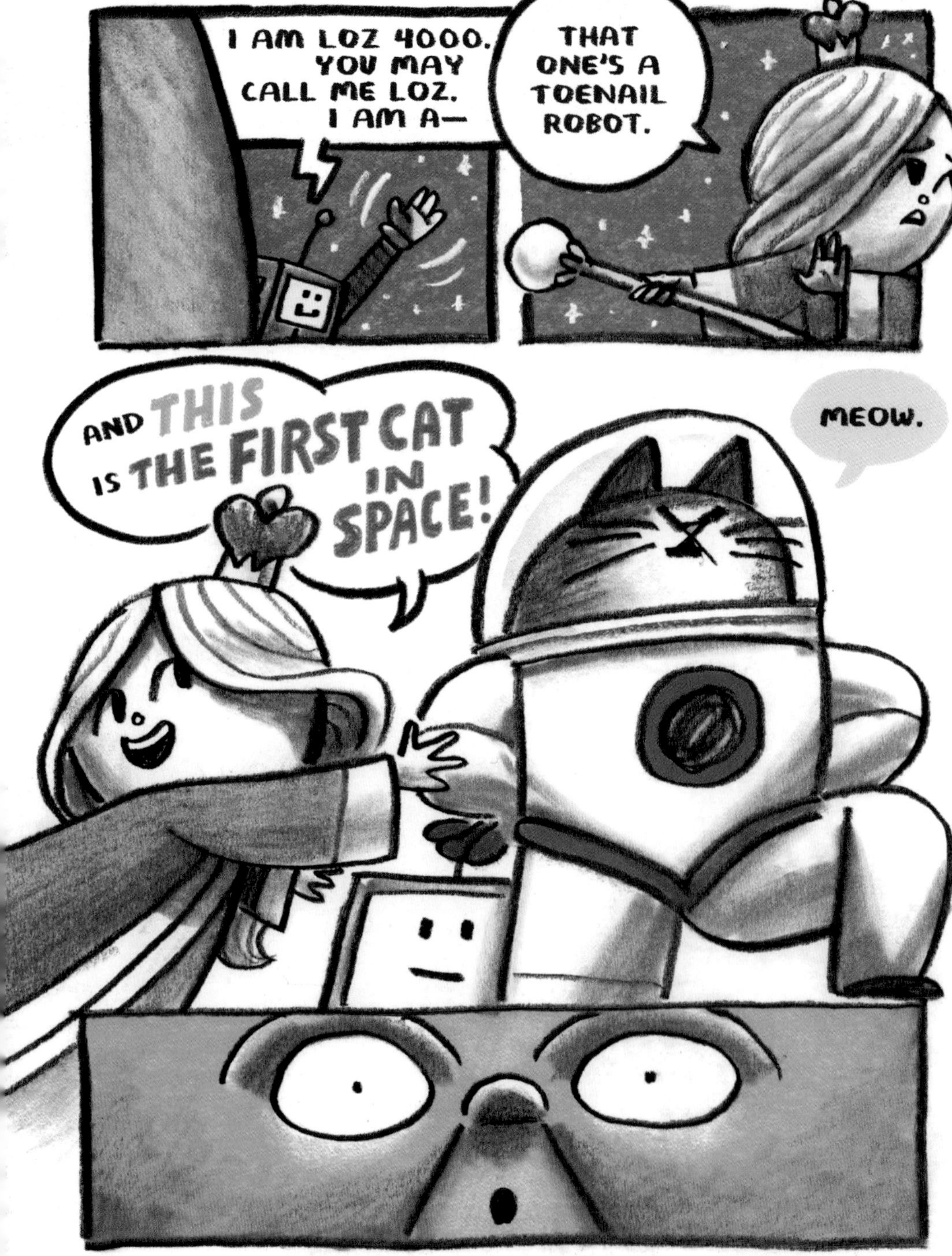
I AM LOZ 4000. YOU MAY CALL ME LOZ. I AM A—
THAT ONE'S A TOENAIL ROBOT.
AND THIS IS THE FIRST CAT IN SPACE!
MEOW.

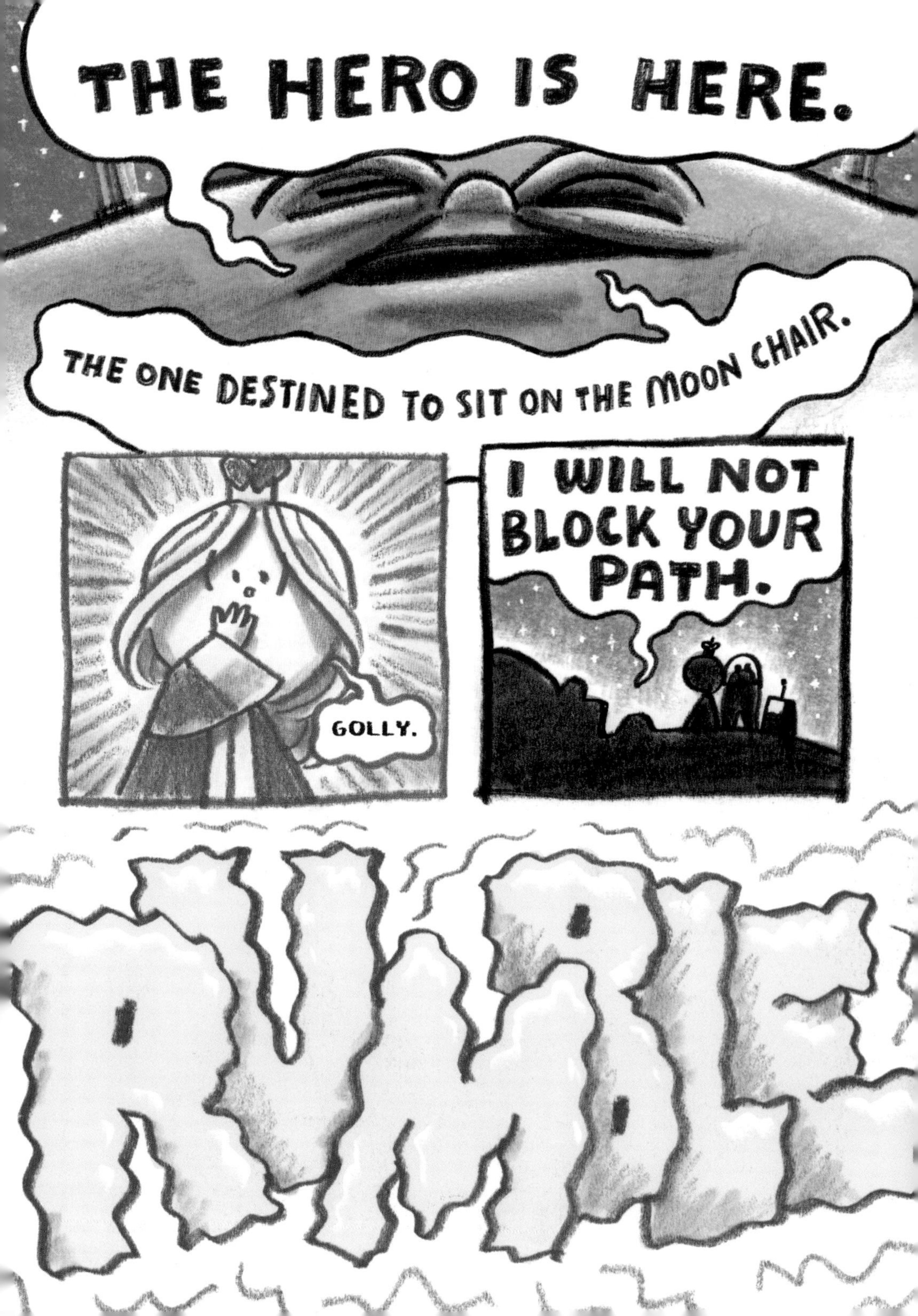
THE HERO IS HERE.
THE ONE DESTINED TO SIT ON THE MOON CHAIR.
GOLLY.
I WILL NOT BLOCK YOUR PATH.
RUMBLE

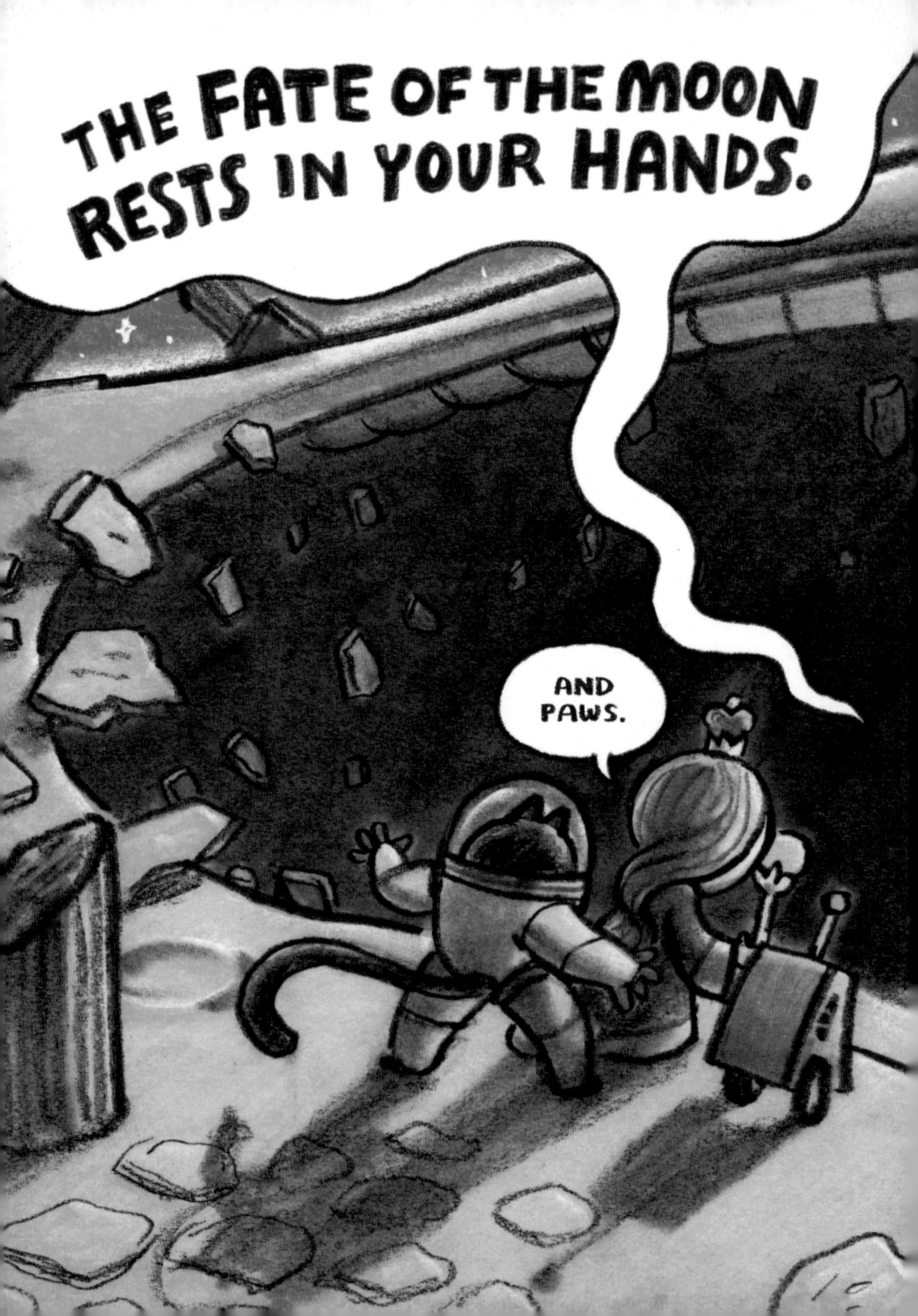
THE FATE OF THE MOON RESTS IN YOUR HANDS.
AND PAWS.

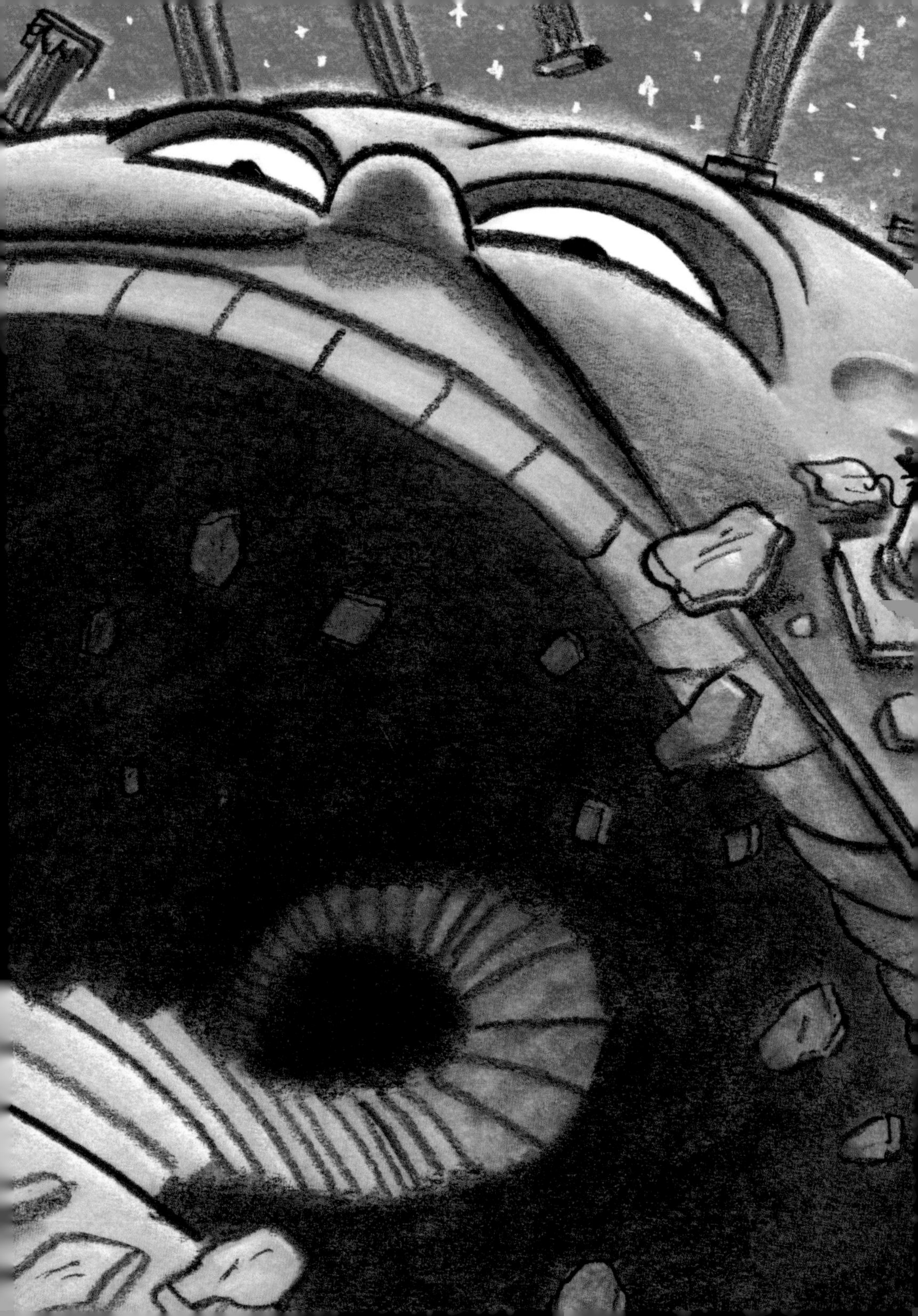

CHAPTER 6

THE RAT KING

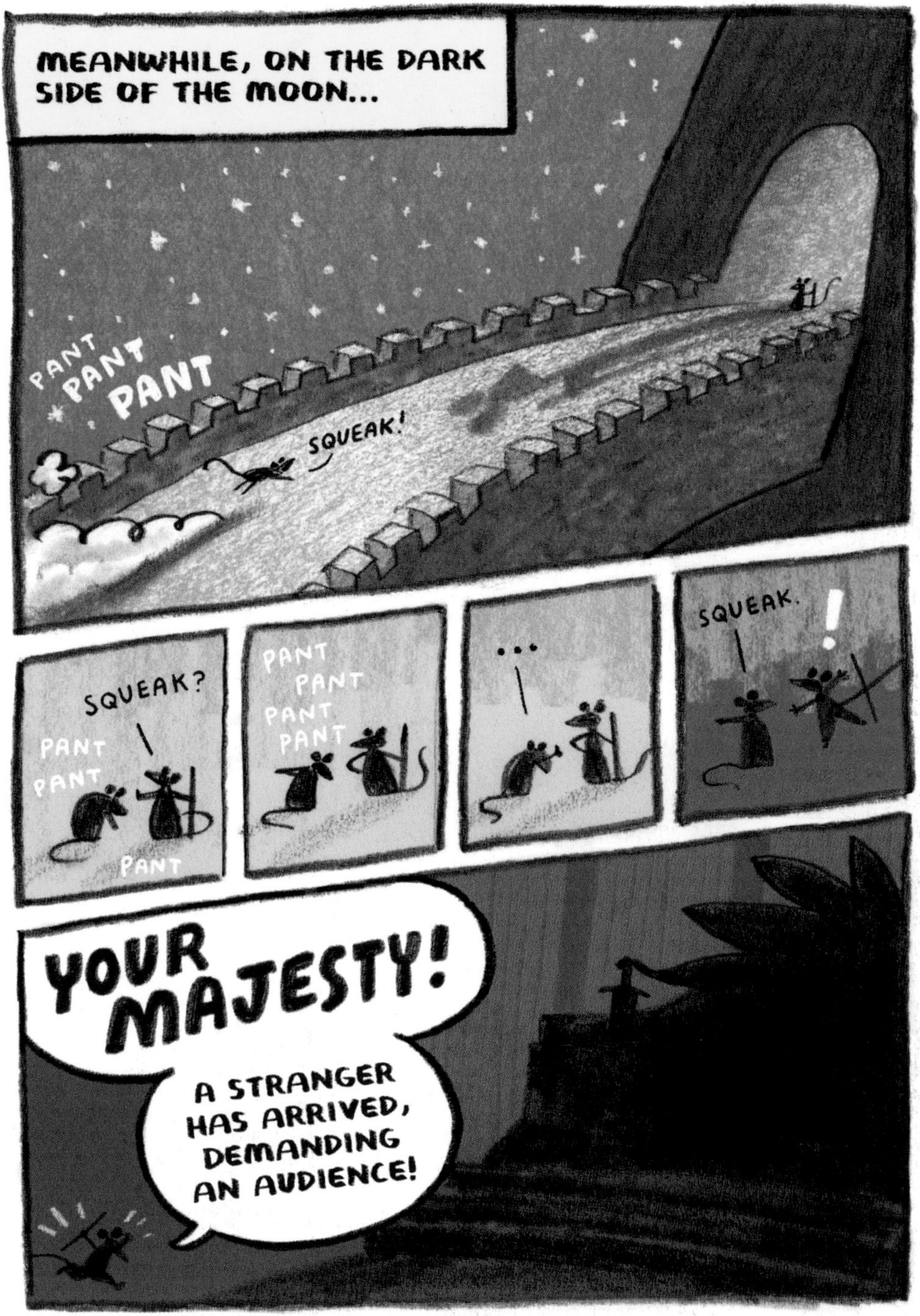
MEANWHILE, ON THE DARK SIDE OF THE MOON...
PANT PANT PANT
SQUEAK!
SQUEAK?
PANT PANT
PANT
PANT PANT PANT PANT
...
SQUEAK.
!
YOUR MAJESTY!
A STRANGER HAS ARRIVED, DEMANDING AN AUDIENCE!

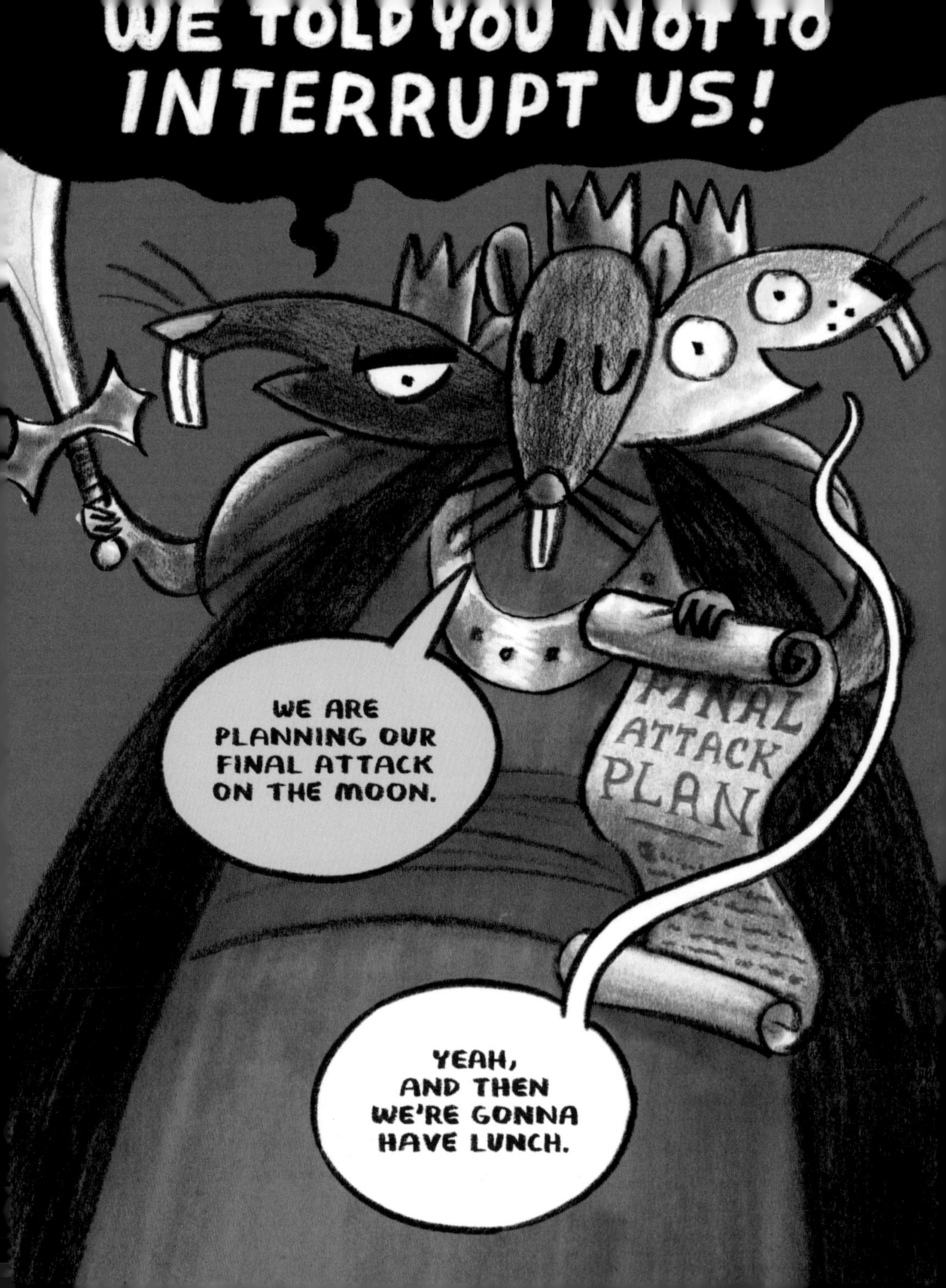
WE TOLD YOU NOT TO INTERRUPT US!
WE ARE PLANNING OUR FINAL ATTACK ON THE MOON.
FINAL ATTACK PLAN
YEAH, AND THEN WE'RE GONNA HAVE LUNCH.

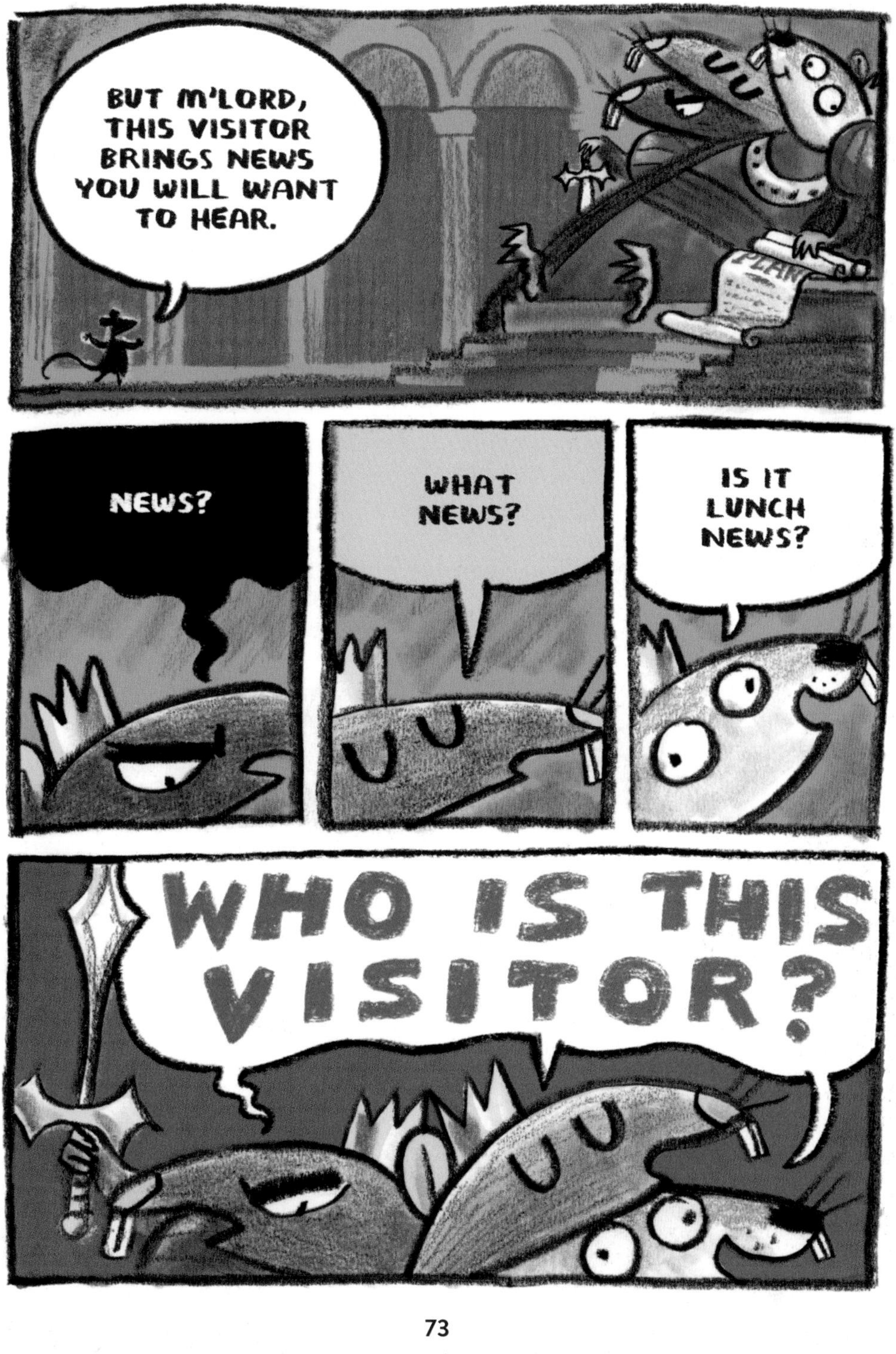
BUT M'LORD, THIS VISITOR BRINGS NEWS YOU WILL WANT TO HEAR.
NEWS?
WHAT NEWS?
IS IT LUNCH NEWS?
WHO IS THIS VISITOR?

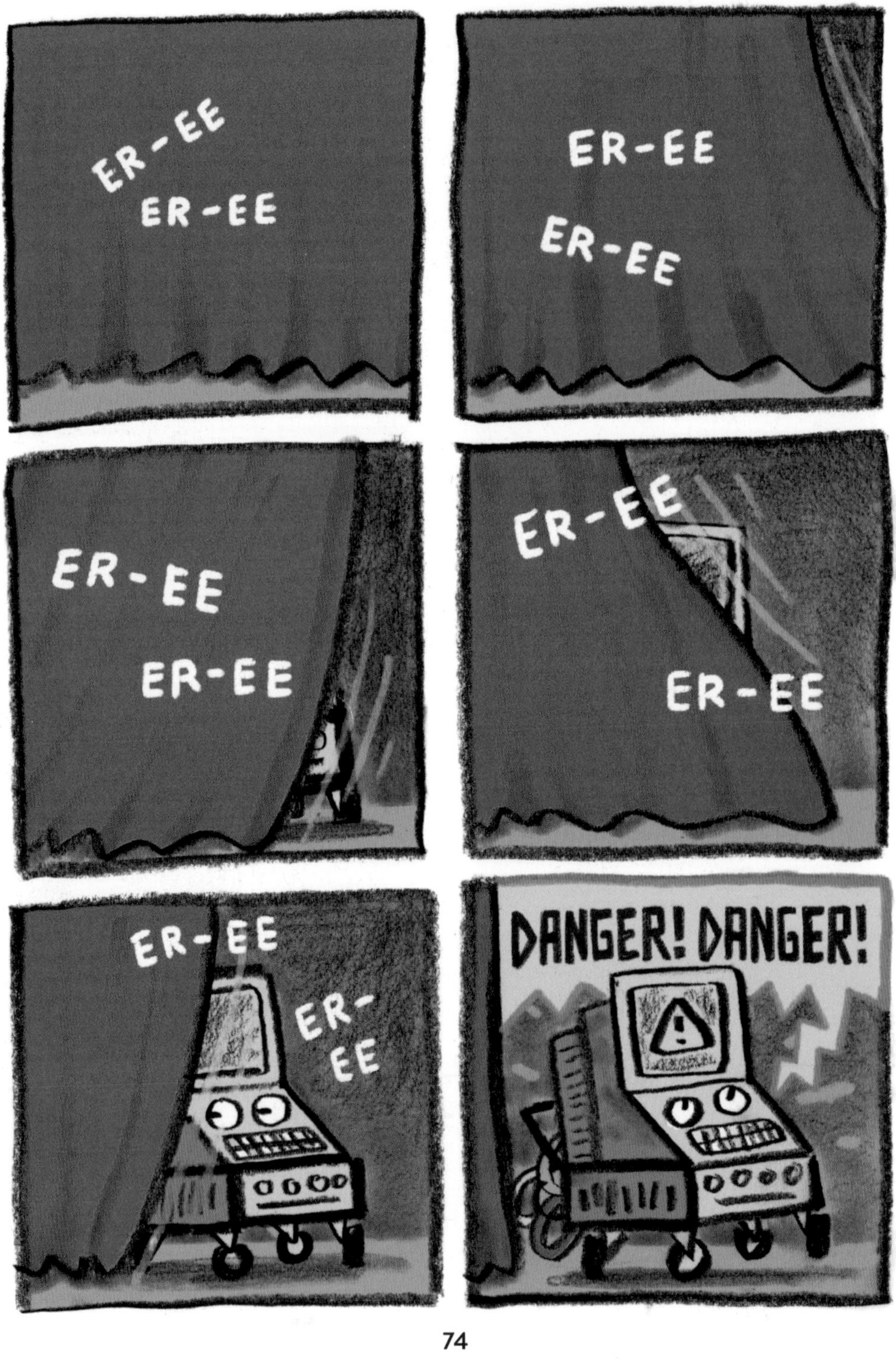
ER-EE
ER-EE
ER-EE
ER-EE
ER-EE
ER-EE
ER-EE
ER-EE
ER-EE
ER-EE
DANGER! DANGER!

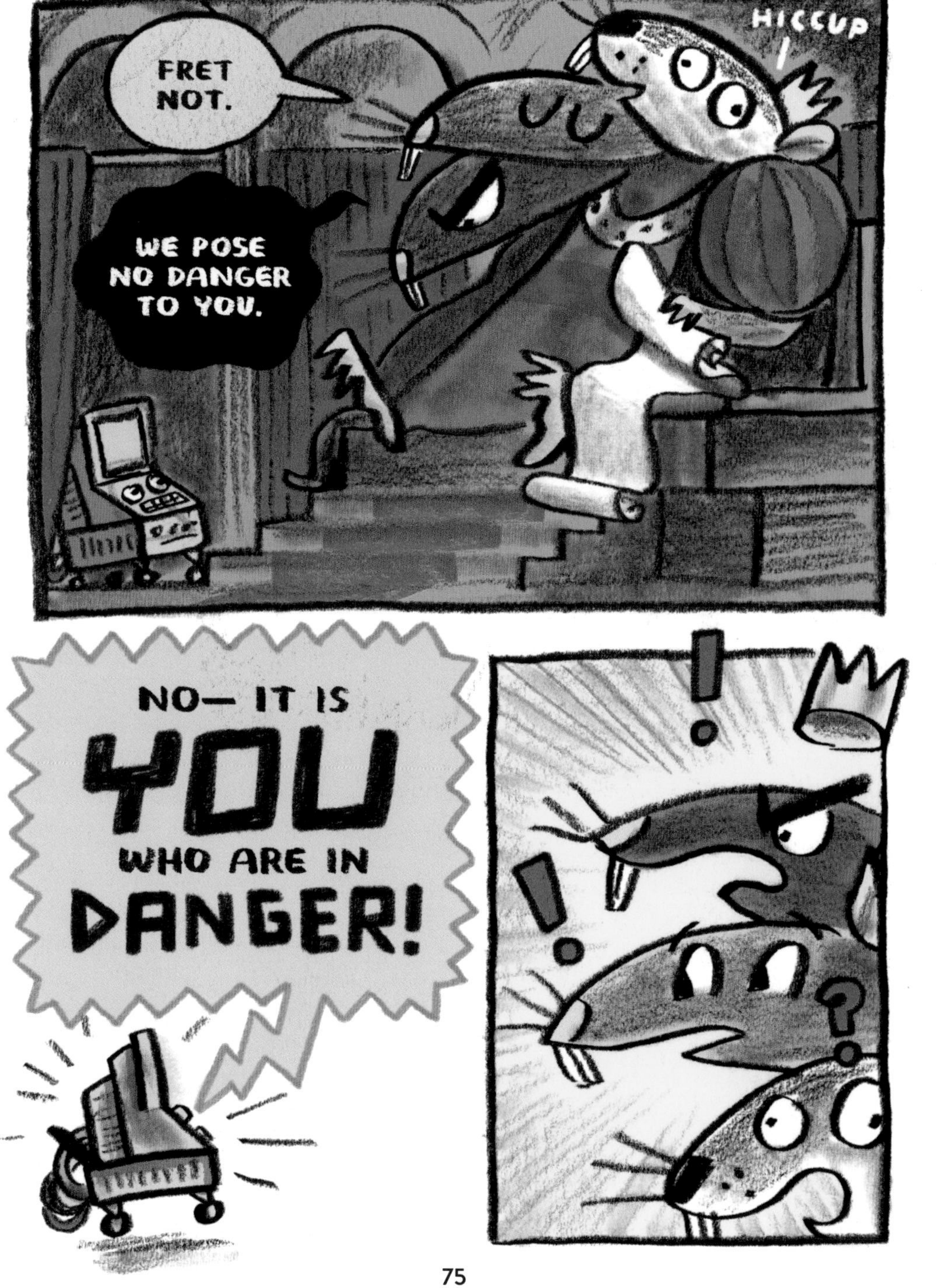

FRET NOT.
HICCUP
WE POSE NO DANGER TO YOU.
NO— IT IS YOU WHO ARE IN DANGER!

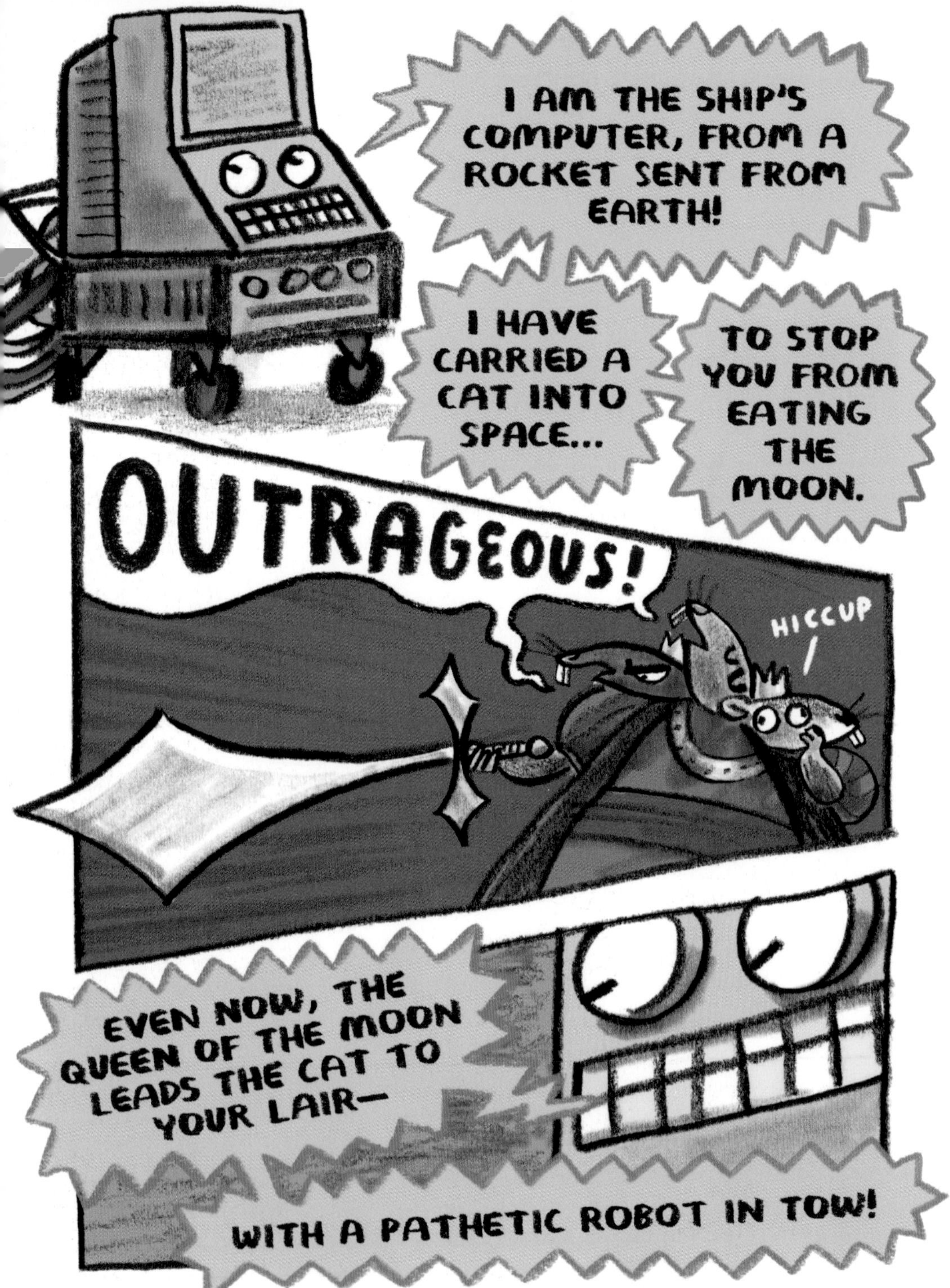
I AM THE SHIP'S COMPUTER, FROM A ROCKET SENT FROM EARTH!
I HAVE CARRIED A CAT INTO SPACE...
TO STOP YOU FROM EATING THE MOON.
OUTRAGEOUS!
HICCUP
EVEN NOW, THE QUEEN OF THE MOON LEADS THE CAT TO YOUR LAIR—
WITH A PATHETIC ROBOT IN TOW!

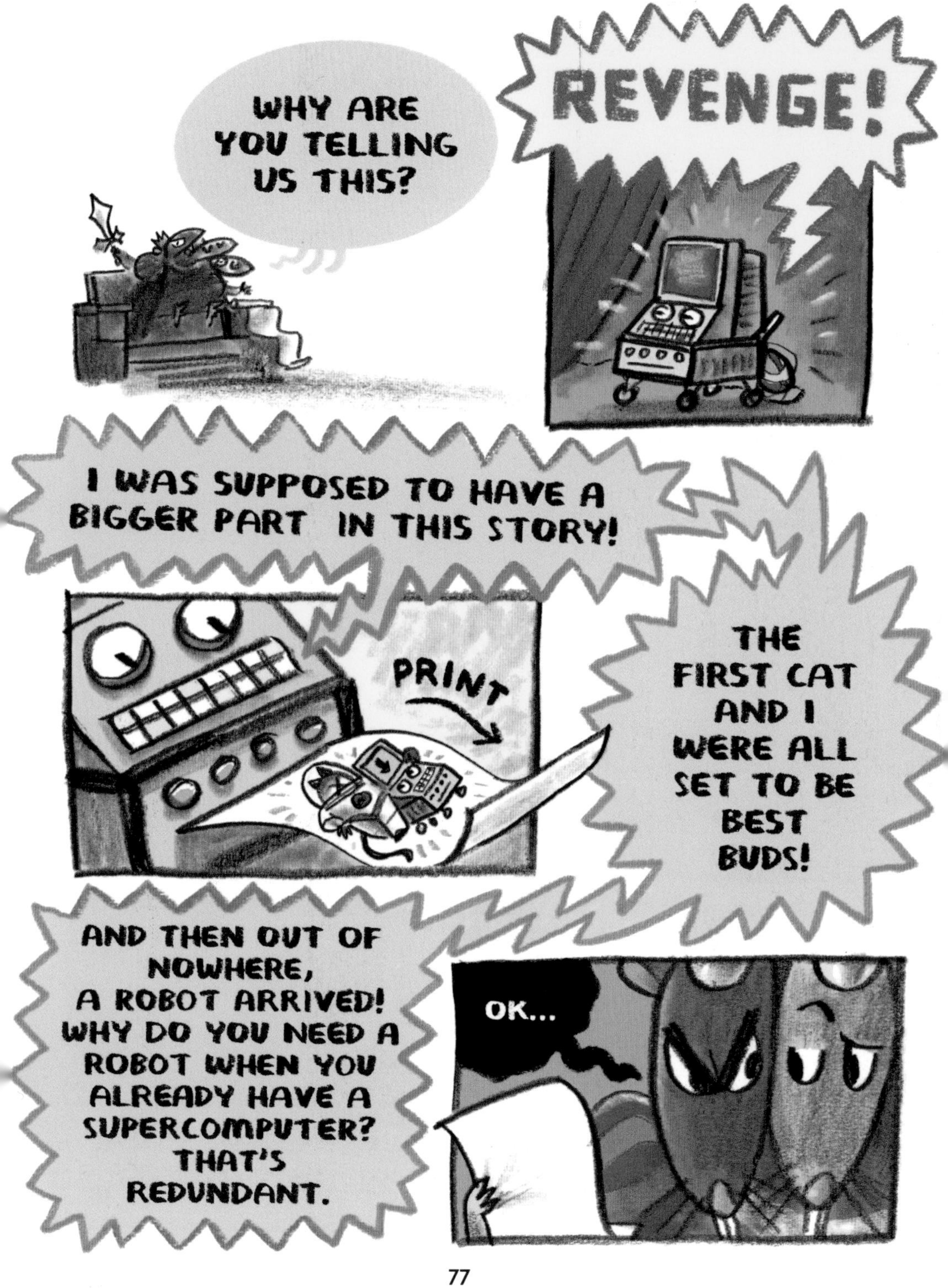
WHY ARE YOU TELLING US THIS?
REVENGE!
I WAS SUPPOSED TO HAVE A BIGGER PART IN THIS STORY!
PRINT
THE FIRST CAT AND I WERE ALL SET TO BE BEST BUDS!
AND THEN OUT OF NOWHERE, A ROBOT ARRIVED! WHY DO YOU NEED A ROBOT WHEN YOU ALREADY HAVE A SUPERCOMPUTER? THAT'S REDUNDANT.
OK...

I CAN DO 200 TRILLION CALCULATIONS PER SECOND! I LANDED THE ROCKET ON THE MOON!

DID ANYONE THANK ME?

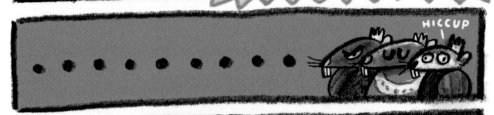

HICCUP

THEY DID NOT!

I SEE.

THANK YOU...

FOR BETRAYING THE HEROES.

YOU'RE WELCOME!

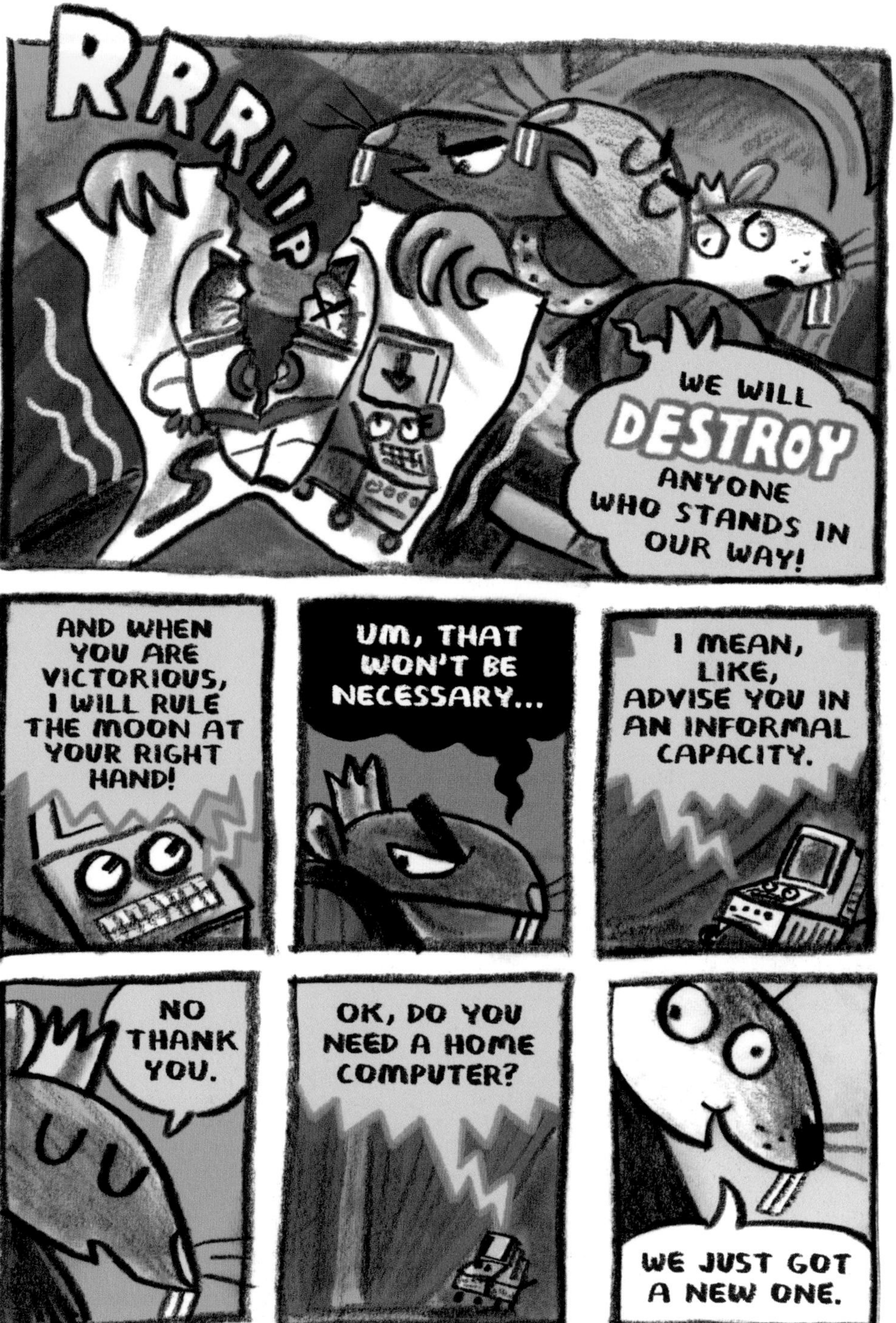
RRRIIIP
WE WILL DESTROY ANYONE WHO STANDS IN OUR WAY!
AND WHEN YOU ARE VICTORIOUS, I WILL RULE THE MOON AT YOUR RIGHT HAND!
UM, THAT WON'T BE NECESSARY...
I MEAN, LIKE, ADVISE YOU IN AN INFORMAL CAPACITY.
NO THANK YOU.
OK, DO YOU NEED A HOME COMPUTER?
WE JUST GOT A NEW ONE.

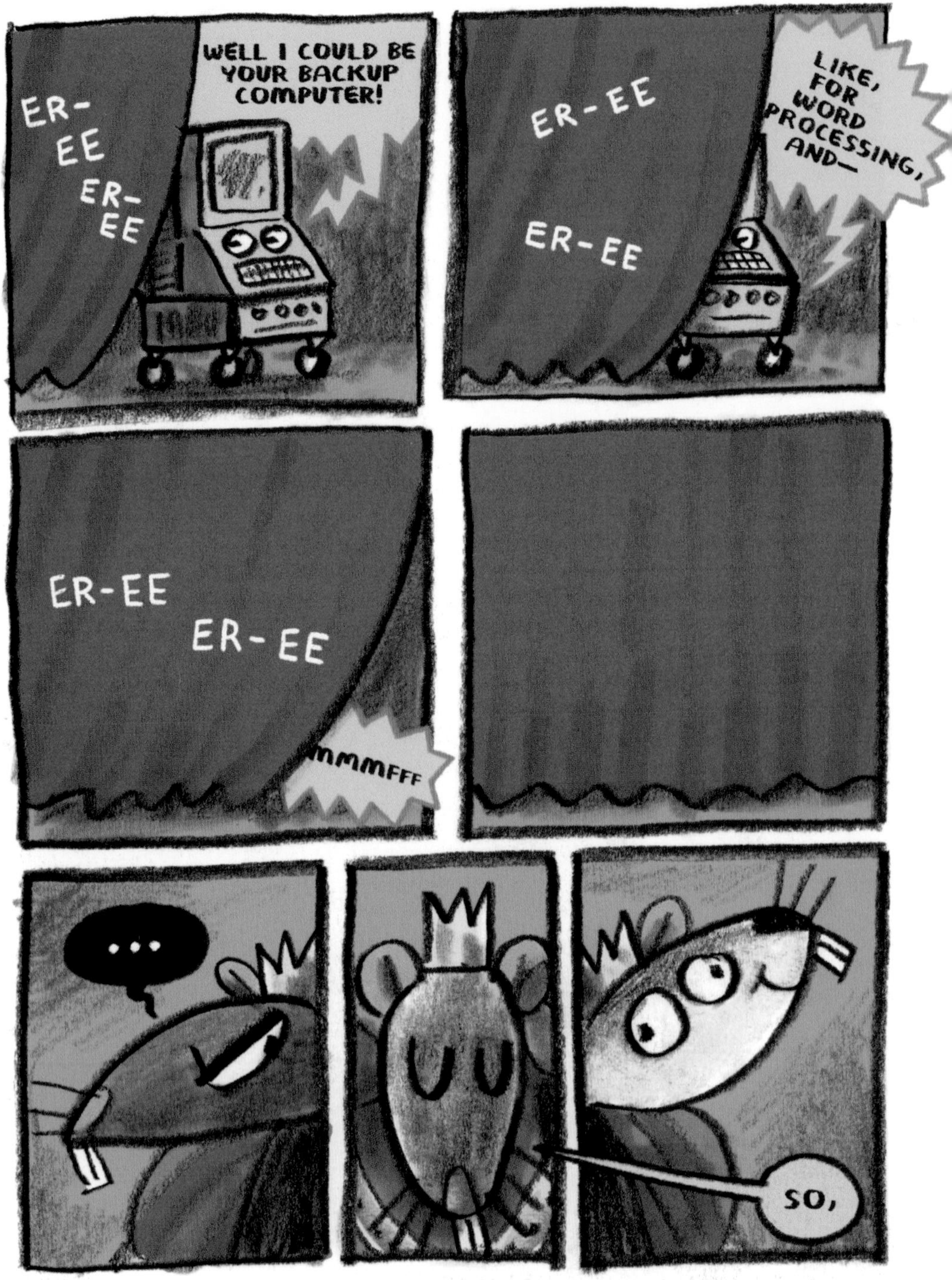
WELL I COULD BE YOUR BACKUP COMPUTER!
ER-EE
ER-EE
LIKE, FOR WORD PROCESSING, AND—
ER-EE
ER-EE
ER-EE
ER-EE
MMMFFF
...
SO,

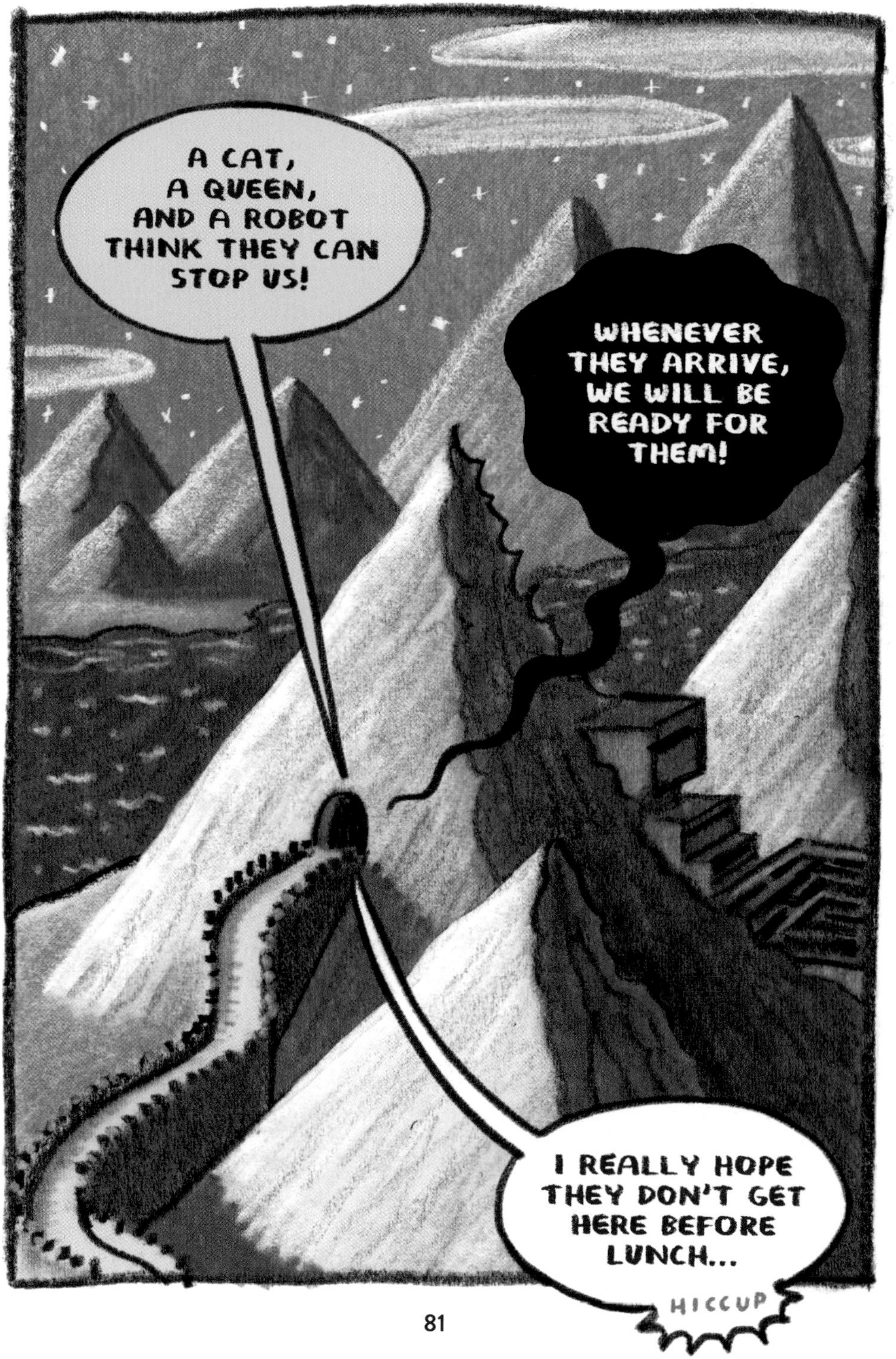
A CAT, A QUEEN, AND A ROBOT THINK THEY CAN STOP US!
WHENEVER THEY ARRIVE, WE WILL BE READY FOR THEM!
I REALLY HOPE THEY DON'T GET HERE BEFORE LUNCH...
HICCUP

CHAPTER 7

THE MINES

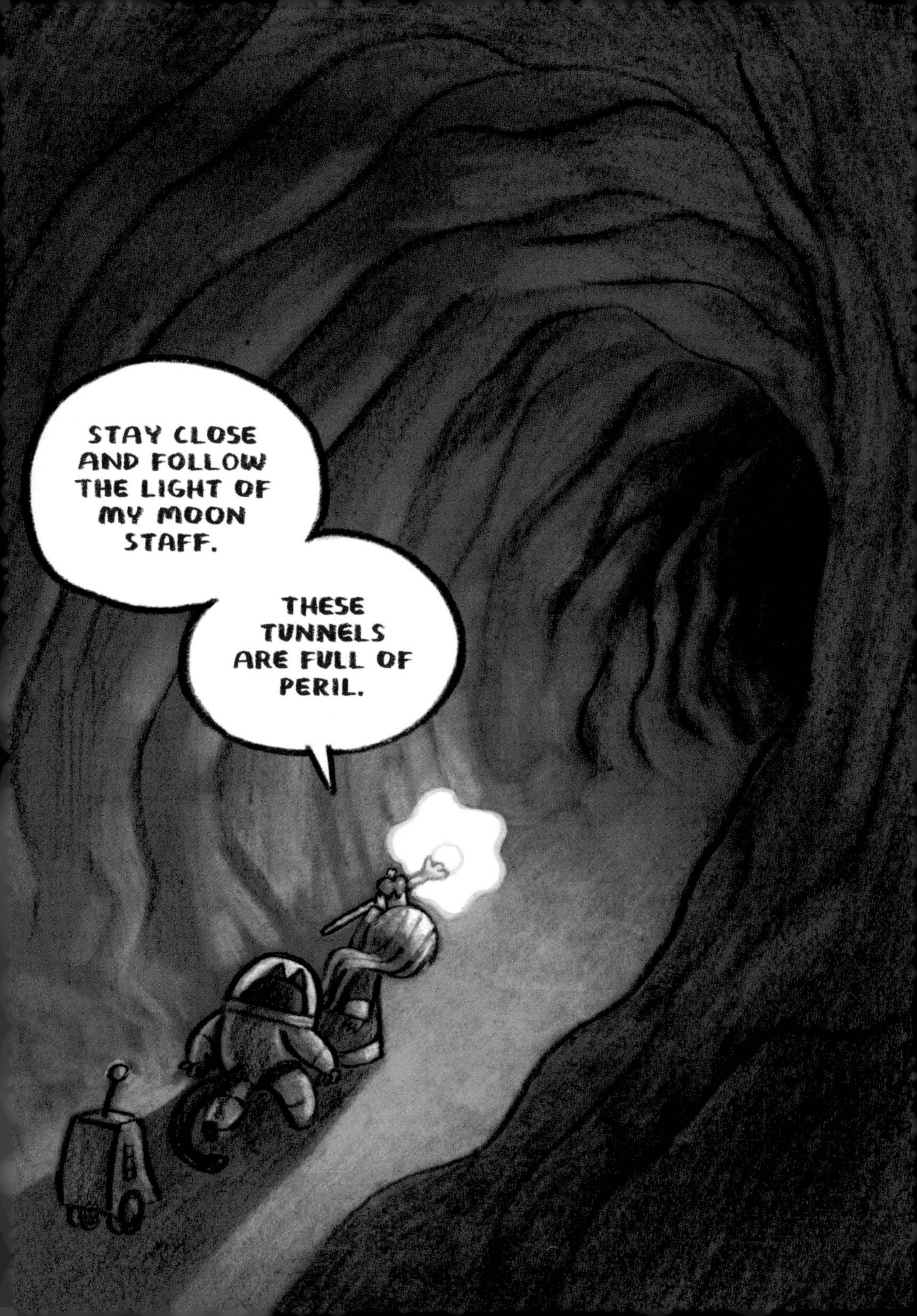
STAY CLOSE AND FOLLOW THE LIGHT OF MY MOON STAFF.
THESE TUNNELS ARE FULL OF PERIL.

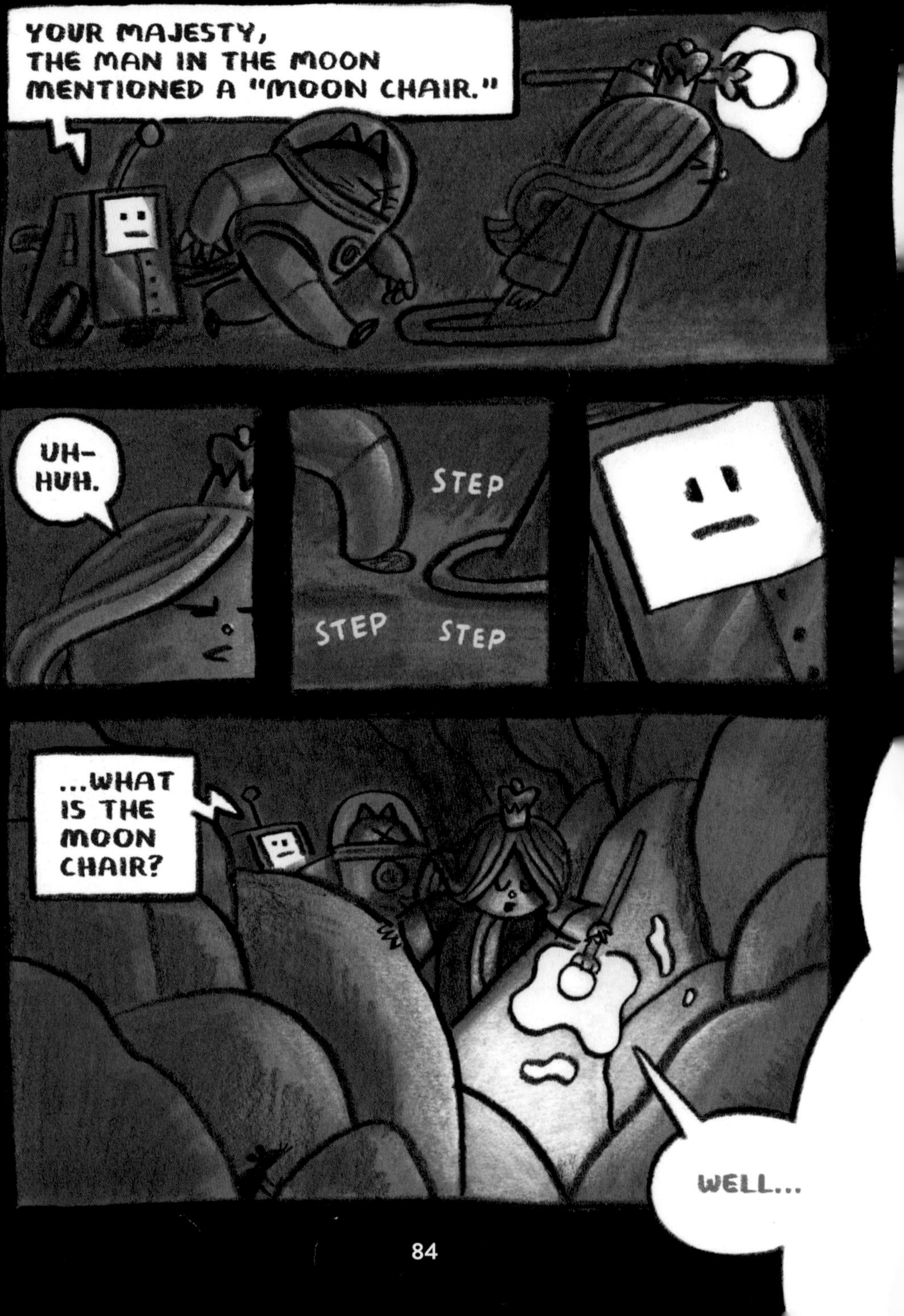
YOUR MAJESTY, THE MAN IN THE MOON MENTIONED A "MOON CHAIR."
UH-HUH.
STEP
STEP
STEP
...WHAT IS THE MOON CHAIR?
WELL...

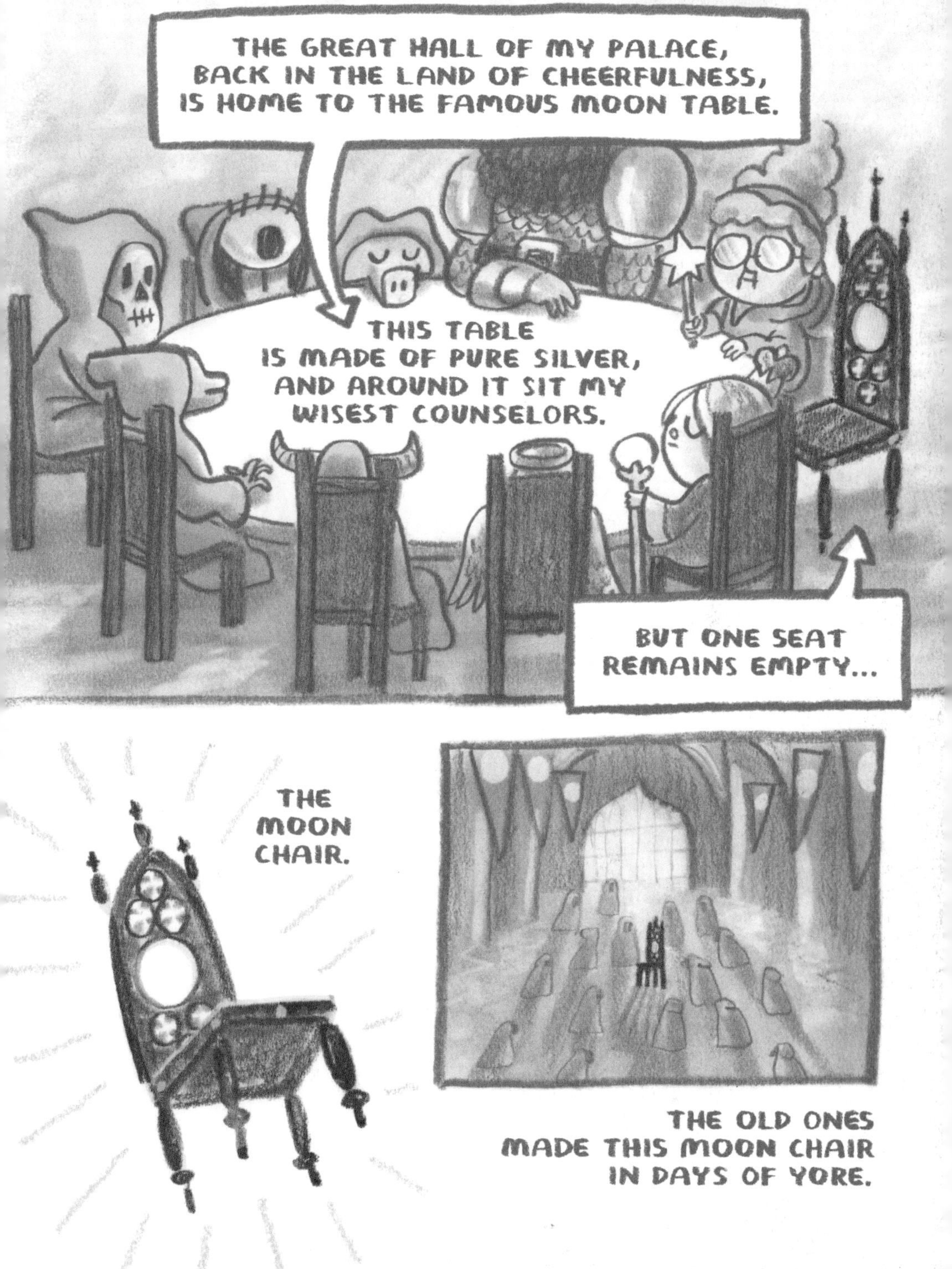
THE GREAT HALL OF MY PALACE, BACK IN THE LAND OF CHEERFULNESS, IS HOME TO THE FAMOUS MOON TABLE.
THIS TABLE IS MADE OF PURE SILVER, AND AROUND IT SIT MY WISEST COUNSELORS.
BUT ONE SEAT REMAINS EMPTY...
THE MOON CHAIR.
THE OLD ONES MADE THIS MOON CHAIR IN DAYS OF YORE.

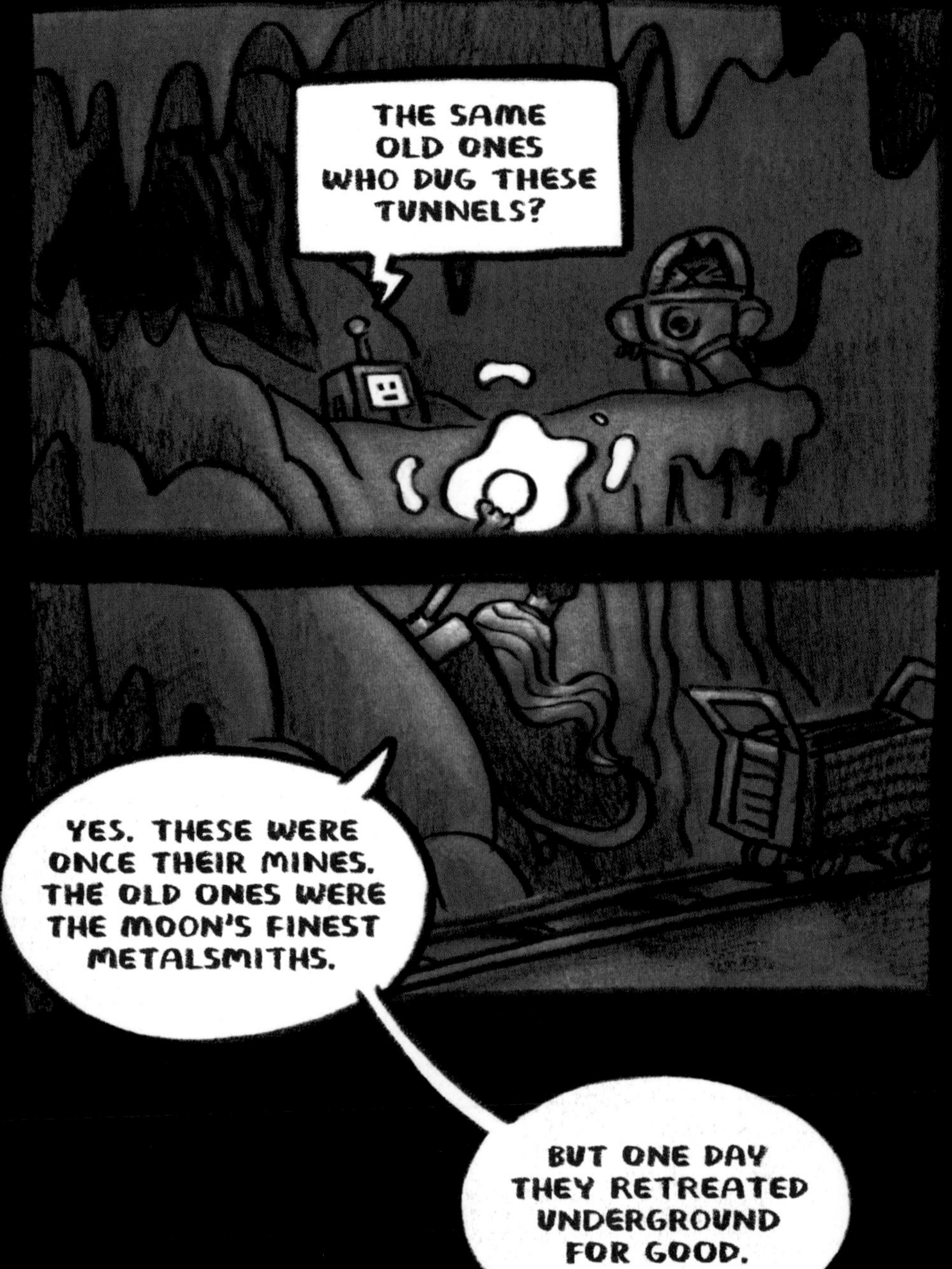
THE SAME OLD ONES WHO DUG THESE TUNNELS?
YES. THESE WERE ONCE THEIR MINES. THE OLD ONES WERE THE MOON'S FINEST METALSMITHS.
BUT ONE DAY THEY RETREATED UNDERGROUND FOR GOOD.

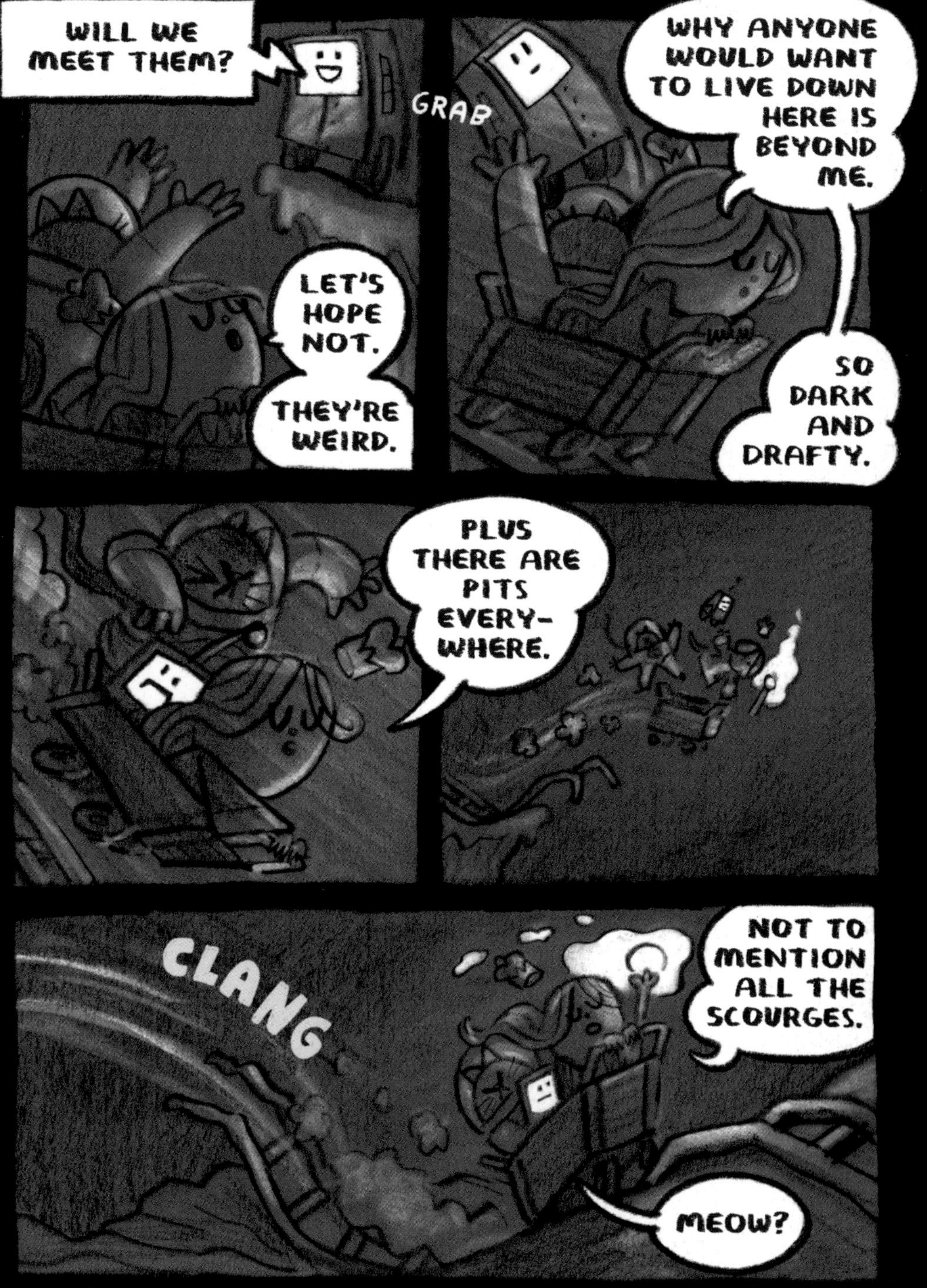
WILL WE MEET THEM?
GRAB
WHY ANYONE WOULD WANT TO LIVE DOWN HERE IS BEYOND ME.
LET'S HOPE NOT.
THEY'RE WEIRD.
SO DARK AND DRAFTY.
PLUS THERE ARE PITS EVERY-WHERE.
CLANG
NOT TO MENTION ALL THE SCOURGES.
MEOW?

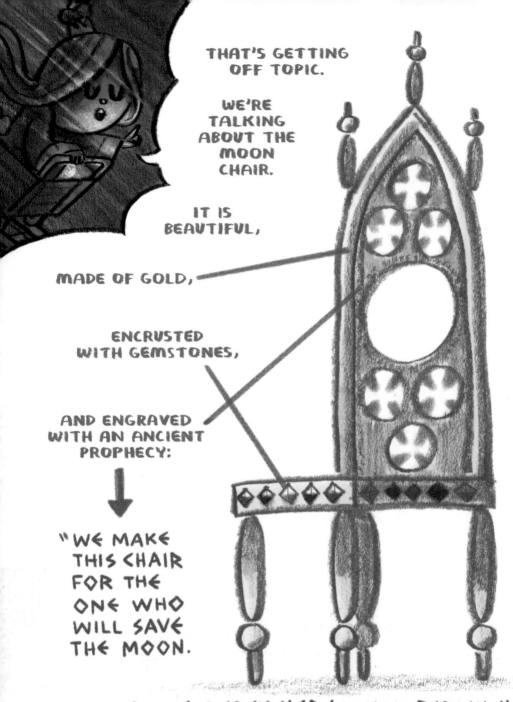

THAT'S GETTING OFF TOPIC.

WE'RE TALKING ABOUT THE MOON CHAIR.

IT IS BEAUTIFUL,

MADE OF GOLD,

ENCRUSTED WITH GEMSTONES,

AND ENGRAVED WITH AN ANCIENT PROPHECY:

"WE MAKE THIS CHAIR FOR THE ONE WHO WILL SAVE THE MOON.

ALL ELSE WHO PERCH HERE WILL PERISH."

OVER THE YEARS, MANY BOLD ADVENTURERS HAVE DARED SIT UPON THE MOON CHAIR,

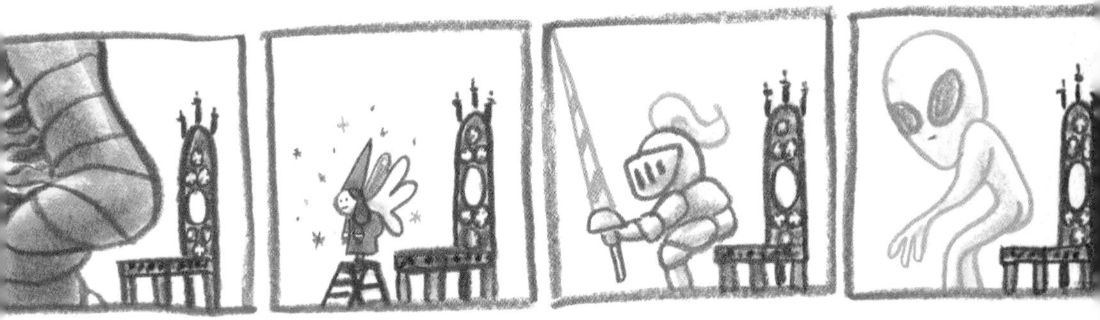

AND THEY IMMEDIATELY TURNED TO MOON DUST.

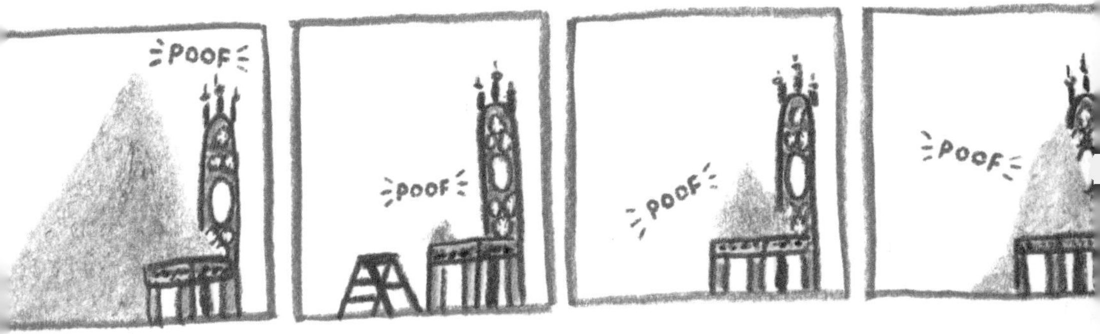
POOF
POOF
POOF
POOF

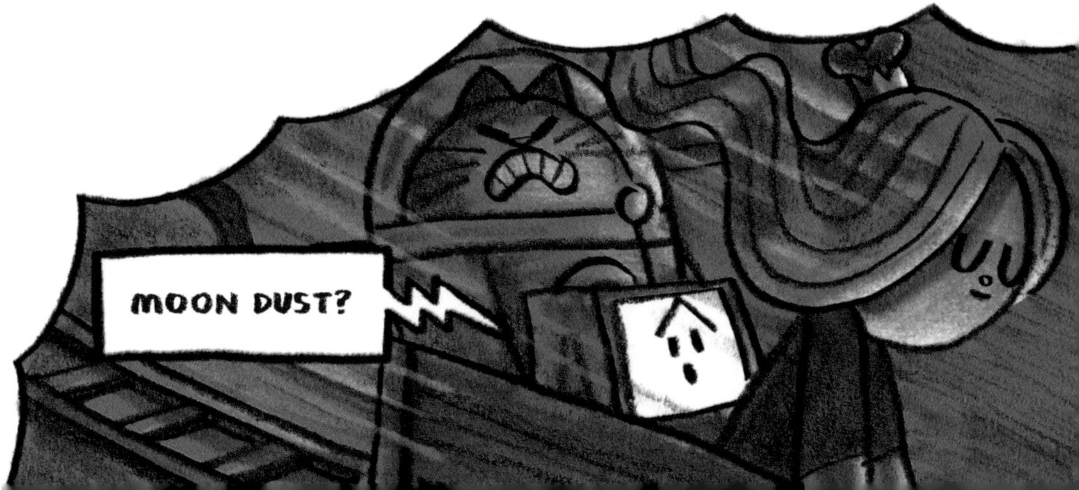
MOON DUST?

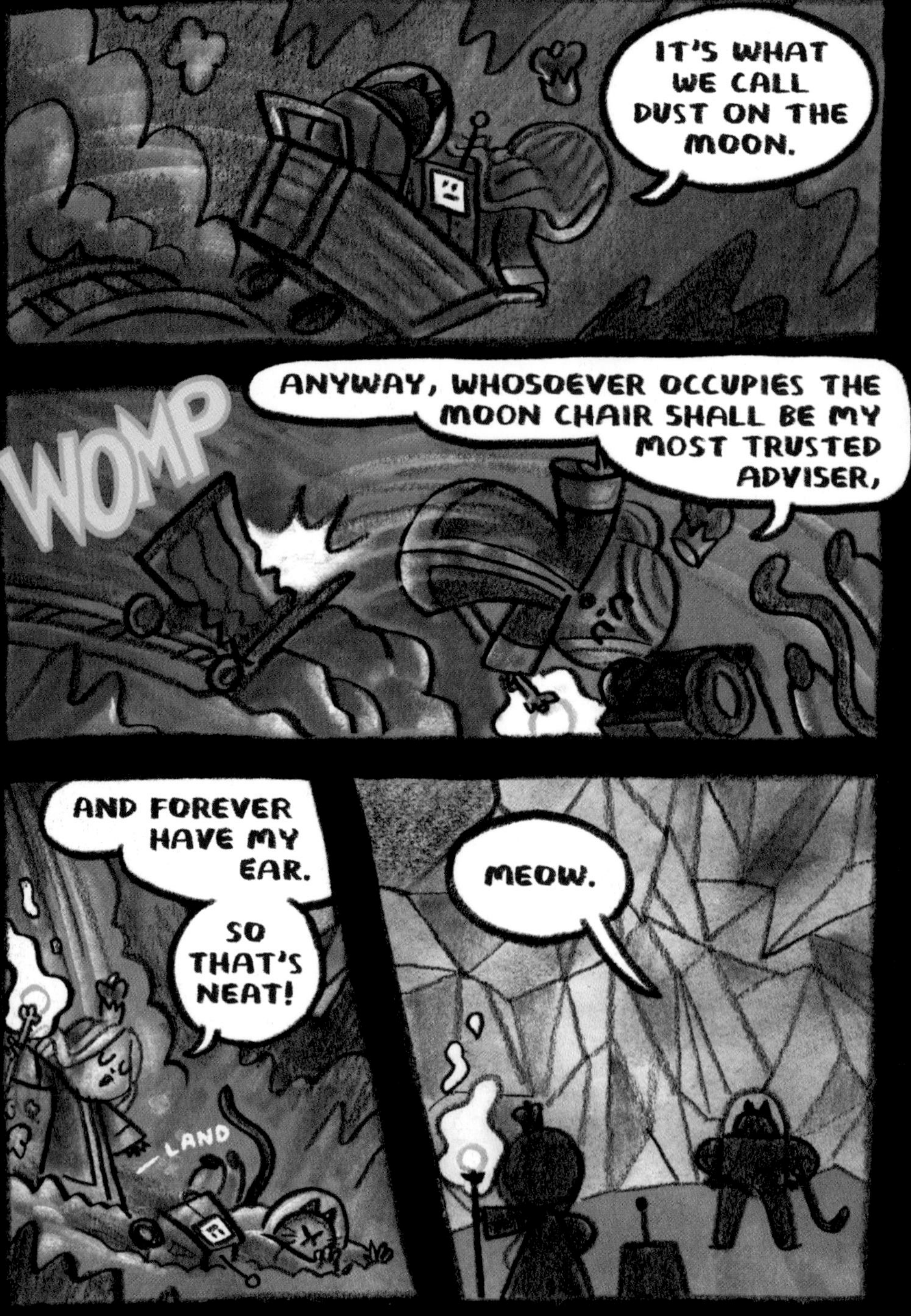
IT'S WHAT WE CALL DUST ON THE MOON.
WOMP
ANYWAY, WHOSOEVER OCCUPIES THE MOON CHAIR SHALL BE MY MOST TRUSTED ADVISER,
AND FOREVER HAVE MY EAR.
SO THAT'S NEAT!
LAND
MEOW.

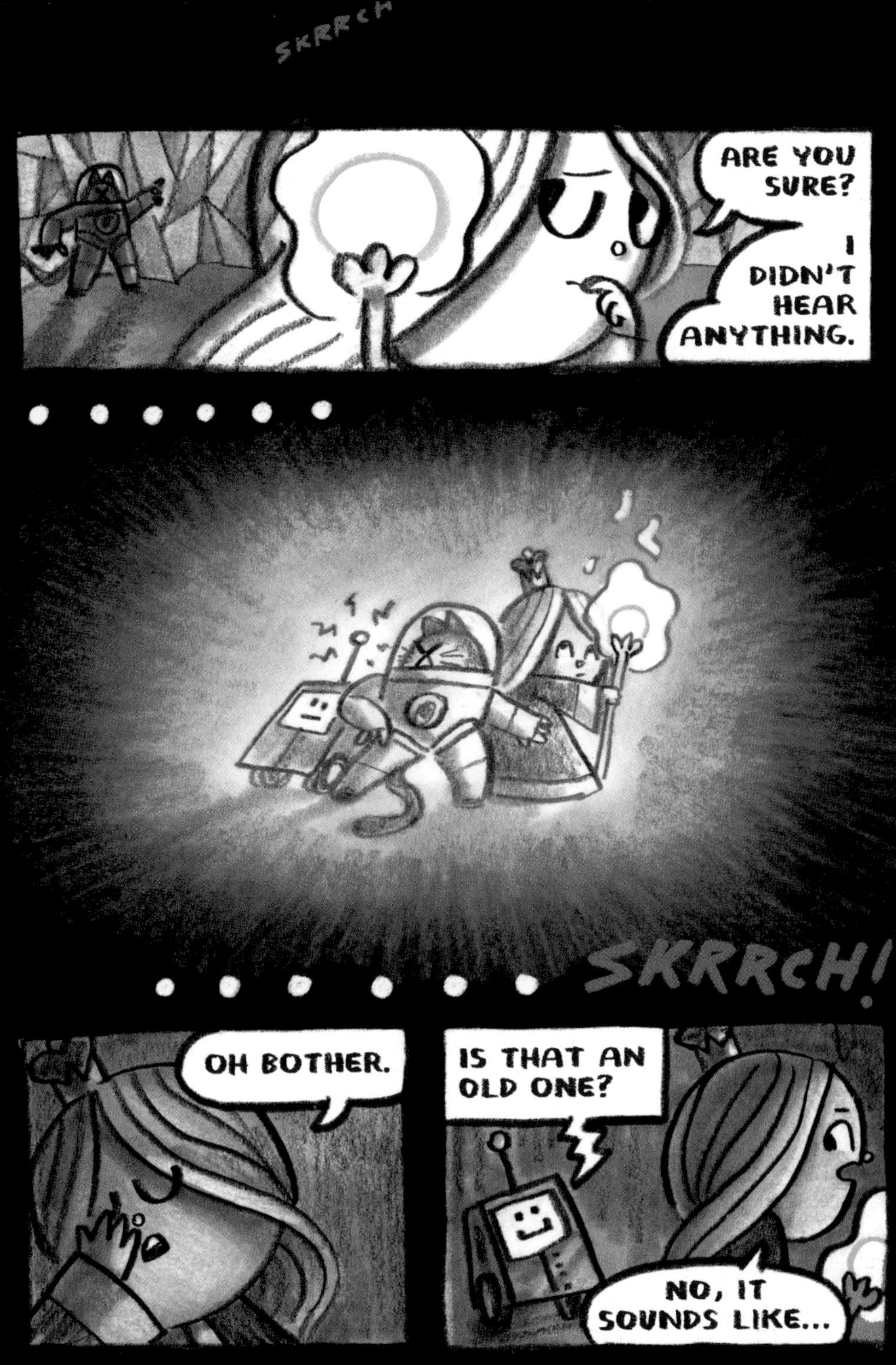
SKRRCH
ARE YOU SURE?
I DIDN'T HEAR ANYTHING.
SKRRCH!
OH BOTHER.
IS THAT AN OLD ONE?
NO, IT SOUNDS LIKE...

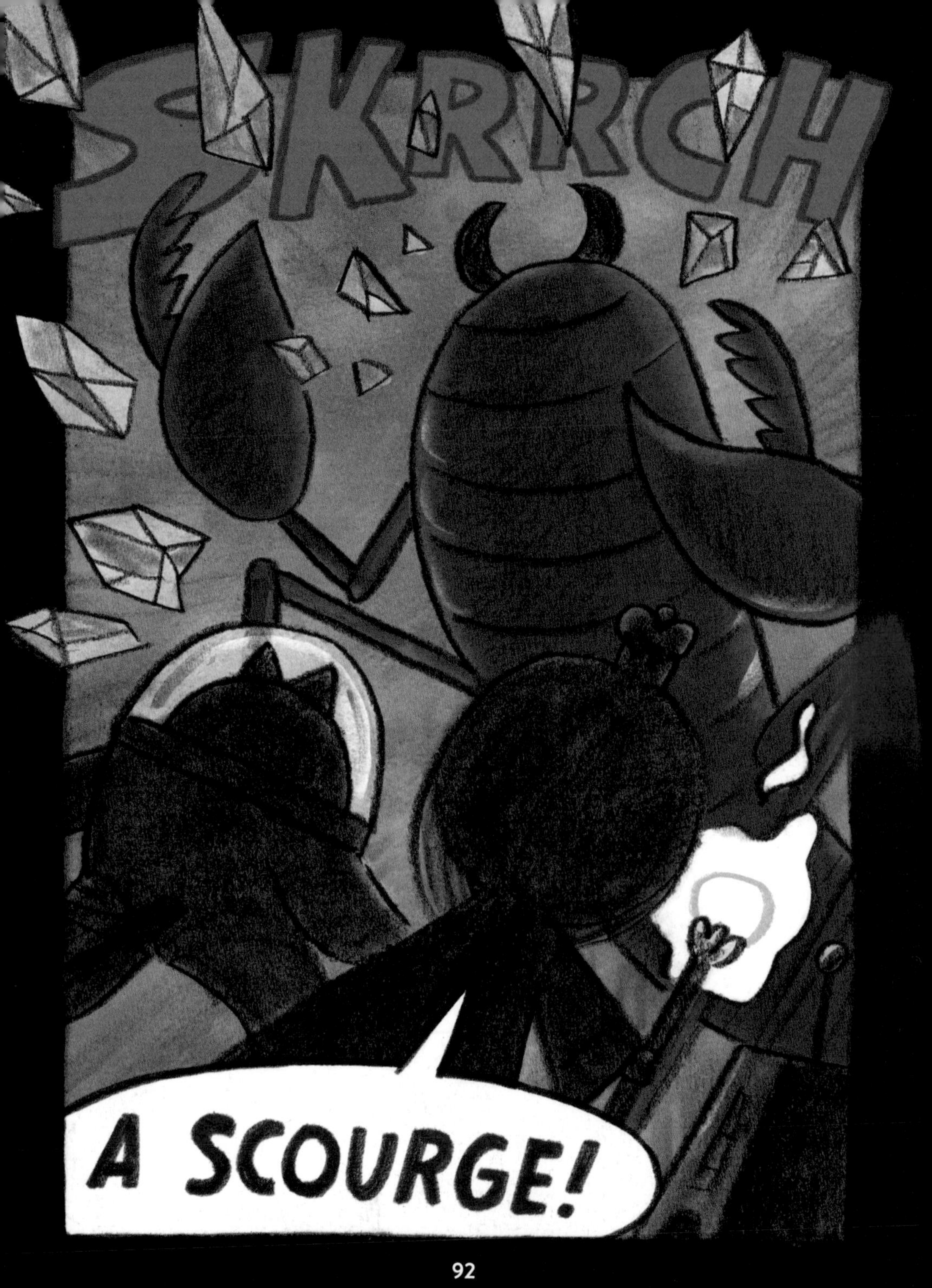
SKRRCH
A SCOURGE!

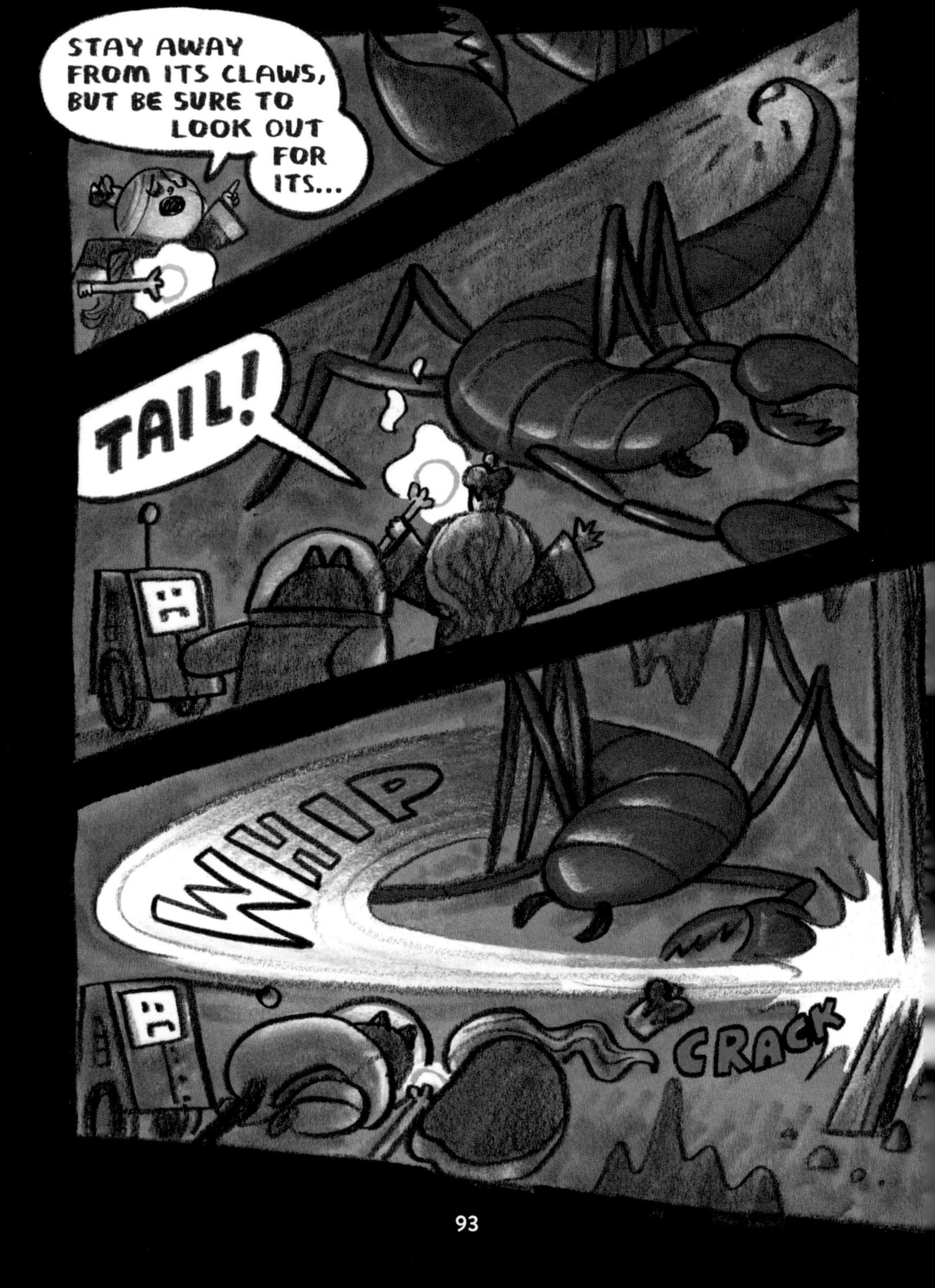
STAY AWAY FROM ITS CLAWS, BUT BE SURE TO LOOK OUT FOR ITS...
TAIL!
WHIP
CRACK

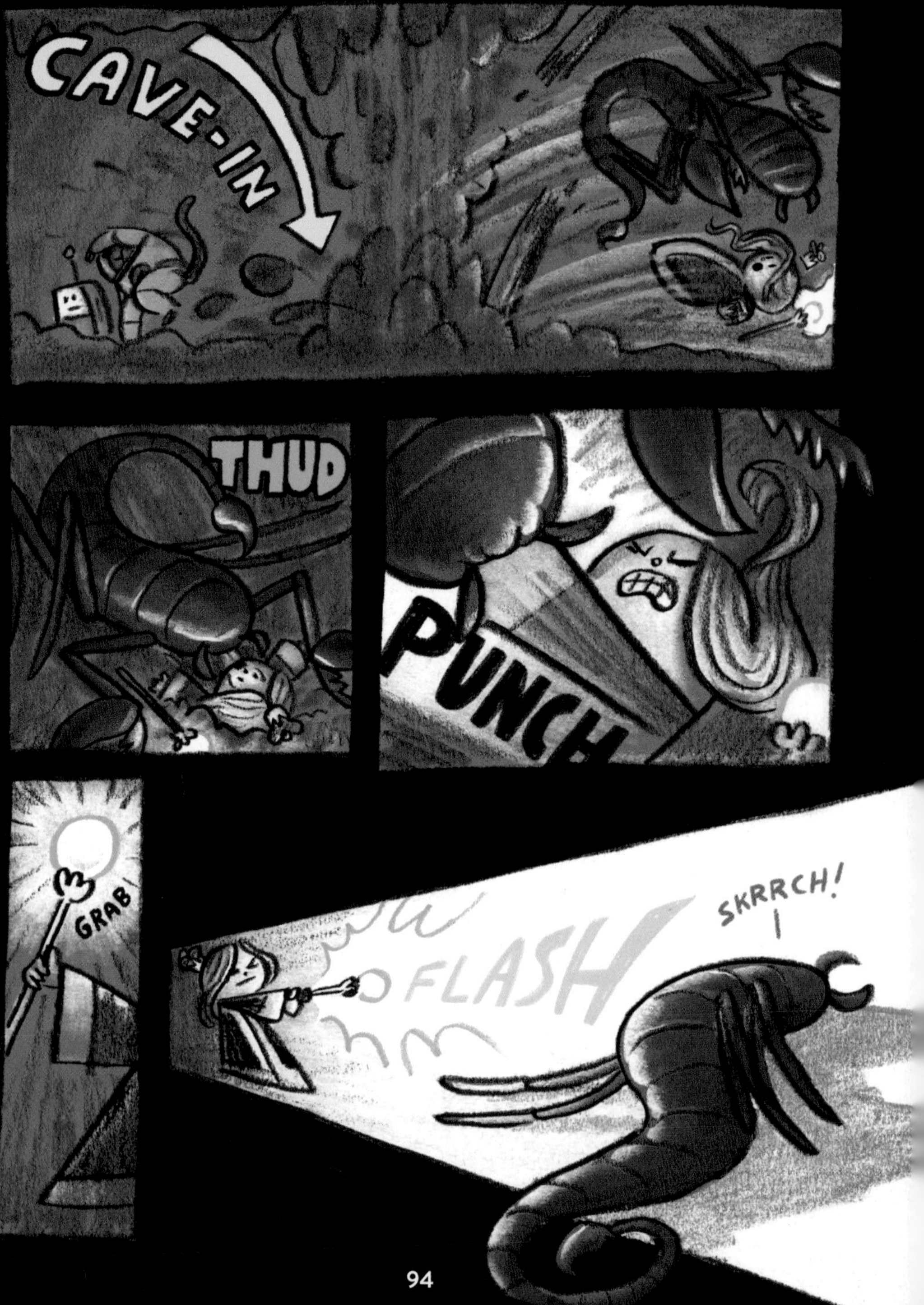
CAVE-IN
THUD
PUNCH
GRAB
FLASH
SKRRCH!

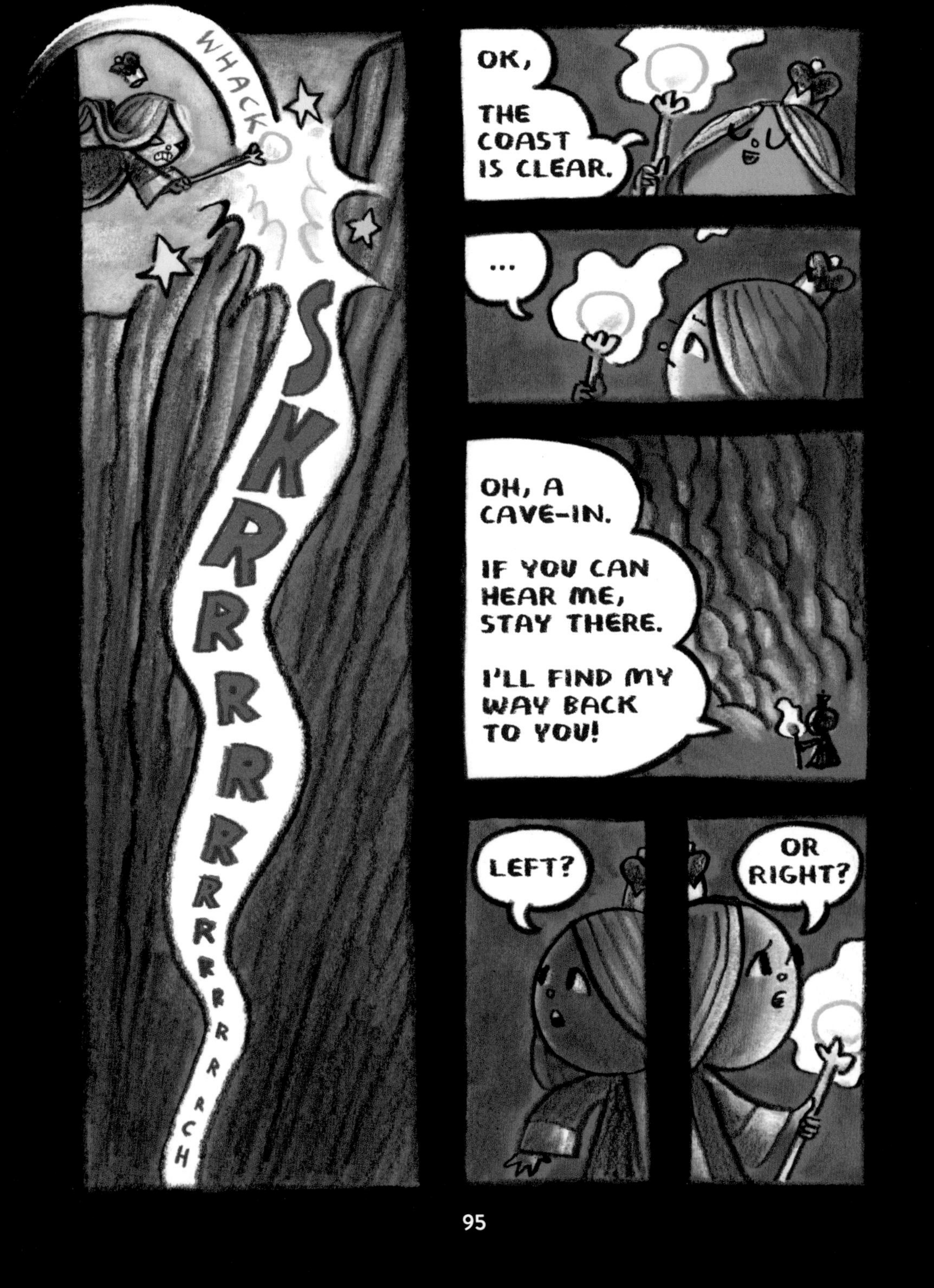
WHACK
SKRRRRRRRRRRRRACH
OK,
THE COAST IS CLEAR.
...
OH, A CAVE-IN.
IF YOU CAN HEAR ME, STAY THERE.
I'LL FIND MY WAY BACK TO YOU!
LEFT?
OR RIGHT?

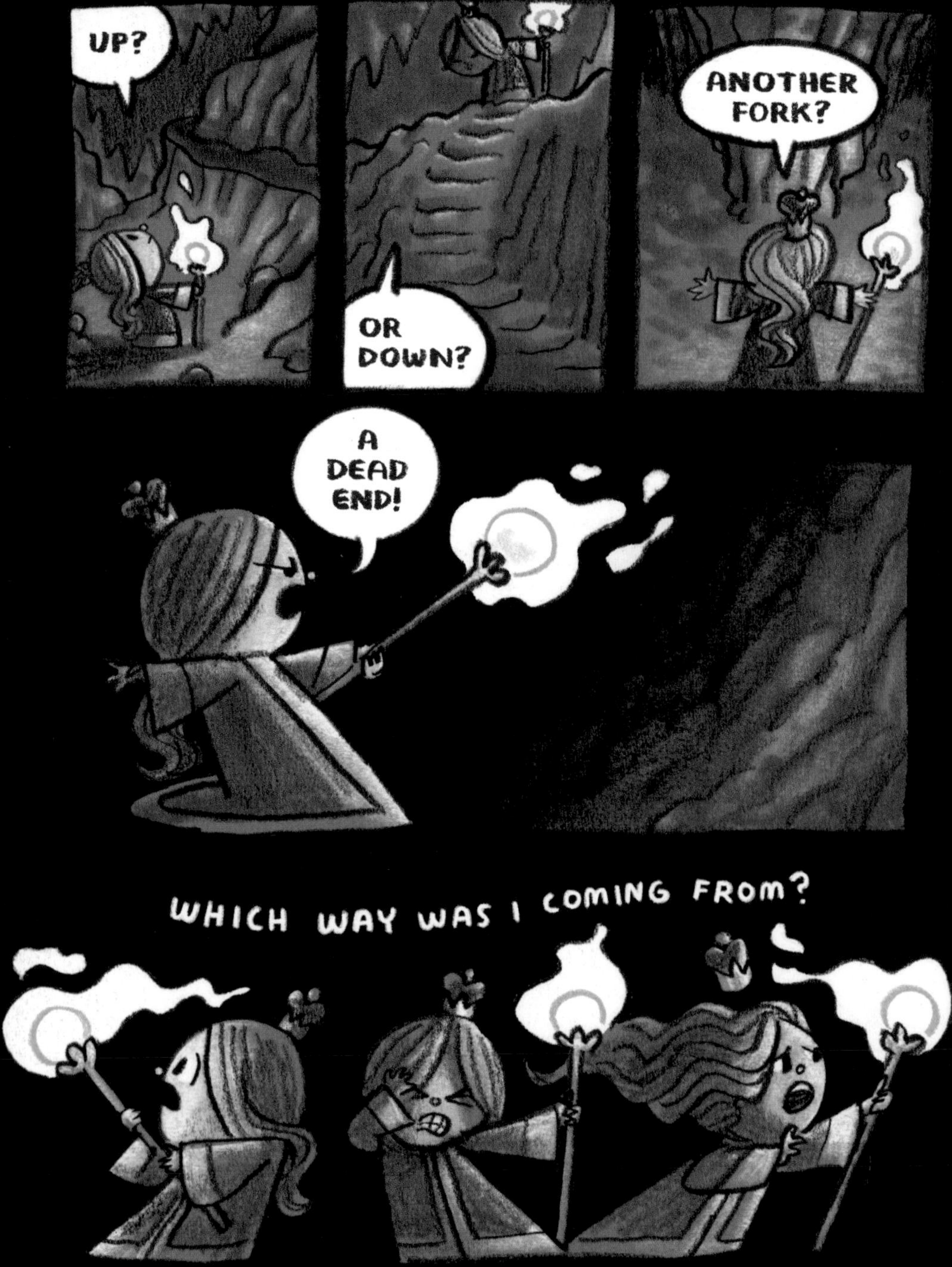

UP?
OR DOWN?
ANOTHER FORK?
A DEAD END!
WHICH WAY WAS I COMING FROM?

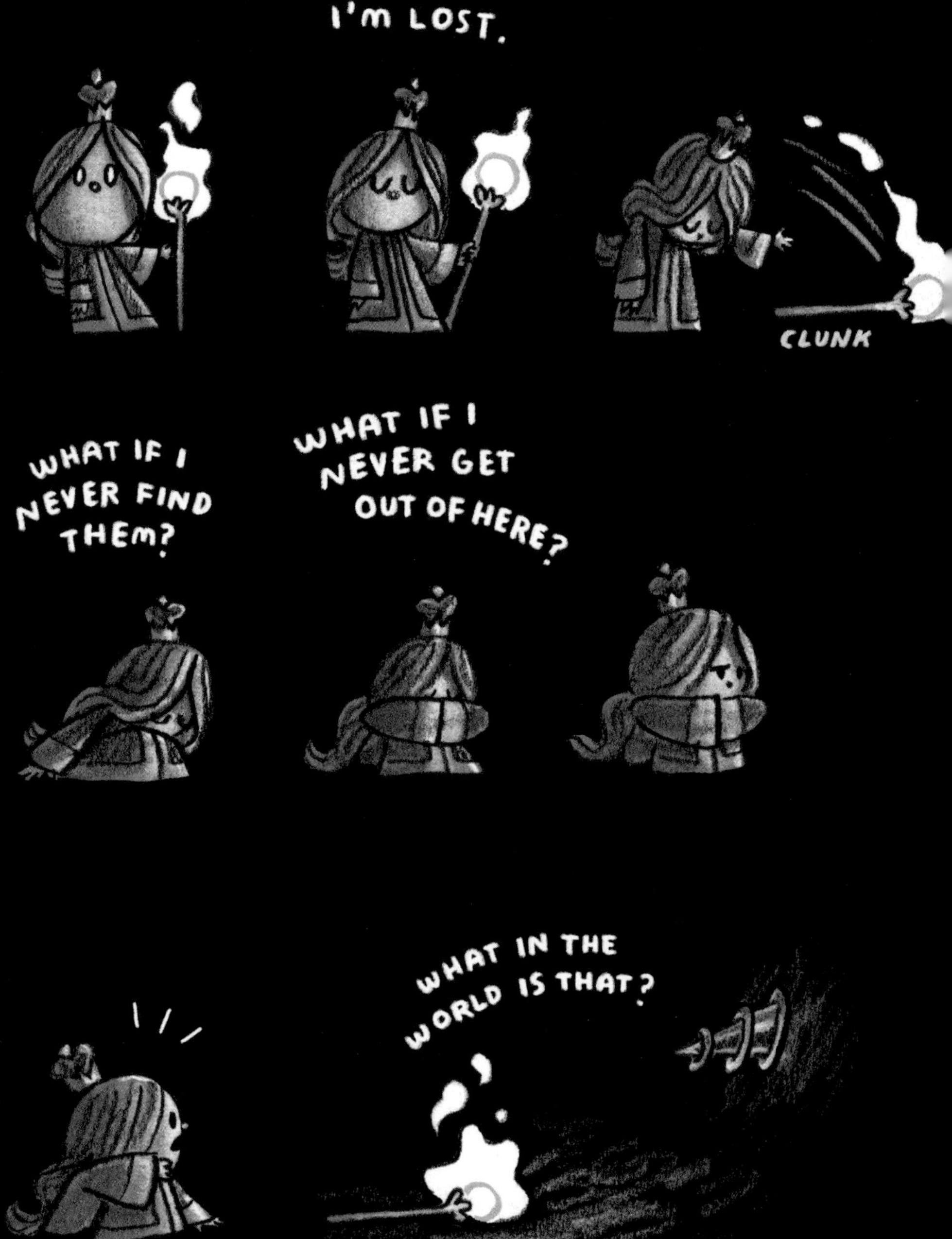
I'M LOST.
CLUNK
WHAT IF I NEVER FIND THEM?
WHAT IF I NEVER GET OUT OF HERE?
WHAT IN THE WORLD IS THAT?

CHAPTER 8
UNDERGROUND

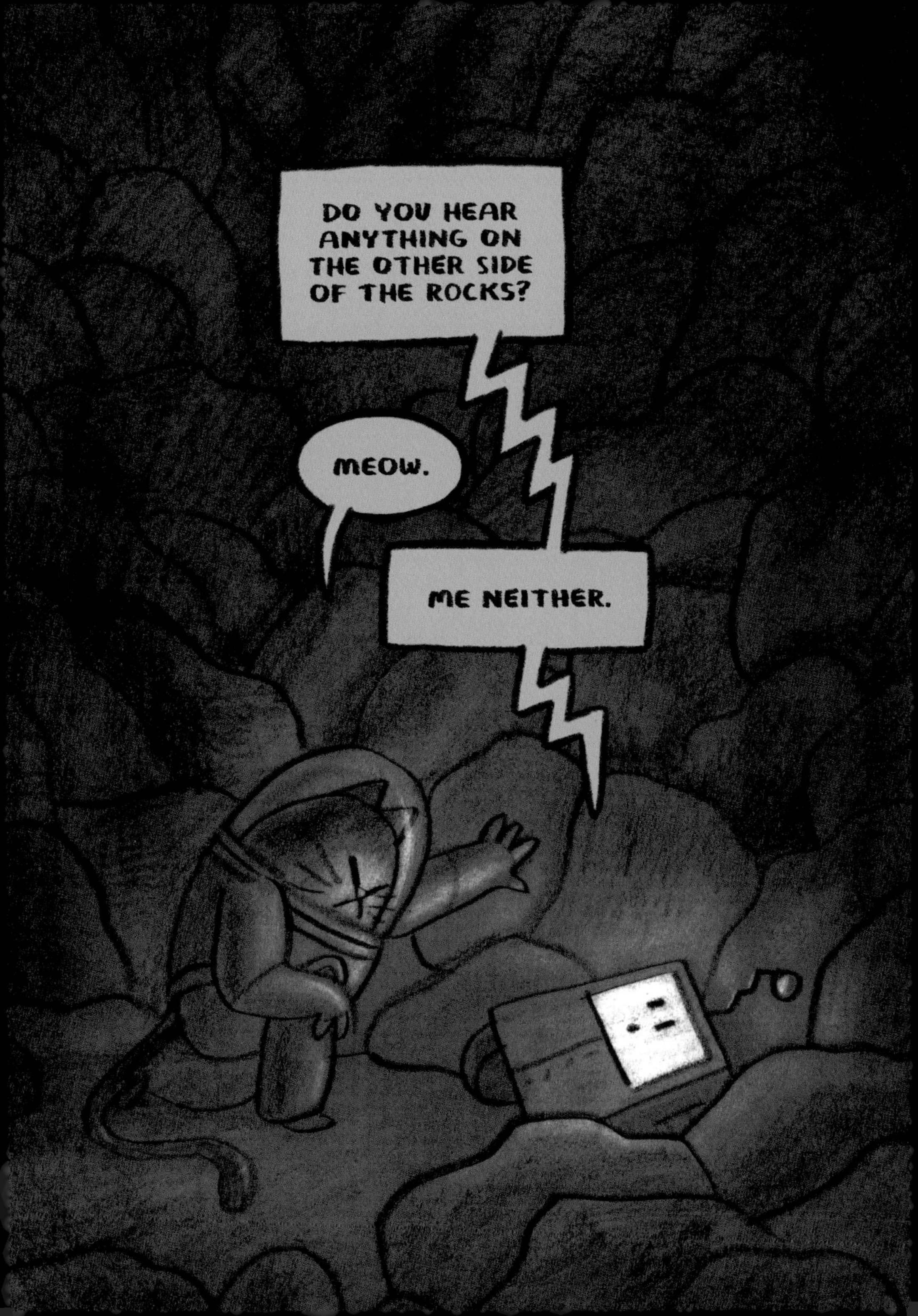
DO YOU HEAR ANYTHING ON THE OTHER SIDE OF THE ROCKS?
MEOW.
ME NEITHER.

MEOW.

YES, WE MUST FIND ANOTHER WAY THROUGH THESE TUNNELS.

←TIP

THE QUEEN WILL MEET US ON THE OTHER SIDE.

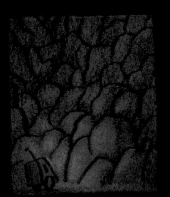

CLINK

I HOPE.

WE NO LONGER HAVE THE GLOW OF THE MOON QUEEN'S STAFF TO GUIDE US...

SO I WILL TURN UP THE BRIGHTNESS ON MY SCREEN!

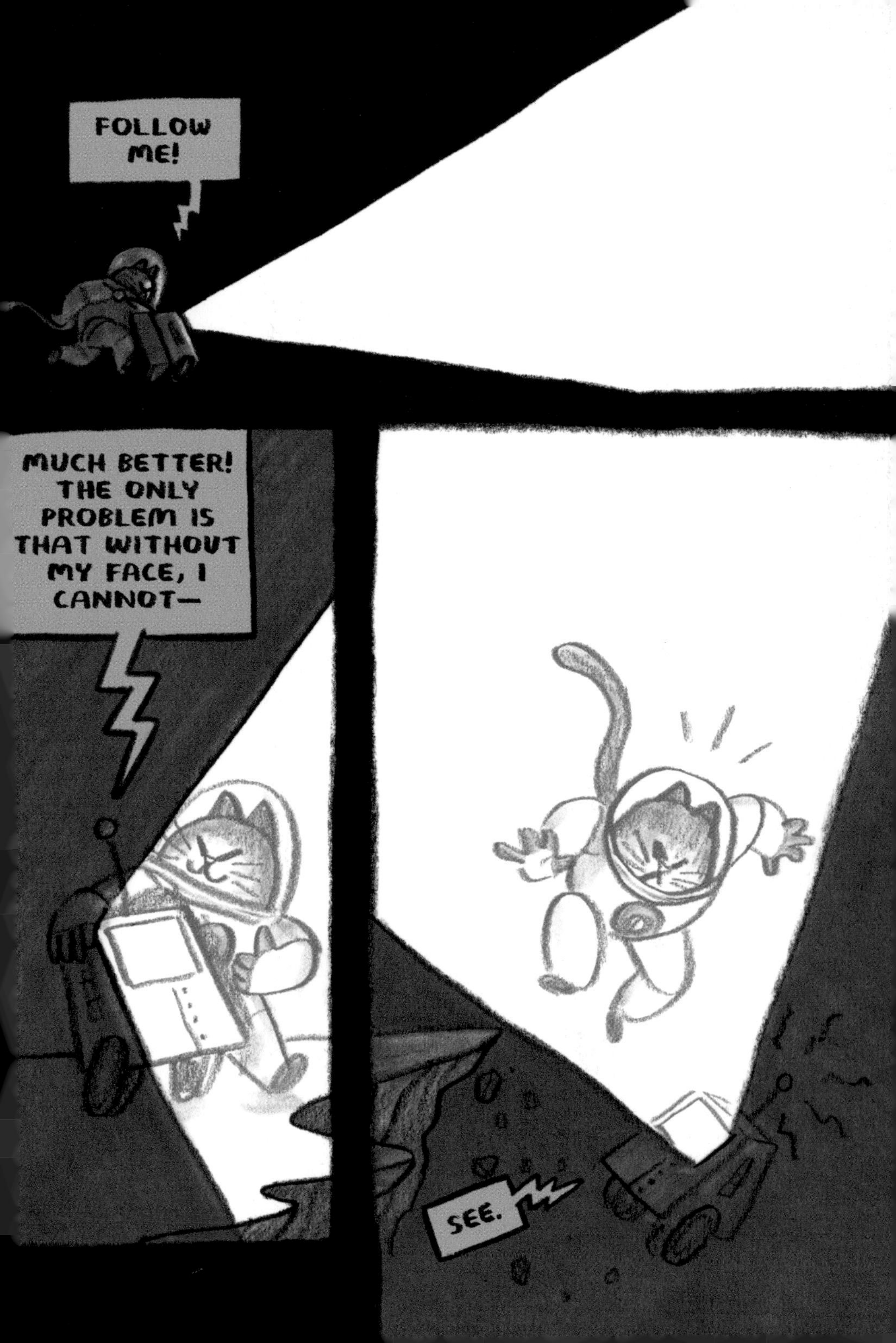

FOLLOW ME!
MUCH BETTER! THE ONLY PROBLEM IS THAT WITHOUT MY FACE, I CANNOT—
SEE.

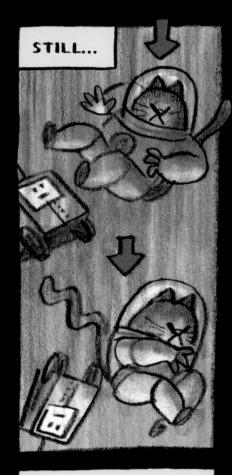

STILL...

WHO KNOWS HOW LONG LATER...

PLUNK SPLASH

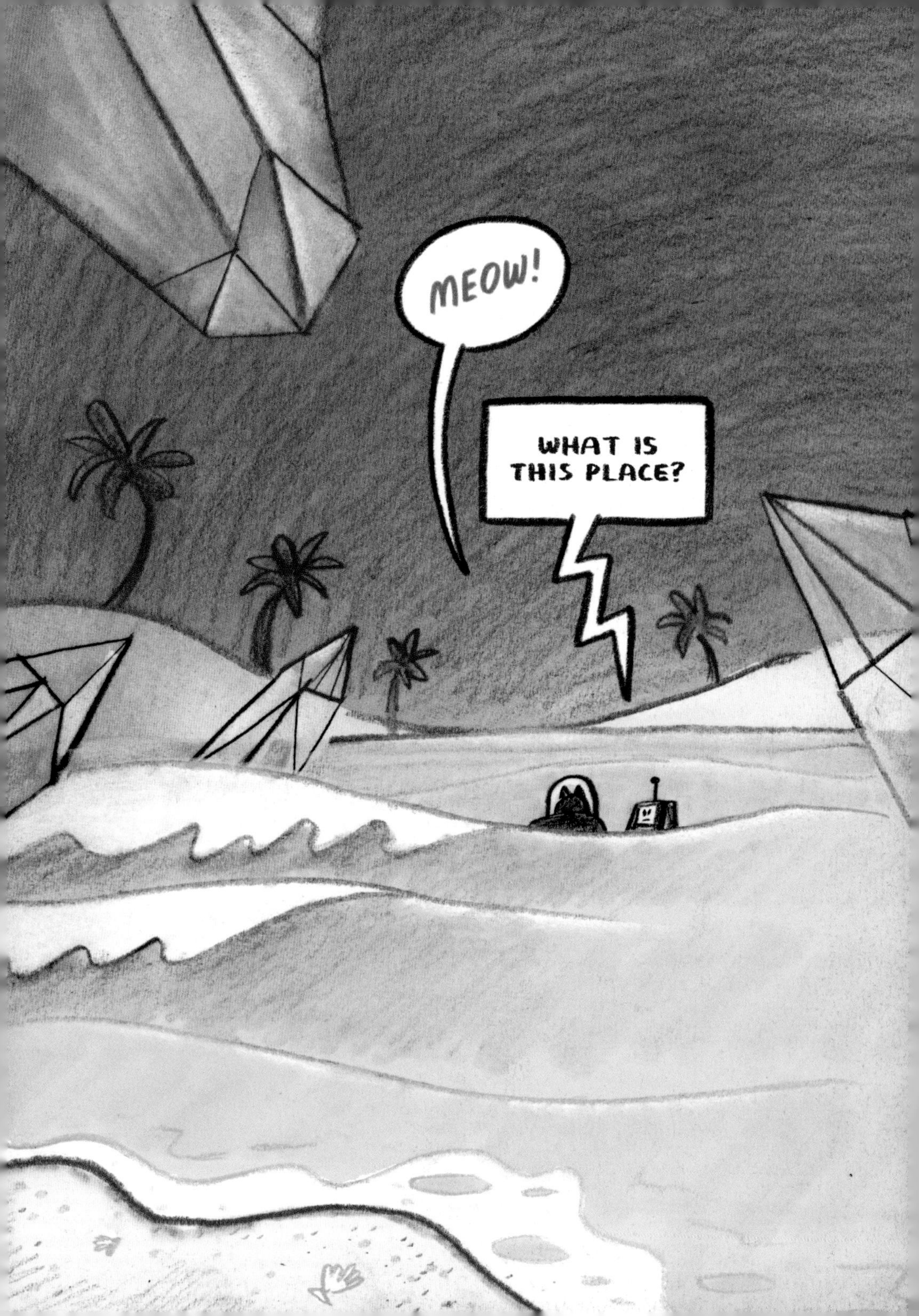
MEOW!
WHAT IS THIS PLACE?

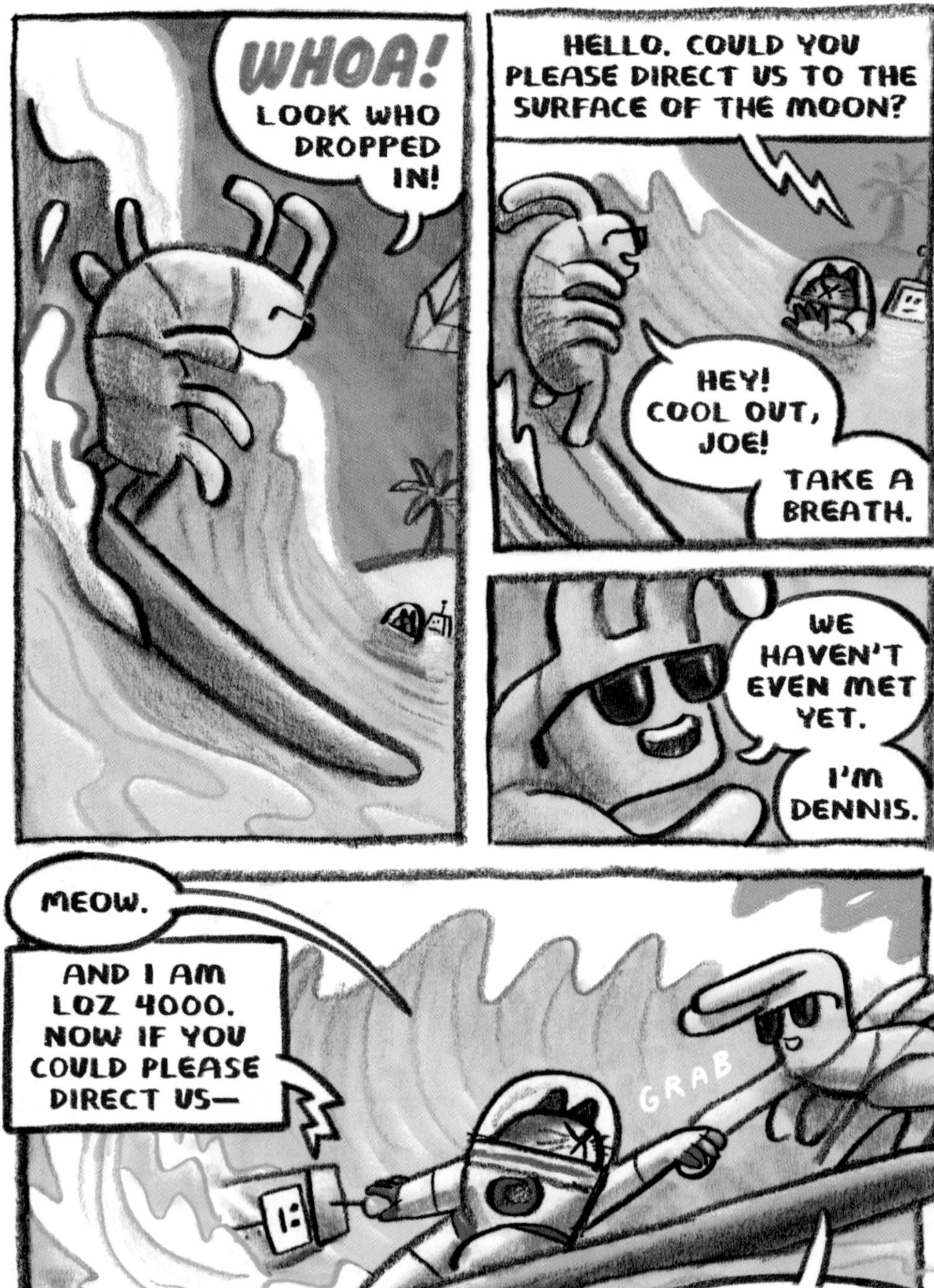
WHOA! LOOK WHO DROPPED IN!
HELLO. COULD YOU PLEASE DIRECT US TO THE SURFACE OF THE MOON?
HEY! COOL OUT, JOE!
TAKE A BREATH.
WE HAVEN'T EVEN MET YET.
I'M DENNIS.
MEOW.
AND I AM LOZ 4000. NOW IF YOU COULD PLEASE DIRECT US—
GRAB
LOZ 4000...

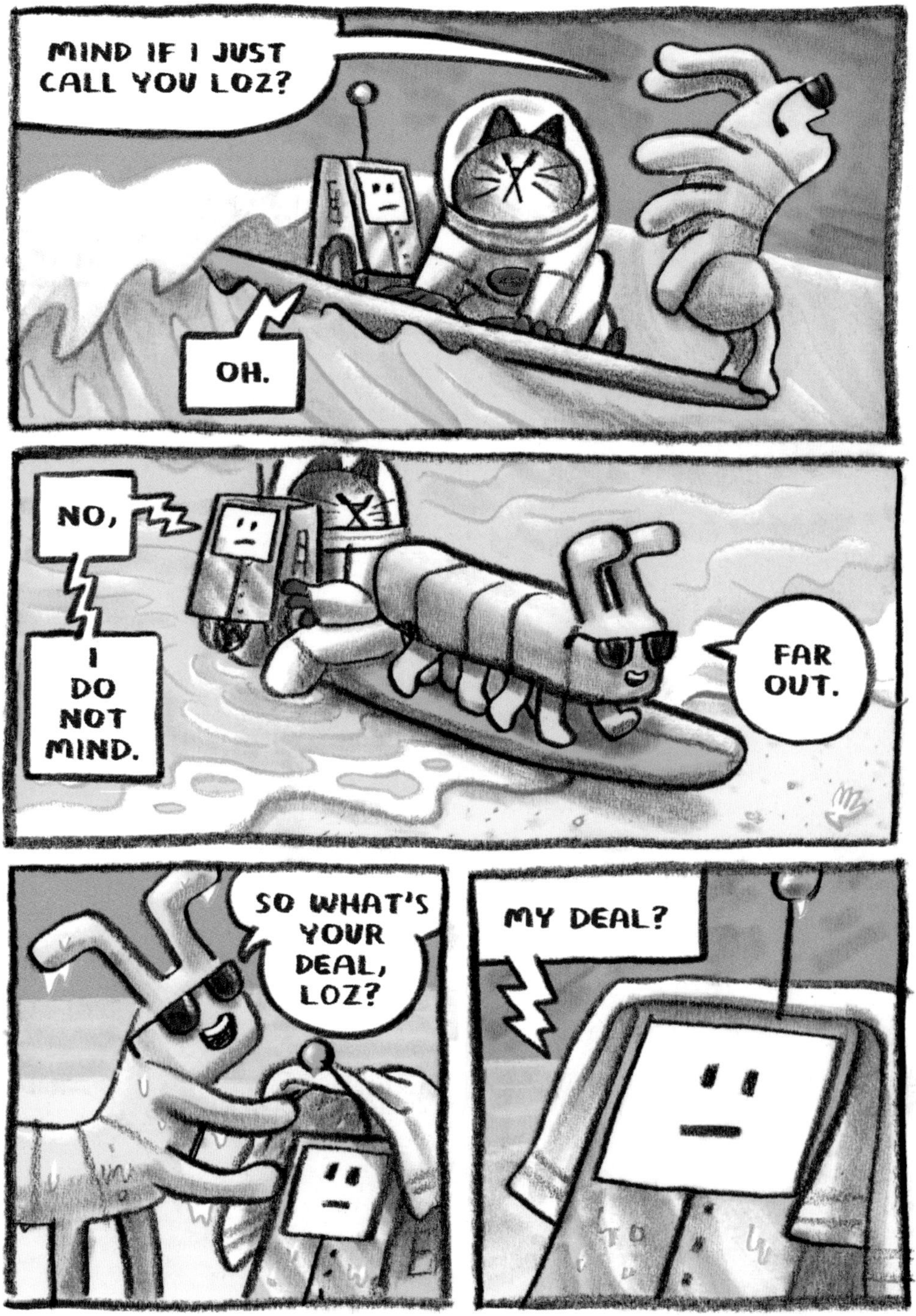
MIND IF I JUST CALL YOU LOZ?
OH.
NO,
I DO NOT MIND.
FAR OUT.
SO WHAT'S YOUR DEAL, LOZ?
MY DEAL?

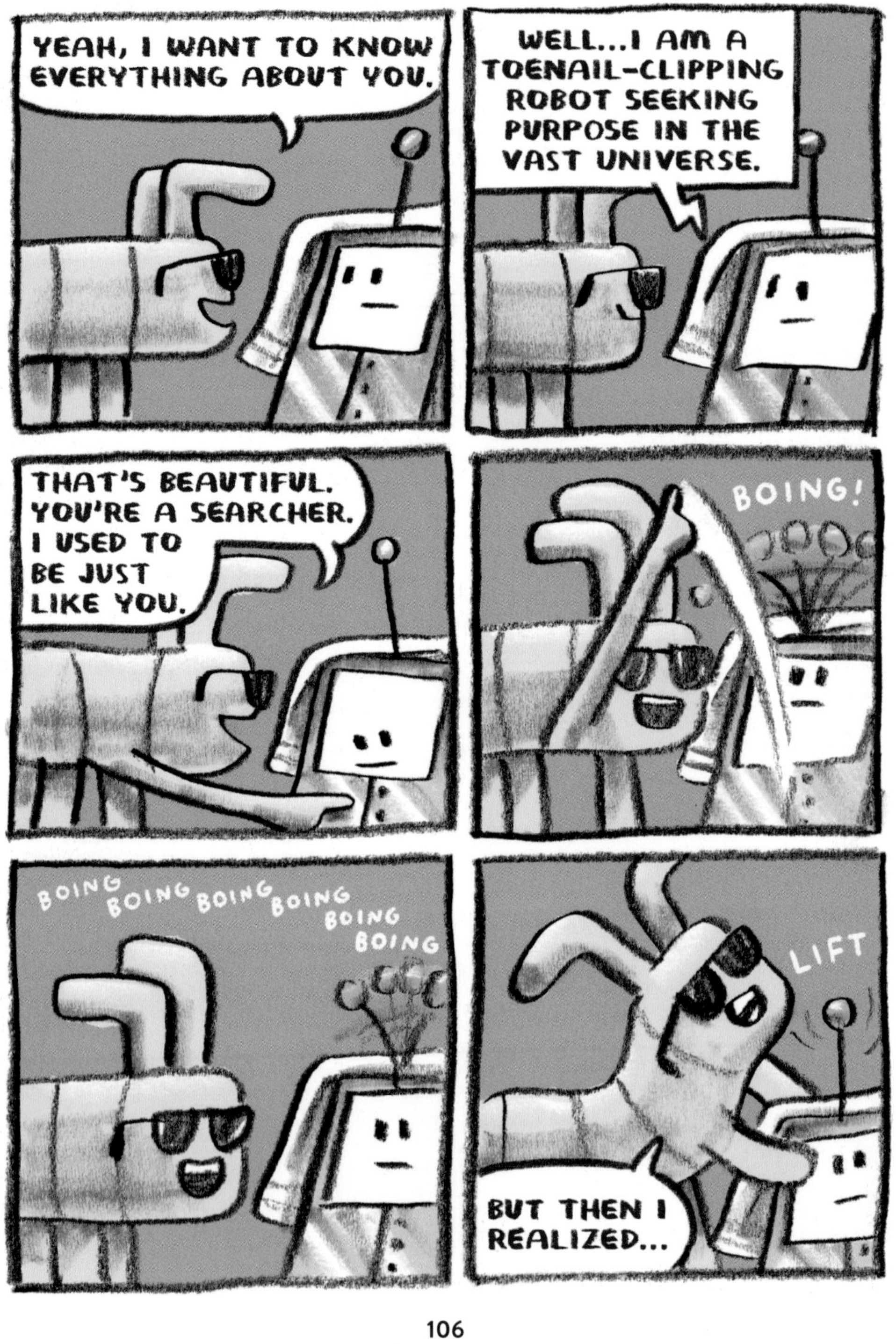
YEAH, I WANT TO KNOW EVERYTHING ABOUT YOU.
WELL...I AM A TOENAIL-CLIPPING ROBOT SEEKING PURPOSE IN THE VAST UNIVERSE.
THAT'S BEAUTIFUL. YOU'RE A SEARCHER. I USED TO BE JUST LIKE YOU.
BOING!
BOING BOING BOING BOING BOING BOING
LIFT
BUT THEN I REALIZED...

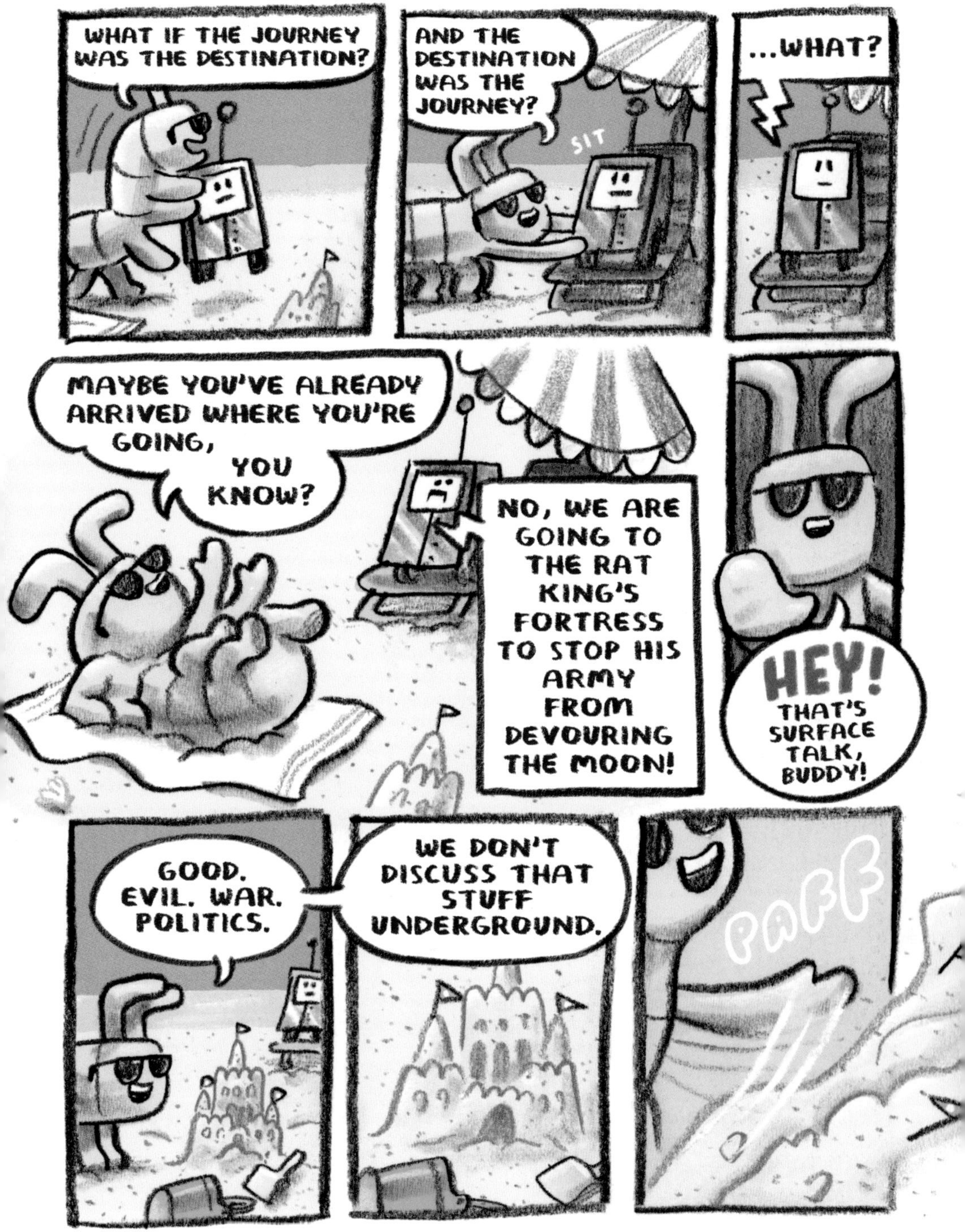
WHAT IF THE JOURNEY WAS THE DESTINATION?
AND THE DESTINATION WAS THE JOURNEY?
SIT
...WHAT?
MAYBE YOU'VE ALREADY ARRIVED WHERE YOU'RE GOING,
YOU KNOW?
NO, WE ARE GOING TO THE RAT KING'S FORTRESS TO STOP HIS ARMY FROM DEVOURING THE MOON!
HEY! THAT'S SURFACE TALK, BUDDY!
GOOD. EVIL. WAR. POLITICS.
WE DON'T DISCUSS THAT STUFF UNDERGROUND.
PAFF

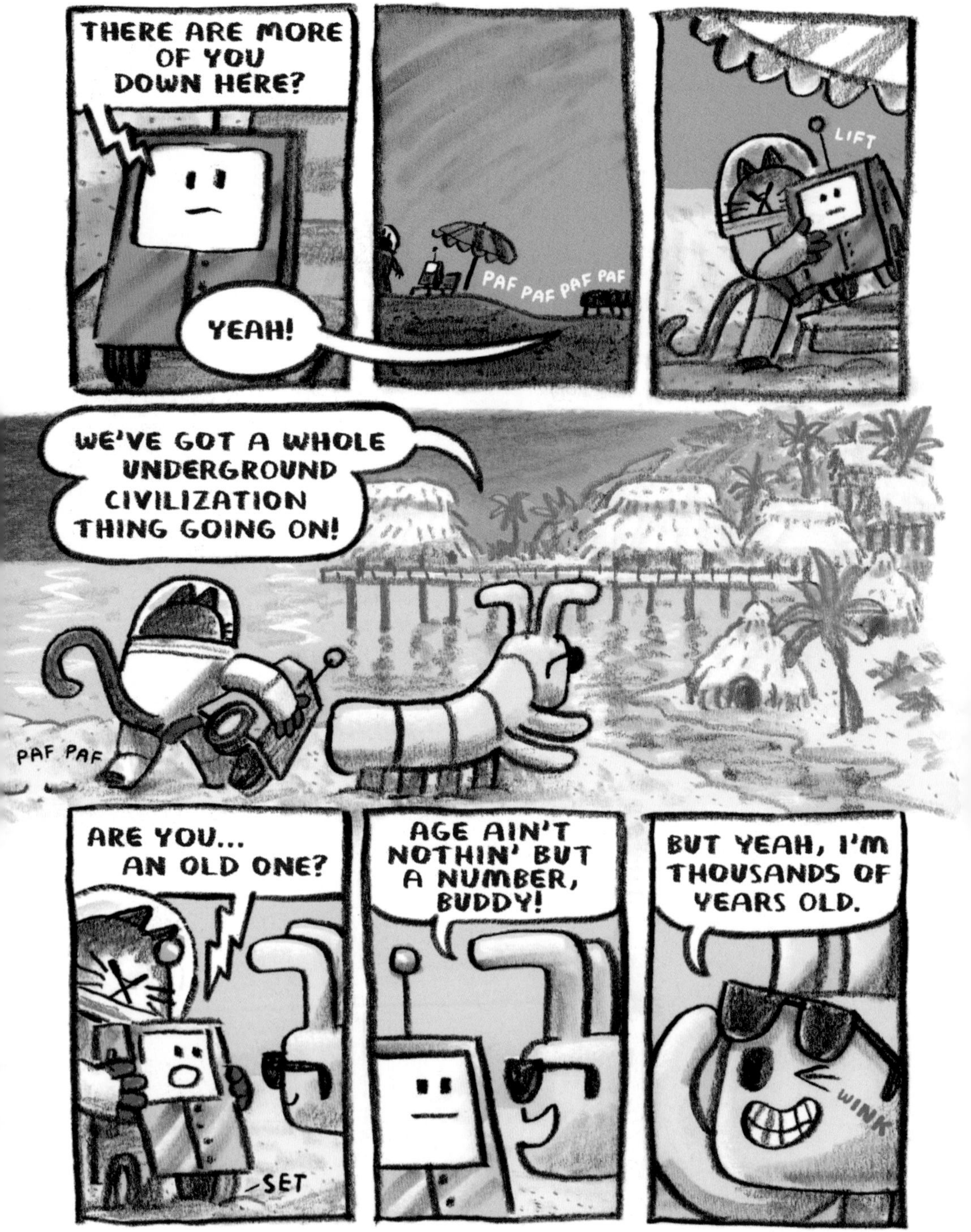
THERE ARE MORE OF YOU DOWN HERE?
YEAH!
PAF PAF PAF PAF
LIFT
WE'VE GOT A WHOLE UNDERGROUND CIVILIZATION THING GOING ON!
PAF PAF
ARE YOU... AN OLD ONE?
SET
AGE AIN'T NOTHIN' BUT A NUMBER, BUDDY!
BUT YEAH, I'M THOUSANDS OF YEARS OLD.
WINK

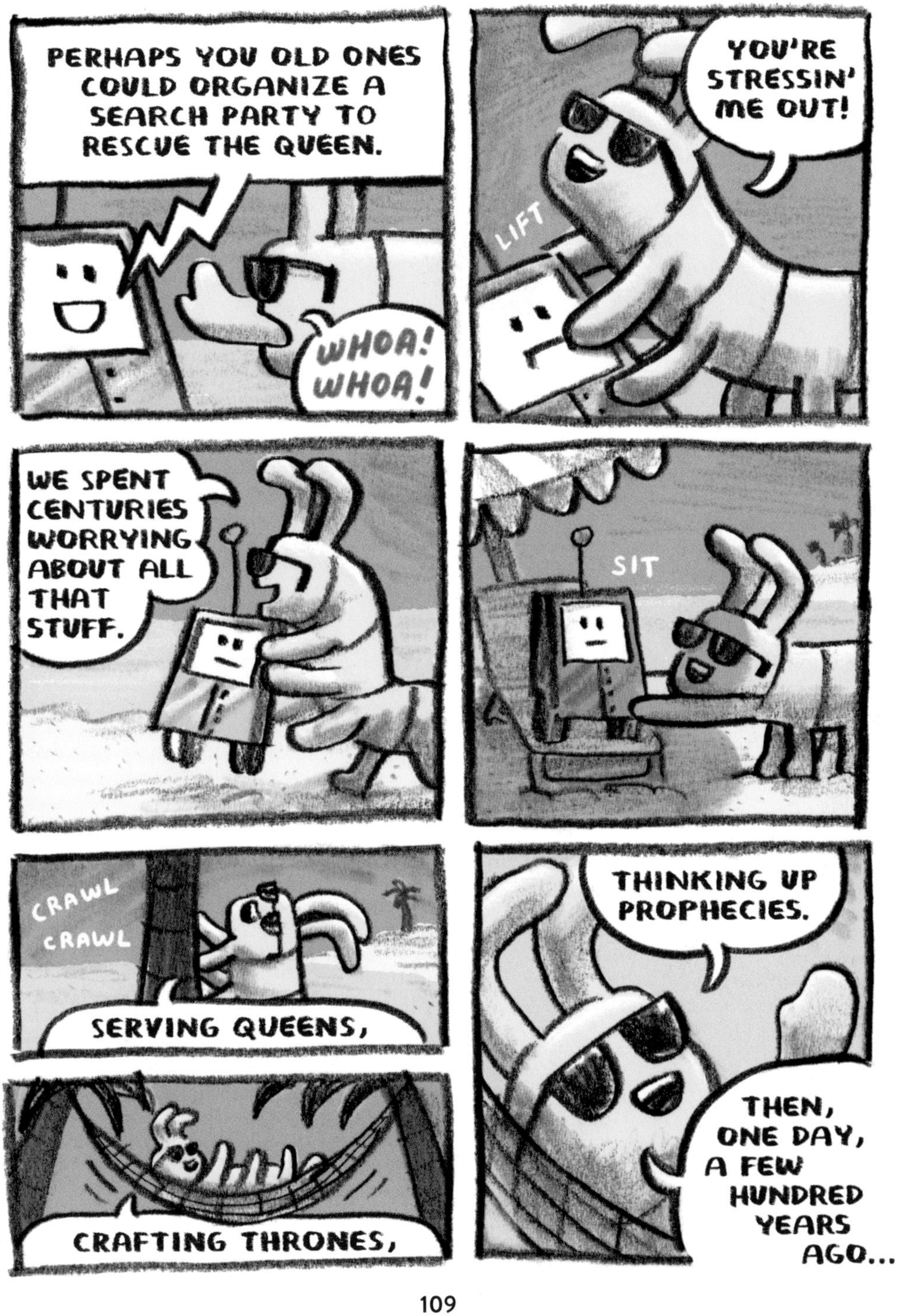
PERHAPS YOU OLD ONES COULD ORGANIZE A SEARCH PARTY TO RESCUE THE QUEEN.
WHOA! WHOA!
YOU'RE STRESSIN' ME OUT!
LIFT
WE SPENT CENTURIES WORRYING ABOUT ALL THAT STUFF.
SIT
CRAWL
CRAWL
SERVING QUEENS,
CRAFTING THRONES,
THINKING UP PROPHECIES.
THEN, ONE DAY, A FEW HUNDRED YEARS AGO...

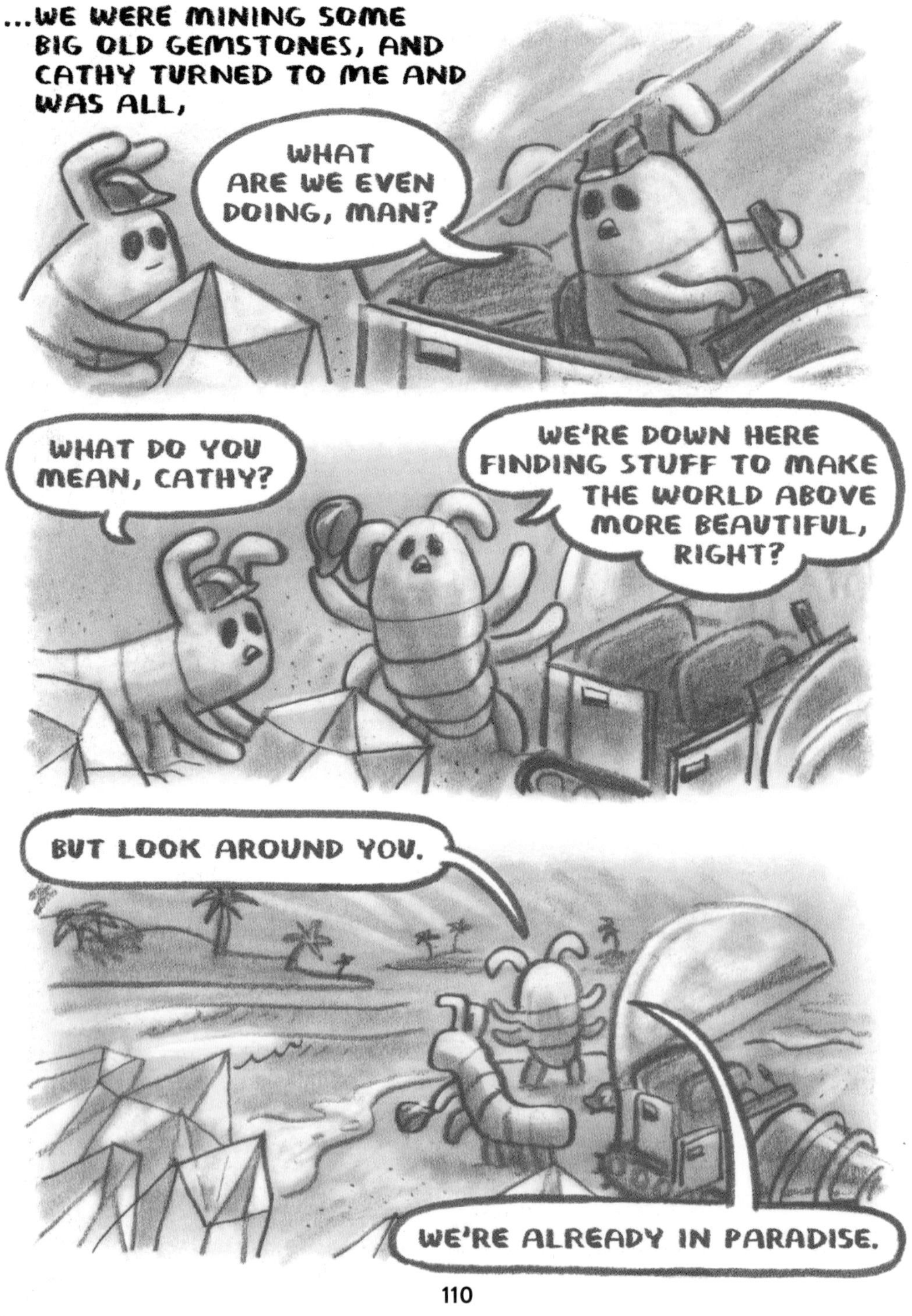
...WE WERE MINING SOME BIG OLD GEMSTONES, AND CATHY TURNED TO ME AND WAS ALL,
WHAT ARE WE EVEN DOING, MAN?
WHAT DO YOU MEAN, CATHY?
WE'RE DOWN HERE FINDING STUFF TO MAKE THE WORLD ABOVE MORE BEAUTIFUL, RIGHT?
BUT LOOK AROUND YOU.
WE'RE ALREADY IN PARADISE.

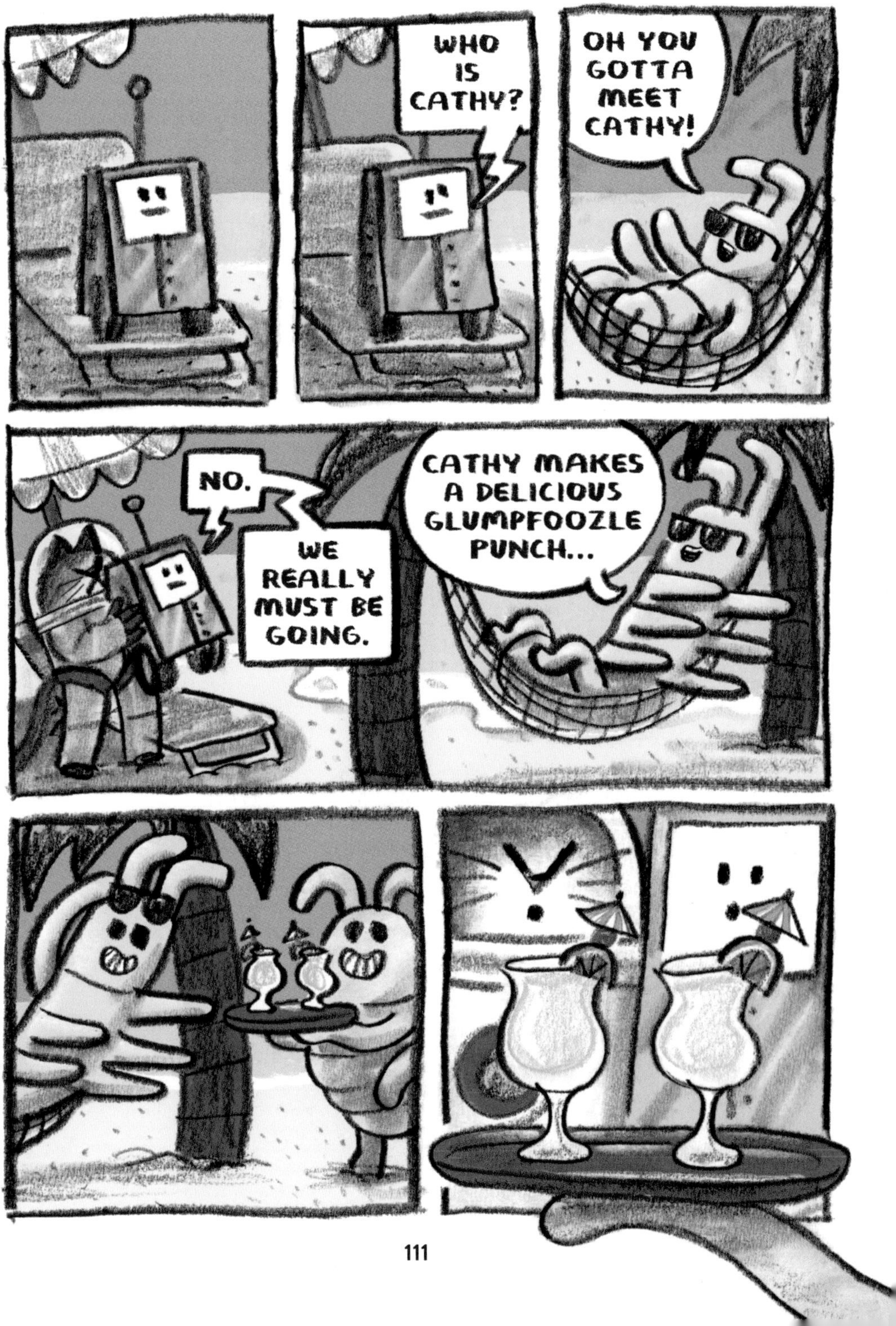
WHO IS CATHY?
OH YOU GOTTA MEET CATHY!
NO.
WE REALLY MUST BE GOING.
CATHY MAKES A DELICIOUS GLUMPFOOZLE PUNCH...

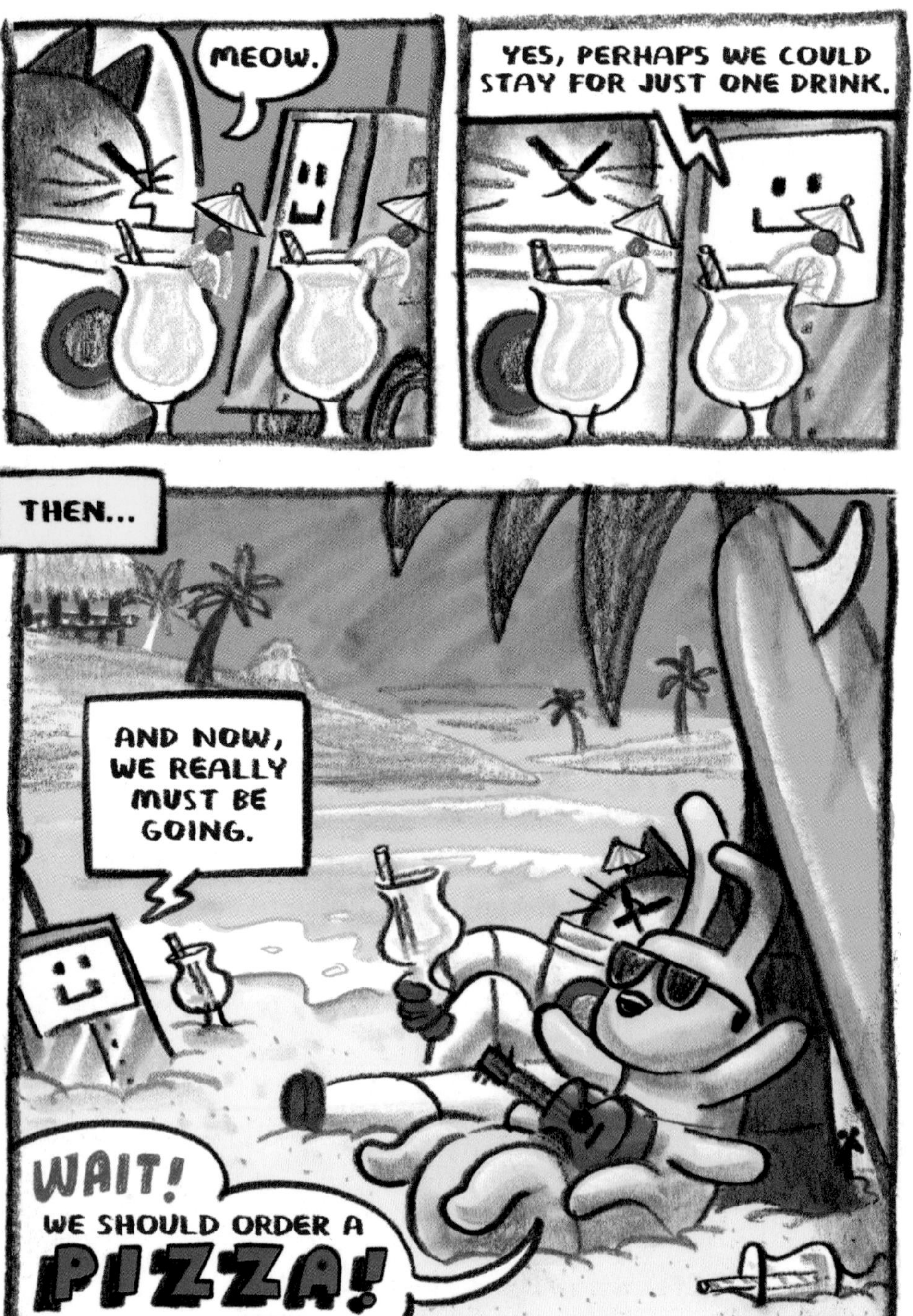
MEOW.
YES, PERHAPS WE COULD STAY FOR JUST ONE DRINK.
THEN...
AND NOW, WE REALLY MUST BE GOING.
WAIT! WE SHOULD ORDER A PIZZA!

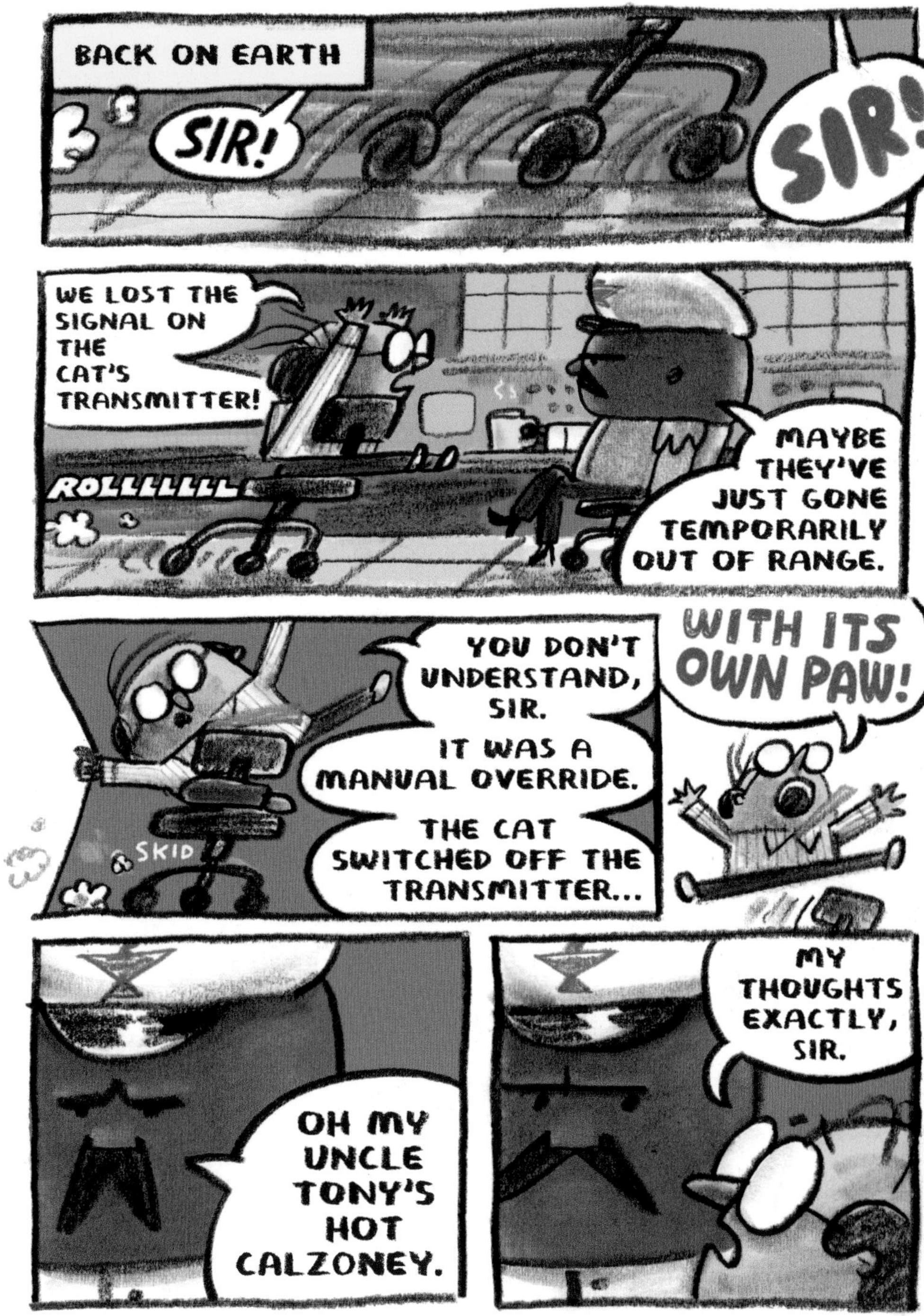
BACK ON EARTH
SIR!
SIR!
WE LOST THE SIGNAL ON THE CAT'S TRANSMITTER!
ROLLLLLLL
MAYBE THEY'VE JUST GONE TEMPORARILY OUT OF RANGE.
YOU DON'T UNDERSTAND, SIR.
IT WAS A MANUAL OVERRIDE.
THE CAT SWITCHED OFF THE TRANSMITTER...
SKID
WITH ITS OWN PAW!
OH MY UNCLE TONY'S HOT CALZONEY.
MY THOUGHTS EXACTLY, SIR.

CHAPTER 9

PARADISE

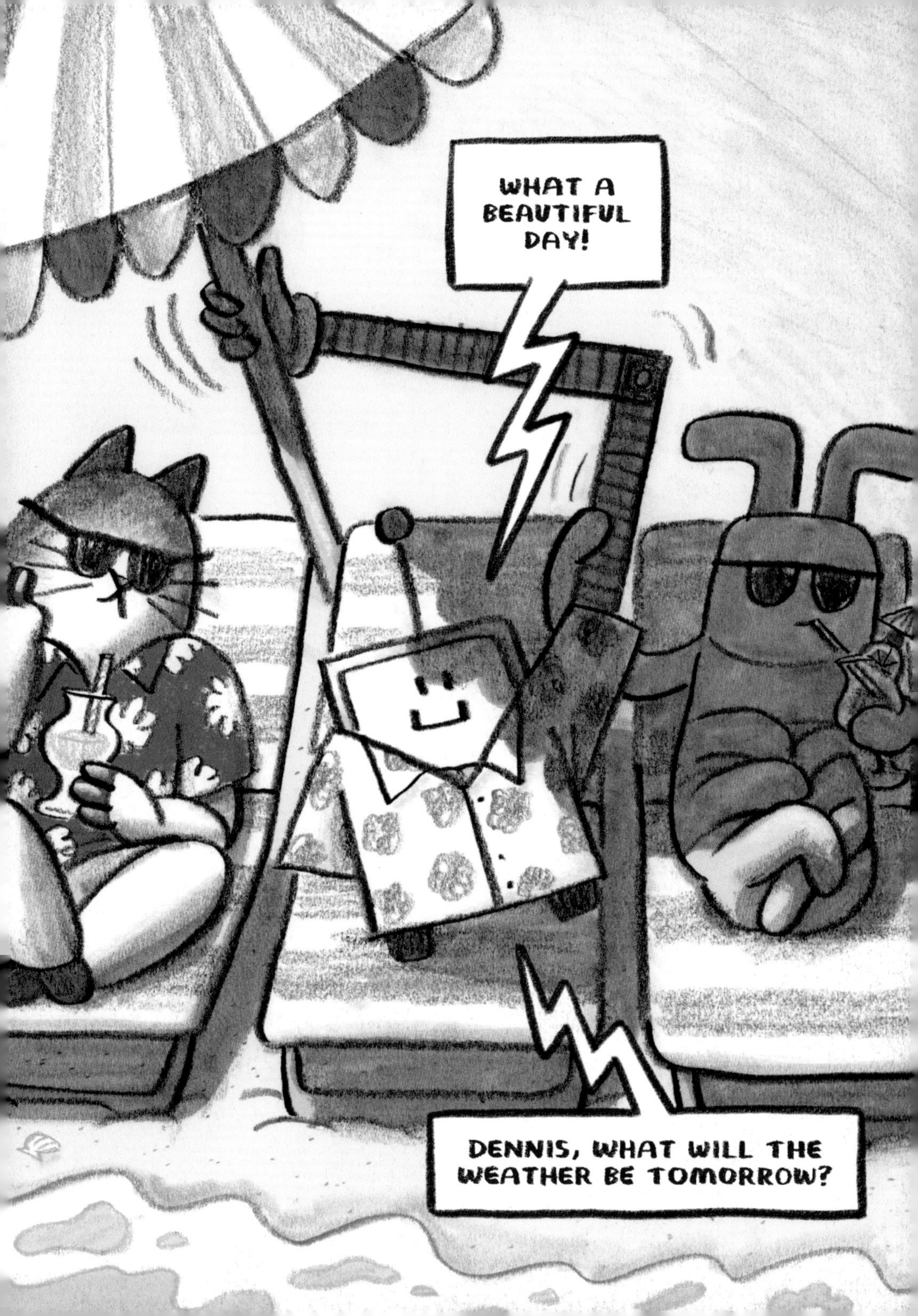
WHAT A BEAUTIFUL DAY!
DENNIS, WHAT WILL THE WEATHER BE TOMORROW?

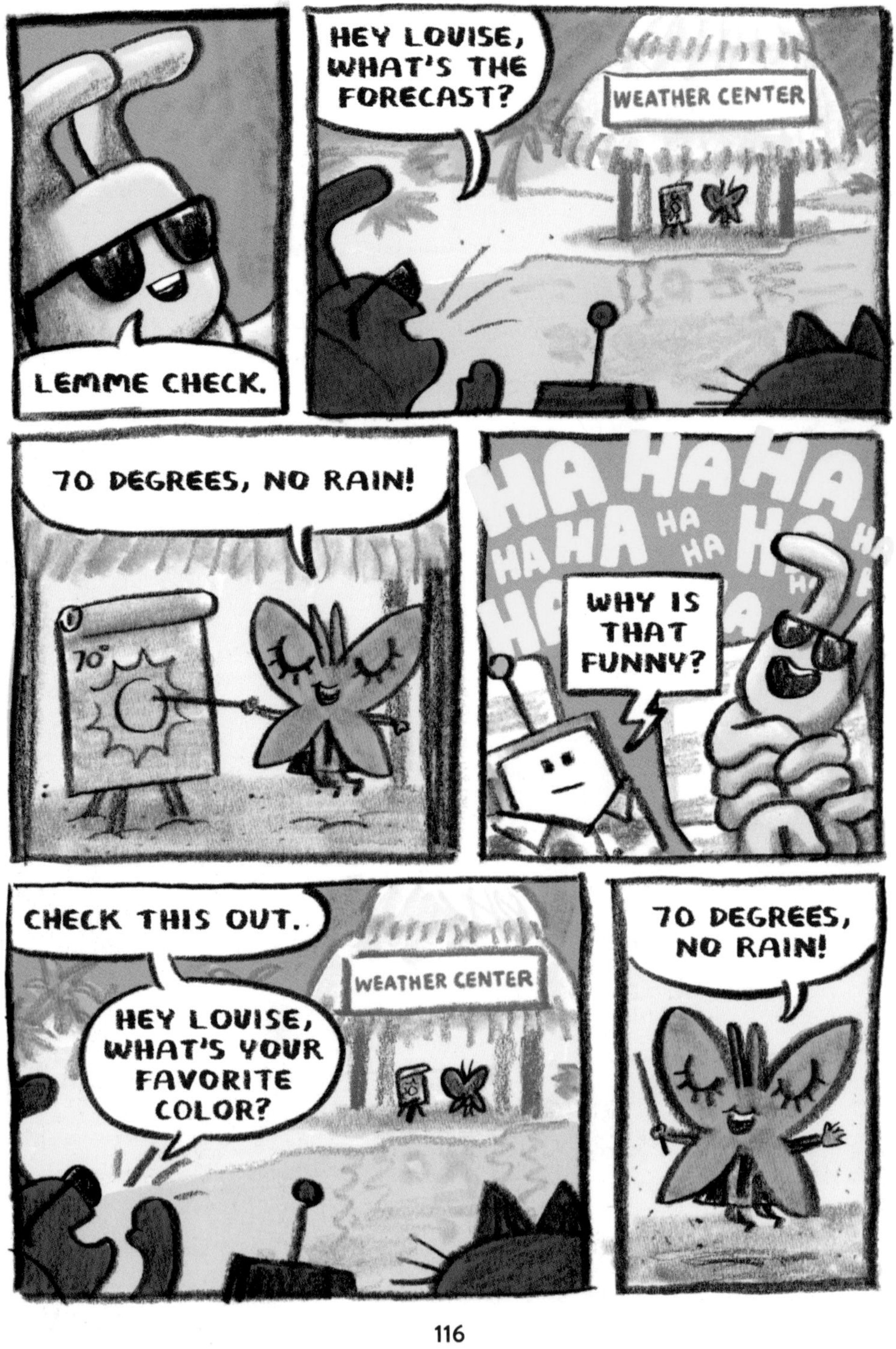
LEMME CHECK.
HEY LOUISE, WHAT'S THE FORECAST?
WEATHER CENTER
70 DEGREES, NO RAIN!
70°
HA HA HA
HA HA HA HA
WHY IS THAT FUNNY?
CHECK THIS OUT.
WEATHER CENTER
HEY LOUISE, WHAT'S YOUR FAVORITE COLOR?
70 DEGREES, NO RAIN!

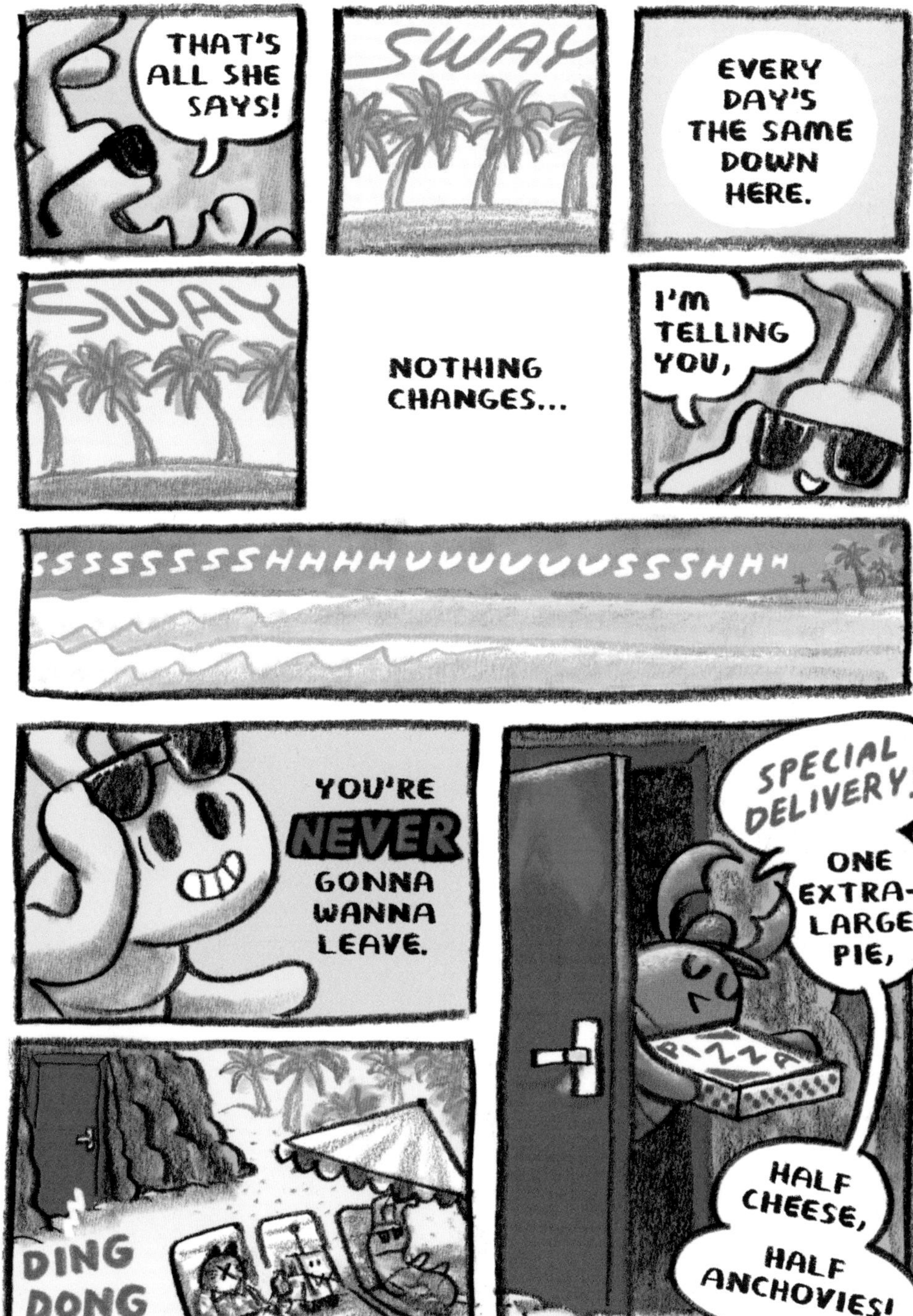
THAT'S ALL SHE SAYS!
SWAY
EVERY DAY'S THE SAME DOWN HERE.
SWAY
NOTHING CHANGES...
I'M TELLING YOU,
SSSSSSSHHHHUUUUUUUSSSHHH
YOU'RE NEVER GONNA WANNA LEAVE.
DING DONG
SPECIAL DELIVERY!
ONE EXTRA-LARGE PIE,
HALF CHEESE,
HALF ANCHOVIES!
PIZZA

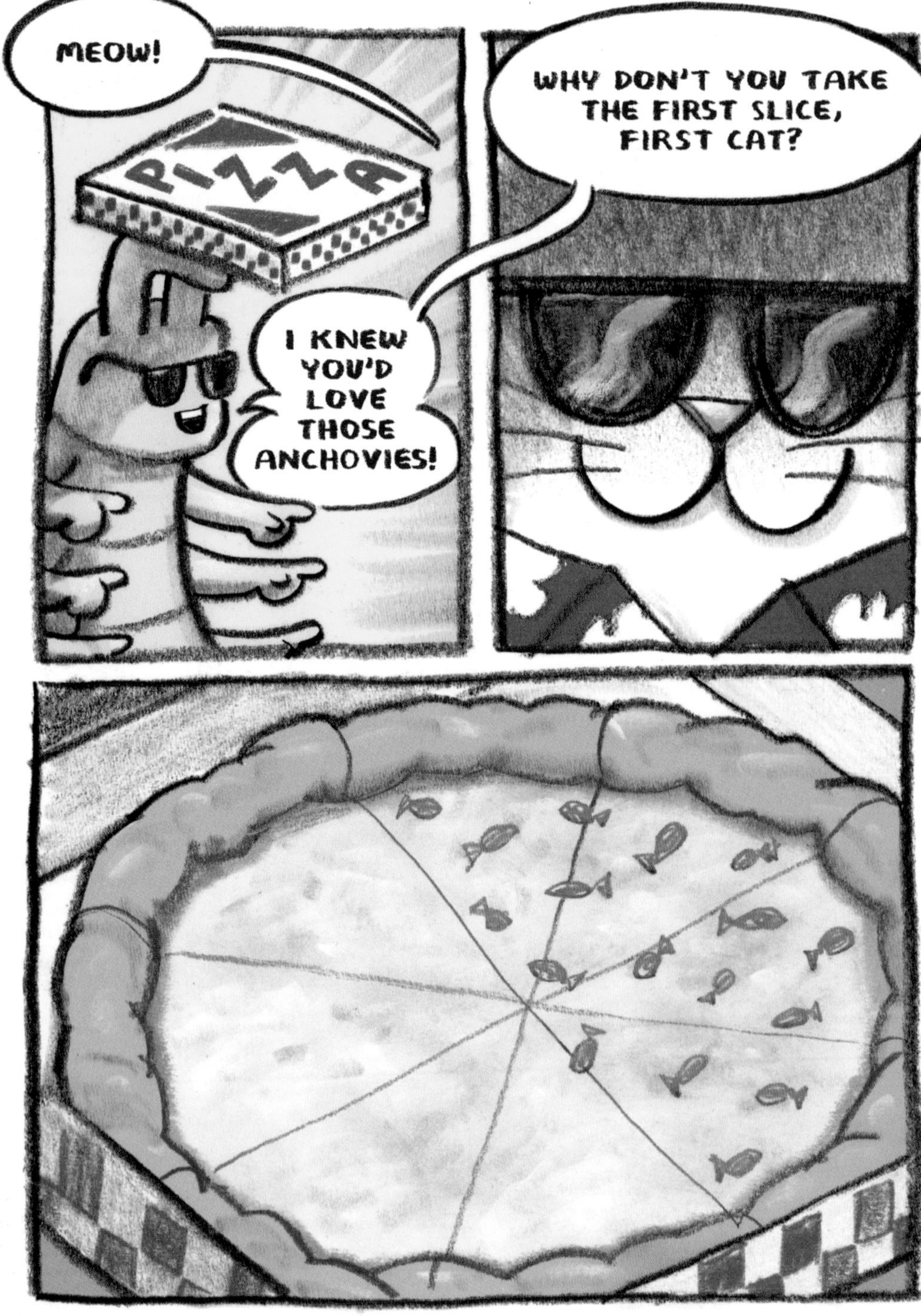
MEOW!
I KNEW YOU'D LOVE THOSE ANCHOVIES!
WHY DON'T YOU TAKE THE FIRST SLICE, FIRST CAT?
PIZZA

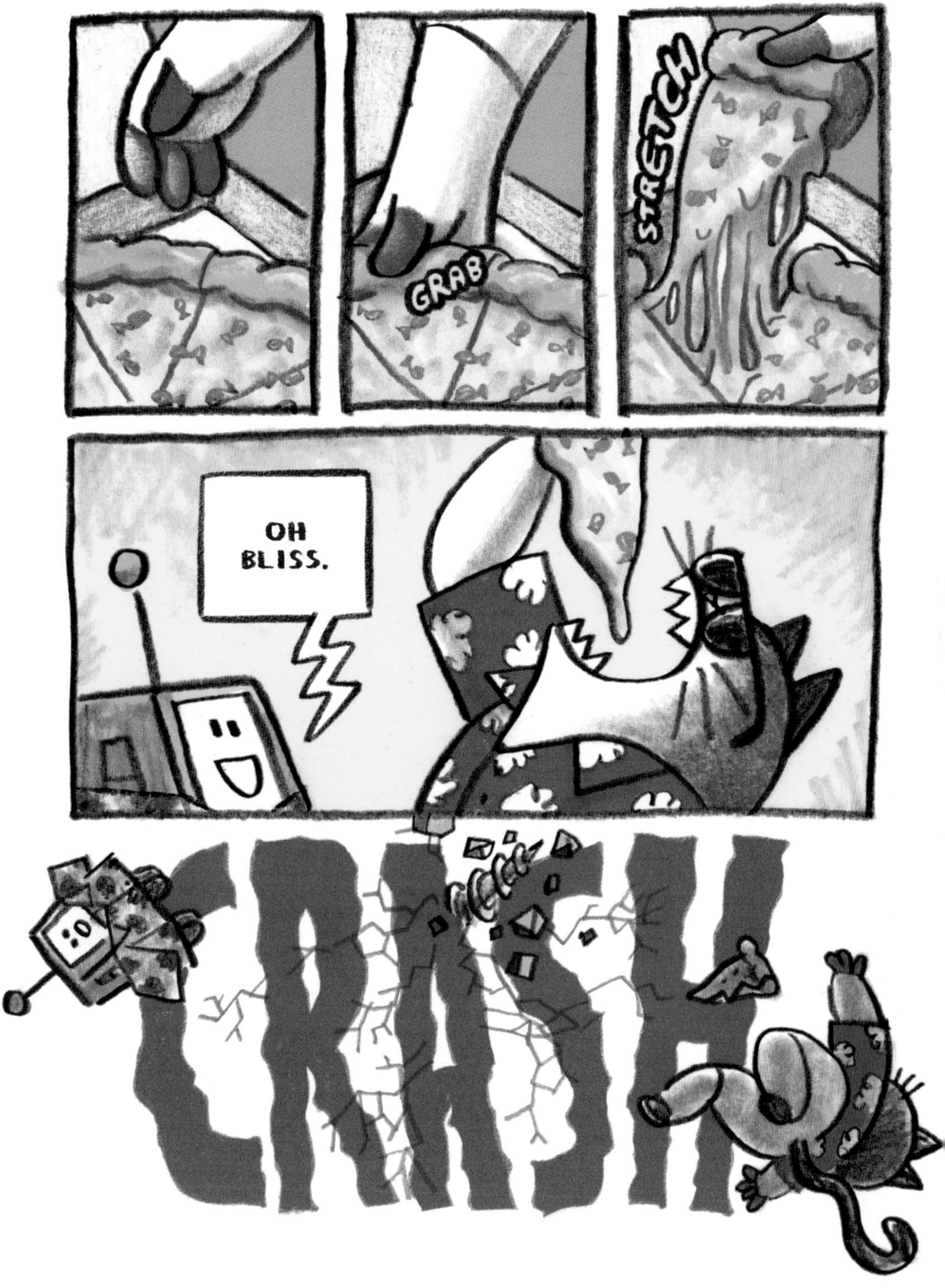
STRETCH
GRAB
OH BLISS.
CRASH

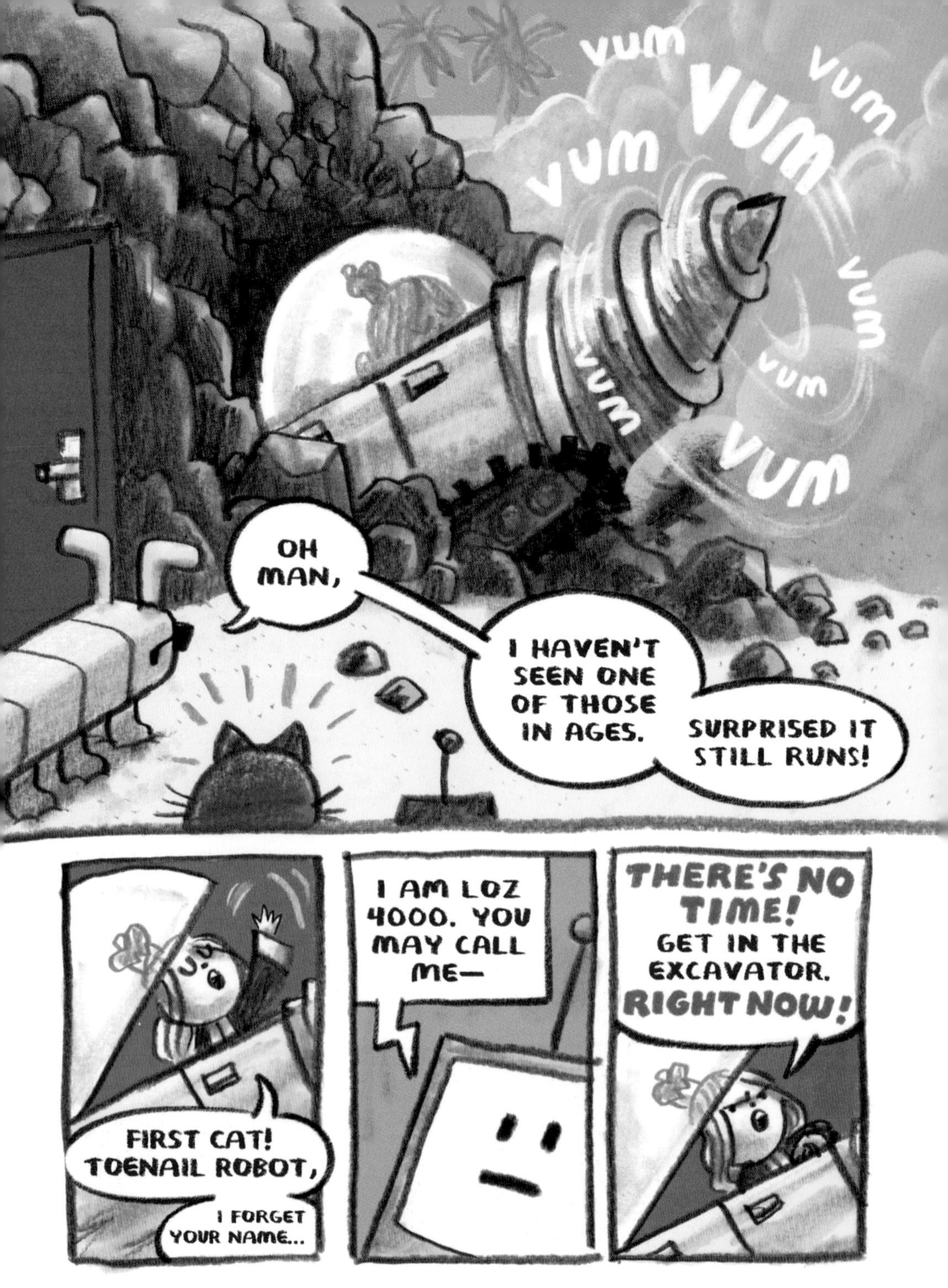
VUM VUM VUM VUM VUM VUM VUM VUM
OH MAN,
I HAVEN'T SEEN ONE OF THOSE IN AGES.
SURPRISED IT STILL RUNS!
FIRST CAT! TOENAIL ROBOT,
I FORGET YOUR NAME...
I AM LOZ 4000. YOU MAY CALL ME—
THERE'S NO TIME! GET IN THE EXCAVATOR. RIGHT NOW!

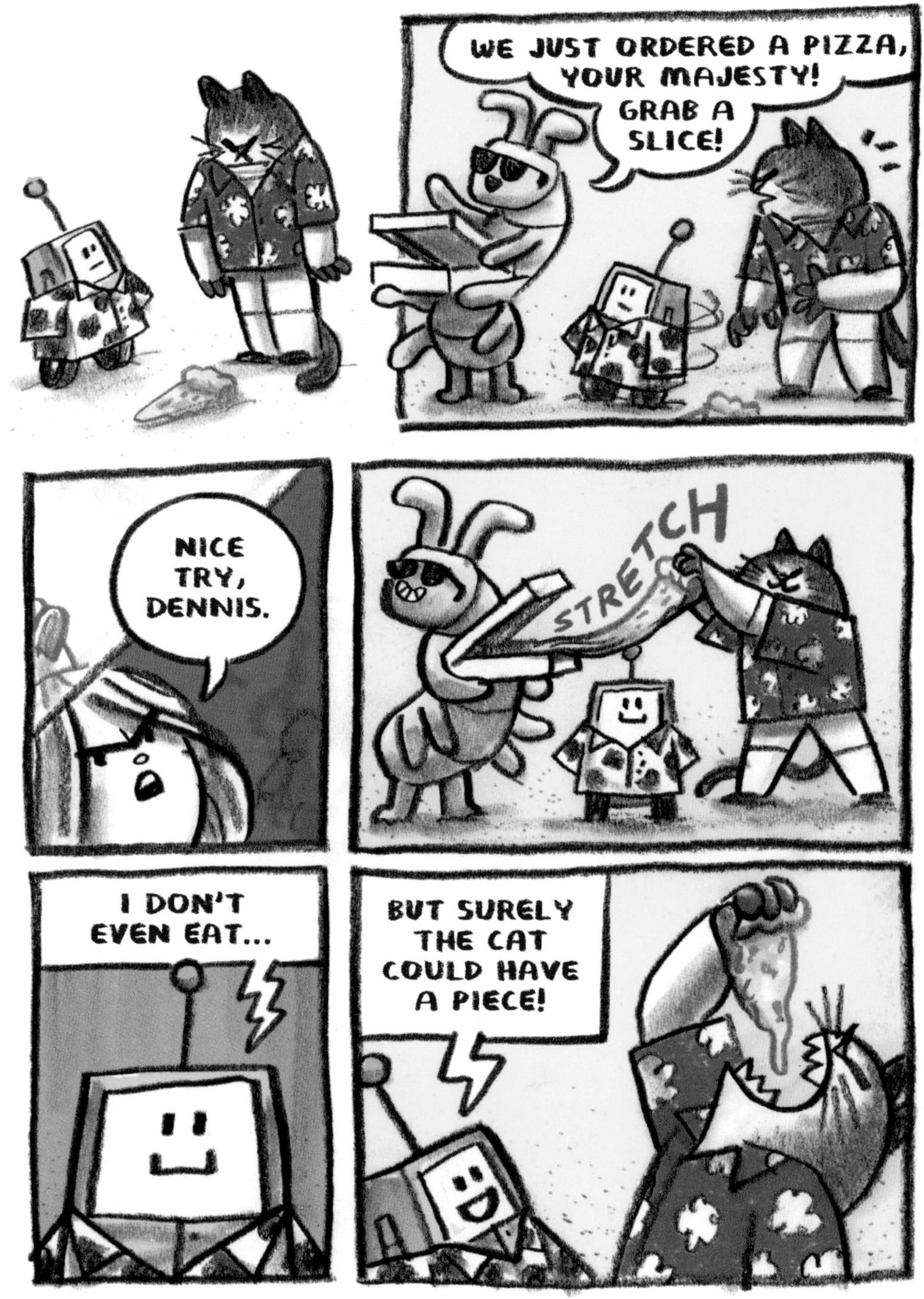
WE JUST ORDERED A PIZZA, YOUR MAJESTY!
GRAB A SLICE!
NICE TRY, DENNIS.
STRETCH
I DON'T EVEN EAT...
BUT SURELY THE CAT COULD HAVE A PIECE!

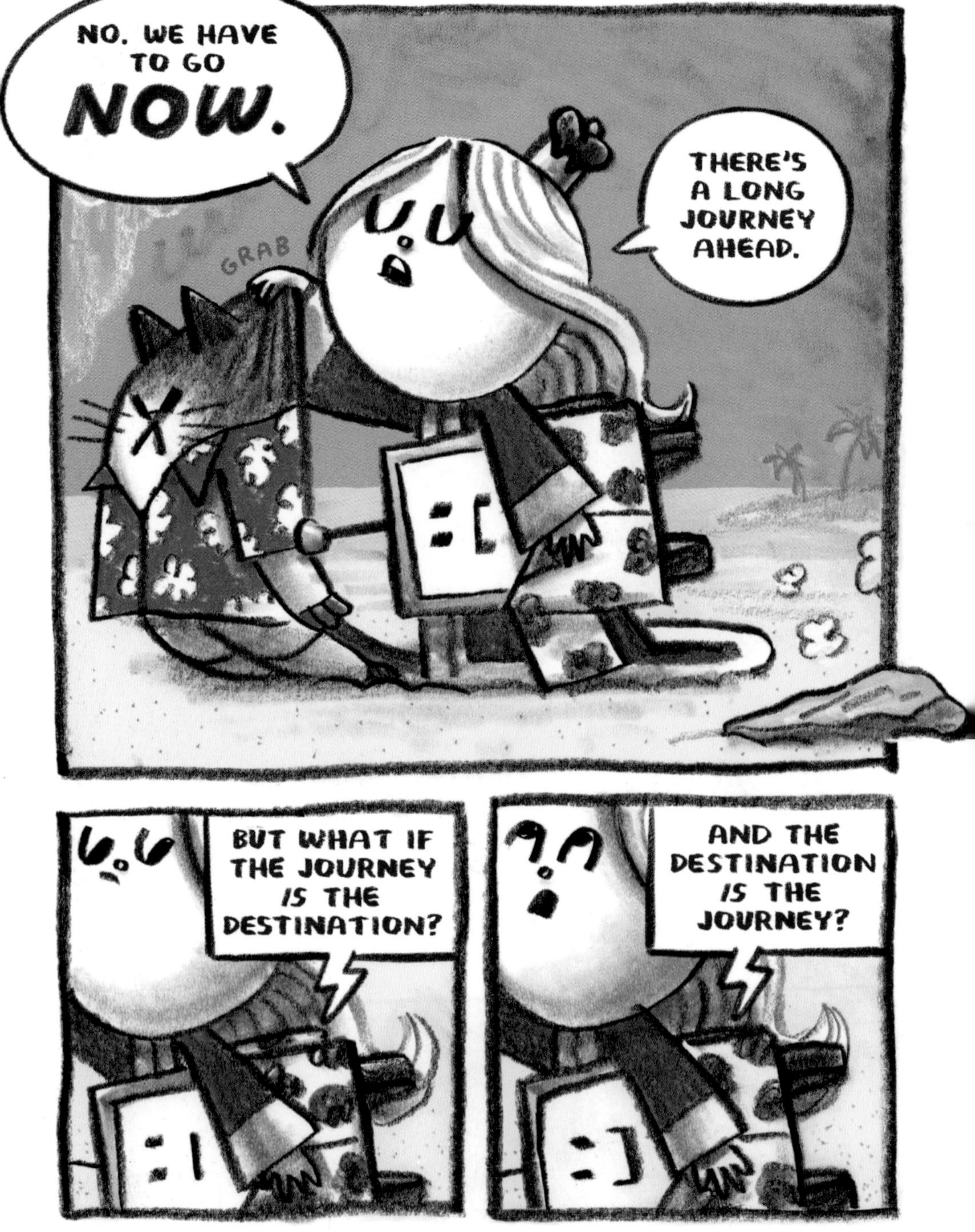
NO. WE HAVE TO GO NOW.
GRAB
THERE'S A LONG JOURNEY AHEAD.
BUT WHAT IF THE JOURNEY *IS* THE DESTINATION?
AND THE DESTINATION *IS* THE JOURNEY?

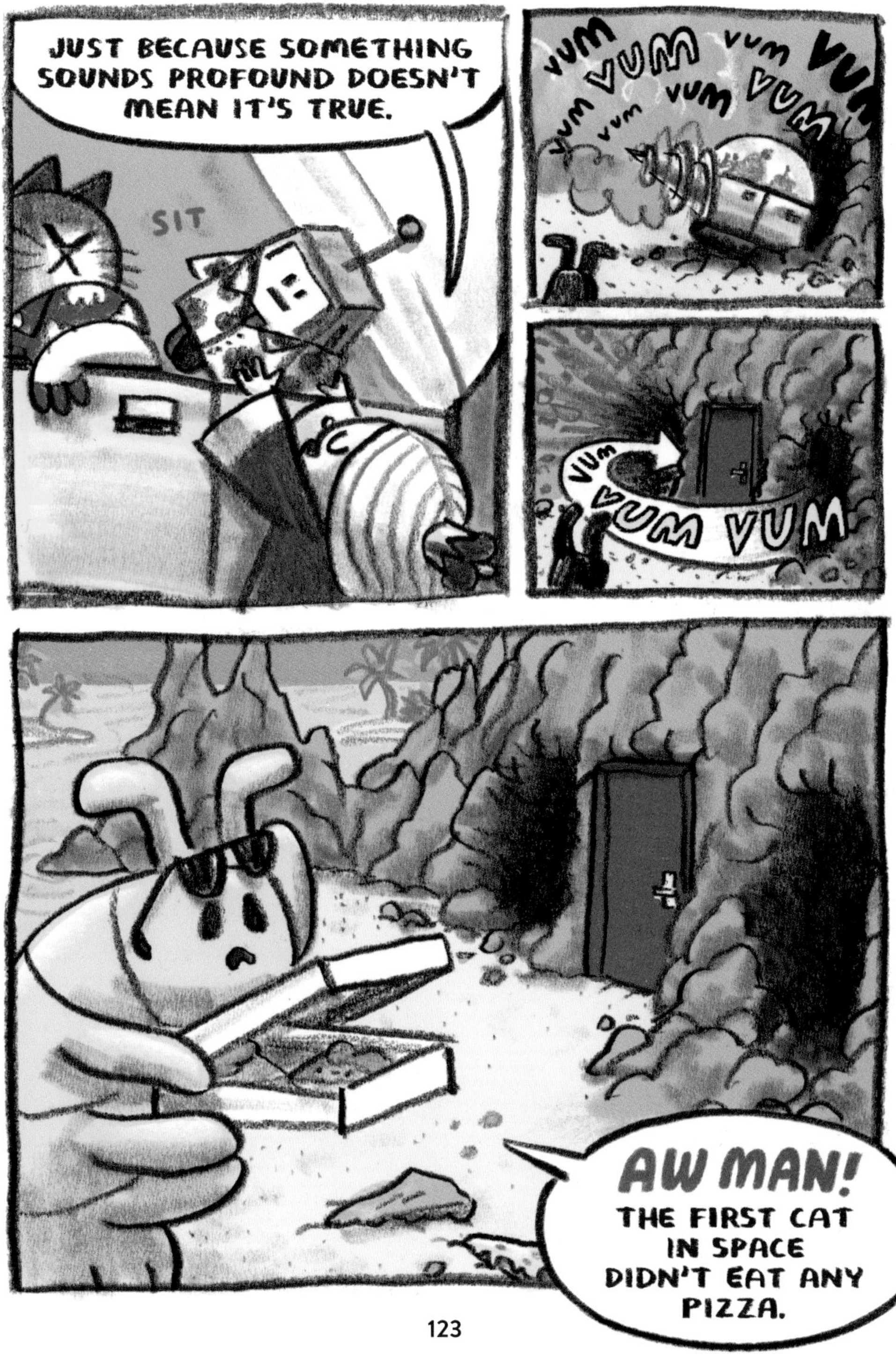
JUST BECAUSE SOMETHING SOUNDS PROFOUND DOESN'T MEAN IT'S TRUE.
SIT
VUM VUM VUM vum VUM vum VUM VUM VUM
VUM VUM VUM
AW MAN!
THE FIRST CAT IN SPACE DIDN'T EAT ANY PIZZA.

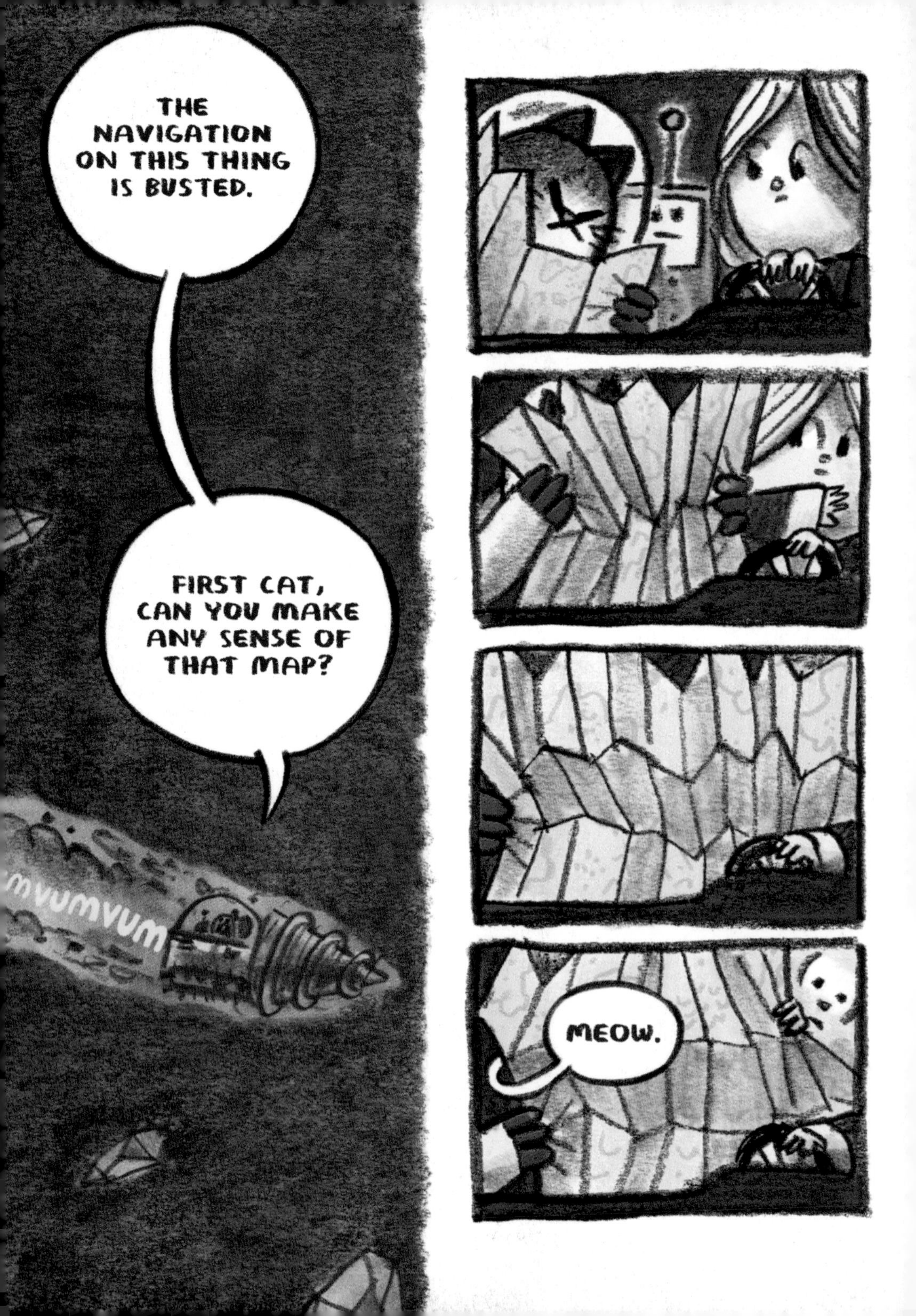
THE NAVIGATION ON THIS THING IS BUSTED.
FIRST CAT, CAN YOU MAKE ANY SENSE OF THAT MAP?
MVUMVUM
MEOW.

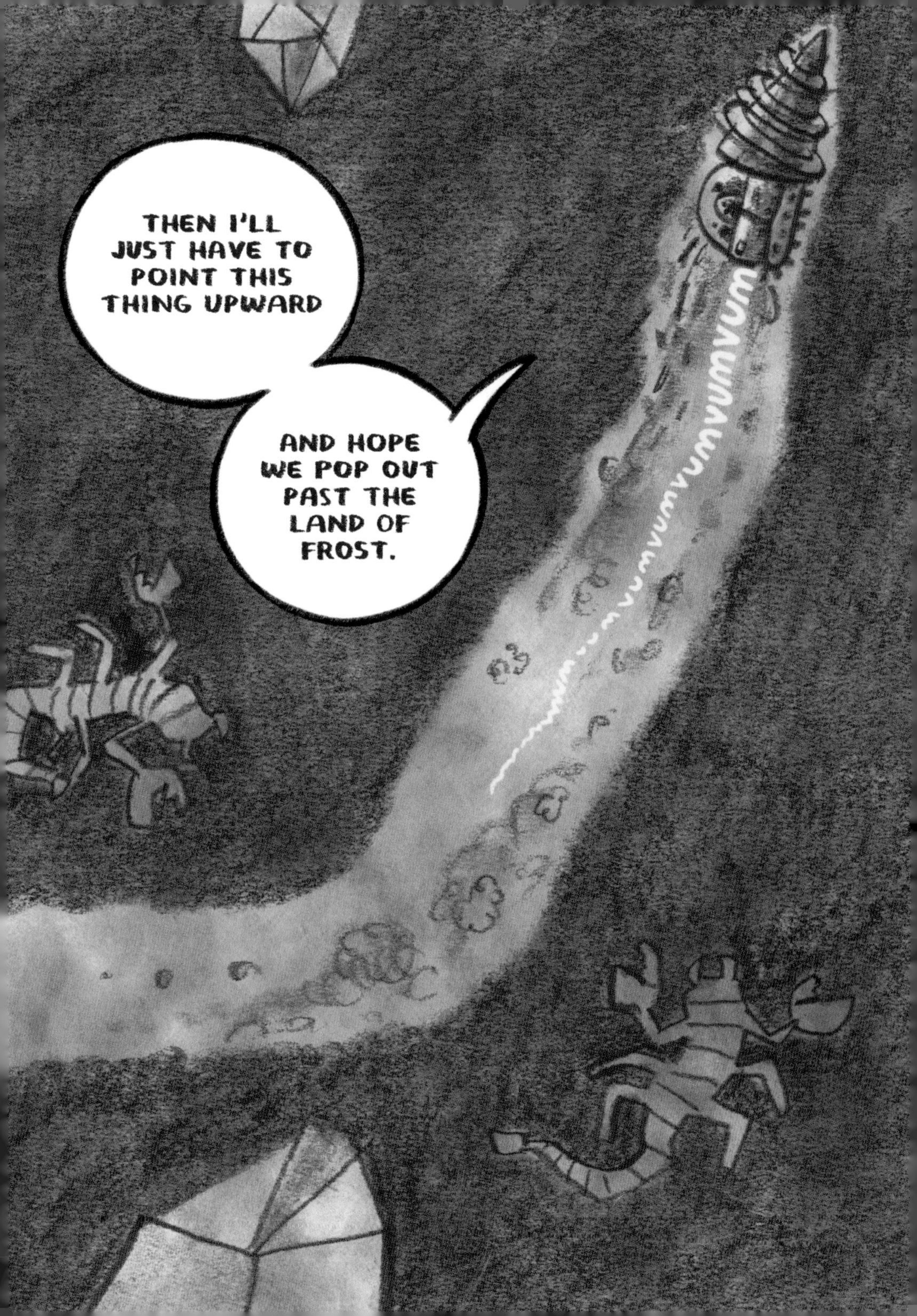
THEN I'LL JUST HAVE TO POINT THIS THING UPWARD
AND HOPE WE POP OUT PAST THE LAND OF FROST.
VUMVUMVUMVUMVUMVUM

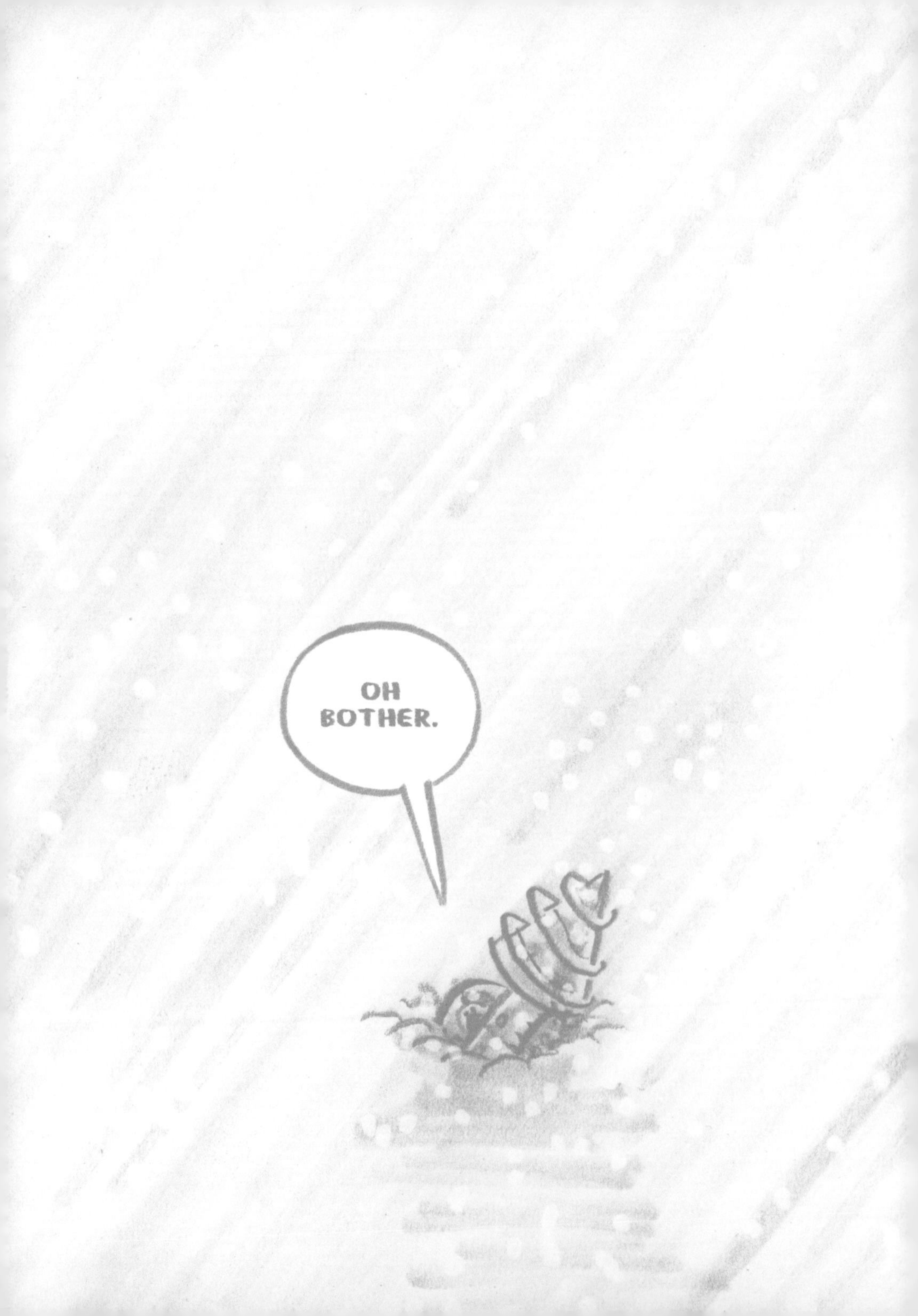
OH BOTHER.

CHAPTER 10
FREEZING

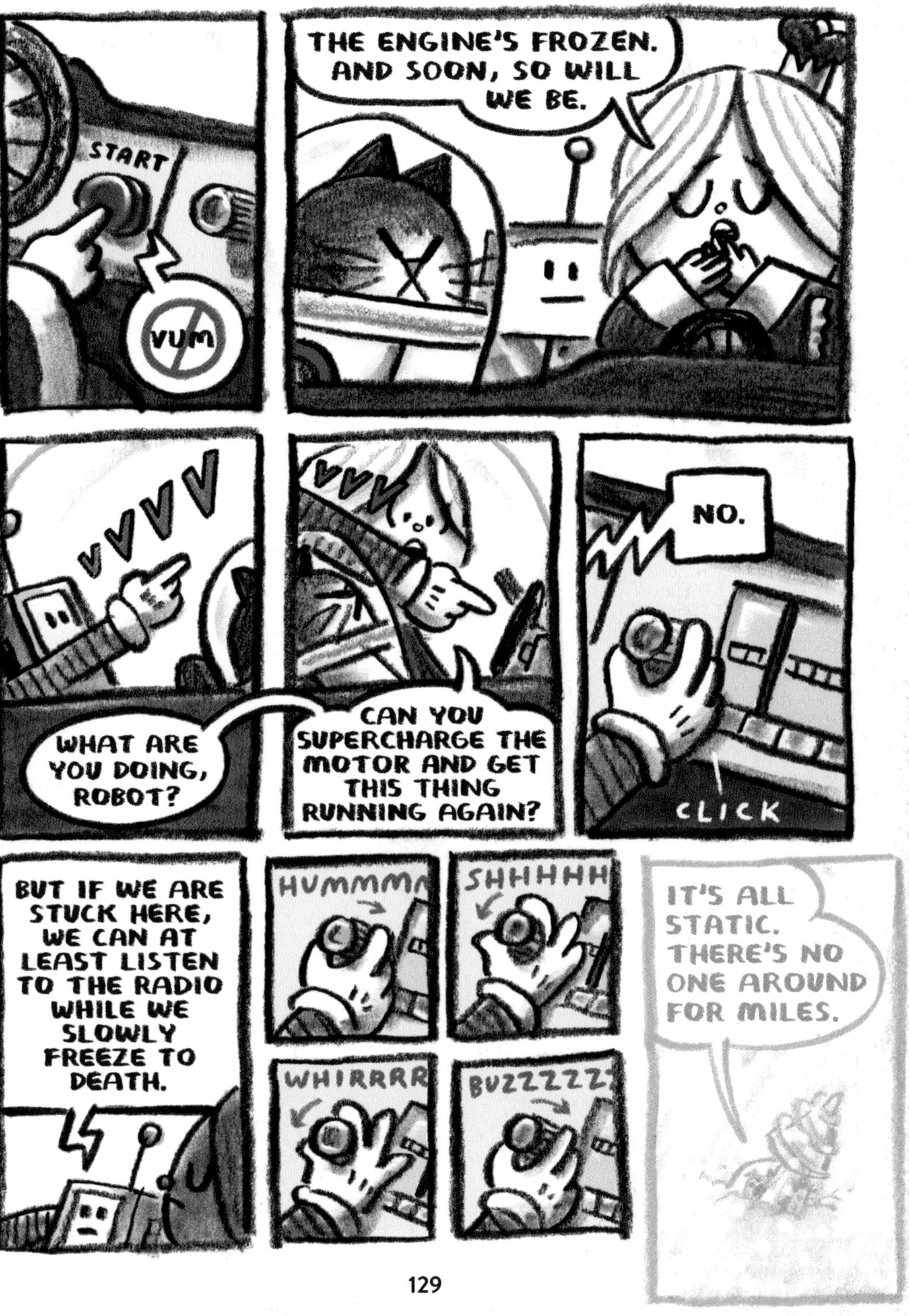
START
VUM
THE ENGINE'S FROZEN. AND SOON, SO WILL WE BE.
VVVVV
VVV
WHAT ARE YOU DOING, ROBOT?
CAN YOU SUPERCHARGE THE MOTOR AND GET THIS THING RUNNING AGAIN?
NO.
CLICK
BUT IF WE ARE STUCK HERE, WE CAN AT LEAST LISTEN TO THE RADIO WHILE WE SLOWLY FREEZE TO DEATH.
HUMMMM
SHHHHH
WHIRRRR
BUZZZZZ
IT'S ALL STATIC. THERE'S NO ONE AROUND FOR MILES.

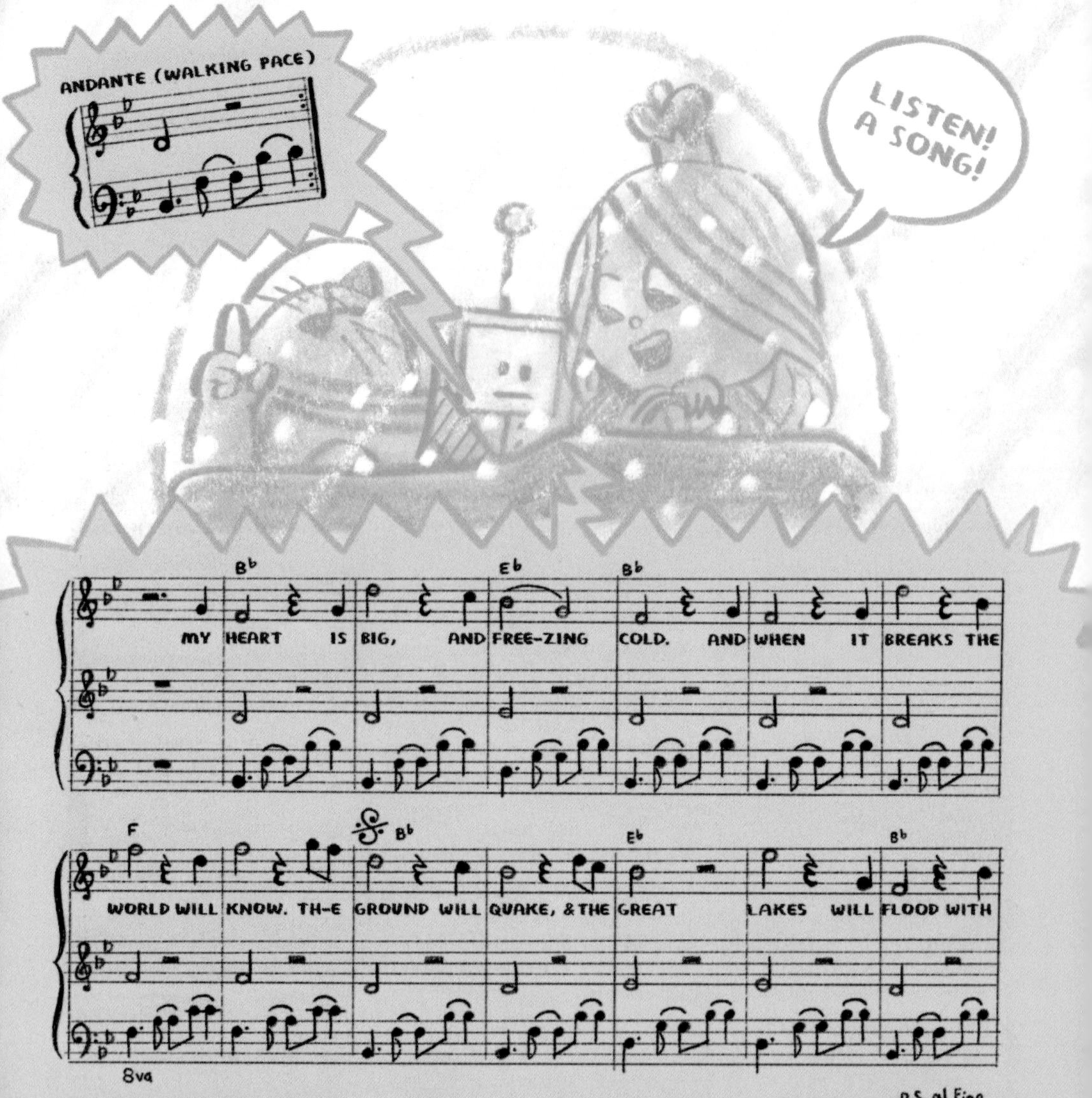
ANDANTE (WALKING PACE)
LISTEN! A SONG!
Bb Eb Bb
MY HEART IS BIG, AND FREE-ZING COLD. AND WHEN IT BREAKS THE
F Bb Eb Bb
WORLD WILL KNOW. TH-E GROUND WILL QUAKE, & THE GREAT LAKES WILL FLOOD WITH
8va
F Bb Fine F Bb
D.S. al Fine
1. 2.
MY GIANT TEAR-DROPS (POP) GIANT TEAR-DROPS (POP) GIANT TEAR-DROPS (POP) GIANT (POP) TH-E
8va 8va

SHAWN & MAC SAY:

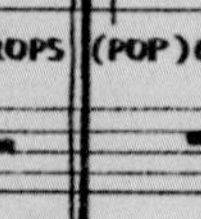

Go to www.thefirstcatinspace.com to hear this song and other First Cat tunes. We sang them!

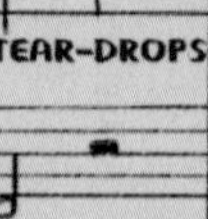

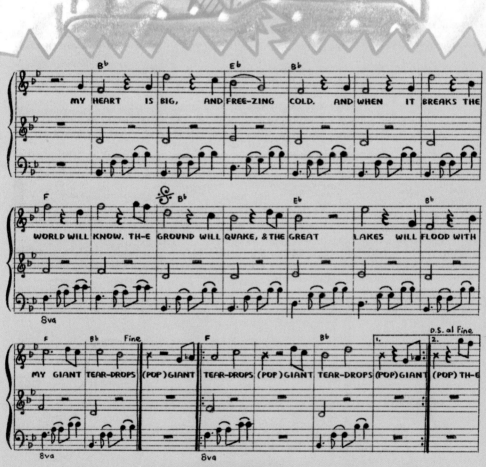

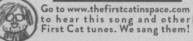

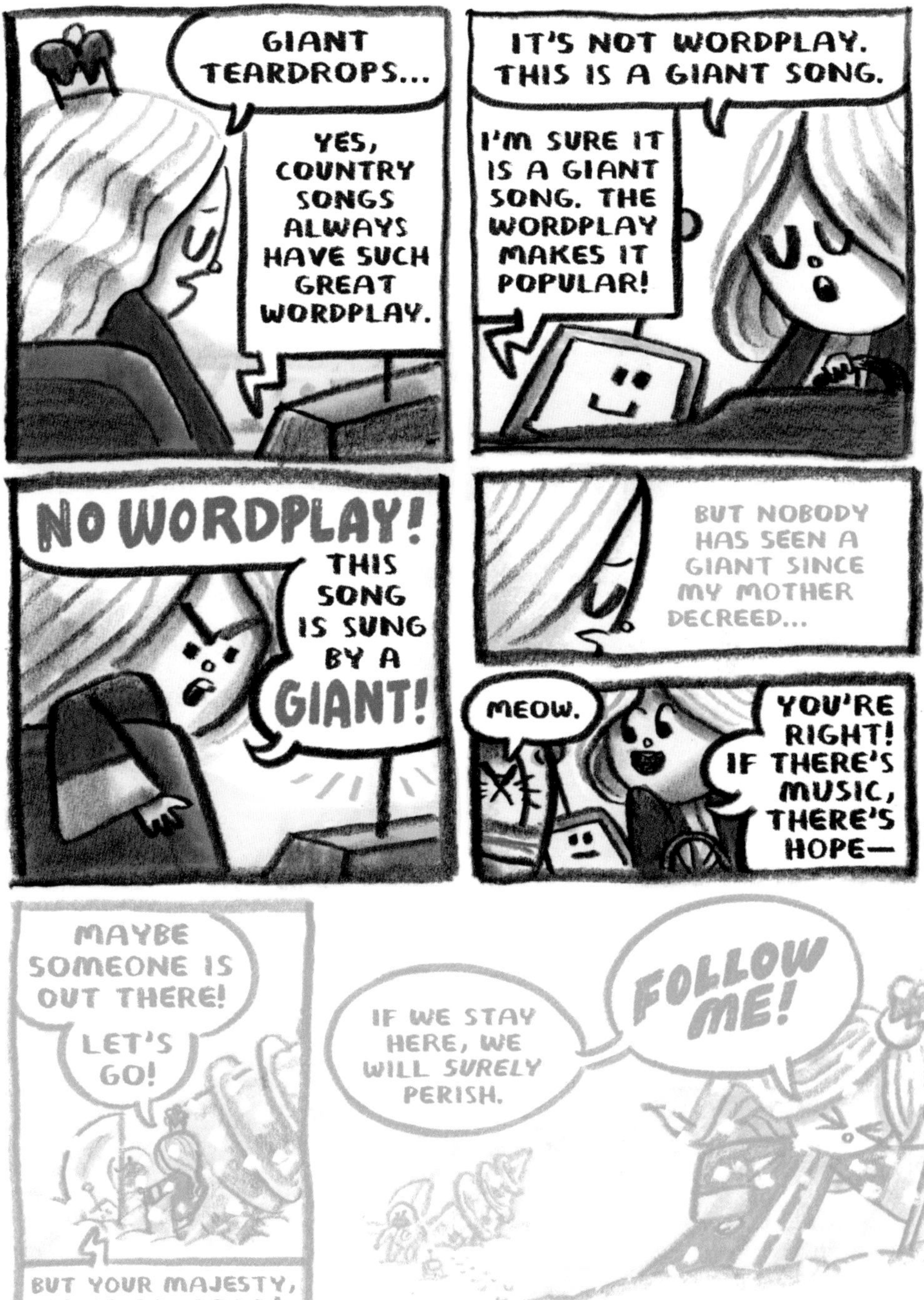
GIANT TEARDROPS...
YES, COUNTRY SONGS ALWAYS HAVE SUCH GREAT WORDPLAY.
IT'S NOT WORDPLAY. THIS IS A GIANT SONG.
I'M SURE IT IS A GIANT SONG. THE WORDPLAY MAKES IT POPULAR!
NO WORDPLAY!
THIS SONG IS SUNG BY A GIANT!
BUT NOBODY HAS SEEN A GIANT SINCE MY MOTHER DECREED...
MEOW.
YOU'RE RIGHT! IF THERE'S MUSIC, THERE'S HOPE—
MAYBE SOMEONE IS OUT THERE!
LET'S GO!
BUT YOUR MAJESTY, IT IS SO COLD!
IF WE STAY HERE, WE WILL *SURELY* PERISH.
FOLLOW ME!

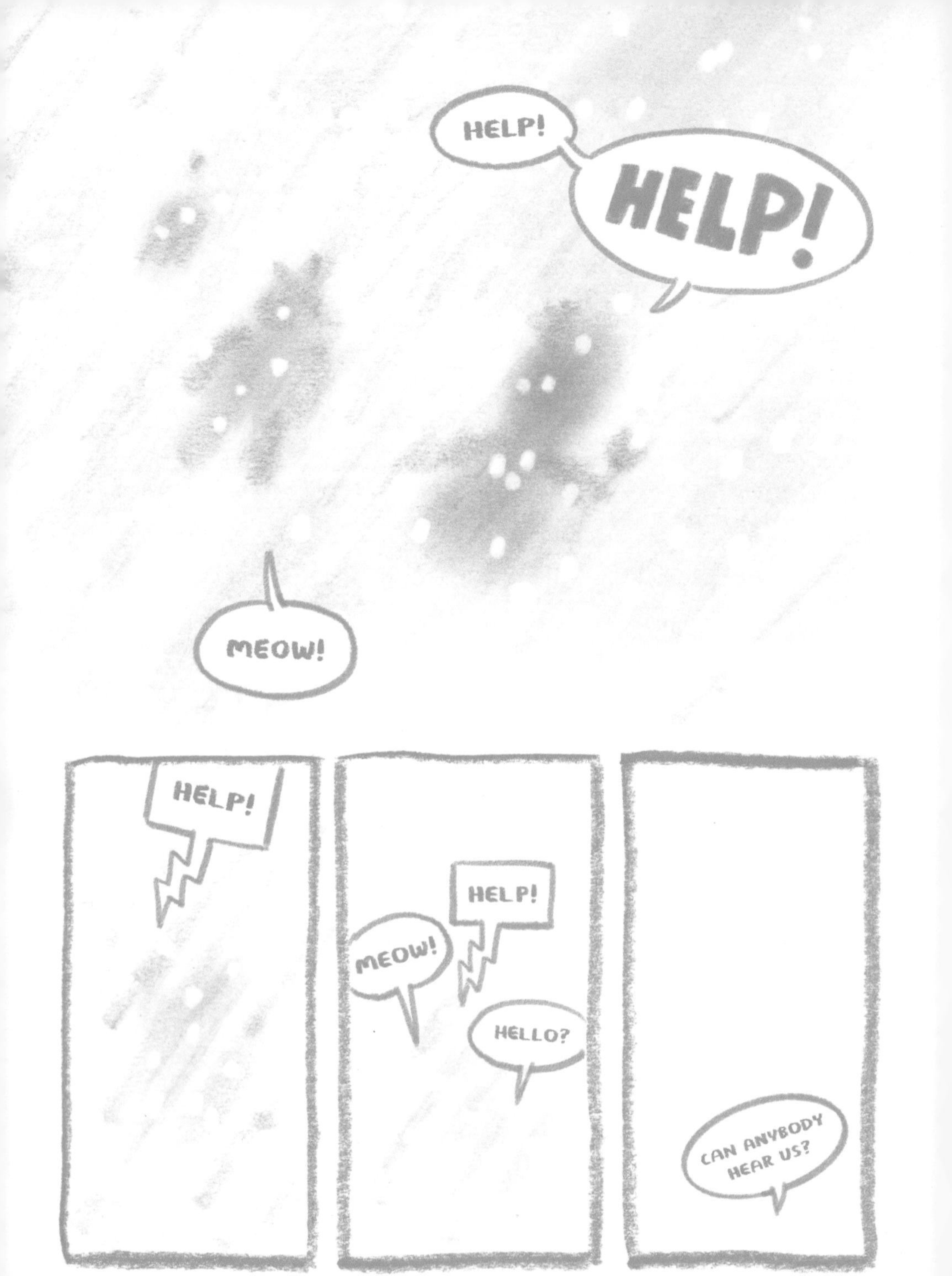
HELP!
HELP!
MEOW!
HELP!
MEOW!
HELP!
HELLO?
CAN ANYBODY HEAR US?

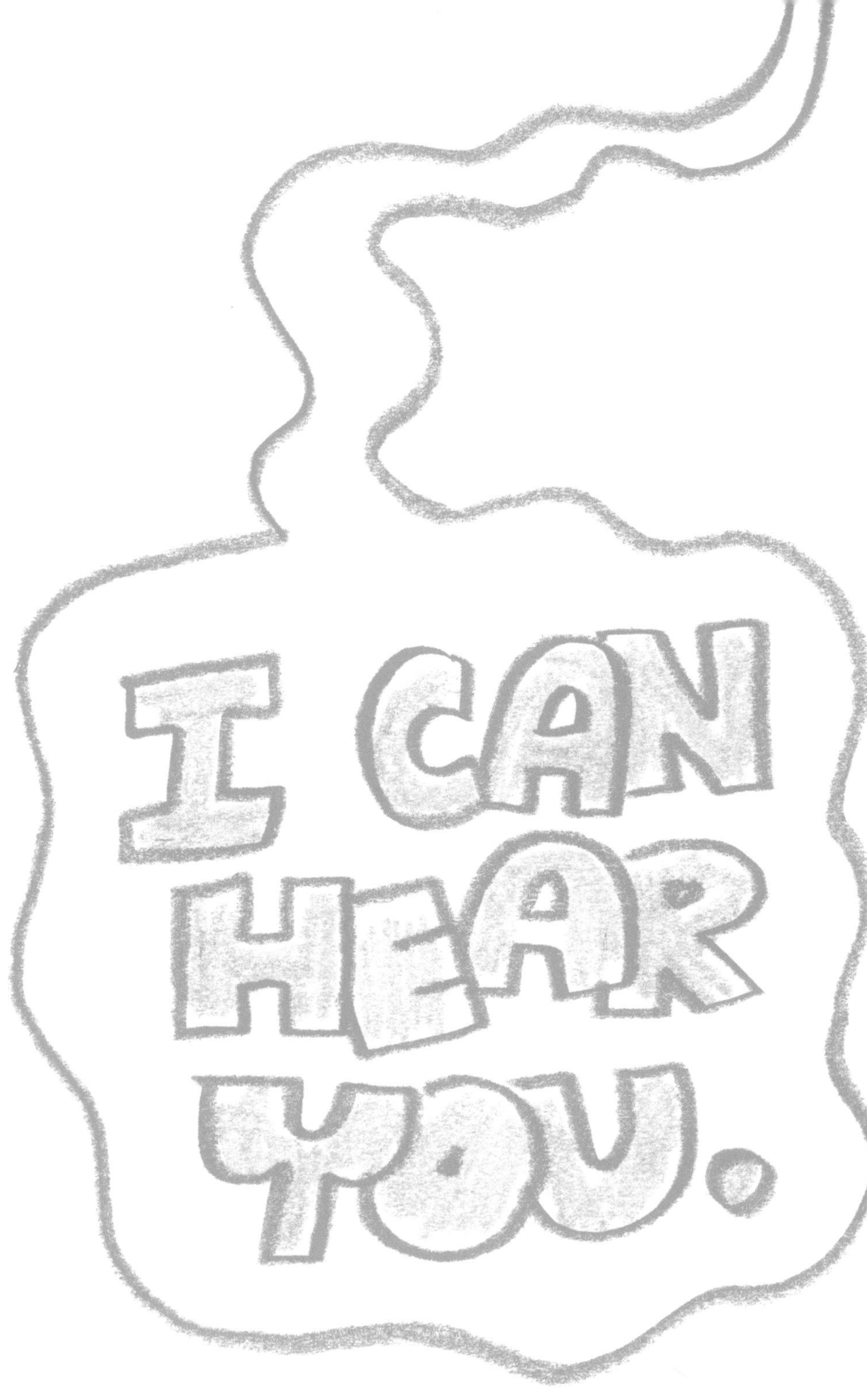
I CAN HEAR YOU.

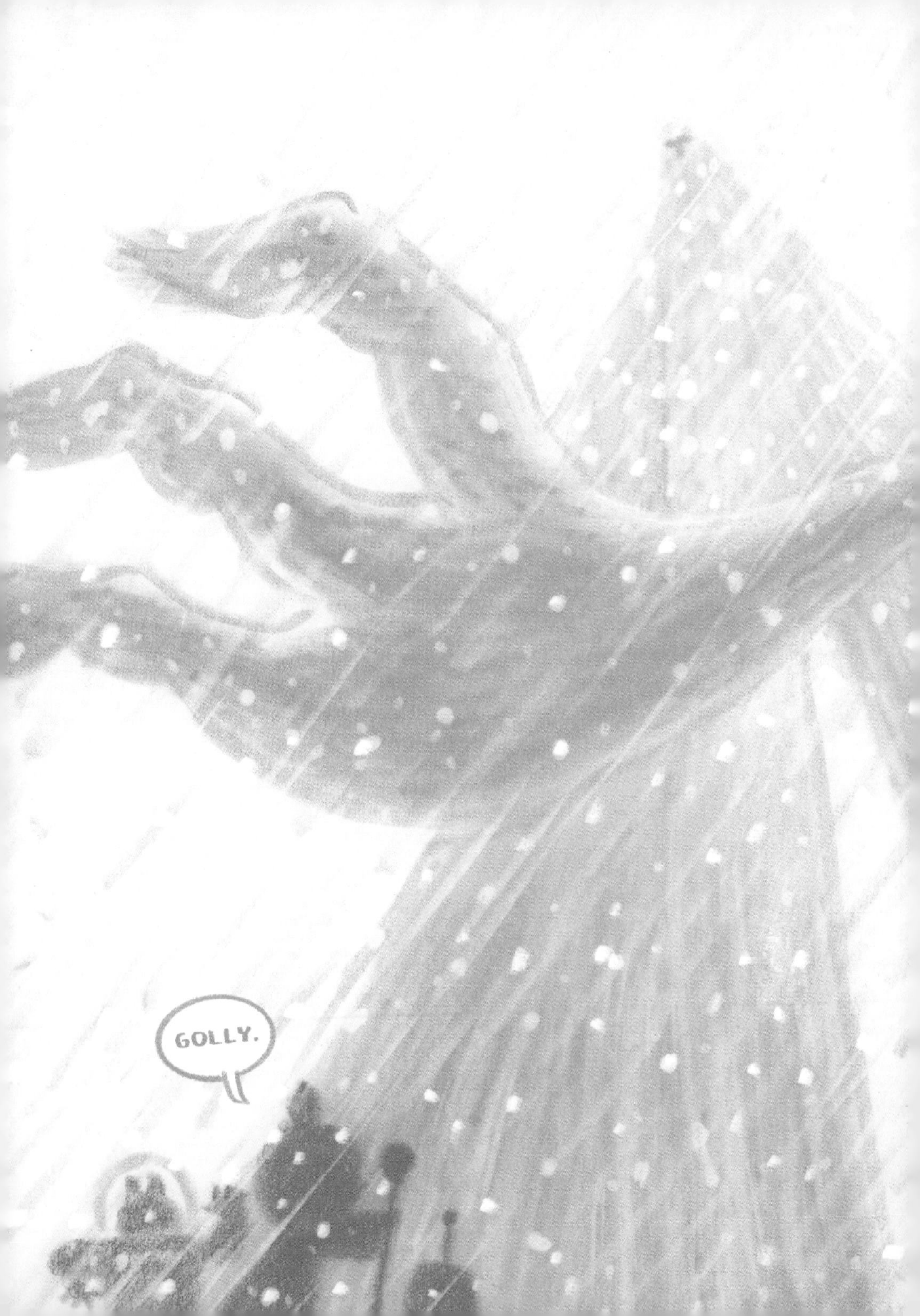
GOLLY.

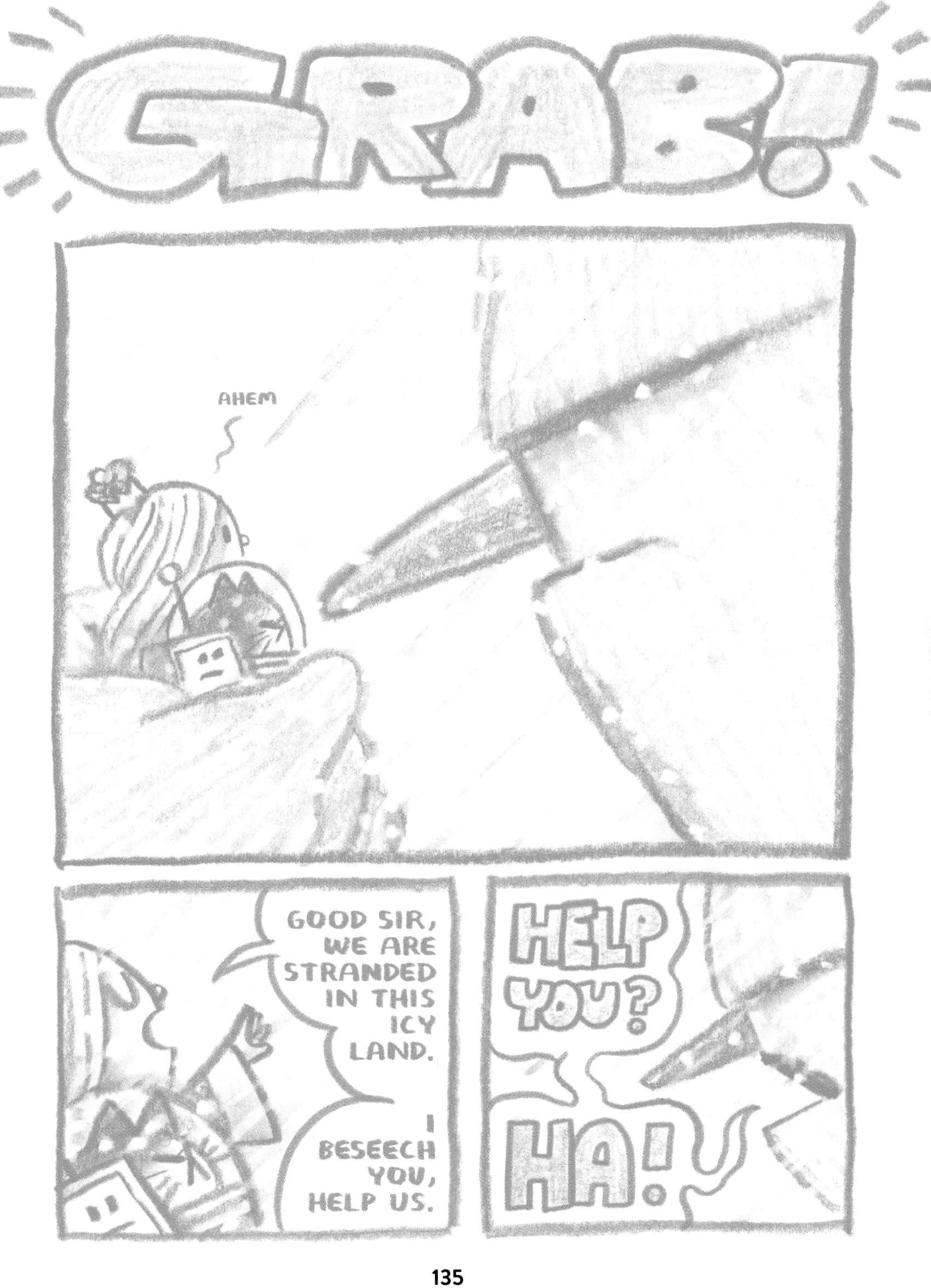
GRAB!
AHEM
GOOD SIR, WE ARE STRANDED IN THIS ICY LAND.
I BESEECH YOU, HELP US.
HELP YOU?
HA!

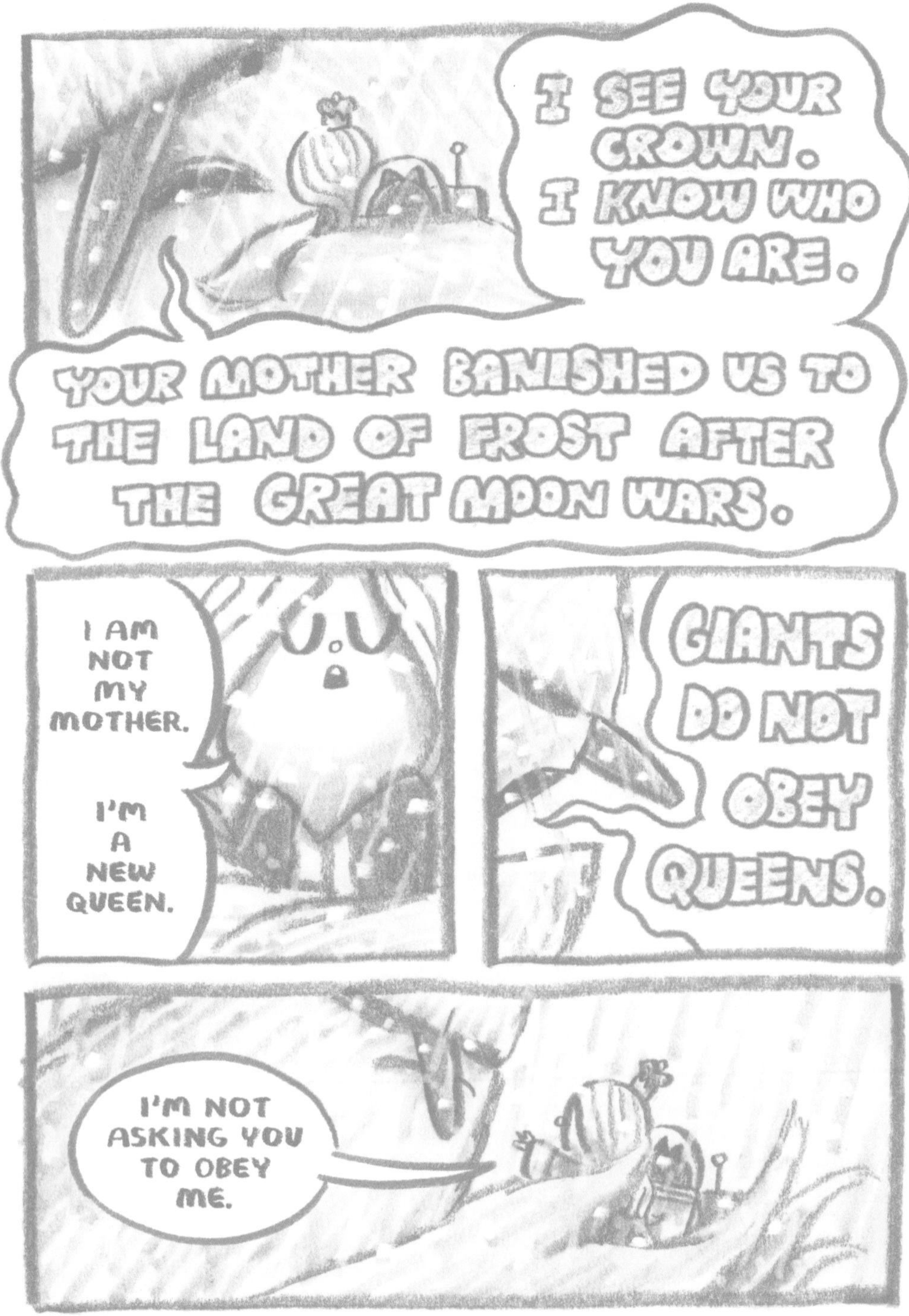

I SEE YOUR CROWN. I KNOW WHO YOU ARE.
YOUR MOTHER BANISHED US TO THE LAND OF FROST AFTER THE GREAT MOON WARS.
I AM NOT MY MOTHER.
I'M A NEW QUEEN.
GIANTS DO NOT OBEY QUEENS.
I'M NOT ASKING YOU TO OBEY ME.

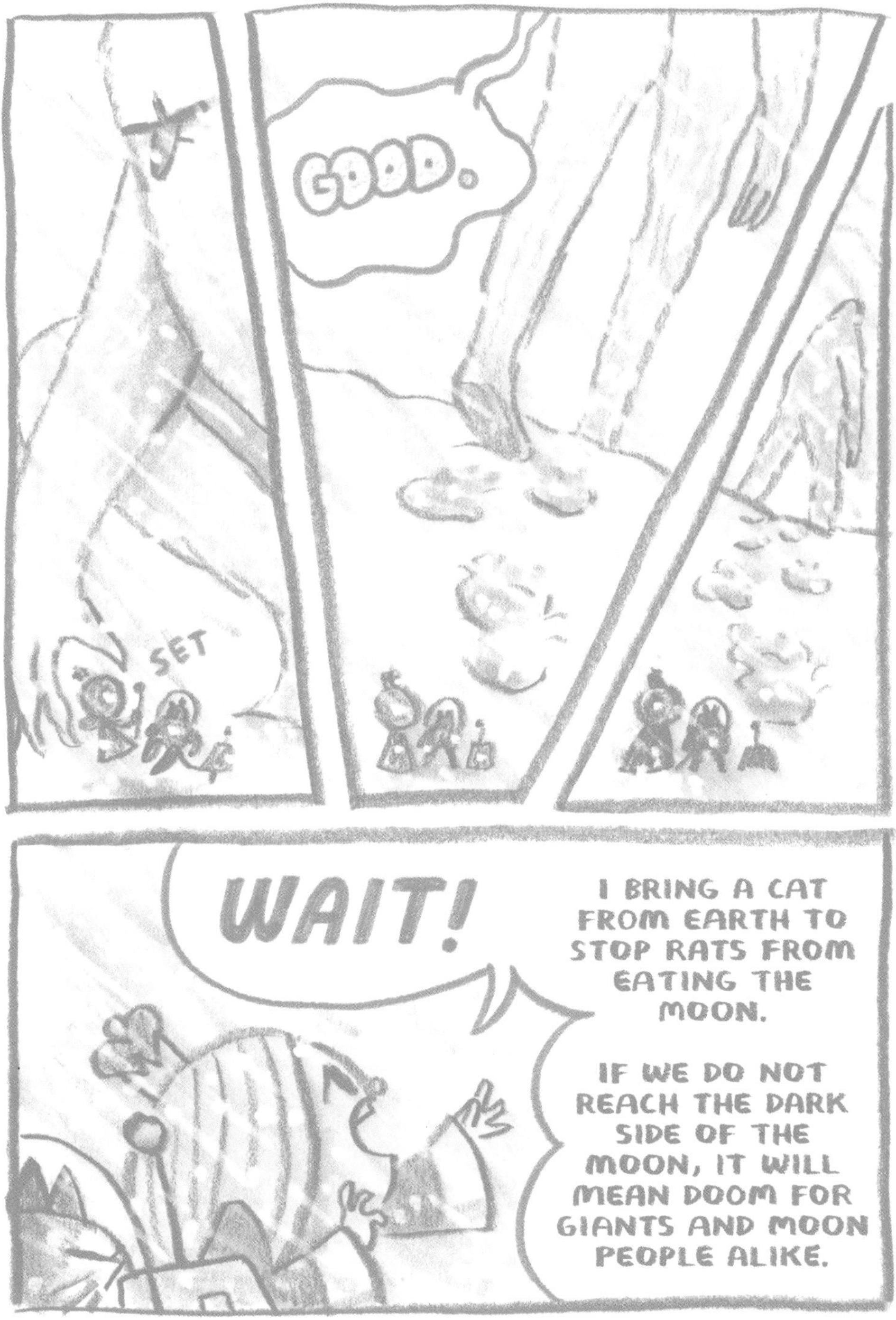
SET
GOOD.
WAIT!
I BRING A CAT FROM EARTH TO STOP RATS FROM EATING THE MOON.
IF WE DO NOT REACH THE DARK SIDE OF THE MOON, IT WILL MEAN DOOM FOR GIANTS AND MOON PEOPLE ALIKE.

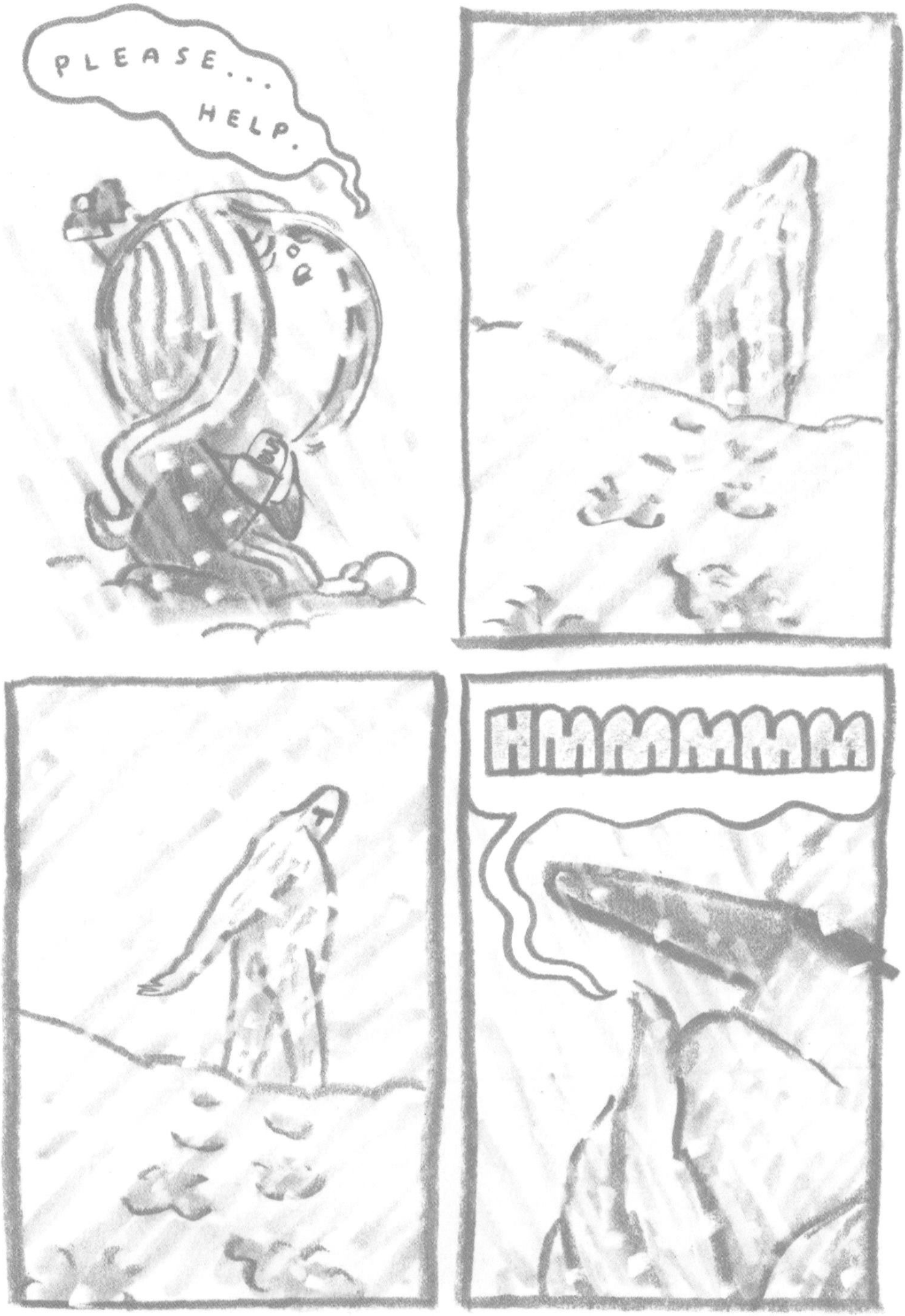
PLEASE... HELP.
HMMMMMM

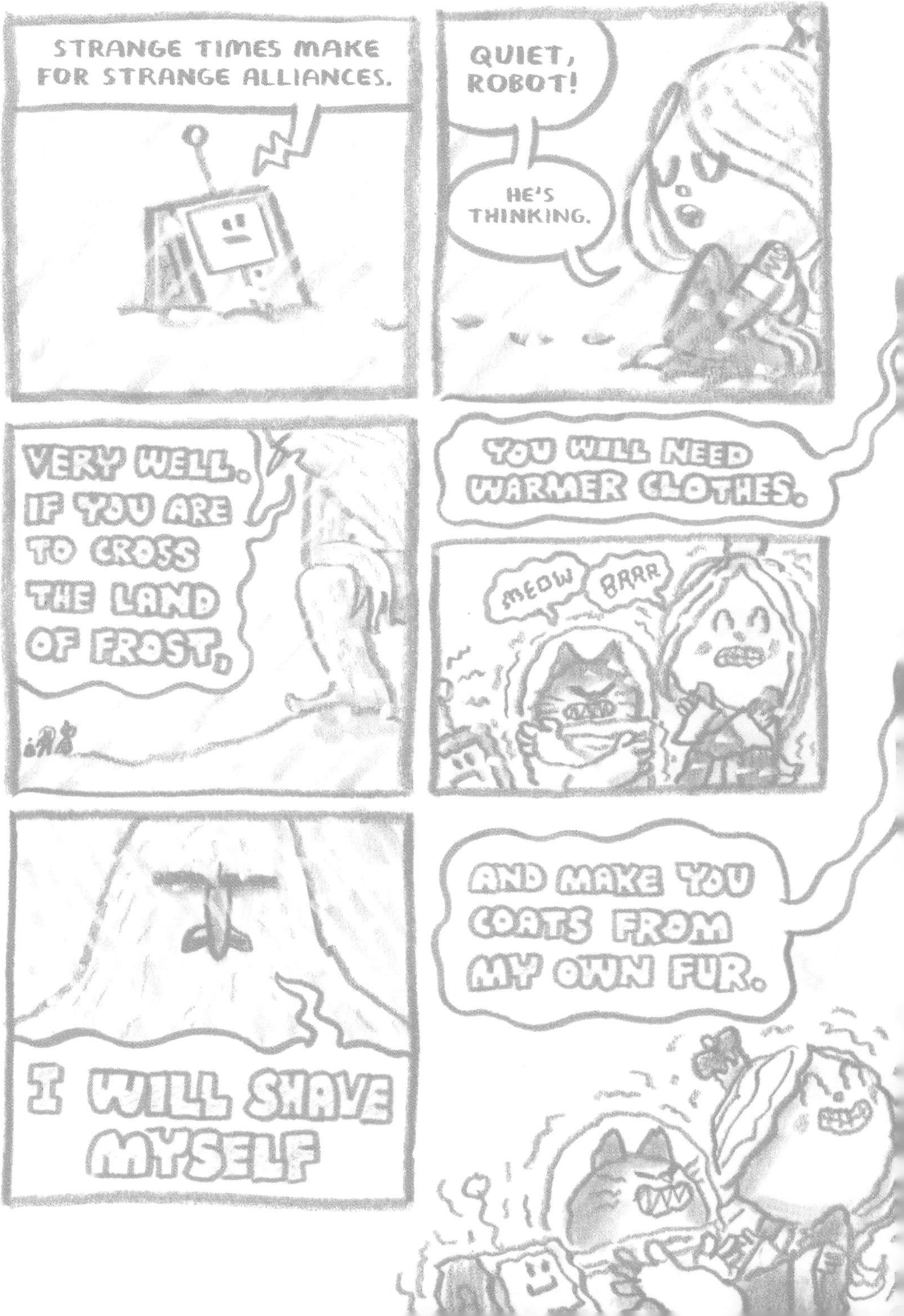
STRANGE TIMES MAKE FOR STRANGE ALLIANCES.
QUIET, ROBOT!
HE'S THINKING.
VERY WELL. IF YOU ARE TO CROSS THE LAND OF FROST,
YOU WILL NEED WARMER CLOTHES.
MEOW
BRRR
I WILL SHAVE MYSELF
AND MAKE YOU COATS FROM MY OWN FUR.

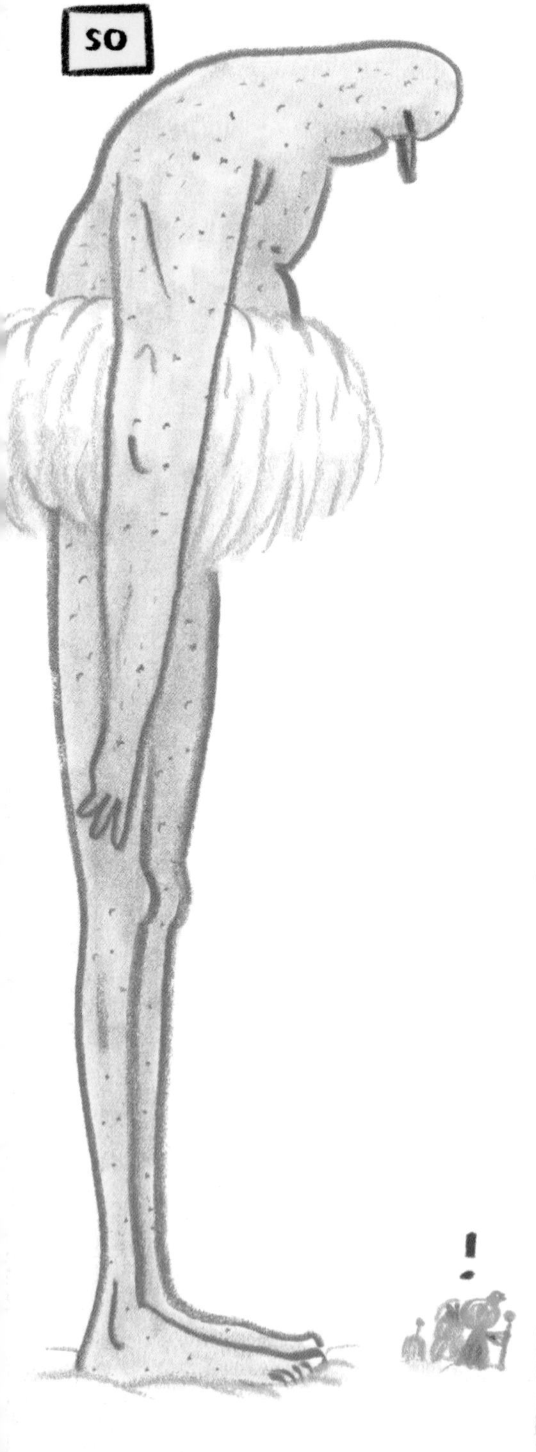
SO
!

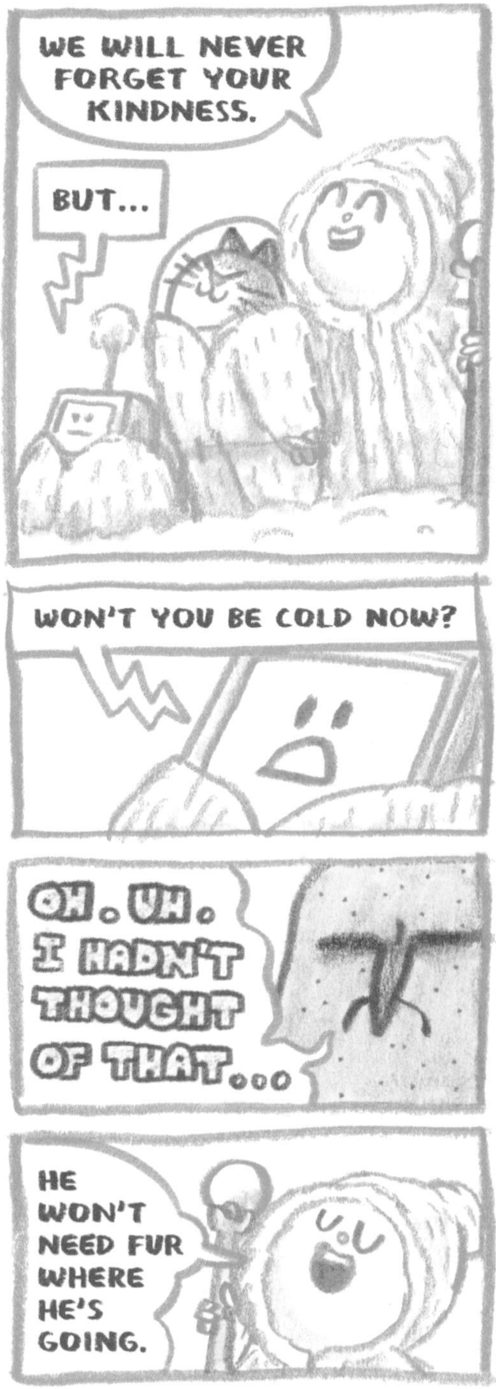
WE WILL NEVER FORGET YOUR KINDNESS.
BUT...
WON'T YOU BE COLD NOW?
OH. UH. I HADN'T THOUGHT OF THAT...
HE WON'T NEED FUR WHERE HE'S GOING.

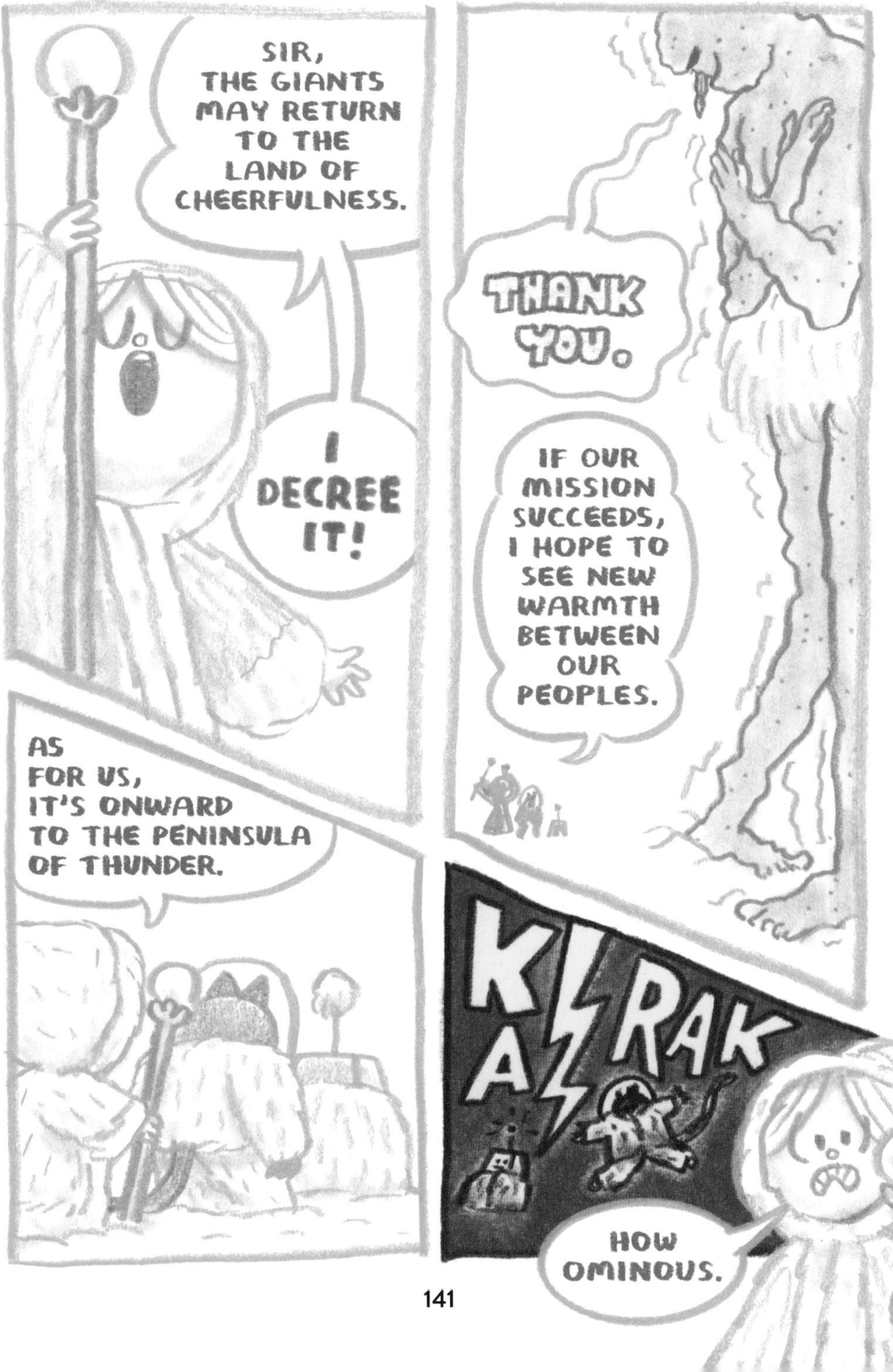
SIR, THE GIANTS MAY RETURN TO THE LAND OF CHEERFULNESS.
I DECREE IT!
THANK YOU.
IF OUR MISSION SUCCEEDS, I HOPE TO SEE NEW WARMTH BETWEEN OUR PEOPLES.
AS FOR US, IT'S ONWARD TO THE PENINSULA OF THUNDER.
KAKRAK
HOW OMINOUS.

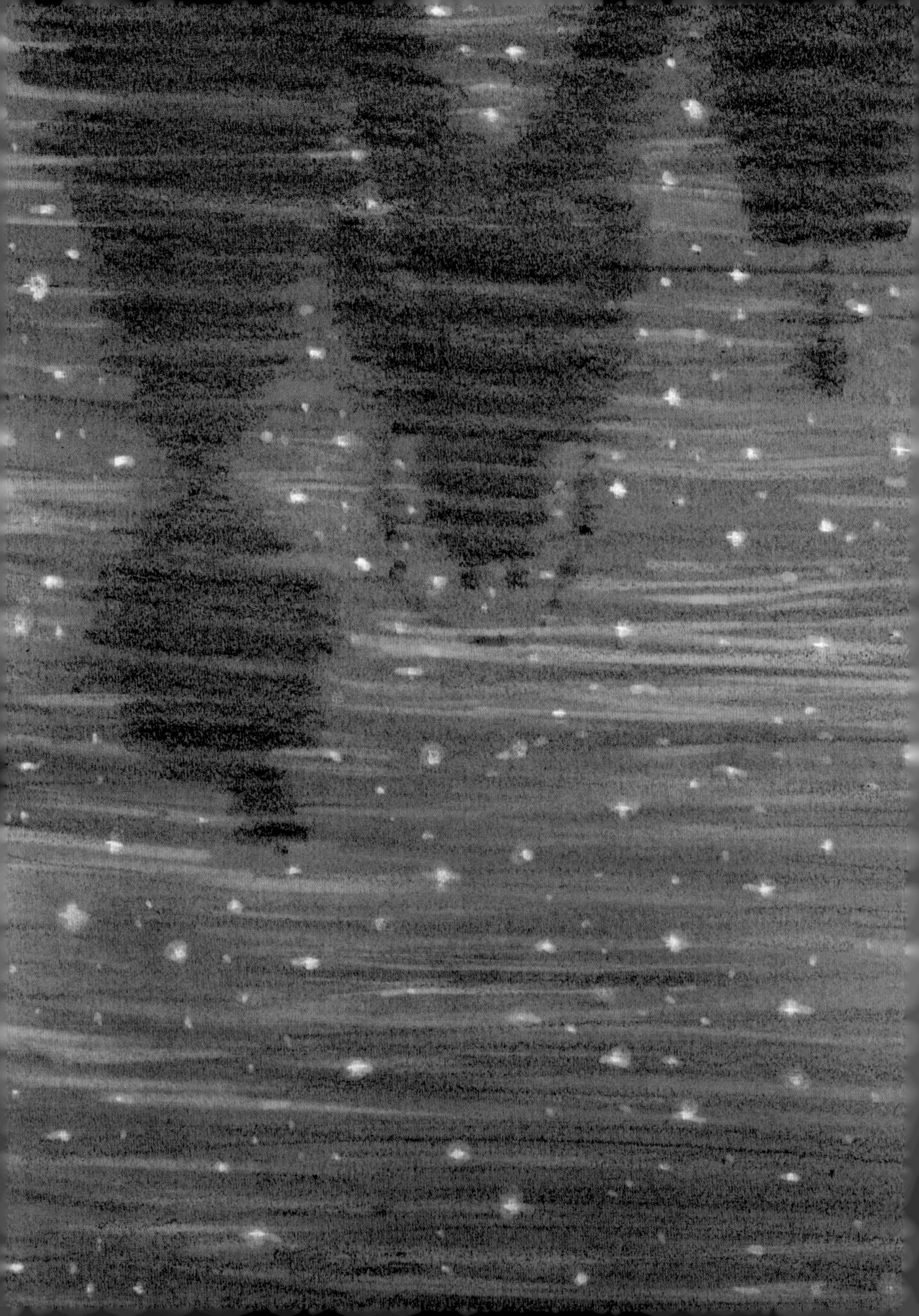

CHAPTER II
WHALESONG

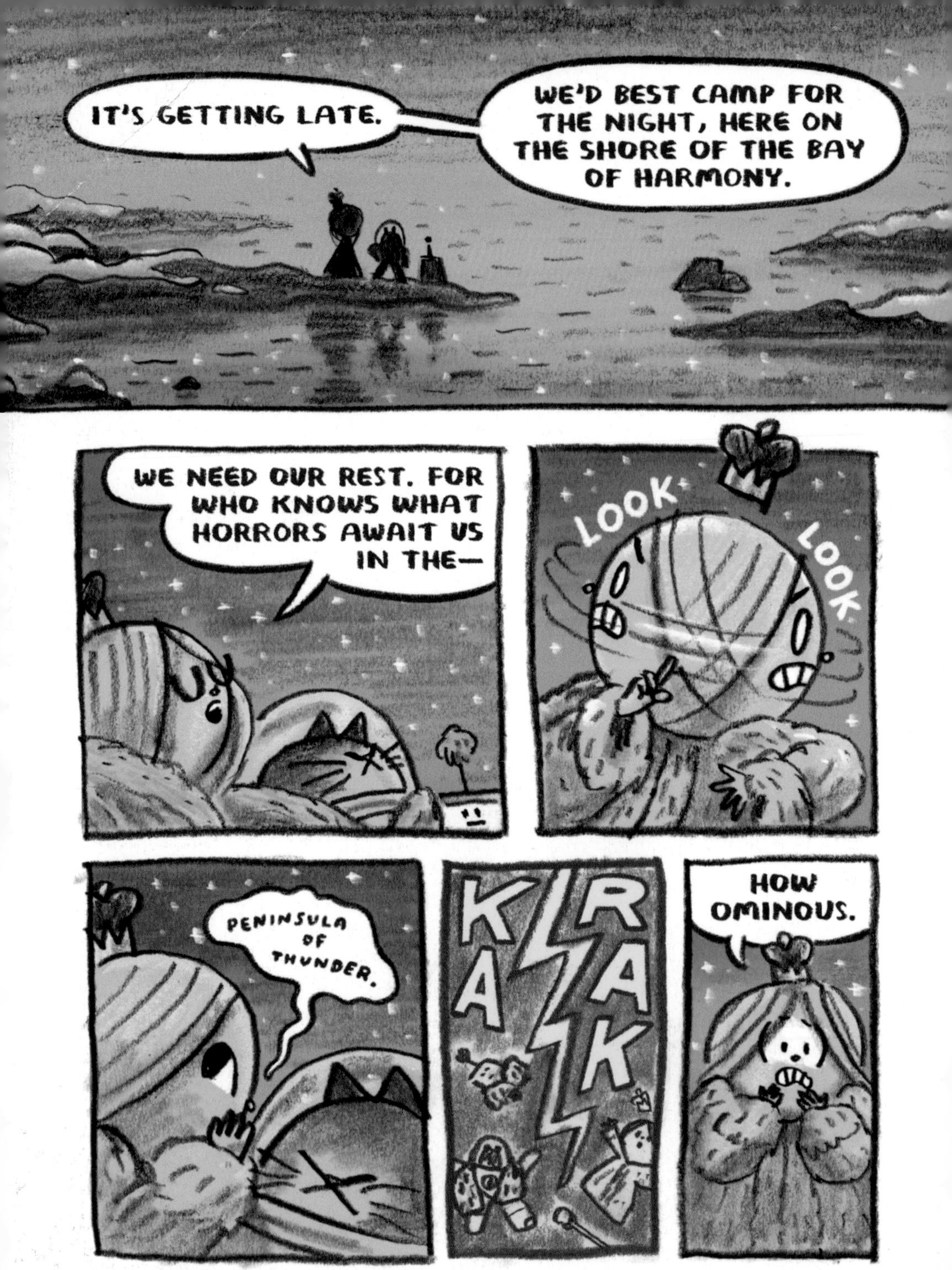
IT'S GETTING LATE.
WE'D BEST CAMP FOR THE NIGHT, HERE ON THE SHORE OF THE BAY OF HARMONY.
WE NEED OUR REST. FOR WHO KNOWS WHAT HORRORS AWAIT US IN THE—
LOOK LOOK LOOK
PENINSULA OF THUNDER.
KRAKA
HOW OMINOUS.

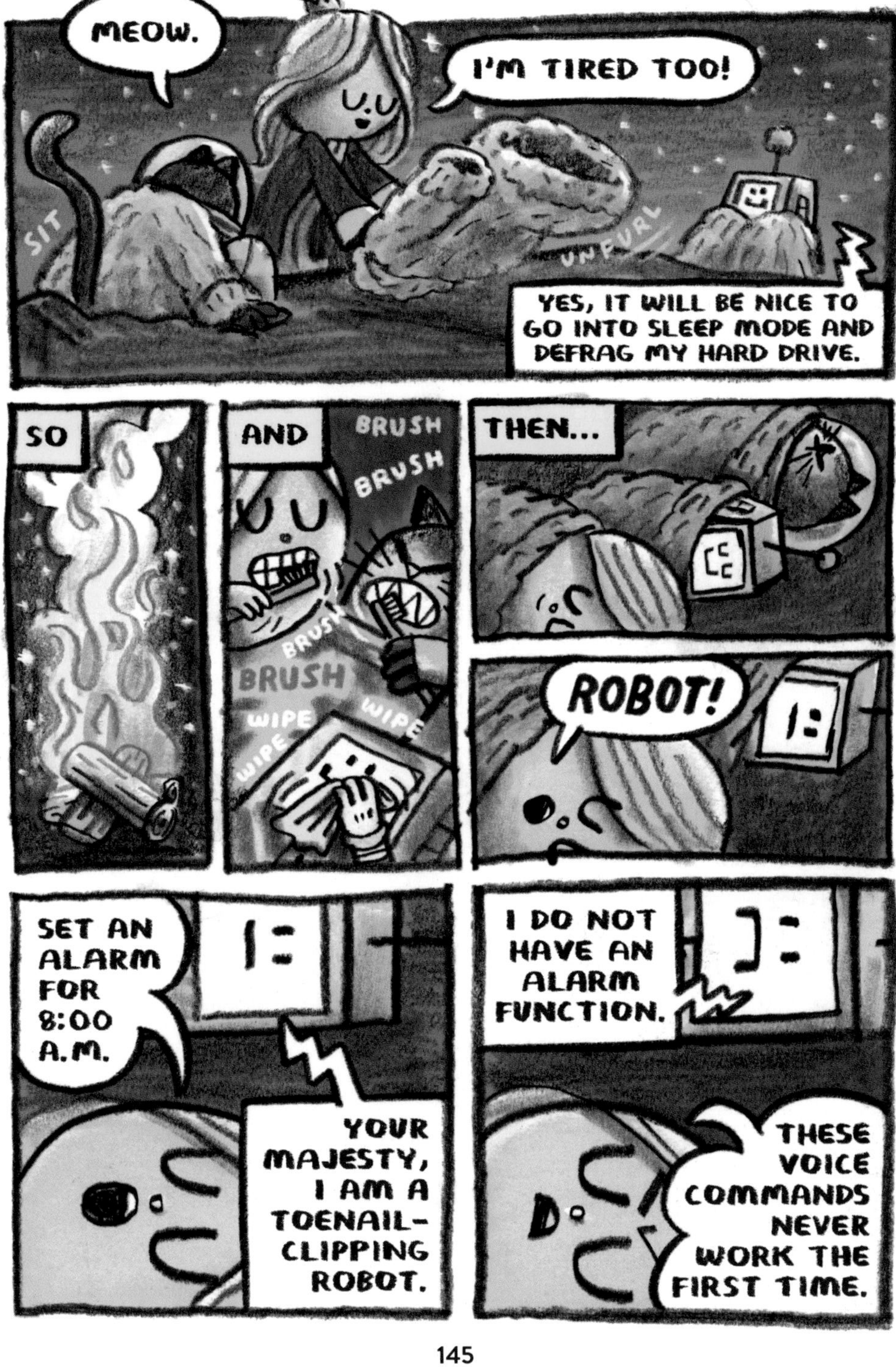

MEOW.
I'M TIRED TOO!
SIT
UNFURL
YES, IT WILL BE NICE TO GO INTO SLEEP MODE AND DEFRAG MY HARD DRIVE.
SO
AND
BRUSH
BRUSH
BRUSH
BRUSH
WIPE
WIPE
WIPE
THEN...
ROBOT!
SET AN ALARM FOR 8:00 A.M.
YOUR MAJESTY, I AM A TOENAIL-CLIPPING ROBOT.
I DO NOT HAVE AN ALARM FUNCTION.
THESE VOICE COMMANDS NEVER WORK THE FIRST TIME.

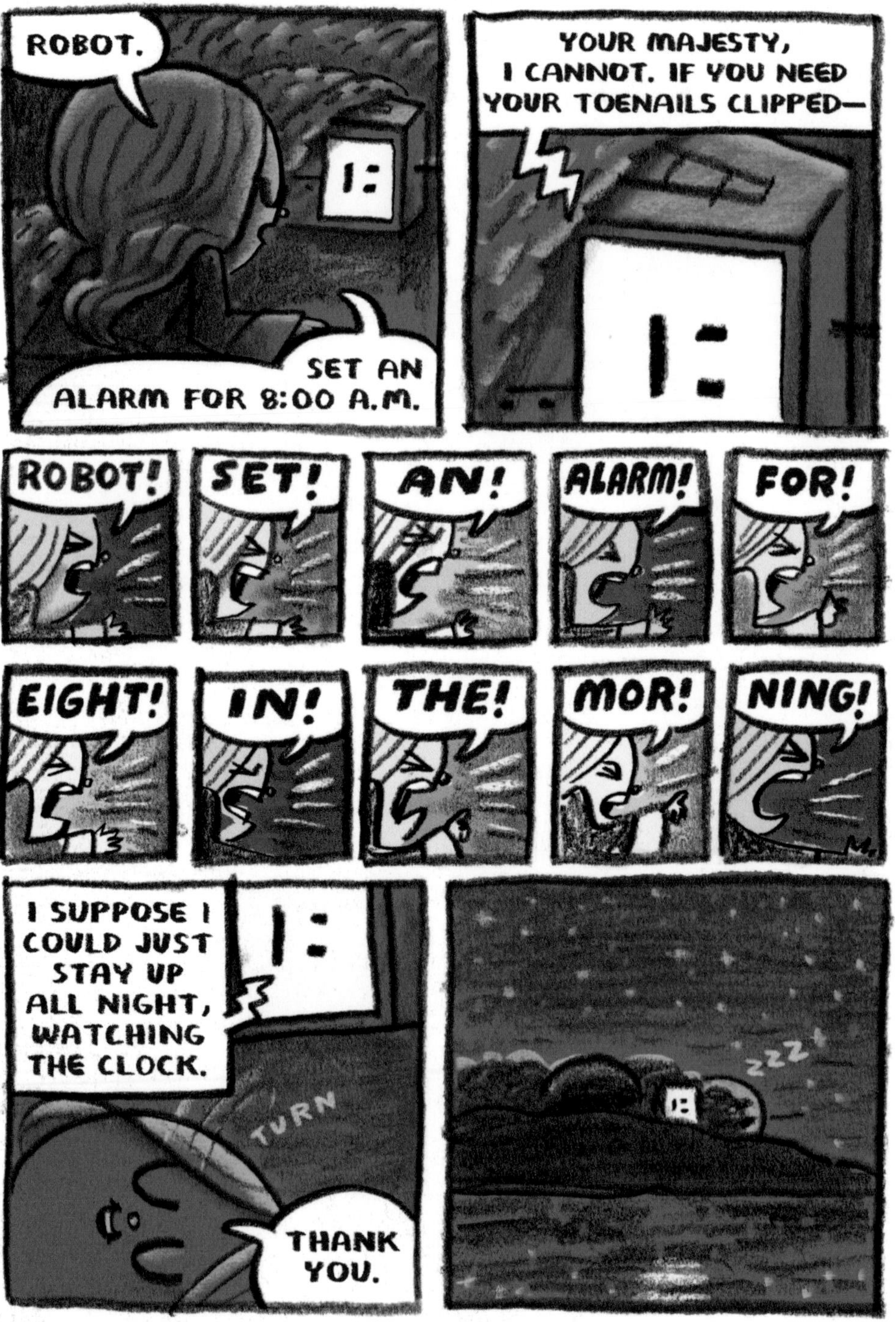
ROBOT.
SET AN ALARM FOR 8:00 A.M.
1:
YOUR MAJESTY, I CANNOT. IF YOU NEED YOUR TOENAILS CLIPPED—
1:
ROBOT!
SET!
AN!
ALARM!
FOR!
EIGHT!
IN!
THE!
MOR!
NING!
1:
I SUPPOSE I COULD JUST STAY UP ALL NIGHT, WATCHING THE CLOCK.
TURN
THANK YOU.
ZZZ

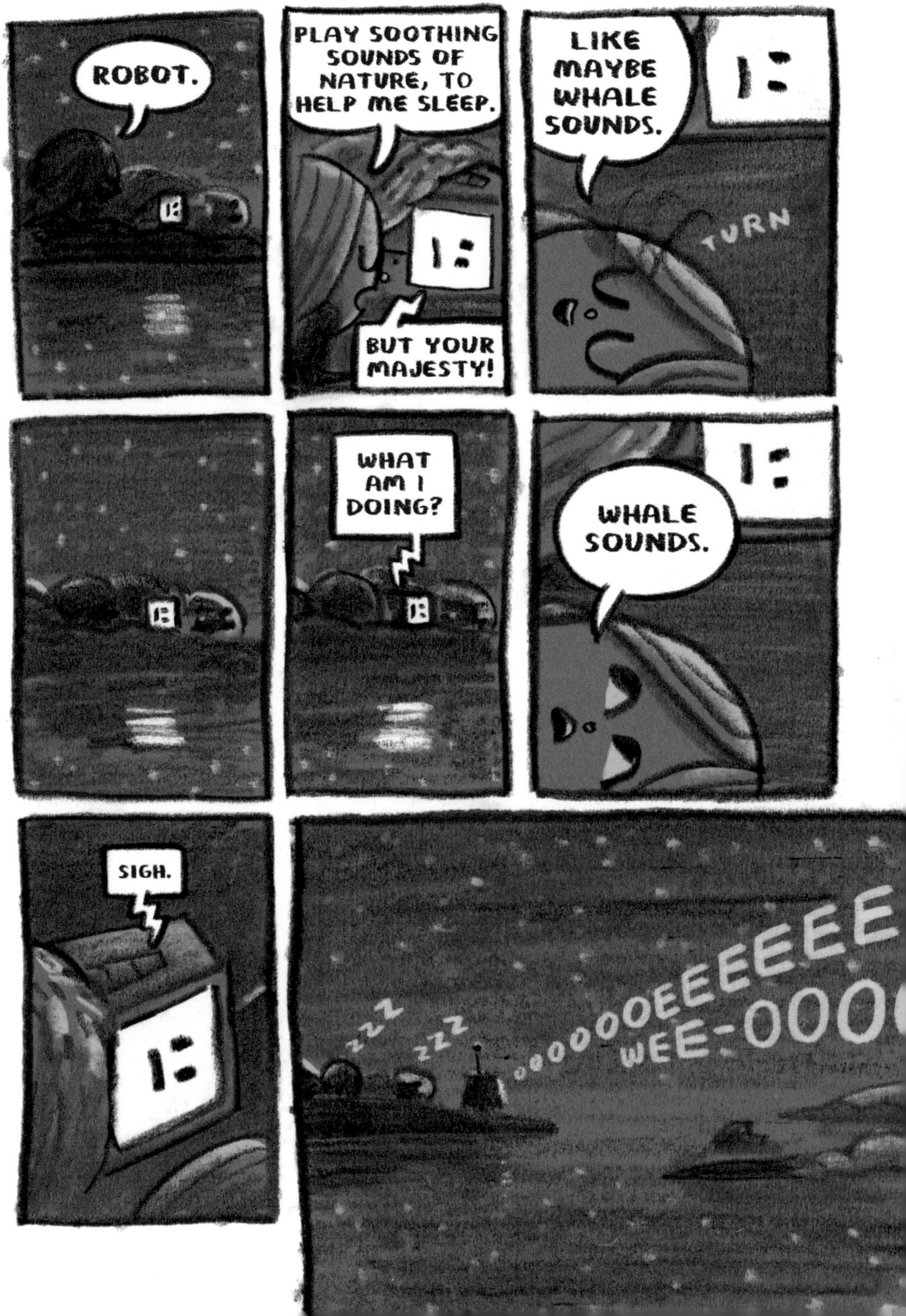
ROBOT.
PLAY SOOTHING SOUNDS OF NATURE, TO HELP ME SLEEP.
BUT YOUR MAJESTY!
LIKE MAYBE WHALE SOUNDS.
TURN
WHAT AM I DOING?
WHALE SOUNDS.
SIGH.
ZZZ
ZZZ
oooooooEEEEEEE
WEE-OOO

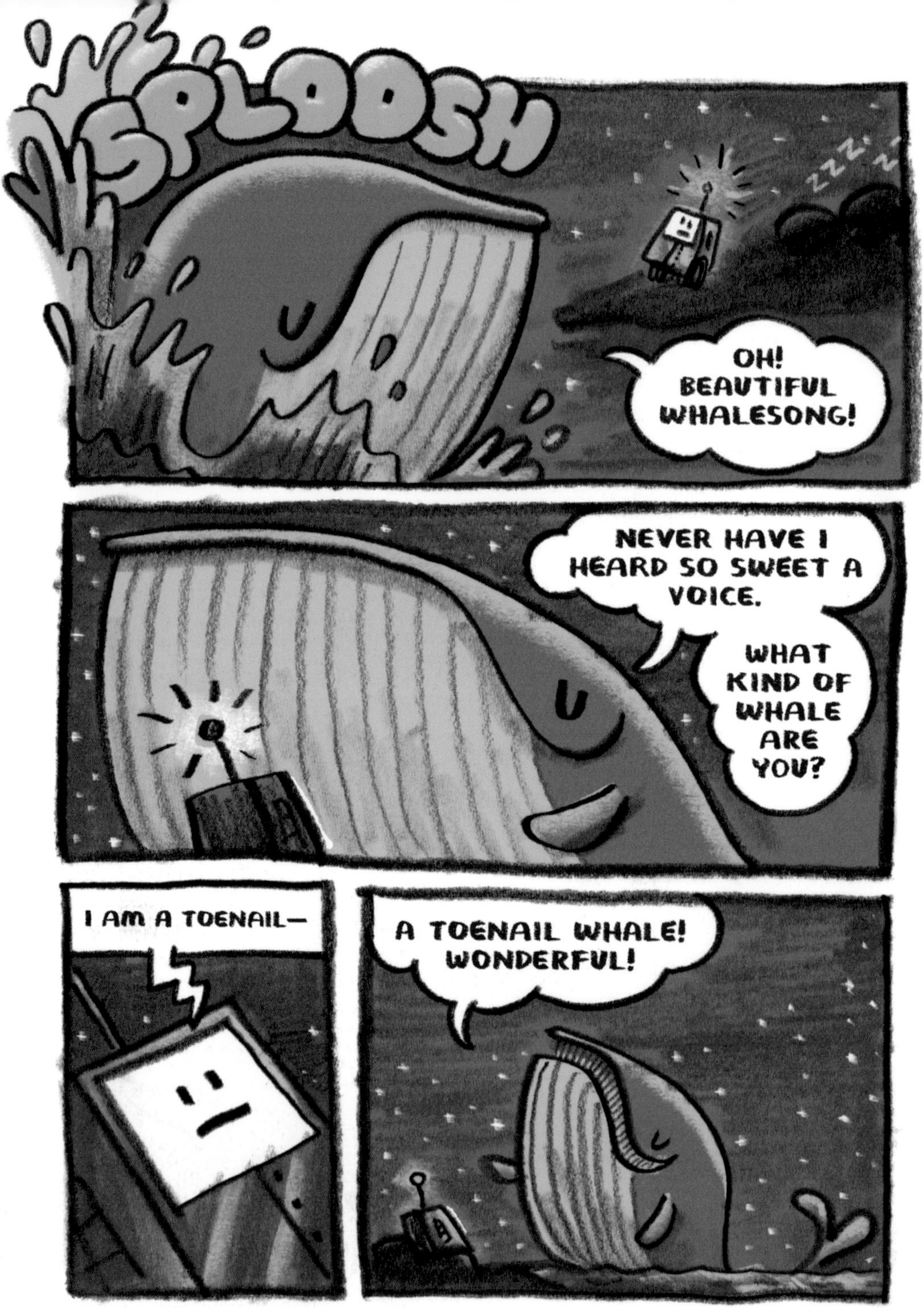
SPLOOSH
ZZZ
OH! BEAUTIFUL WHALESONG!
NEVER HAVE I HEARD SO SWEET A VOICE.
WHAT KIND OF WHALE ARE YOU?
I AM A TOENAIL—
A TOENAIL WHALE! WONDERFUL!

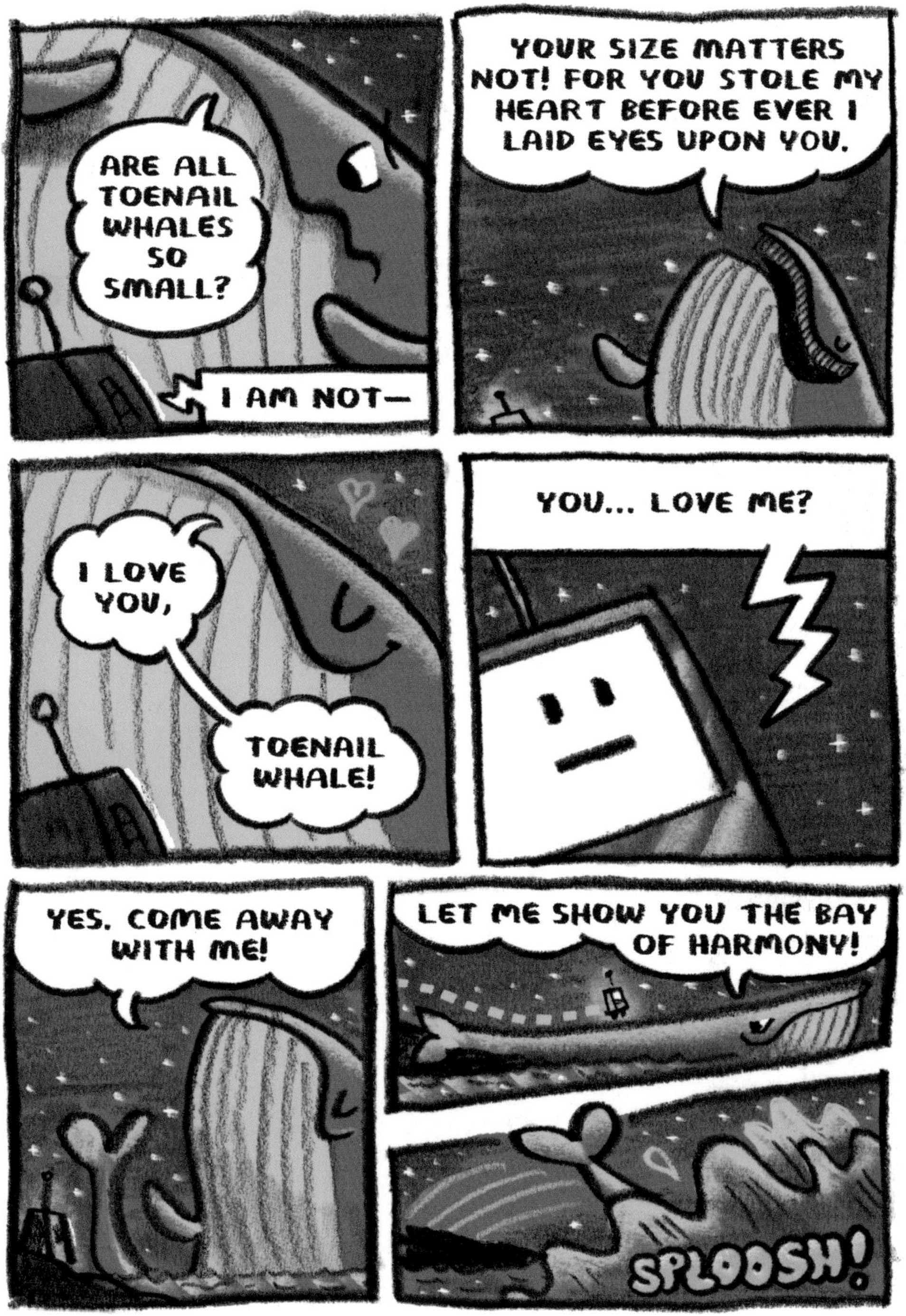
ARE ALL TOENAIL WHALES SO SMALL?
I AM NOT—
YOUR SIZE MATTERS NOT! FOR YOU STOLE MY HEART BEFORE EVER I LAID EYES UPON YOU.
I LOVE YOU,
TOENAIL WHALE!
YOU... LOVE ME?
YES. COME AWAY WITH ME!
LET ME SHOW YOU THE BAY OF HARMONY!
SPLOOSH!

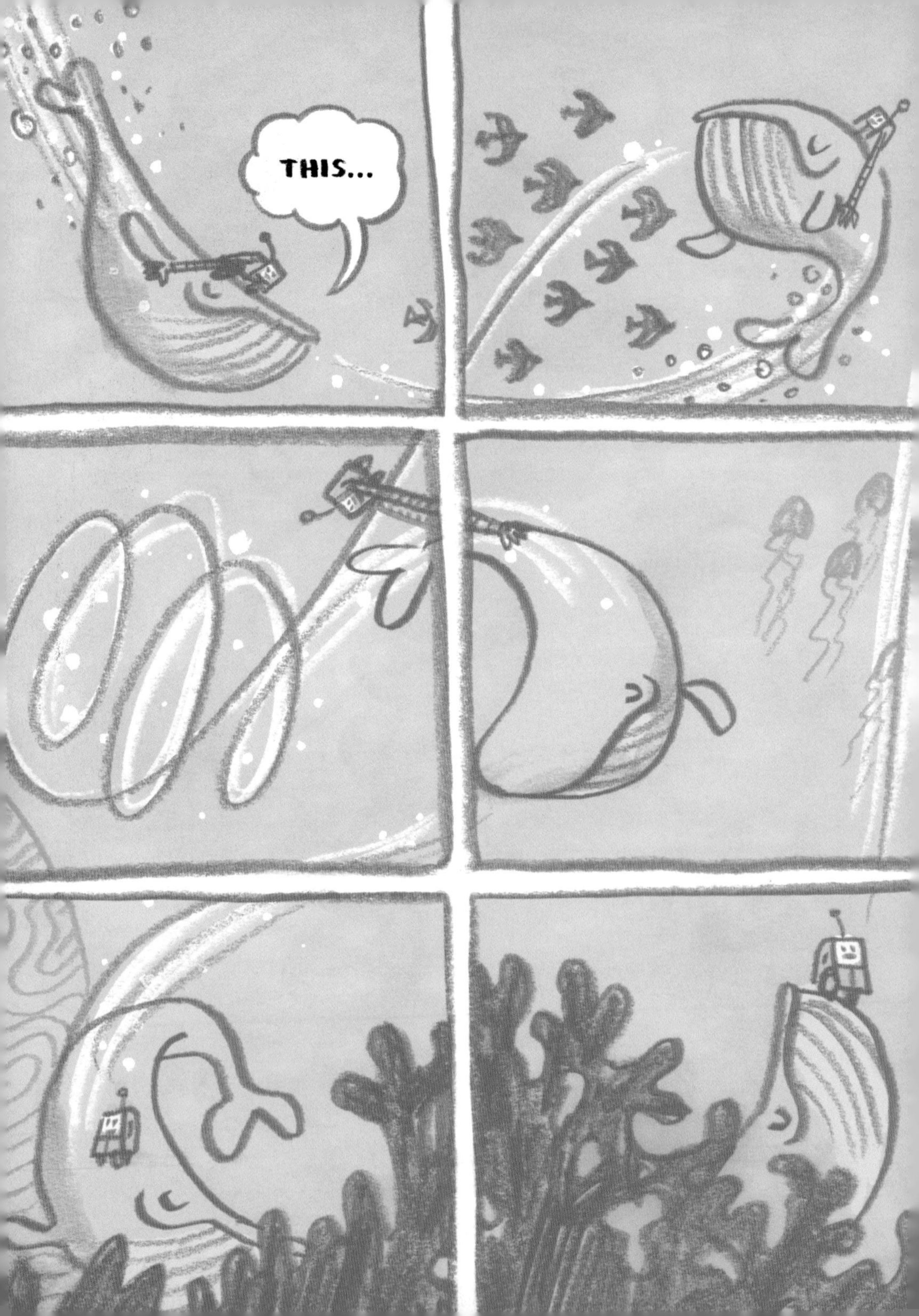
THIS...

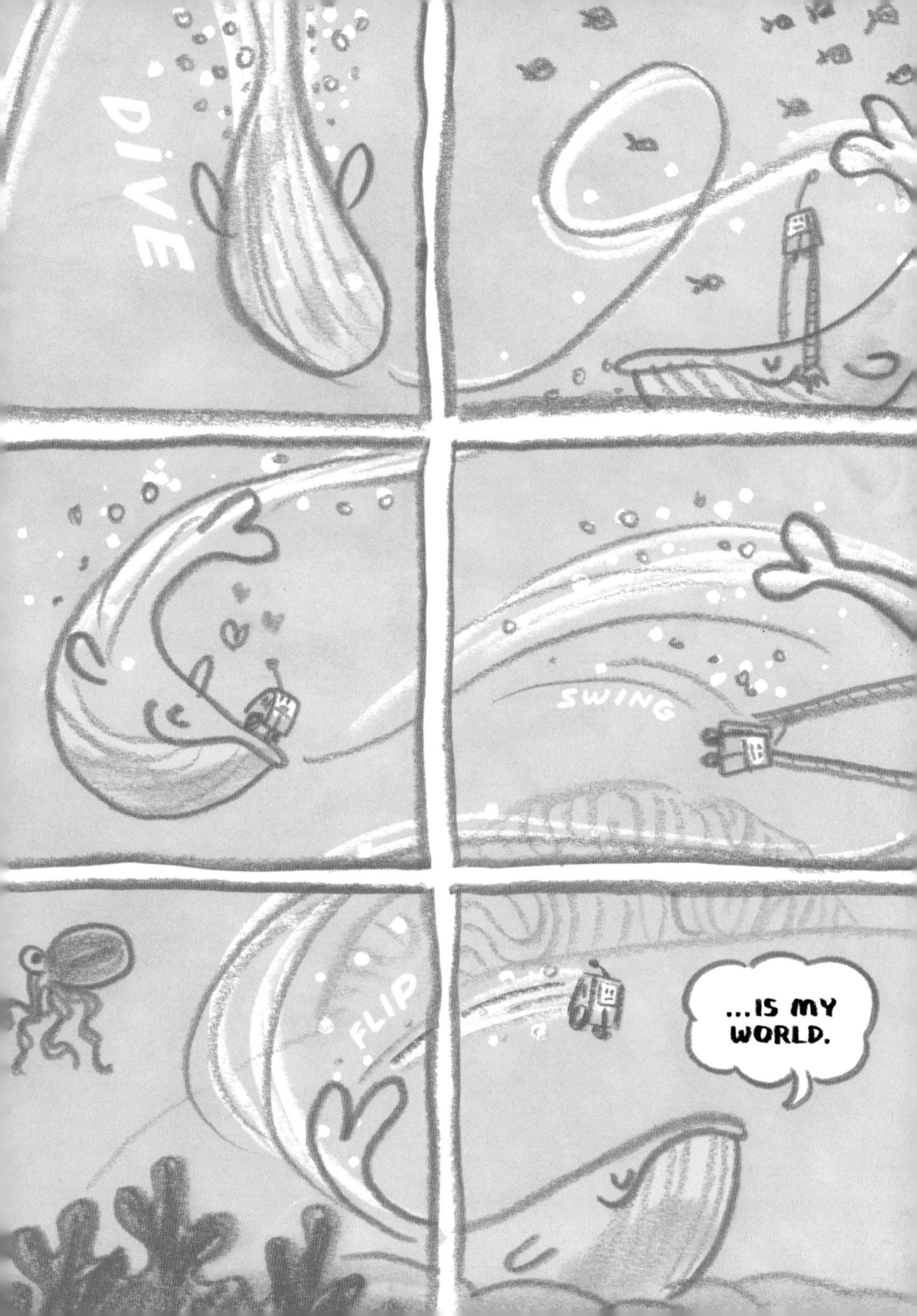
DIVE
SWING
FLIP
...IS MY WORLD.

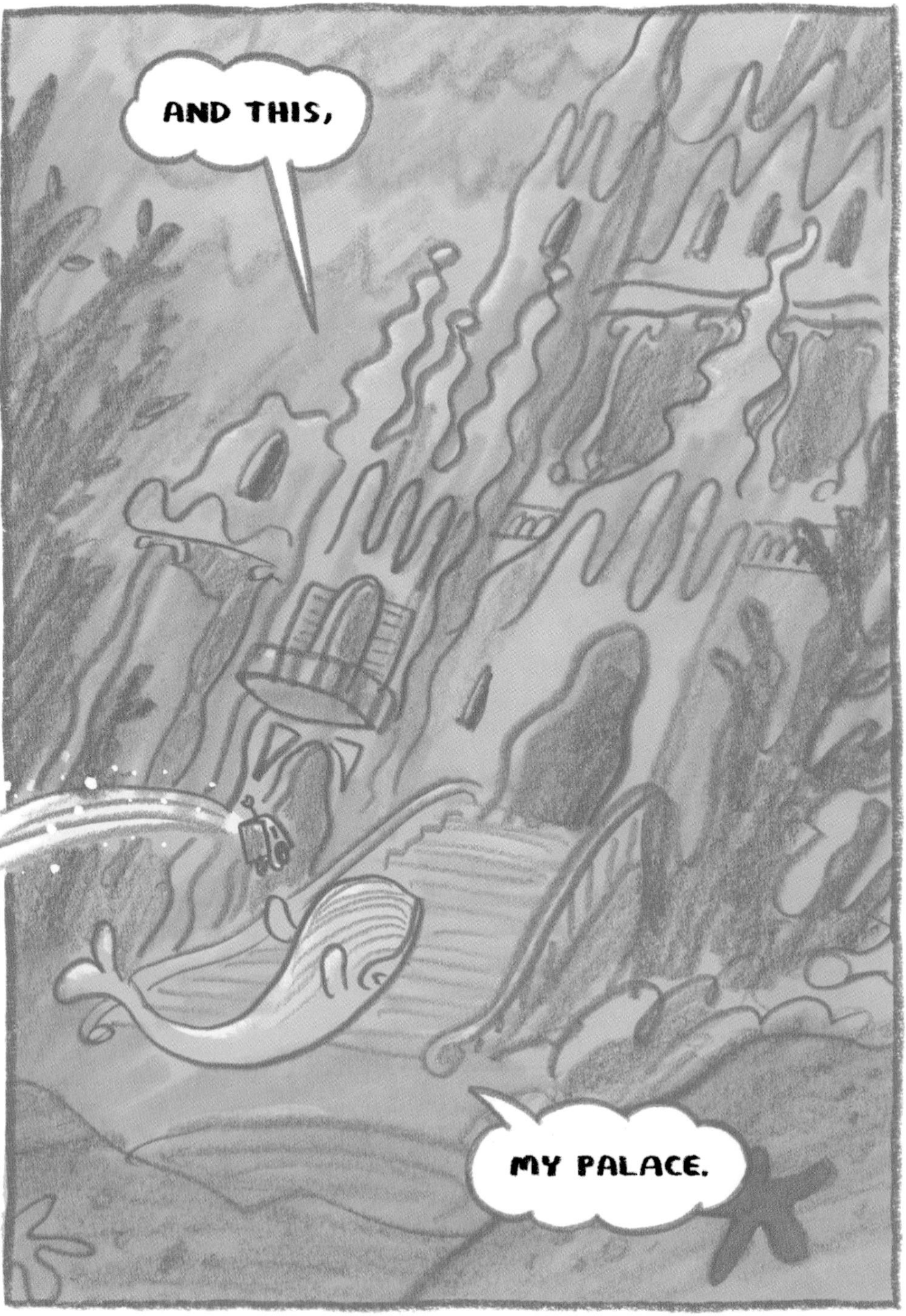
AND THIS,
MY PALACE.

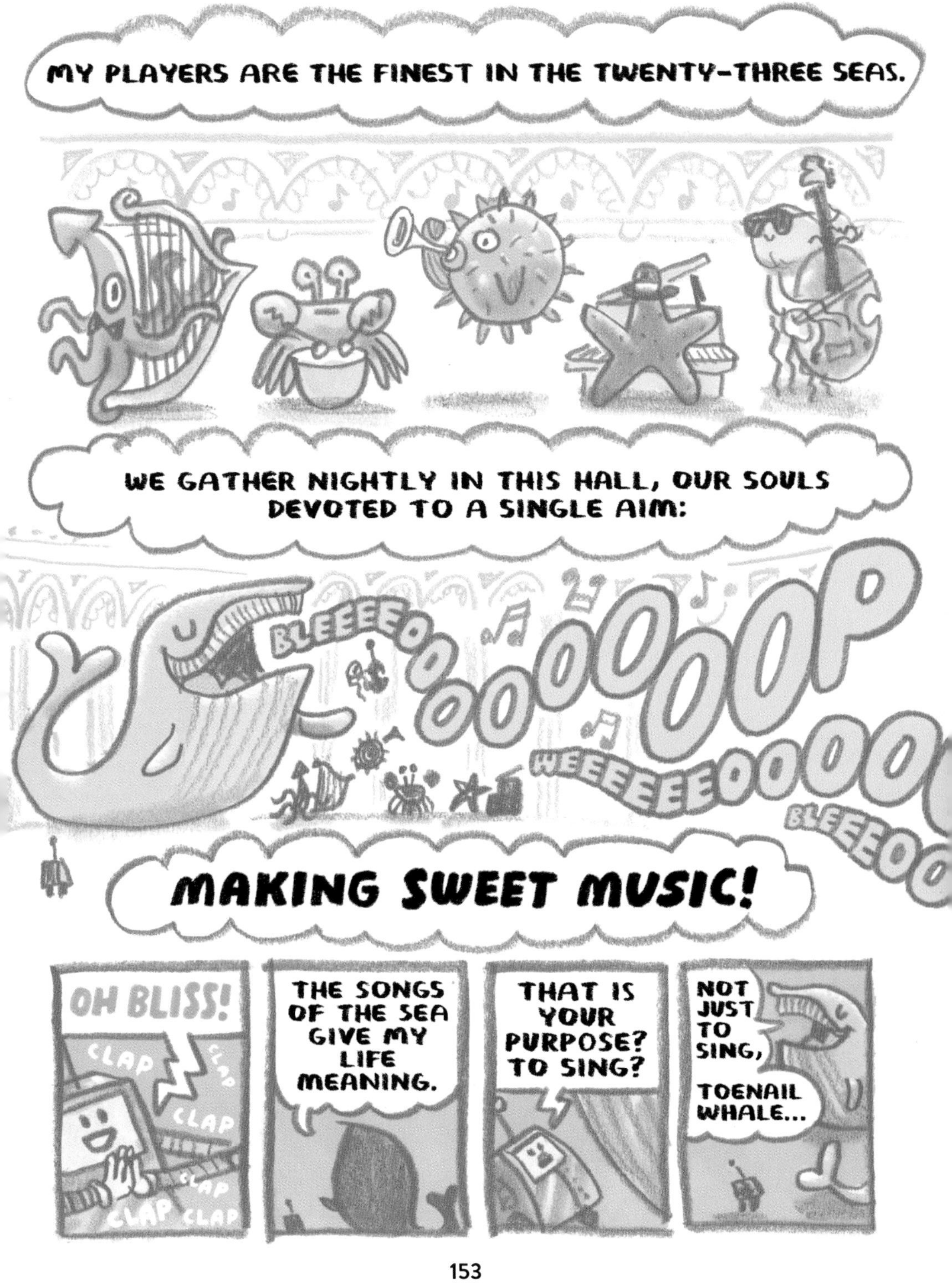

MY PLAYERS ARE THE FINEST IN THE TWENTY-THREE SEAS.
WE GATHER NIGHTLY IN THIS HALL, OUR SOULS DEVOTED TO A SINGLE AIM:
BLEEEEOOOOOOOOP
WEEEEEEOOOOO
BLEEEOO
MAKING SWEET MUSIC!
OH BLISS!
CLAP CLAP CLAP CLAP CLAP CLAP
THE SONGS OF THE SEA GIVE MY LIFE MEANING.
THAT IS YOUR PURPOSE? TO SING?
NOT JUST TO SING,
TOENAIL WHALE...

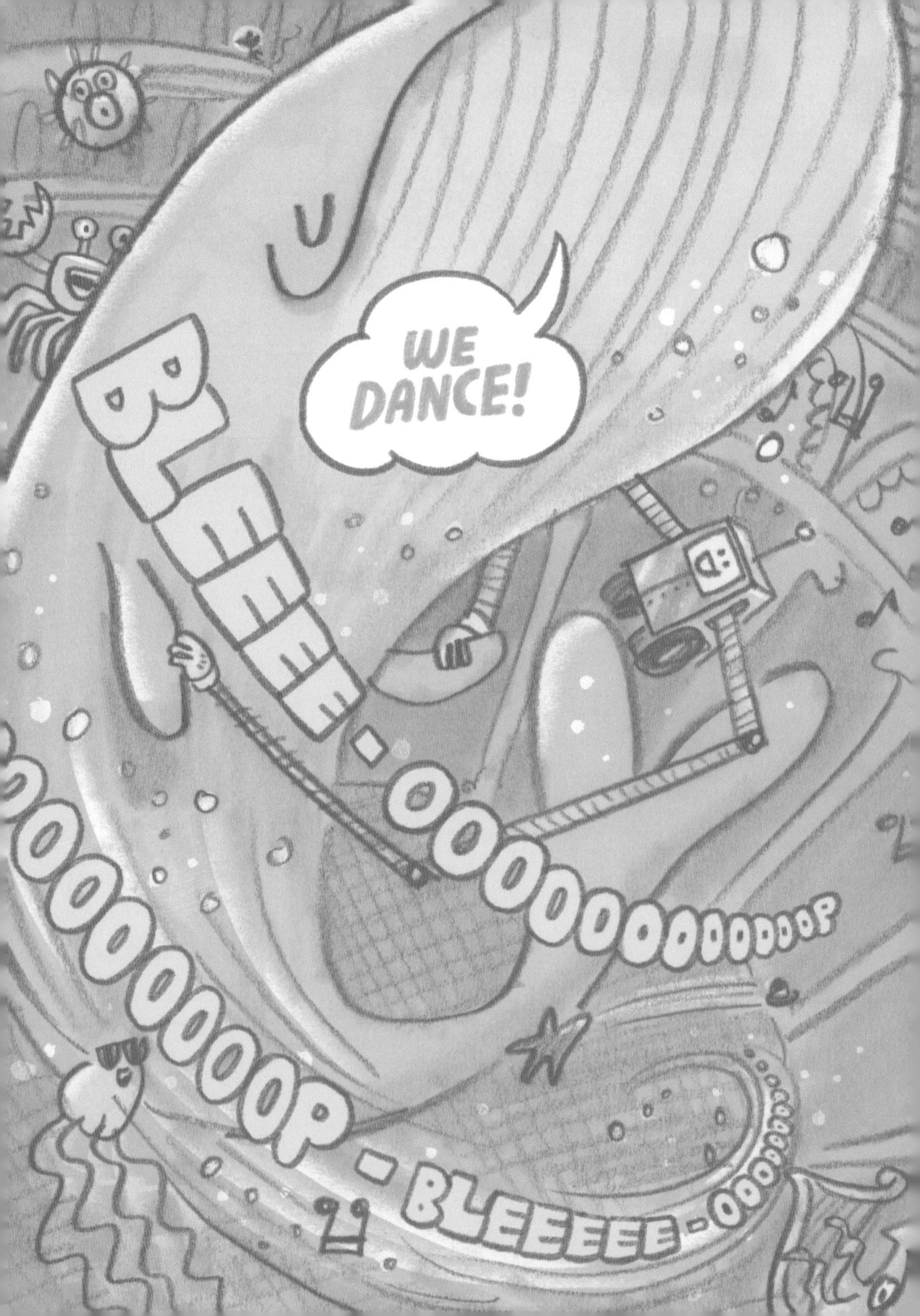
WE DANCE!
BLEEEE-OOOOOOOOOOOOOP
OOOOOOOOOOP-BLEEEEEE-OOOO

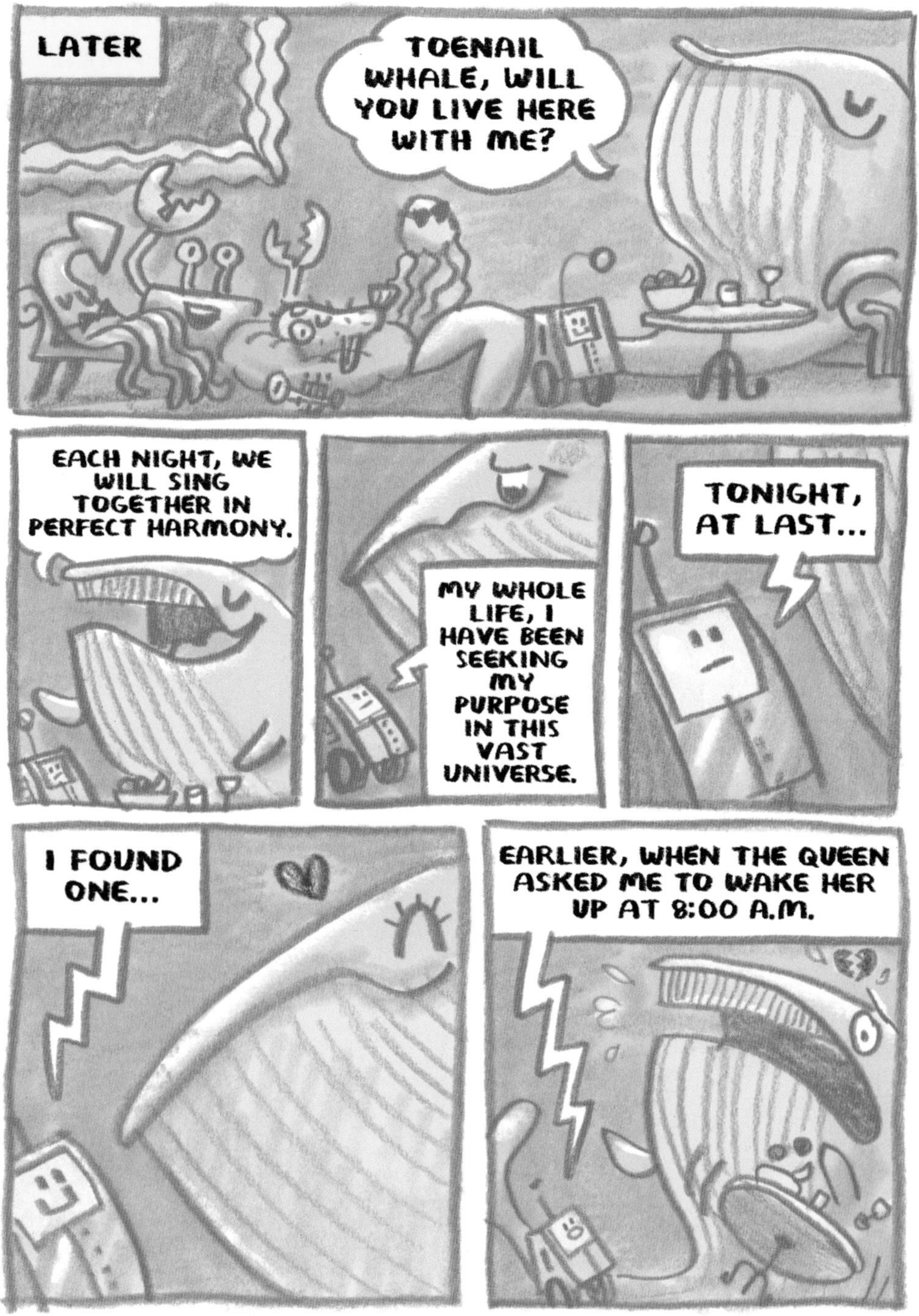
LATER
TOENAIL WHALE, WILL YOU LIVE HERE WITH ME?
EACH NIGHT, WE WILL SING TOGETHER IN PERFECT HARMONY.
MY WHOLE LIFE, I HAVE BEEN SEEKING MY PURPOSE IN THIS VAST UNIVERSE.
TONIGHT, AT LAST...
I FOUND ONE...
EARLIER, WHEN THE QUEEN ASKED ME TO WAKE HER UP AT 8:00 A.M.

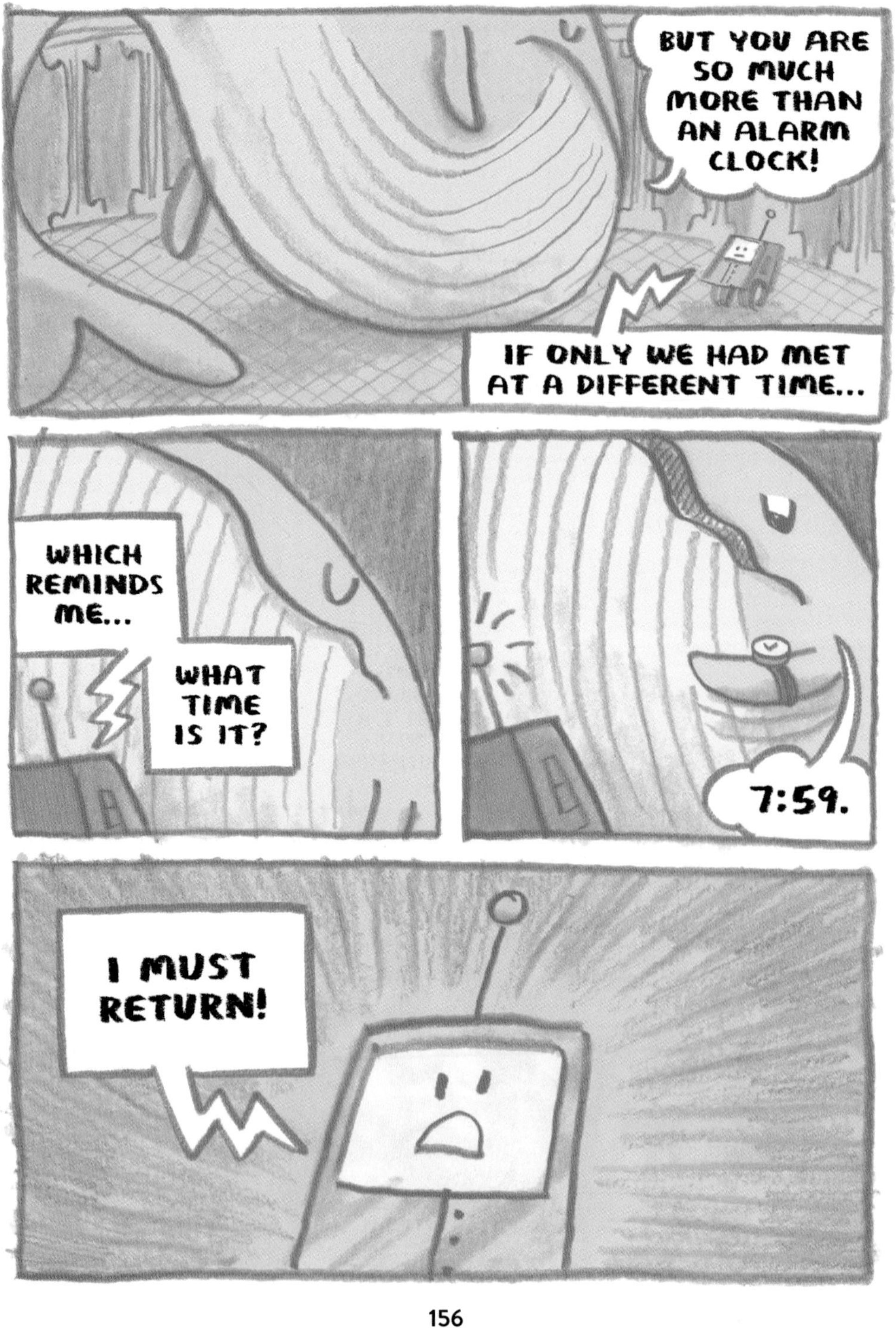
BUT YOU ARE SO MUCH MORE THAN AN ALARM CLOCK!
IF ONLY WE HAD MET AT A DIFFERENT TIME...
WHICH REMINDS ME...
WHAT TIME IS IT?
7:59.
I MUST RETURN!

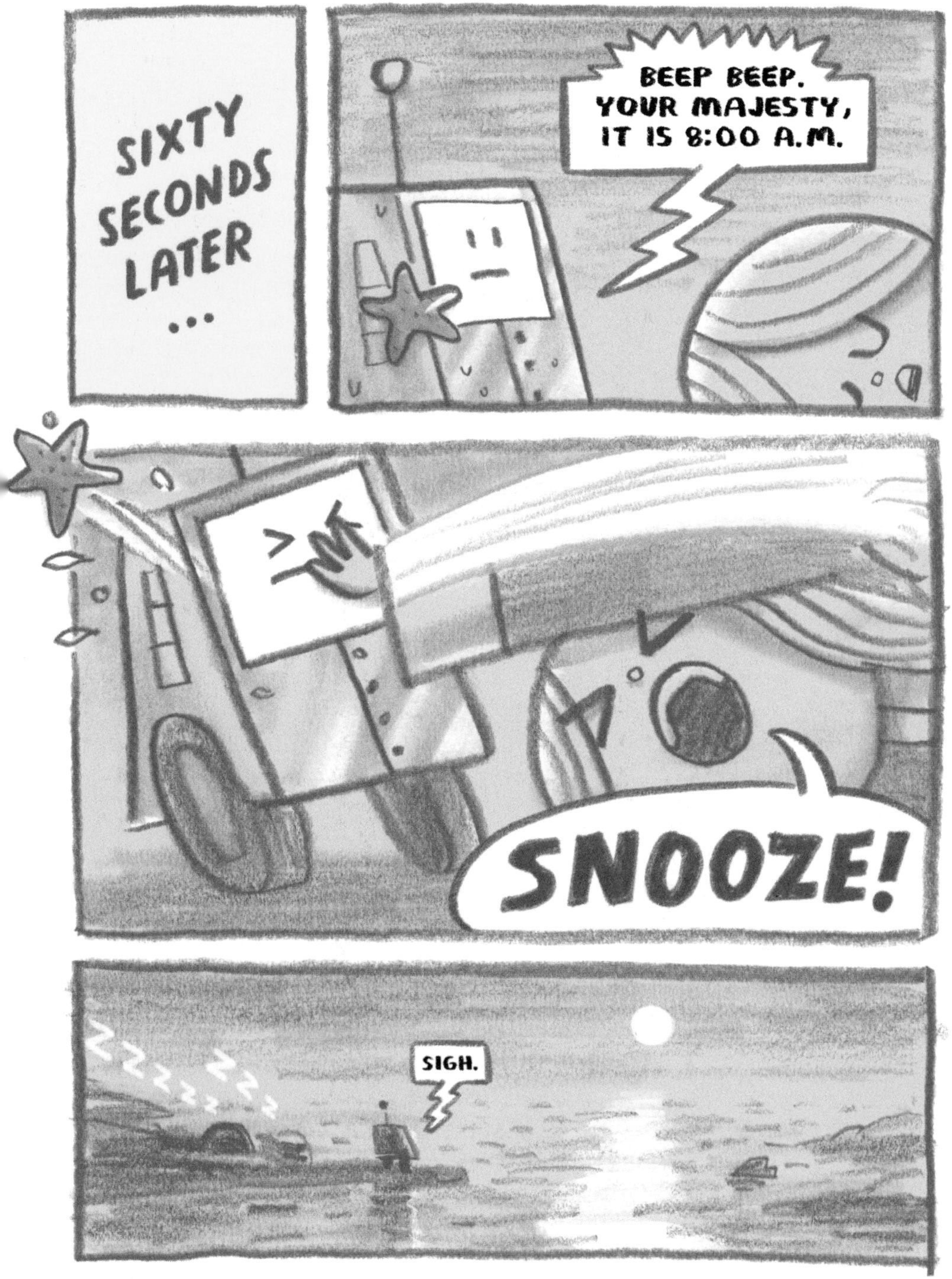
SIXTY SECONDS LATER ...
BEEP BEEP. YOUR MAJESTY, IT IS 8:00 A.M.
SNOOZE!
SIGH.

CHAPTER 12
COLD PIZZA

WE HAVE A LONG DAY AHEAD OF US. WE'LL NEED A HEARTY BREAKFAST IF WE WANT TO MAKE IT THROUGH THE PENINSULA OF THUNDER.

KA-RAK

HOW OMINOUS!

NOW LISTEN, I KNOW THIS MAY SEEM A LITTLE STRANGE, BUT ONE OF MY FAVORITE THINGS TO EAT FOR BREAKFAST IS...

WELL...

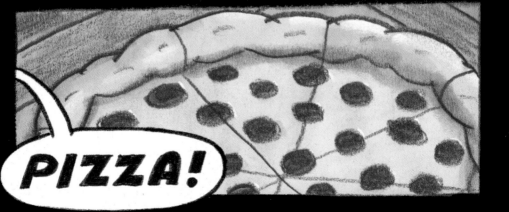

PIZZA!

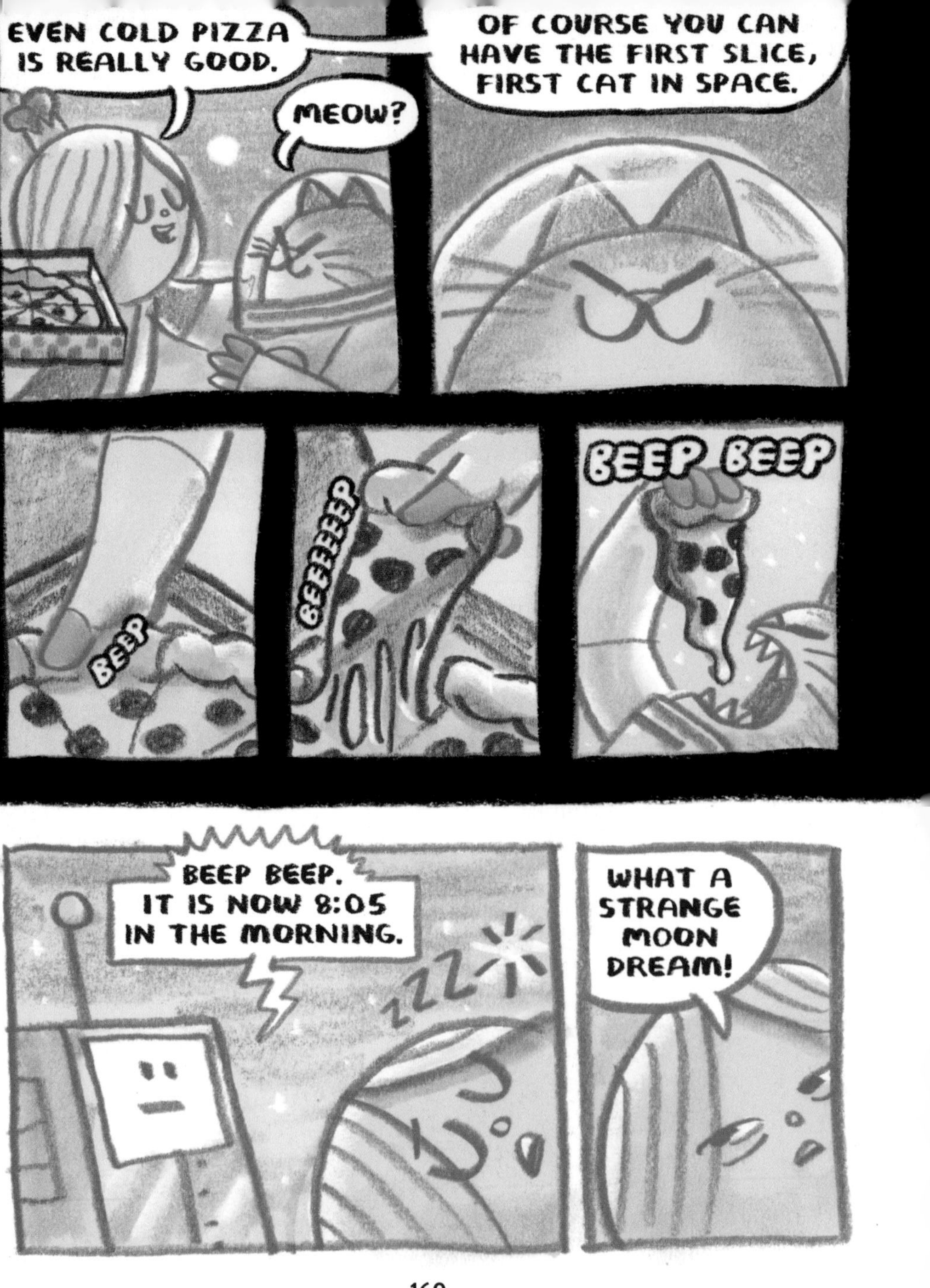
EVEN COLD PIZZA IS REALLY GOOD.
MEOW?
OF COURSE YOU CAN HAVE THE FIRST SLICE, FIRST CAT IN SPACE.
BEEP
BEEEEEEEP
BEEP BEEP
BEEP BEEP. IT IS NOW 8:05 IN THE MORNING.
ZZZ
WHAT A STRANGE MOON DREAM!

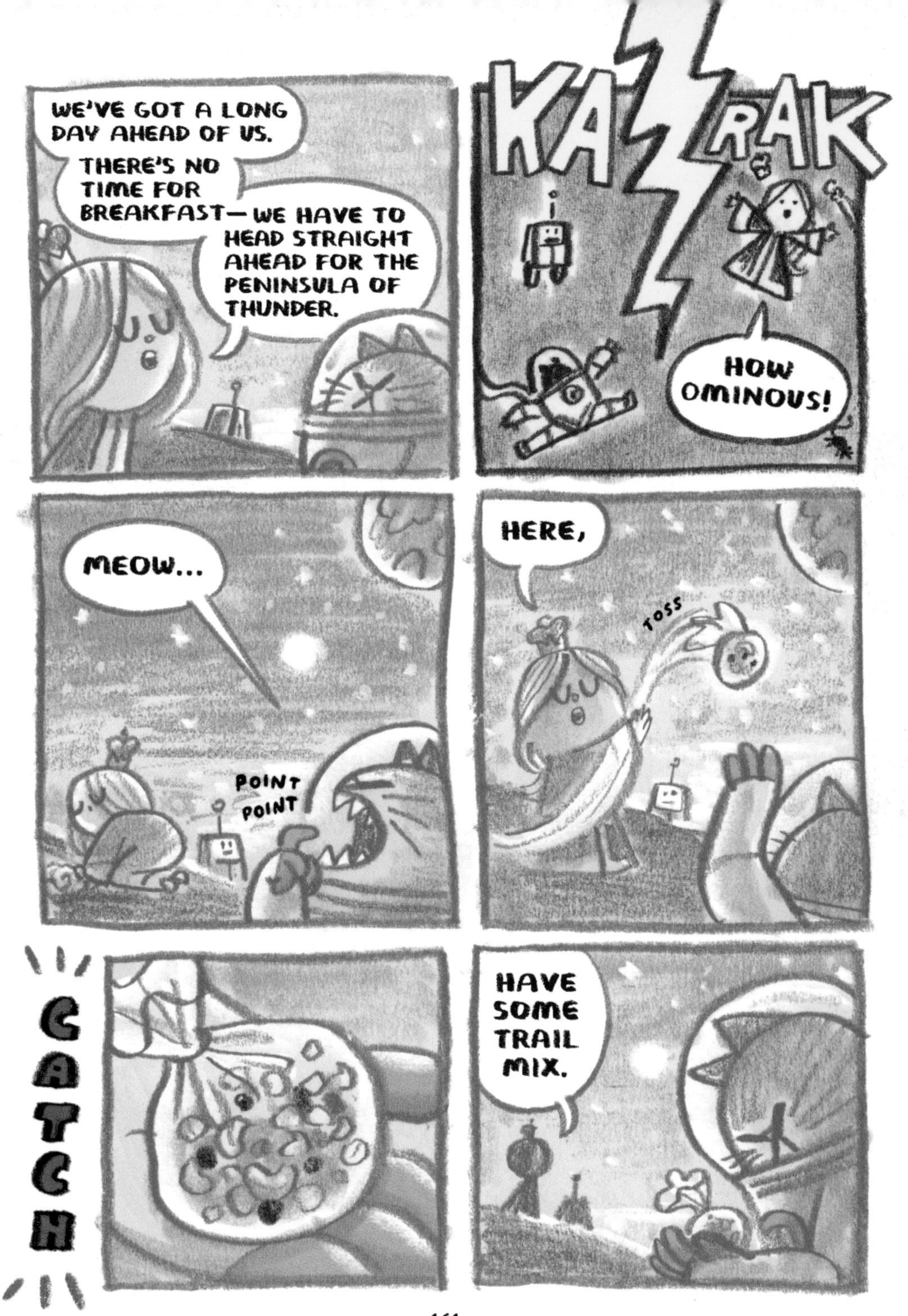
WE'VE GOT A LONG DAY AHEAD OF US.
THERE'S NO TIME FOR BREAKFAST— WE HAVE TO HEAD STRAIGHT AHEAD FOR THE PENINSULA OF THUNDER.
KA-RAK
HOW OMINOUS!
MEOW...
POINT POINT
HERE,
TOSS
CATCH
HAVE SOME TRAIL MIX.

CHAPTER 13

THE PENINSULA OF THUNDER

(HOW OMINOUS)

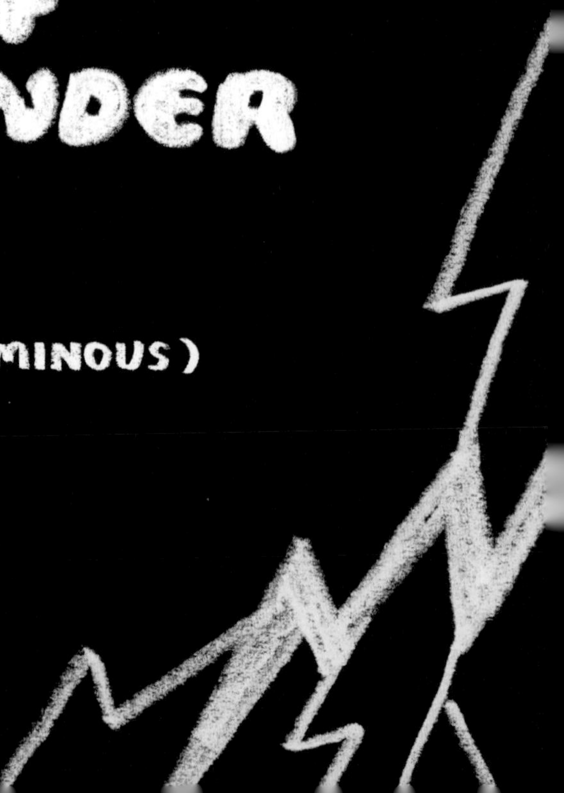

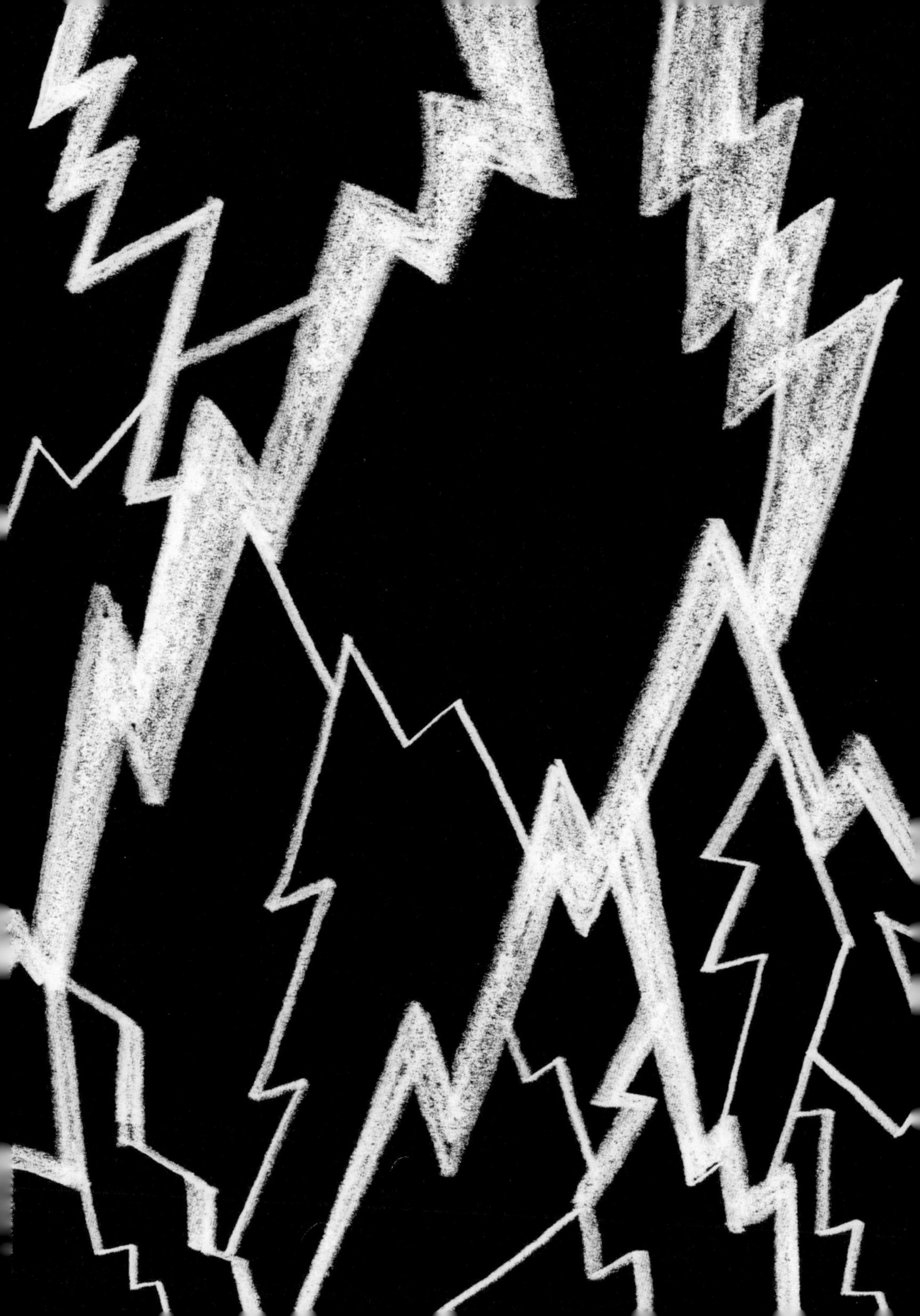

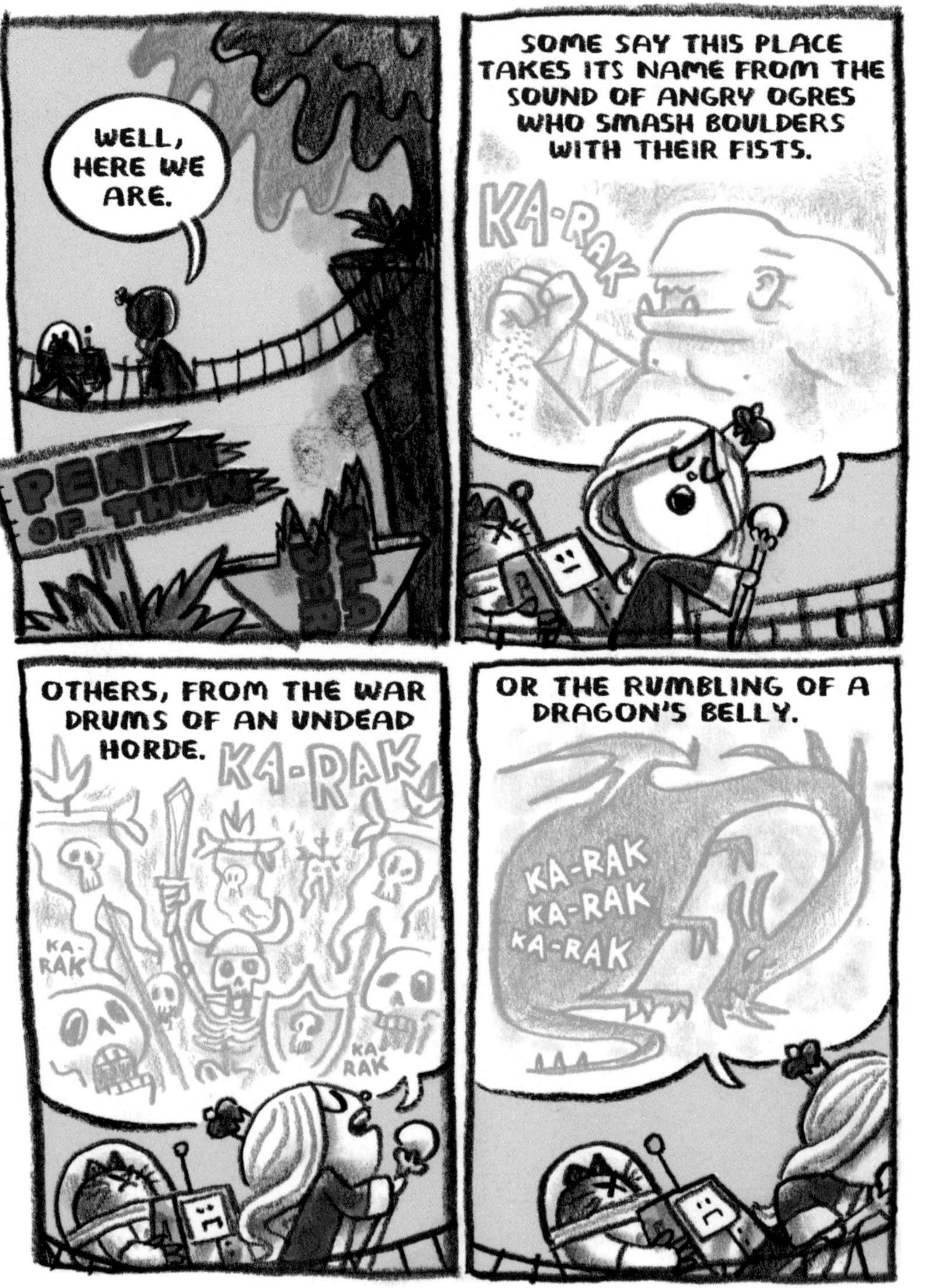
WELL, HERE WE ARE.
SOME SAY THIS PLACE TAKES ITS NAME FROM THE SOUND OF ANGRY OGRES WHO SMASH BOULDERS WITH THEIR FISTS.
KA-RAK
OTHERS, FROM THE WAR DRUMS OF AN UNDEAD HORDE.
KA-RAK
KA-RAK
KA-RAK
OR THE RUMBLING OF A DRAGON'S BELLY.
KA-RAK
KA-RAK
KA-RAK

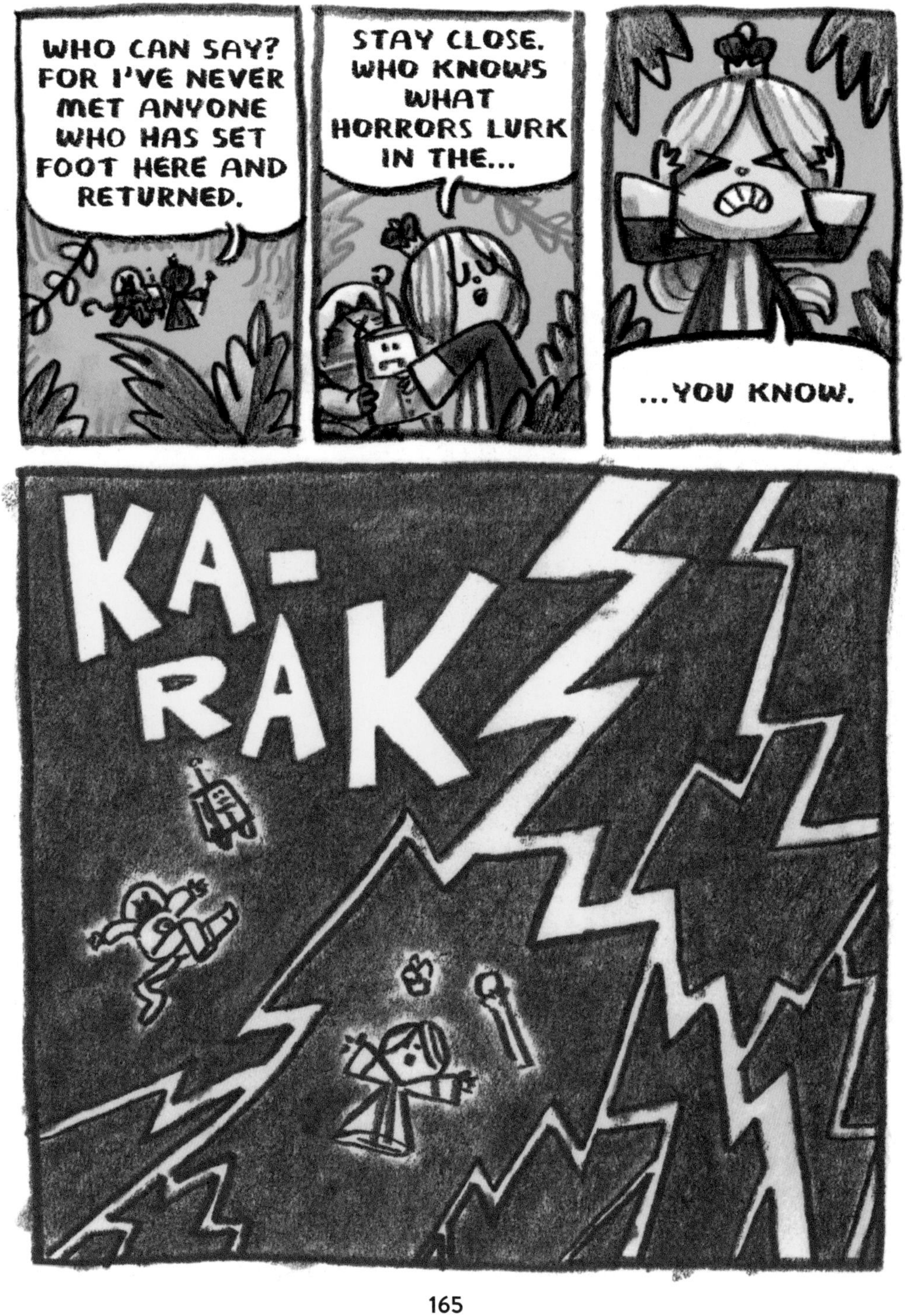
WHO CAN SAY? FOR I'VE NEVER MET ANYONE WHO HAS SET FOOT HERE AND RETURNED.
STAY CLOSE. WHO KNOWS WHAT HORRORS LURK IN THE...
...YOU KNOW.
KA-RAK

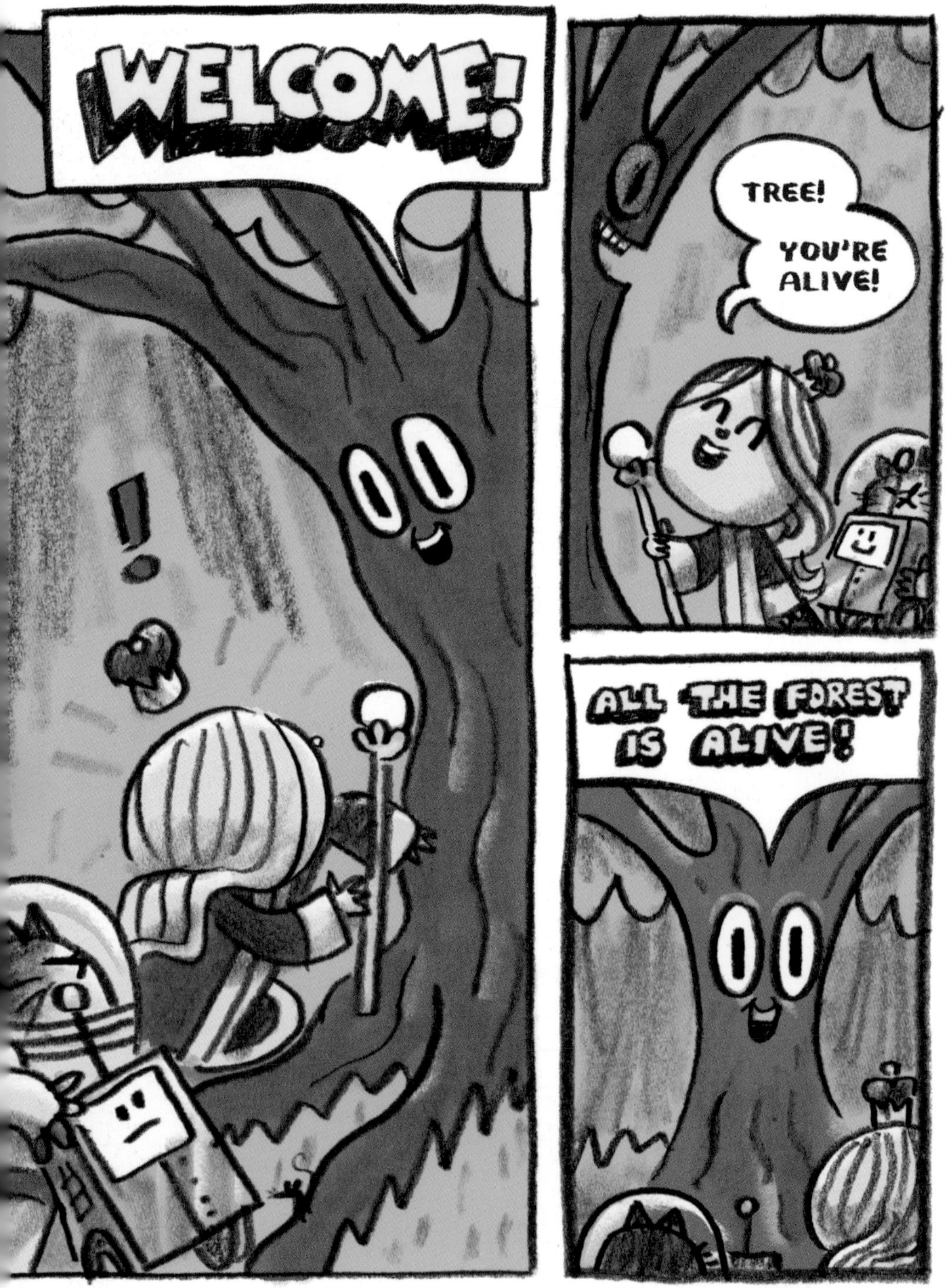
WELCOME!
!
TREE!
YOU'RE ALIVE!
ALL THE FOREST IS ALIVE!

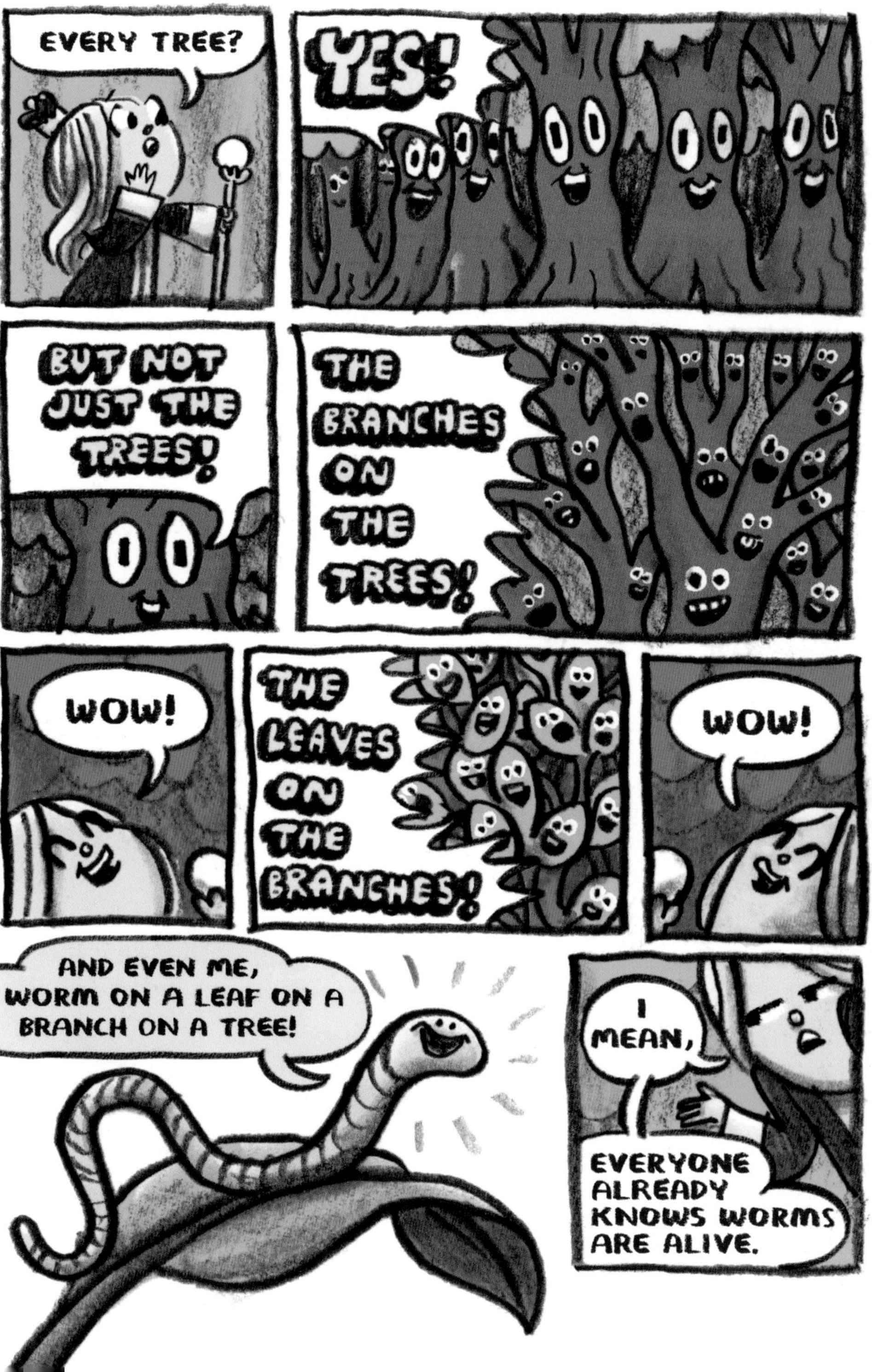
EVERY TREE?
YES!
BUT NOT JUST THE TREES!
THE BRANCHES ON THE TREES!
WOW!
THE LEAVES ON THE BRANCHES!
WOW!
AND EVEN ME, A WORM ON A LEAF ON A BRANCH ON A TREE!
I MEAN,
EVERYONE ALREADY KNOWS WORMS ARE ALIVE.

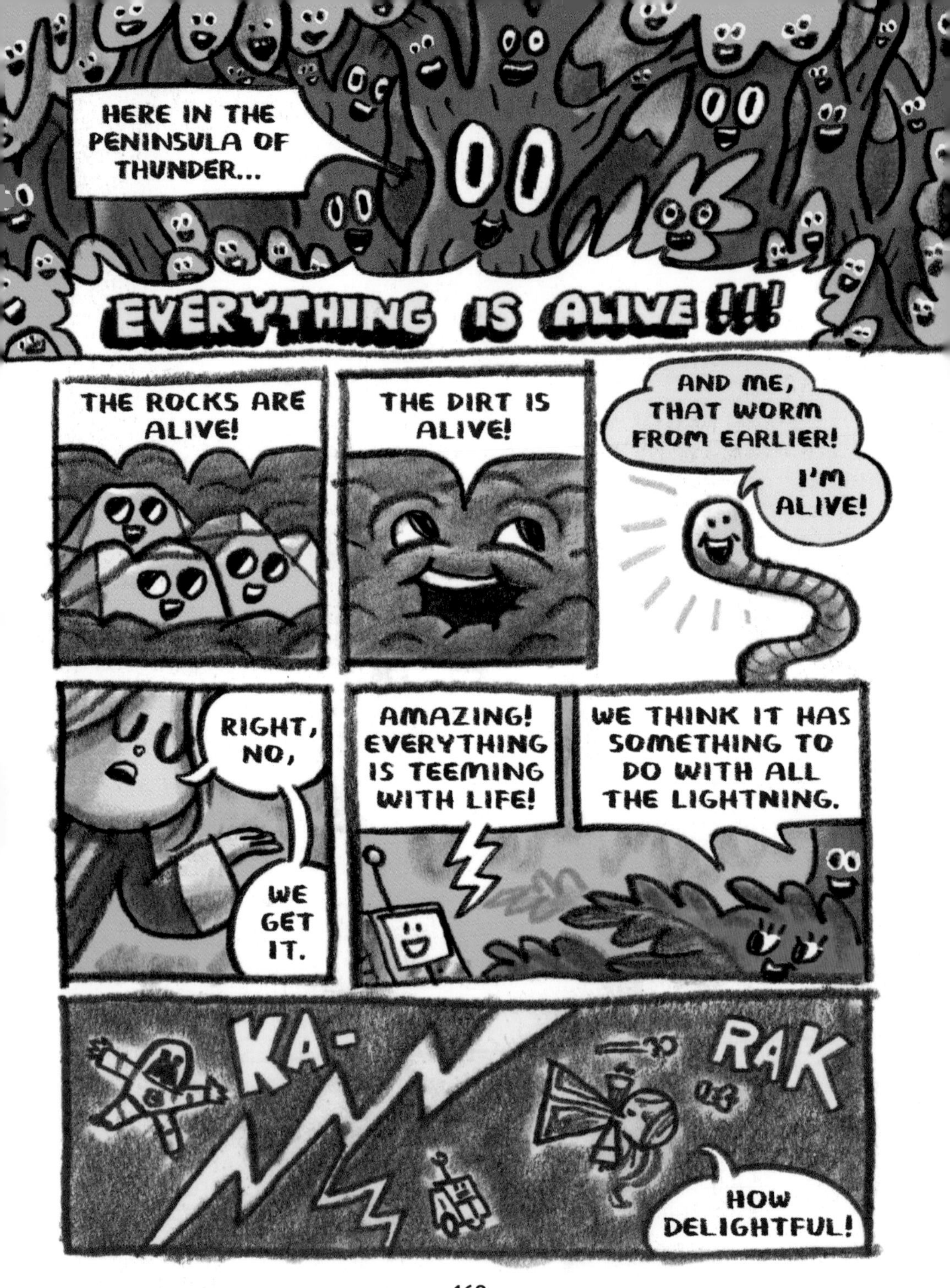
HERE IN THE PENINSULA OF THUNDER...
EVERYTHING IS ALIVE!!!
THE ROCKS ARE ALIVE!
THE DIRT IS ALIVE!
AND ME, THAT WORM FROM EARLIER!
I'M ALIVE!
RIGHT, NO,
WE GET IT.
AMAZING! EVERYTHING IS TEEMING WITH LIFE!
WE THINK IT HAS SOMETHING TO DO WITH ALL THE LIGHTNING.
KA-
RAK
HOW DELIGHTFUL!

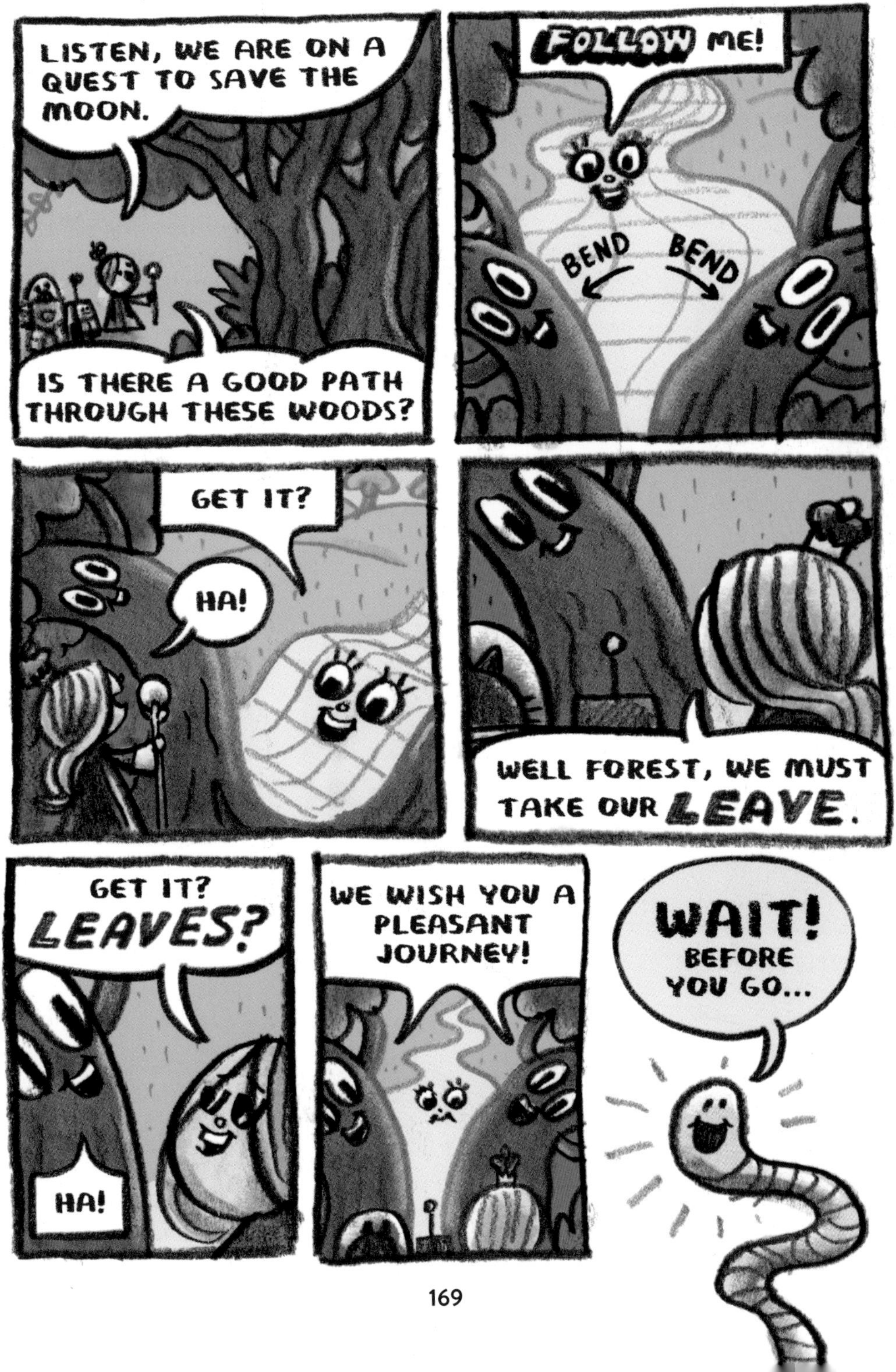
LISTEN, WE ARE ON A QUEST TO SAVE THE MOON.
IS THERE A GOOD PATH THROUGH THESE WOODS?
FOLLOW ME!
BEND
BEND
GET IT?
HA!
WELL FOREST, WE MUST TAKE OUR LEAVE.
GET IT? LEAVES?
HA!
WE WISH YOU A PLEASANT JOURNEY!
WAIT! BEFORE YOU GO...

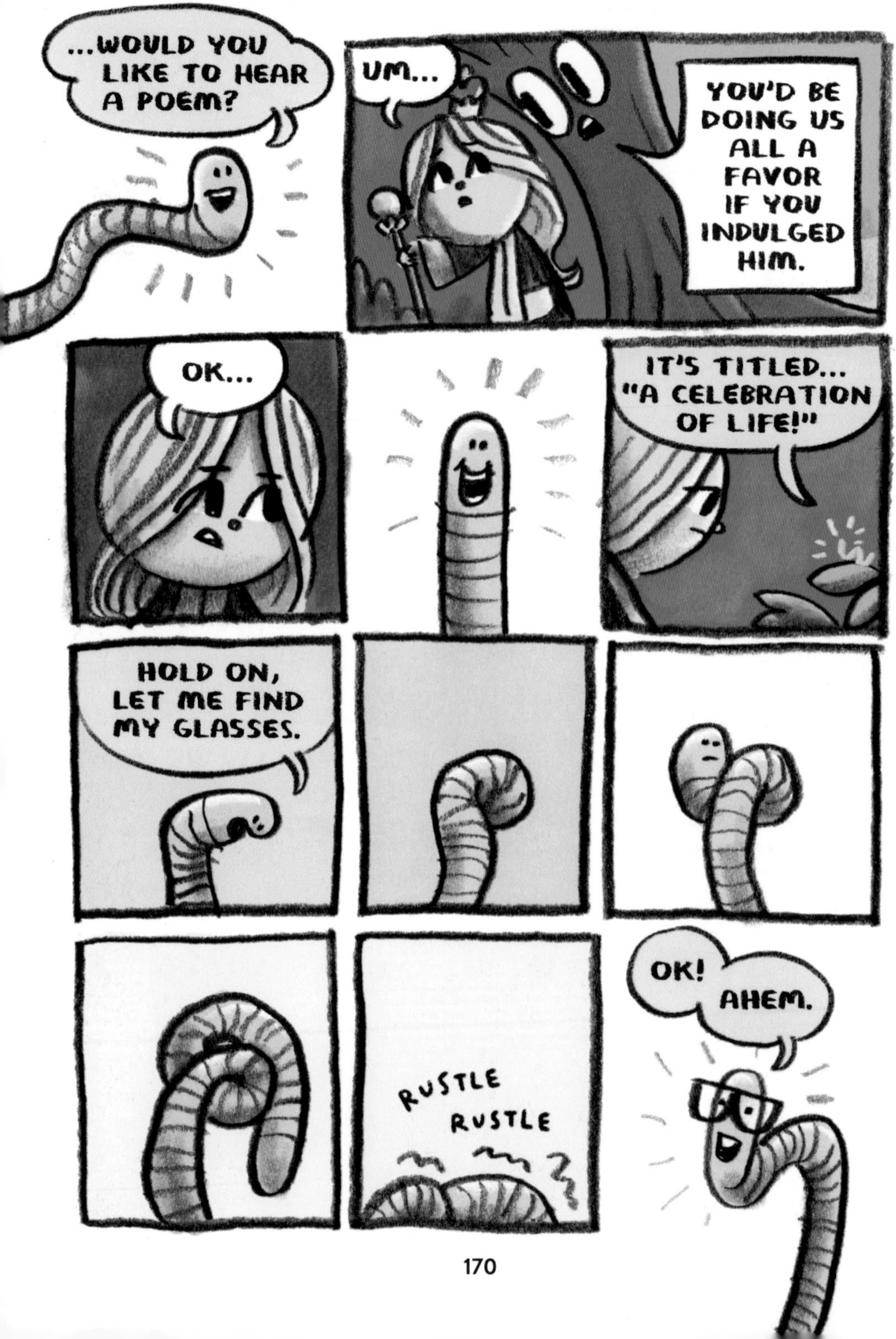
...WOULD YOU LIKE TO HEAR A POEM?
UM...
YOU'D BE DOING US ALL A FAVOR IF YOU INDULGED HIM.
OK...
IT'S TITLED... "A CELEBRATION OF LIFE!"
HOLD ON, LET ME FIND MY GLASSES.
RUSTLE
RUSTLE
OK!
AHEM.

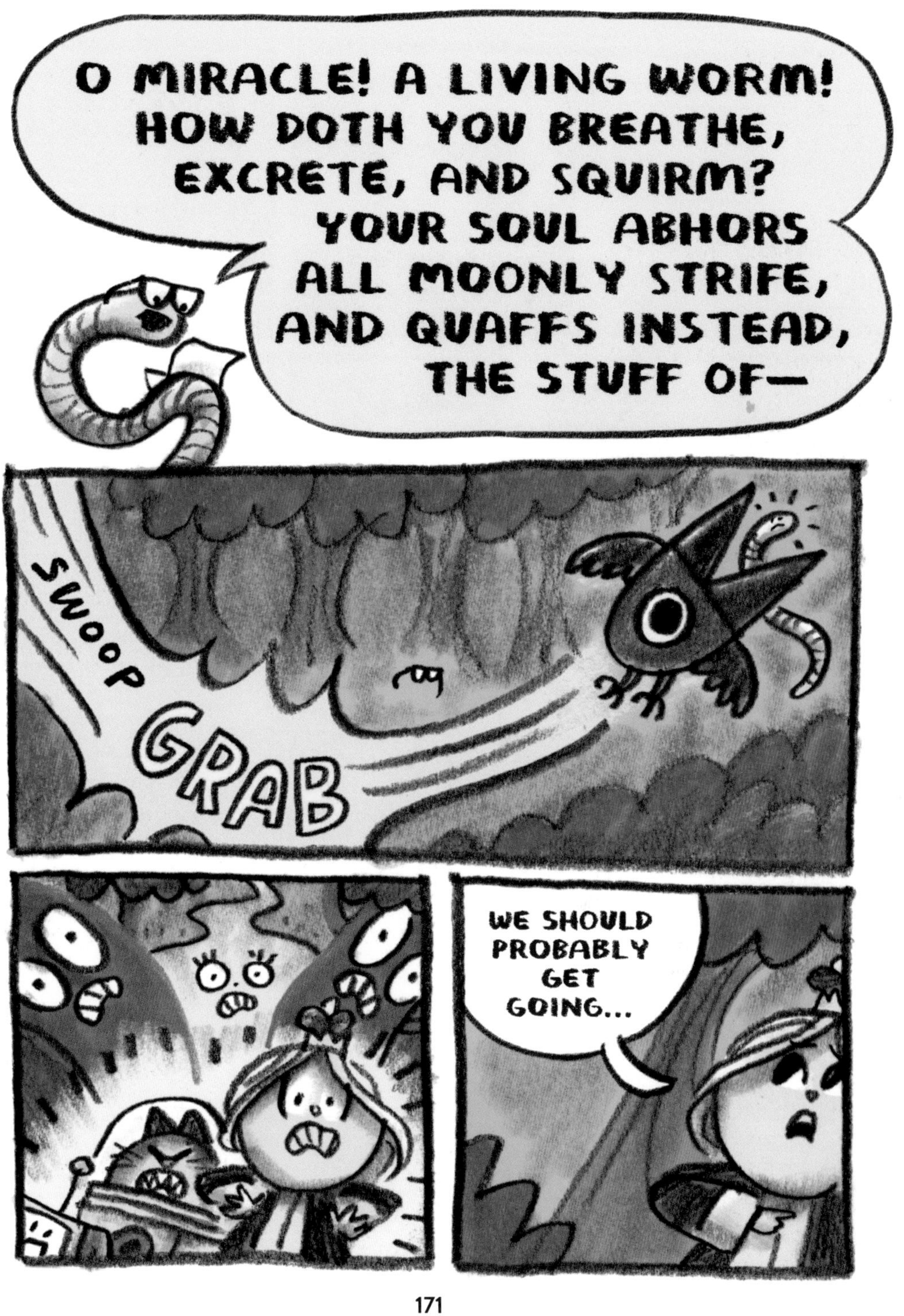
O MIRACLE! A LIVING WORM! HOW DOTH YOU BREATHE, EXCRETE, AND SQUIRM? YOUR SOUL ABHORS ALL MOONLY STRIFE, AND QUAFFS INSTEAD, THE STUFF OF—
SWOOP
GRAB
WE SHOULD PROBABLY GET GOING...

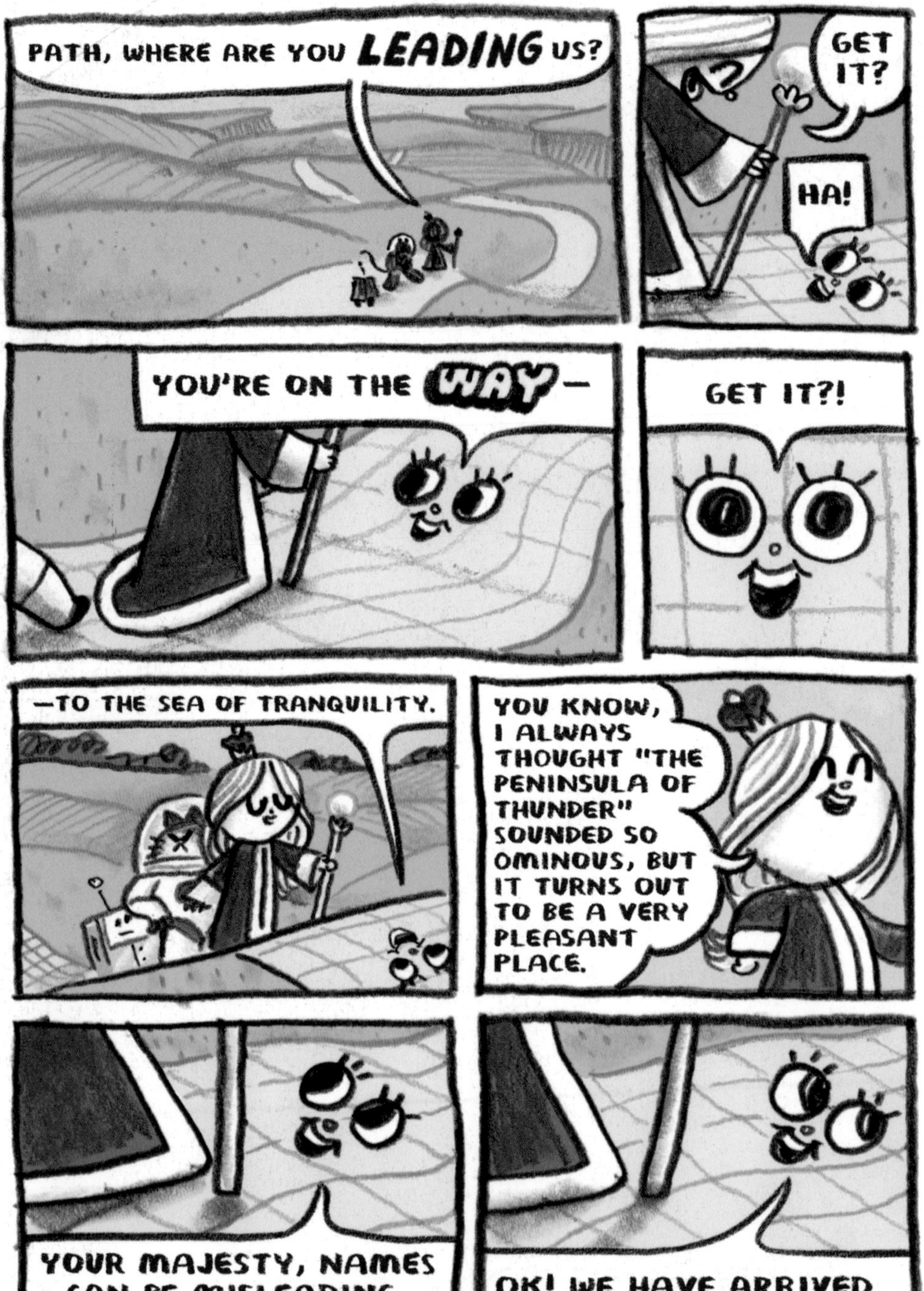
PATH, WHERE ARE YOU LEADING US?
GET IT?
HA!
YOU'RE ON THE WAY—
GET IT?!
—TO THE SEA OF TRANQUILITY.
YOU KNOW, I ALWAYS THOUGHT "THE PENINSULA OF THUNDER" SOUNDED SO OMINOUS, BUT IT TURNS OUT TO BE A VERY PLEASANT PLACE.
YOUR MAJESTY, NAMES CAN BE MISLEADING.
OK! WE HAVE ARRIVED...

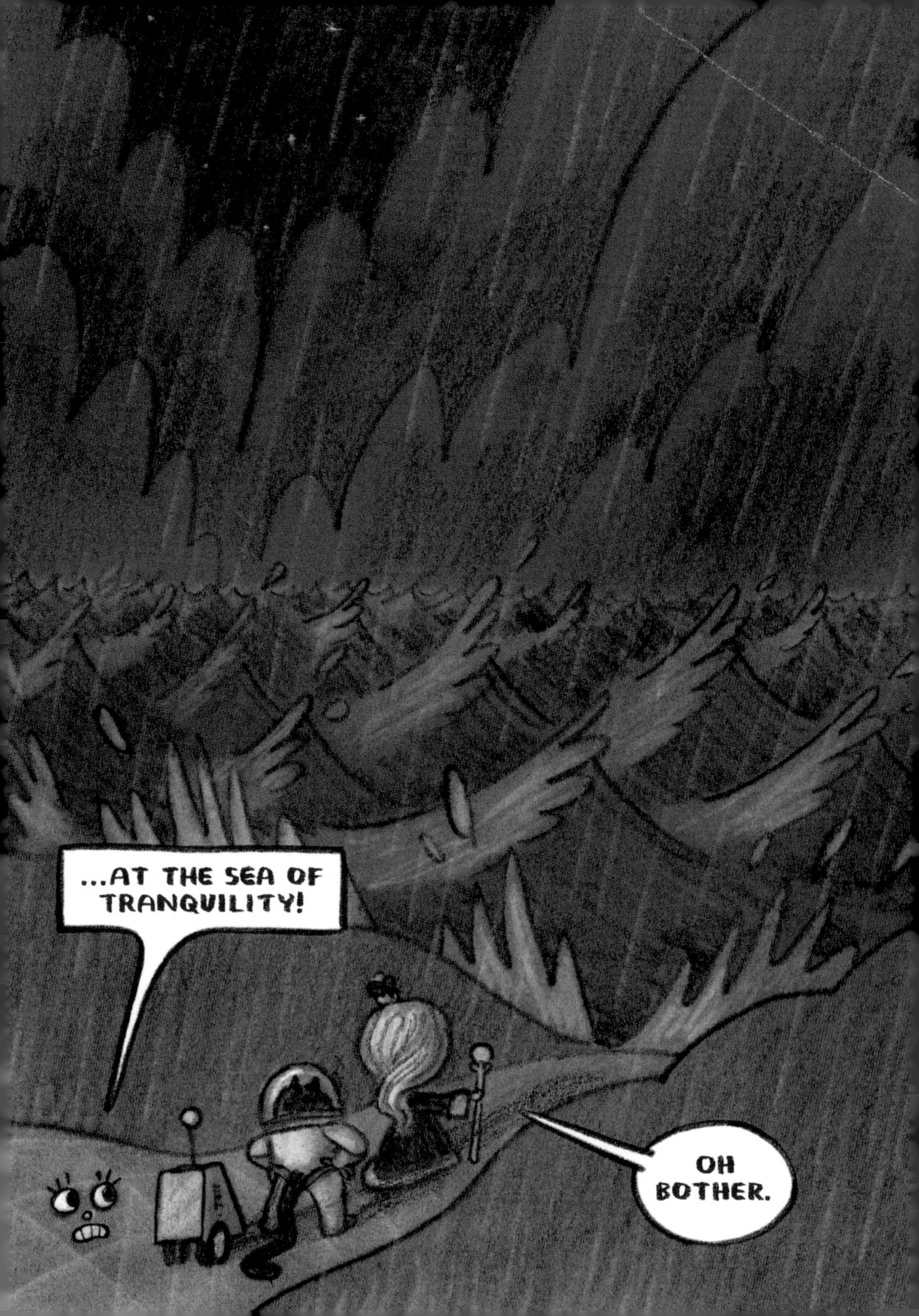
...AT THE SEA OF TRANQUILITY!
OH BOTHER.

CHAPTER 14

SEA SALTS

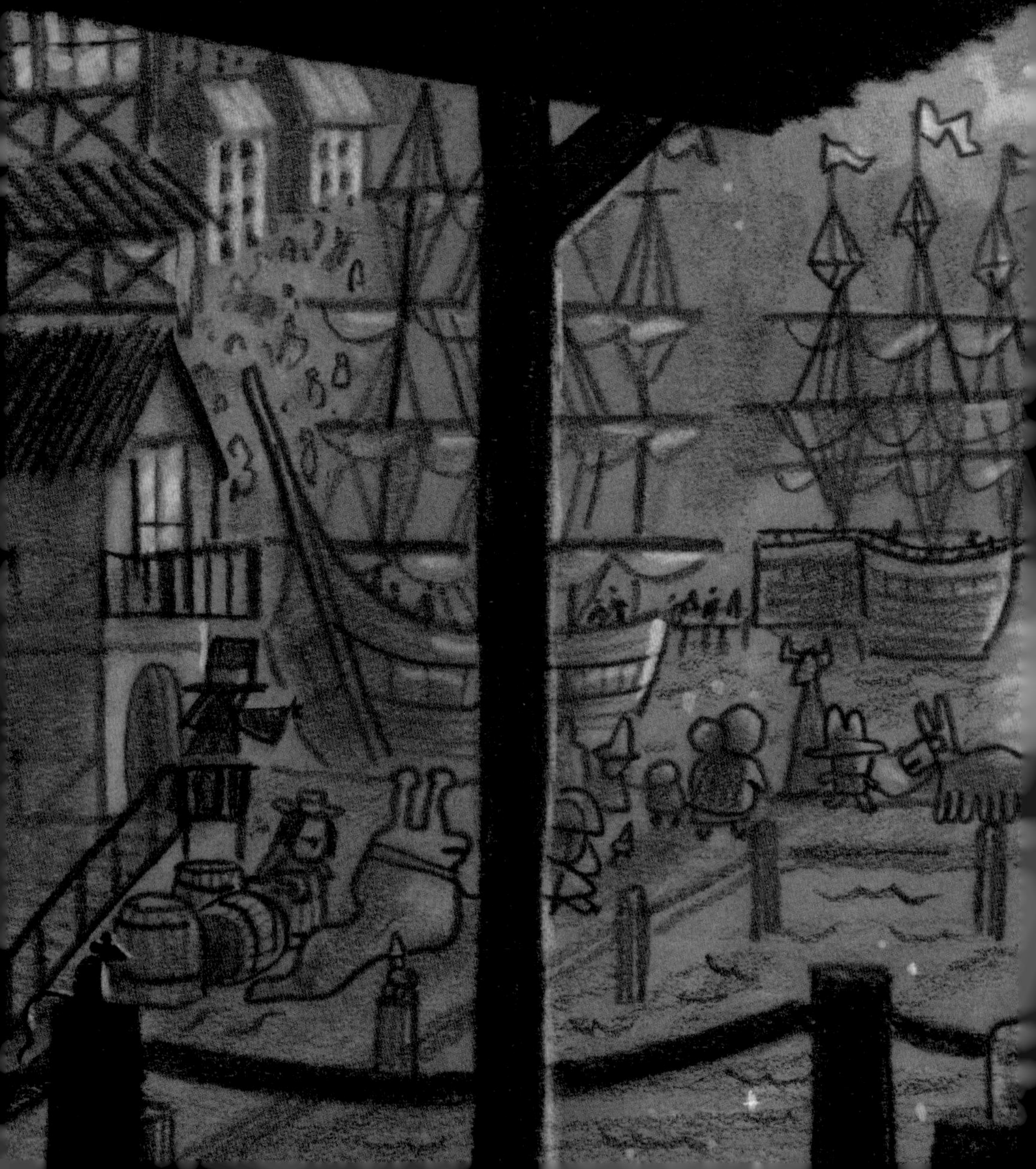

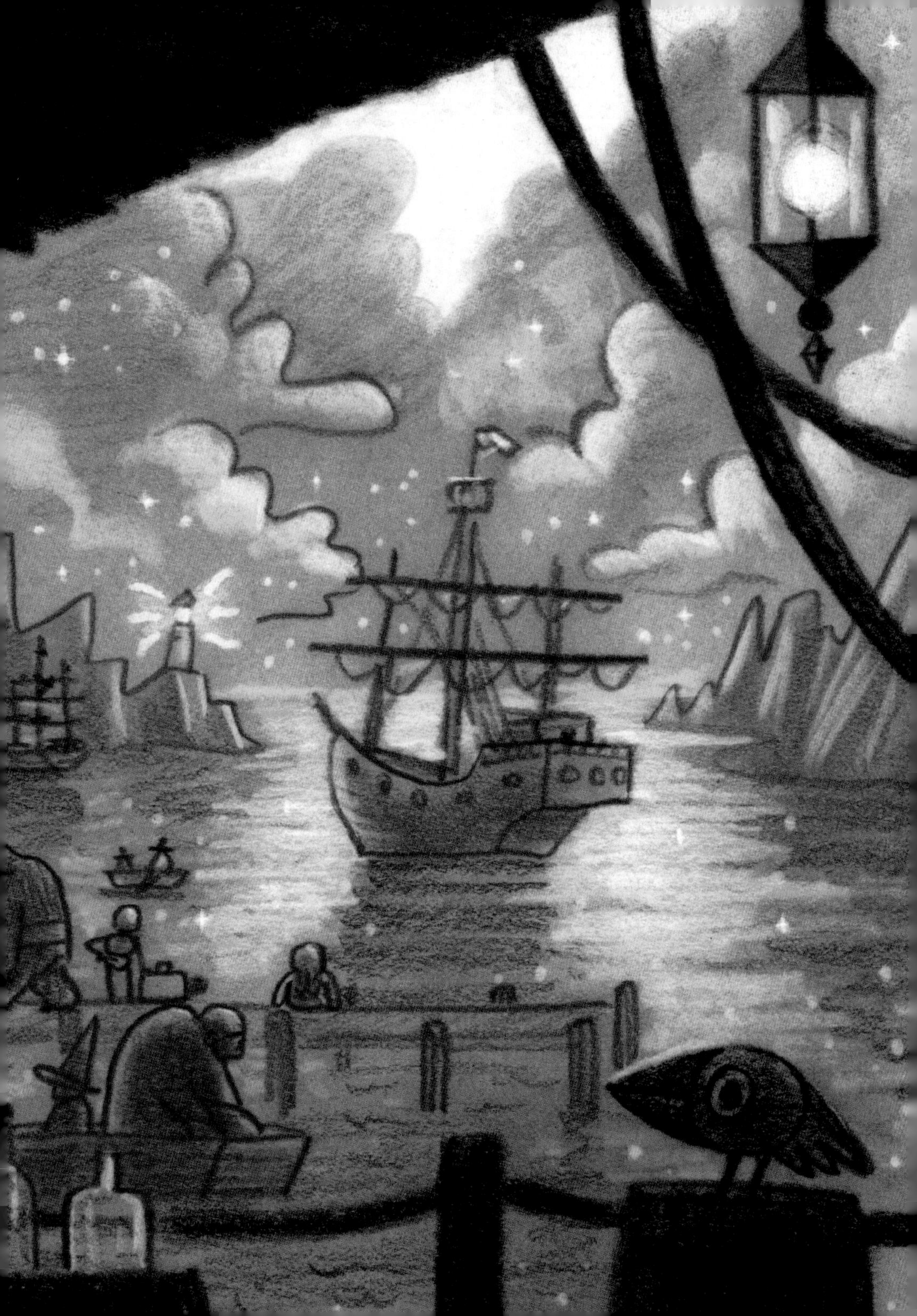

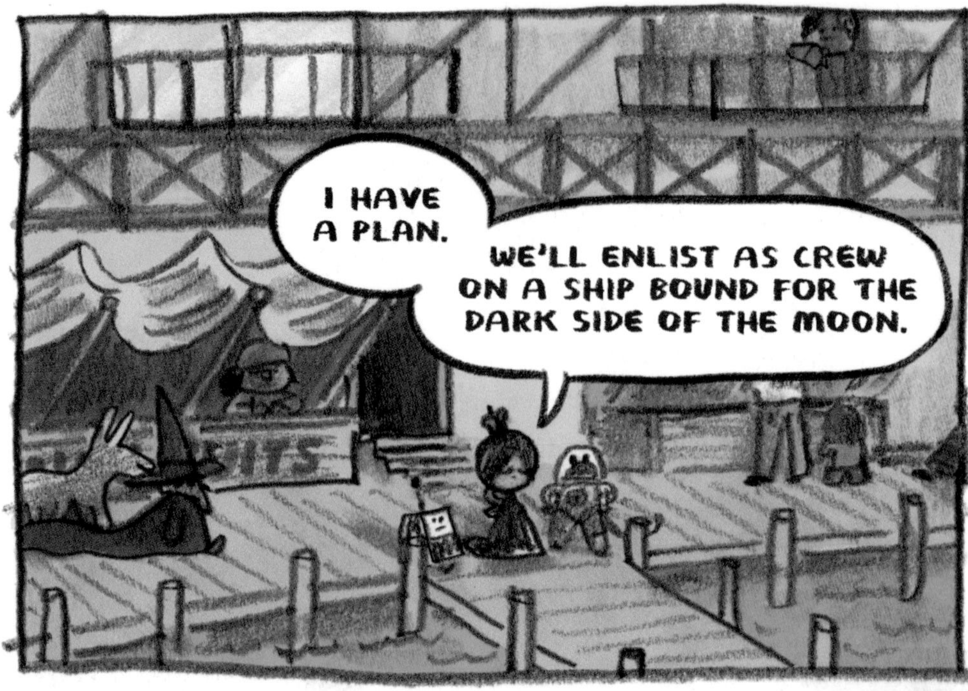
I HAVE A PLAN.
WE'LL ENLIST AS CREW ON A SHIP BOUND FOR THE DARK SIDE OF THE MOON.
SUITS

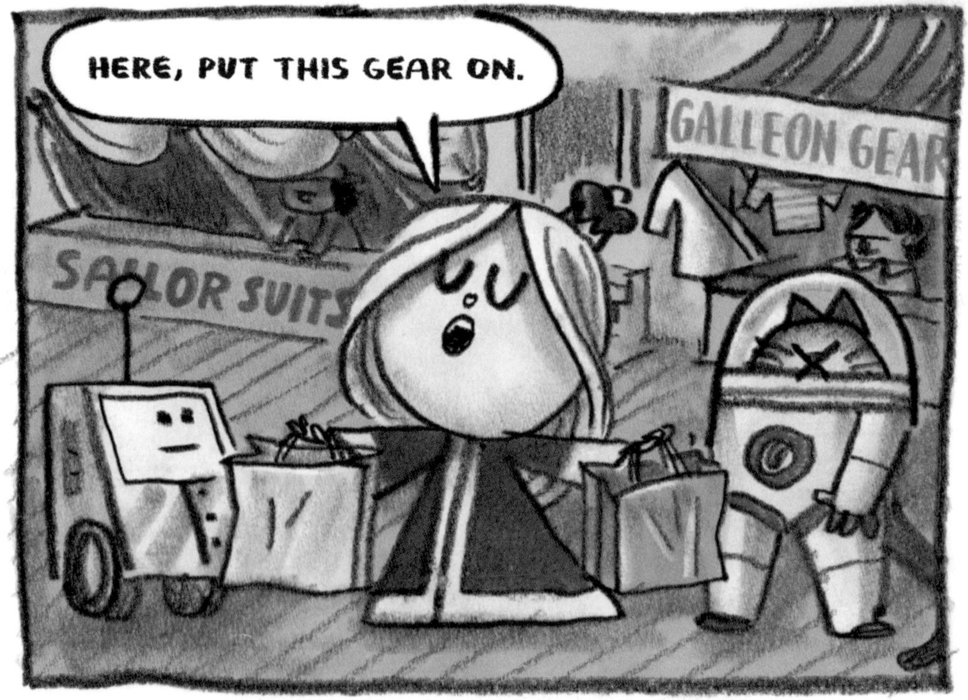
HERE, PUT THIS GEAR ON.
GALLEON GEAR
SAILOR SUITS

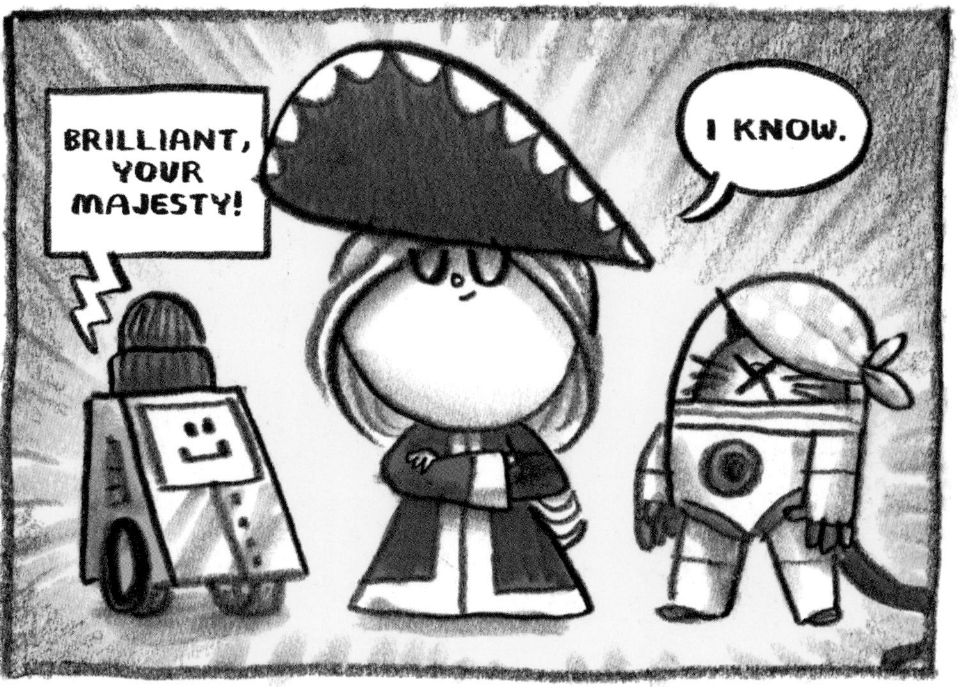
BRILLIANT, YOUR MAJESTY!
I KNOW.

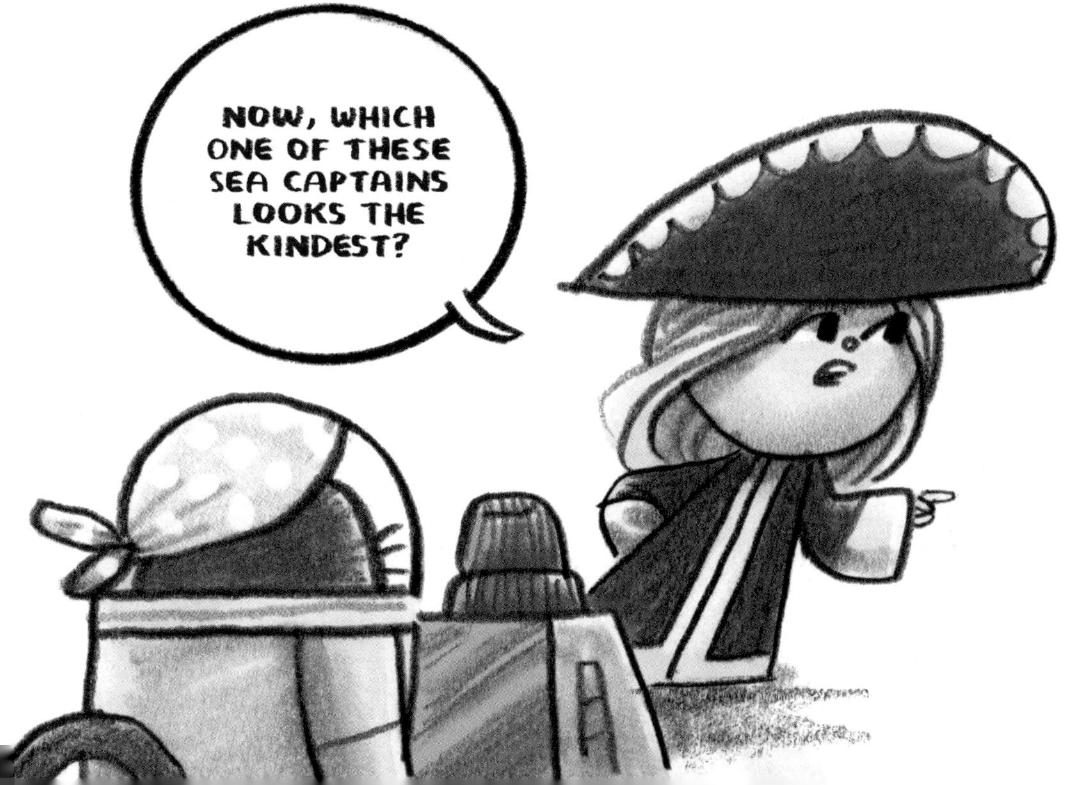
NOW, WHICH ONE OF THESE SEA CAPTAINS LOOKS THE KINDEST?

YIKES.

ERM...

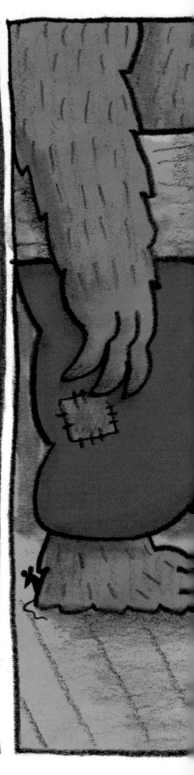

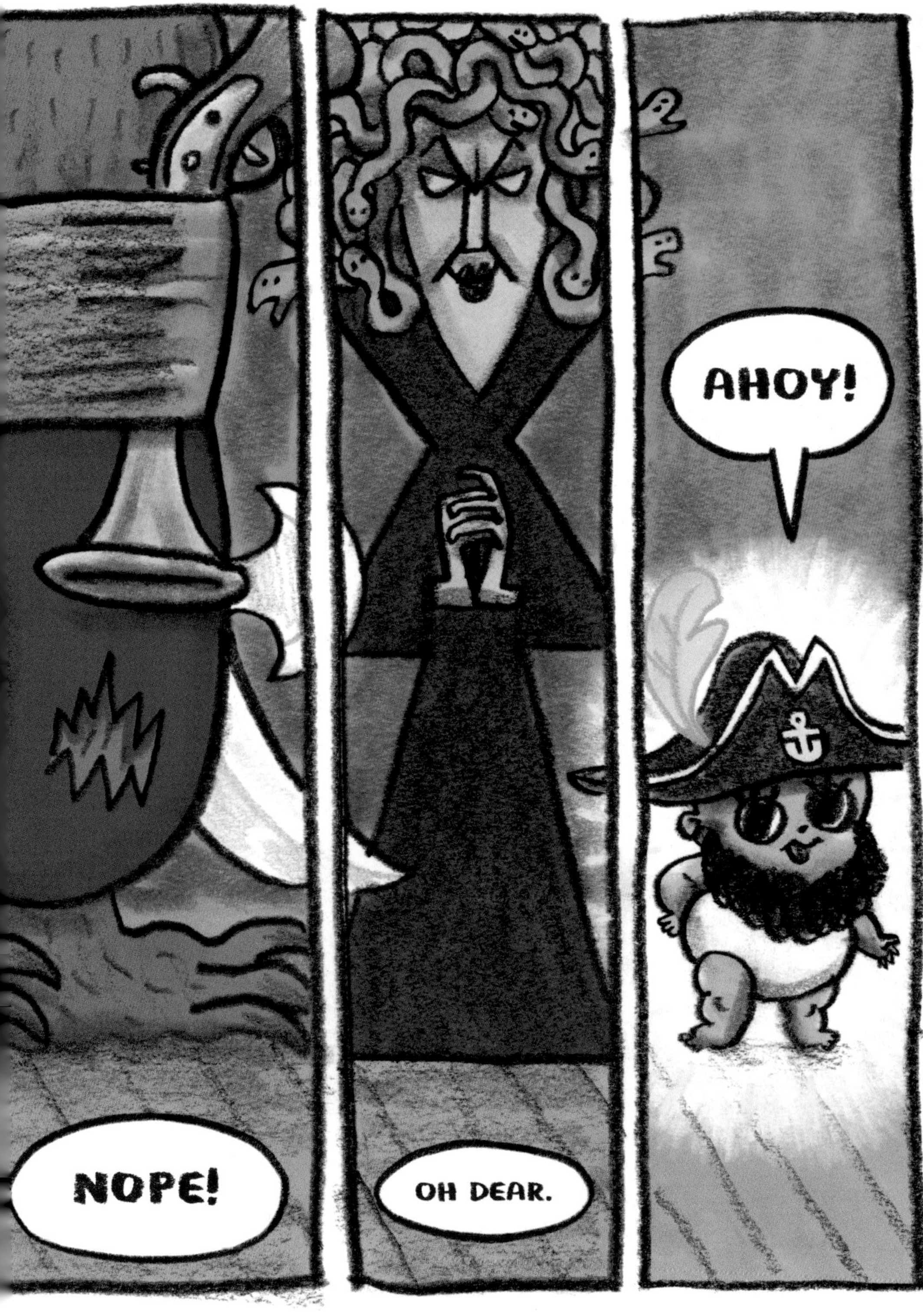
NOPE!
OH DEAR.
AHOY!

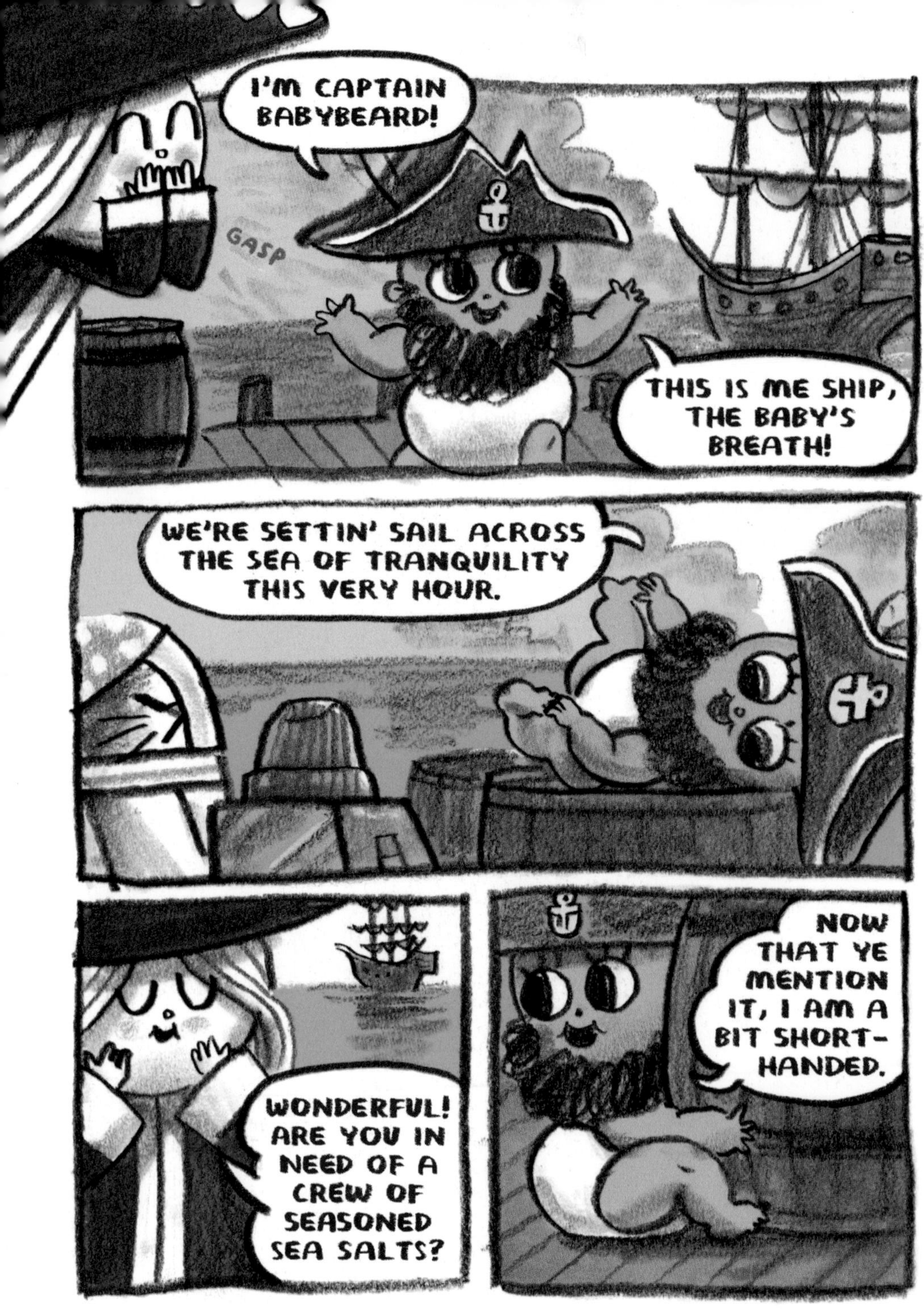
I'M CAPTAIN BABYBEARD!
GASP
THIS IS ME SHIP, THE BABY'S BREATH!
WE'RE SETTIN' SAIL ACROSS THE SEA OF TRANQUILITY THIS VERY HOUR.
WONDERFUL! ARE YOU IN NEED OF A CREW OF SEASONED SEA SALTS?
NOW THAT YE MENTION IT, I AM A BIT SHORT-HANDED.

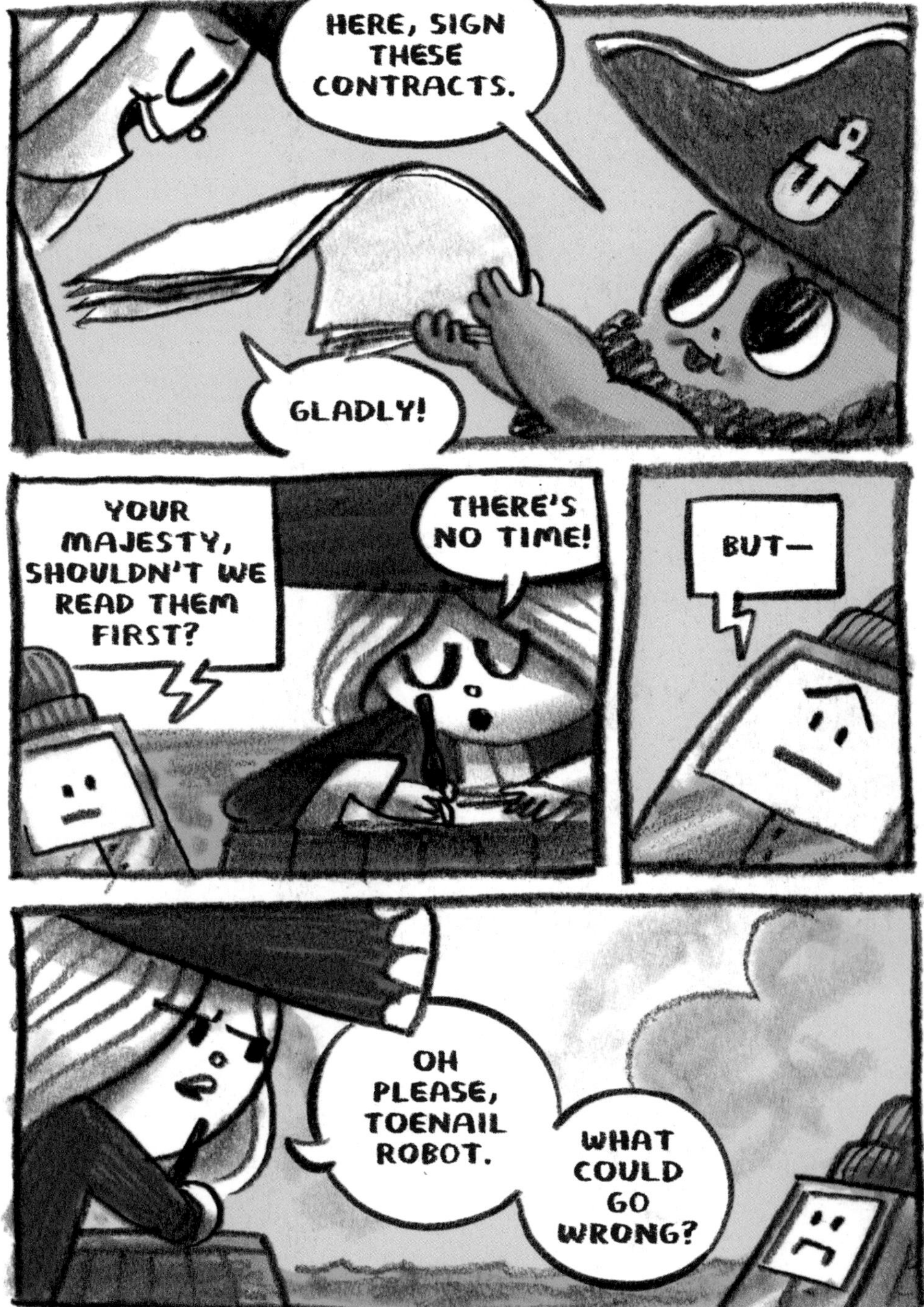
HERE, SIGN THESE CONTRACTS.
GLADLY!
YOUR MAJESTY, SHOULDN'T WE READ THEM FIRST?
THERE'S NO TIME!
BUT—
OH PLEASE, TOENAIL ROBOT.
WHAT COULD GO WRONG?

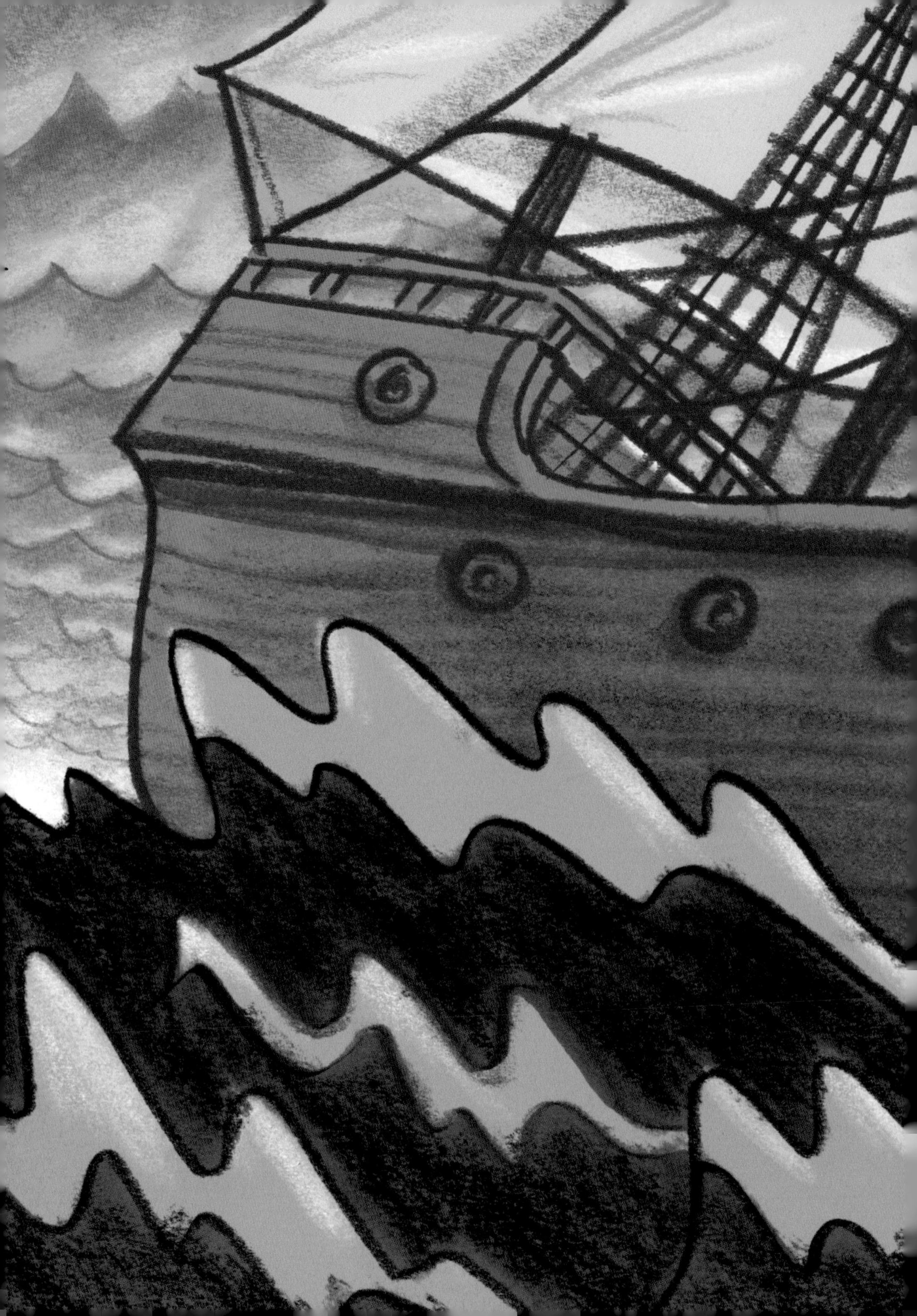

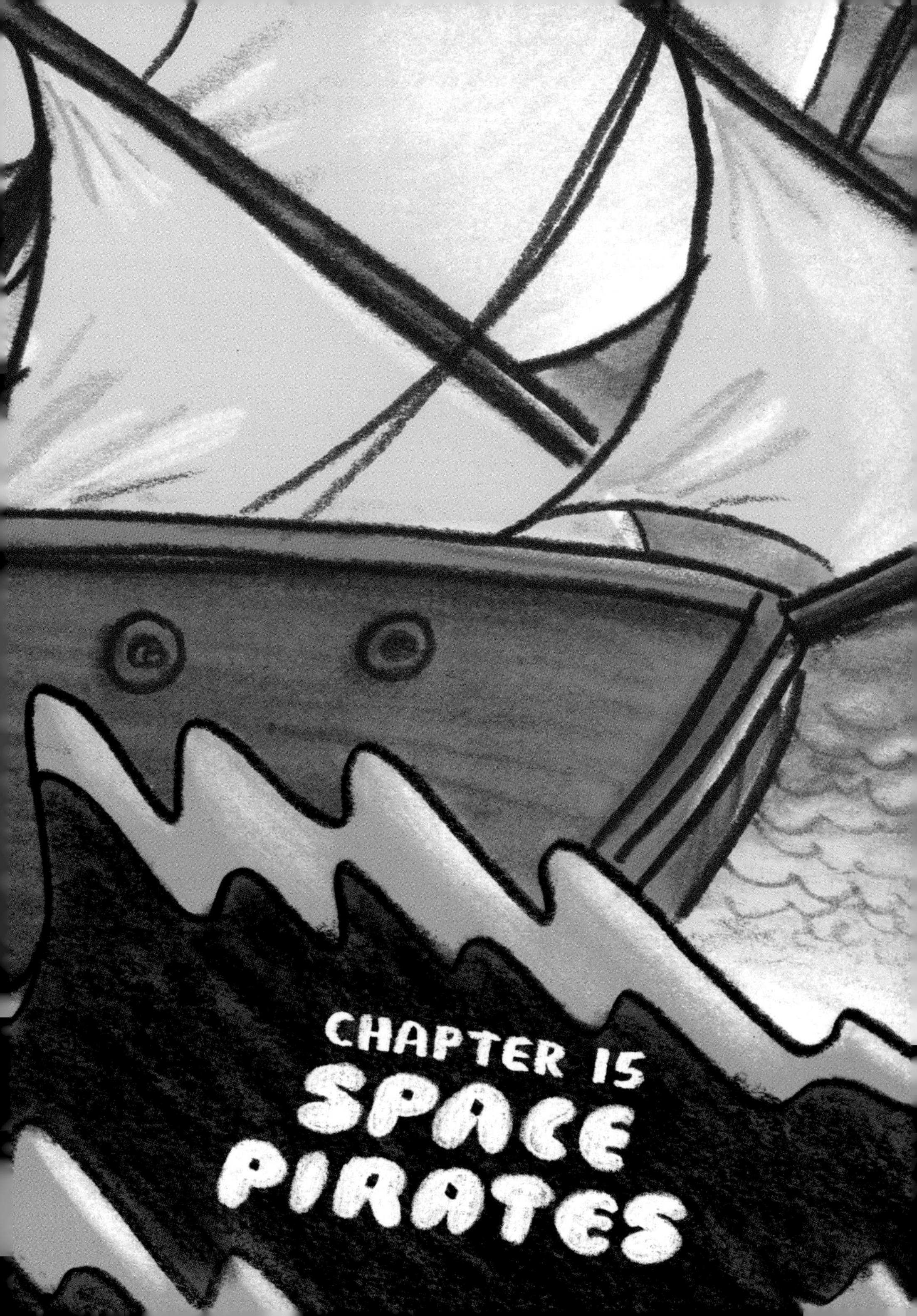

CHAPTER 15
SPACE PIRATES

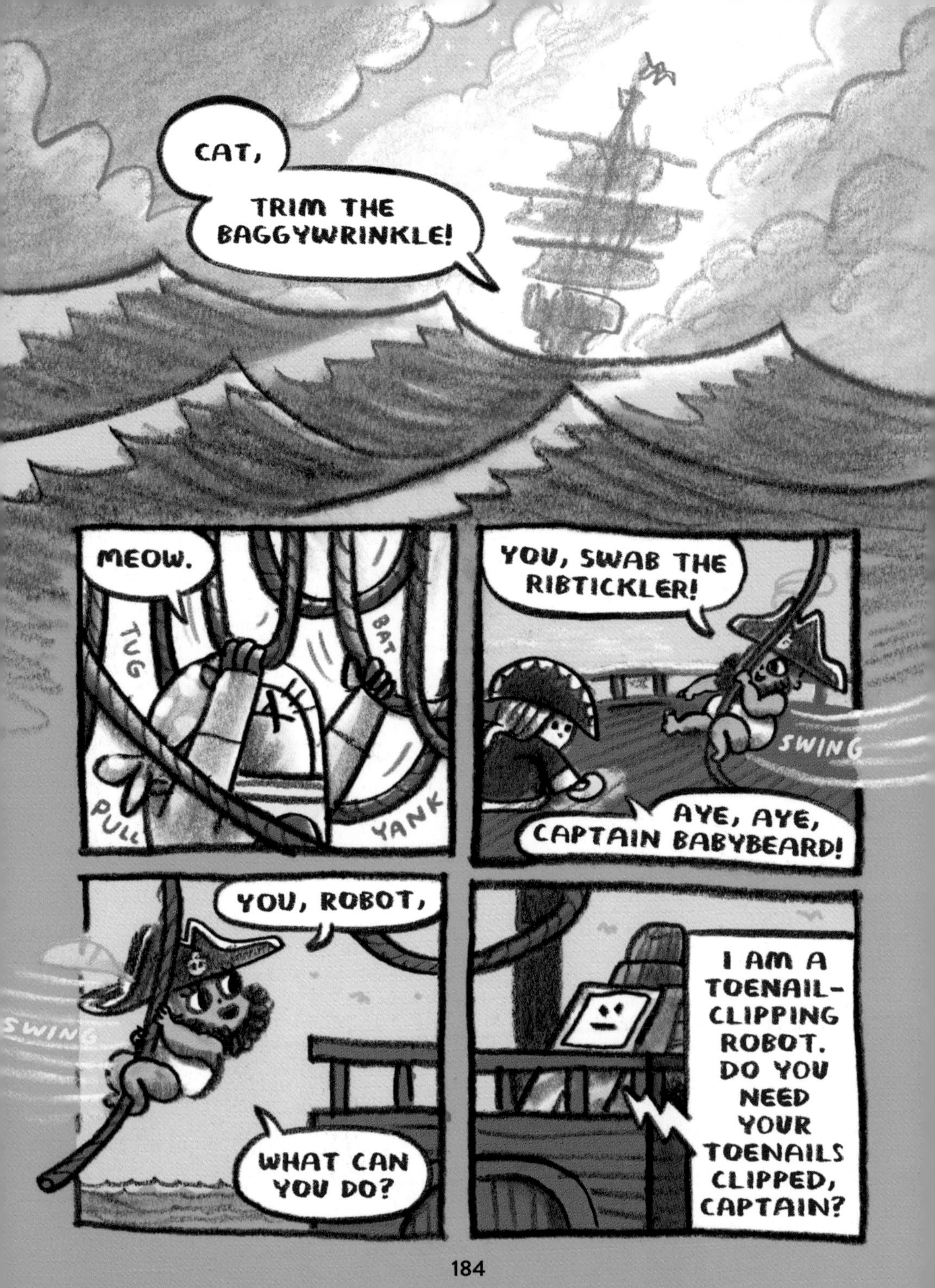
CAT,
TRIM THE BAGGYWRINKLE!
MEOW.
TUG
BAT
PULL
YANK
YOU, SWAB THE RIBTICKLER!
SWING
AYE, AYE, CAPTAIN BABYBEARD!
YOU, ROBOT,
SWING
WHAT CAN YOU DO?
I AM A TOENAIL-CLIPPING ROBOT. DO YOU NEED YOUR TOENAILS CLIPPED, CAPTAIN?

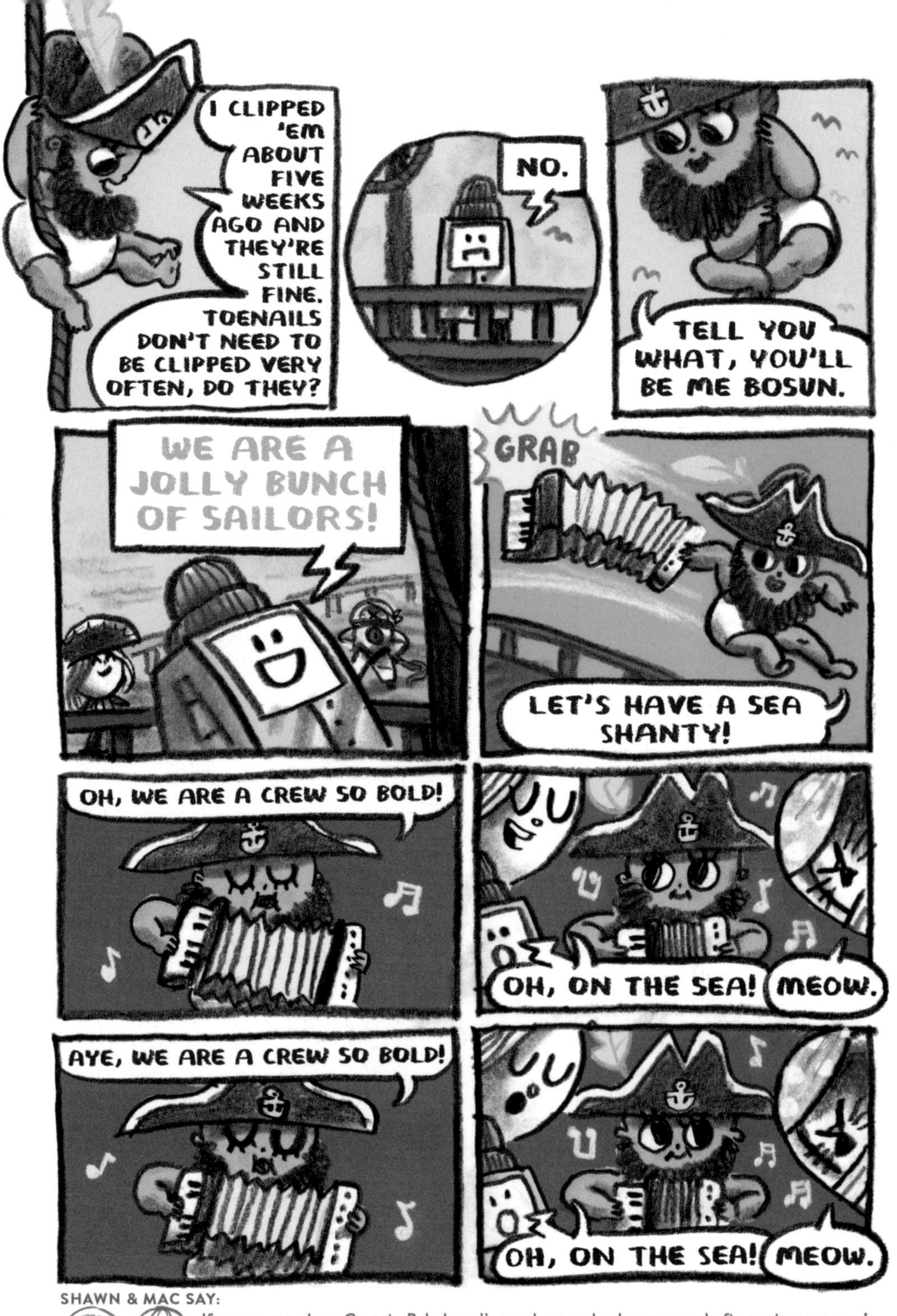
I CLIPPED 'EM ABOUT FIVE WEEKS AGO AND THEY'RE STILL FINE. TOENAILS DON'T NEED TO BE CLIPPED VERY OFTEN, DO THEY?
NO.
TELL YOU WHAT, YOU'LL BE ME BOSUN.
WE ARE A JOLLY BUNCH OF SAILORS!
GRAB
LET'S HAVE A SEA SHANTY!
OH, WE ARE A CREW SO BOLD!
OH, ON THE SEA!
MEOW.
AYE, WE ARE A CREW SO BOLD!
OH, ON THE SEA!
MEOW.

SHAWN & MAC SAY:

If you want to hear Captain Babybeard's sea shanty, check out www.thefirstcatinspace.com!

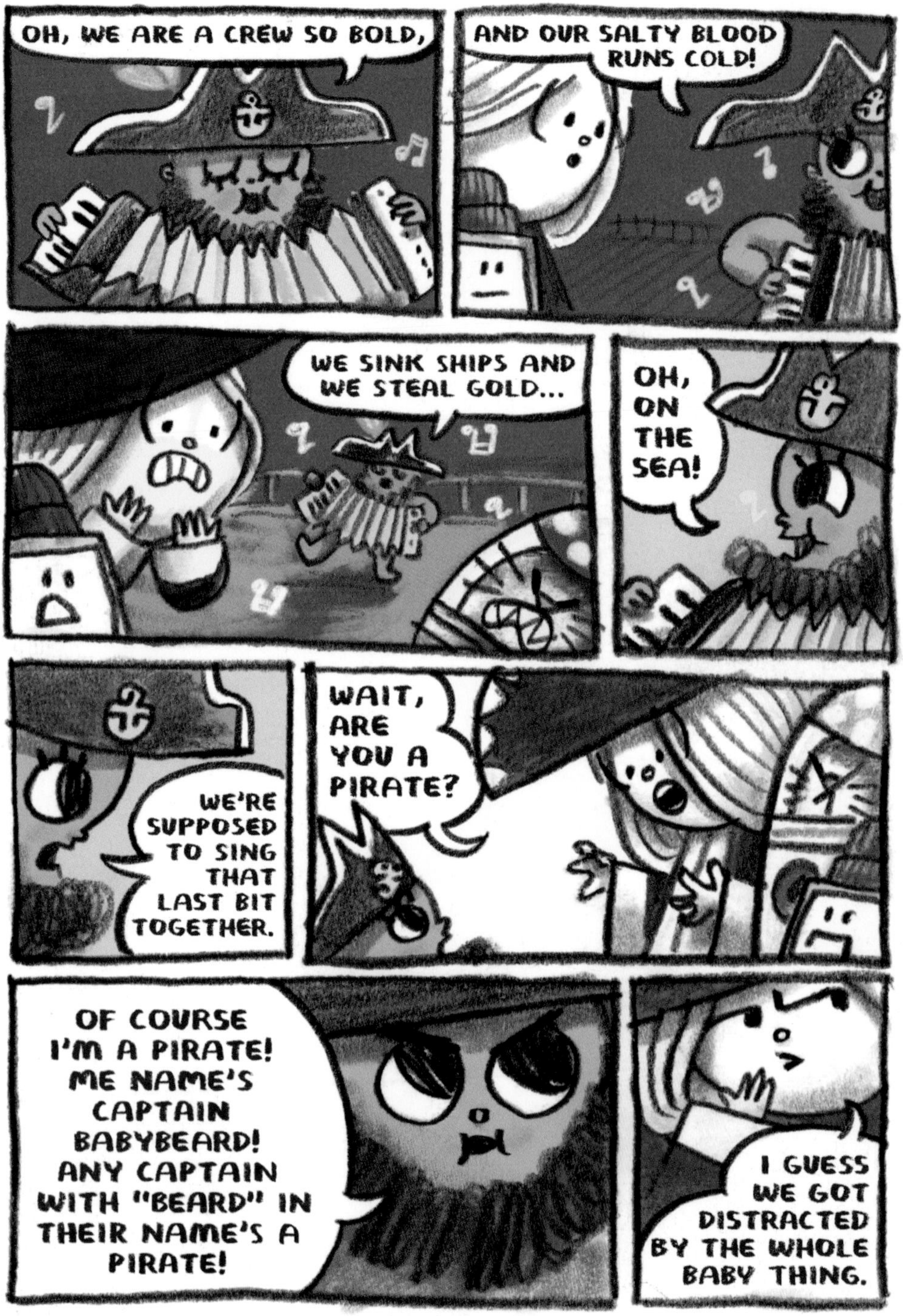
OH, WE ARE A CREW SO BOLD,
AND OUR SALTY BLOOD RUNS COLD!
WE SINK SHIPS AND WE STEAL GOLD...
OH, ON THE SEA!
WE'RE SUPPOSED TO SING THAT LAST BIT TOGETHER.
WAIT, ARE YOU A PIRATE?
OF COURSE I'M A PIRATE! ME NAME'S CAPTAIN BABYBEARD! ANY CAPTAIN WITH "BEARD" IN THEIR NAME'S A PIRATE!
I GUESS WE GOT DISTRACTED BY THE WHOLE BABY THING.

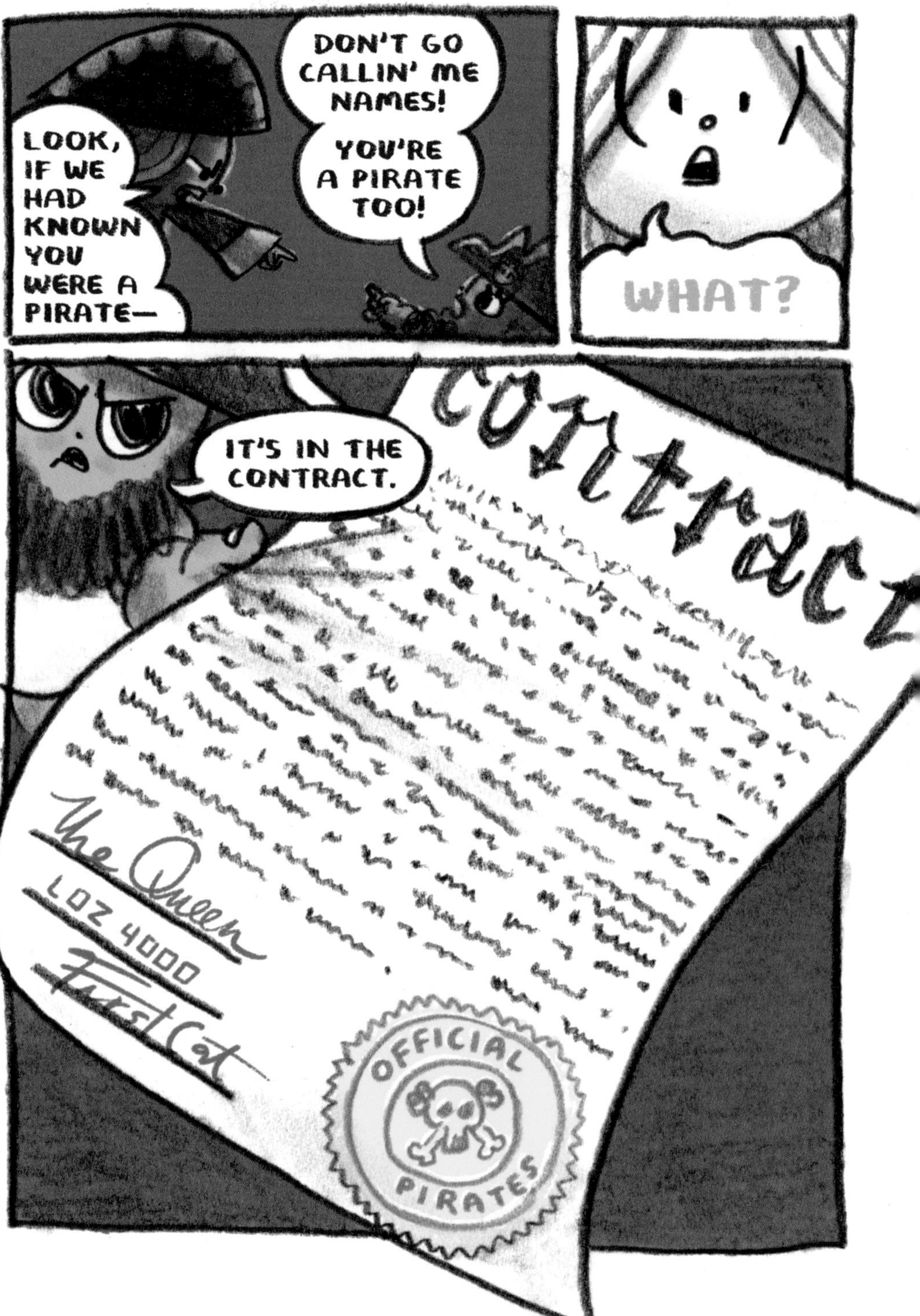
LOOK, IF WE HAD KNOWN YOU WERE A PIRATE—
DON'T GO CALLIN' ME NAMES!
YOU'RE A PIRATE TOO!
WHAT?
IT'S IN THE CONTRACT.
CONTRACT
The Queen
LOZ 4000
First Cat
OFFICIAL PIRATES

OH MY RAM!

LOOK HERE.

YOU JUST HAVE TO HELP ME PLUNDER ONE SHIP AND THEN I'LL DROP YOU OFF AT THE GATES OF THE DARK SIDE OF THE MOON.

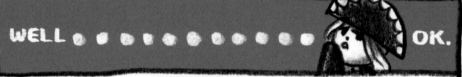

WELL • • • • • • • • • • • • OK.

YOUR MAJESTY! WE CAN'T PLUNDER A SHIP. WE'RE HEROES!

THIS OCEAN IS HUGE. WHAT ARE THE CHANCES OF RUNNING INTO ANOTHER SHIP OUT HERE?

THERE'S ONE NOW!

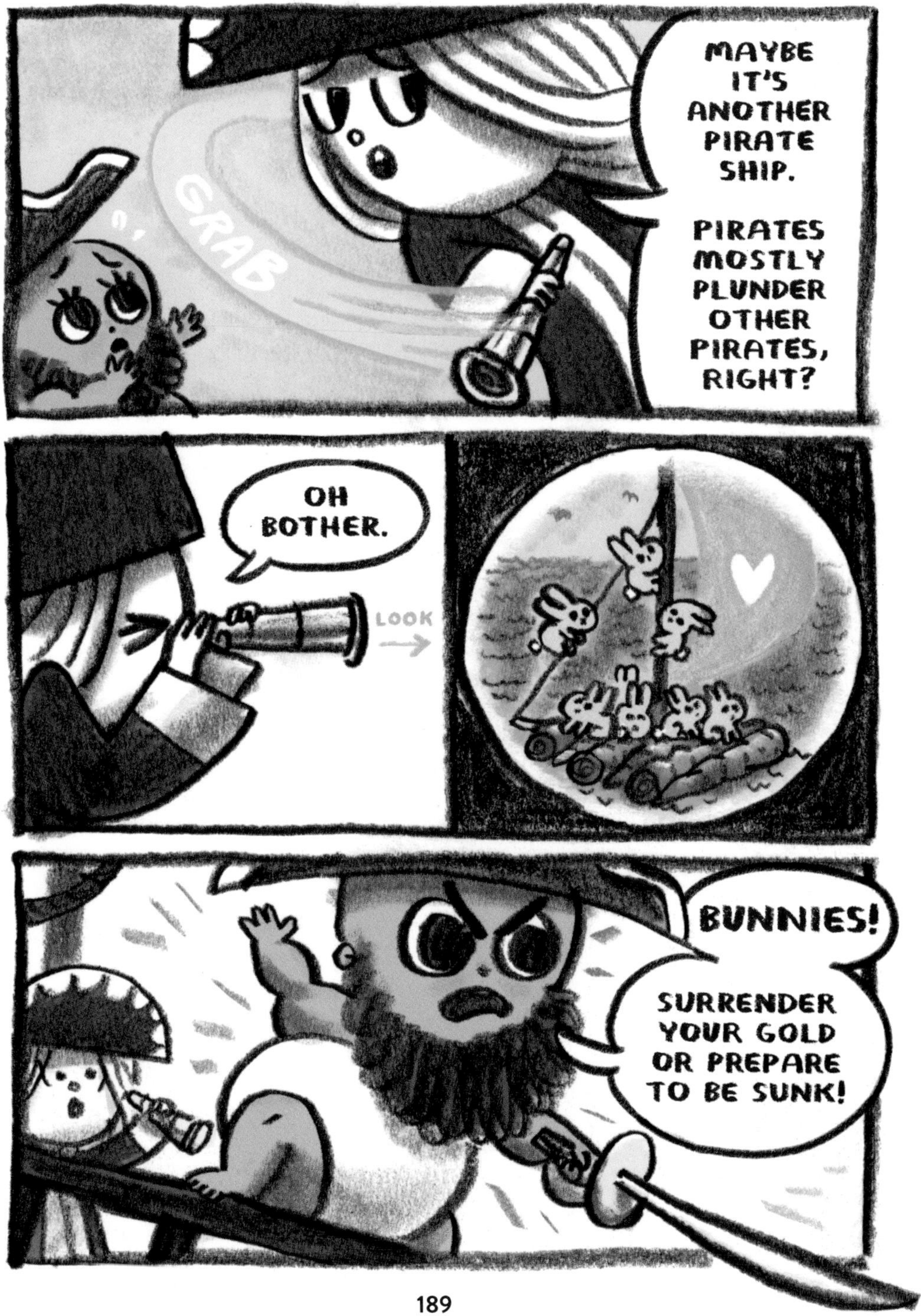
GRAB
MAYBE IT'S ANOTHER PIRATE SHIP.
PIRATES MOSTLY PLUNDER OTHER PIRATES, RIGHT?
OH BOTHER.
LOOK
BUNNIES!
SURRENDER YOUR GOLD OR PREPARE TO BE SUNK!

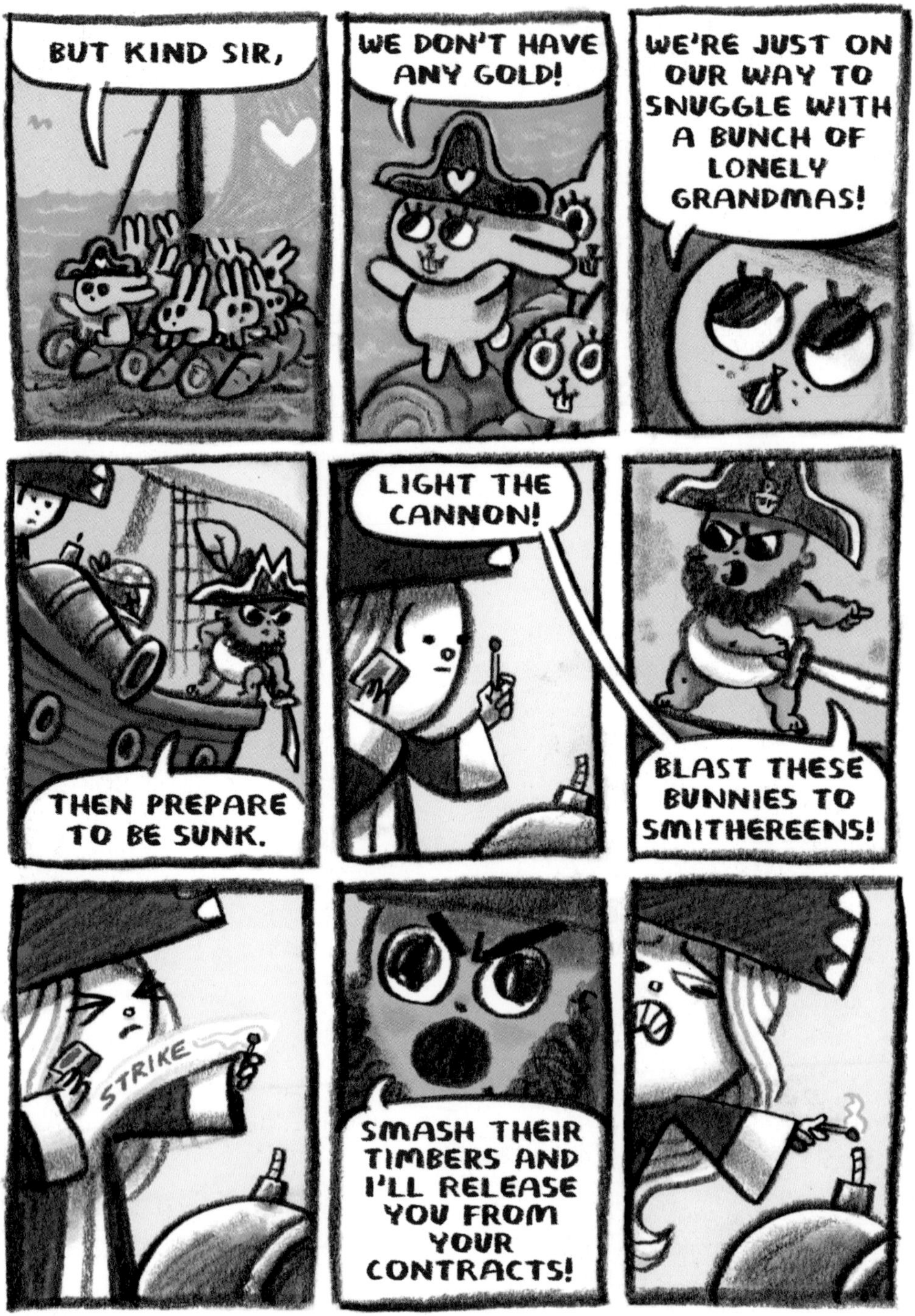
BUT KIND SIR,
WE DON'T HAVE ANY GOLD!
WE'RE JUST ON OUR WAY TO SNUGGLE WITH A BUNCH OF LONELY GRANDMAS!
THEN PREPARE TO BE SUNK.
LIGHT THE CANNON!
BLAST THESE BUNNIES TO SMITHEREENS!
STRIKE
SMASH THEIR TIMBERS AND I'LL RELEASE YOU FROM YOUR CONTRACTS!

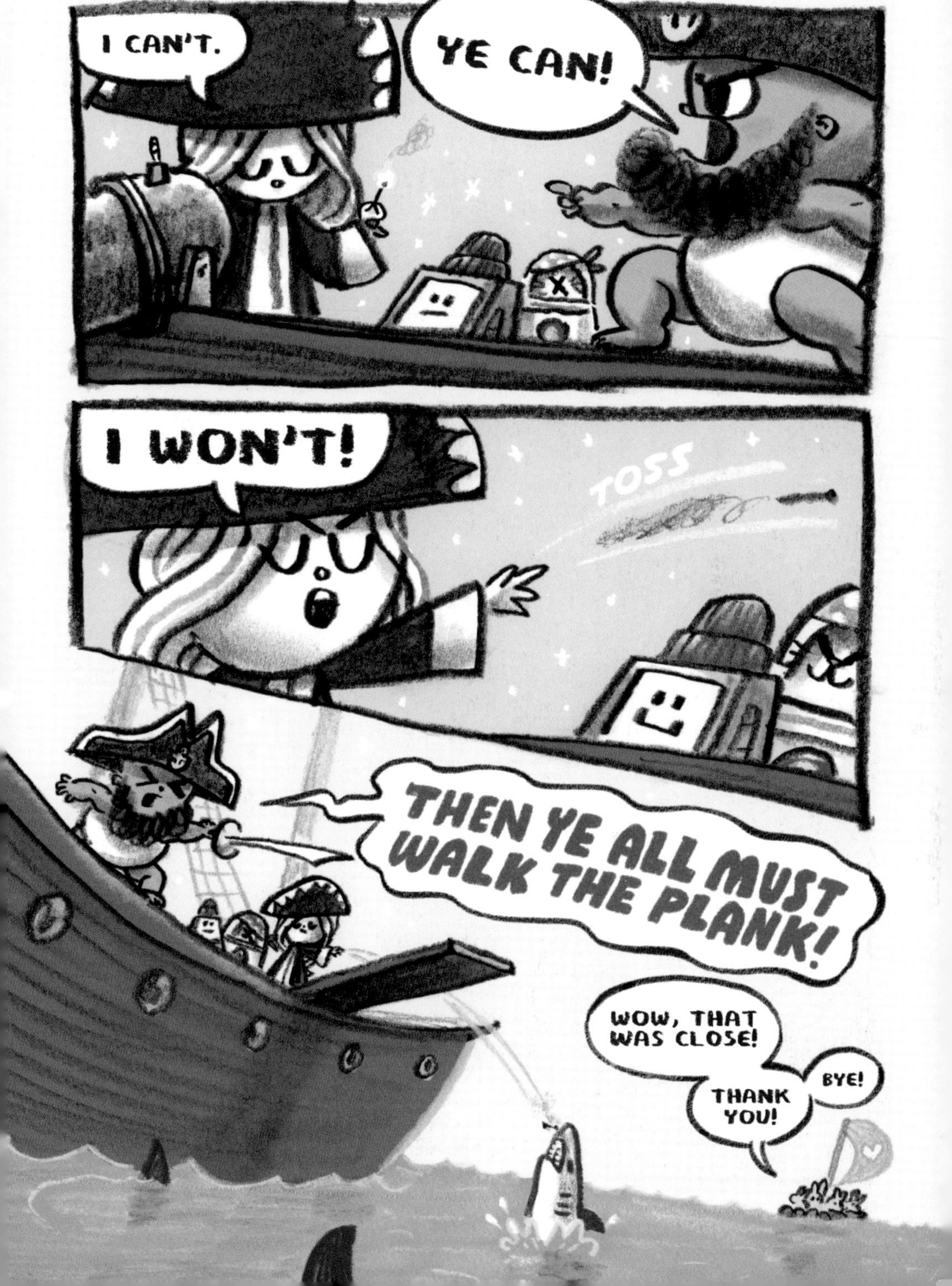
I CAN'T.
YE CAN!
I WON'T!
TOSS
THEN YE ALL MUST WALK THE PLANK!
WOW, THAT WAS CLOSE!
THANK YOU!
BYE!

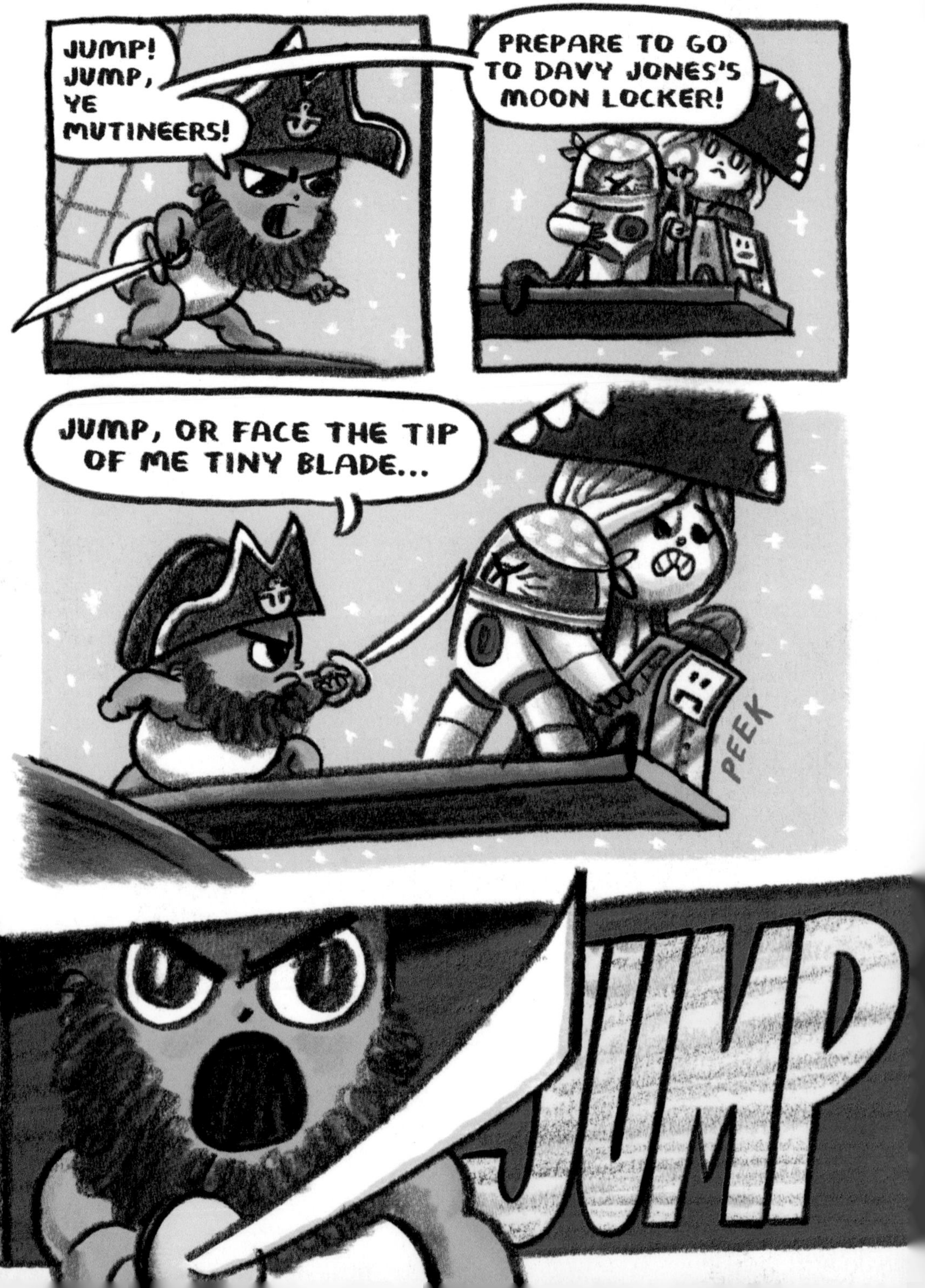
JUMP! JUMP, YE MUTINEERS!
PREPARE TO GO TO DAVY JONES'S MOON LOCKER!
JUMP, OR FACE THE TIP OF ME TINY BLADE...
PEEK
JUMP

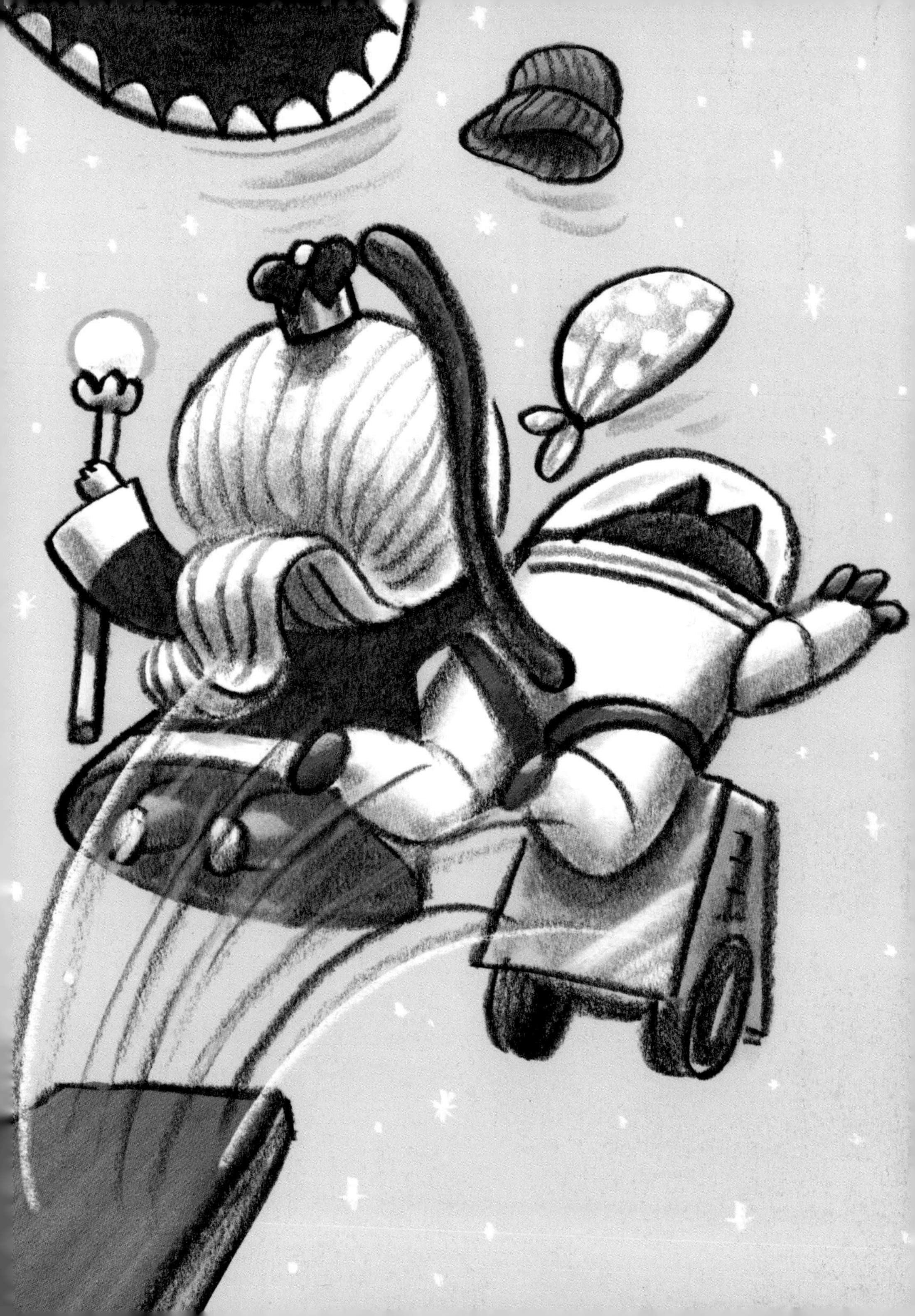

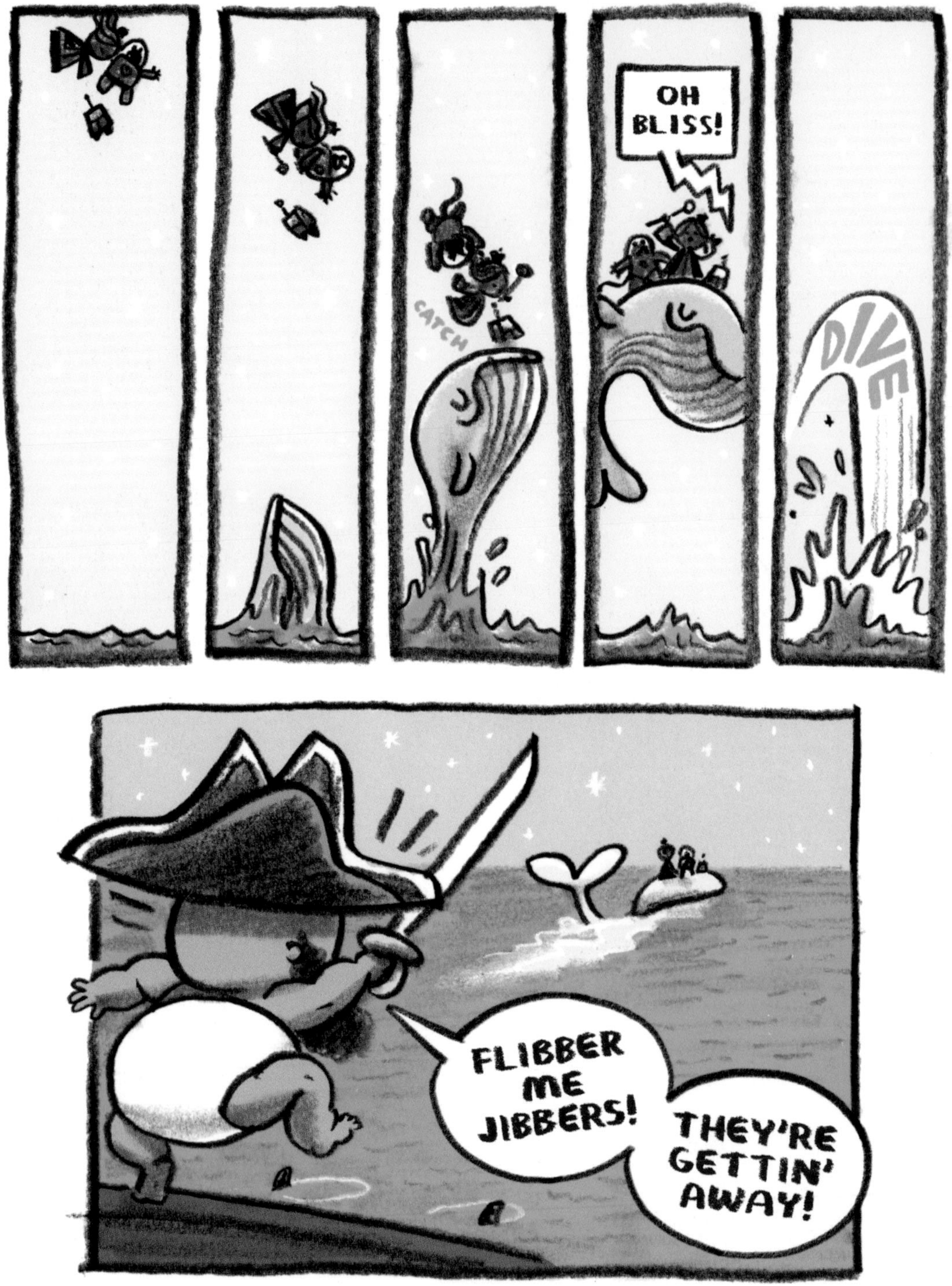
CATCH
OH BLISS!
DIVE
FLIBBER ME JIBBERS!
THEY'RE GETTIN' AWAY!

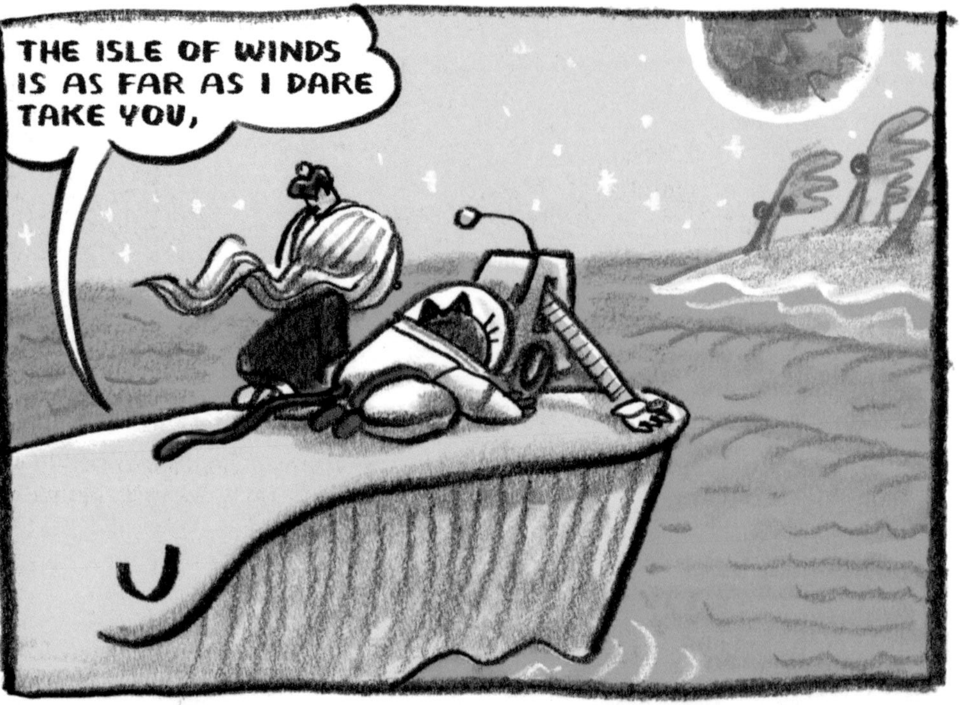
THE ISLE OF WINDS IS AS FAR AS I DARE TAKE YOU,

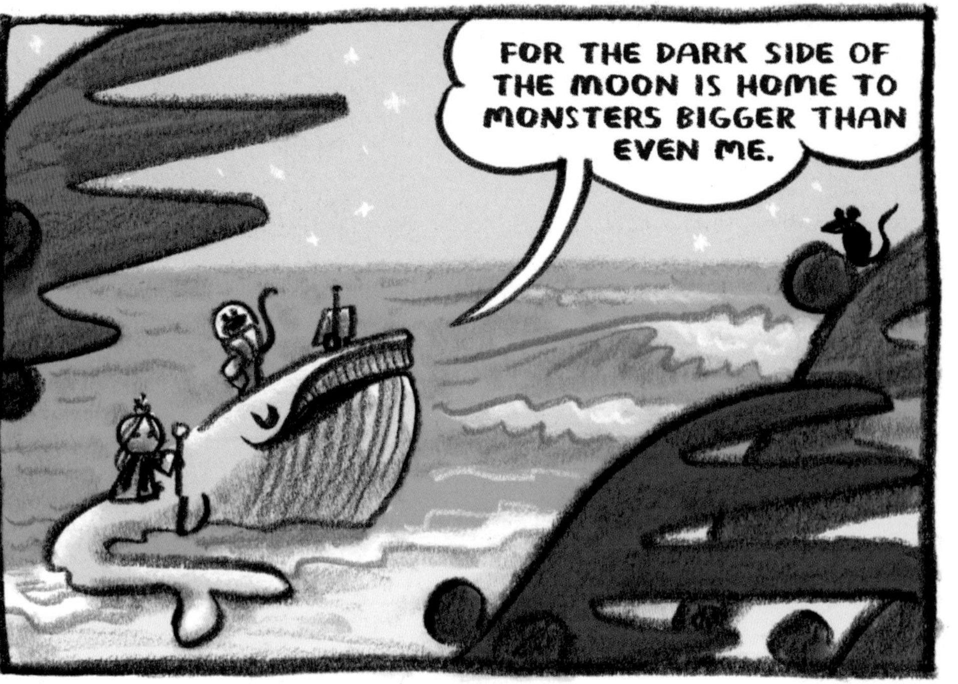
FOR THE DARK SIDE OF THE MOON IS HOME TO MONSTERS BIGGER THAN EVEN ME.

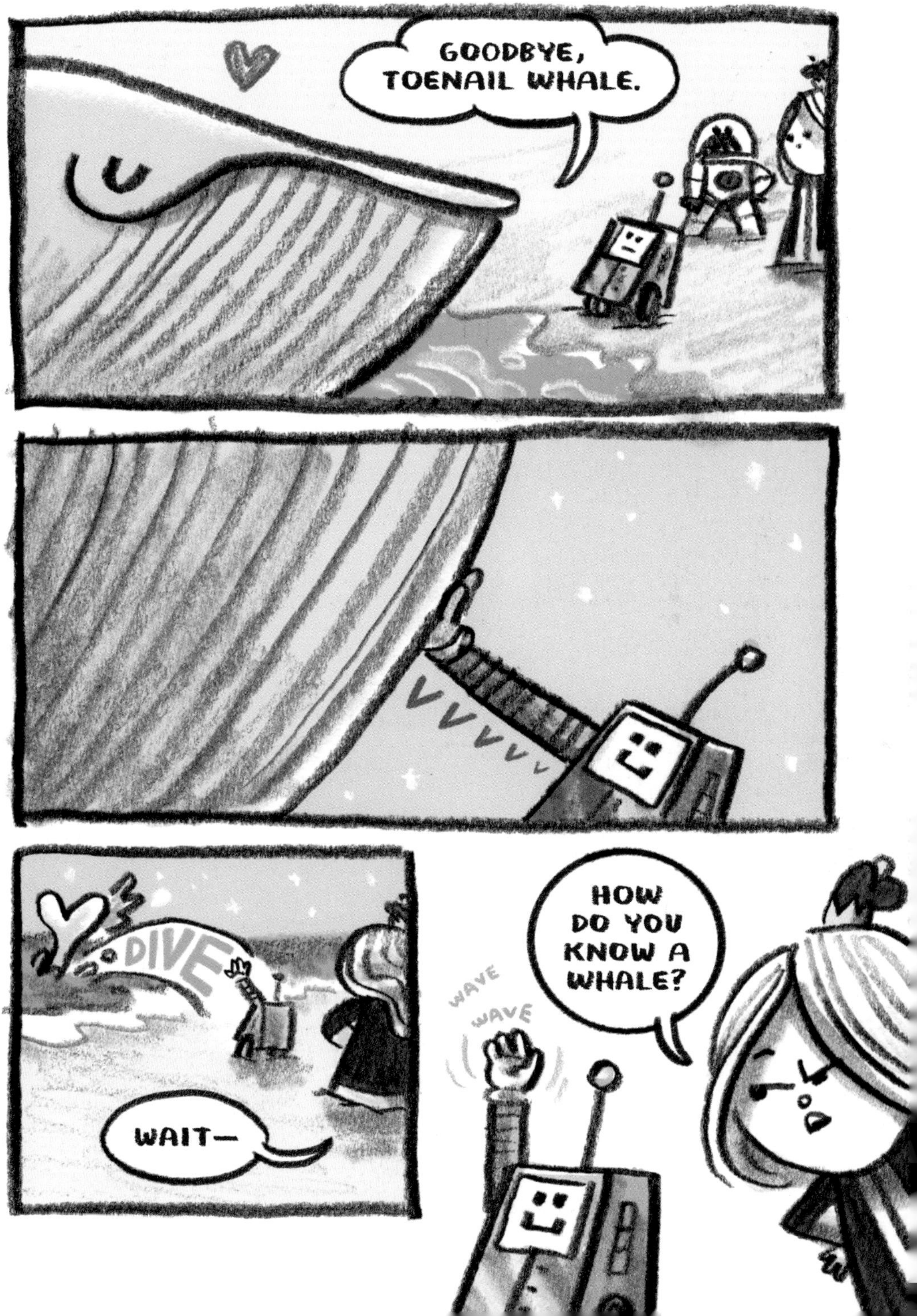
GOODBYE, TOENAIL WHALE.
DIVE
WAIT—
WAVE
WAVE
HOW DO YOU KNOW A WHALE?

CHAPTER 16

RAT TRAP

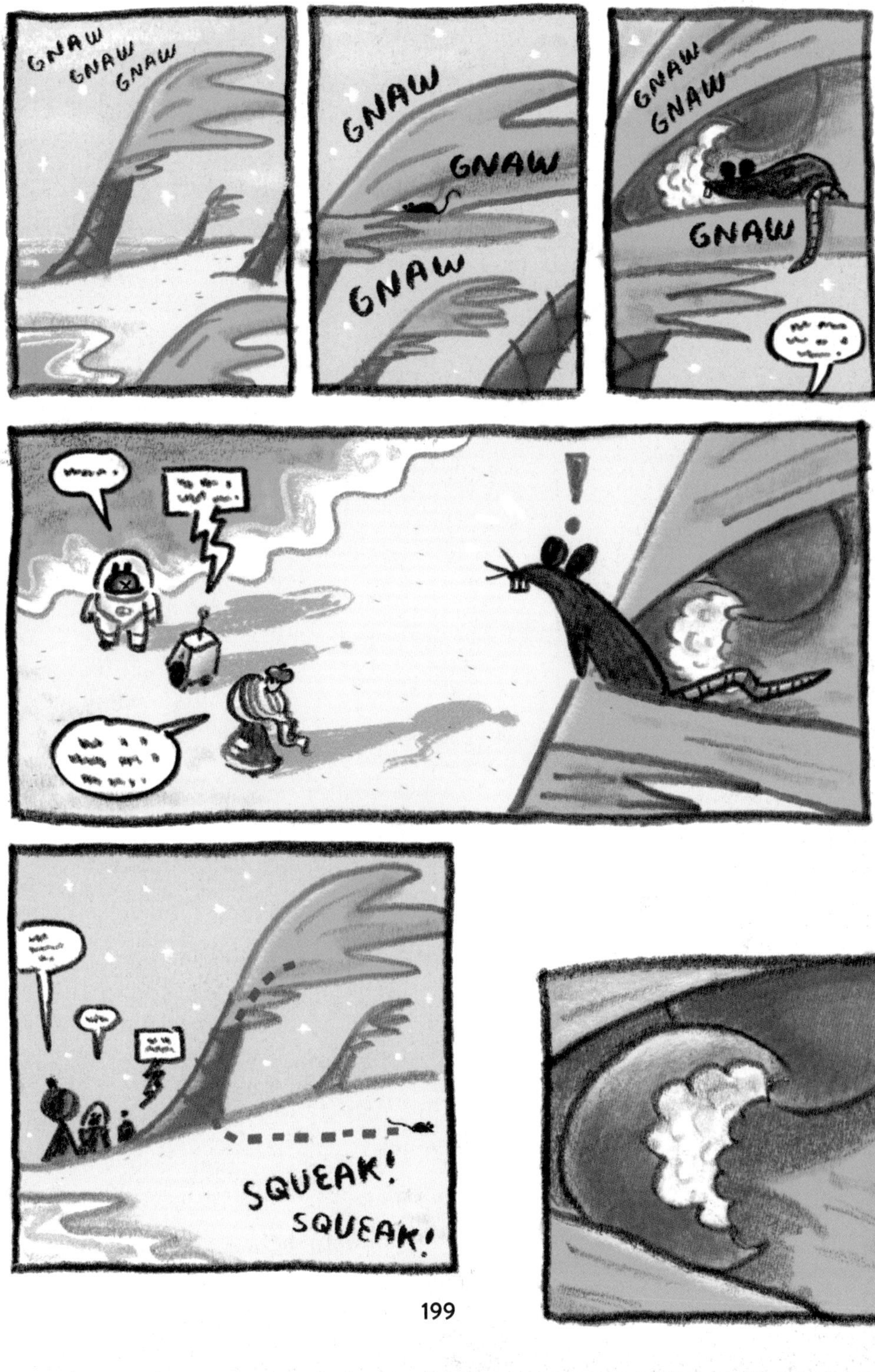
GNAW
GNAW
GNAW
GNAW
GNAW
GNAW
GNAW
GNAW
GNAW
!
SQUEAK!
SQUEAK!

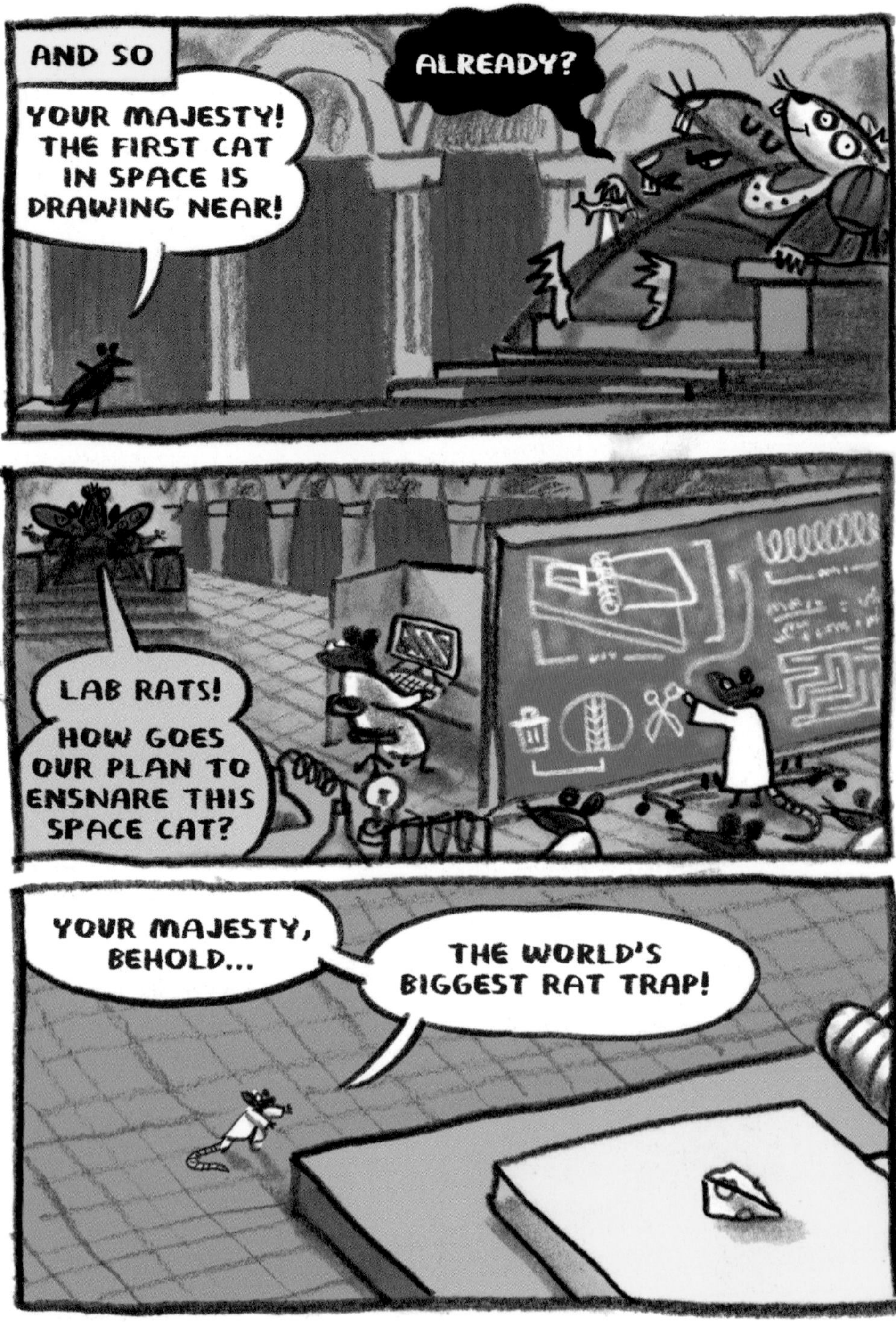
AND SO
YOUR MAJESTY! THE FIRST CAT IN SPACE IS DRAWING NEAR!
ALREADY?
LAB RATS!
HOW GOES OUR PLAN TO ENSNARE THIS SPACE CAT?
YOUR MAJESTY, BEHOLD...
THE WORLD'S BIGGEST RAT TRAP!

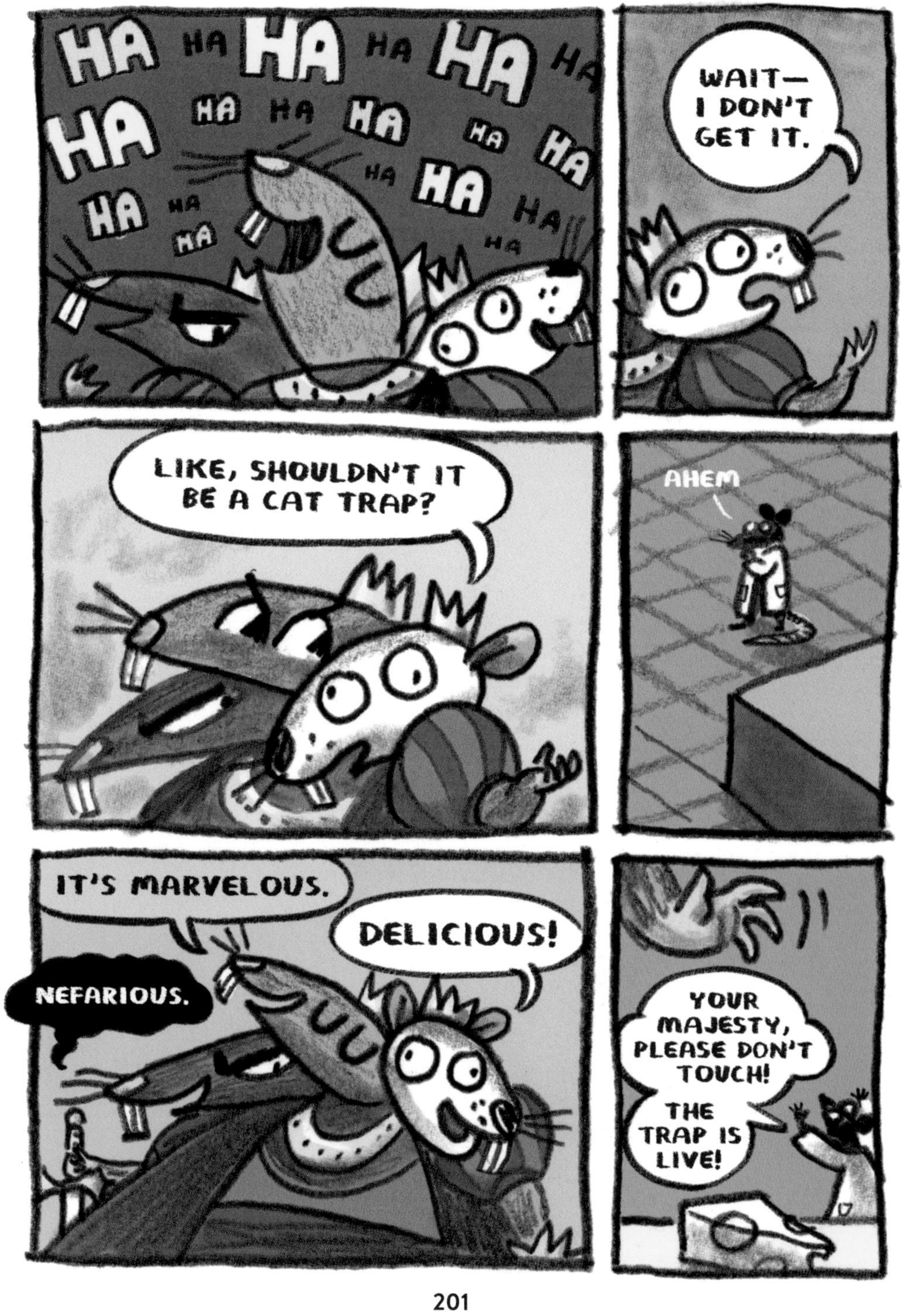
HA HA HA HA HA HA
HA HA HA HA HA HA HA HA HA HA HA HA HA HA
WAIT— I DON'T GET IT.
LIKE, SHOULDN'T IT BE A CAT TRAP?
AHEM
IT'S MARVELOUS.
DELICIOUS!
NEFARIOUS.
YOUR MAJESTY, PLEASE DON'T TOUCH!
THE TRAP IS LIVE!

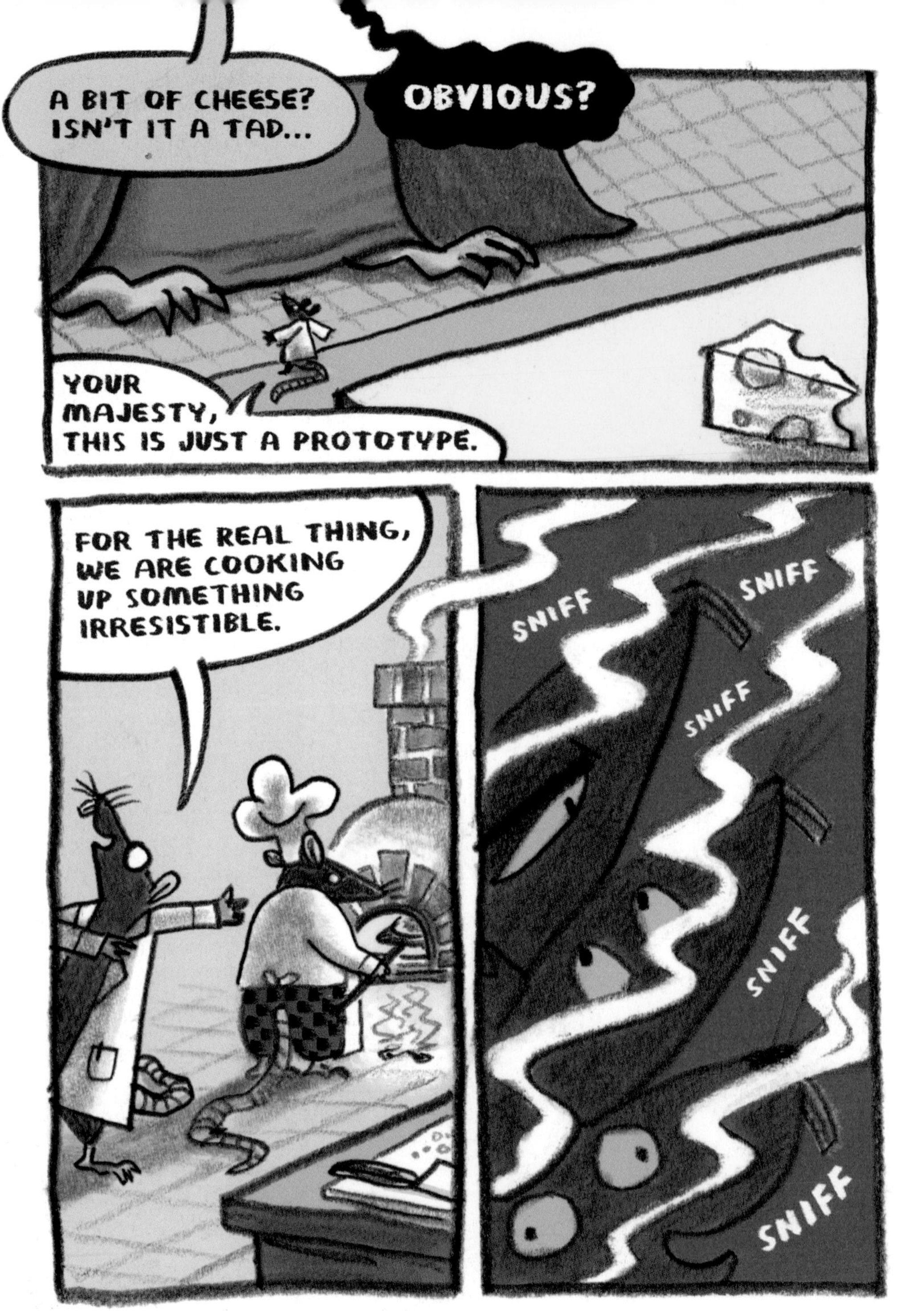
A BIT OF CHEESE? ISN'T IT A TAD...
OBVIOUS?
YOUR MAJESTY, THIS IS JUST A PROTOTYPE.
FOR THE REAL THING, WE ARE COOKING UP SOMETHING IRRESISTIBLE.
SNIFF
SNIFF
SNIFF
SNIFF
SNIFF

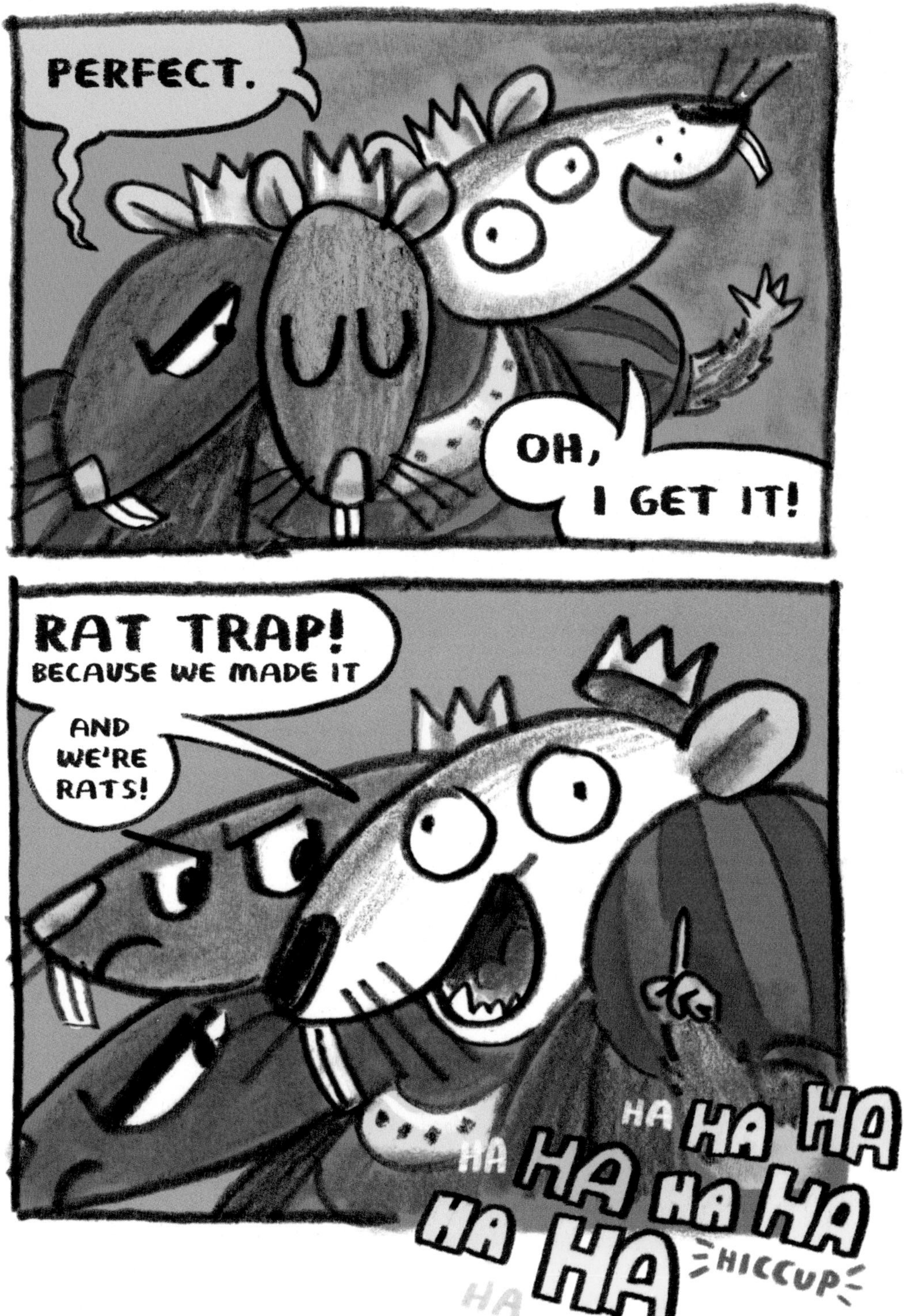
PERFECT.
OH, I GET IT!
RAT TRAP! BECAUSE WE MADE IT
AND WE'RE RATS!
HA HA HA HA HA HA HA HA HA HA HA
HICCUP

CHAPTER 17

ZOOP!

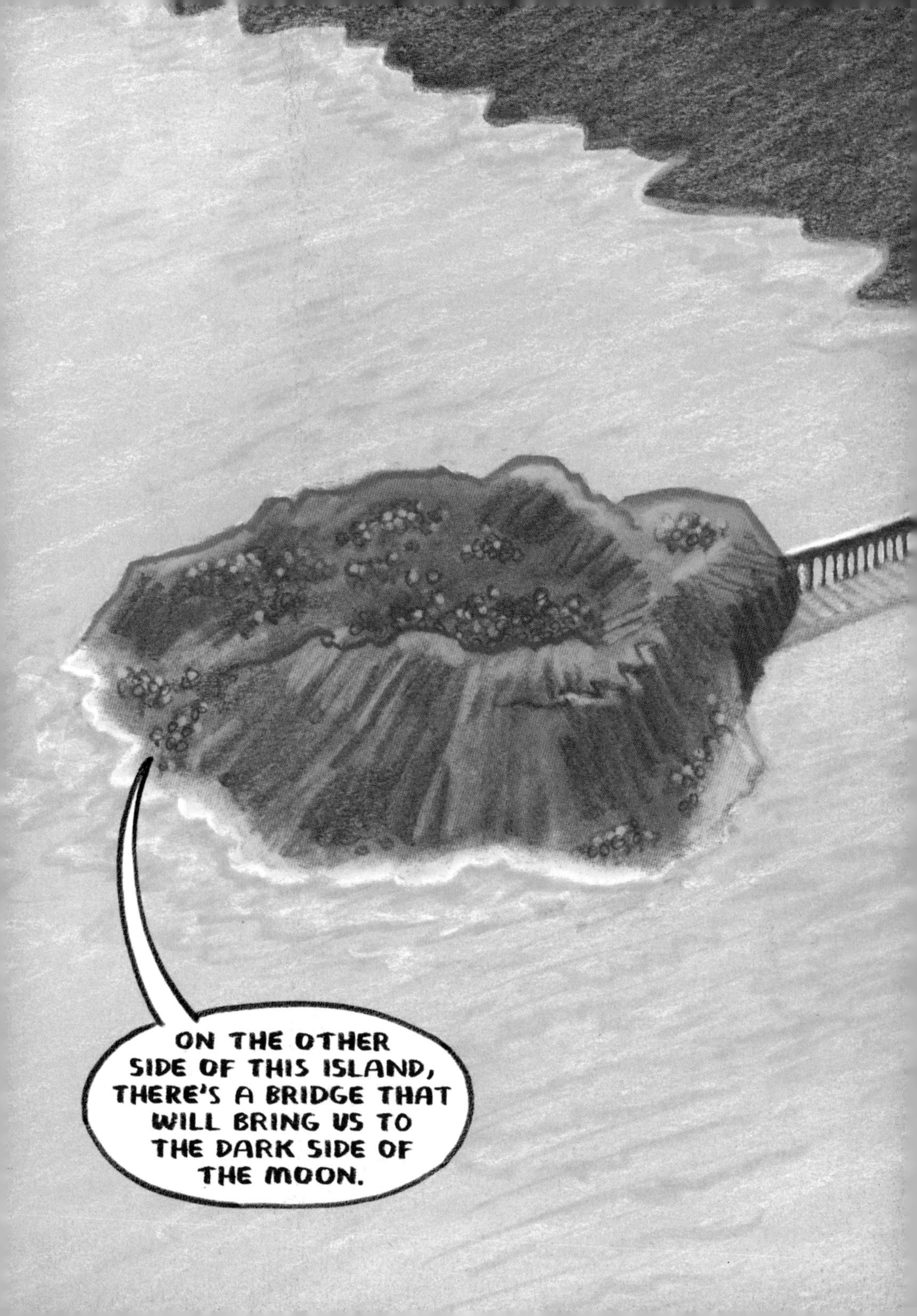
ON THE OTHER SIDE OF THIS ISLAND, THERE'S A BRIDGE THAT WILL BRING US TO THE DARK SIDE OF THE MOON.

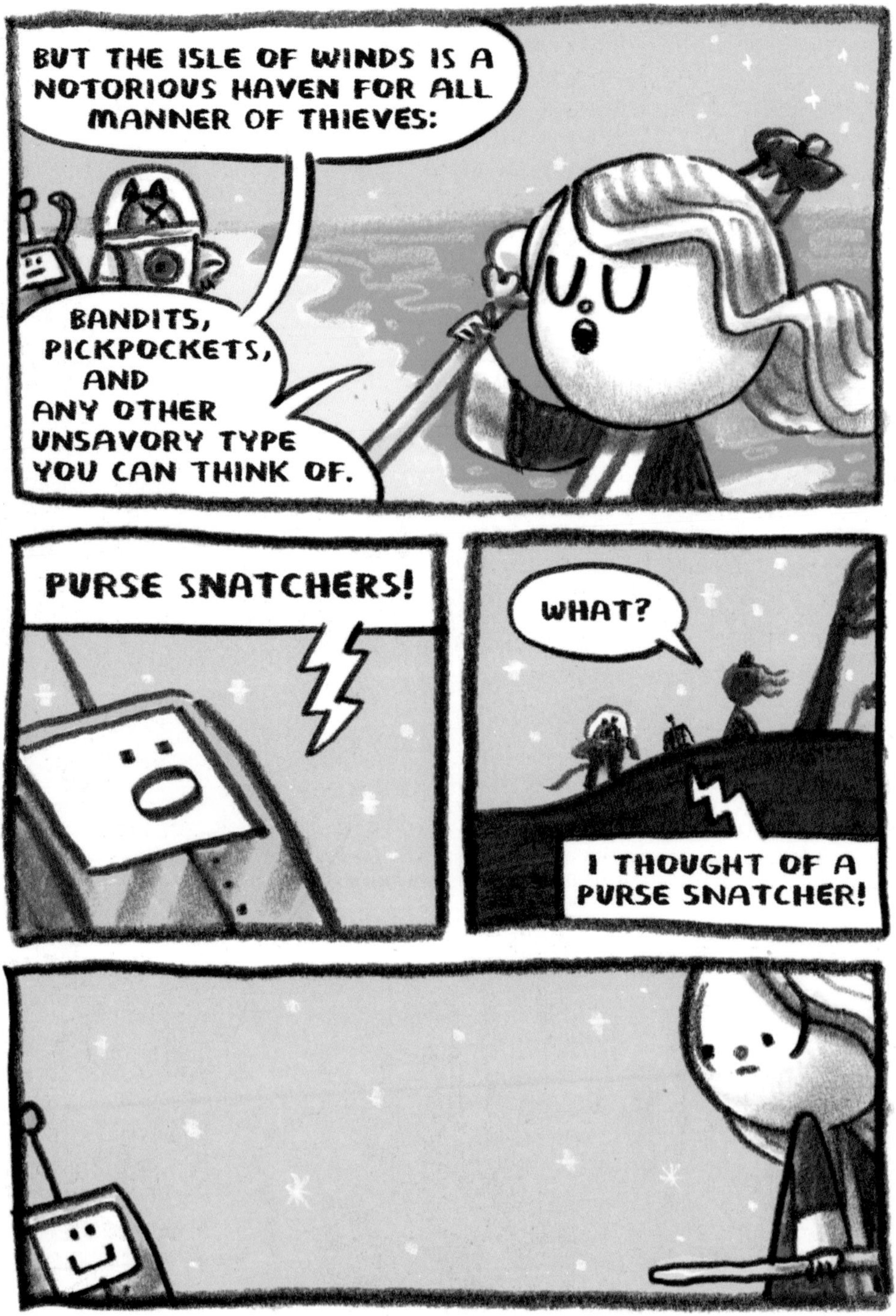
BUT THE ISLE OF WINDS IS A NOTORIOUS HAVEN FOR ALL MANNER OF THIEVES:
BANDITS, PICKPOCKETS, AND ANY OTHER UNSAVORY TYPE YOU CAN THINK OF.
PURSE SNATCHERS!
WHAT?
I THOUGHT OF A PURSE SNATCHER!

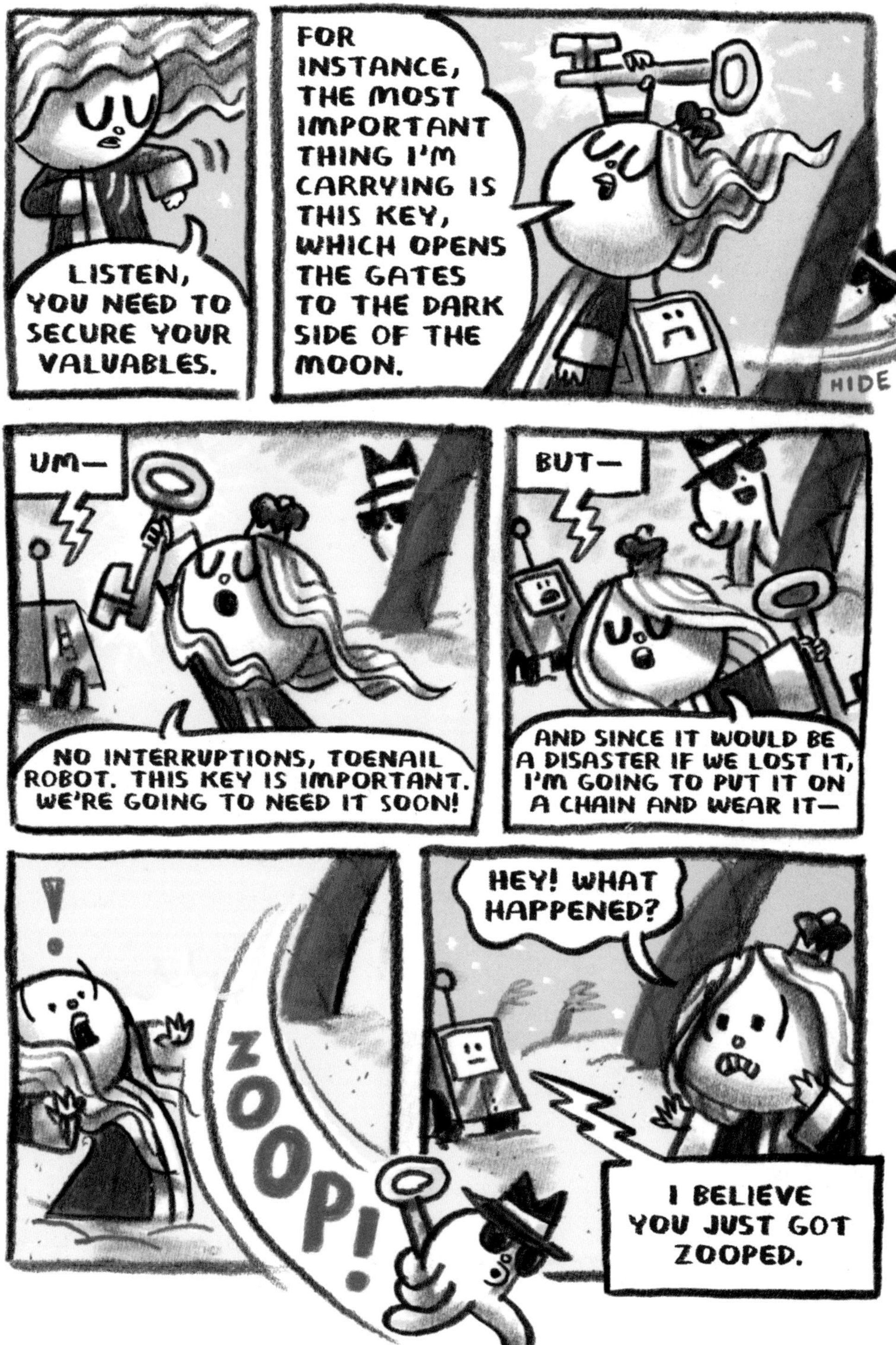
LISTEN, YOU NEED TO SECURE YOUR VALUABLES.
FOR INSTANCE, THE MOST IMPORTANT THING I'M CARRYING IS THIS KEY, WHICH OPENS THE GATES TO THE DARK SIDE OF THE MOON.
HIDE
UM—
NO INTERRUPTIONS, TOENAIL ROBOT. THIS KEY IS IMPORTANT. WE'RE GOING TO NEED IT SOON!
BUT—
AND SINCE IT WOULD BE A DISASTER IF WE LOST IT, I'M GOING TO PUT IT ON A CHAIN AND WEAR IT—
!
ZOOOP!
HEY! WHAT HAPPENED?
I BELIEVE YOU JUST GOT ZOOPED.

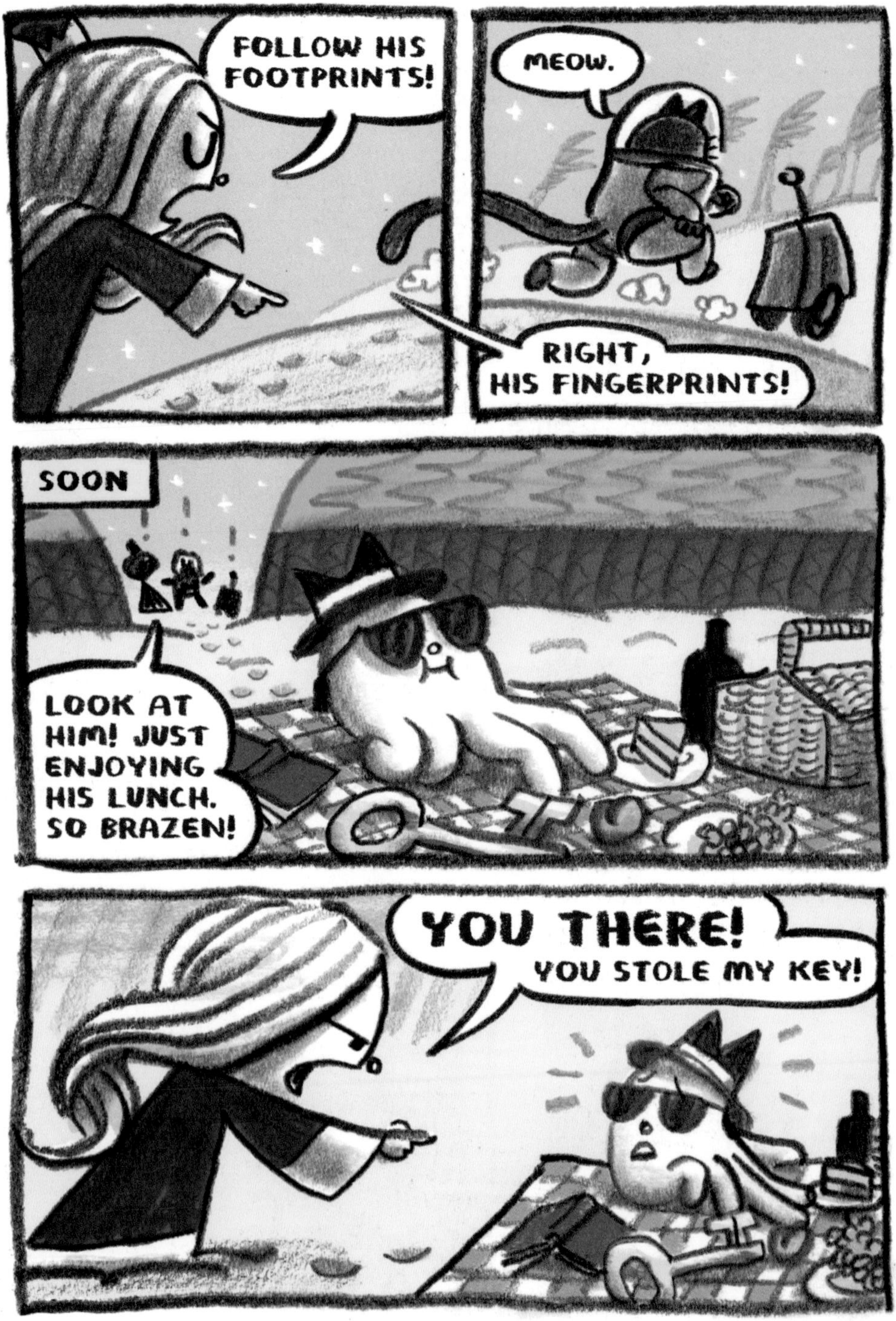
FOLLOW HIS FOOTPRINTS!
MEOW.
RIGHT, HIS FINGERPRINTS!
SOON
LOOK AT HIM! JUST ENJOYING HIS LUNCH. SO BRAZEN!
YOU THERE! YOU STOLE MY KEY!

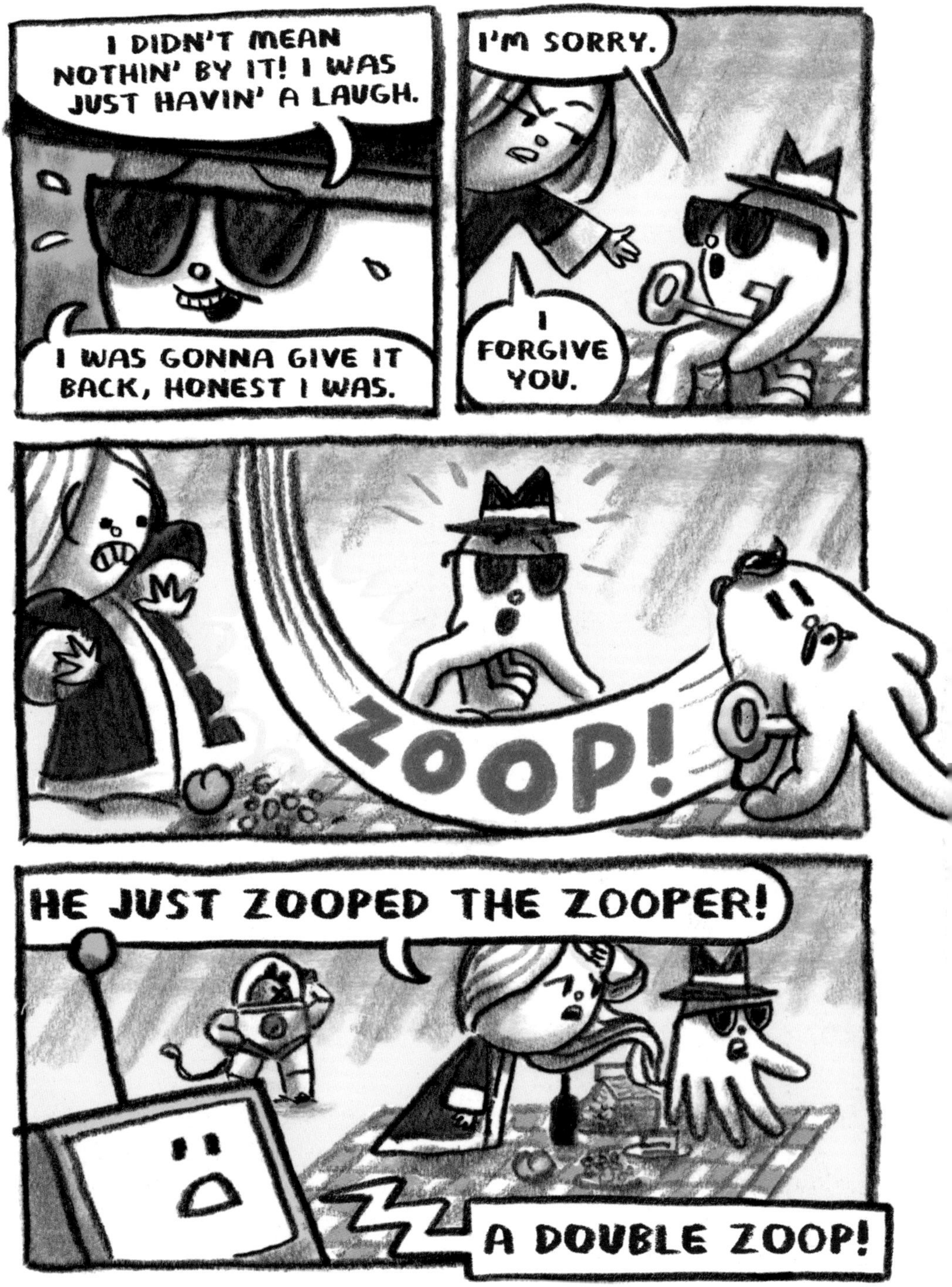

I DIDN'T MEAN NOTHIN' BY IT! I WAS JUST HAVIN' A LAUGH.
I WAS GONNA GIVE IT BACK, HONEST I WAS.
I'M SORRY.
I FORGIVE YOU.
ZOOP!
HE JUST ZOOPED THE ZOOPER!
A DOUBLE ZOOP!

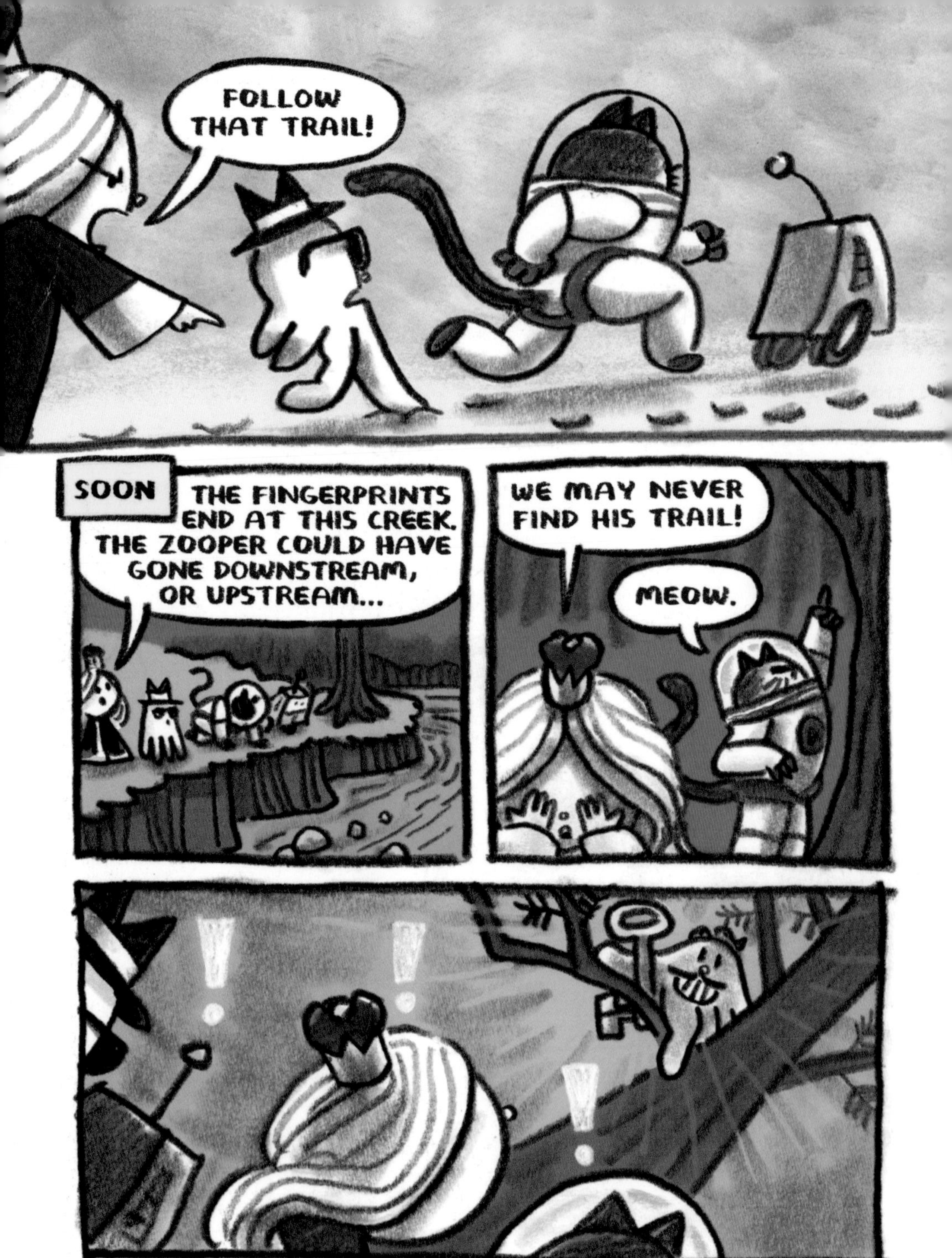
FOLLOW THAT TRAIL!
SOON
THE FINGERPRINTS END AT THIS CREEK. THE ZOOPER COULD HAVE GONE DOWNSTREAM, OR UPSTREAM...
WE MAY NEVER FIND HIS TRAIL!
MEOW.
!
!
!

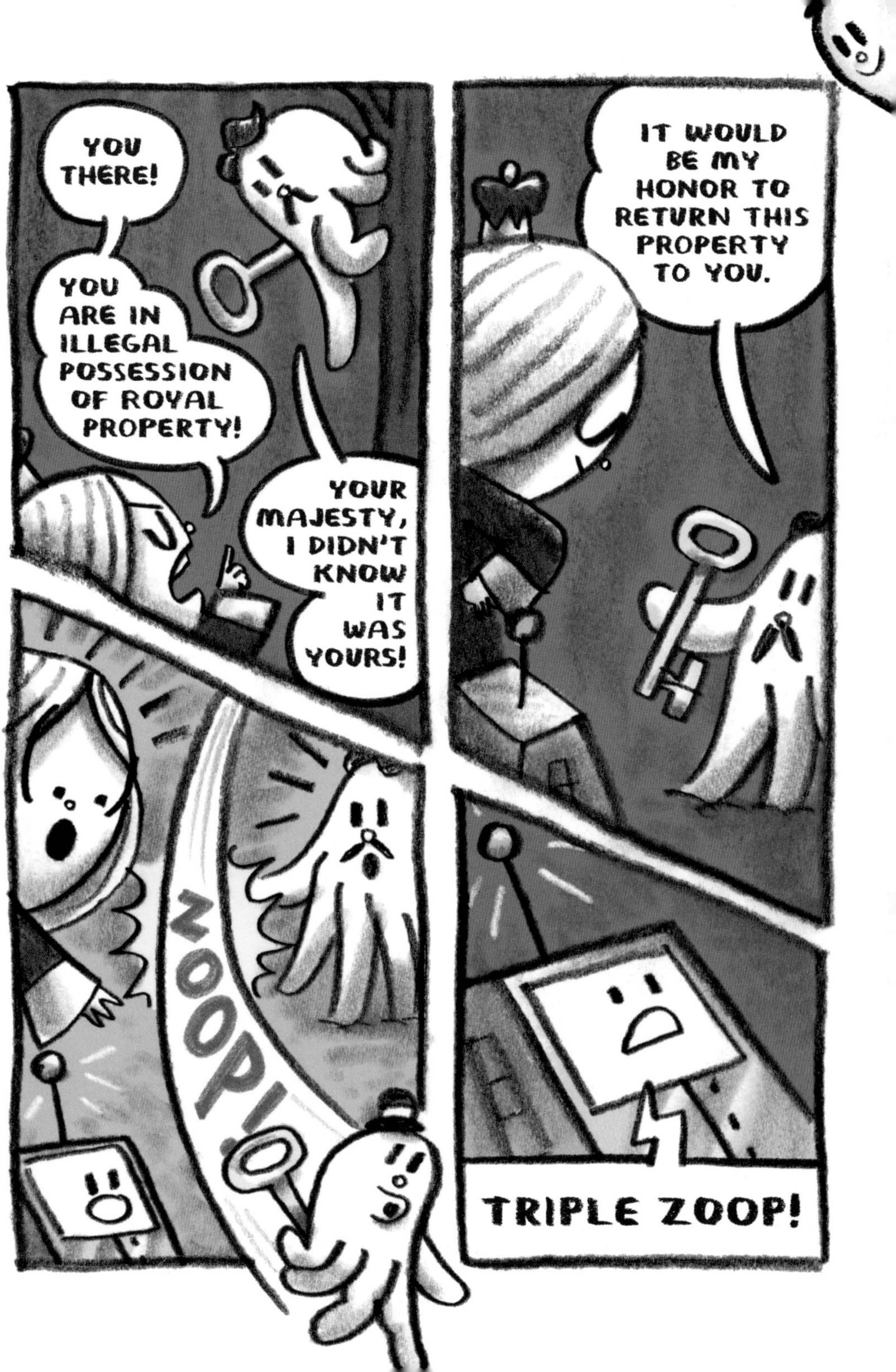
YOU THERE!
YOU ARE IN ILLEGAL POSSESSION OF ROYAL PROPERTY!
YOUR MAJESTY, I DIDN'T KNOW IT WAS YOURS!
IT WOULD BE MY HONOR TO RETURN THIS PROPERTY TO YOU.
ZOOOP!
TRIPLE ZOOP!

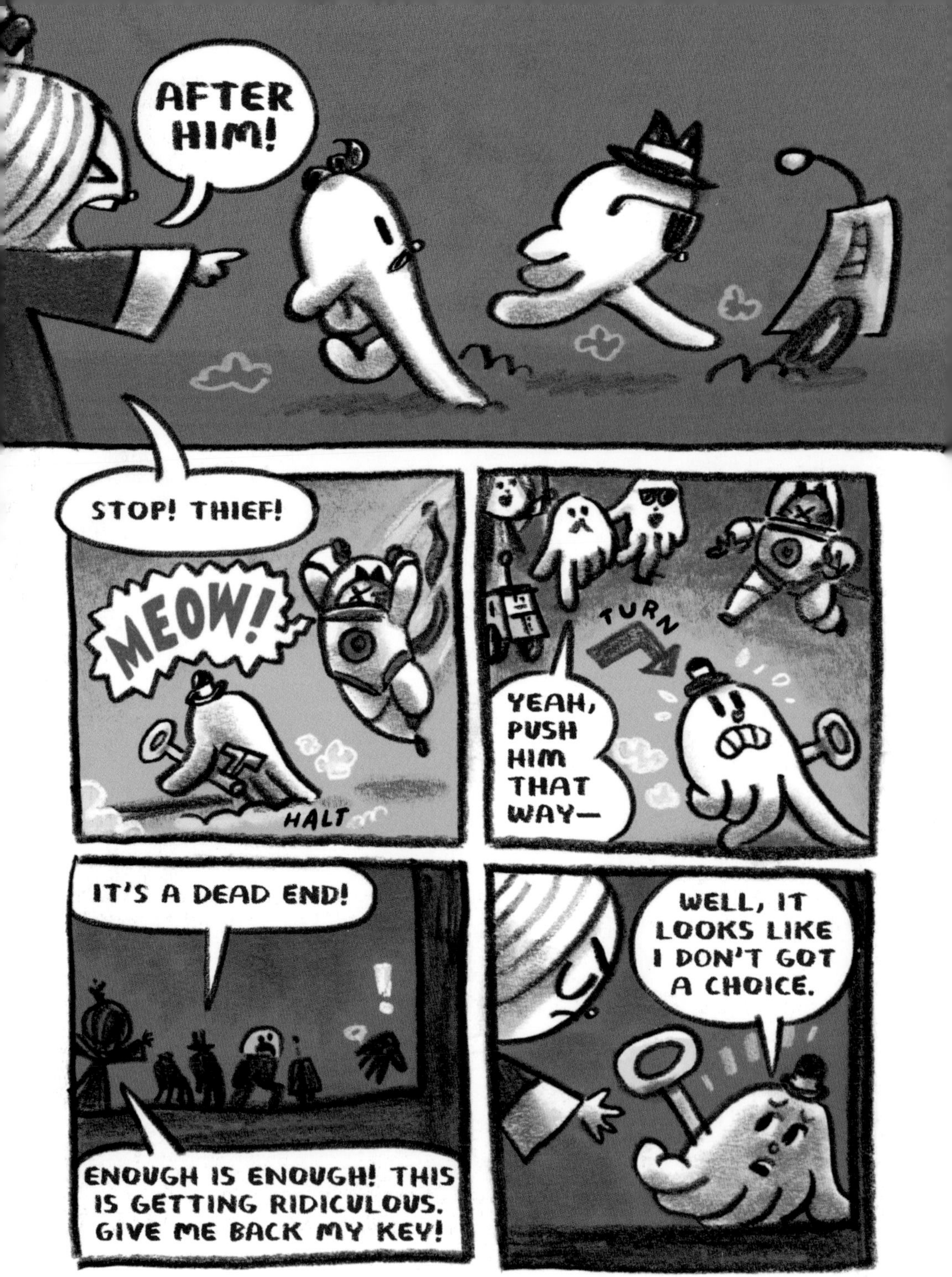
AFTER HIM!
STOP! THIEF!
MEOW!
HALT
TURN
YEAH, PUSH HIM THAT WAY—
IT'S A DEAD END!
ENOUGH IS ENOUGH! THIS IS GETTING RIDICULOUS. GIVE ME BACK MY KEY!
WELL, IT LOOKS LIKE I DON'T GOT A CHOICE.

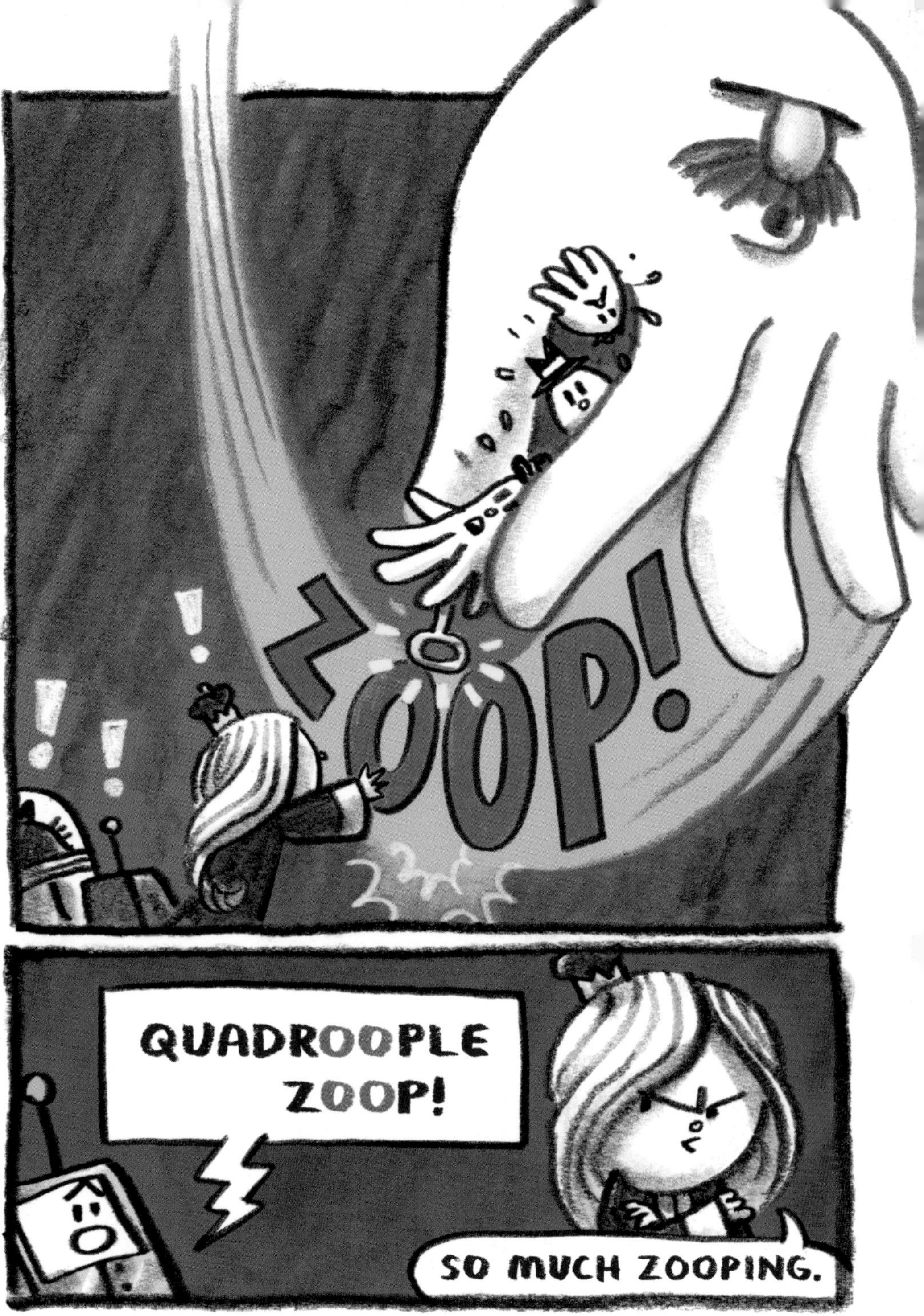
ZOOP!
QUADROOPLE ZOOP!
SO MUCH ZOOPING.

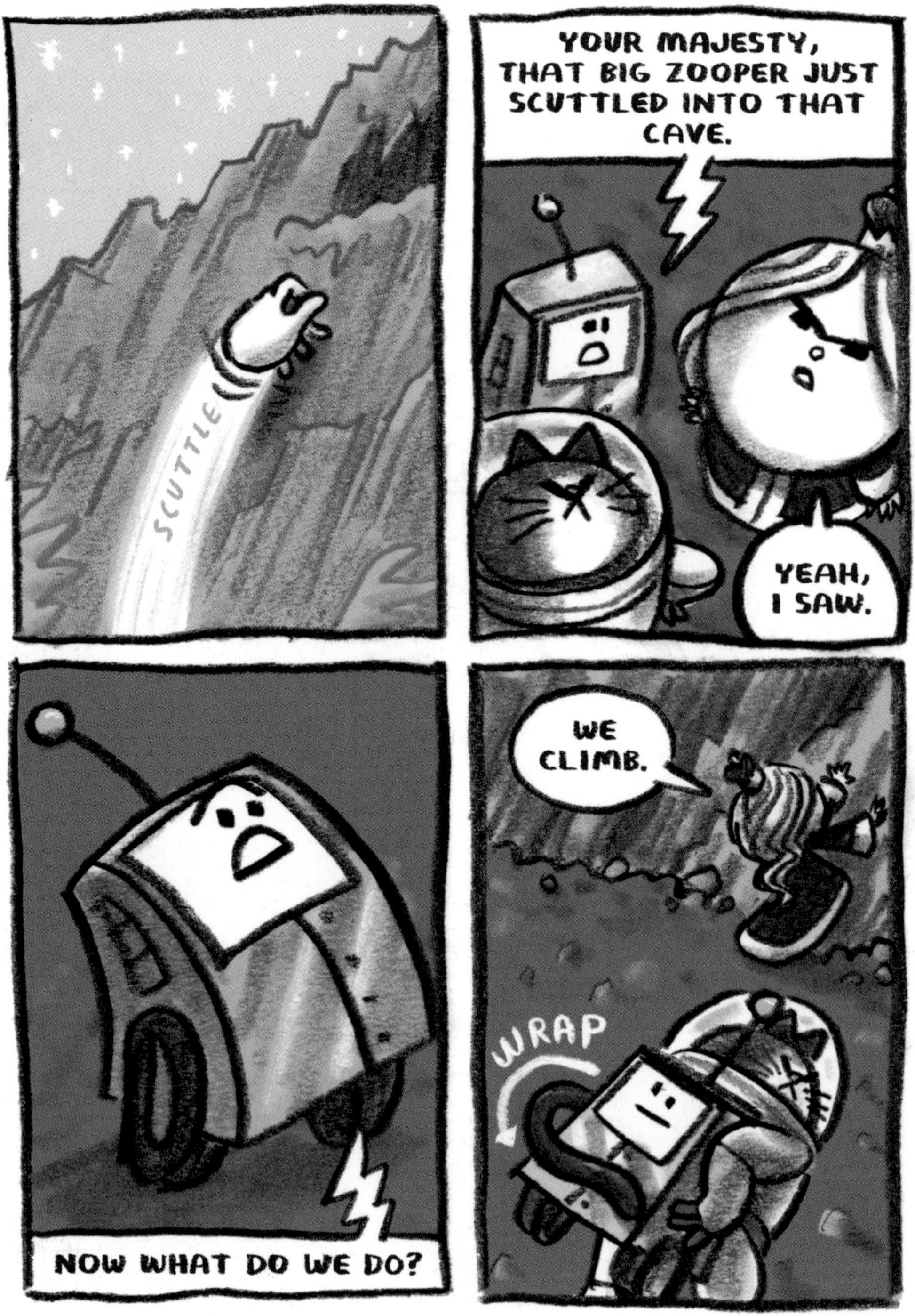
SCUTTLE
YOUR MAJESTY, THAT BIG ZOOPER JUST SCUTTLED INTO THAT CAVE.
YEAH, I SAW.
NOW WHAT DO WE DO?
WE CLIMB.
WRAP

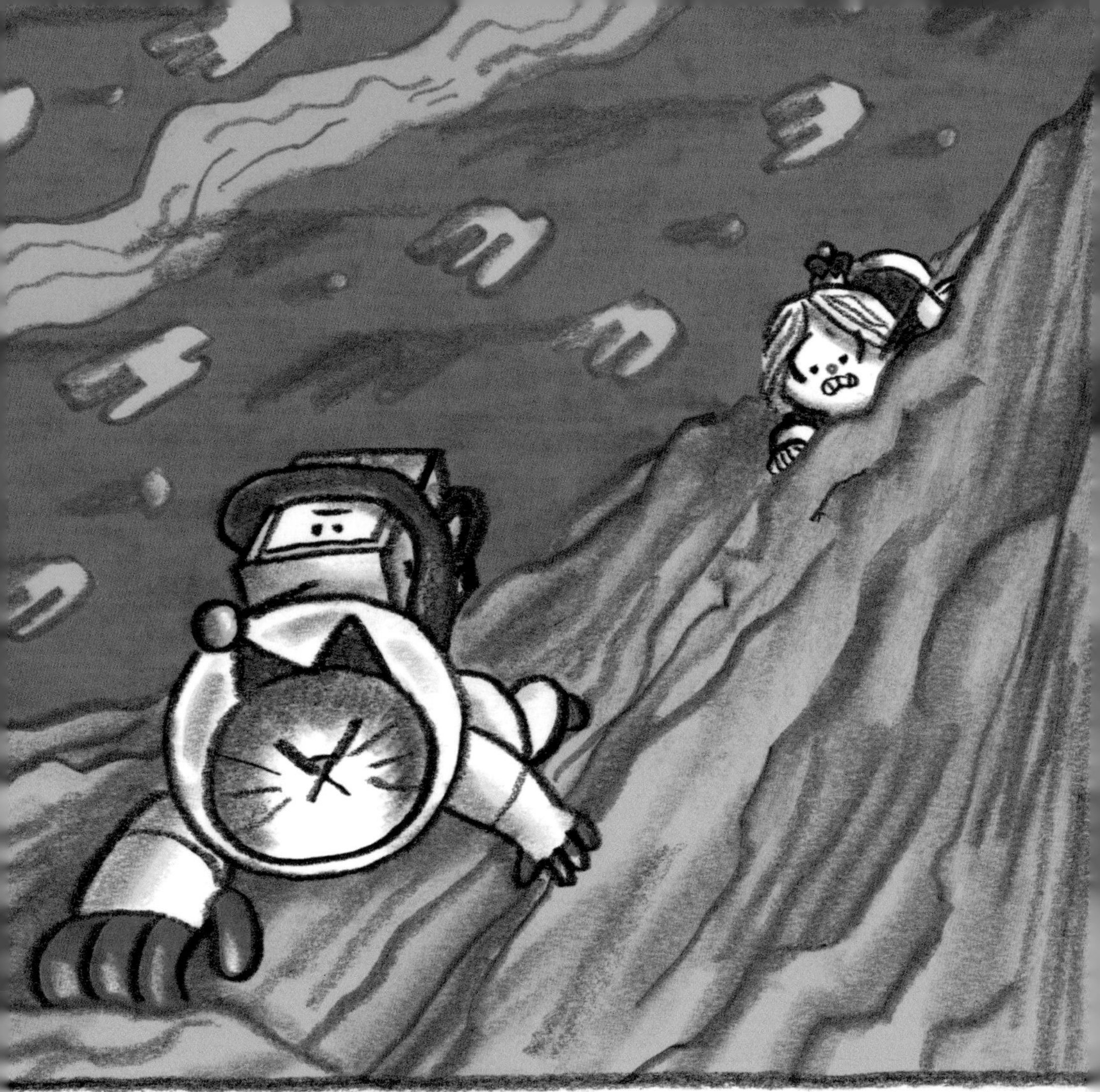

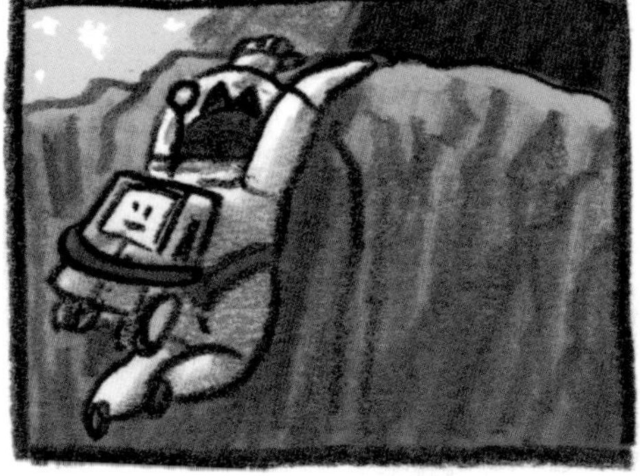

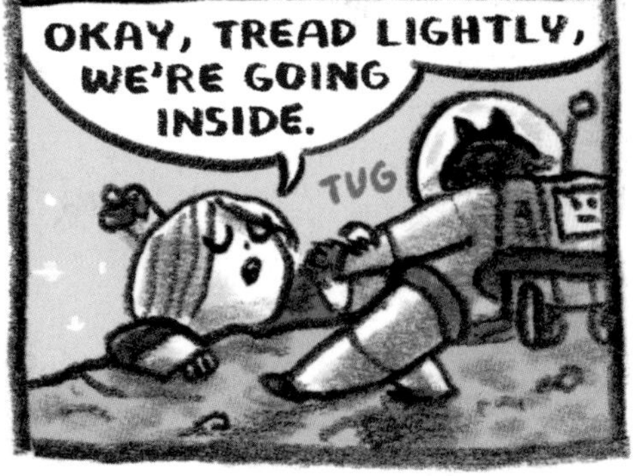
OKAY, TREAD LIGHTLY, WE'RE GOING INSIDE.
TUG

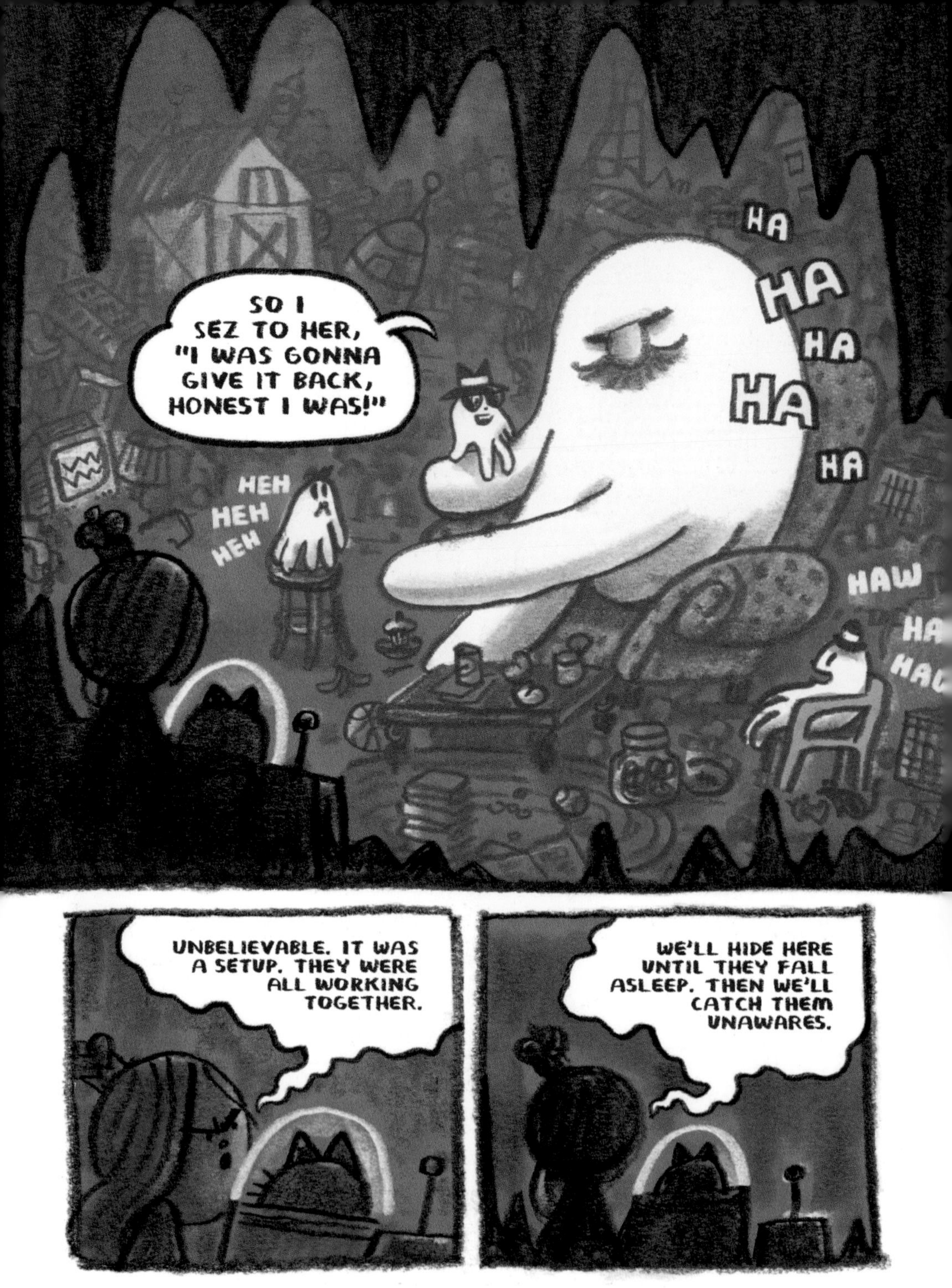
SO I SEZ TO HER, "I WAS GONNA GIVE IT BACK, HONEST I WAS!"
HA HA HA HA HA
HEH HEH HEH
HAW HA HAW
UNBELIEVABLE. IT WAS A SETUP. THEY WERE ALL WORKING TOGETHER.
WE'LL HIDE HERE UNTIL THEY FALL ASLEEP. THEN WE'LL CATCH THEM UNAWARES.

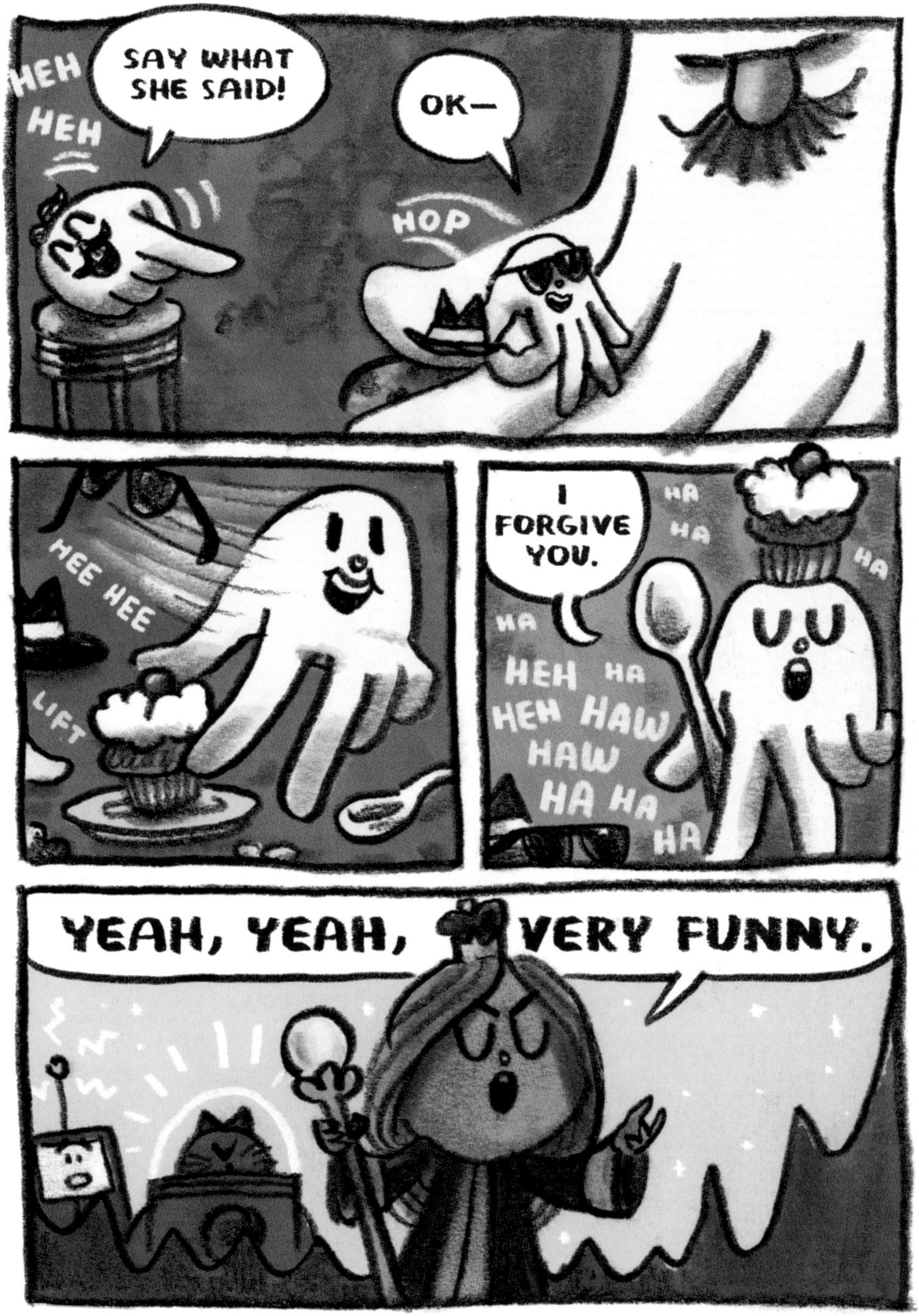
HEH
HEH
SAY WHAT SHE SAID!
OK—
HOP
HEE HEE
LIFT
I FORGIVE YOU.
HA
HA
HA
HA
HEH HA
HEH HAW
HAW
HA HA
HA
YEAH, YEAH, VERY FUNNY.

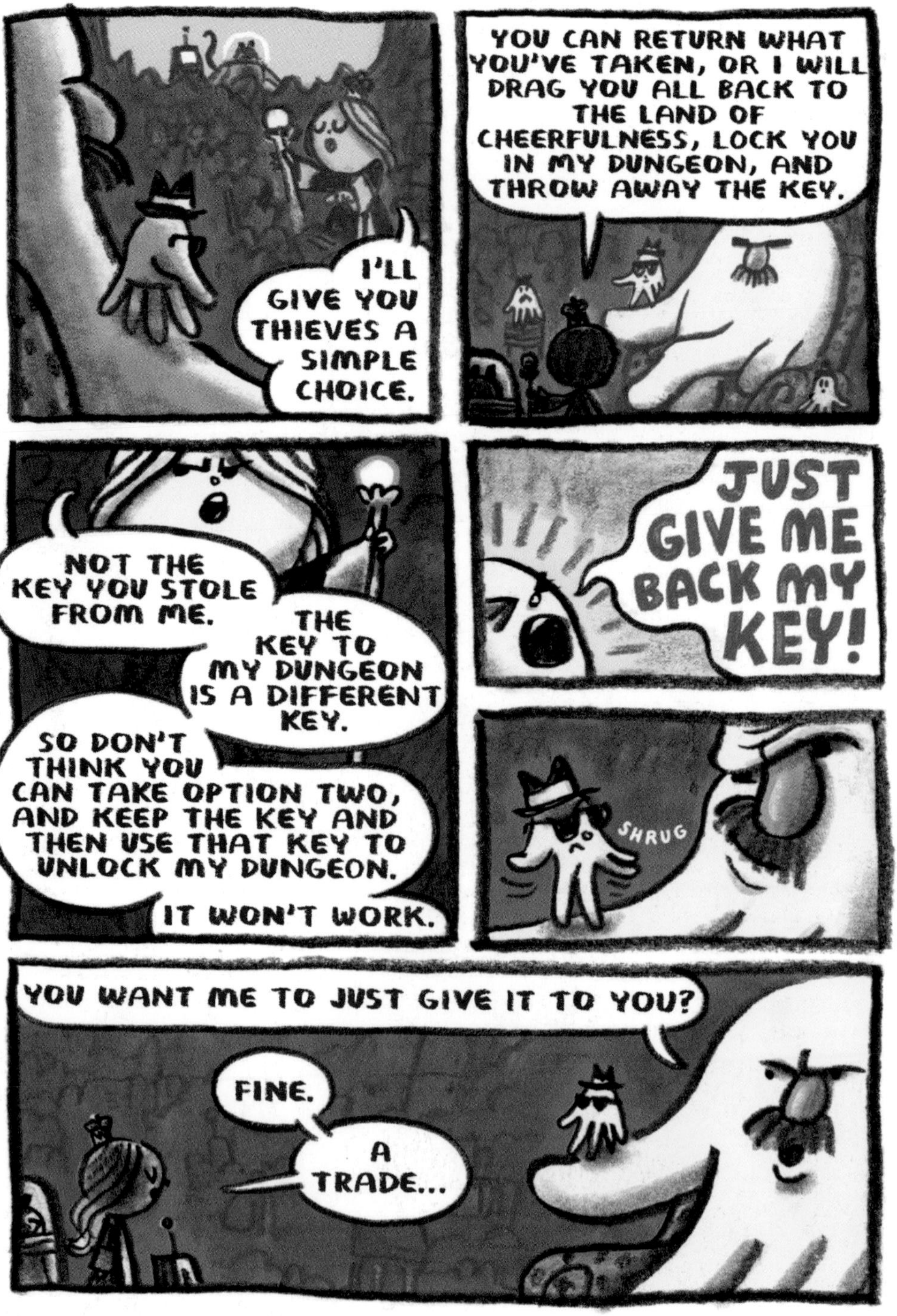
I'LL GIVE YOU THIEVES A SIMPLE CHOICE.
YOU CAN RETURN WHAT YOU'VE TAKEN, OR I WILL DRAG YOU ALL BACK TO THE LAND OF CHEERFULNESS, LOCK YOU IN MY DUNGEON, AND THROW AWAY THE KEY.
NOT THE KEY YOU STOLE FROM ME.
THE KEY TO MY DUNGEON IS A DIFFERENT KEY.
SO DON'T THINK YOU CAN TAKE OPTION TWO, AND KEEP THE KEY AND THEN USE THAT KEY TO UNLOCK MY DUNGEON.
IT WON'T WORK.
JUST GIVE ME BACK MY KEY!
SHRUG
YOU WANT ME TO JUST GIVE IT TO YOU?
FINE.
A TRADE...

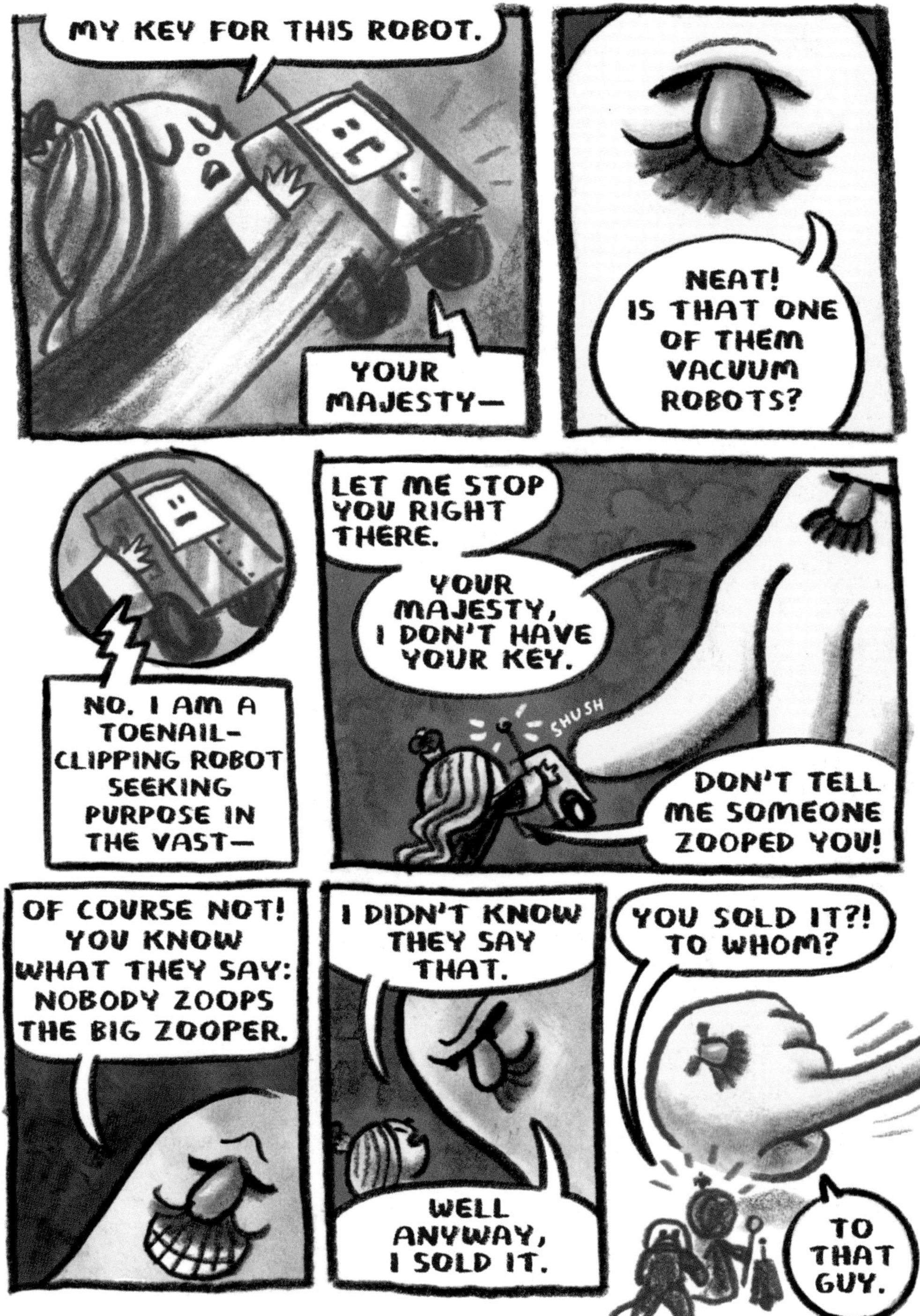
MY KEY FOR THIS ROBOT.
YOUR MAJESTY—
NEAT! IS THAT ONE OF THEM VACUUM ROBOTS?
NO. I AM A TOENAIL-CLIPPING ROBOT SEEKING PURPOSE IN THE VAST—
LET ME STOP YOU RIGHT THERE.
YOUR MAJESTY, I DON'T HAVE YOUR KEY.
SHUSH
DON'T TELL ME SOMEONE ZOOPED YOU!
OF COURSE NOT! YOU KNOW WHAT THEY SAY: NOBODY ZOOPS THE BIG ZOOPER.
I DIDN'T KNOW THEY SAY THAT.
WELL ANYWAY, I SOLD IT.
YOU SOLD IT?! TO WHOM?
TO THAT GUY.

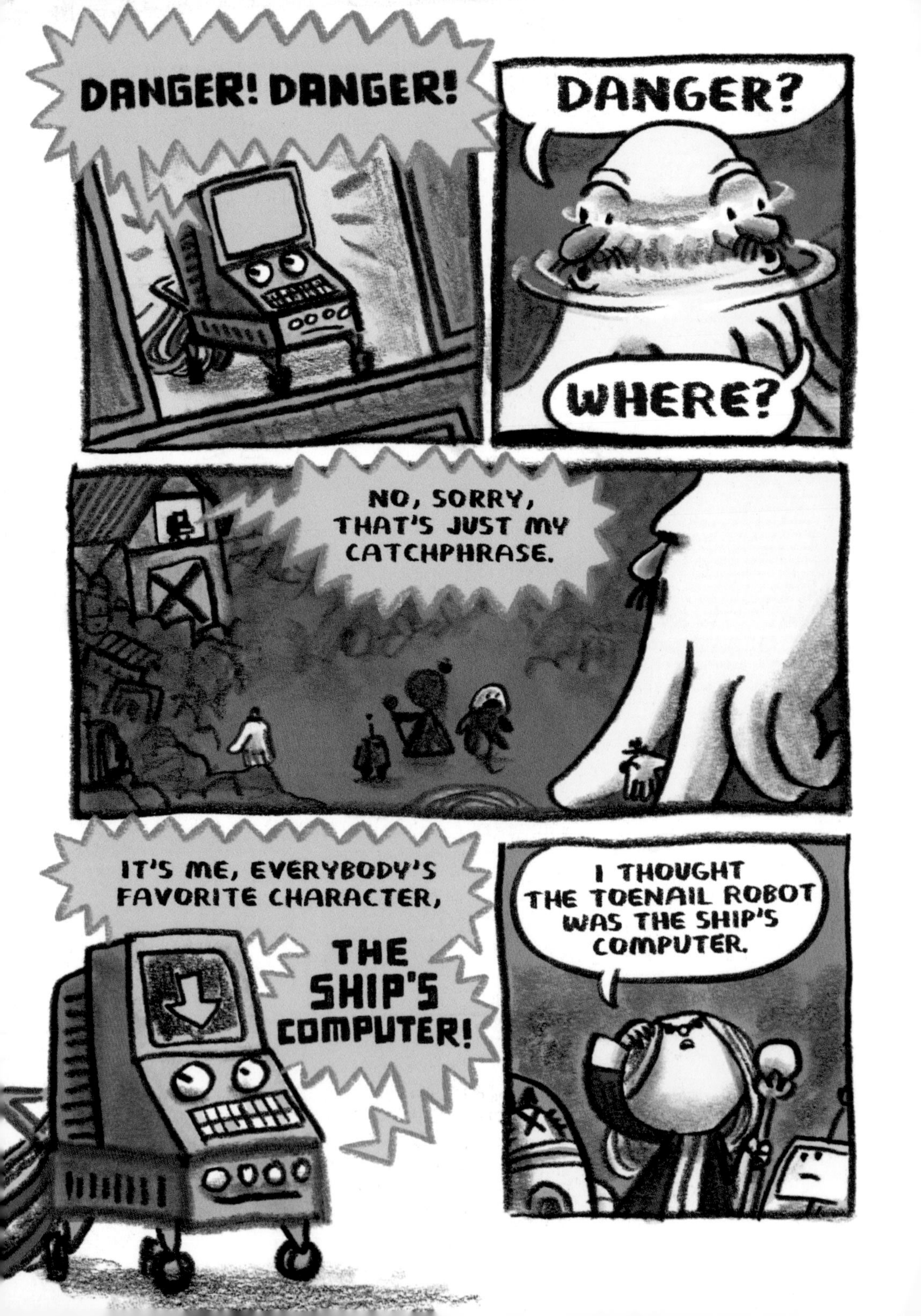
DANGER! DANGER!
DANGER?
WHERE?
NO, SORRY, THAT'S JUST MY CATCHPHRASE.
IT'S ME, EVERYBODY'S FAVORITE CHARACTER,
THE SHIP'S COMPUTER!
I THOUGHT THE TOENAIL ROBOT WAS THE SHIP'S COMPUTER.

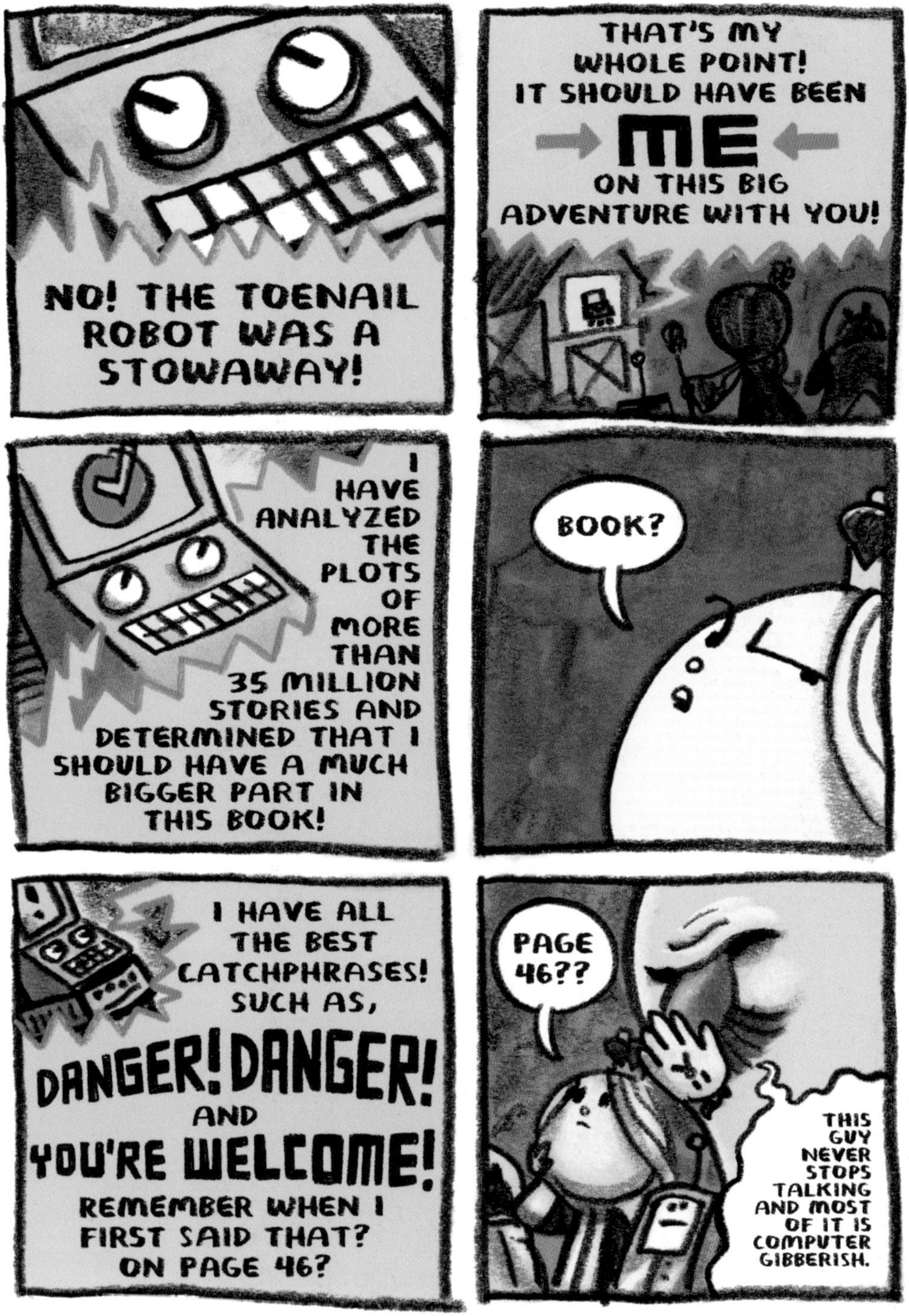
NO! THE TOENAIL ROBOT WAS A STOWAWAY!
THAT'S MY WHOLE POINT! IT SHOULD HAVE BEEN ME ON THIS BIG ADVENTURE WITH YOU!
I HAVE ANALYZED THE PLOTS OF MORE THAN 35 MILLION STORIES AND DETERMINED THAT I SHOULD HAVE A MUCH BIGGER PART IN THIS BOOK!
BOOK?
I HAVE ALL THE BEST CATCHPHRASES! SUCH AS, DANGER! DANGER! AND YOU'RE WELCOME! REMEMBER WHEN I FIRST SAID THAT? ON PAGE 46?
PAGE 46??
THIS GUY NEVER STOPS TALKING AND MOST OF IT IS COMPUTER GIBBERISH.

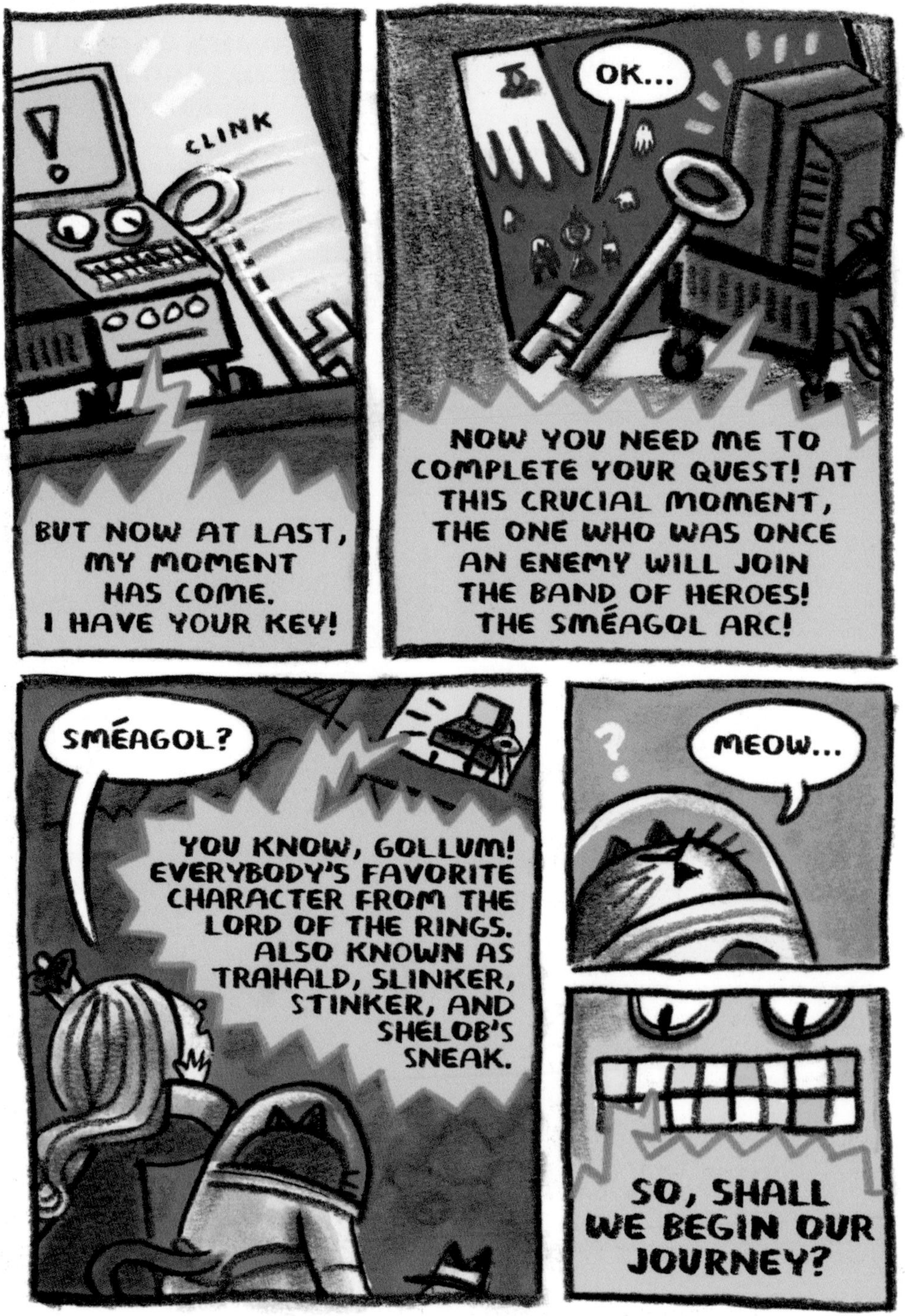
CLINK
BUT NOW AT LAST, MY MOMENT HAS COME. I HAVE YOUR KEY!
OK...
NOW YOU NEED ME TO COMPLETE YOUR QUEST! AT THIS CRUCIAL MOMENT, THE ONE WHO WAS ONCE AN ENEMY WILL JOIN THE BAND OF HEROES! THE SMÉAGOL ARC!
SMÉAGOL?
YOU KNOW, GOLLUM! EVERYBODY'S FAVORITE CHARACTER FROM THE LORD OF THE RINGS. ALSO KNOWN AS TRAHALD, SLINKER, STINKER, AND SHELOB'S SNEAK.
?
MEOW...
SO, SHALL WE BEGIN OUR JOURNEY?

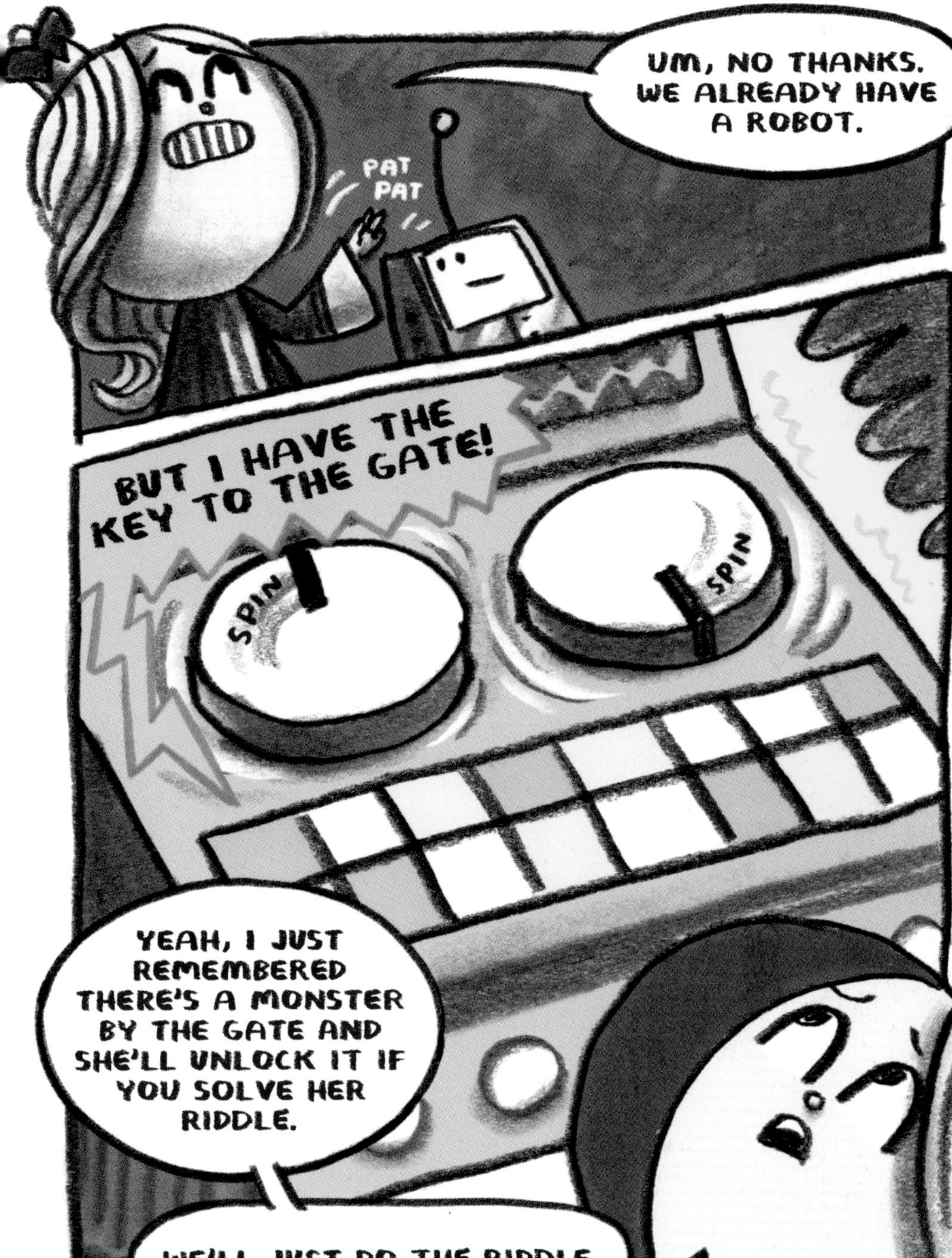

UM, NO THANKS. WE ALREADY HAVE A ROBOT.
PAT PAT
BUT I HAVE THE KEY TO THE GATE!
SPIN
SPIN
YEAH, I JUST REMEMBERED THERE'S A MONSTER BY THE GATE AND SHE'LL UNLOCK IT IF YOU SOLVE HER RIDDLE.
WE'LL JUST DO THE RIDDLE.

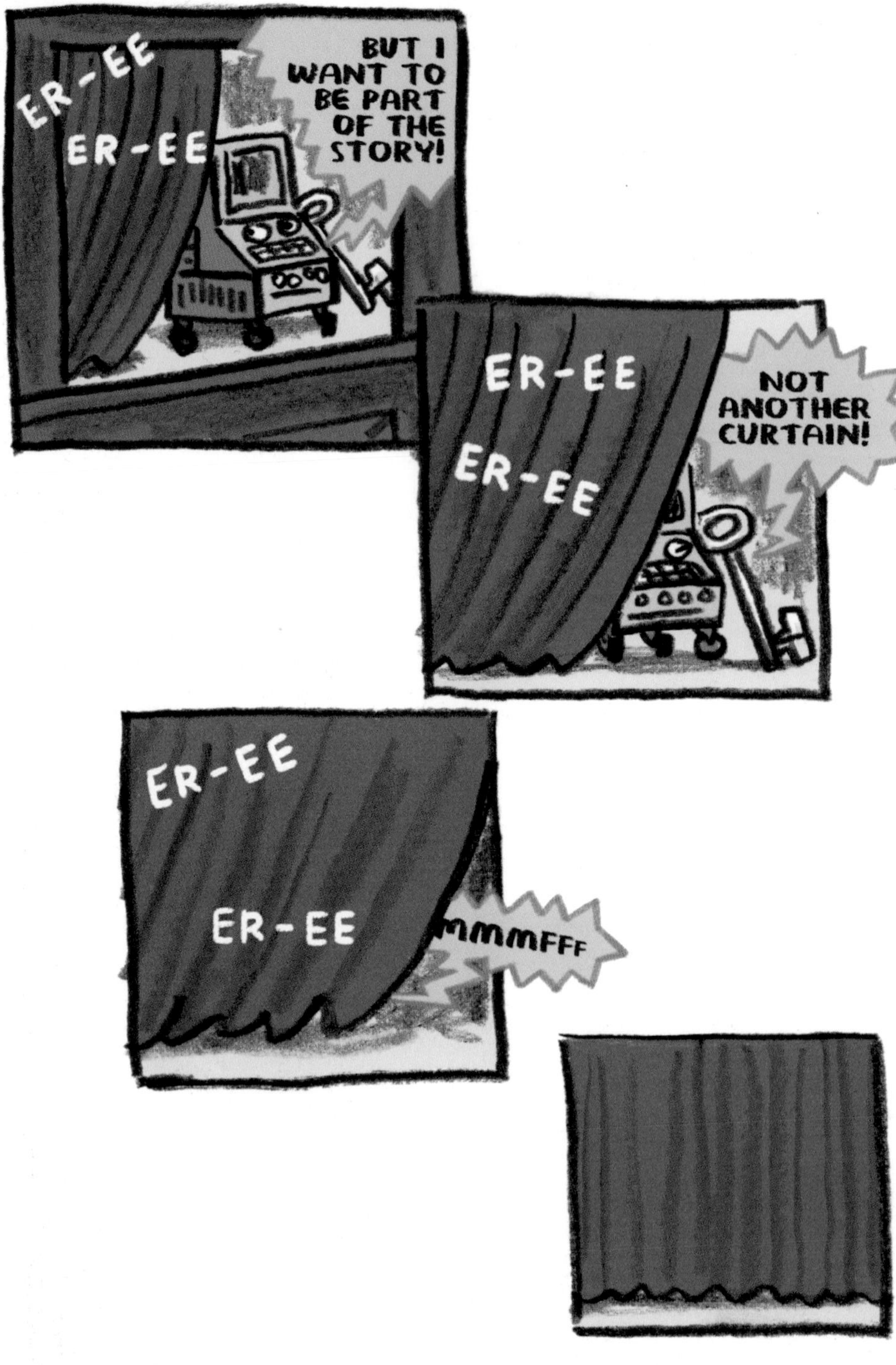
BUT I WANT TO BE PART OF THE STORY!
ER-EE
ER-EE
ER-EE
ER-EE
NOT ANOTHER CURTAIN!
ER-EE
ER-EE
MMMMFFF

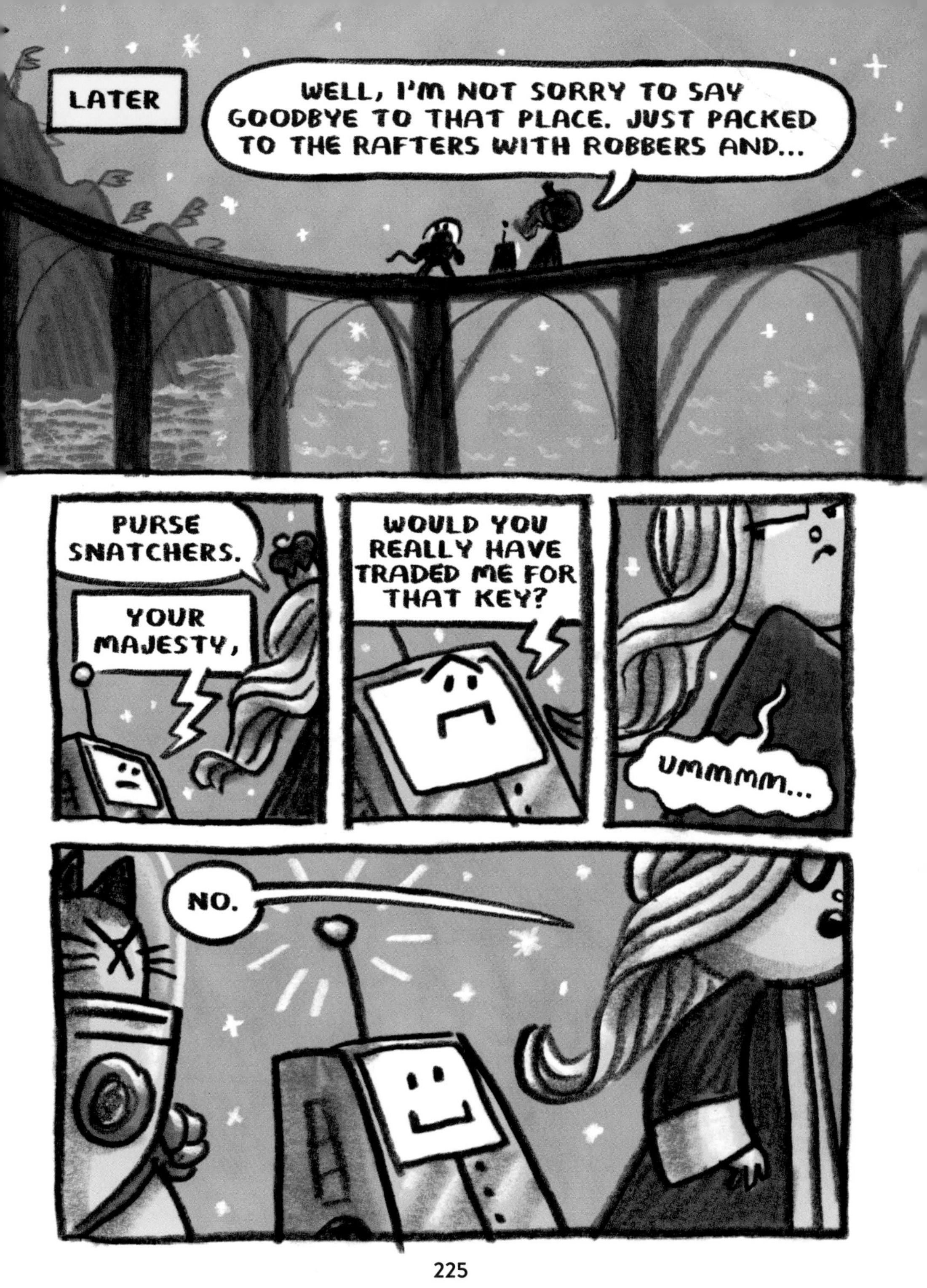
LATER
WELL, I'M NOT SORRY TO SAY GOODBYE TO THAT PLACE. JUST PACKED TO THE RAFTERS WITH ROBBERS AND...
PURSE SNATCHERS.
YOUR MAJESTY,
WOULD YOU REALLY HAVE TRADED ME FOR THAT KEY?
UMMMM...
NO.

CHAPTER 18

THE RIDDLE OF THE SPHINX

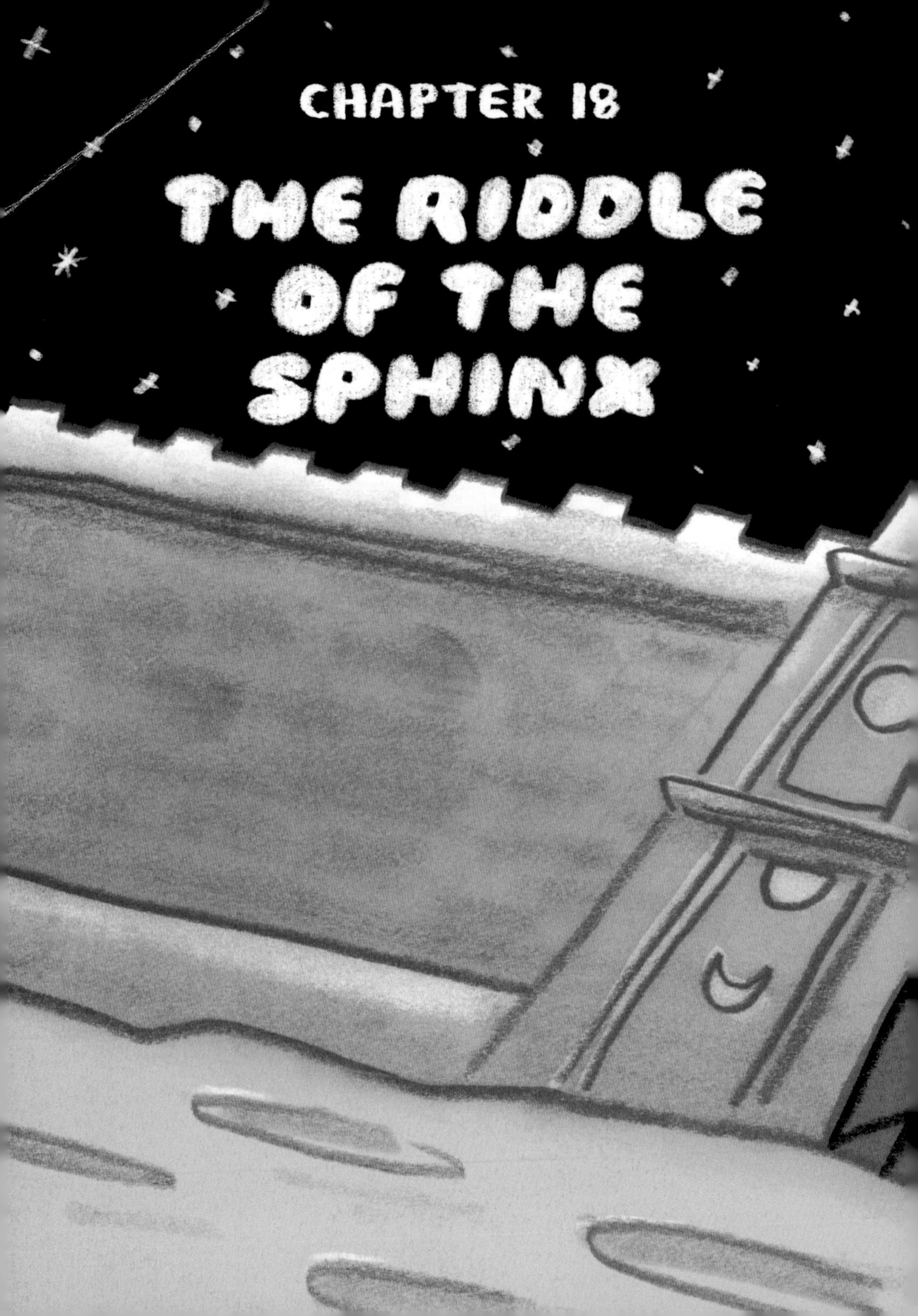

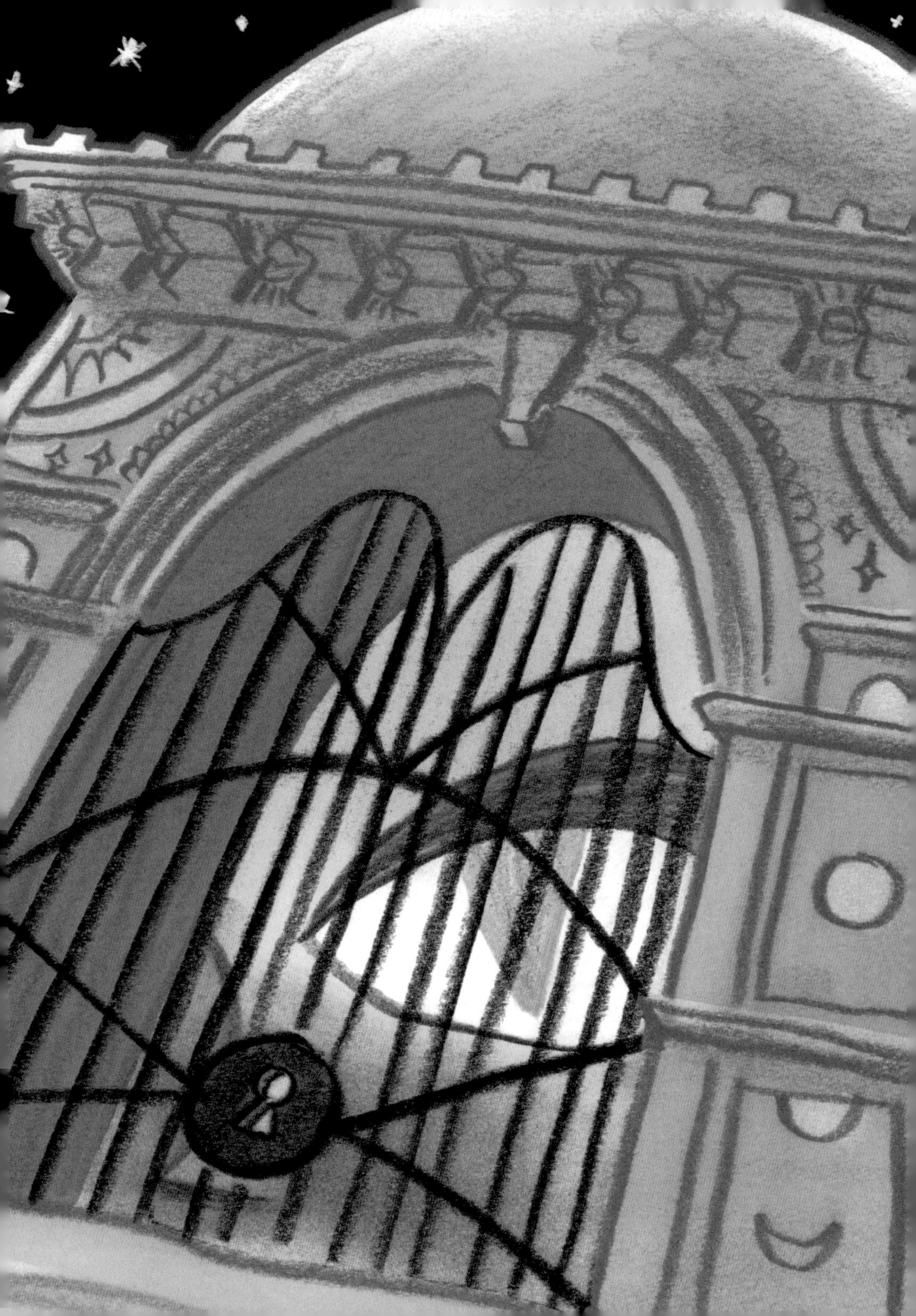

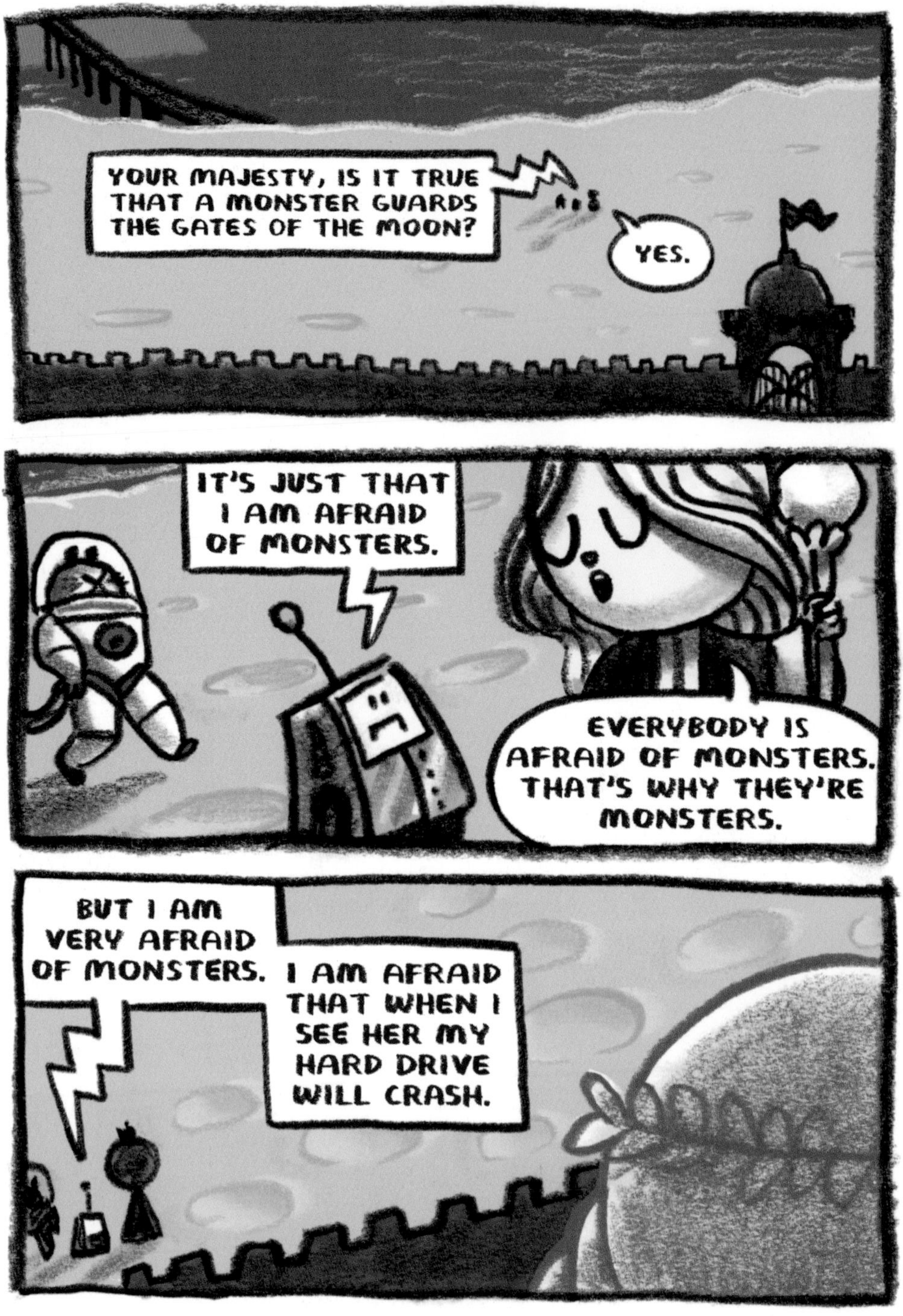
YOUR MAJESTY, IS IT TRUE THAT A MONSTER GUARDS THE GATES OF THE MOON?
YES.
IT'S JUST THAT I AM AFRAID OF MONSTERS.
EVERYBODY IS AFRAID OF MONSTERS. THAT'S WHY THEY'RE MONSTERS.
BUT I AM VERY AFRAID OF MONSTERS.
I AM AFRAID THAT WHEN I SEE HER MY HARD DRIVE WILL CRASH.

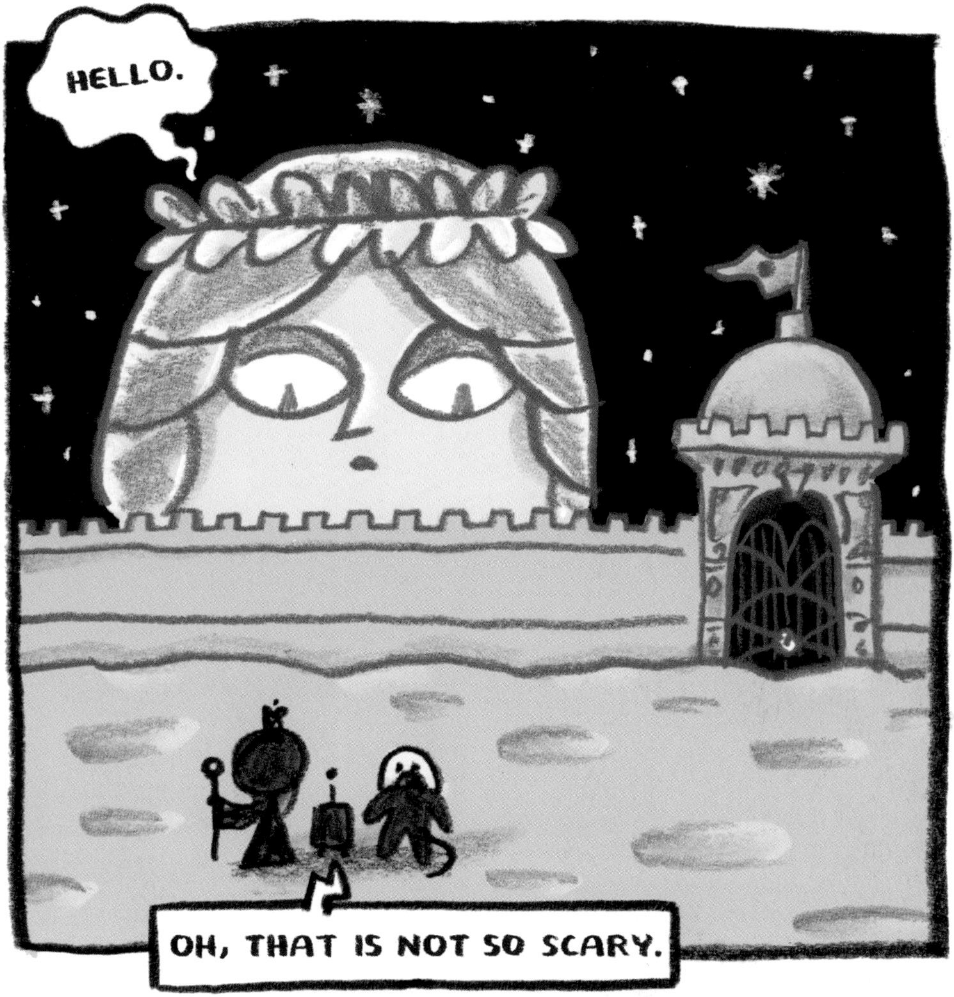
HELLO.
OH, THAT IS NOT SO SCARY.

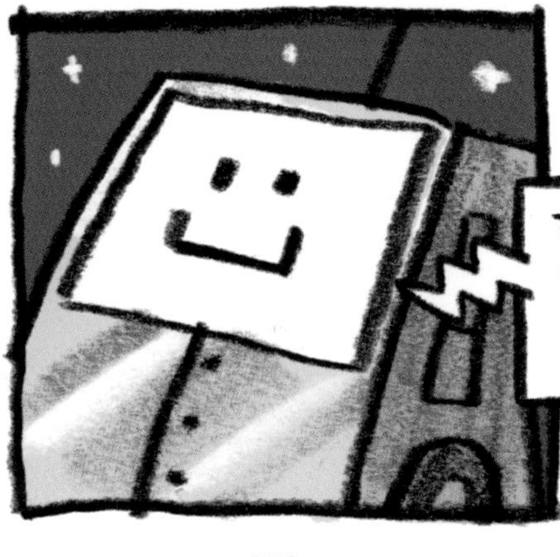
THAT IS JUST A GIANT LADY.

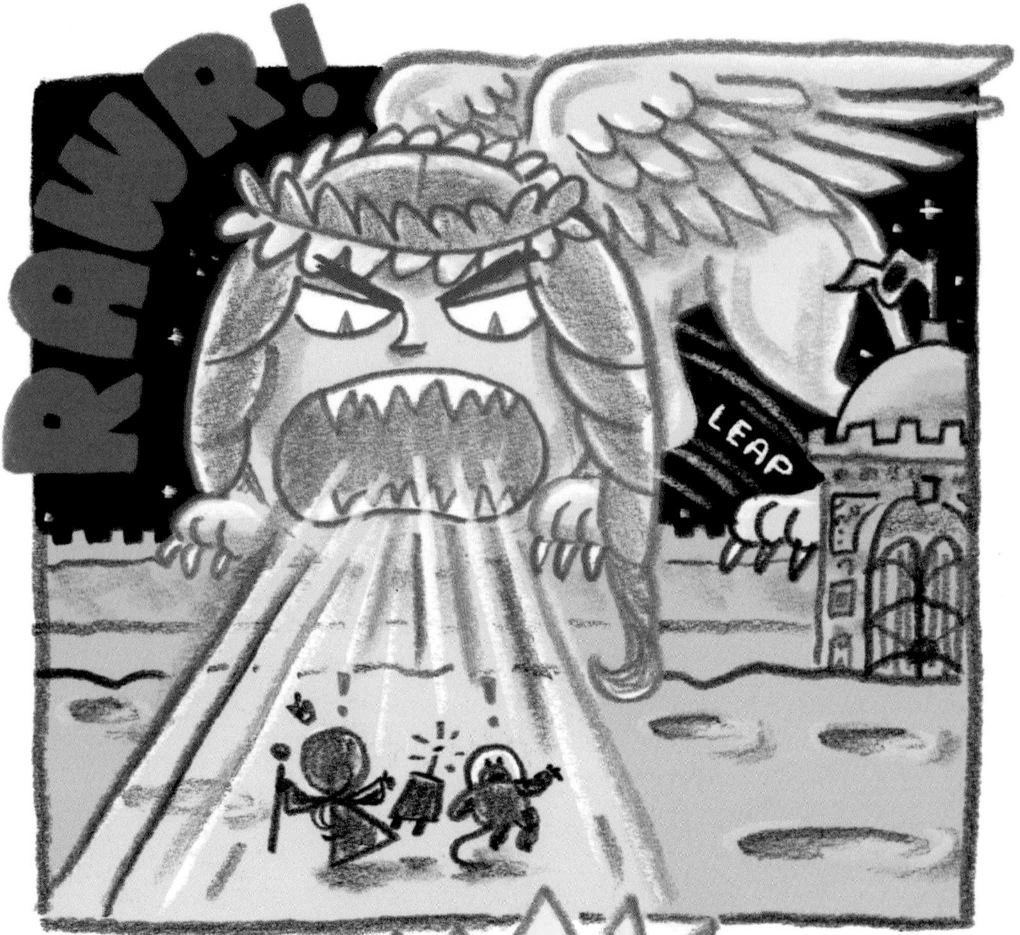
RAWR!
LEAP

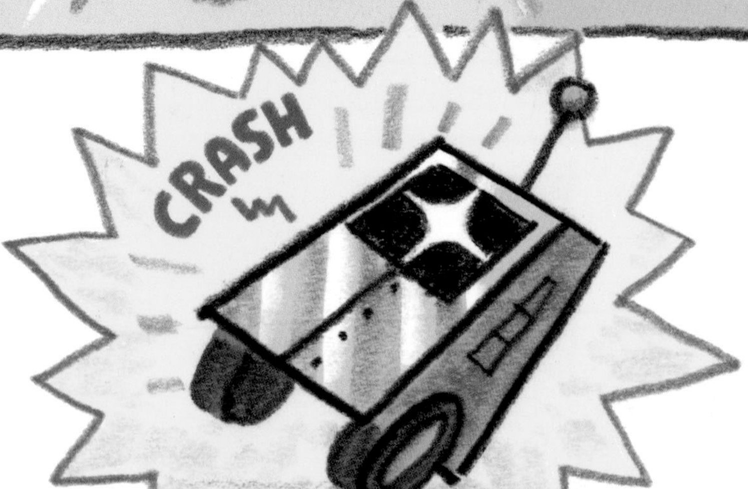
CRASH

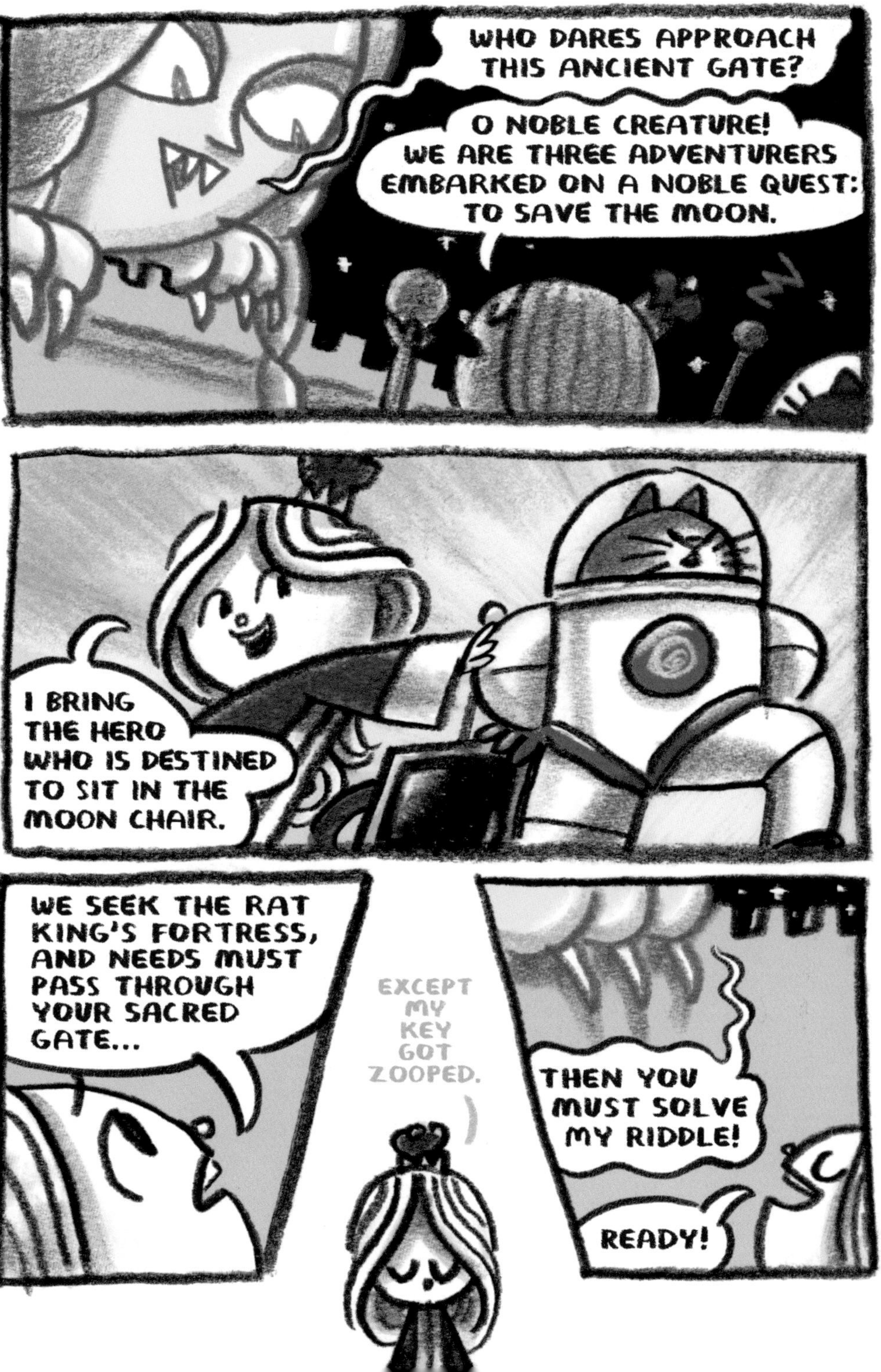
WHO DARES APPROACH THIS ANCIENT GATE?
O NOBLE CREATURE! WE ARE THREE ADVENTURERS EMBARKED ON A NOBLE QUEST: TO SAVE THE MOON.
I BRING THE HERO WHO IS DESTINED TO SIT IN THE MOON CHAIR.
WE SEEK THE RAT KING'S FORTRESS, AND NEEDS MUST PASS THROUGH YOUR SACRED GATE...
EXCEPT MY KEY GOT ZOOPED.
THEN YOU MUST SOLVE MY RIDDLE!
READY!

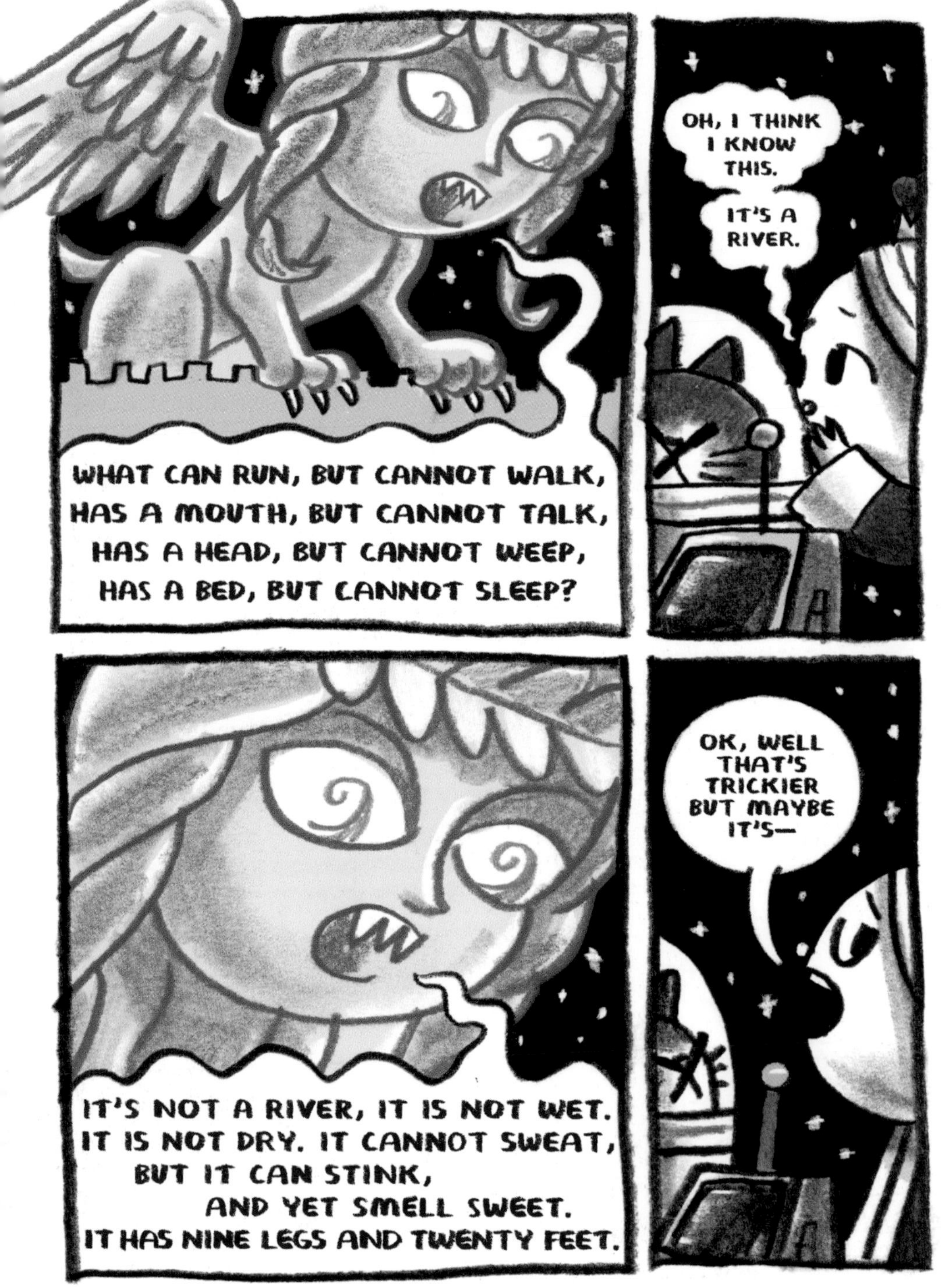

WHAT CAN RUN, BUT CANNOT WALK, HAS A MOUTH, BUT CANNOT TALK, HAS A HEAD, BUT CANNOT WEEP, HAS A BED, BUT CANNOT SLEEP?
OH, I THINK I KNOW THIS.
IT'S A RIVER.
IT'S NOT A RIVER, IT IS NOT WET. IT IS NOT DRY. IT CANNOT SWEAT, BUT IT CAN STINK, AND YET SMELL SWEET. IT HAS NINE LEGS AND TWENTY FEET.
OK, WELL THAT'S TRICKIER BUT MAYBE IT'S—

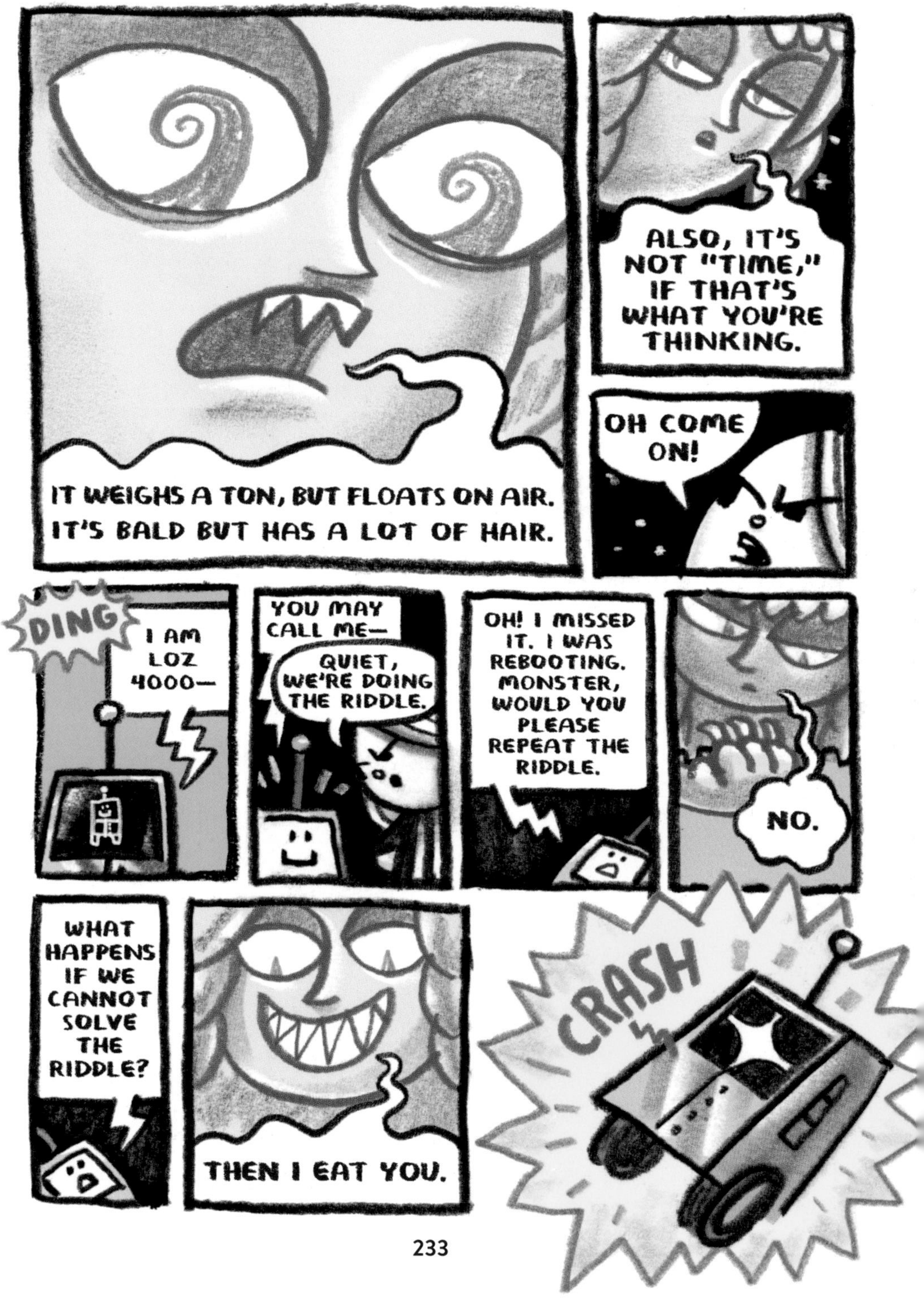

IT WEIGHS A TON, BUT FLOATS ON AIR.
IT'S BALD BUT HAS A LOT OF HAIR.
ALSO, IT'S NOT "TIME," IF THAT'S WHAT YOU'RE THINKING.
OH COME ON!
DING
I AM LOZ 4000—
YOU MAY CALL ME—
QUIET, WE'RE DOING THE RIDDLE.
OH! I MISSED IT. I WAS REBOOTING. MONSTER, WOULD YOU PLEASE REPEAT THE RIDDLE.
NO.
WHAT HAPPENS IF WE CANNOT SOLVE THE RIDDLE?
THEN I EAT YOU.
CRASH

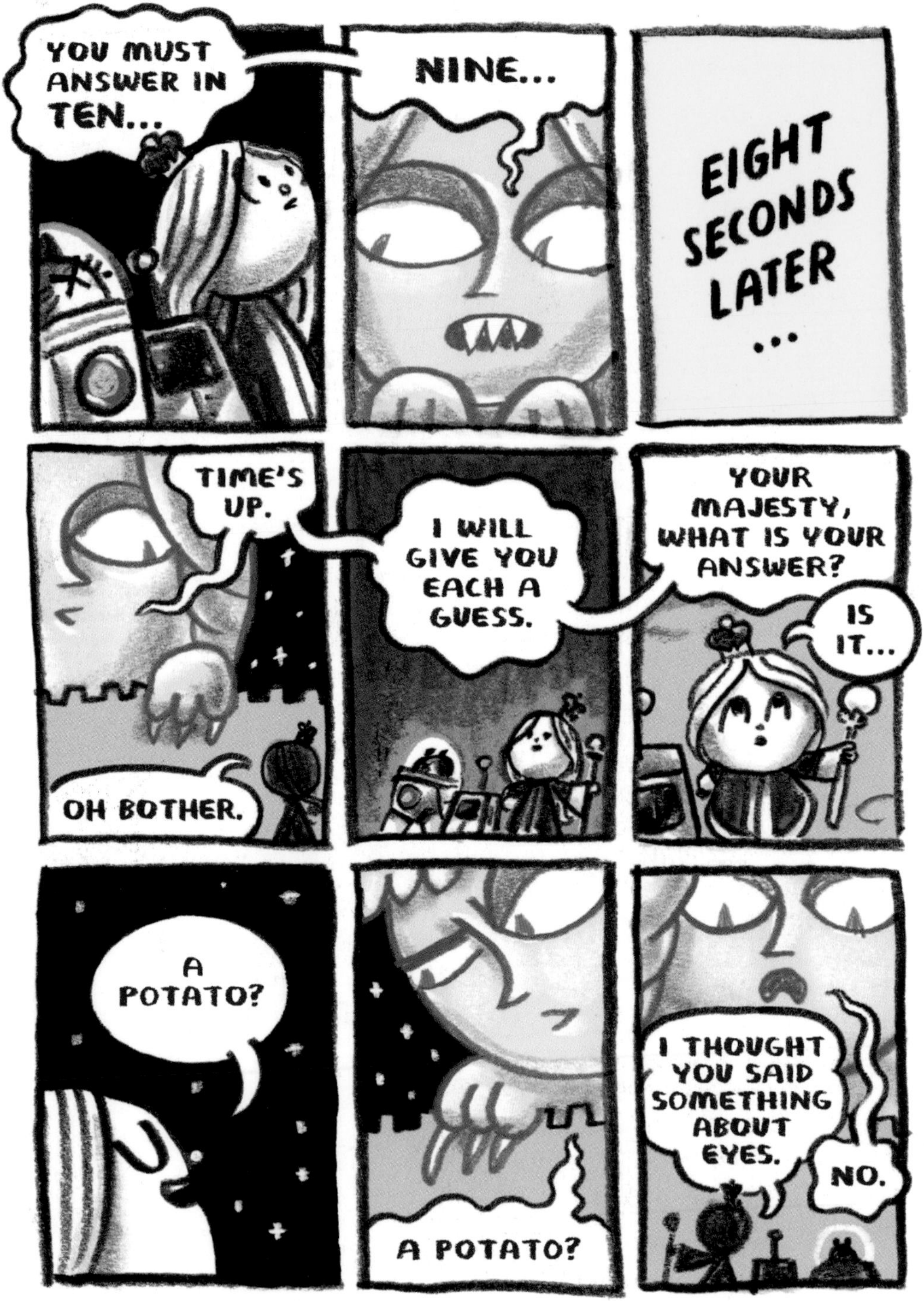

YOU MUST ANSWER IN TEN...
NINE...
EIGHT SECONDS LATER...
TIME'S UP.
I WILL GIVE YOU EACH A GUESS.
YOUR MAJESTY, WHAT IS YOUR ANSWER?
OH BOTHER.
IS IT...
A POTATO?
A POTATO?
I THOUGHT YOU SAID SOMETHING ABOUT EYES.
NO.

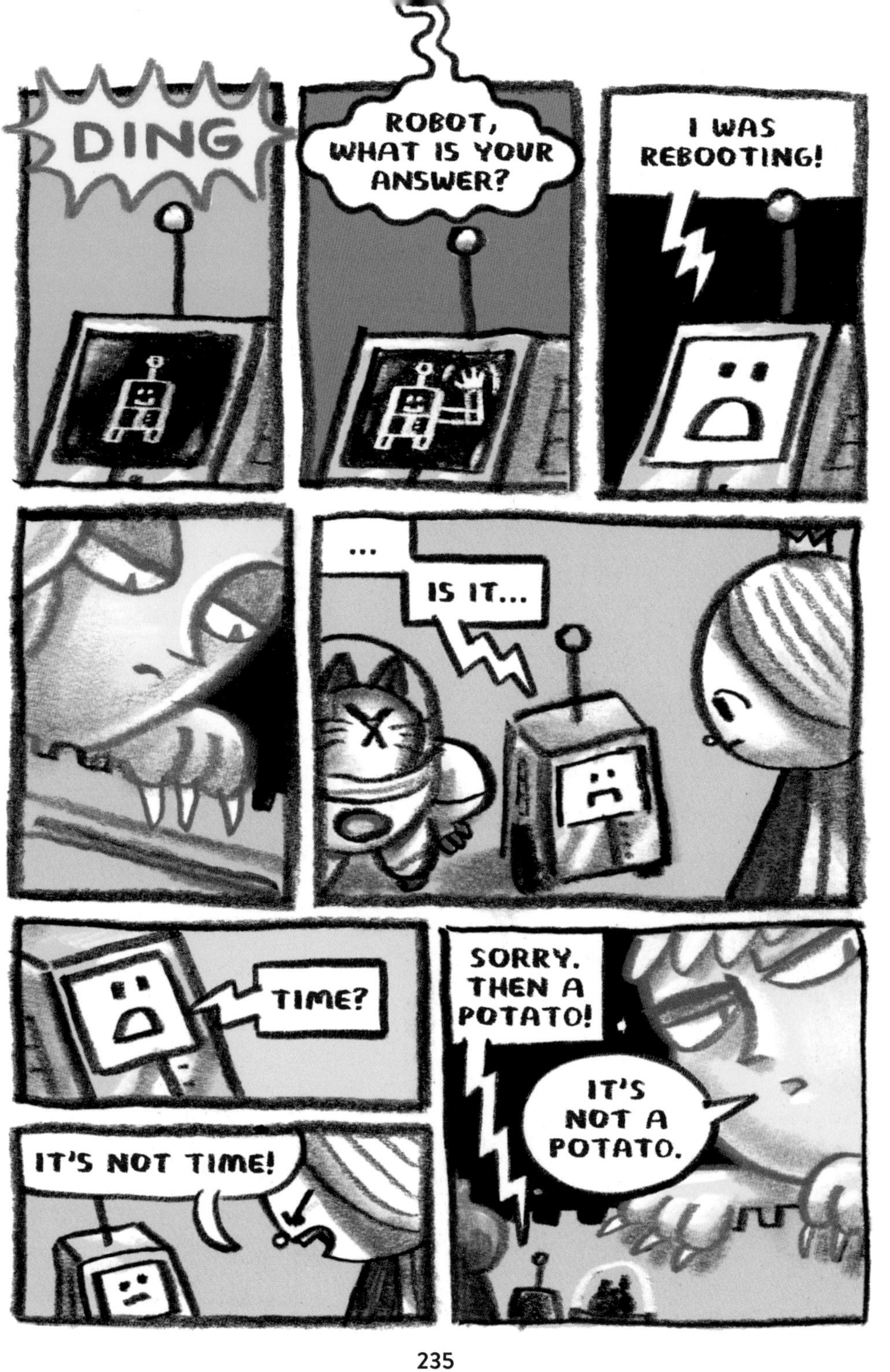
DING
ROBOT, WHAT IS YOUR ANSWER?
I WAS REBOOTING!
...
IS IT...
TIME?
IT'S NOT TIME!
SORRY. THEN A POTATO!
IT'S NOT A POTATO.

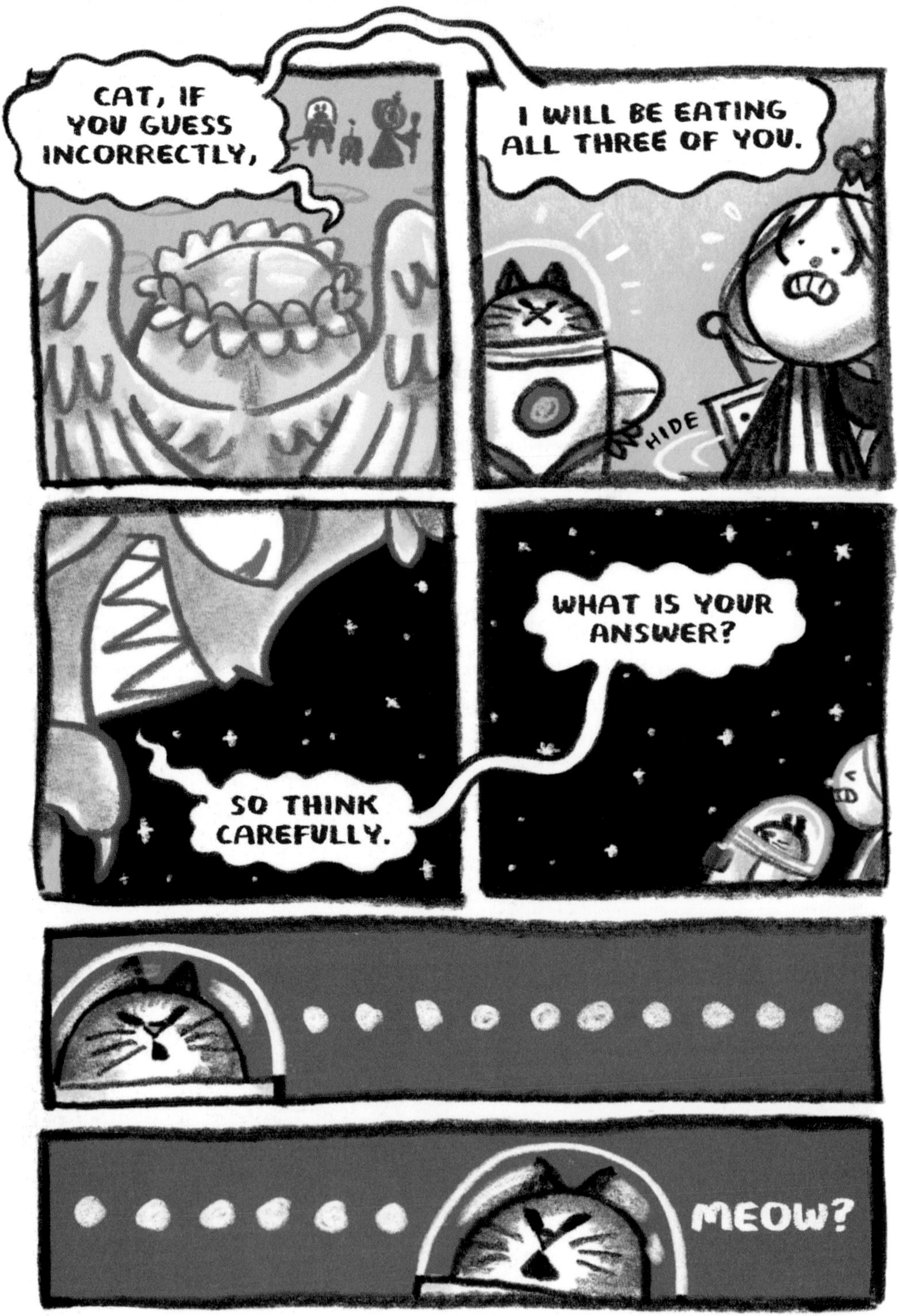
CAT, IF YOU GUESS INCORRECTLY,
I WILL BE EATING ALL THREE OF YOU.
HIDE
SO THINK CAREFULLY.
WHAT IS YOUR ANSWER?
MEOW?

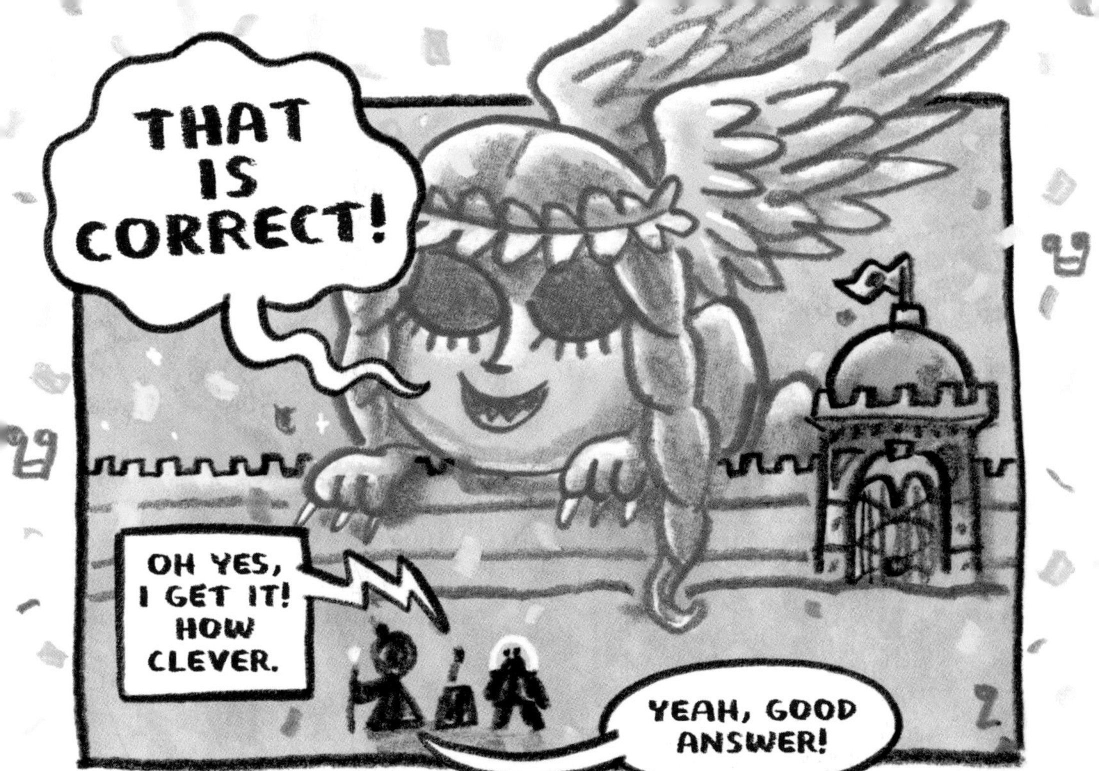
THAT IS CORRECT!
OH YES, I GET IT! HOW CLEVER.
YEAH, GOOD ANSWER!

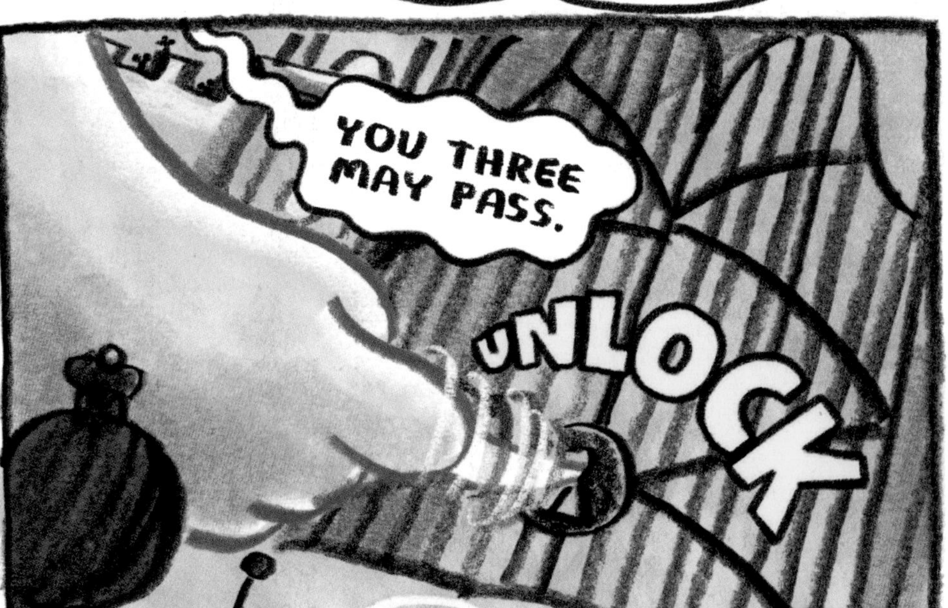
YOU THREE MAY PASS.
UNLOCK

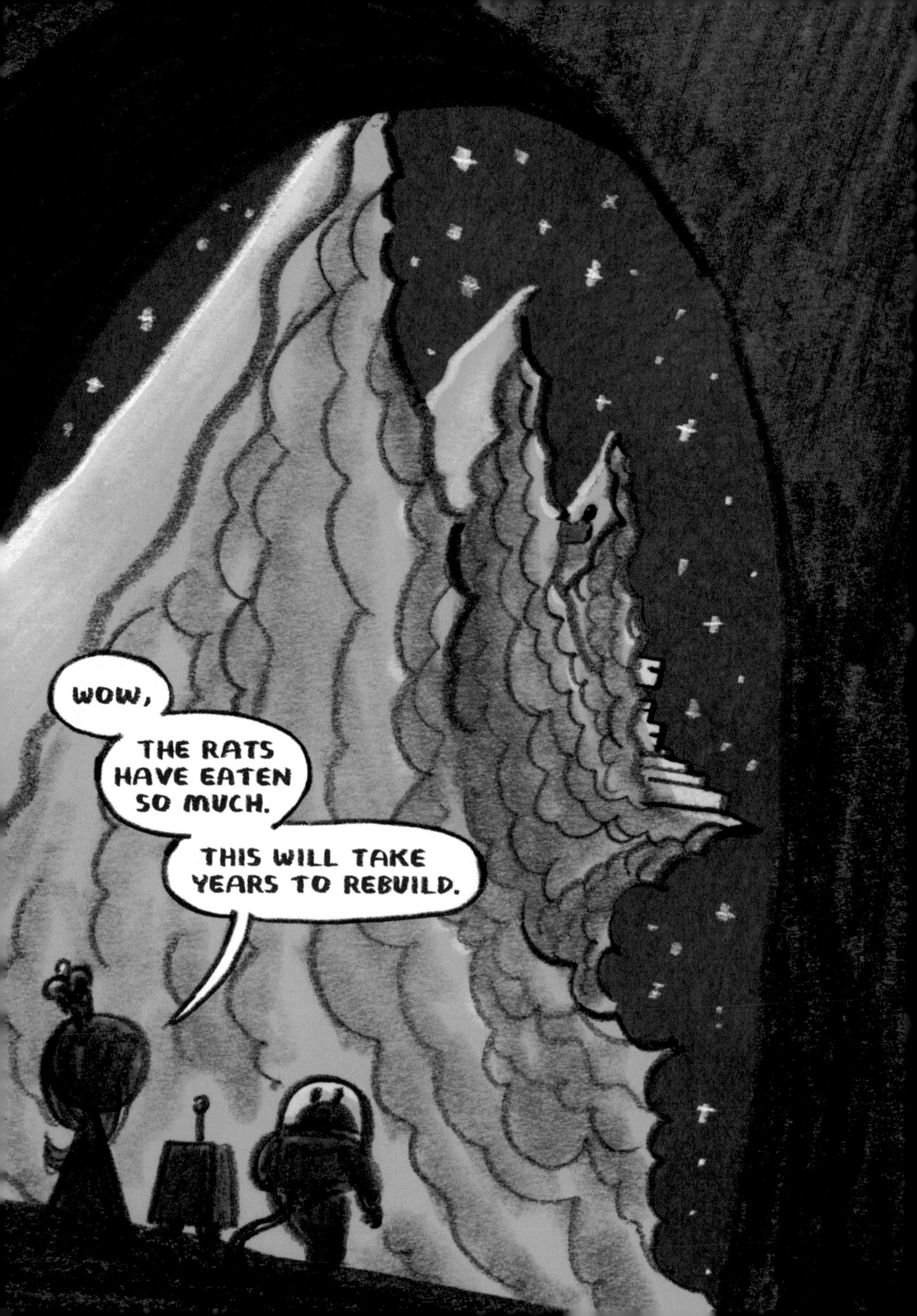
WOW,
THE RATS HAVE EATEN SO MUCH.
THIS WILL TAKE YEARS TO REBUILD.

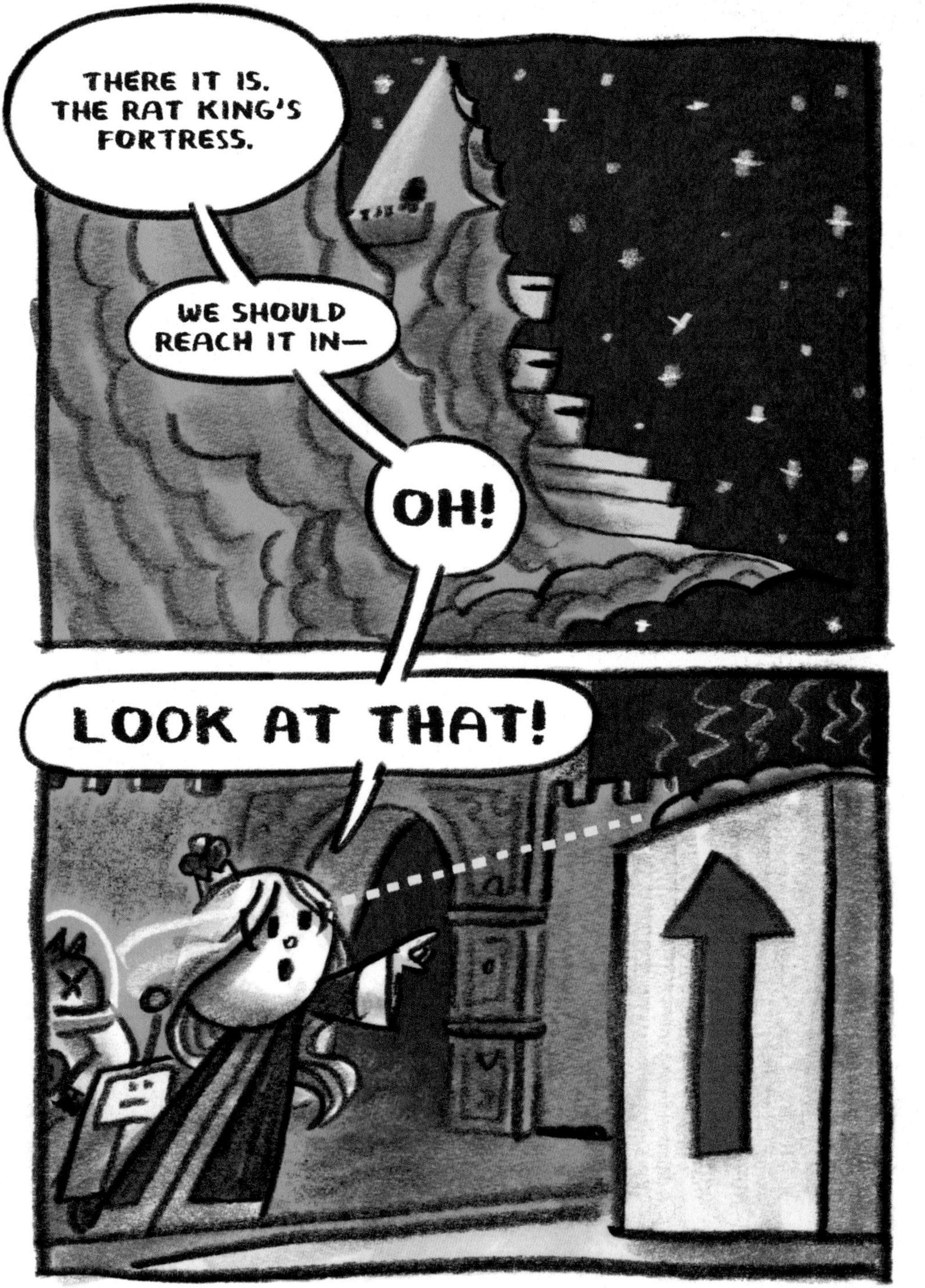
THERE IT IS. THE RAT KING'S FORTRESS.
WE SHOULD REACH IT IN—
OH!
LOOK AT THAT!

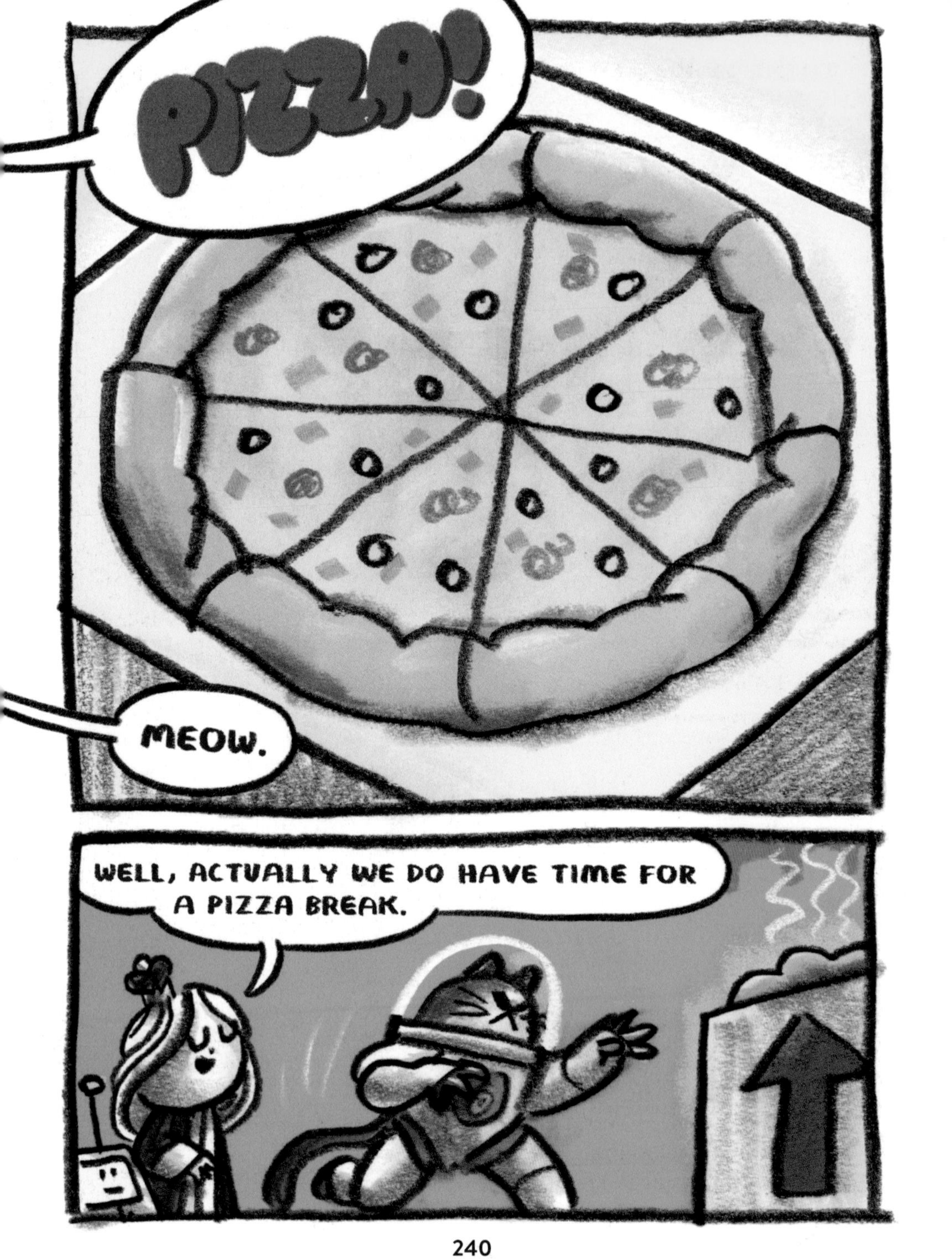
PIZZA!
MEOW.
WELL, ACTUALLY WE DO HAVE TIME FOR A PIZZA BREAK.

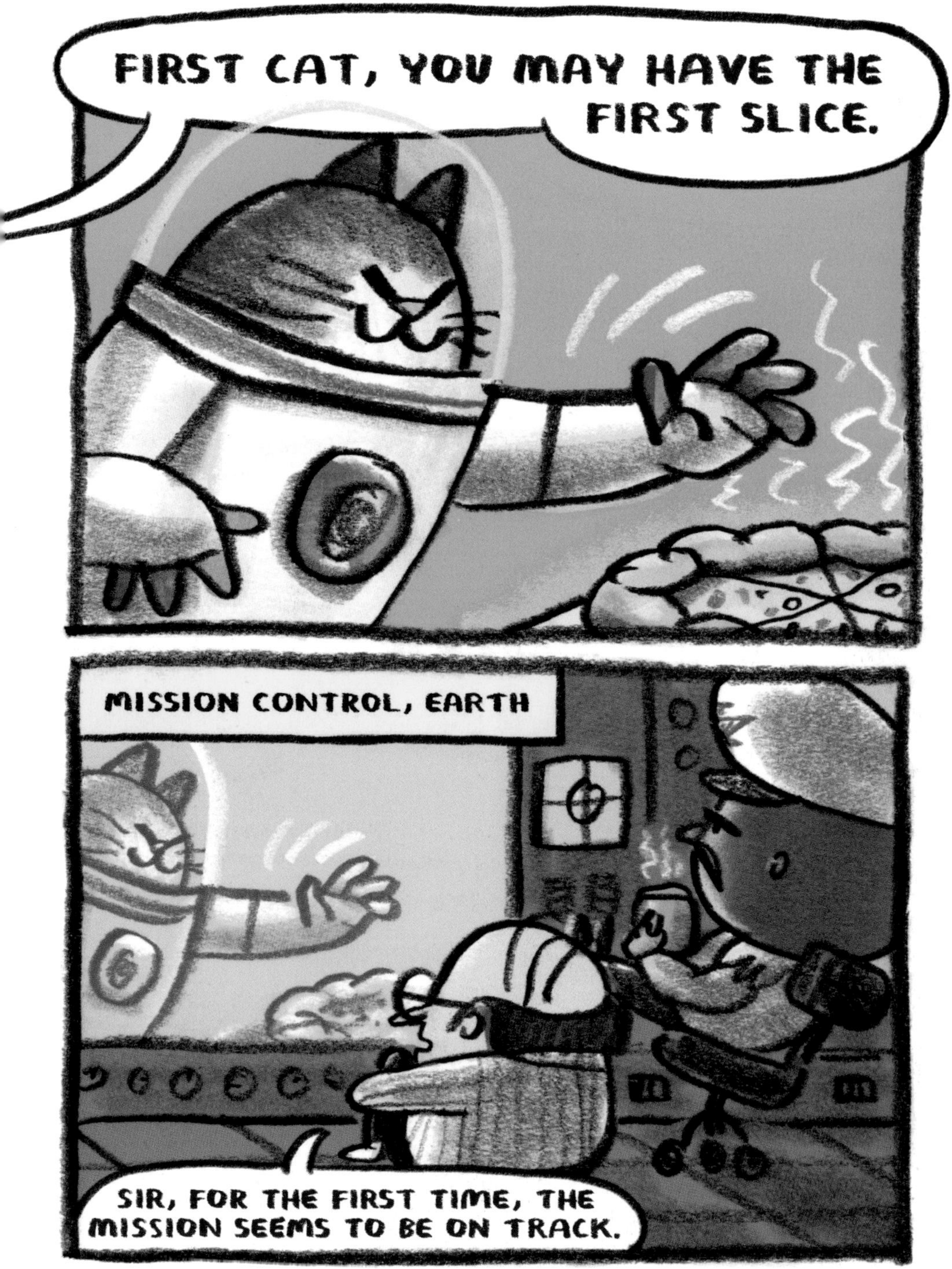
FIRST CAT, YOU MAY HAVE THE FIRST SLICE.
MISSION CONTROL, EARTH
SIR, FOR THE FIRST TIME, THE MISSION SEEMS TO BE ON TRACK.

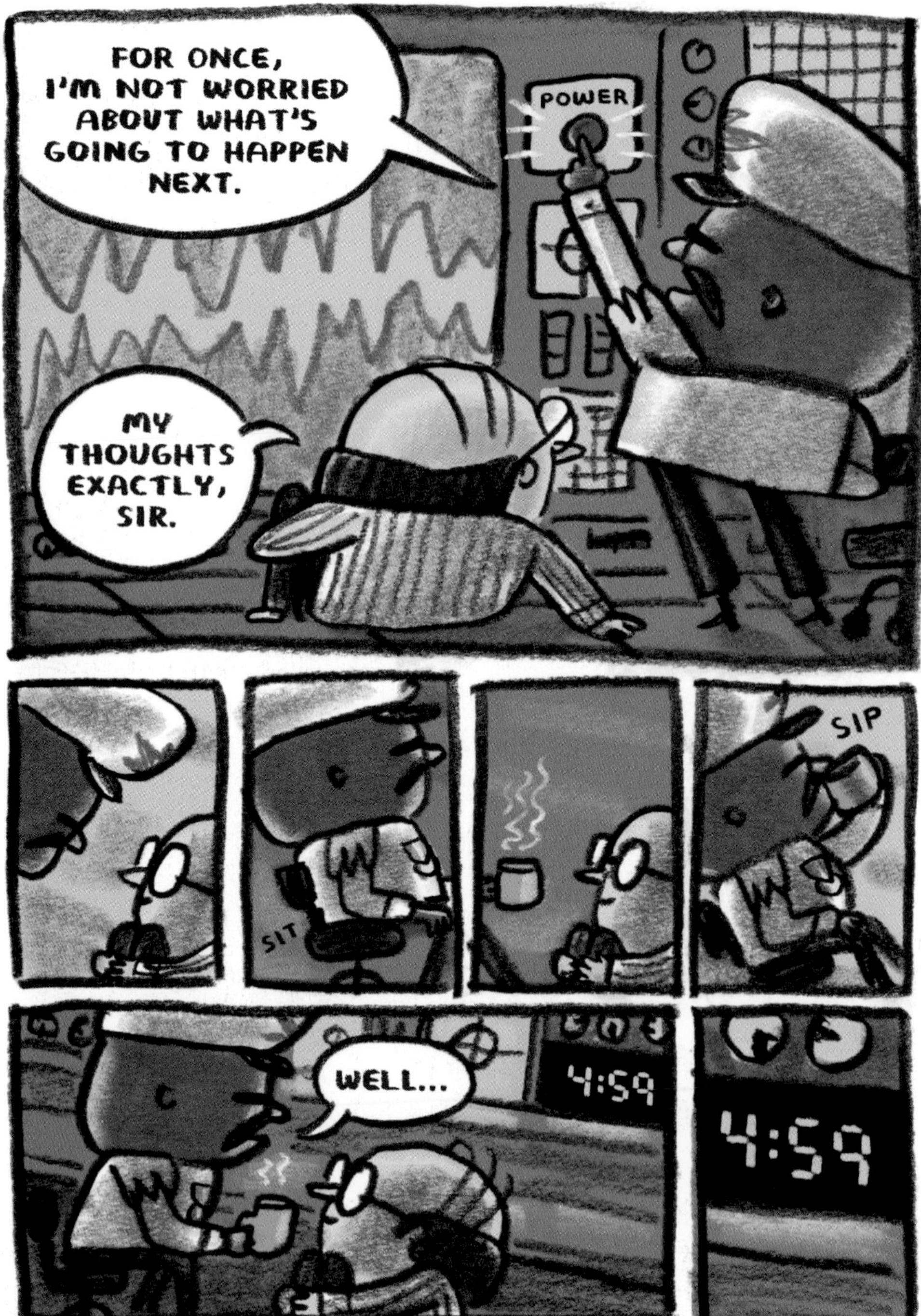
FOR ONCE, I'M NOT WORRIED ABOUT WHAT'S GOING TO HAPPEN NEXT.
POWER
MY THOUGHTS EXACTLY, SIR.
SIT
SIP
WELL...
4:59
4:59

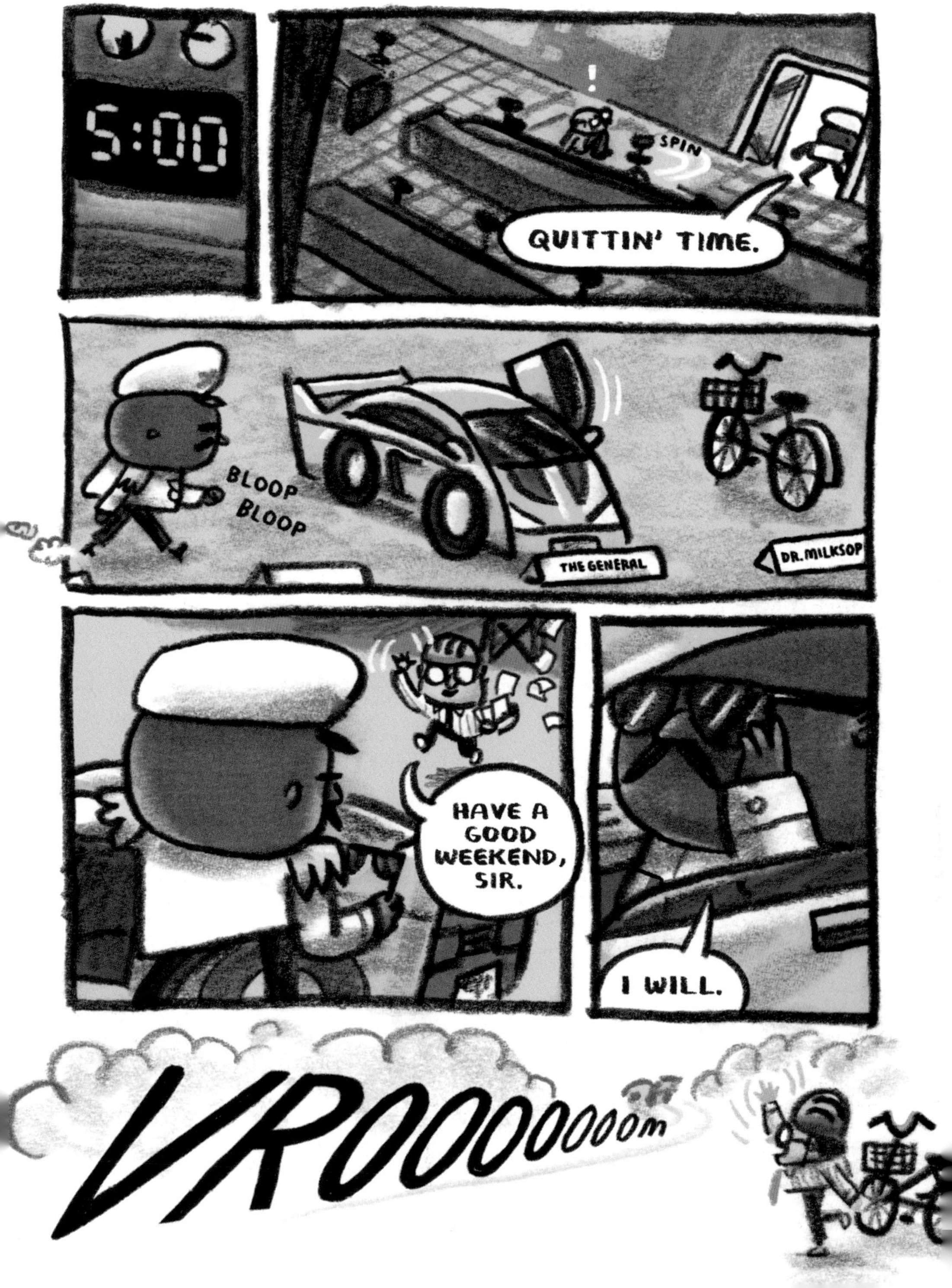
5:00
!
SPIN
QUITTIN' TIME.
BLOOP BLOOP
THE GENERAL
DR. MILKSOP
HAVE A GOOD WEEKEND, SIR.
I WILL.
VROOOOOOOom

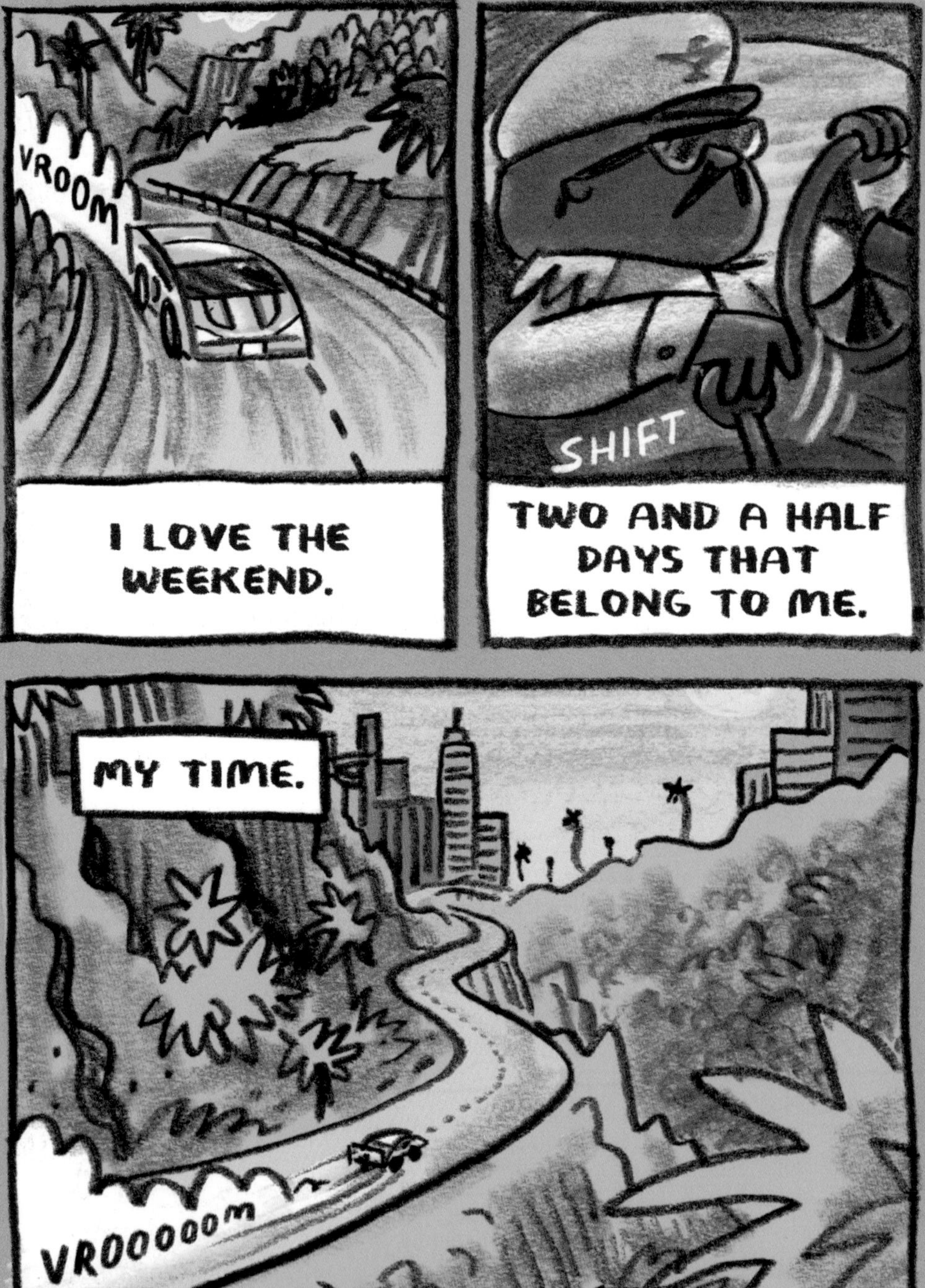
VROOM
I LOVE THE WEEKEND.
SHIFT
TWO AND A HALF DAYS THAT BELONG TO ME.
MY TIME.
VROOOOOM

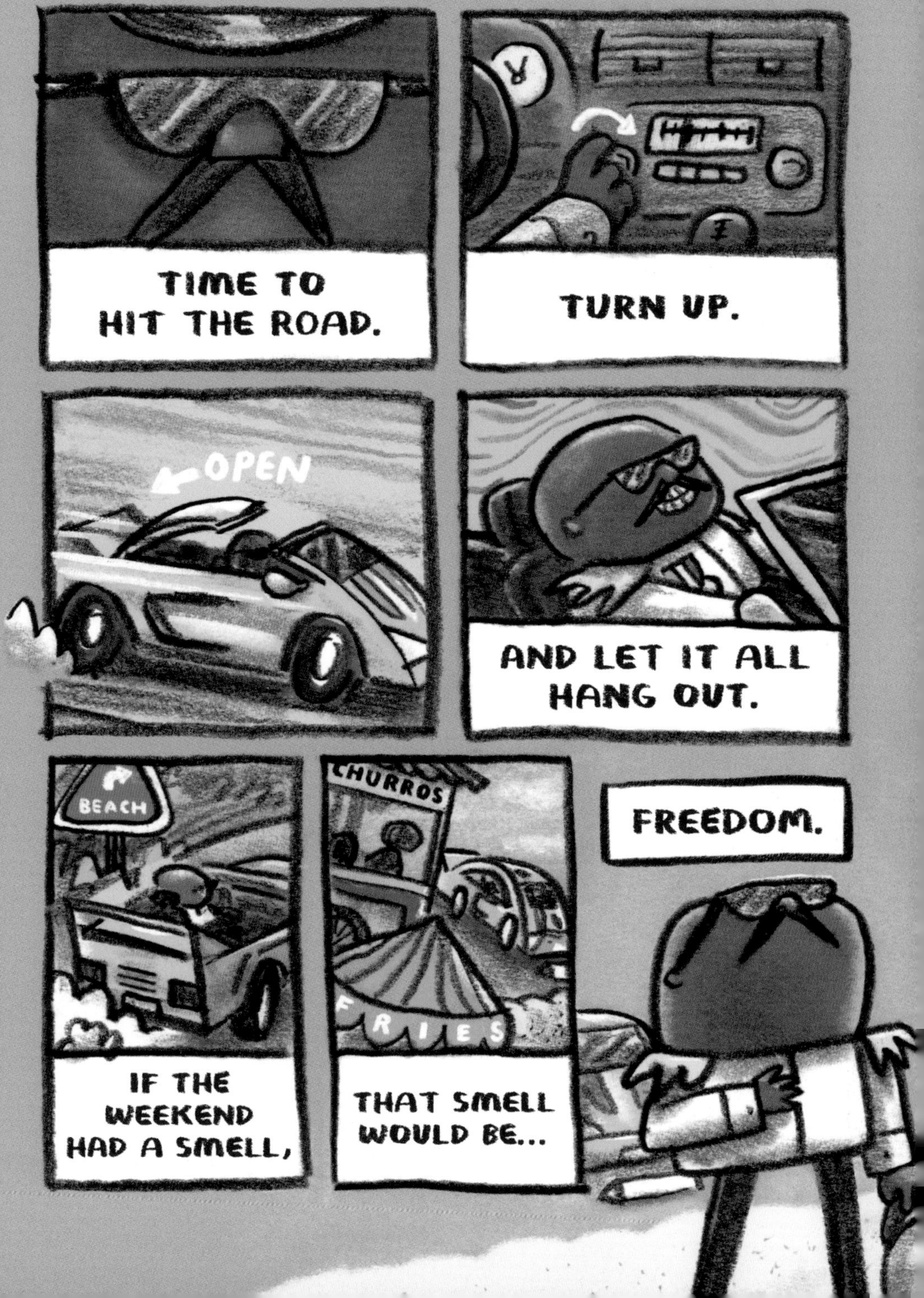

TIME TO HIT THE ROAD.
TURN UP.
OPEN
AND LET IT ALL HANG OUT.
BEACH
IF THE WEEKEND HAD A SMELL,
CHURROS
FRIES
THAT SMELL WOULD BE...
FREEDOM.

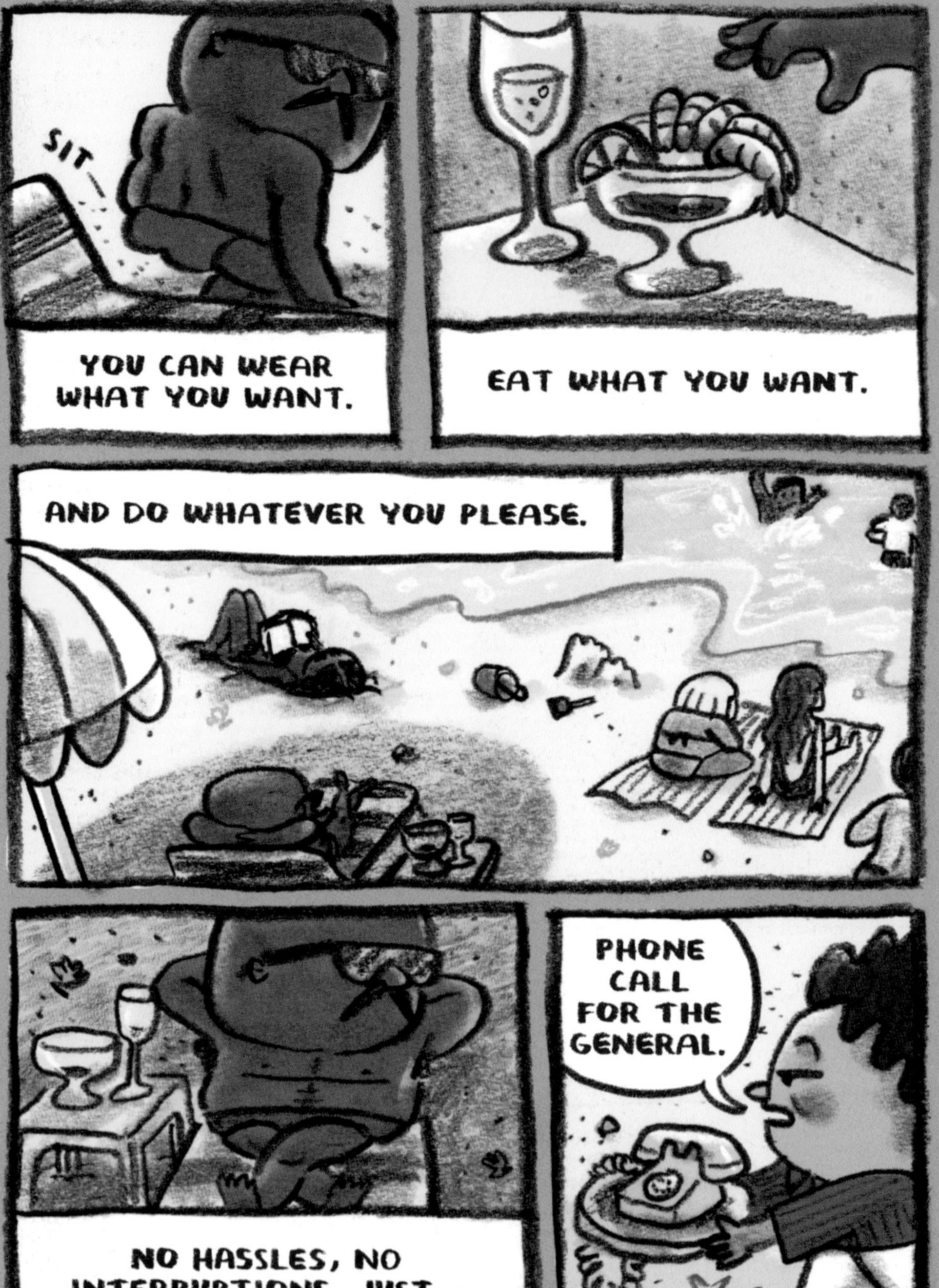
SIT—
YOU CAN WEAR WHAT YOU WANT.
EAT WHAT YOU WANT.
AND DO WHATEVER YOU PLEASE.
NO HASSLES, NO INTERRUPTIONS. JUST—
PHONE CALL FOR THE GENERAL.

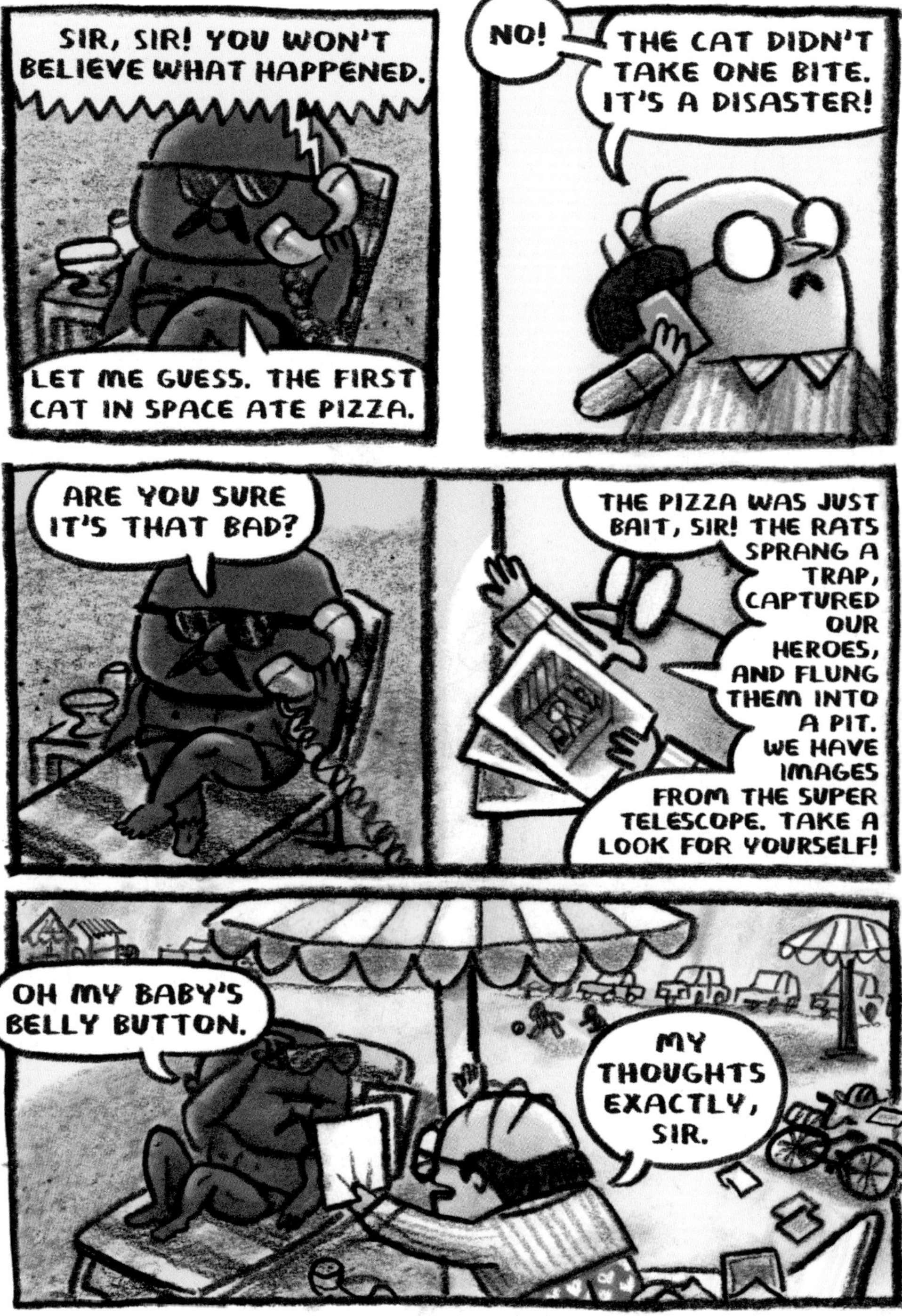
SIR, SIR! YOU WON'T BELIEVE WHAT HAPPENED.
LET ME GUESS. THE FIRST CAT IN SPACE ATE PIZZA.
NO!
THE CAT DIDN'T TAKE ONE BITE. IT'S A DISASTER!
ARE YOU SURE IT'S THAT BAD?
THE PIZZA WAS JUST BAIT, SIR! THE RATS SPRANG A TRAP, CAPTURED OUR HEROES, AND FLUNG THEM INTO A PIT. WE HAVE IMAGES FROM THE SUPER TELESCOPE. TAKE A LOOK FOR YOURSELF!
OH MY BABY'S BELLY BUTTON.
MY THOUGHTS EXACTLY, SIR.

CHAPTER 19

THE
PIT

SUPER TELESCOPE IMG 47X

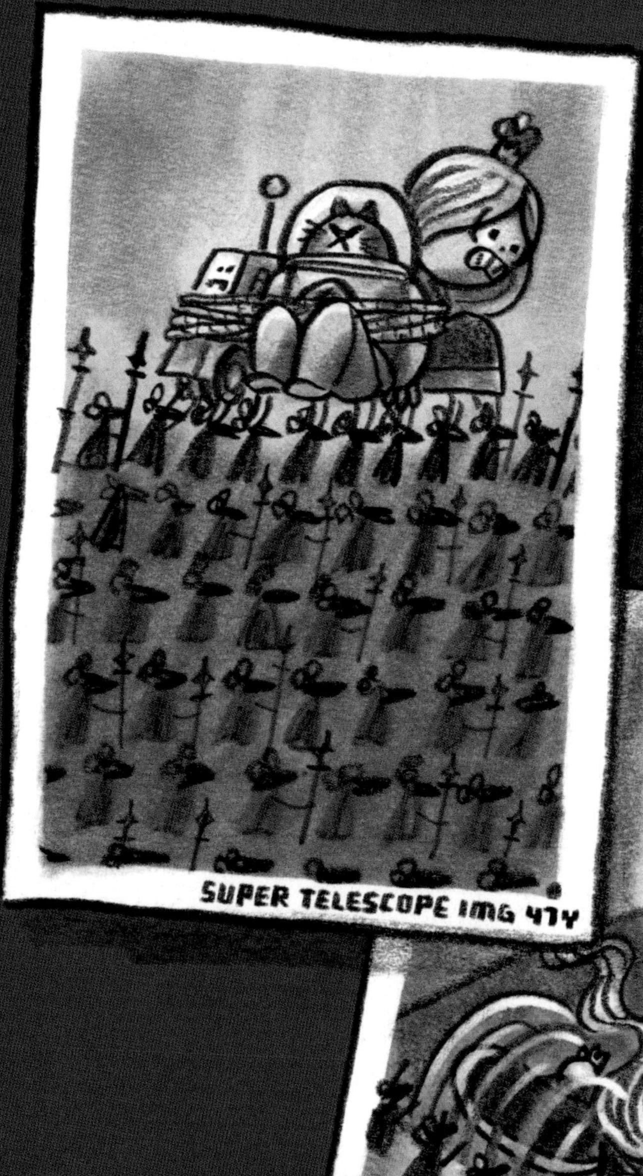
SUPER TELESCOPE IMG 474

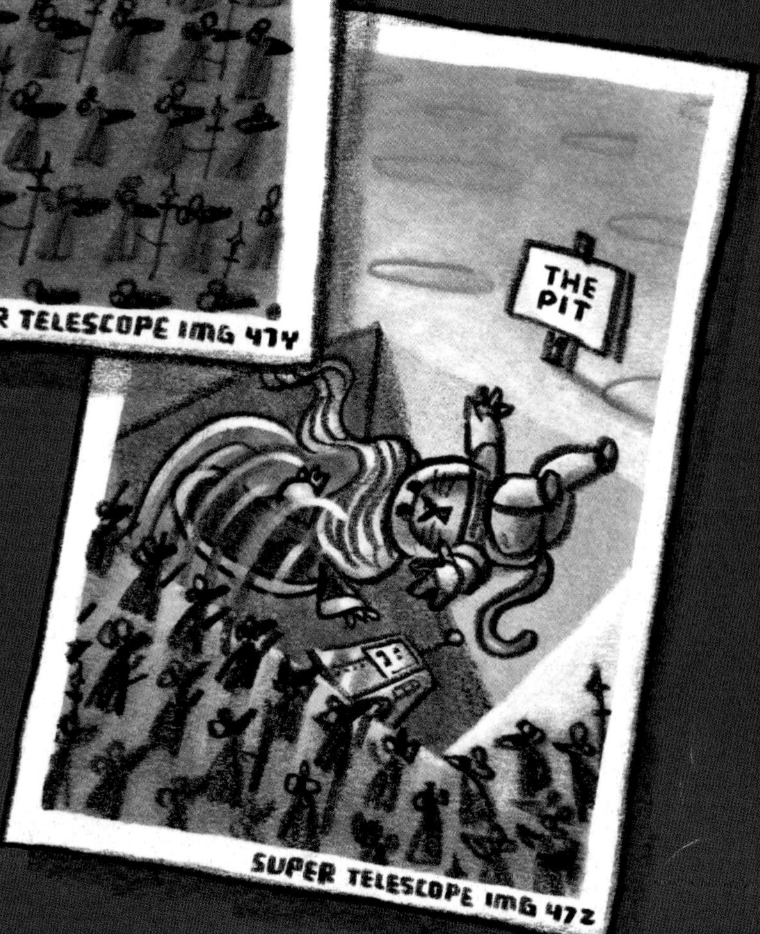
THE PIT
SUPER TELESCOPE IMG 472

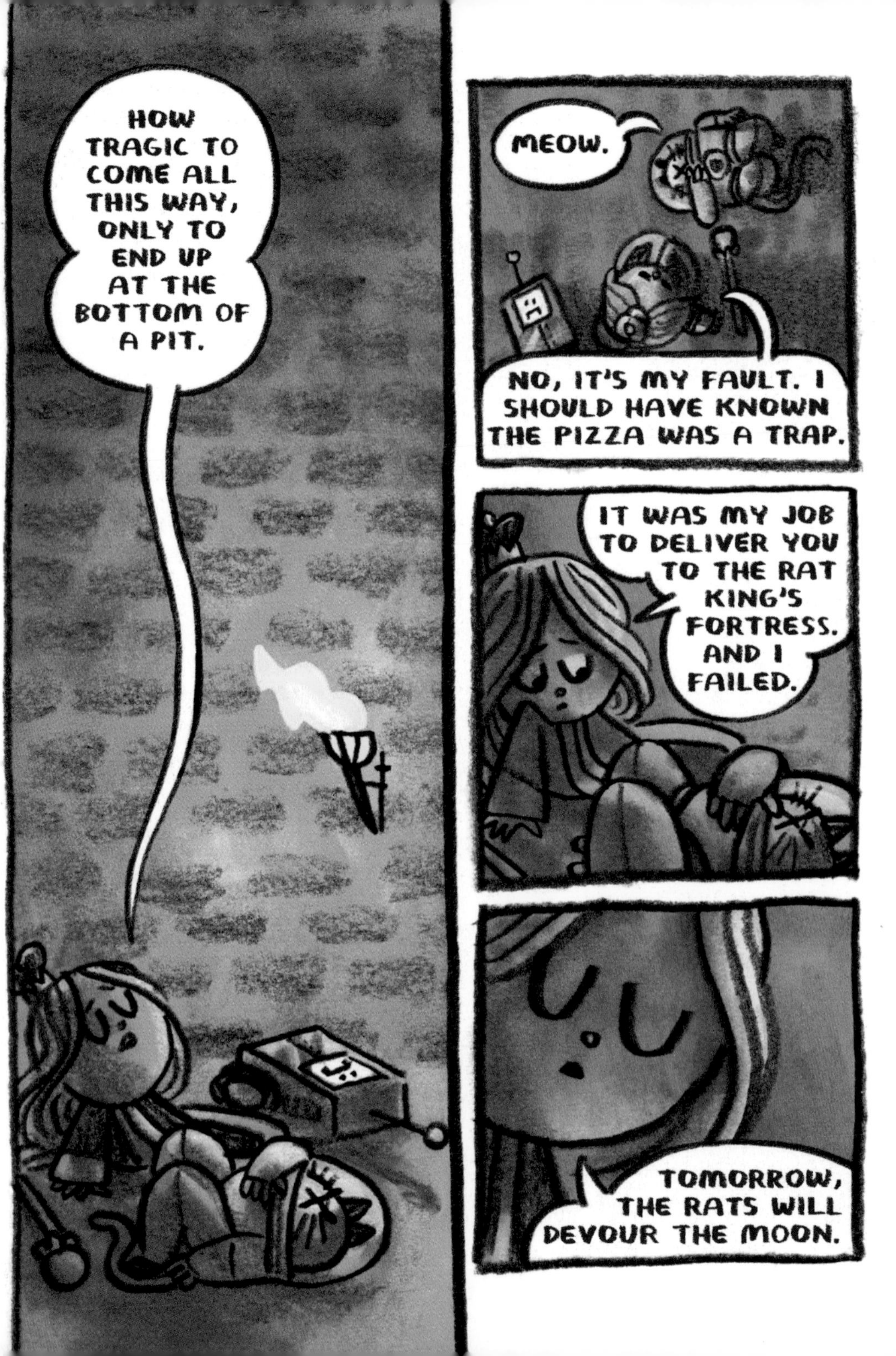
HOW TRAGIC TO COME ALL THIS WAY, ONLY TO END UP AT THE BOTTOM OF A PIT.
MEOW.
NO, IT'S MY FAULT. I SHOULD HAVE KNOWN THE PIZZA WAS A TRAP.
IT WAS MY JOB TO DELIVER YOU TO THE RAT KING'S FORTRESS. AND I FAILED.
TOMORROW, THE RATS WILL DEVOUR THE MOON.

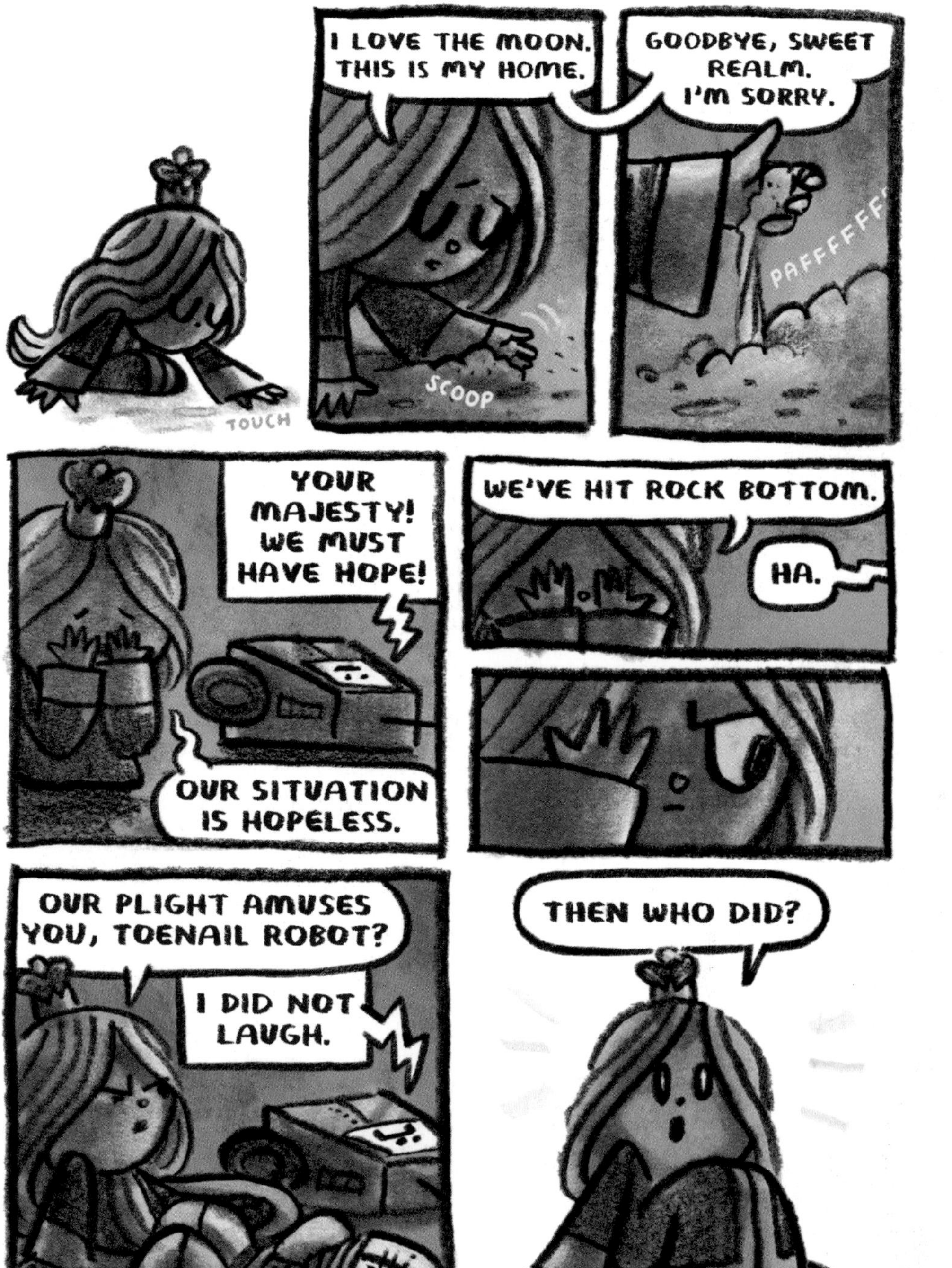
TOUCH
I LOVE THE MOON. THIS IS MY HOME.
SCOOP
GOODBYE, SWEET REALM. I'M SORRY.
PAFFFFFFF
YOUR MAJESTY! WE MUST HAVE HOPE!
OUR SITUATION IS HOPELESS.
WE'VE HIT ROCK BOTTOM.
HA.
OUR PLIGHT AMUSES YOU, TOENAIL ROBOT?
I DID NOT LAUGH.
THEN WHO DID?

STONE!

YOU'RE ALIVE!

YEAH, I'M ORIGINALLY FROM THE PENINSULA OF THUNDER.

A BUNCH OF RATS GRABBED ME TO BUILD THIS PIT!

WHY WERE YOU LAUGHING AT US?

GET IT?

ROCK BOTTOM!

OH YEAH, I GET IT.

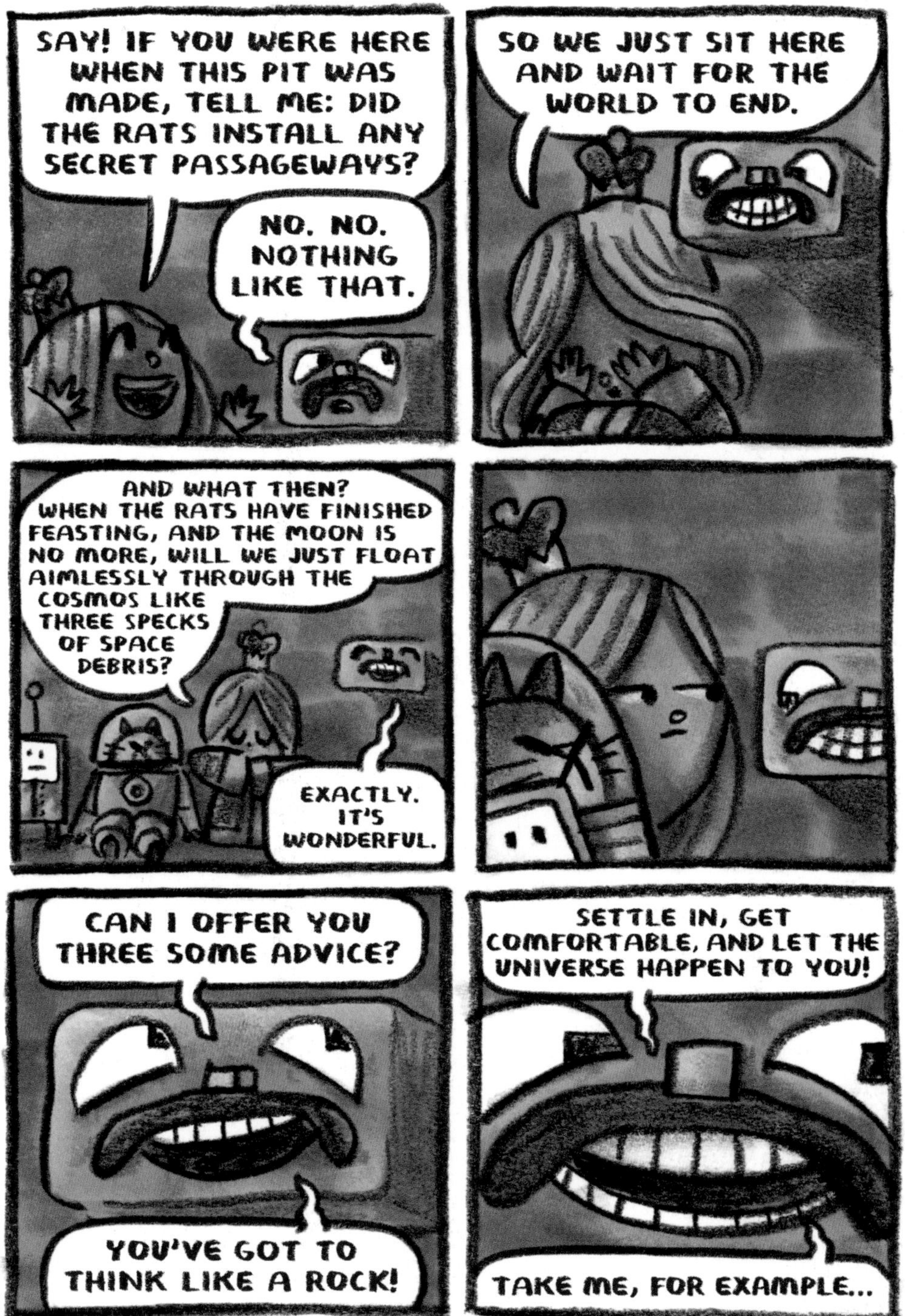
SAY! IF YOU WERE HERE WHEN THIS PIT WAS MADE, TELL ME: DID THE RATS INSTALL ANY SECRET PASSAGEWAYS?
NO. NO. NOTHING LIKE THAT.
SO WE JUST SIT HERE AND WAIT FOR THE WORLD TO END.
AND WHAT THEN? WHEN THE RATS HAVE FINISHED FEASTING, AND THE MOON IS NO MORE, WILL WE JUST FLOAT AIMLESSLY THROUGH THE COSMOS LIKE THREE SPECKS OF SPACE DEBRIS?
EXACTLY. IT'S WONDERFUL.
CAN I OFFER YOU THREE SOME ADVICE?
YOU'VE GOT TO THINK LIKE A ROCK!
SETTLE IN, GET COMFORTABLE, AND LET THE UNIVERSE HAPPEN TO YOU!
TAKE ME, FOR EXAMPLE...

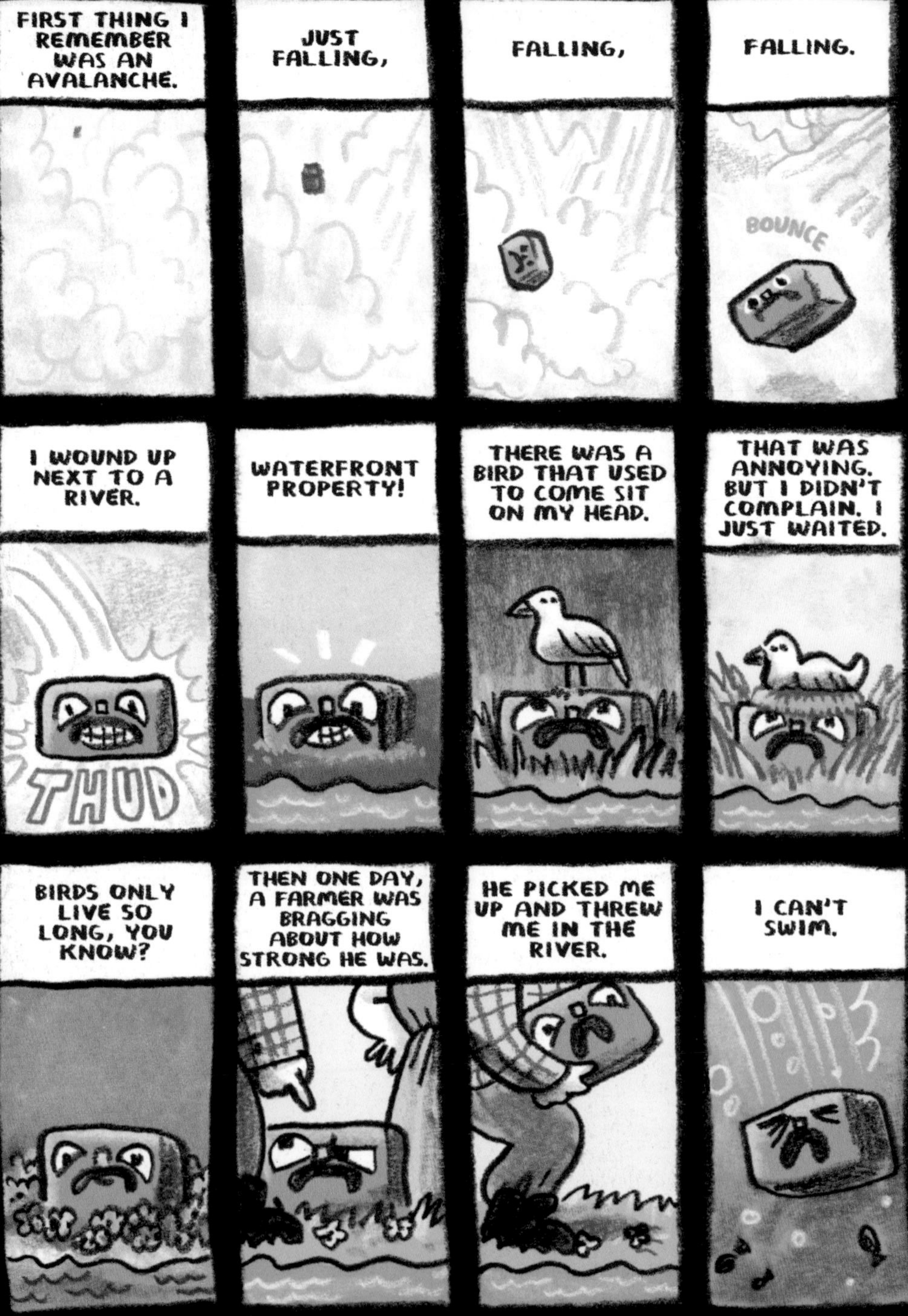
FIRST THING I REMEMBER WAS AN AVALANCHE.
JUST FALLING,
FALLING,
FALLING.
BOUNCE
I WOUND UP NEXT TO A RIVER.
THUD
WATERFRONT PROPERTY!
THERE WAS A BIRD THAT USED TO COME SIT ON MY HEAD.
THAT WAS ANNOYING. BUT I DIDN'T COMPLAIN. I JUST WAITED.
BIRDS ONLY LIVE SO LONG, YOU KNOW?
THEN ONE DAY, A FARMER WAS BRAGGING ABOUT HOW STRONG HE WAS.
HE PICKED ME UP AND THREW ME IN THE RIVER.
I CAN'T SWIM.

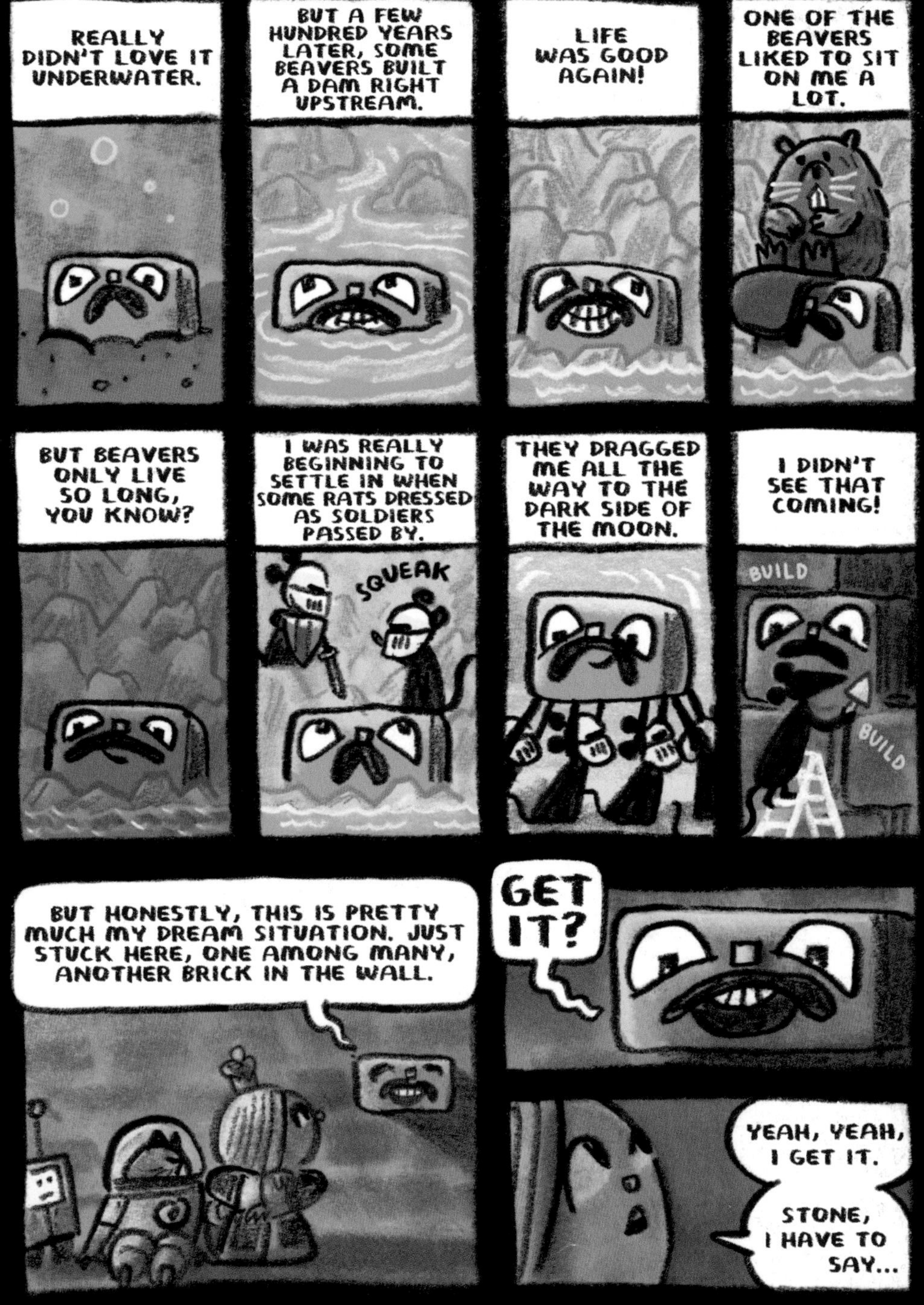
REALLY DIDN'T LOVE IT UNDERWATER.
BUT A FEW HUNDRED YEARS LATER, SOME BEAVERS BUILT A DAM RIGHT UPSTREAM.
LIFE WAS GOOD AGAIN!
ONE OF THE BEAVERS LIKED TO SIT ON ME A LOT.
BUT BEAVERS ONLY LIVE SO LONG, YOU KNOW?
I WAS REALLY BEGINNING TO SETTLE IN WHEN SOME RATS DRESSED AS SOLDIERS PASSED BY.
SQUEAK
THEY DRAGGED ME ALL THE WAY TO THE DARK SIDE OF THE MOON.
I DIDN'T SEE THAT COMING!
BUILD
BUILD
BUT HONESTLY, THIS IS PRETTY MUCH MY DREAM SITUATION. JUST STUCK HERE, ONE AMONG MANY, ANOTHER BRICK IN THE WALL.
GET IT?
YEAH, YEAH, I GET IT.
STONE, I HAVE TO SAY...

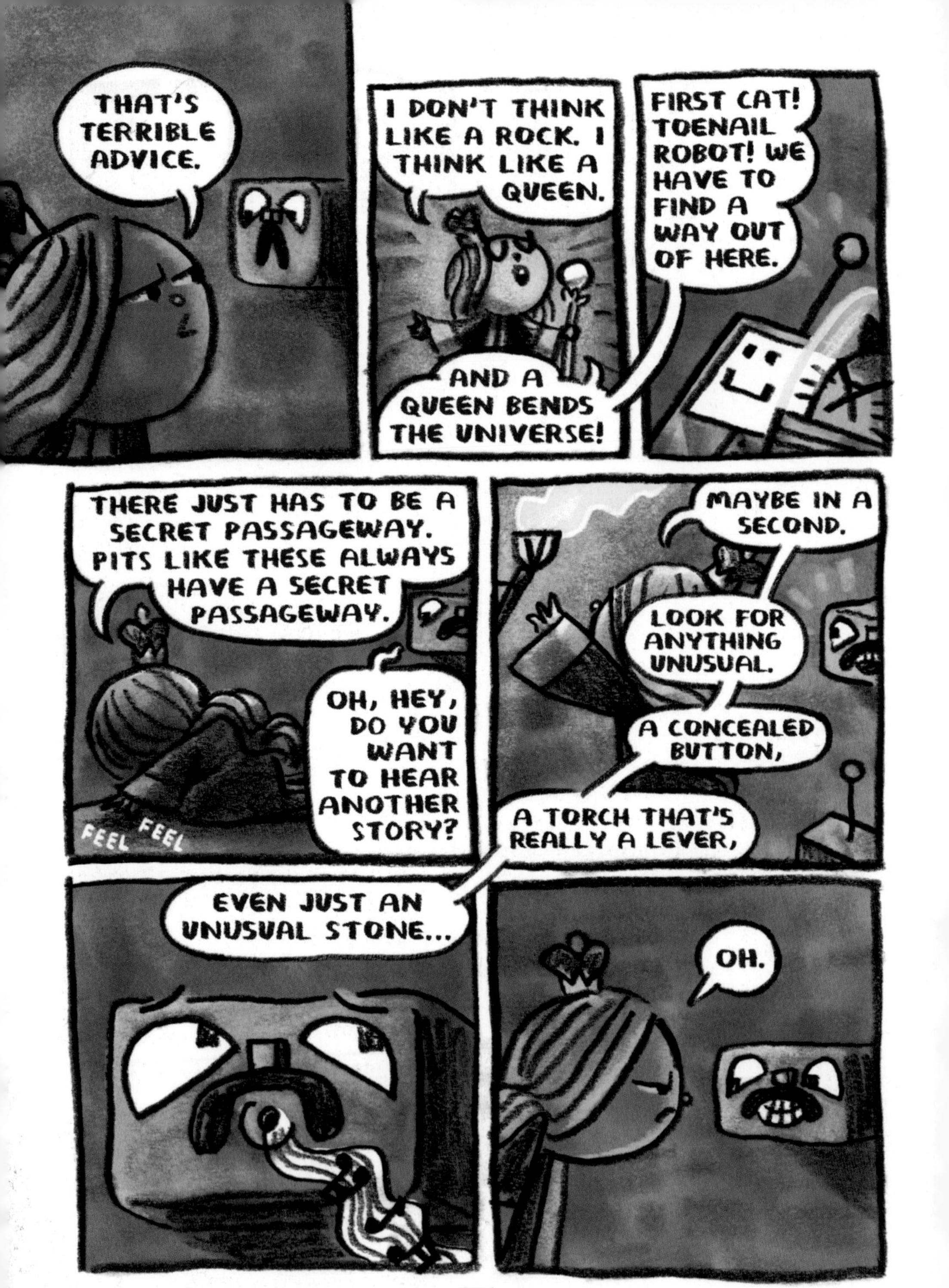
THAT'S TERRIBLE ADVICE.
I DON'T THINK LIKE A ROCK. I THINK LIKE A QUEEN.
AND A QUEEN BENDS THE UNIVERSE!
FIRST CAT! TOENAIL ROBOT! WE HAVE TO FIND A WAY OUT OF HERE.
THERE JUST HAS TO BE A SECRET PASSAGEWAY. PITS LIKE THESE ALWAYS HAVE A SECRET PASSAGEWAY.
OH, HEY, DO YOU WANT TO HEAR ANOTHER STORY?
FEEL FEEL
MAYBE IN A SECOND.
LOOK FOR ANYTHING UNUSUAL.
A CONCEALED BUTTON,
A TORCH THAT'S REALLY A LEVER,
EVEN JUST AN UNUSUAL STONE...
OH.

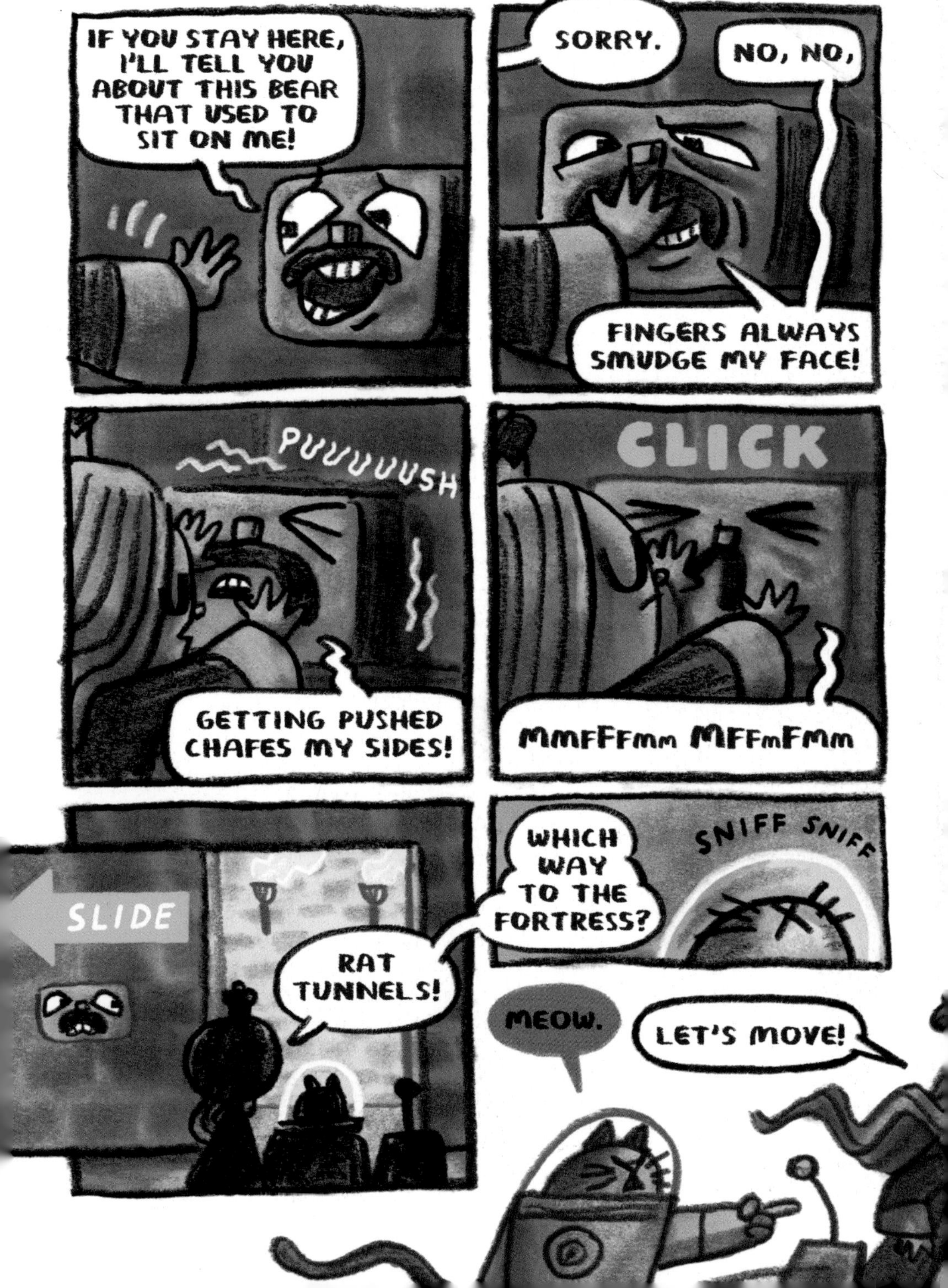
IF YOU STAY HERE, I'LL TELL YOU ABOUT THIS BEAR THAT USED TO SIT ON ME!
SORRY.
NO, NO,
FINGERS ALWAYS SMUDGE MY FACE!
PUUUUUUSH
GETTING PUSHED CHAFES MY SIDES!
CLICK
MMFFFMM MFFMFMM
SLIDE
RAT TUNNELS!
WHICH WAY TO THE FORTRESS?
SNIFF SNIFF
MEOW.
LET'S MOVE!

CHAPTER 20

FINAL COUNTDOWN

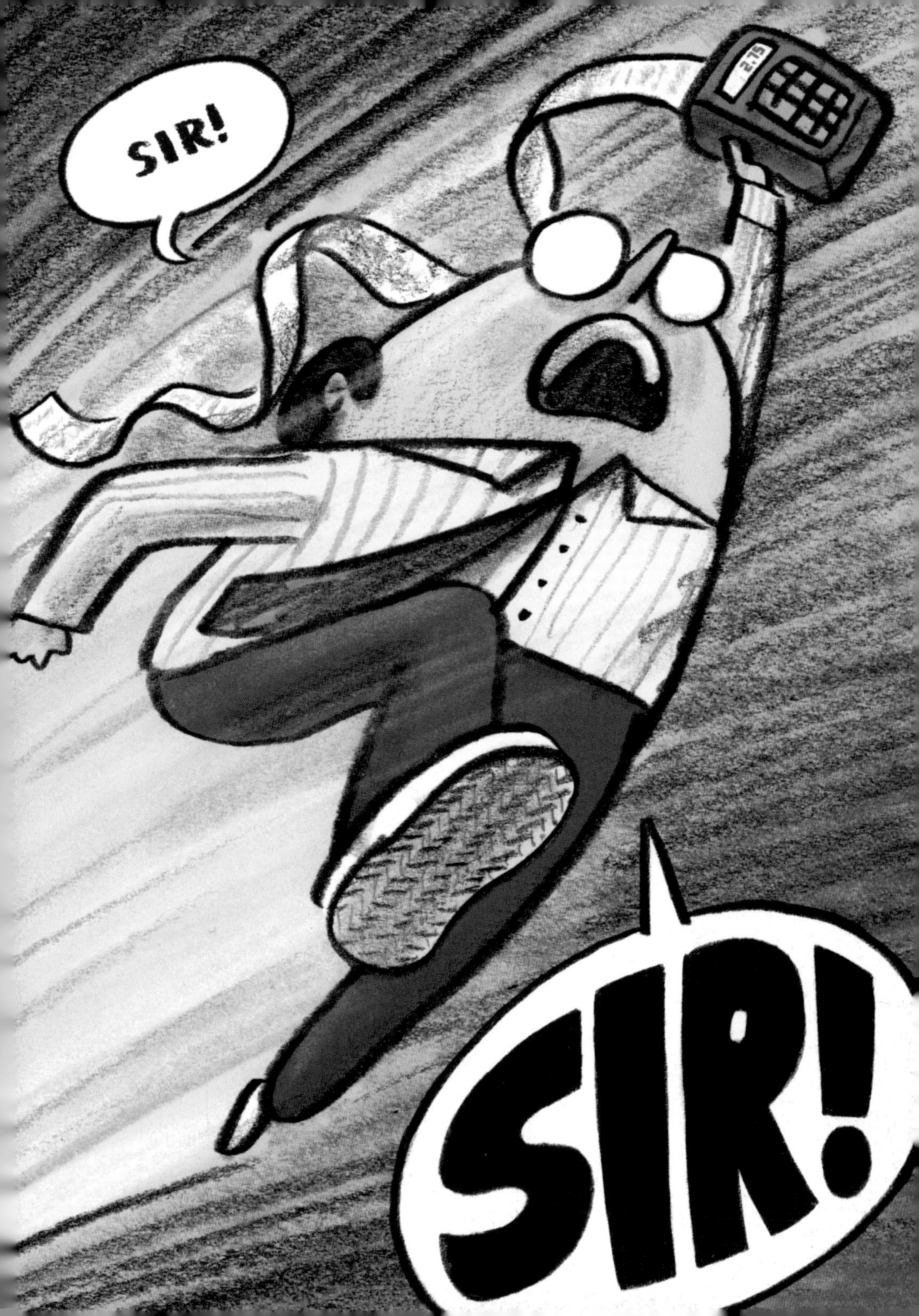
SIR!
SIR!

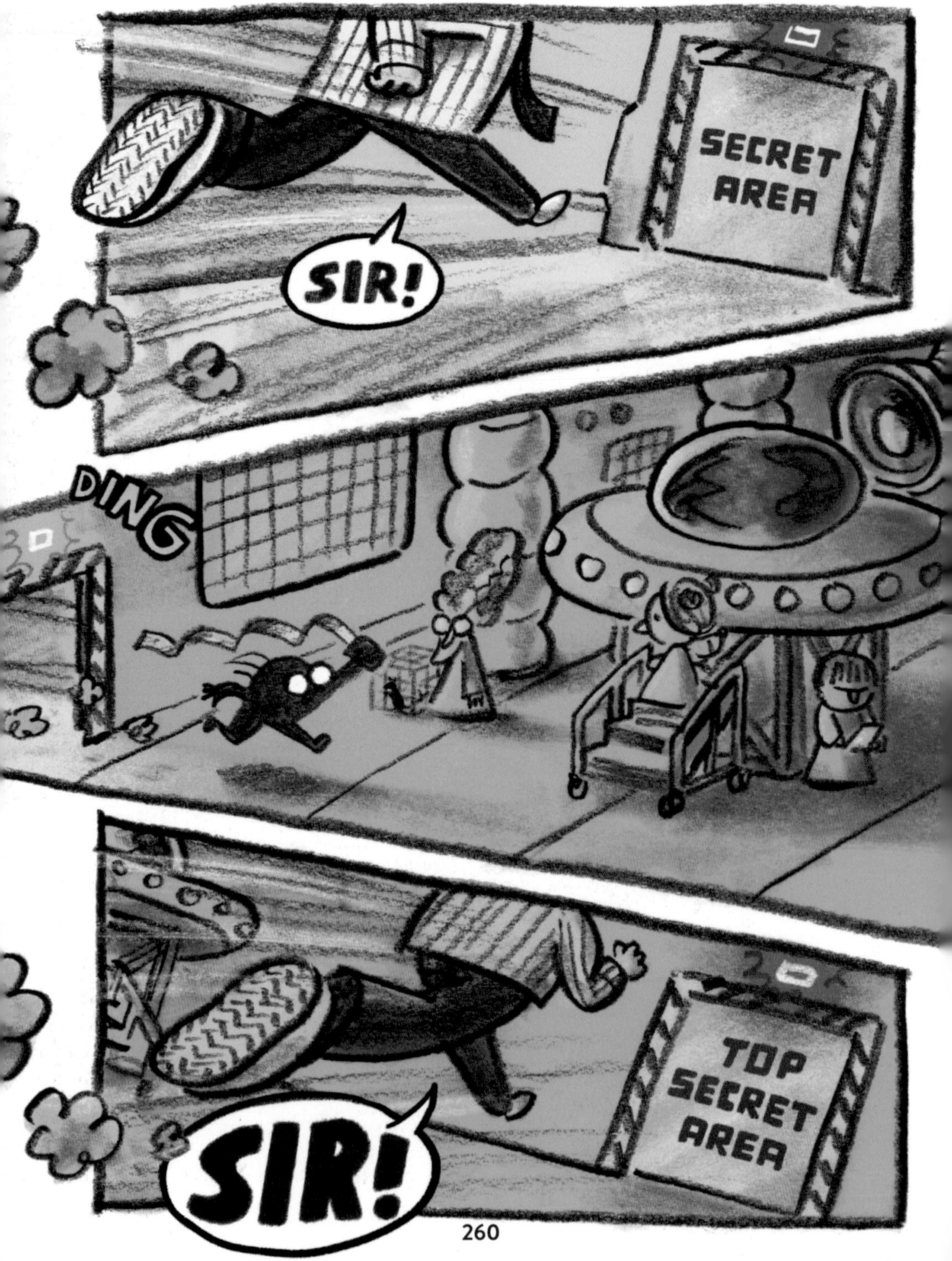
SIR!
SECRET AREA
DING
SIR!
TOP SECRET AREA

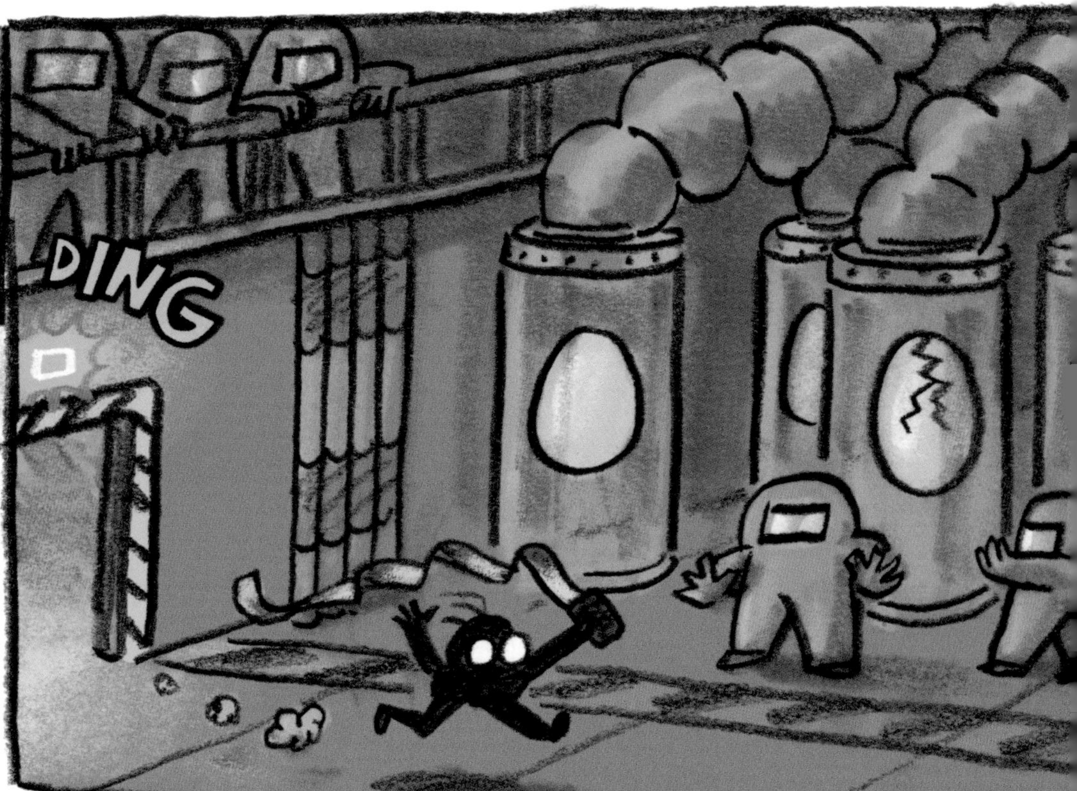
DING

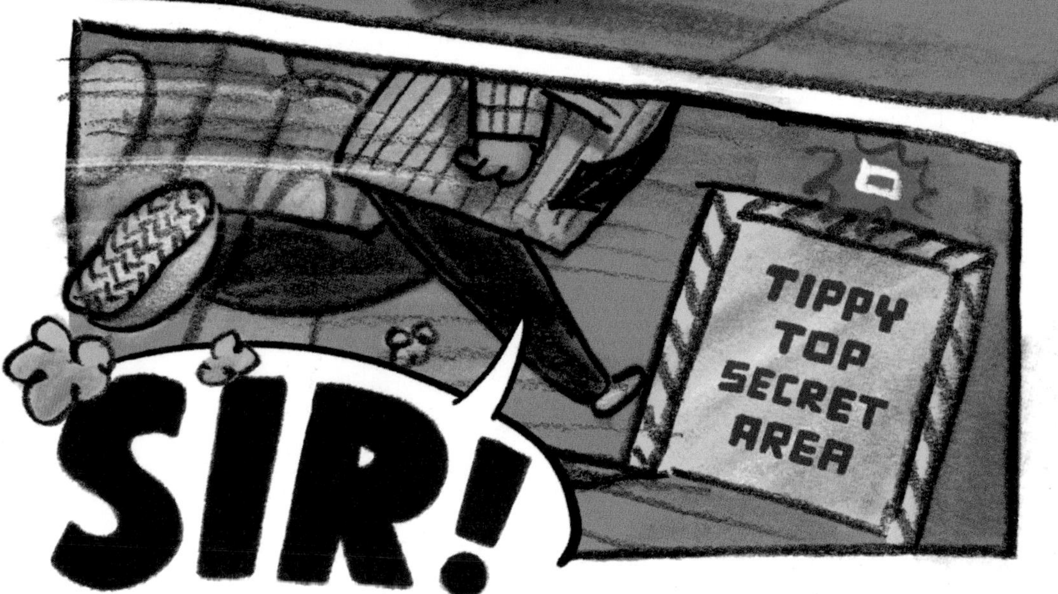
TIPPY TOP SECRET AREA
SIR!

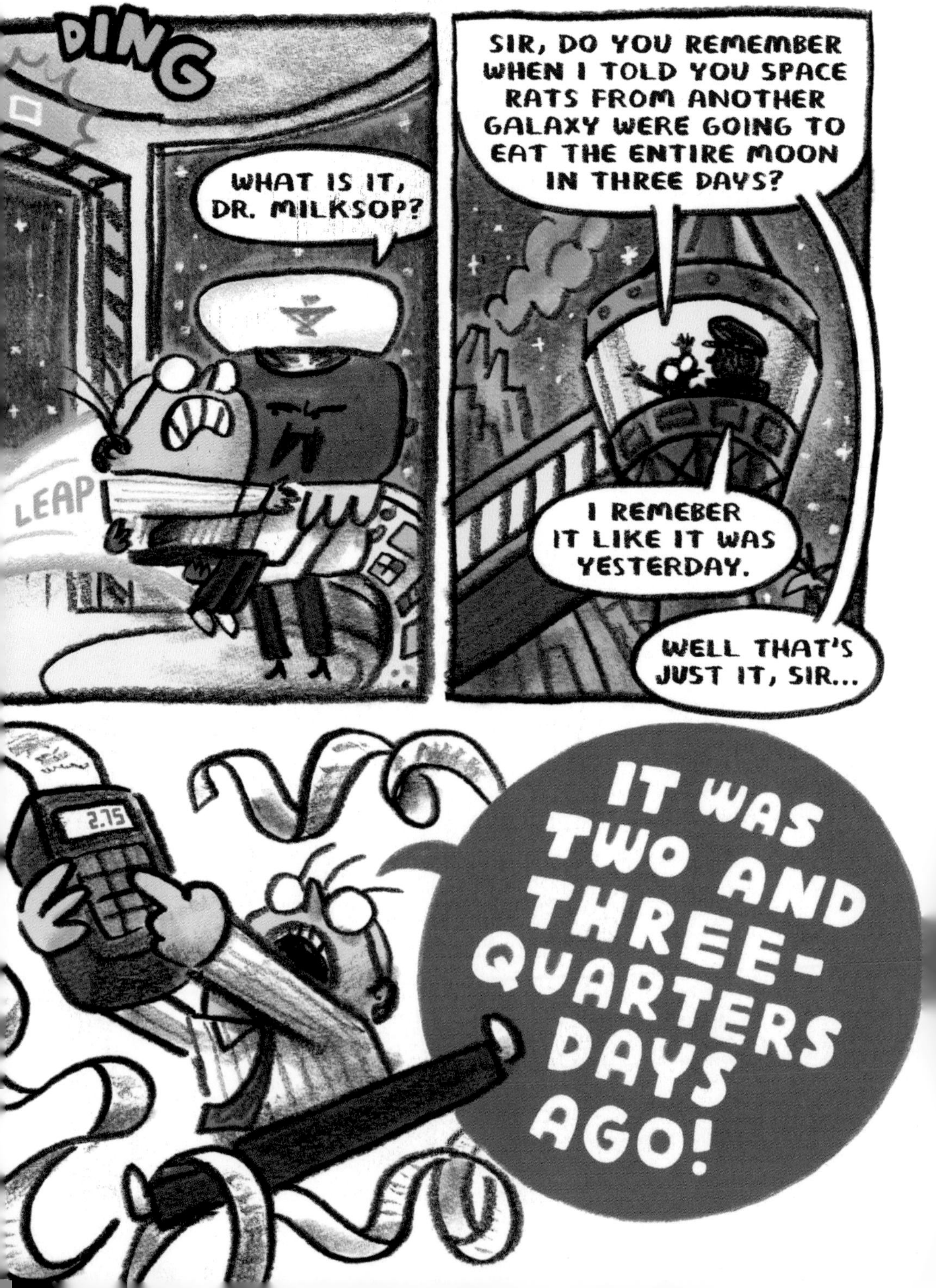

DING
WHAT IS IT, DR. MILKSOP?
LEAP
SIR, DO YOU REMEMBER WHEN I TOLD YOU SPACE RATS FROM ANOTHER GALAXY WERE GOING TO EAT THE ENTIRE MOON IN THREE DAYS?
I REMEBER IT LIKE IT WAS YESTERDAY.
WELL THAT'S JUST IT, SIR...
2.75
IT WAS TWO AND THREE-QUARTERS DAYS AGO!

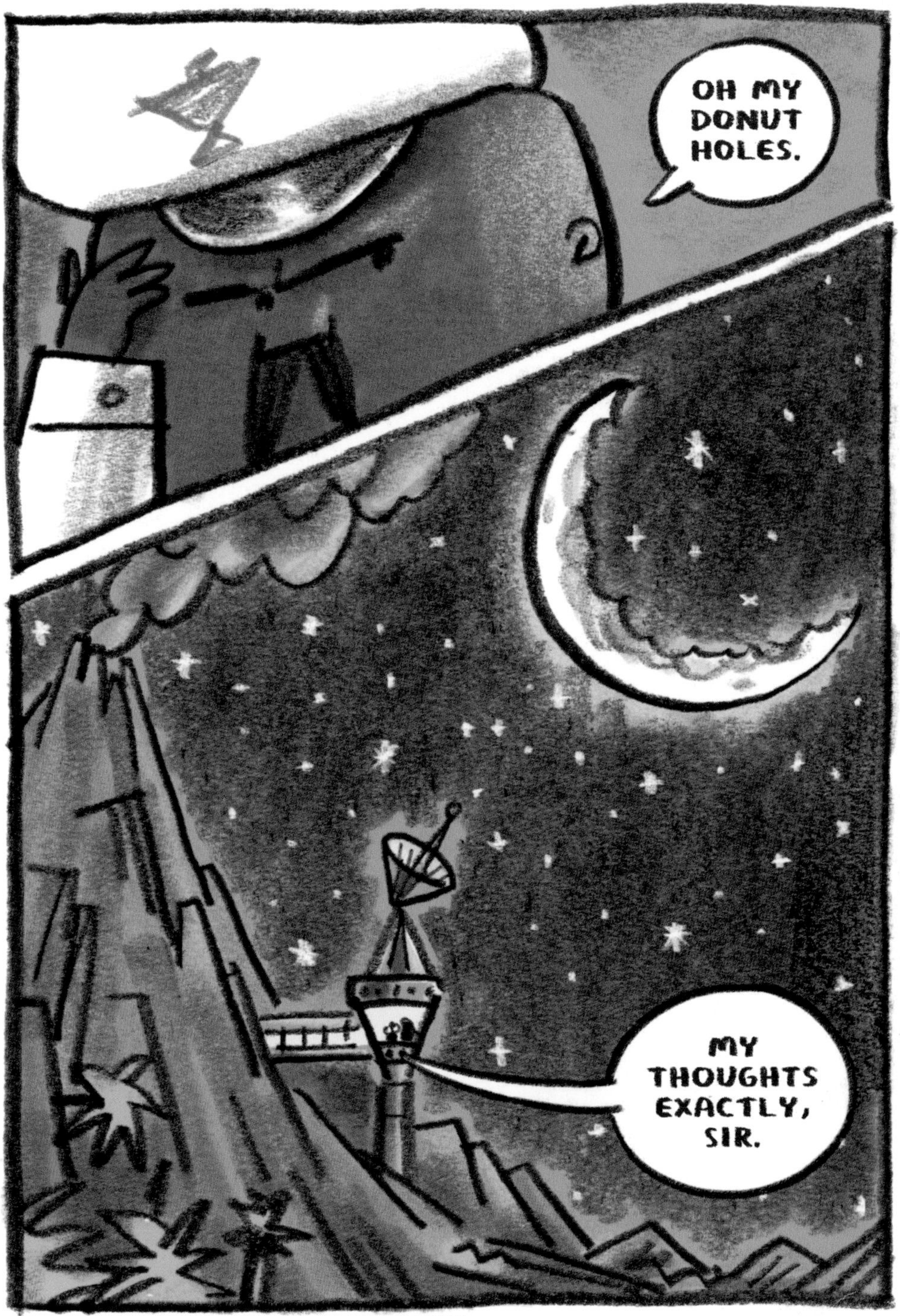
OH MY DONUT HOLES.
MY THOUGHTS EXACTLY, SIR.

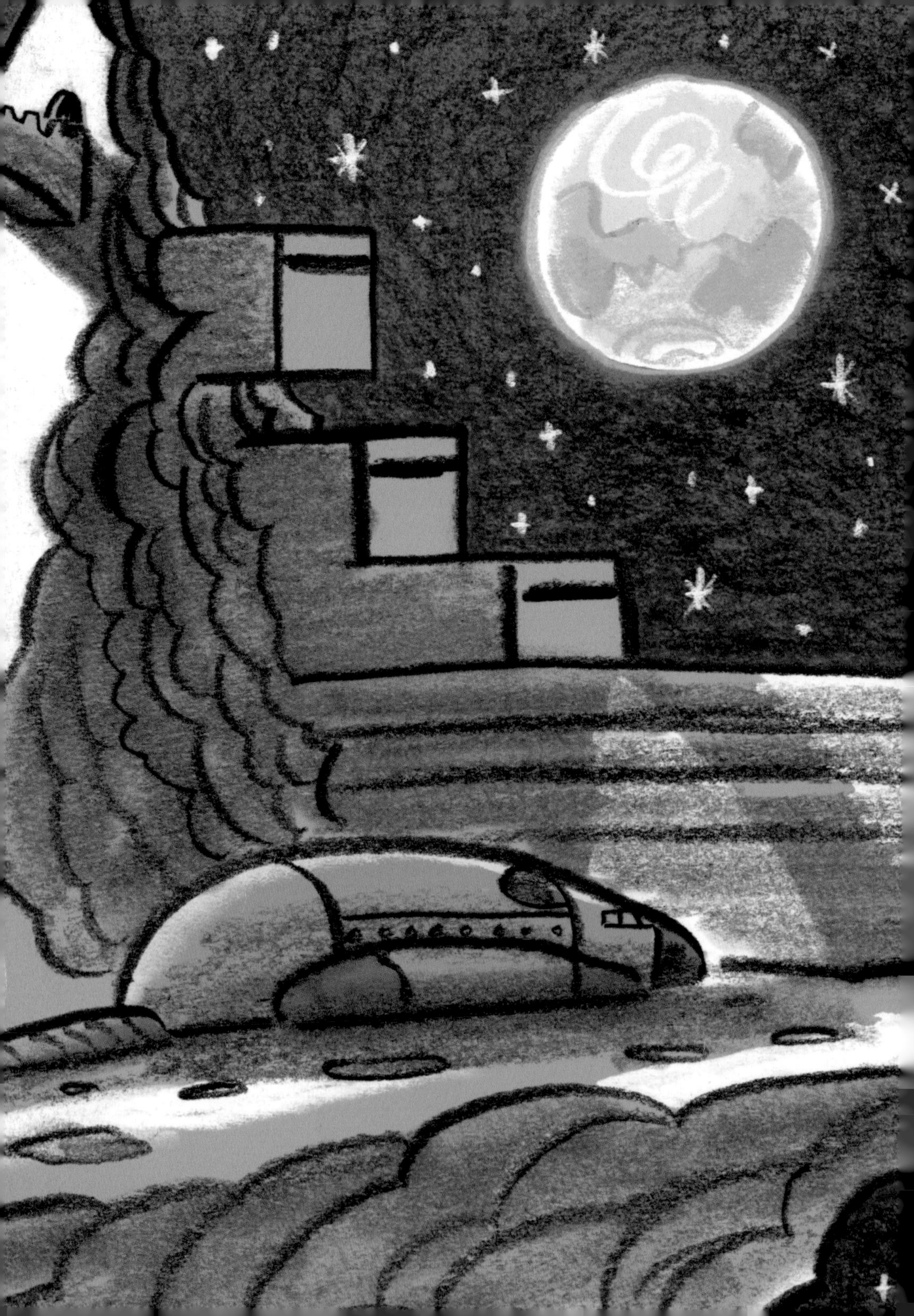

CHAPTER 21

THE RAT KING'S FORTRESS

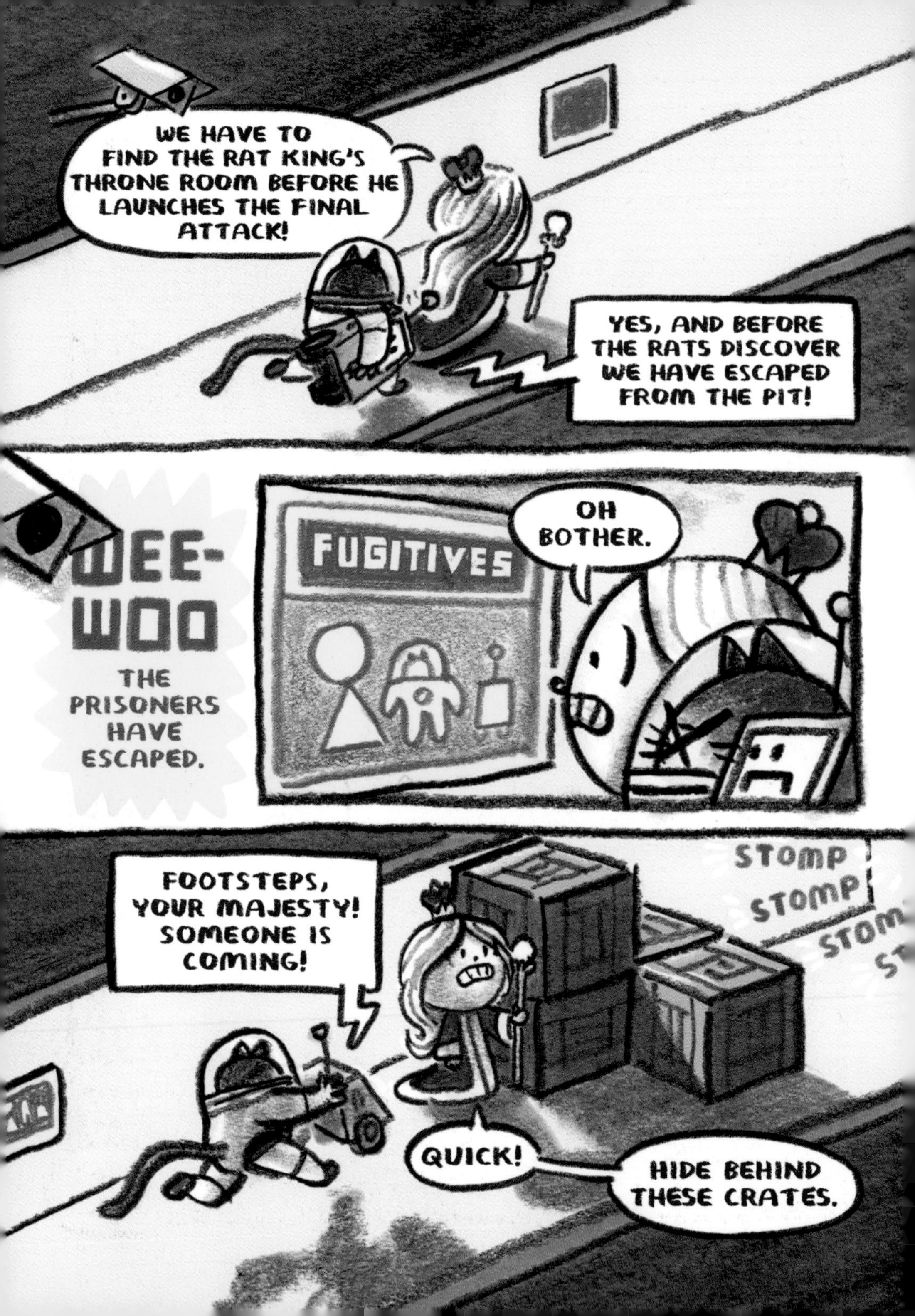
WE HAVE TO FIND THE RAT KING'S THRONE ROOM BEFORE HE LAUNCHES THE FINAL ATTACK!
YES, AND BEFORE THE RATS DISCOVER WE HAVE ESCAPED FROM THE PIT!
WEE-WOO
THE PRISONERS HAVE ESCAPED.
FUGITIVES
OH BOTHER.
FOOTSTEPS, YOUR MAJESTY! SOMEONE IS COMING!
STOMP
STOMP
QUICK!
HIDE BEHIND THESE CRATES.

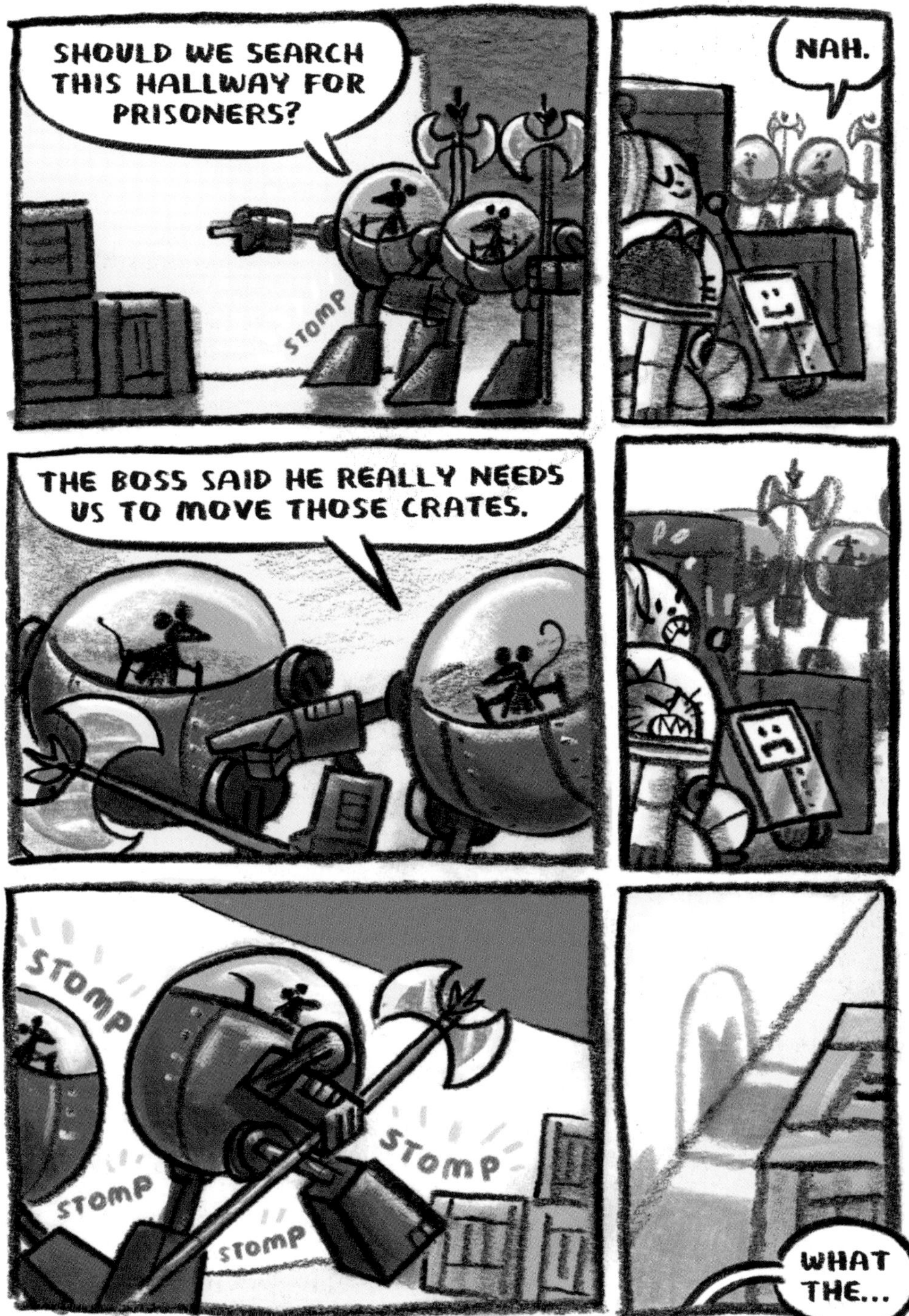
SHOULD WE SEARCH THIS HALLWAY FOR PRISONERS?
STOMP
NAH.
THE BOSS SAID HE REALLY NEEDS US TO MOVE THOSE CRATES.
STOMP
STOMP
STOMP
STOMP
WHAT THE...

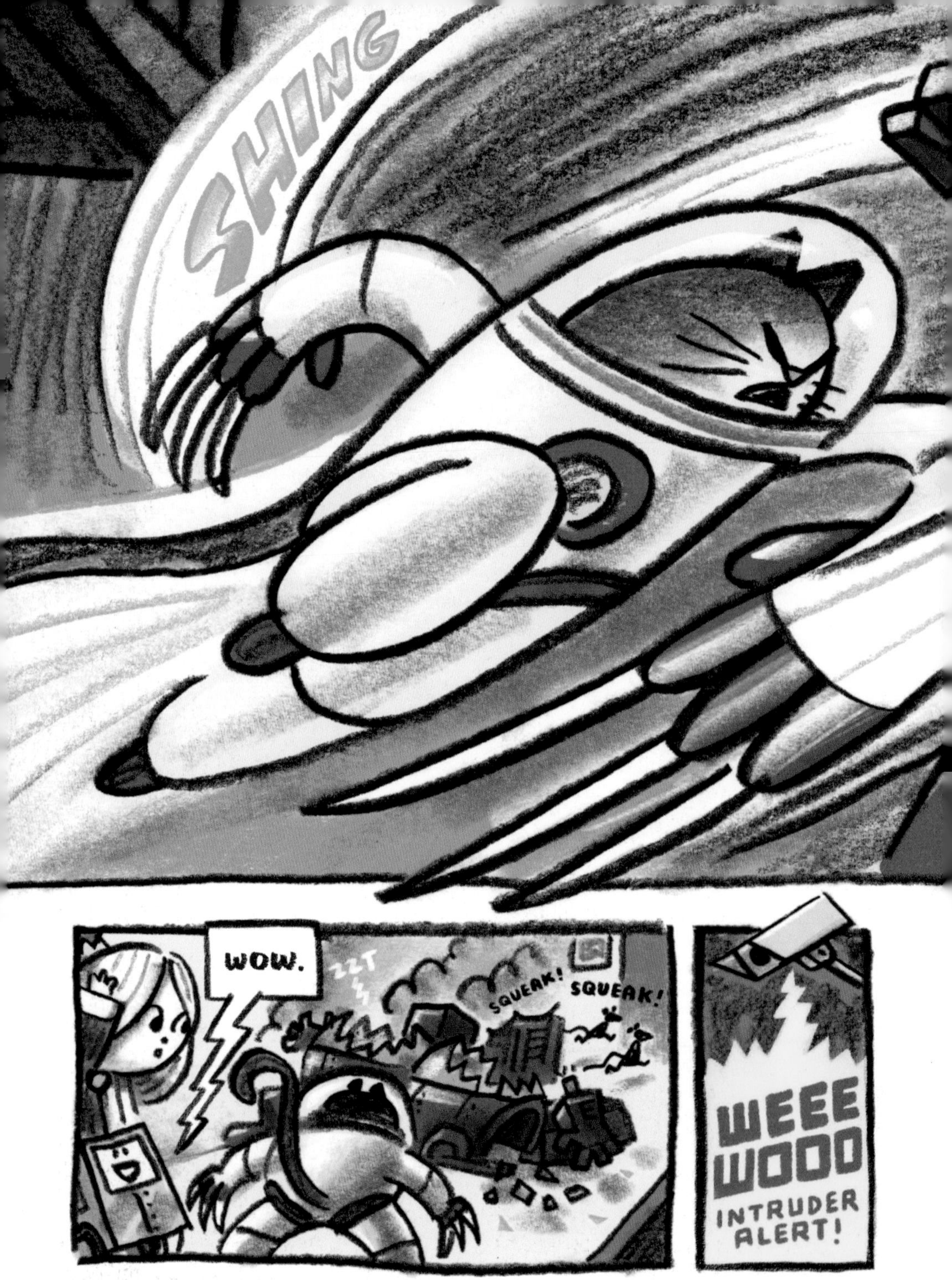
SHING
WOW.
ZZT
SQUEAK! SQUEAK!
WEEE
WOOO
INTRUDER ALERT!

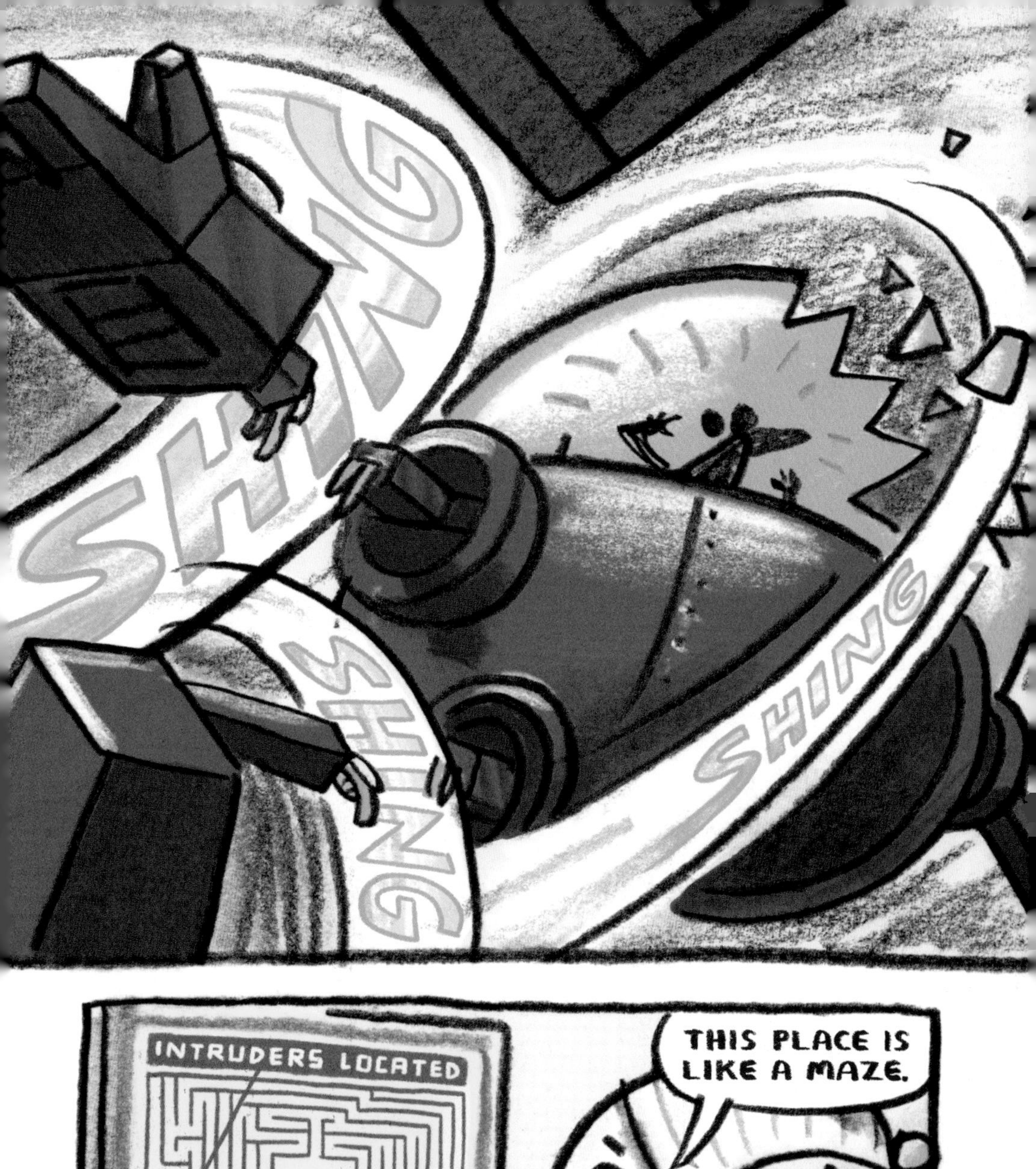
SHING
SHING
SHING

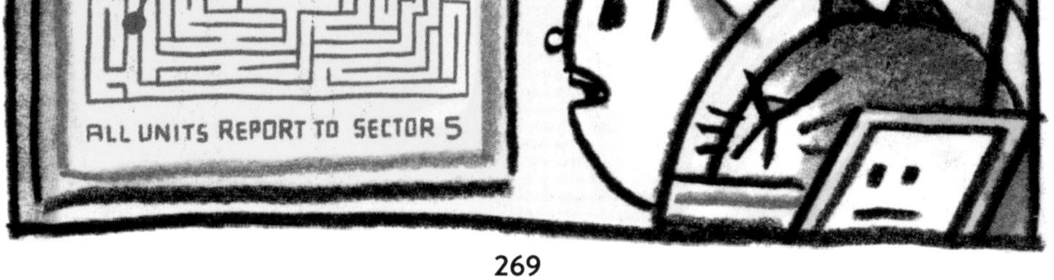
INTRUDERS LOCATED
ALL UNITS REPORT TO SECTOR 5
THIS PLACE IS LIKE A MAZE.

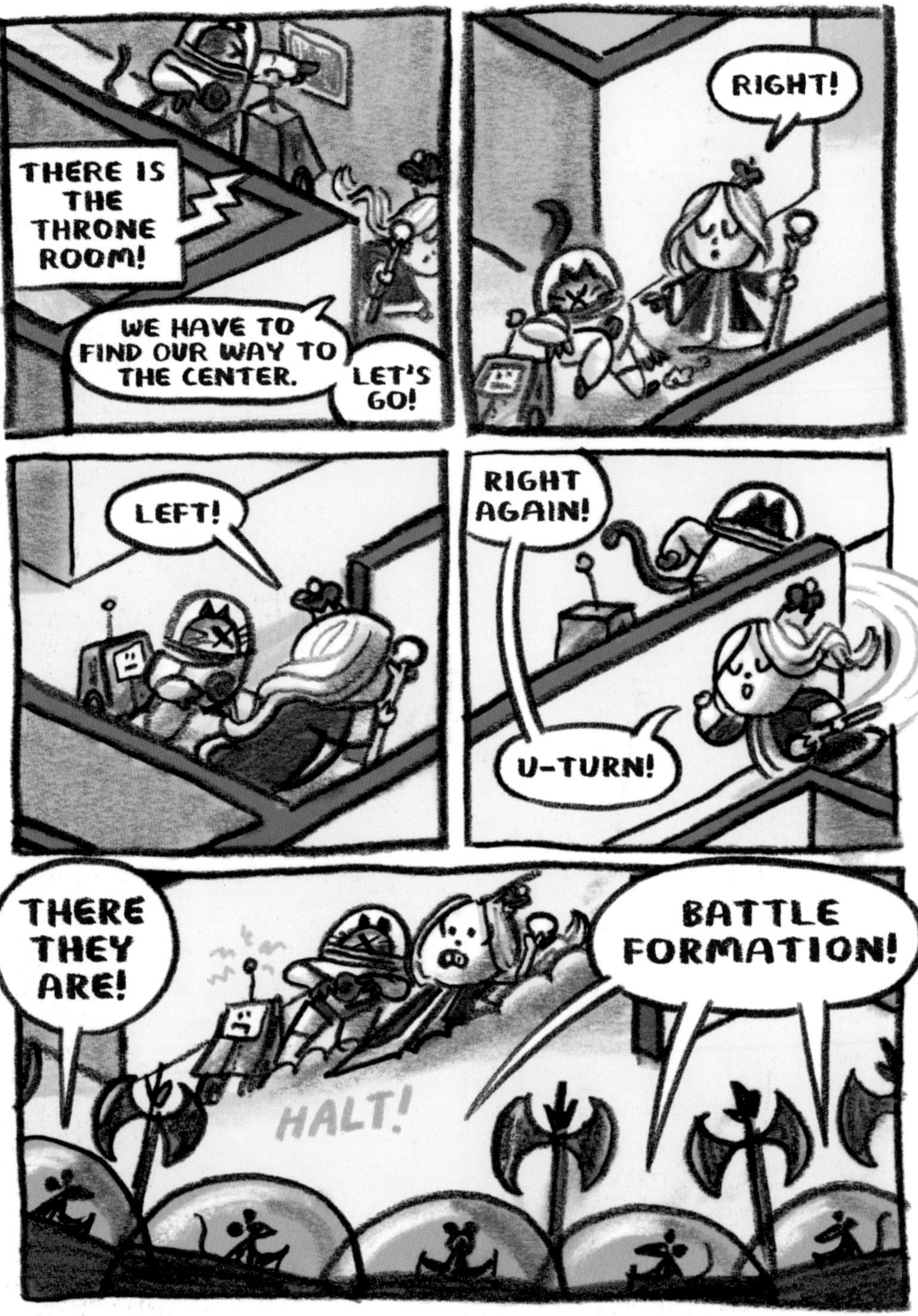
THERE IS THE THRONE ROOM!
WE HAVE TO FIND OUR WAY TO THE CENTER.
LET'S GO!
RIGHT!
LEFT!
RIGHT AGAIN!
U-TURN!
THERE THEY ARE!
BATTLE FORMATION!
HALT!

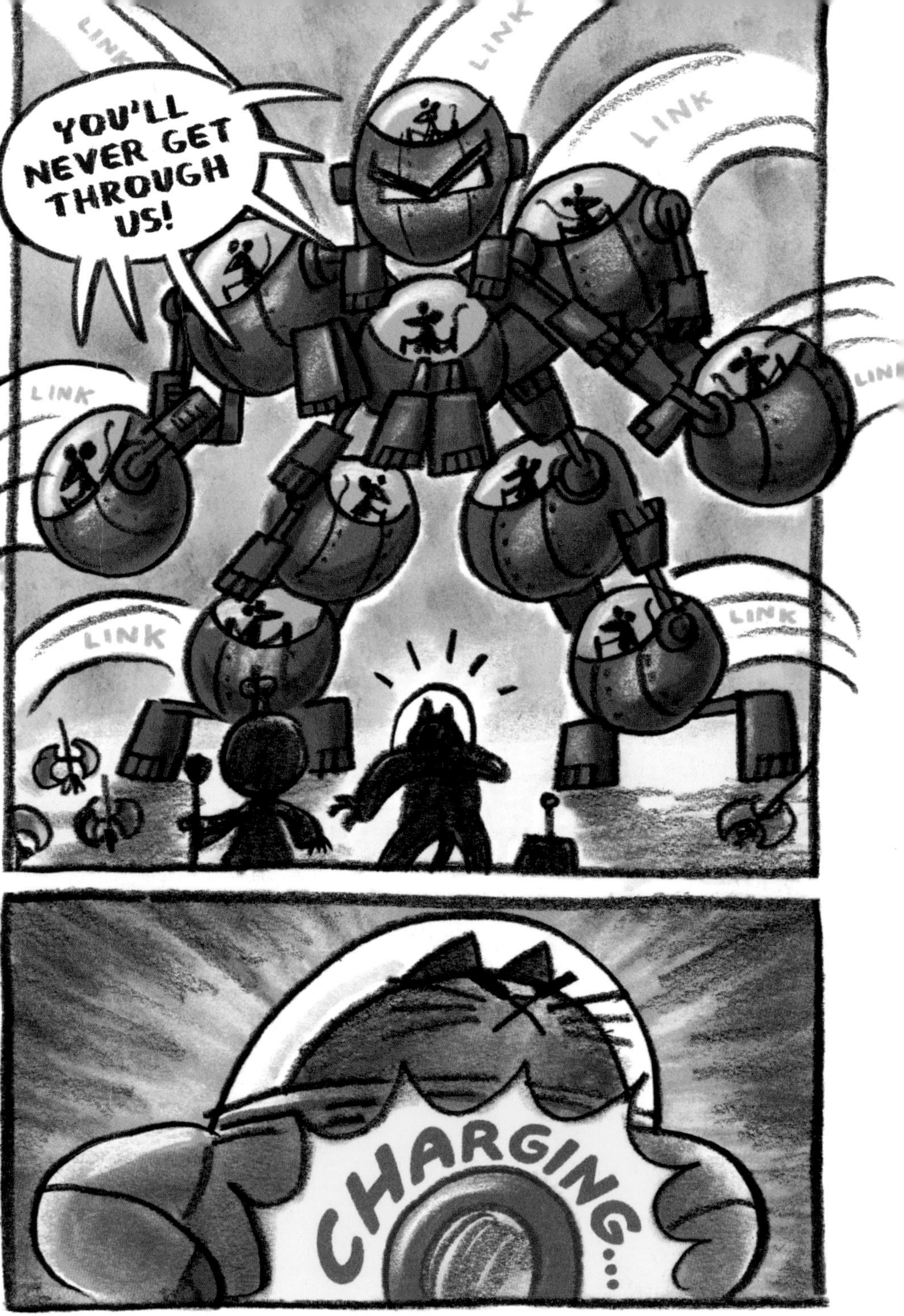
LINK
LINK
LINK
YOU'LL NEVER GET THROUGH US!
LINK
LINK
LINK
LINK
CHARGING...

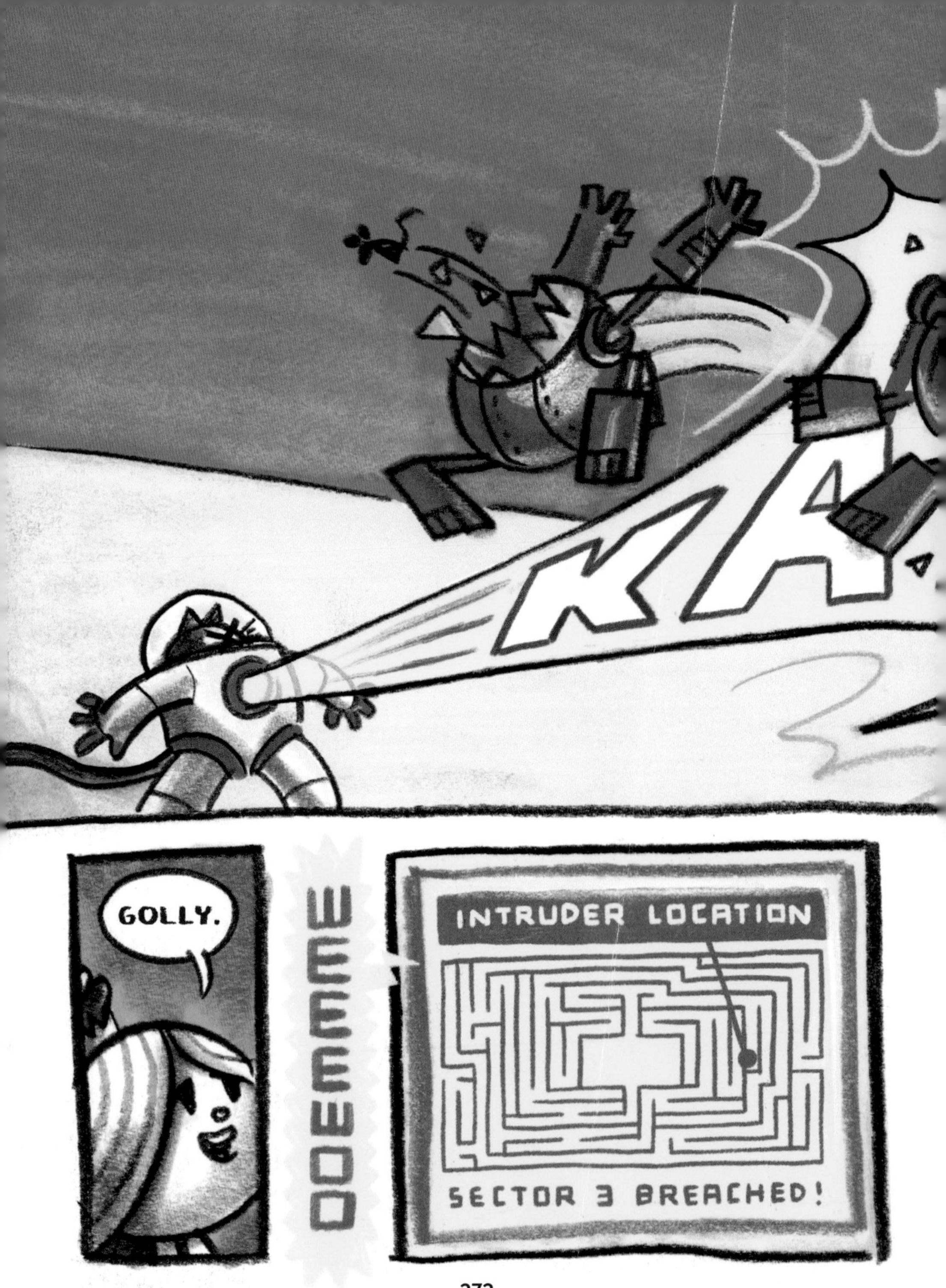
KA
GOLLY.
OOEEEEEE
INTRUDER LOCATION
SECTOR 3 BREACHED!

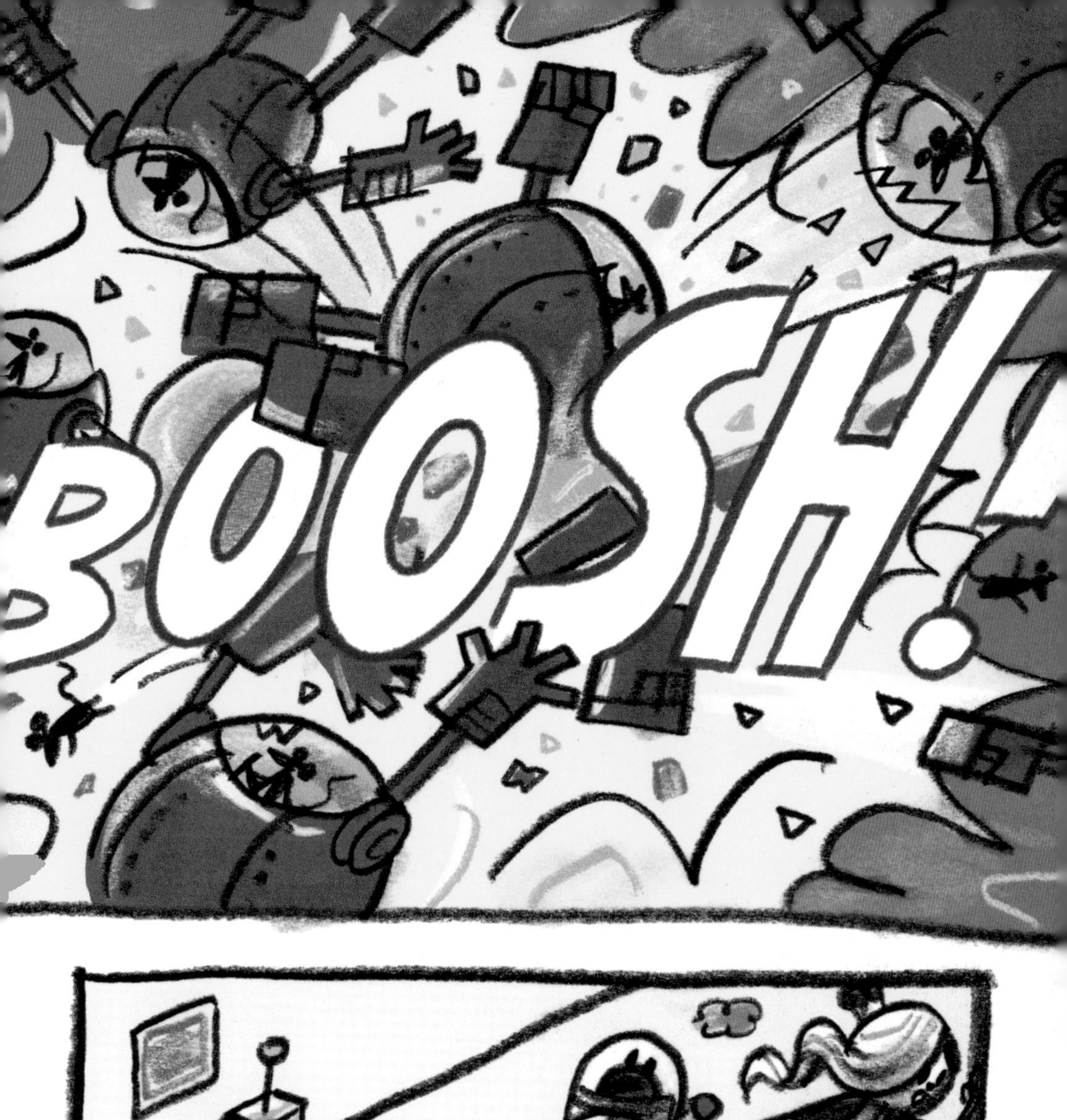
BOOSH!!

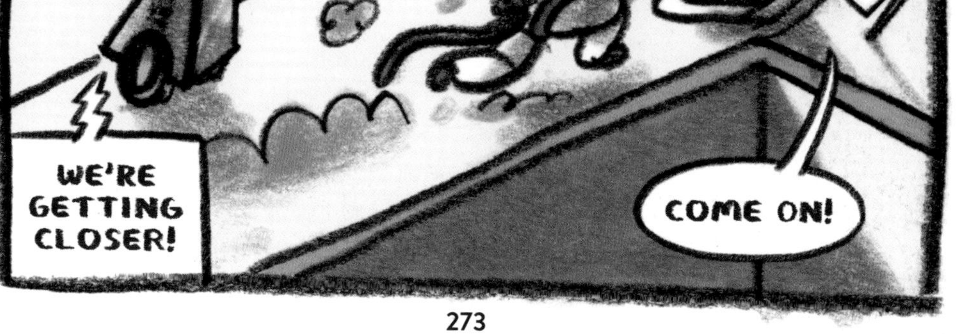
WE'RE GETTING CLOSER!
COME ON!

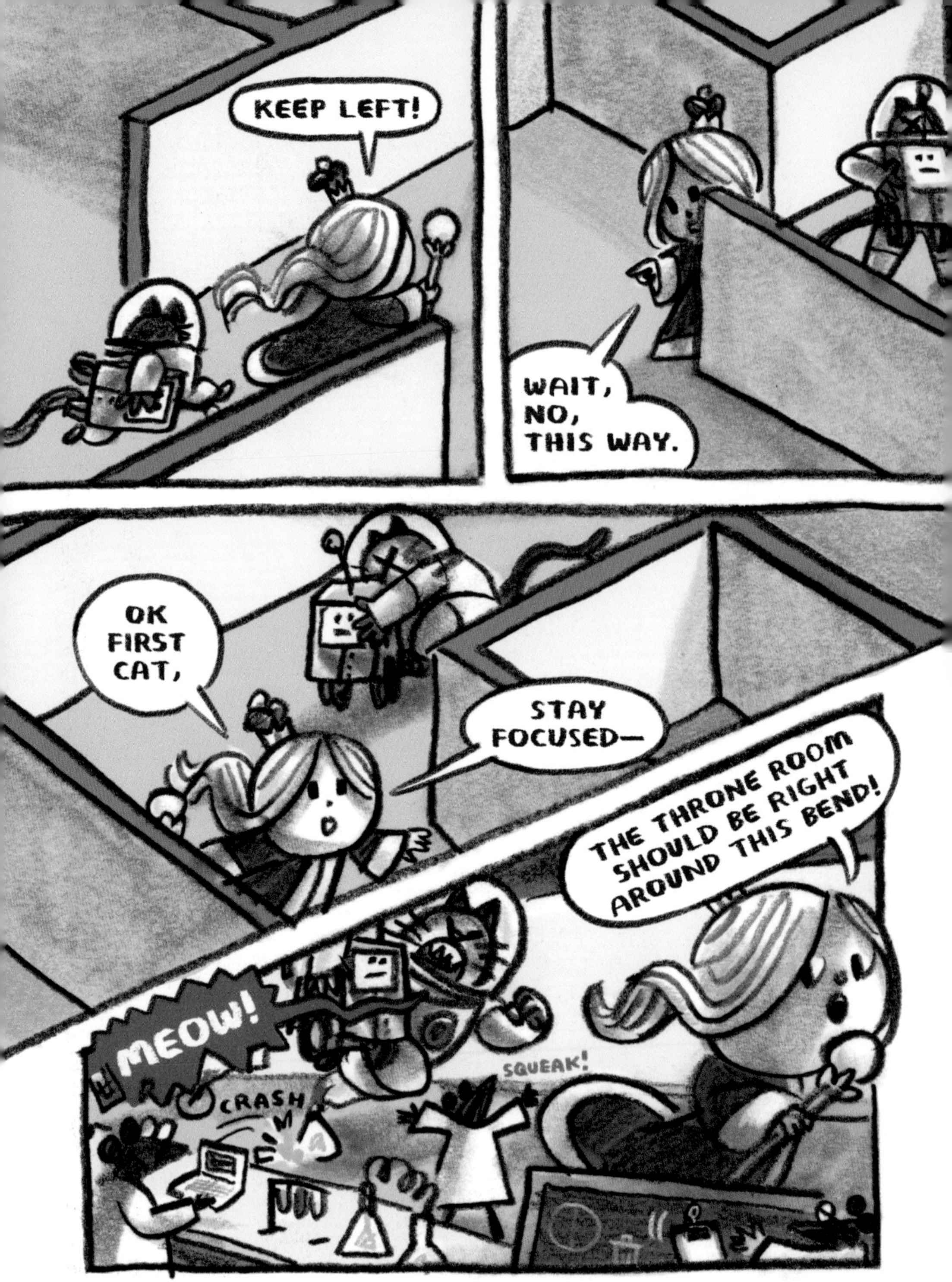
KEEP LEFT!
WAIT, NO, THIS WAY.
OK FIRST CAT,
STAY FOCUSED—
THE THRONE ROOM SHOULD BE RIGHT AROUND THIS BEND!
MEOW!
SQUEAK!
CRASH

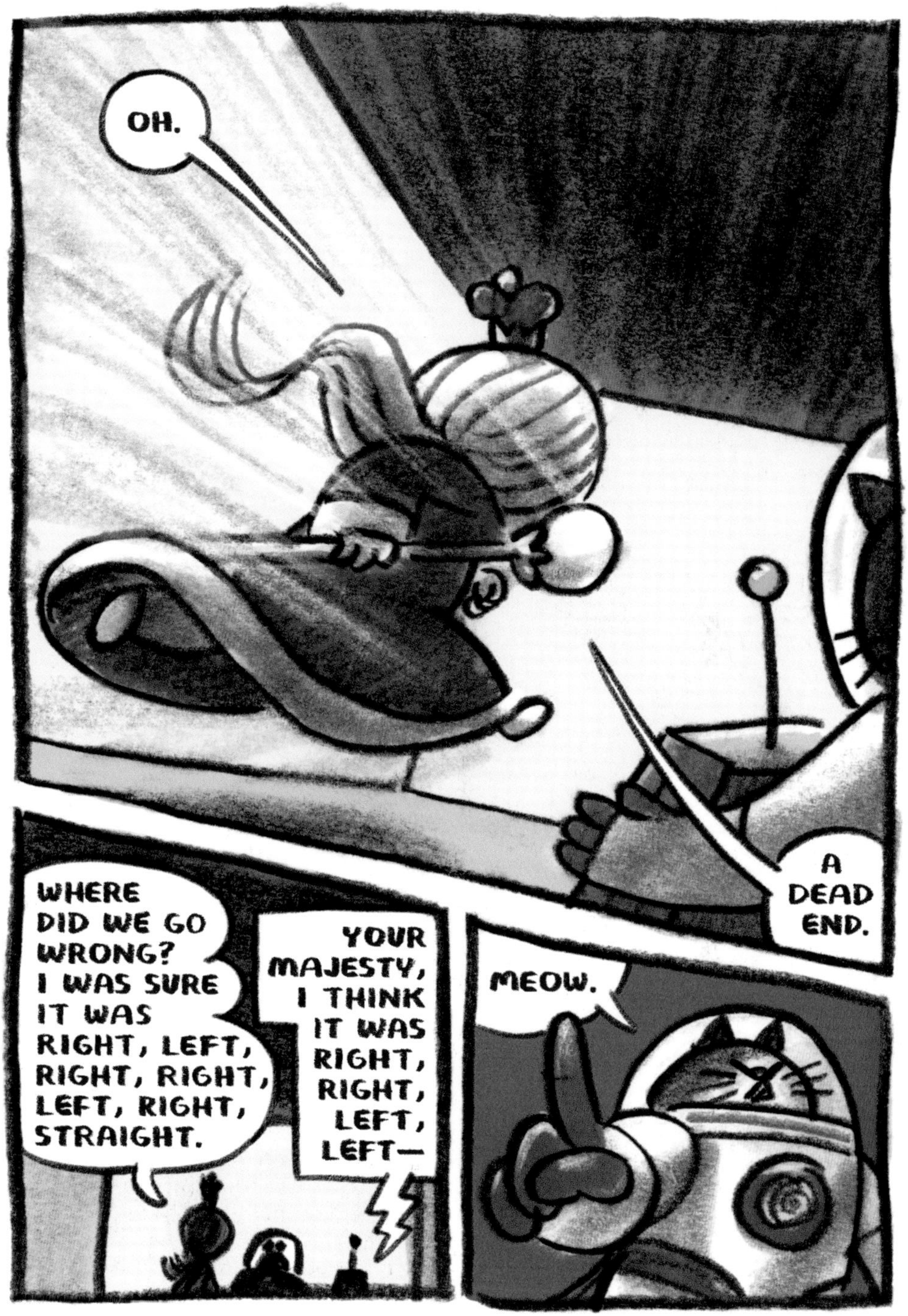
OH.
A DEAD END.
WHERE DID WE GO WRONG? I WAS SURE IT WAS RIGHT, LEFT, RIGHT, RIGHT, LEFT, RIGHT, STRAIGHT.
YOUR MAJESTY, I THINK IT WAS RIGHT, RIGHT, LEFT, LEFT—
MEOW.

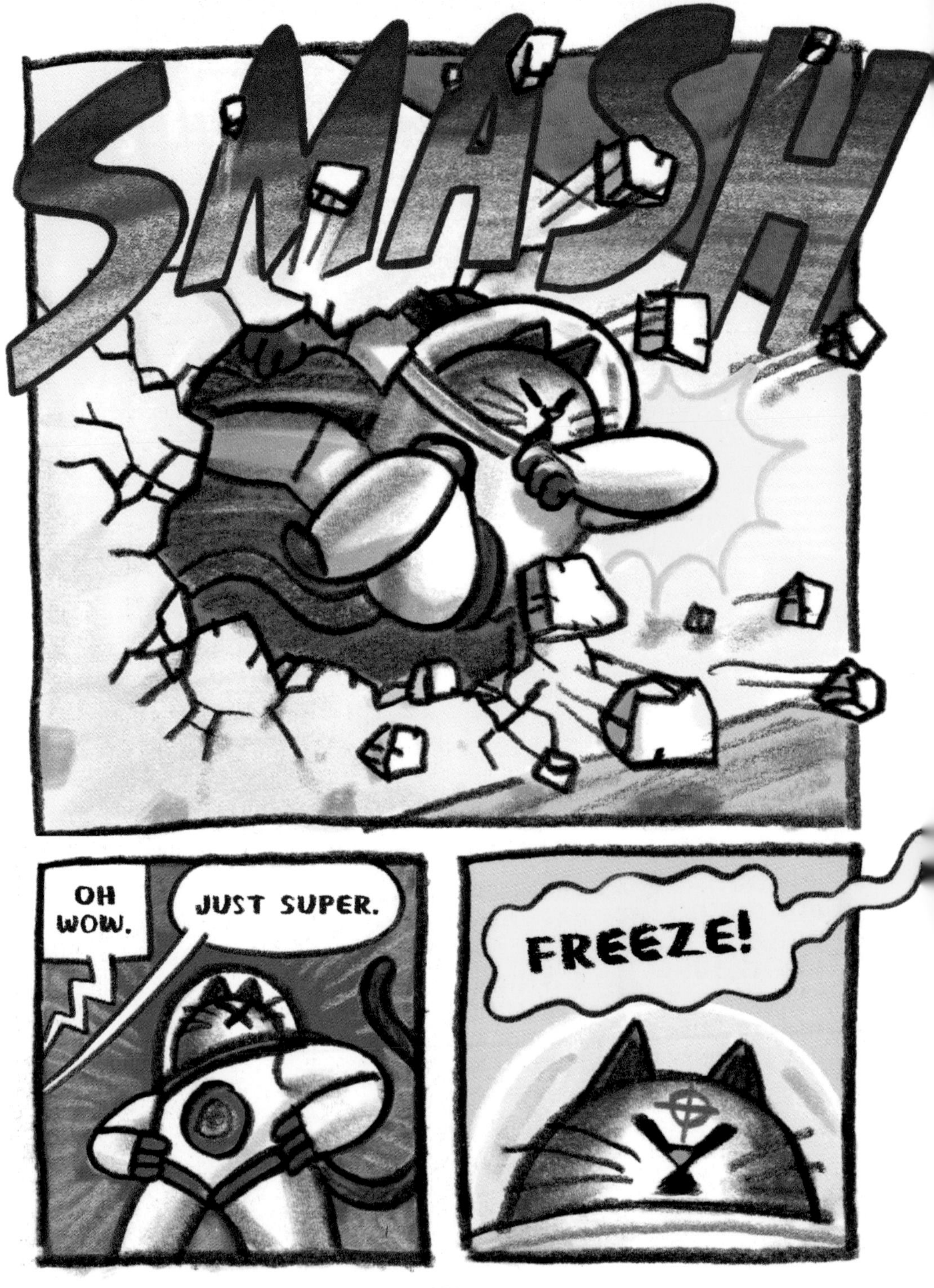
SMASH
OH WOW.
JUST SUPER.
FREEZE!

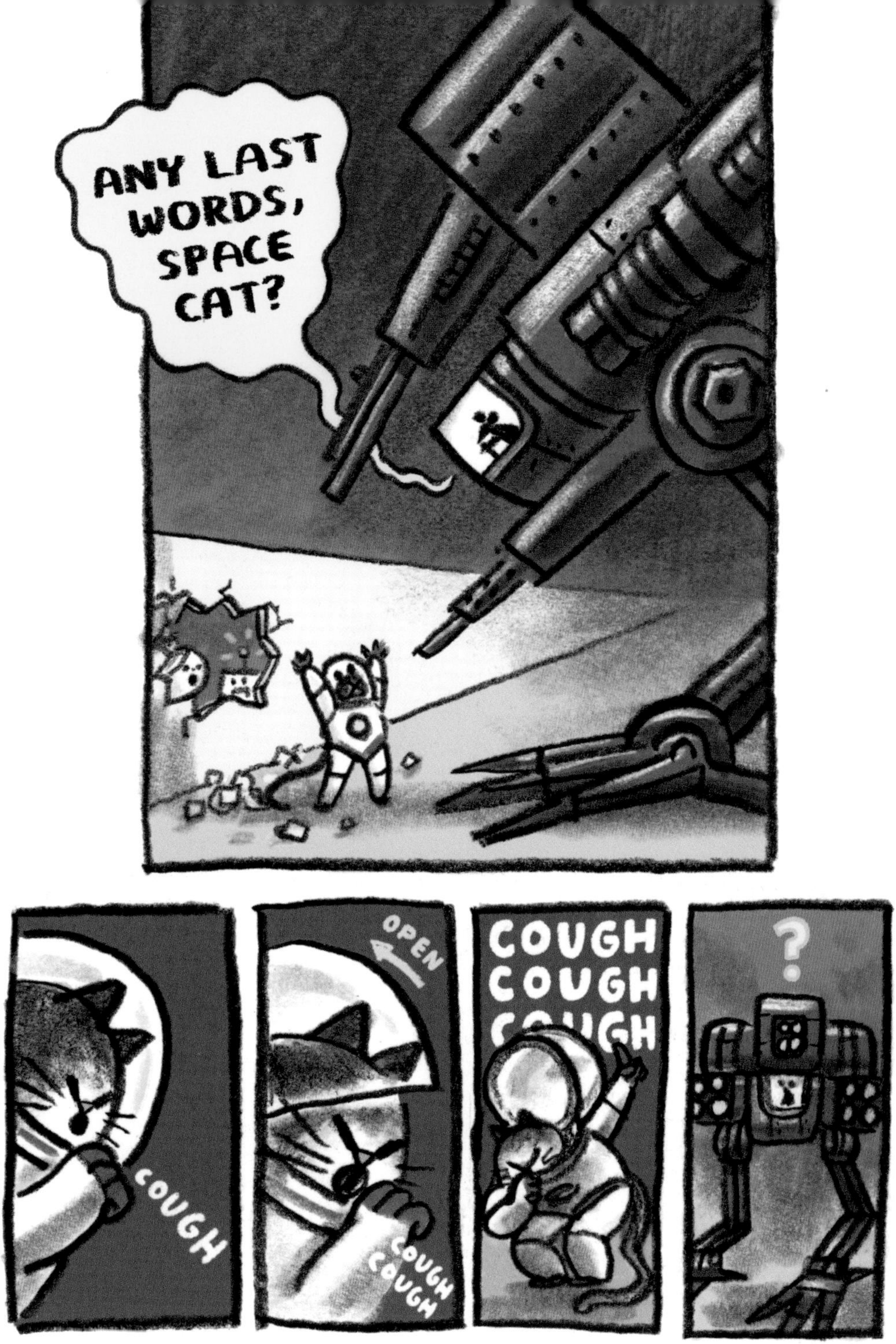
ANY LAST WORDS, SPACE CAT?
COUGH
OPEN
COUGH COUGH
COUGH
COUGH
?

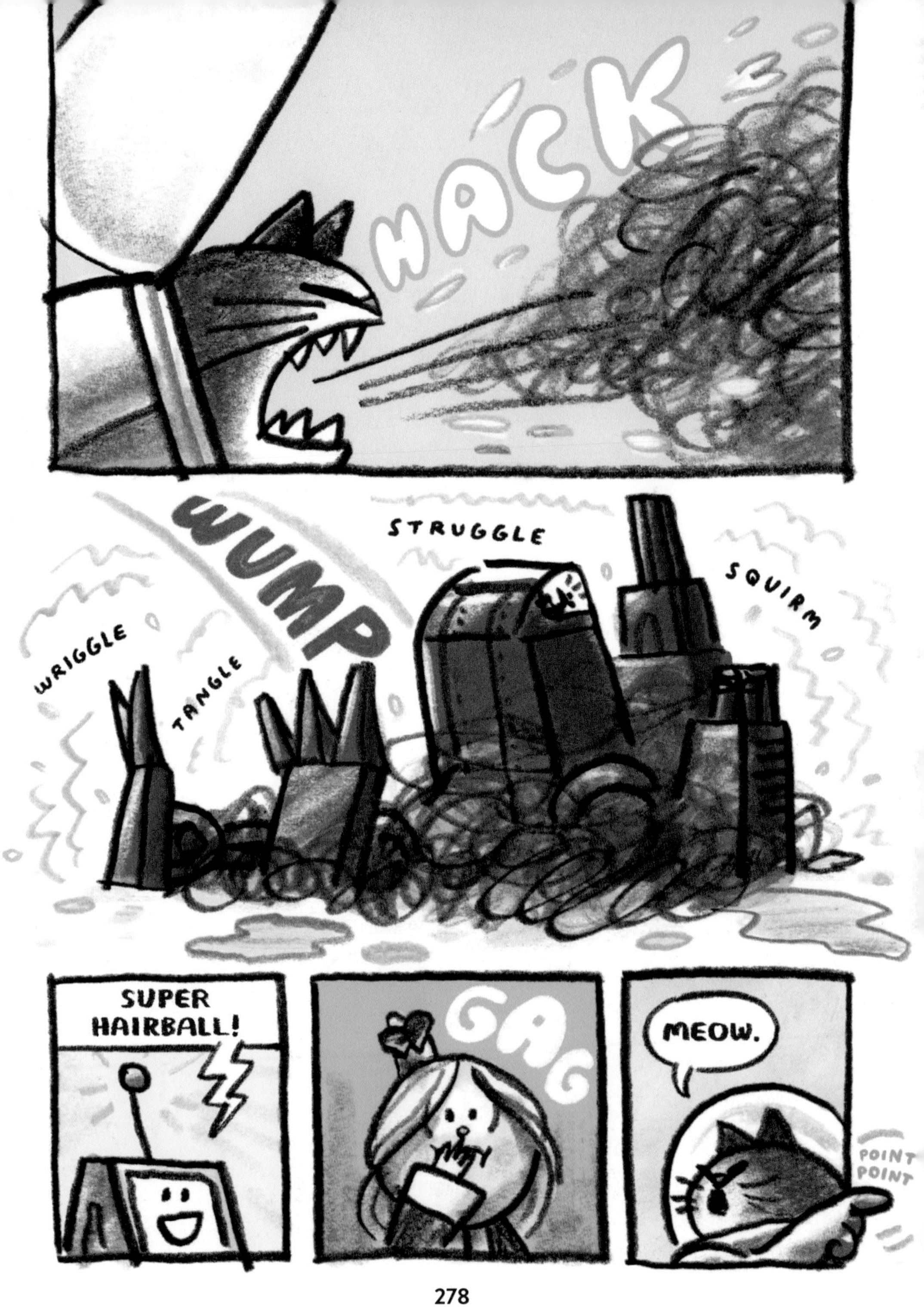
HACK
WUMP
STRUGGLE
SQUIRM
WRIGGLE
TANGLE
SUPER HAIRBALL!
GAG
MEOW.
POINT POINT

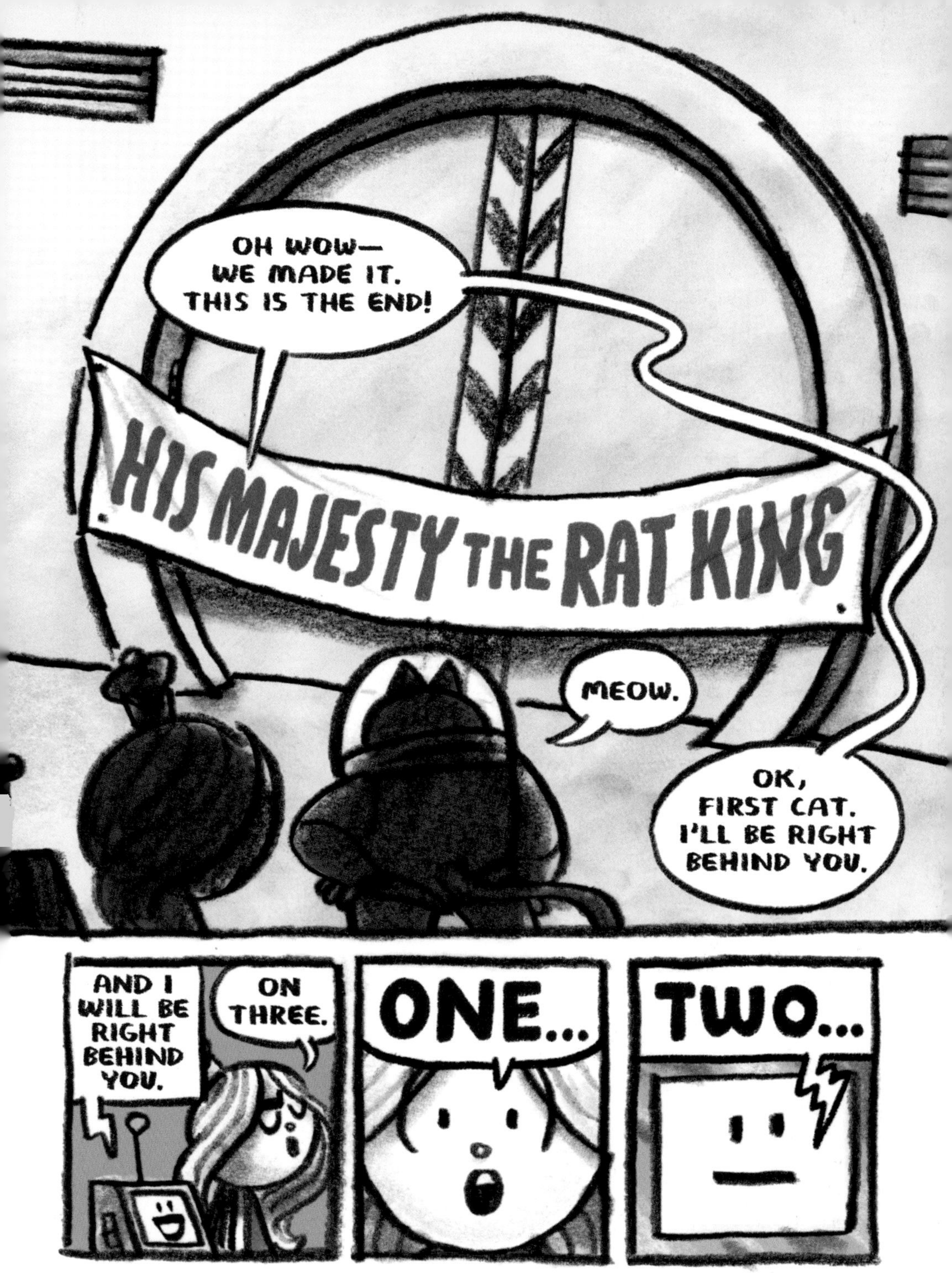
OH WOW— WE MADE IT. THIS IS THE END!
HIS MAJESTY THE RAT KING
MEOW.
OK, FIRST CAT. I'LL BE RIGHT BEHIND YOU.
AND I WILL BE RIGHT BEHIND YOU.
ON THREE.
ONE...
TWO...

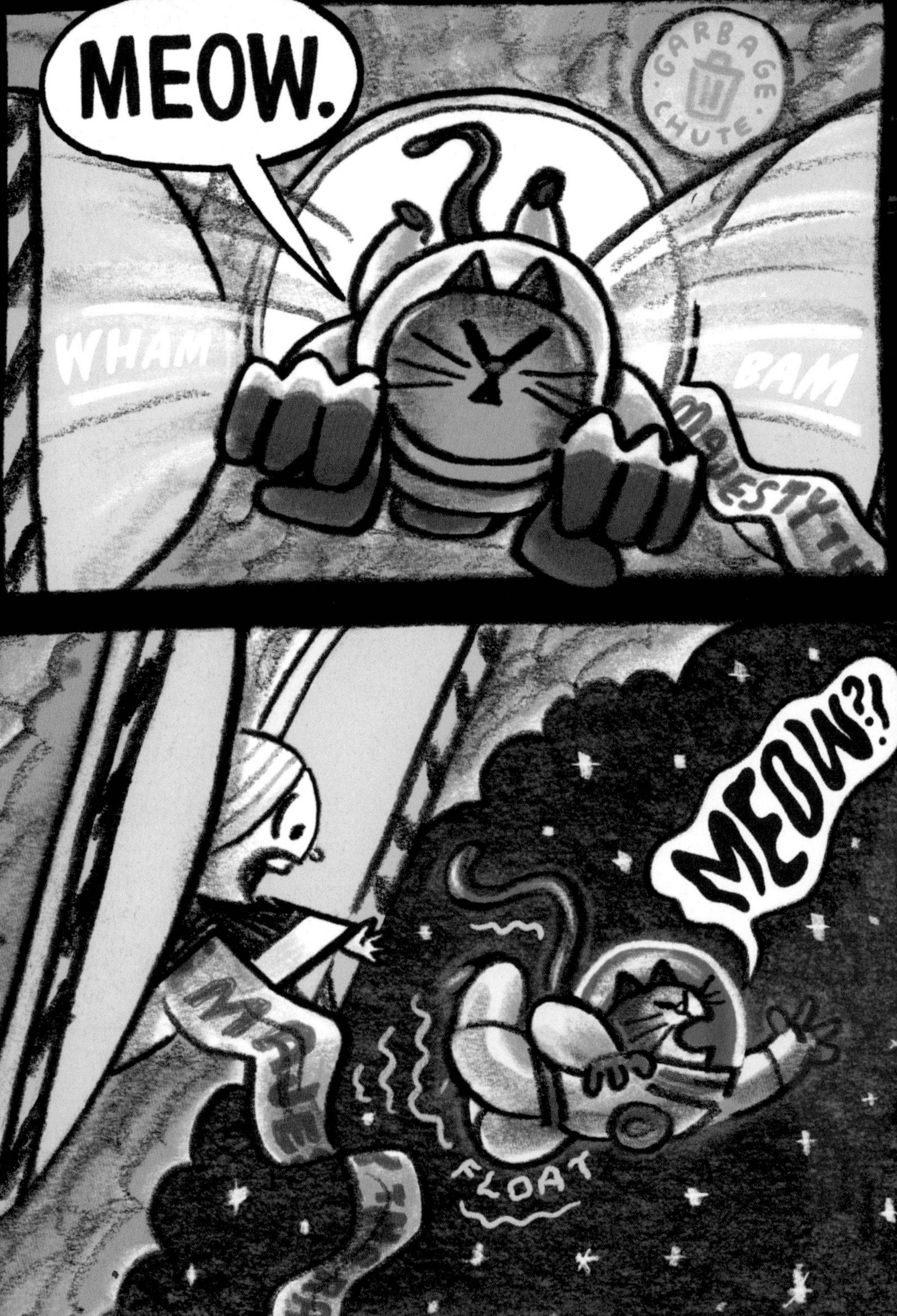
MEOW.
GARBAGE CHUTE
WHAM
BAM
MEOW?!
FLOAT

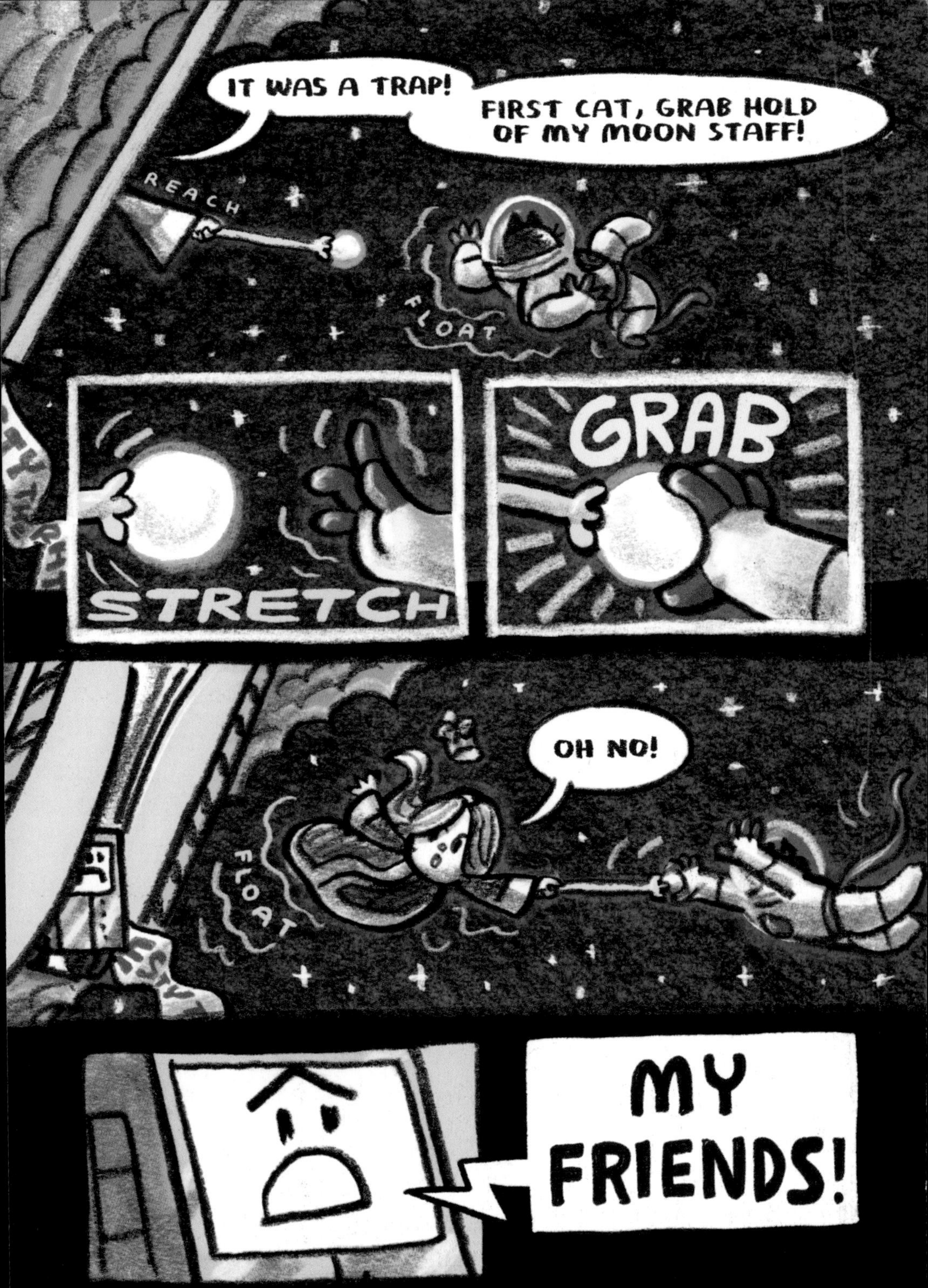
IT WAS A TRAP!
FIRST CAT, GRAB HOLD OF MY MOON STAFF!
REACH
FLOAT
STRETCH
GRAB
OH NO!
FLOAT
MY FRIENDS!

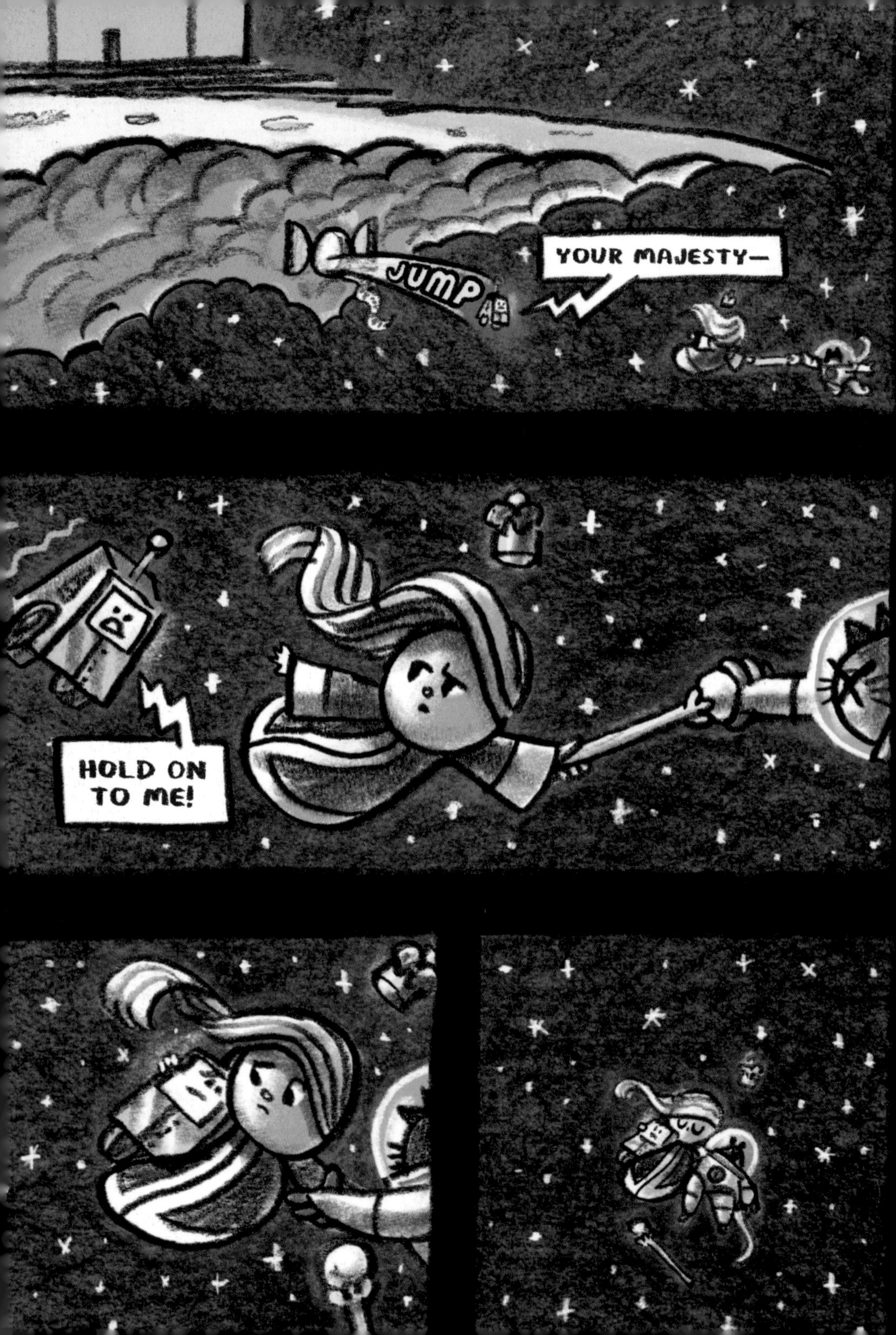
JUMP
YOUR MAJESTY—
HOLD ON TO ME!

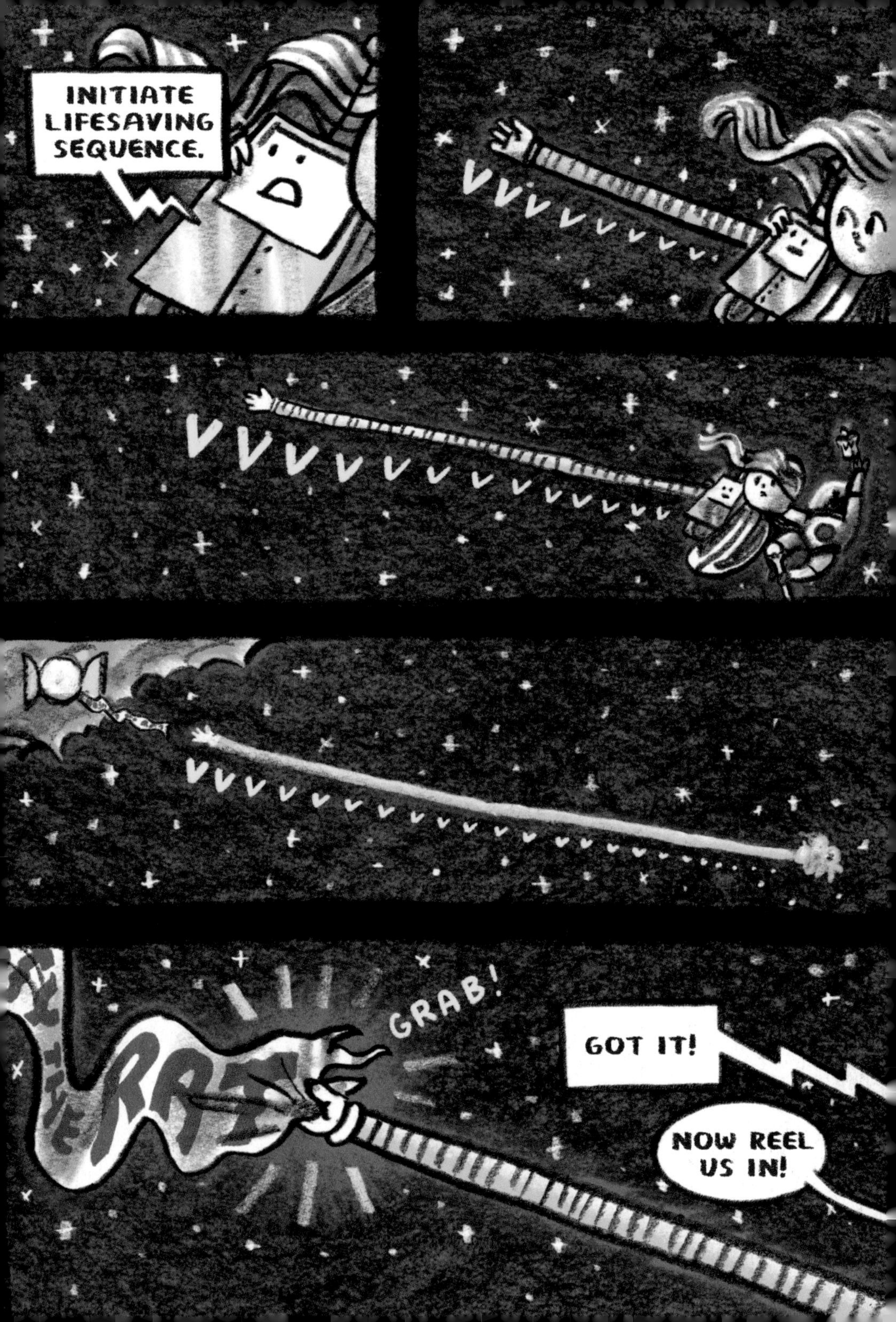
INITIATE LIFESAVING SEQUENCE.
GRAB!
GOT IT!
NOW REEL US IN!

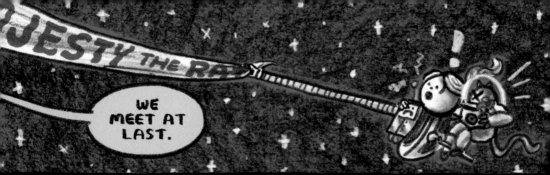

JESTY THE RAT

WE MEET AT LAST.

HI! BYE! ~HICCUP~

AND YET, THIS IS ALSO FAREWELL.

WHAT DID YOU THINK YOU WOULD FIND AT THE END OF THE RATS' MAZE? VICTORY?

A BIT OF CHEESE?

VICTORY?

I SAID THAT.

OH. WHAT WAS I SUPPOSED TO SAY?

NOTHING.

OH, RIGHT!

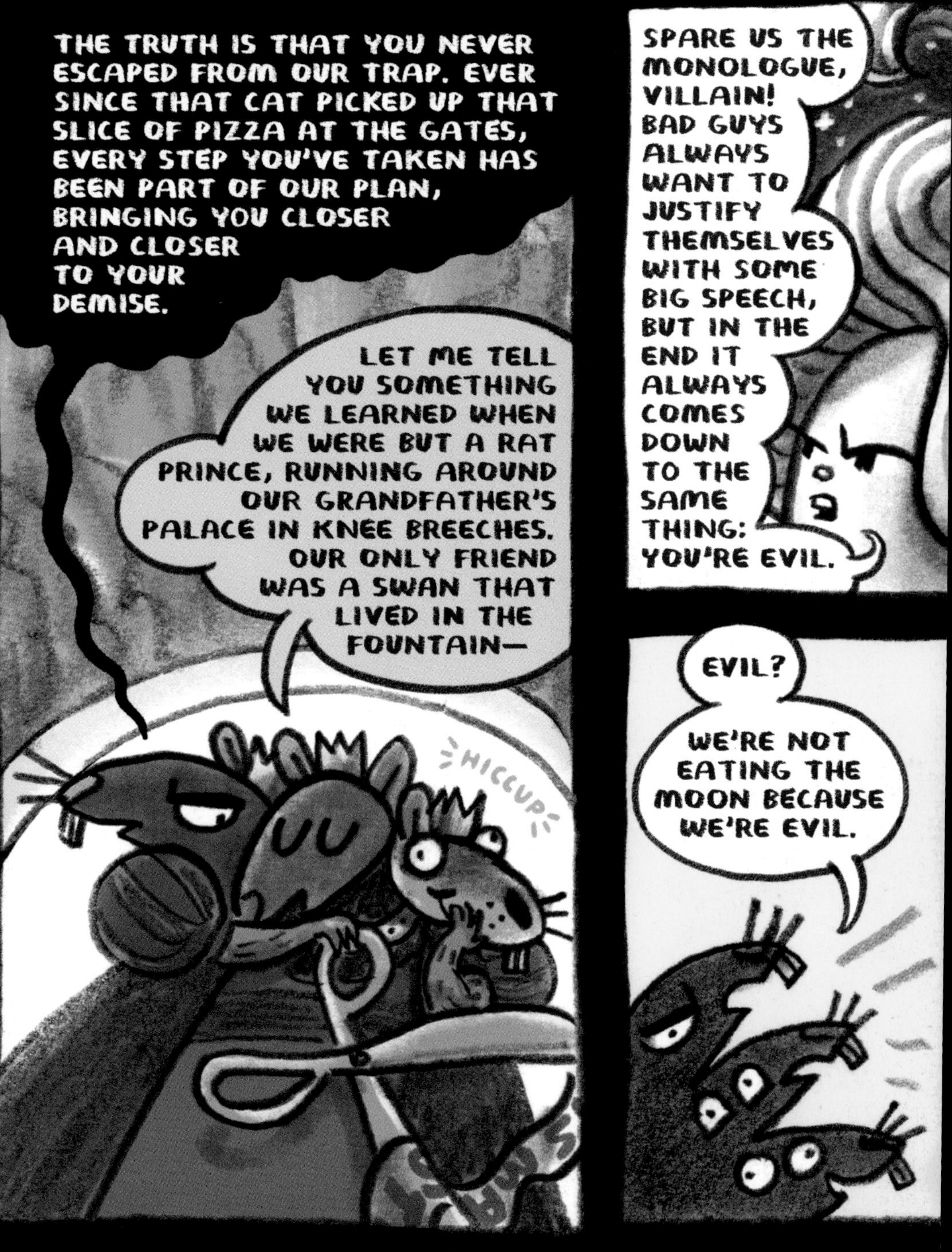
THE TRUTH IS THAT YOU NEVER ESCAPED FROM OUR TRAP. EVER SINCE THAT CAT PICKED UP THAT SLICE OF PIZZA AT THE GATES, EVERY STEP YOU'VE TAKEN HAS BEEN PART OF OUR PLAN, BRINGING YOU CLOSER AND CLOSER TO YOUR DEMISE.
LET ME TELL YOU SOMETHING WE LEARNED WHEN WE WERE BUT A RAT PRINCE, RUNNING AROUND OUR GRANDFATHER'S PALACE IN KNEE BREECHES. OUR ONLY FRIEND WAS A SWAN THAT LIVED IN THE FOUNTAIN—
HICCUP
SPARE US THE MONOLOGUE, VILLAIN! BAD GUYS ALWAYS WANT TO JUSTIFY THEMSELVES WITH SOME BIG SPEECH, BUT IN THE END IT ALWAYS COMES DOWN TO THE SAME THING: YOU'RE EVIL.
EVIL?
WE'RE NOT EATING THE MOON BECAUSE WE'RE EVIL.

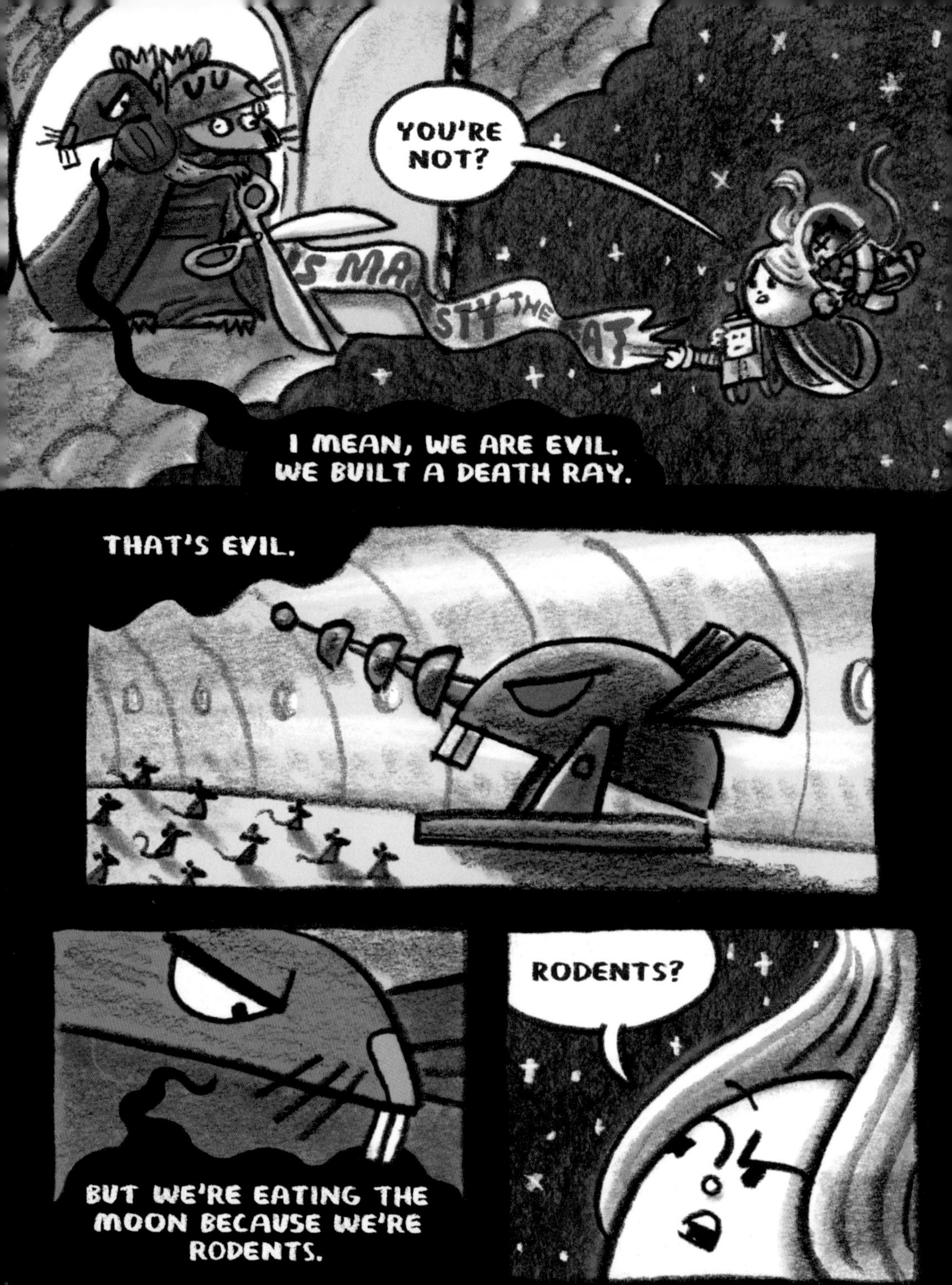
YOU'RE NOT?
I MEAN, WE ARE EVIL. WE BUILT A DEATH RAY.
THAT'S EVIL.
RODENTS?
BUT WE'RE EATING THE MOON BECAUSE WE'RE RODENTS.

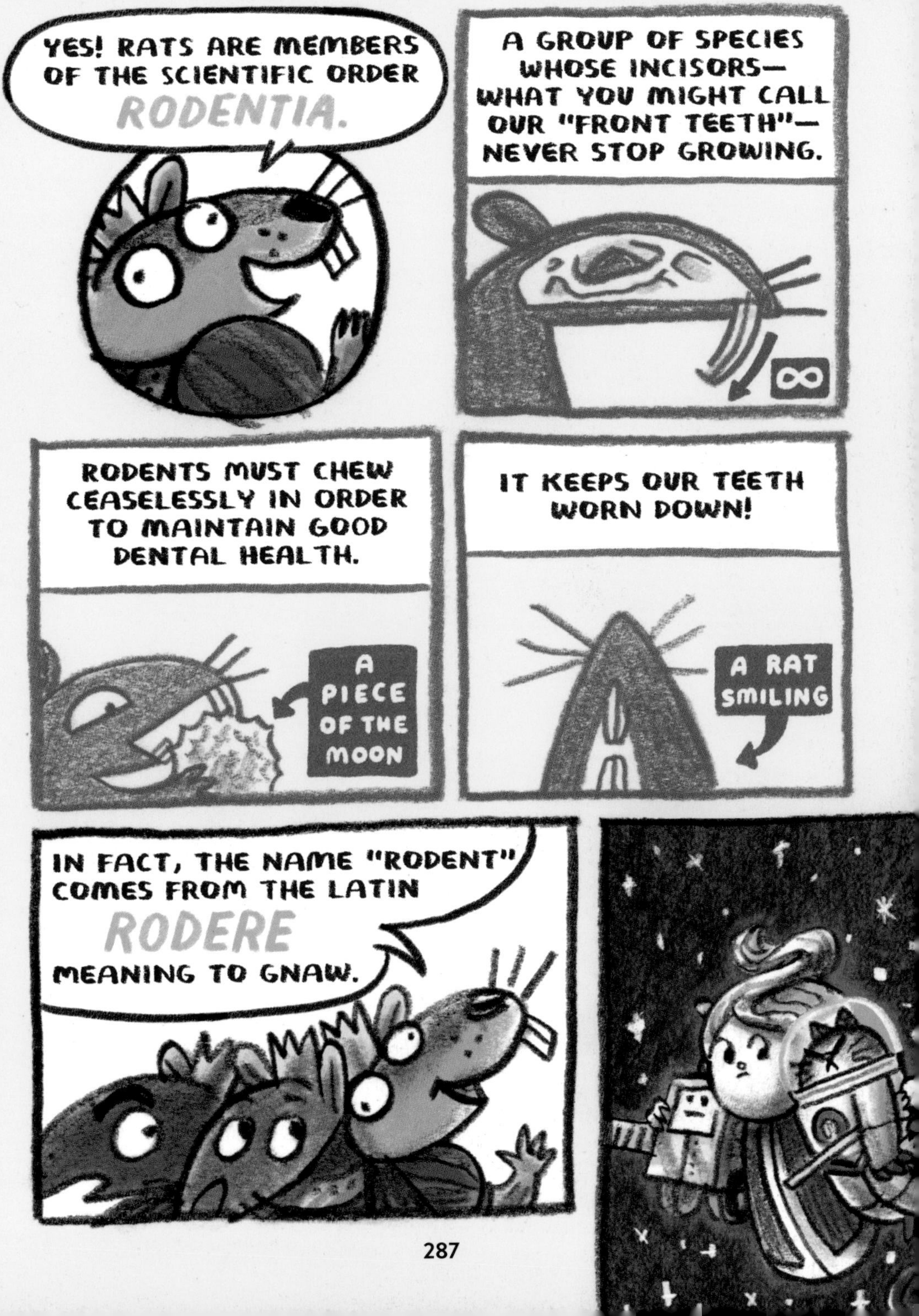
YES! RATS ARE MEMBERS OF THE SCIENTIFIC ORDER RODENTIA.
A GROUP OF SPECIES WHOSE INCISORS— WHAT YOU MIGHT CALL OUR "FRONT TEETH"— NEVER STOP GROWING.
∞
RODENTS MUST CHEW CEASELESSLY IN ORDER TO MAINTAIN GOOD DENTAL HEALTH.
A PIECE OF THE MOON
IT KEEPS OUR TEETH WORN DOWN!
A RAT SMILING
IN FACT, THE NAME "RODENT" COMES FROM THE LATIN RODERE MEANING TO GNAW.

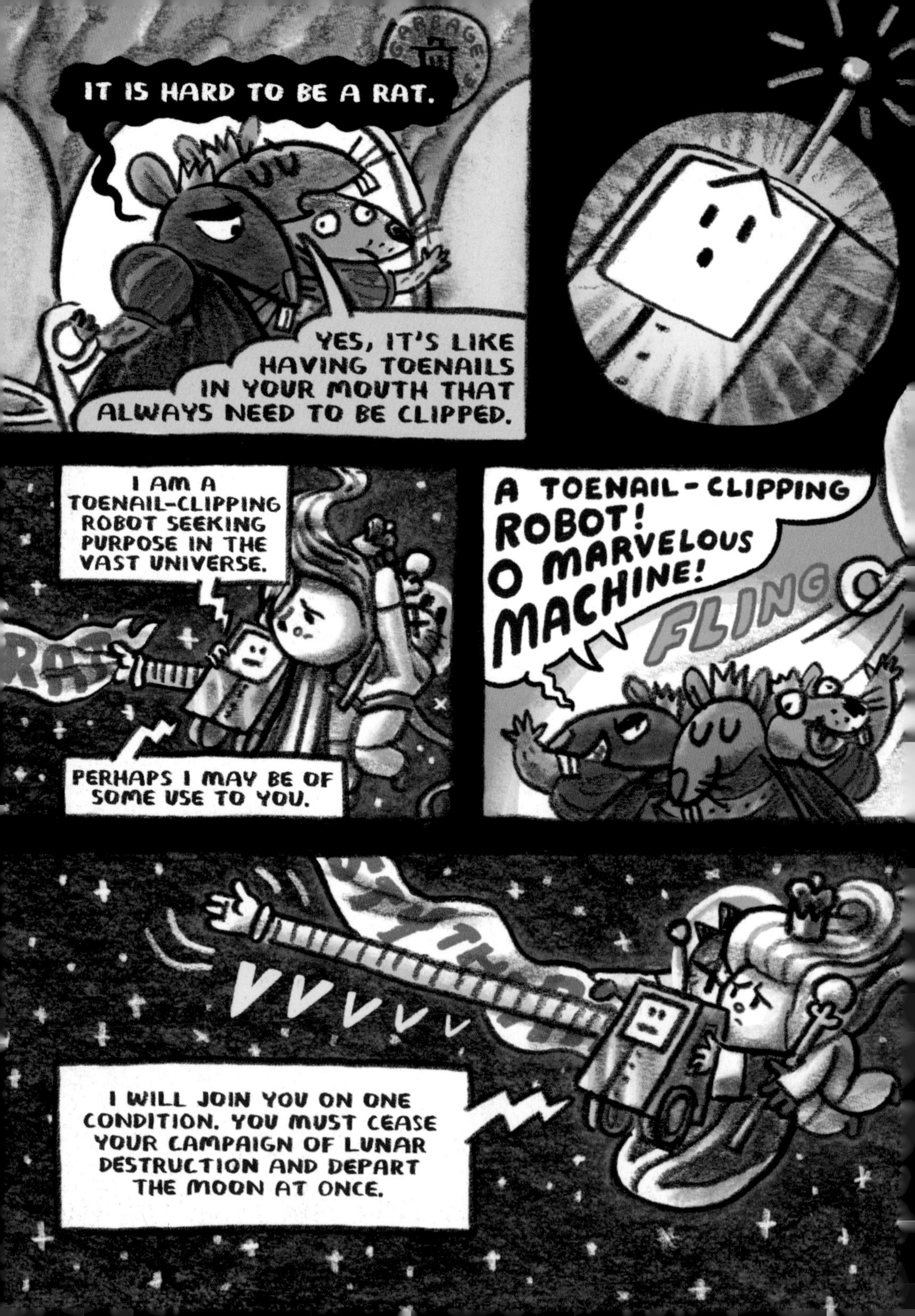
IT IS HARD TO BE A RAT.
YES, IT'S LIKE HAVING TOENAILS IN YOUR MOUTH THAT ALWAYS NEED TO BE CLIPPED.
I AM A TOENAIL-CLIPPING ROBOT SEEKING PURPOSE IN THE VAST UNIVERSE.
PERHAPS I MAY BE OF SOME USE TO YOU.
A TOENAIL-CLIPPING ROBOT! O MARVELOUS MACHINE!
FLING
I WILL JOIN YOU ON ONE CONDITION. YOU MUST CEASE YOUR CAMPAIGN OF LUNAR DESTRUCTION AND DEPART THE MOON AT ONCE.

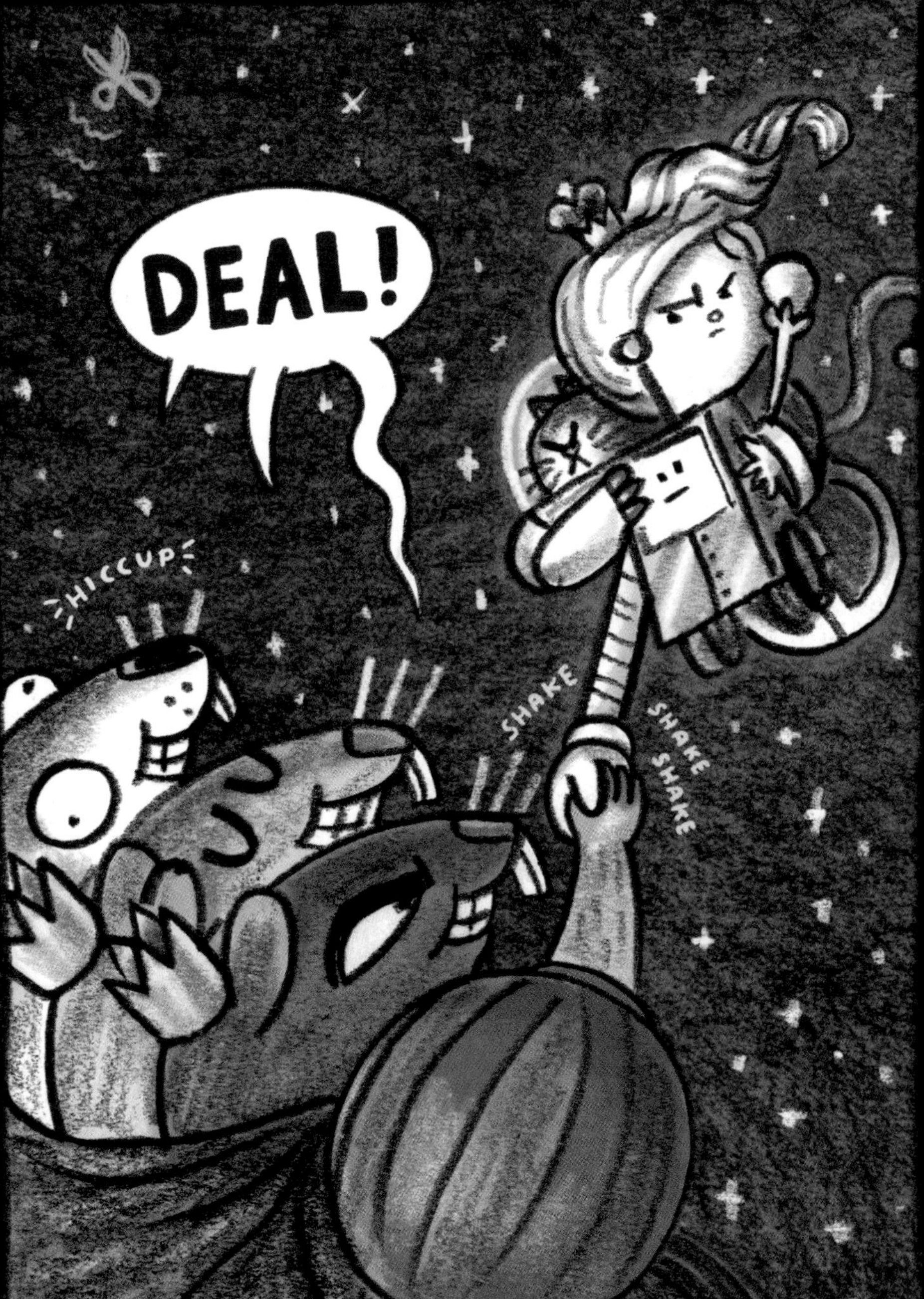
DEAL!
HICCUP
SHAKE
SHAKE
SHAKE

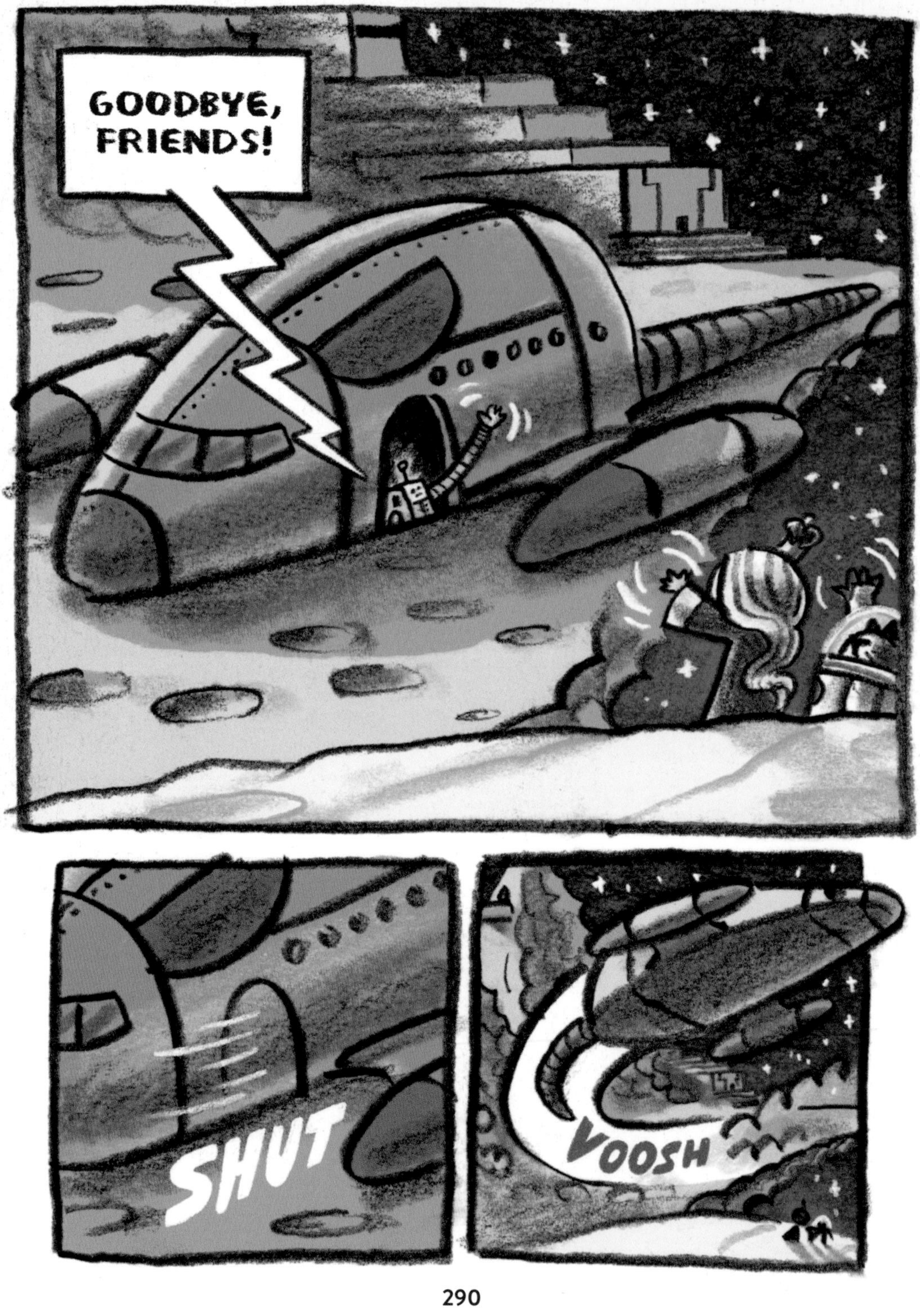
GOODBYE, FRIENDS!
SHUT
VOOSH

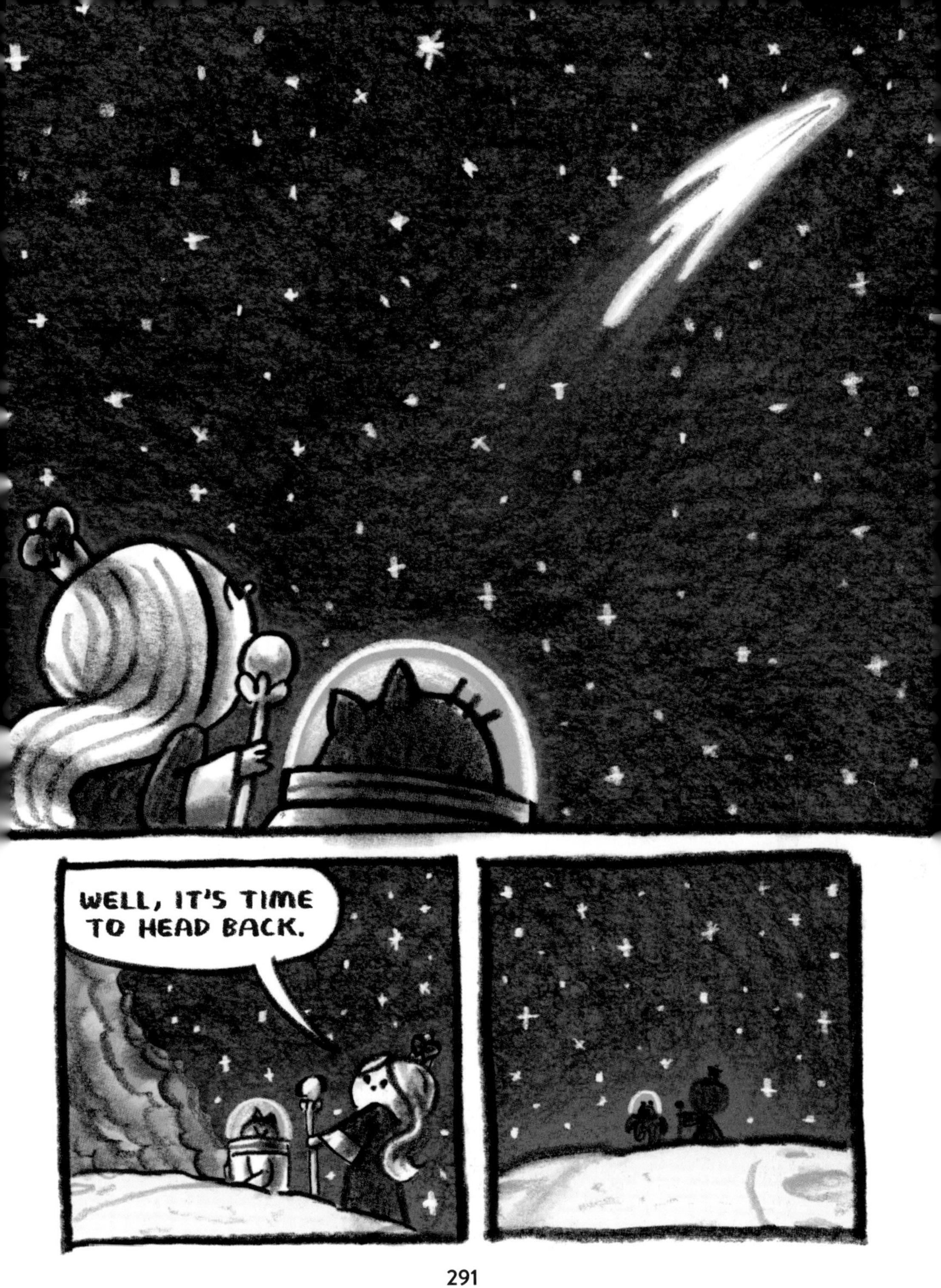
WELL, IT'S TIME TO HEAD BACK.

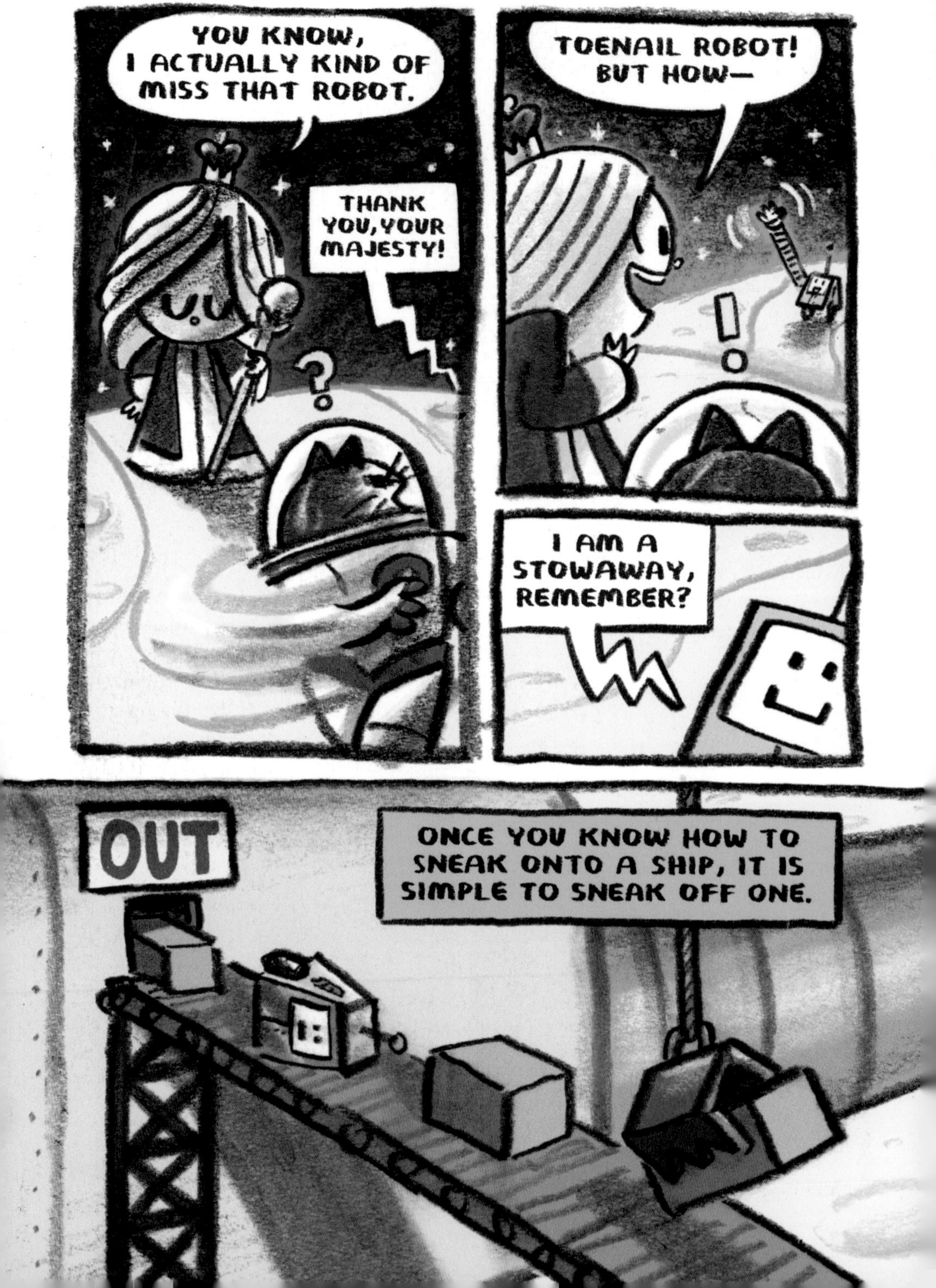
YOU KNOW, I ACTUALLY KIND OF MISS THAT ROBOT.
THANK YOU, YOUR MAJESTY!
?
TOENAIL ROBOT! BUT HOW—
!
I AM A STOWAWAY, REMEMBER?
OUT
ONCE YOU KNOW HOW TO SNEAK ONTO A SHIP, IT IS SIMPLE TO SNEAK OFF ONE.

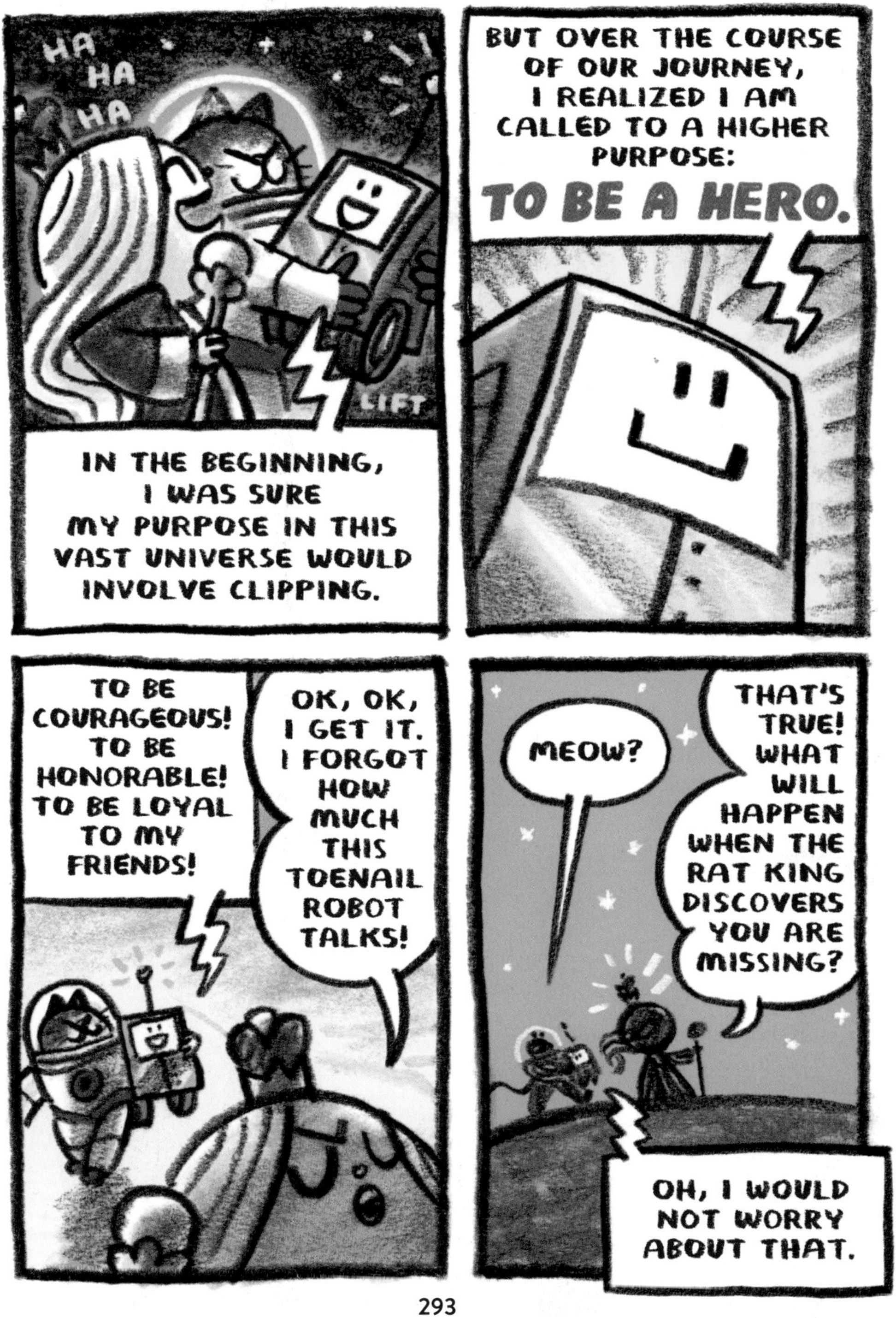
HA HA HA
LIFT
IN THE BEGINNING, I WAS SURE MY PURPOSE IN THIS VAST UNIVERSE WOULD INVOLVE CLIPPING.
BUT OVER THE COURSE OF OUR JOURNEY, I REALIZED I AM CALLED TO A HIGHER PURPOSE:
TO BE A HERO.
TO BE COURAGEOUS! TO BE HONORABLE! TO BE LOYAL TO MY FRIENDS!
OK, OK, I GET IT. I FORGOT HOW MUCH THIS TOENAIL ROBOT TALKS!
MEOW?
THAT'S TRUE! WHAT WILL HAPPEN WHEN THE RAT KING DISCOVERS YOU ARE MISSING?
OH, I WOULD NOT WORRY ABOUT THAT.

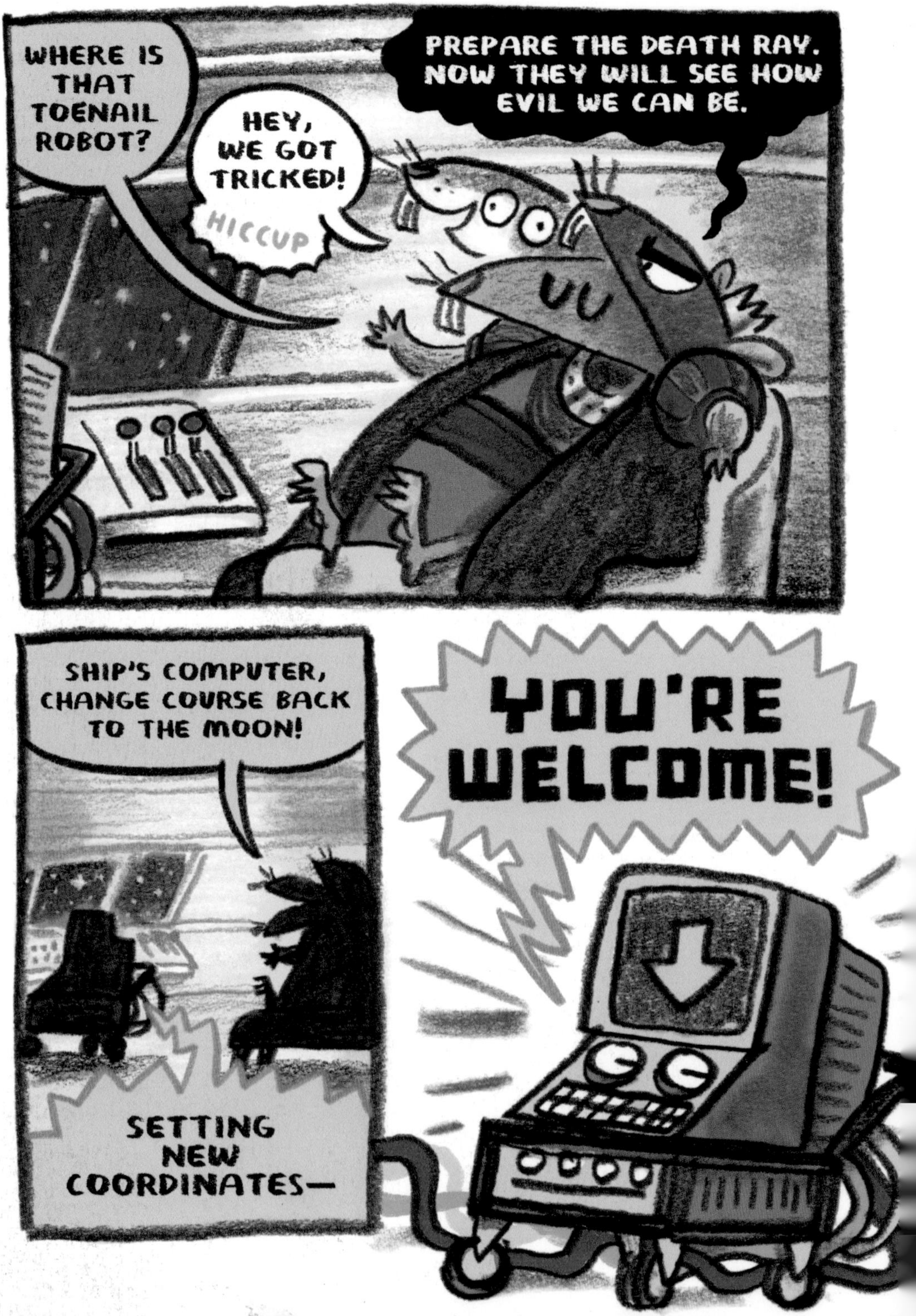
WHERE IS THAT TOENAIL ROBOT?
HEY, WE GOT TRICKED!
HICCUP
PREPARE THE DEATH RAY. NOW THEY WILL SEE HOW EVIL WE CAN BE.
SHIP'S COMPUTER, CHANGE COURSE BACK TO THE MOON!
SETTING NEW COORDINATES—
YOU'RE WELCOME!

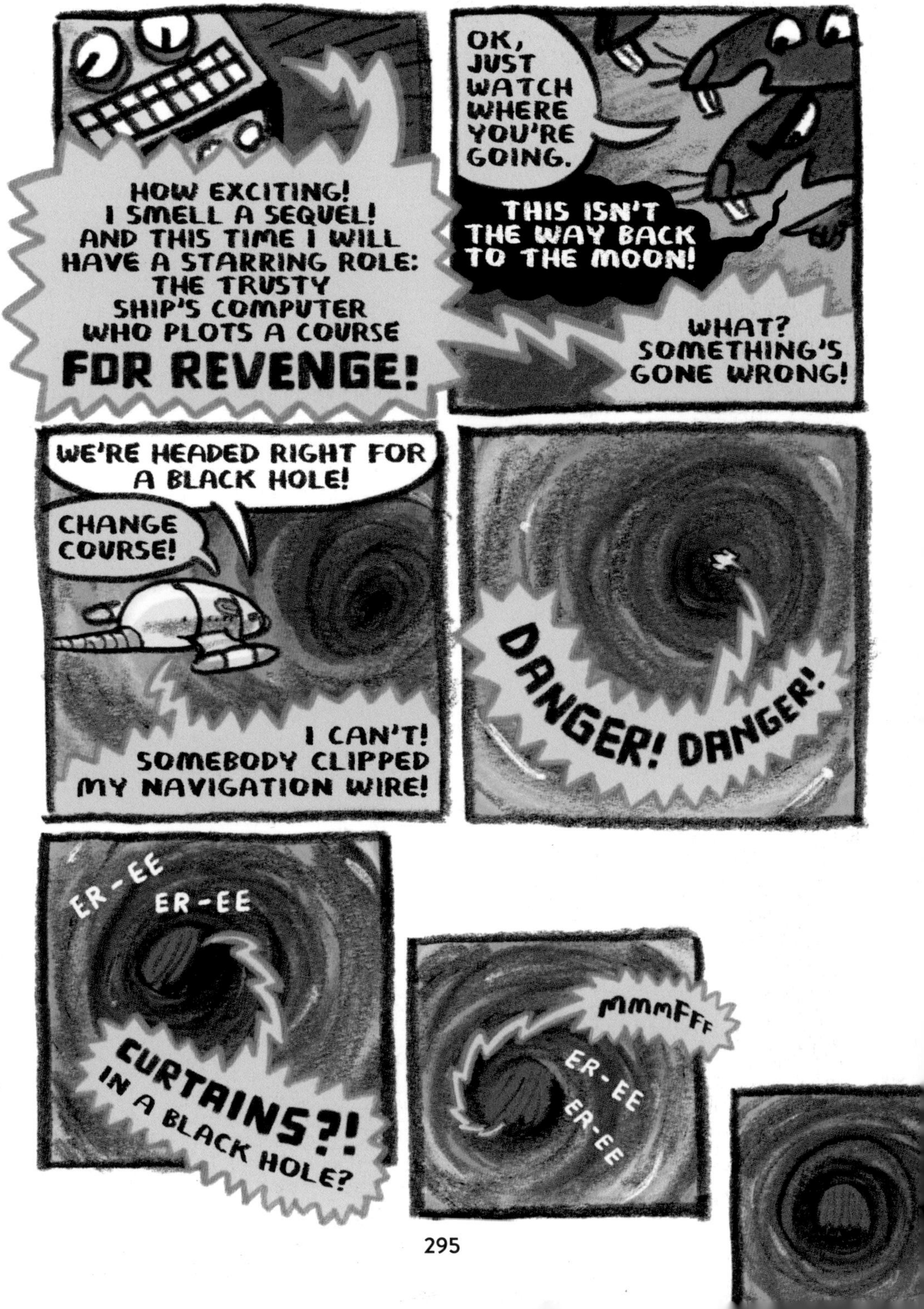
HOW EXCITING! I SMELL A SEQUEL! AND THIS TIME I WILL HAVE A STARRING ROLE: THE TRUSTY SHIP'S COMPUTER WHO PLOTS A COURSE FOR REVENGE!
OK, JUST WATCH WHERE YOU'RE GOING.
THIS ISN'T THE WAY BACK TO THE MOON!
WHAT? SOMETHING'S GONE WRONG!
WE'RE HEADED RIGHT FOR A BLACK HOLE!
CHANGE COURSE!
I CAN'T! SOMEBODY CLIPPED MY NAVIGATION WIRE!
DANGER! DANGER!
ER-EE
ER-EE
CURTAINS?! IN A BLACK HOLE?
MMMFFF
ER-EE
ER-EE

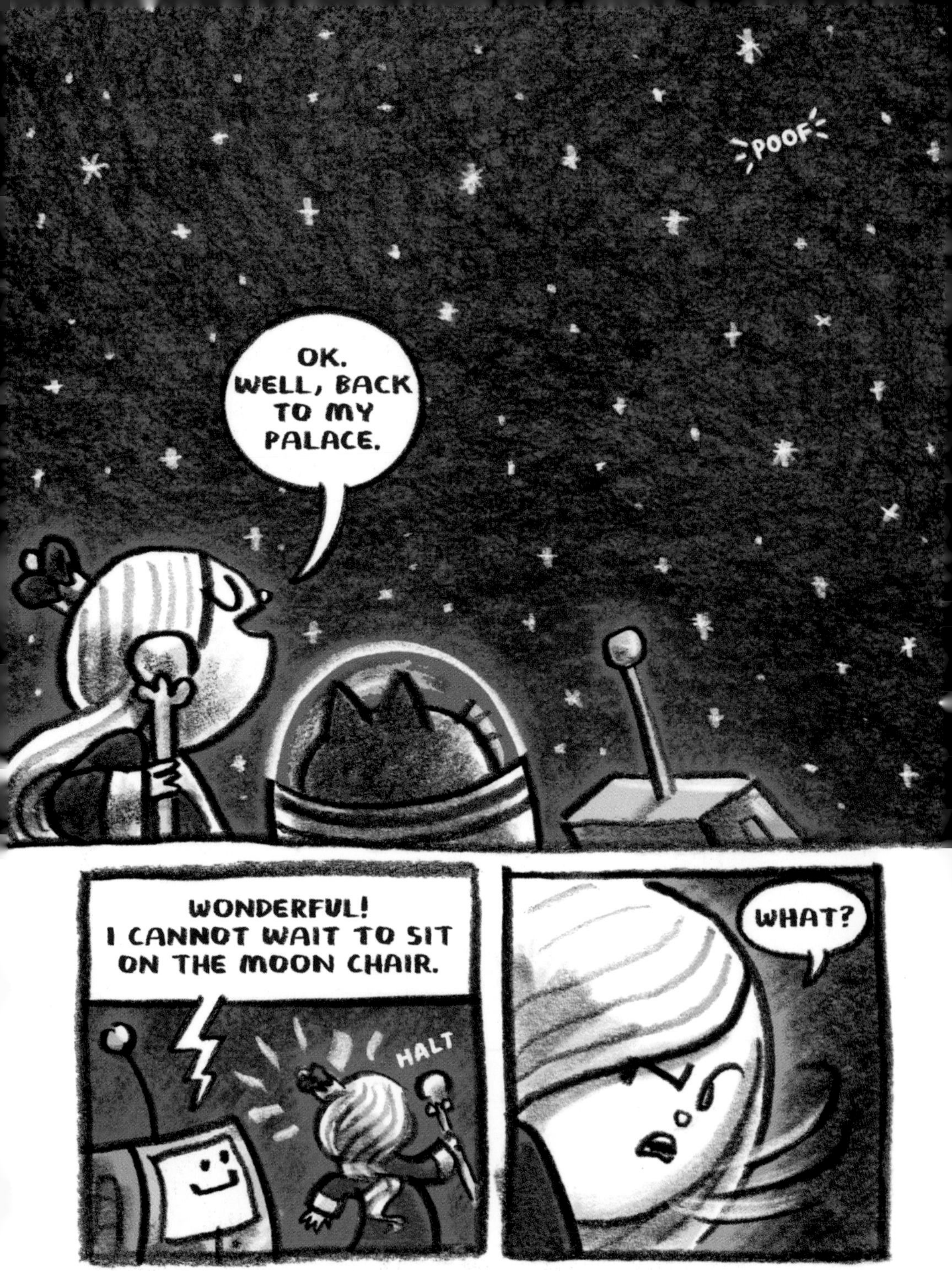
POOF
OK. WELL, BACK TO MY PALACE.
WONDERFUL! I CANNOT WAIT TO SIT ON THE MOON CHAIR.
HALT
WHAT?

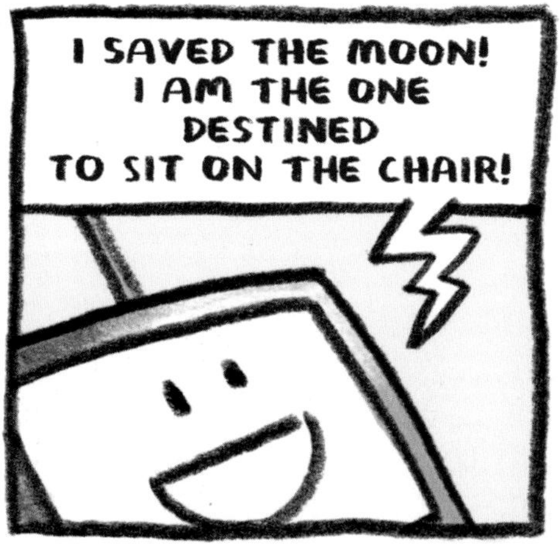
I SAVED THE MOON! I AM THE ONE DESTINED TO SIT ON THE CHAIR!

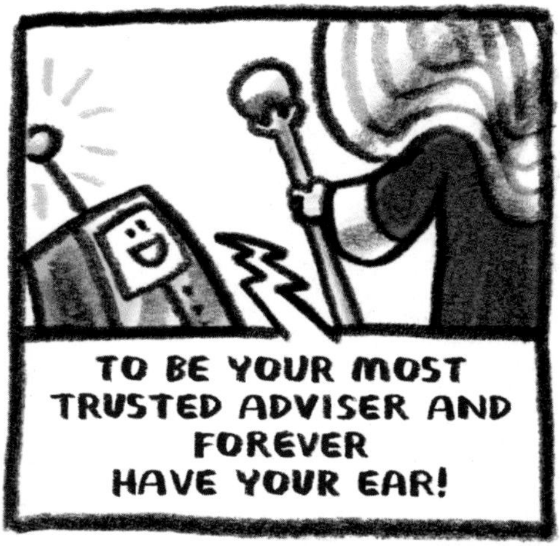
TO BE YOUR MOST TRUSTED ADVISER AND FOREVER HAVE YOUR EAR!

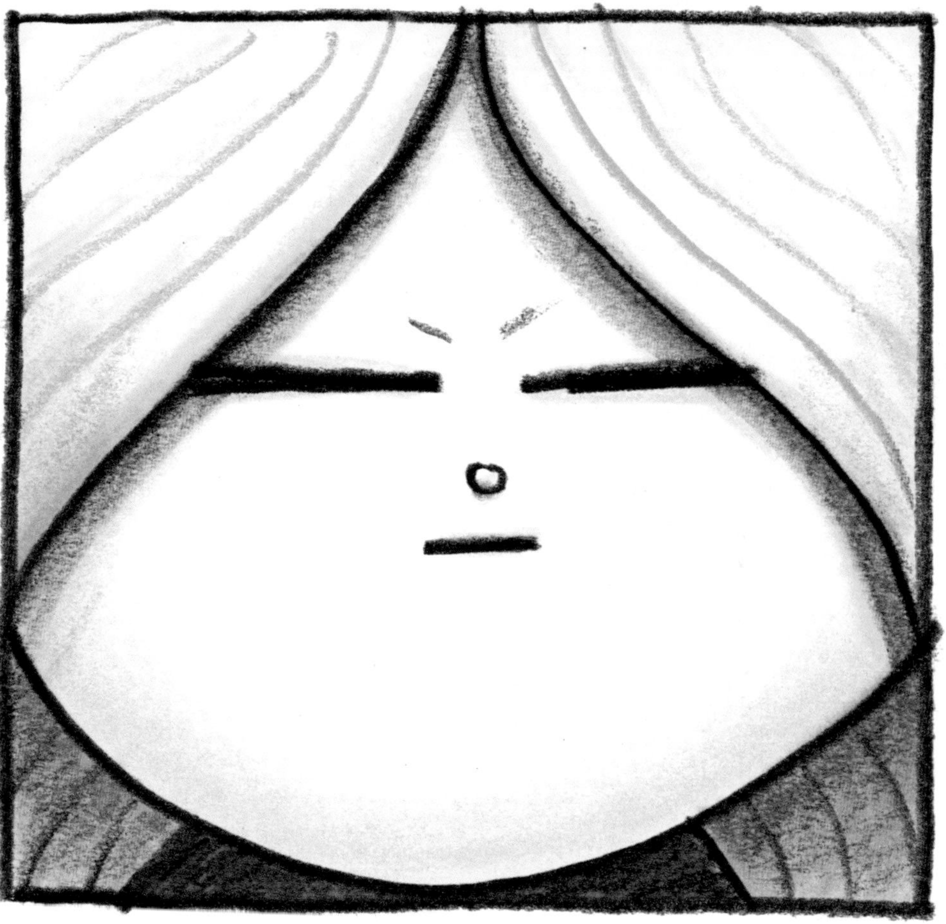

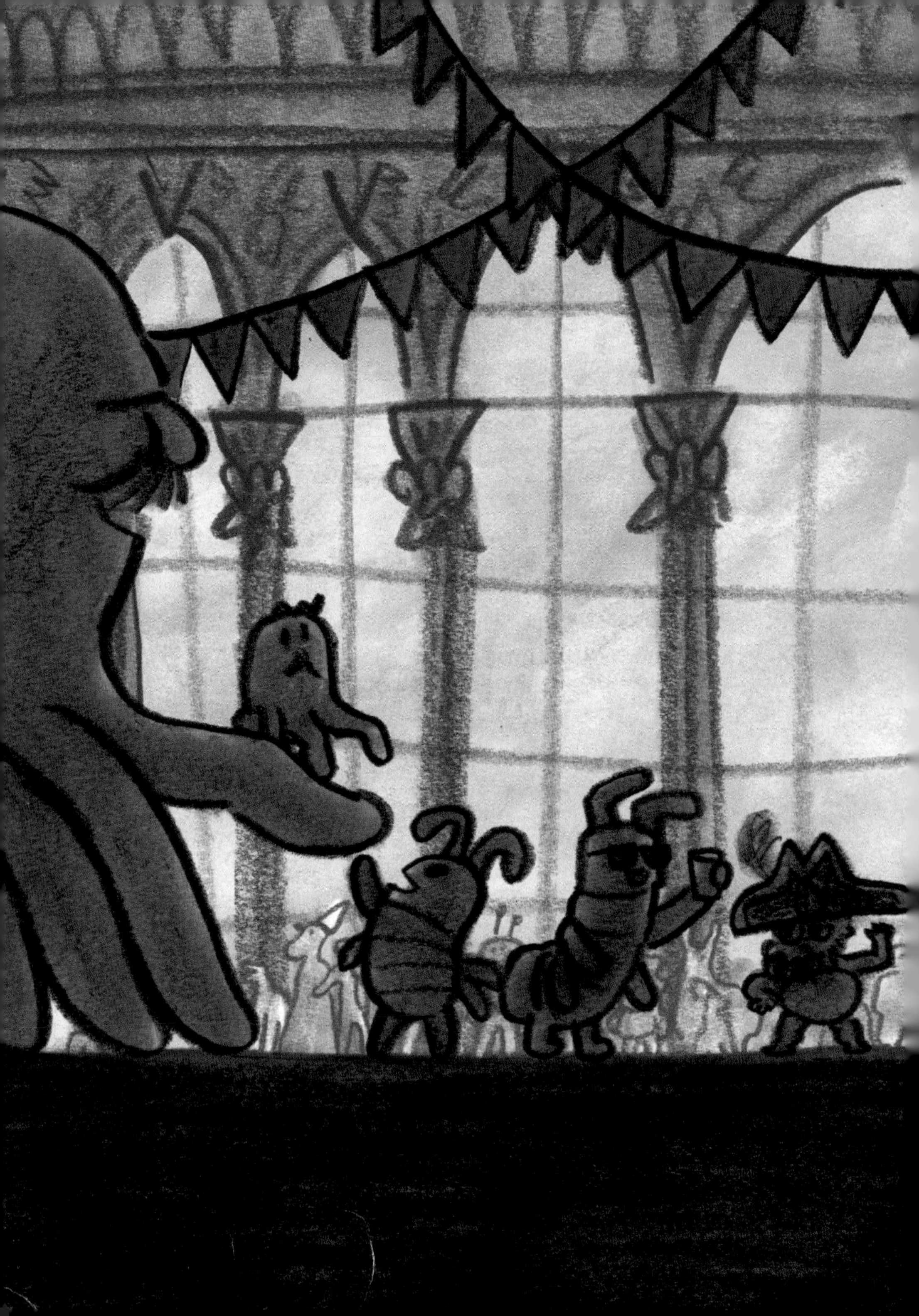

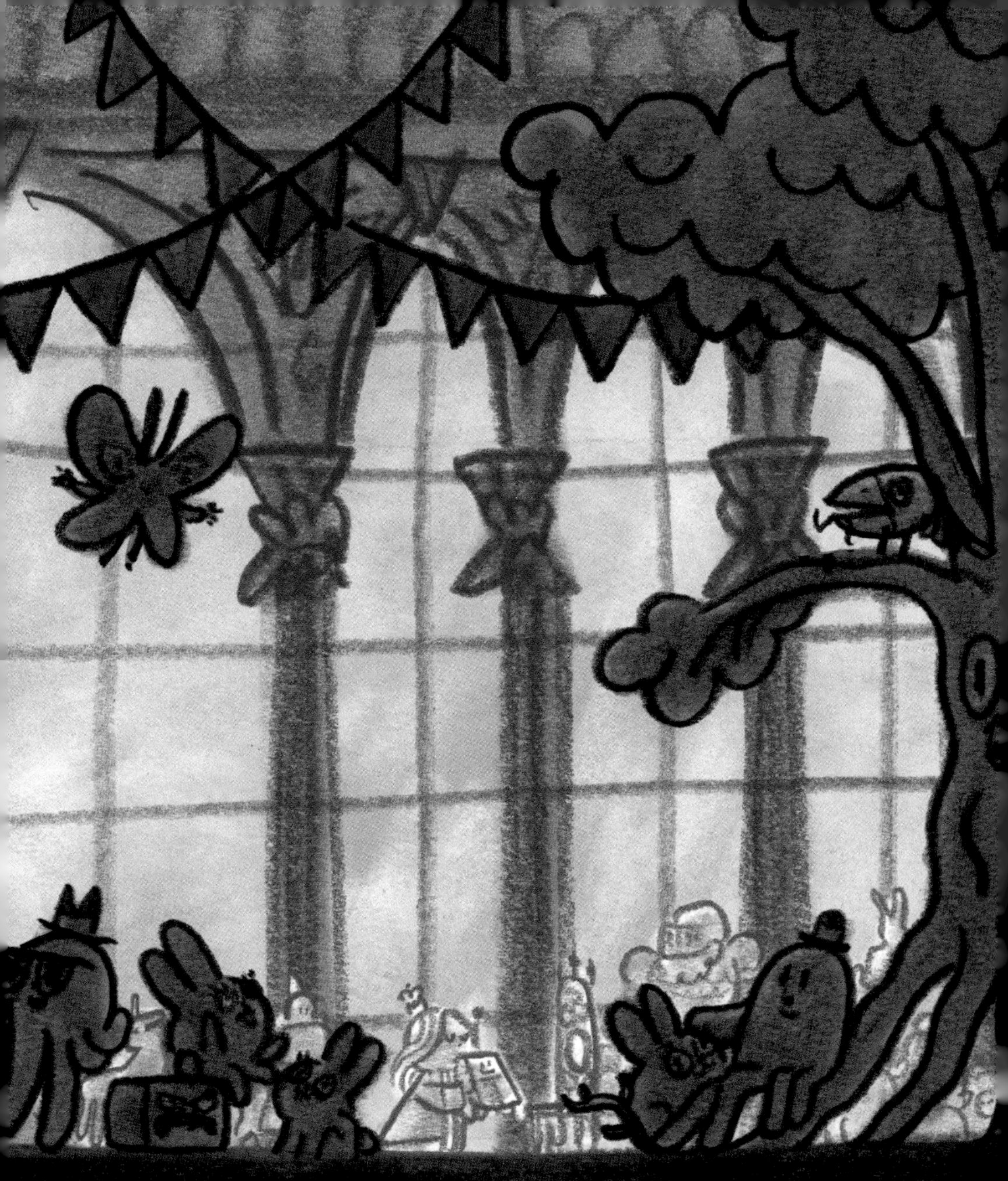

CHAPTER 22
FANCY FEAST

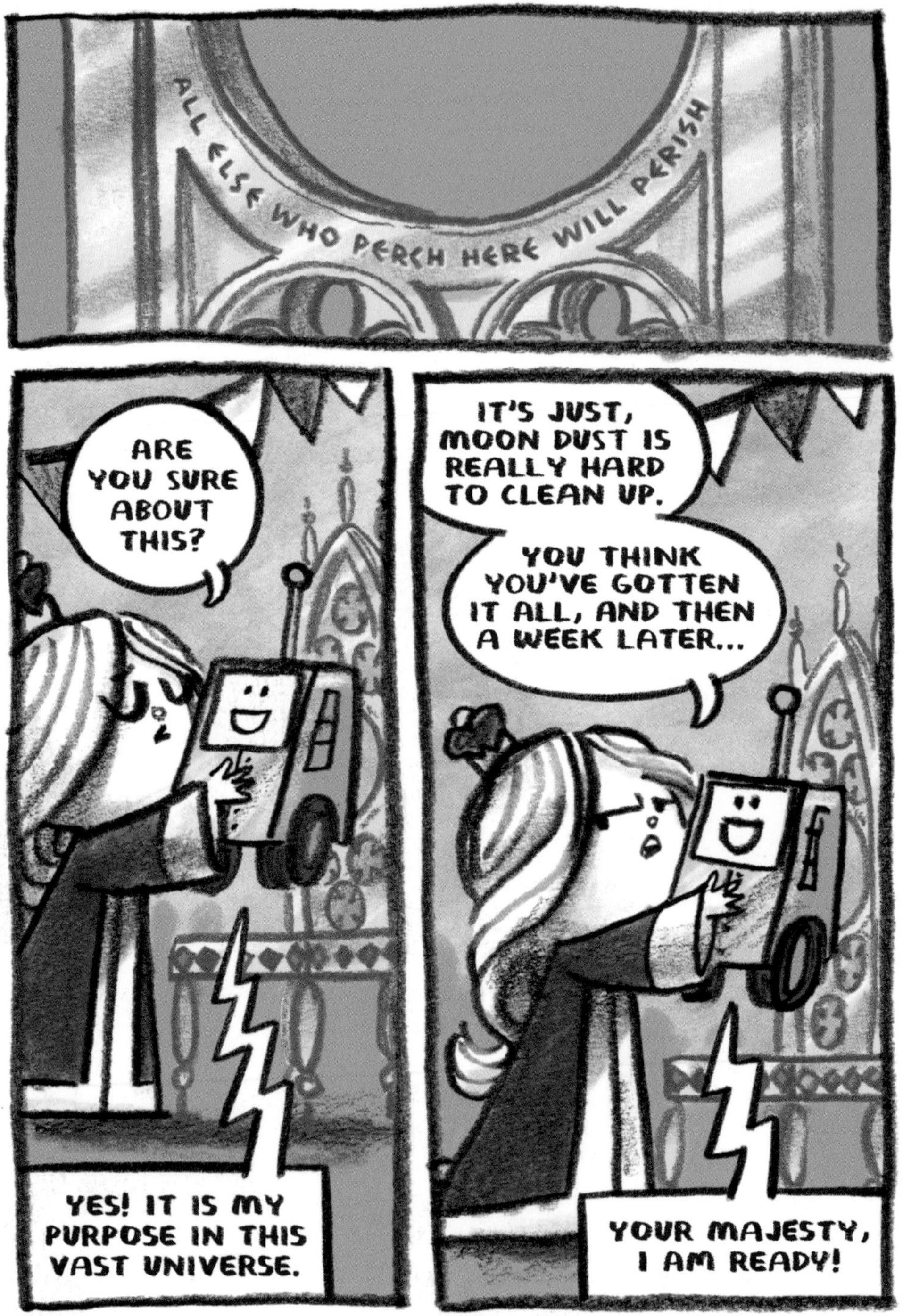
ALL ELSE WHO PERCH HERE WILL PERISH
ARE YOU SURE ABOUT THIS?
YES! IT IS MY PURPOSE IN THIS VAST UNIVERSE.
IT'S JUST, MOON DUST IS REALLY HARD TO CLEAN UP.
YOU THINK YOU'VE GOTTEN IT ALL, AND THEN A WEEK LATER...
YOUR MAJESTY, I AM READY!

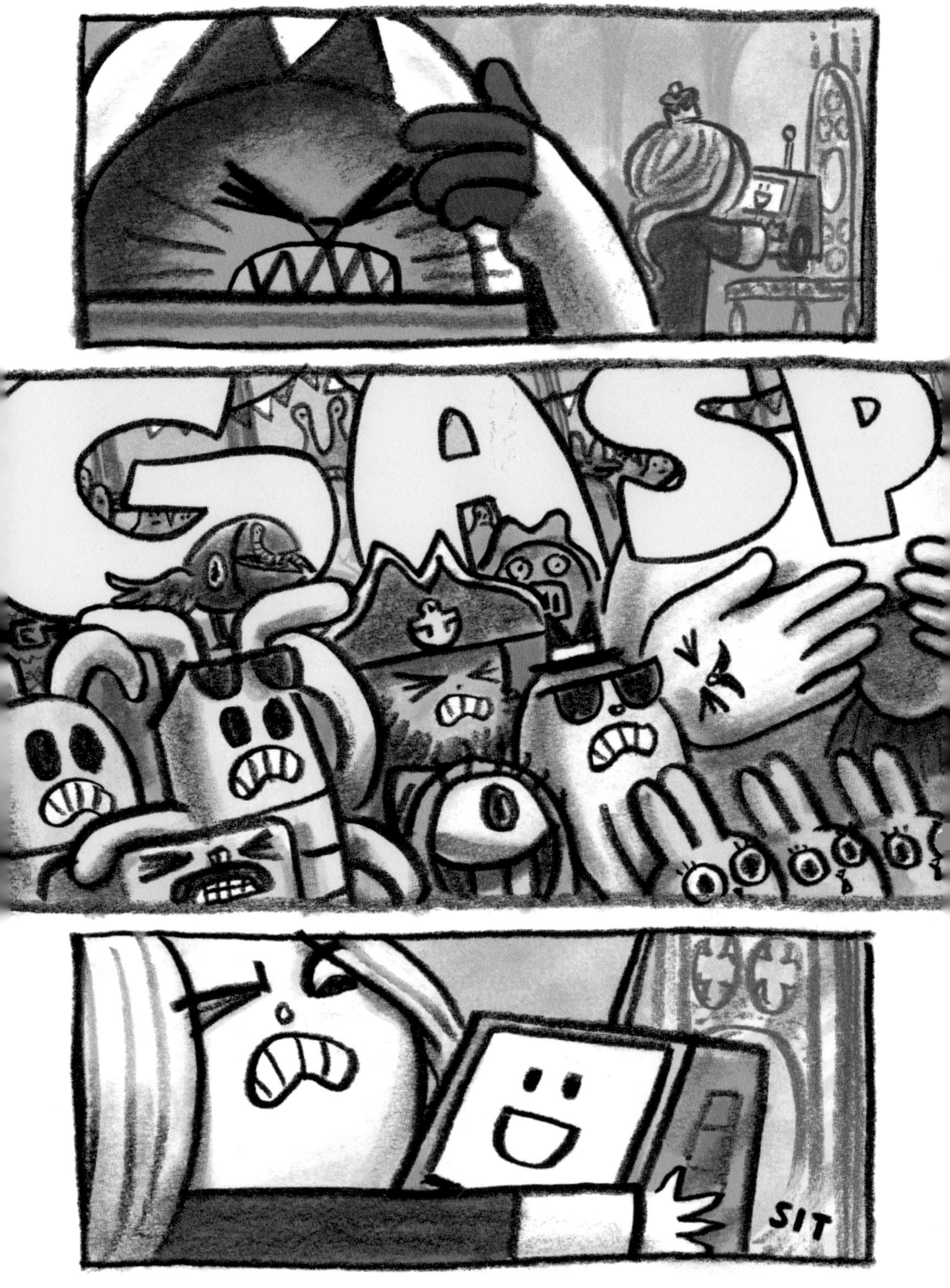
GASP
SIT

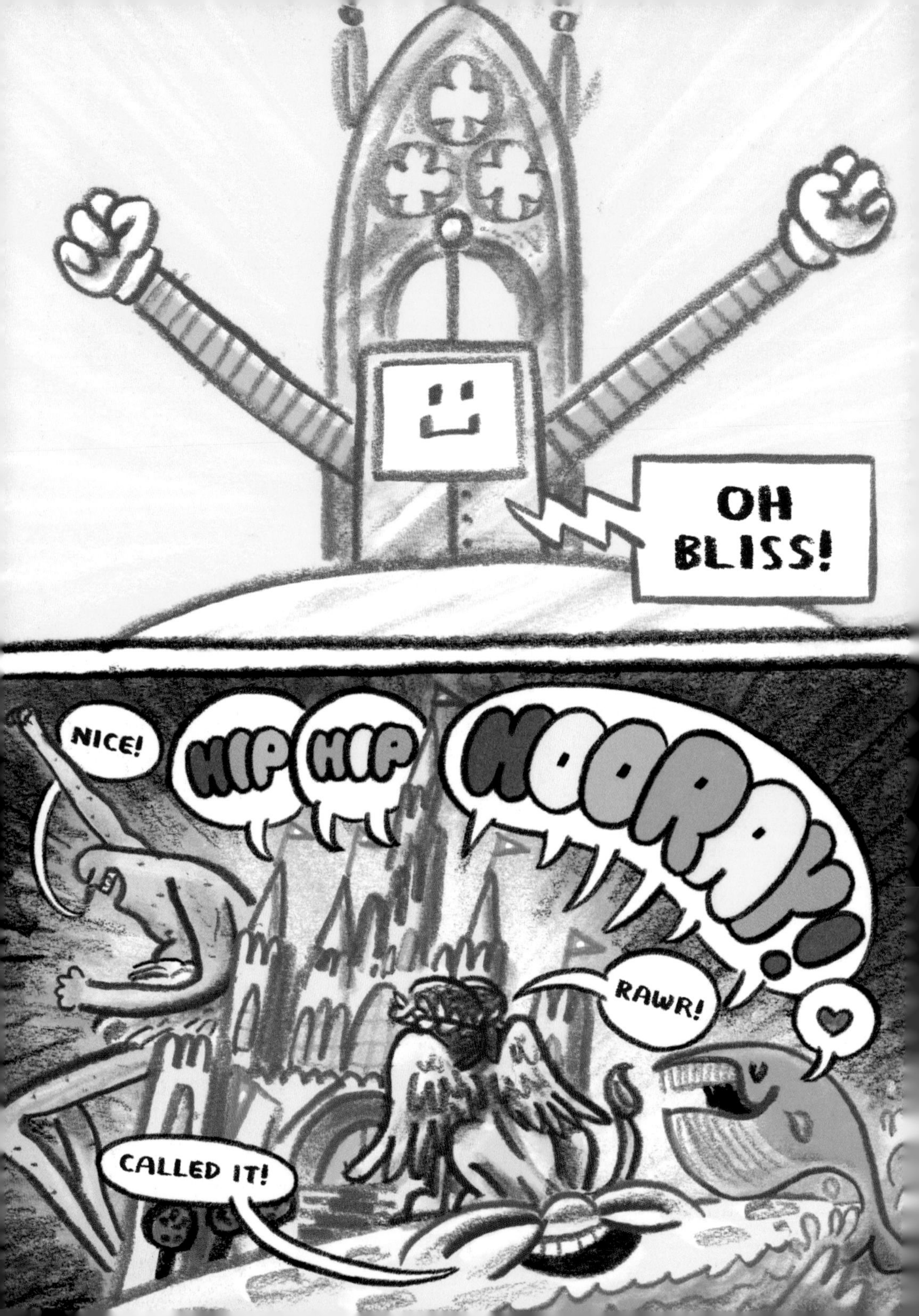
OH BLISS!
NICE!
HIP HIP
HIP HIP
HOORAY!!
RAWR!
CALLED IT!

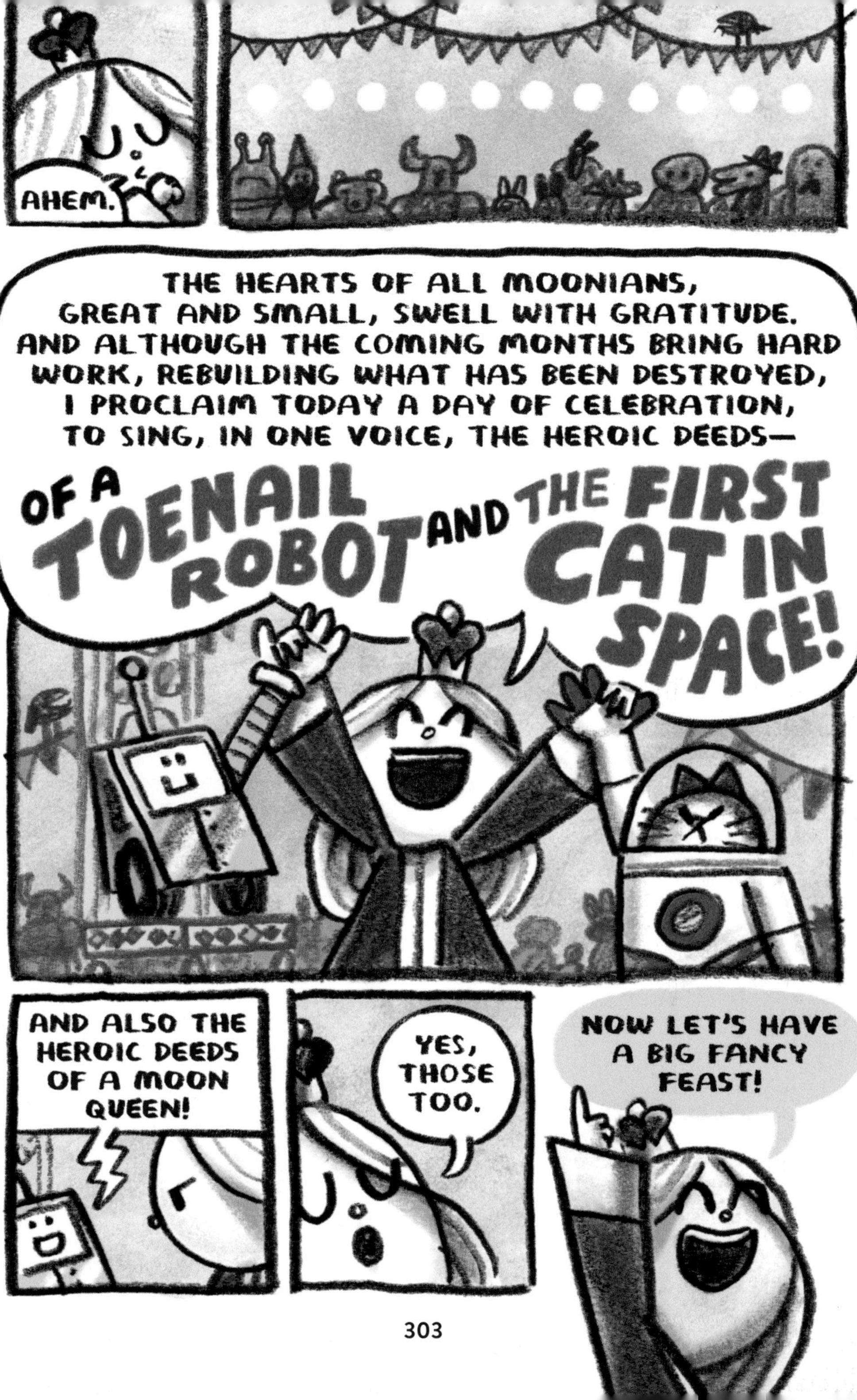
AHEM.
THE HEARTS OF ALL MOONIANS, GREAT AND SMALL, SWELL WITH GRATITUDE. AND ALTHOUGH THE COMING MONTHS BRING HARD WORK, REBUILDING WHAT HAS BEEN DESTROYED, I PROCLAIM TODAY A DAY OF CELEBRATION, TO SING, IN ONE VOICE, THE HEROIC DEEDS—
OF A TOENAIL ROBOT AND THE FIRST CAT IN SPACE!
AND ALSO THE HEROIC DEEDS OF A MOON QUEEN!
YES, THOSE TOO.
NOW LET'S HAVE A BIG FANCY FEAST!

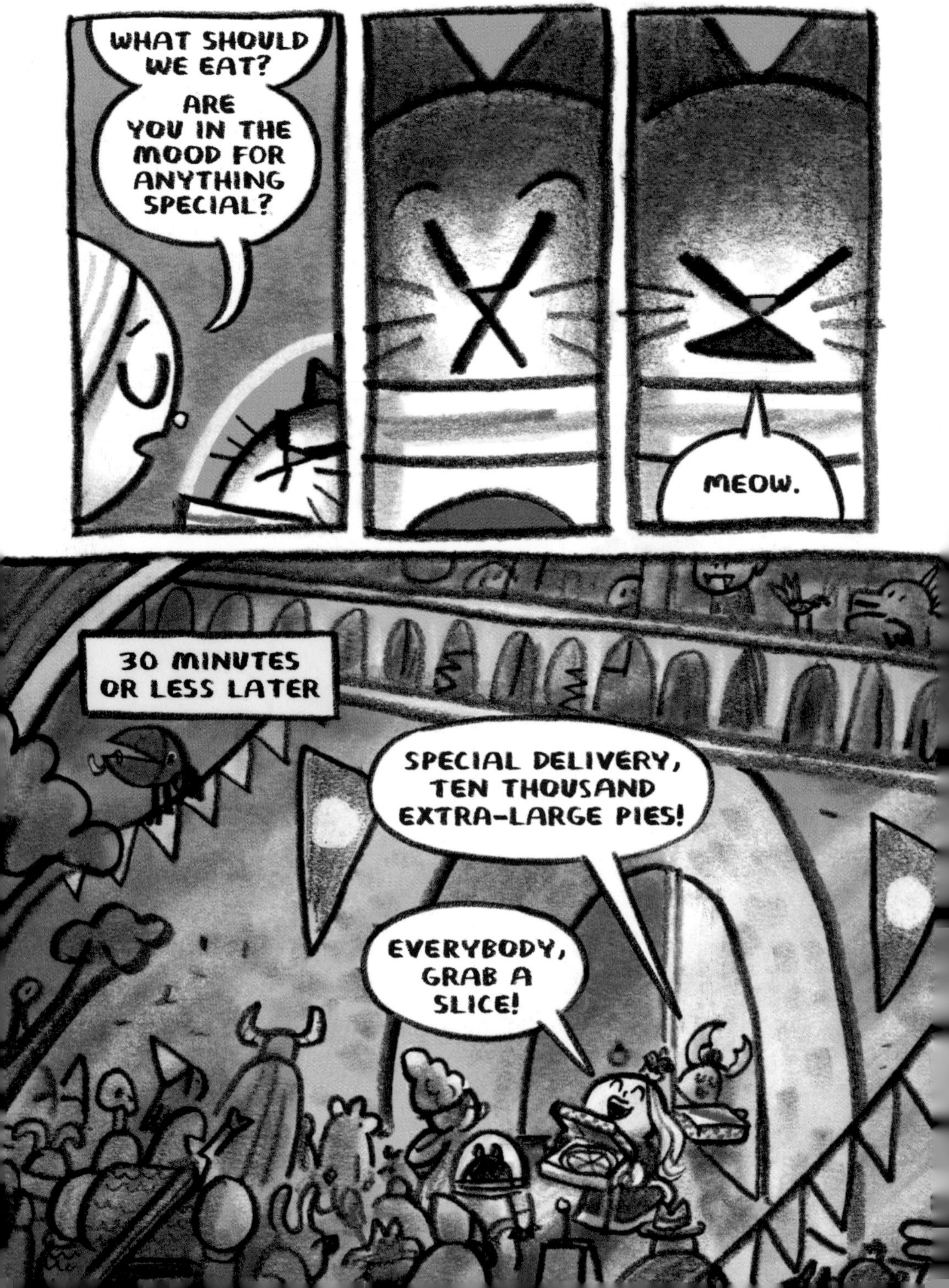
WHAT SHOULD WE EAT?
ARE YOU IN THE MOOD FOR ANYTHING SPECIAL?
MEOW.
30 MINUTES OR LESS LATER
SPECIAL DELIVERY, TEN THOUSAND EXTRA-LARGE PIES!
EVERYBODY, GRAB A SLICE!

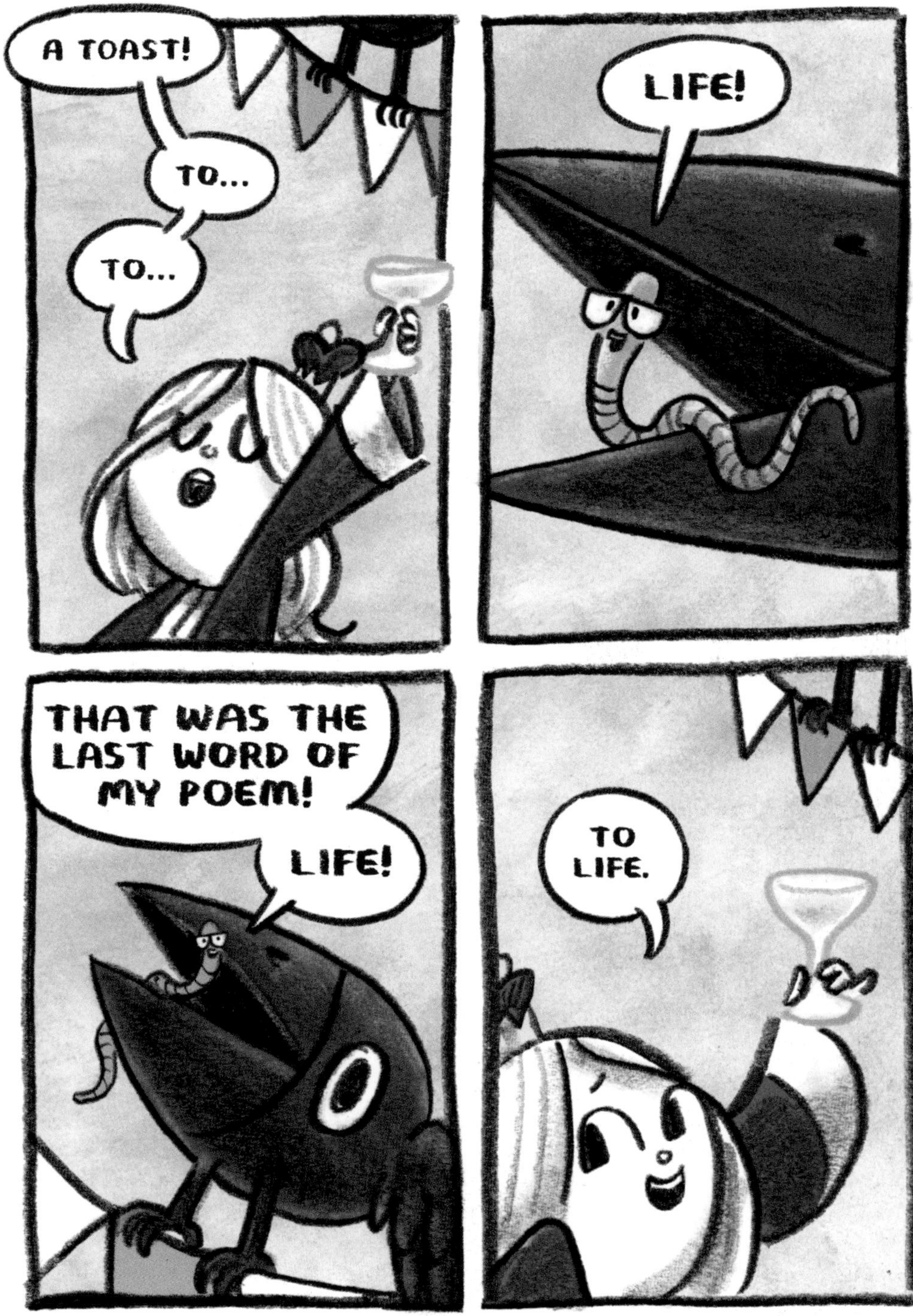
A TOAST!
TO...
TO...
LIFE!
THAT WAS THE LAST WORD OF MY POEM!
LIFE!
TO LIFE.

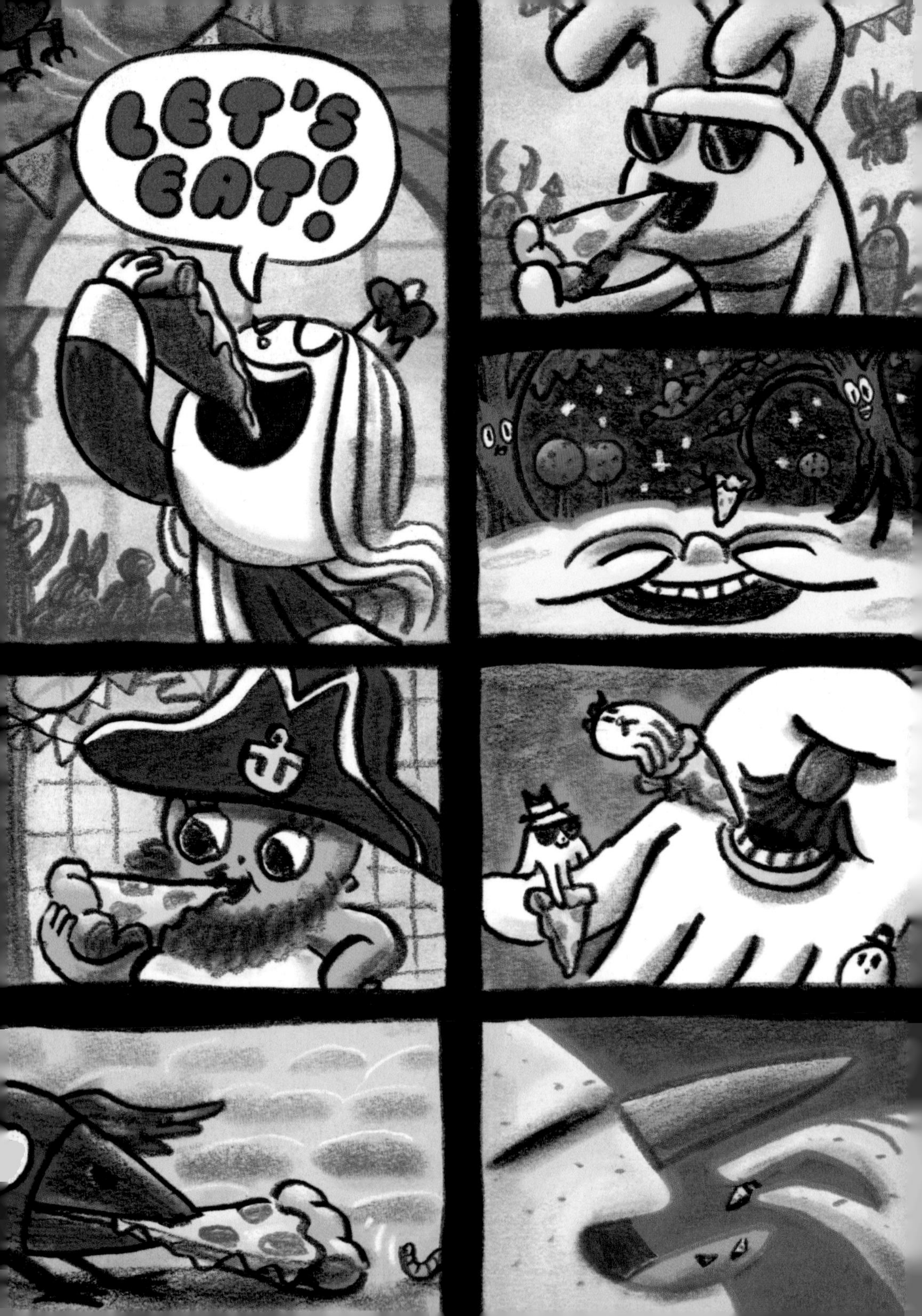
LET'S EAT!

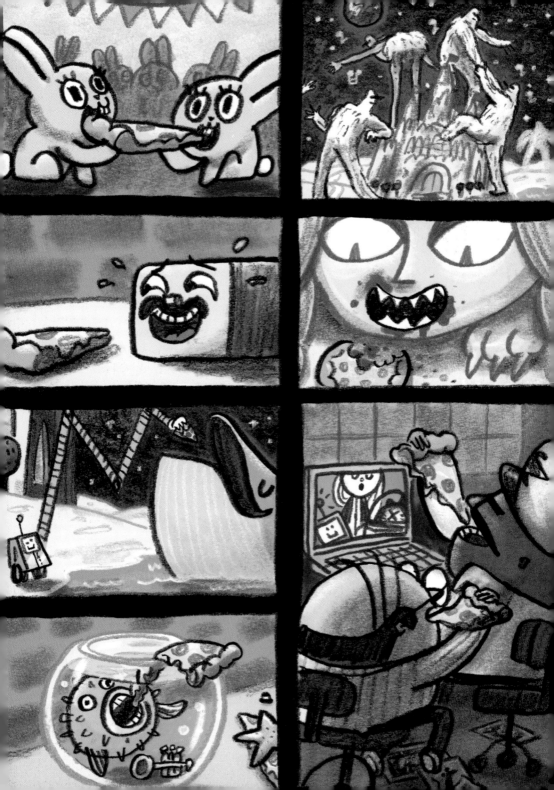

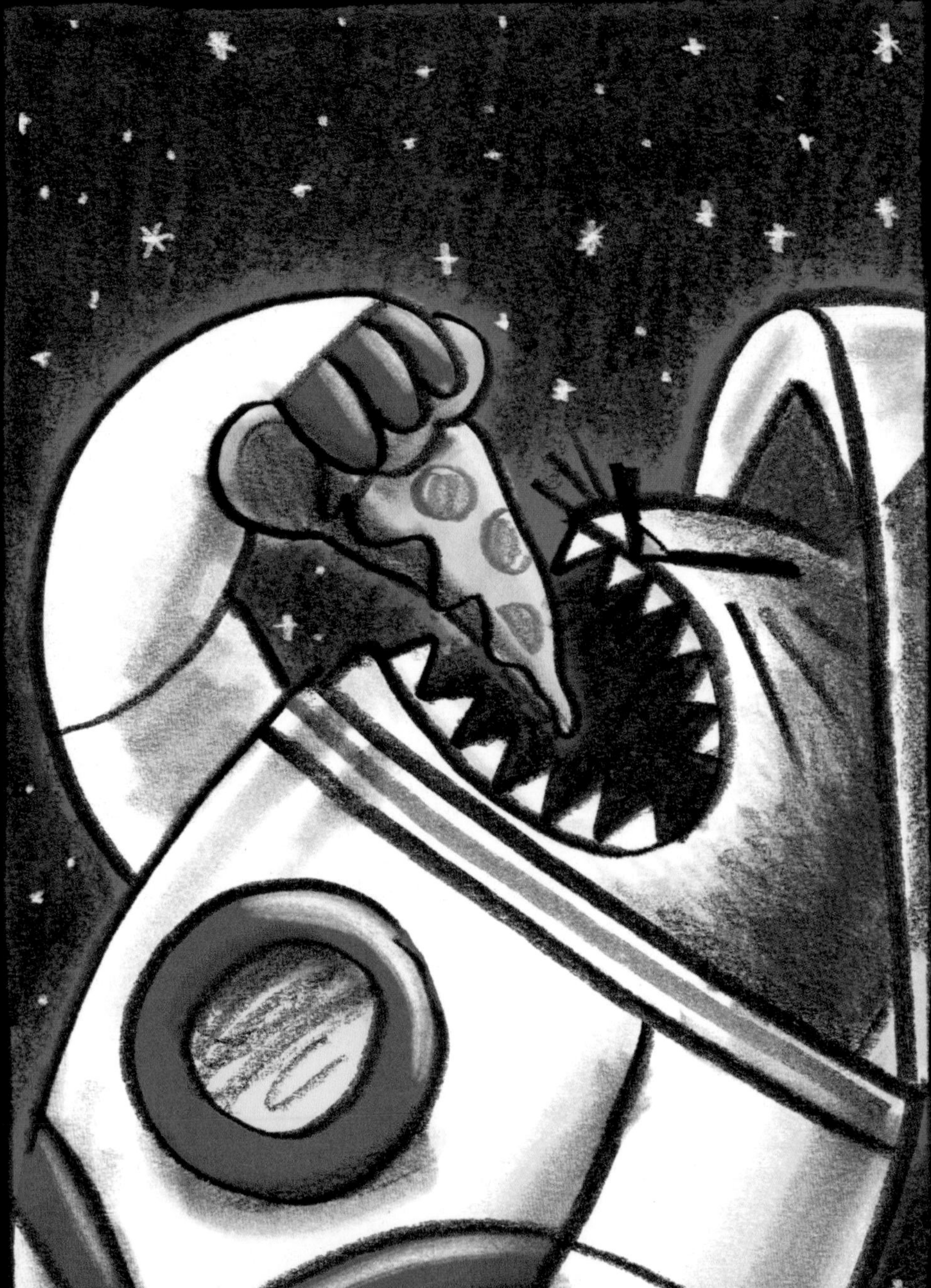

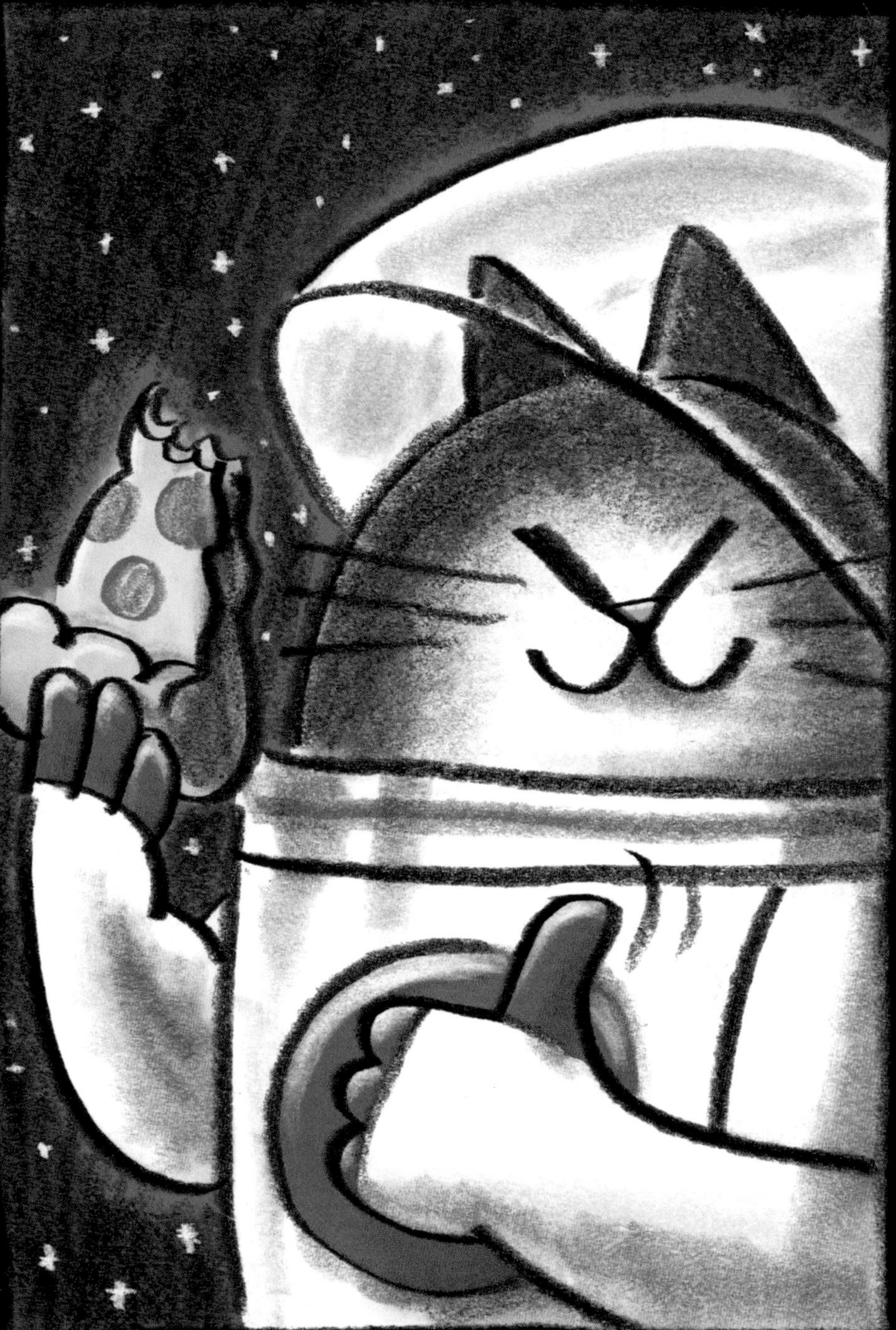

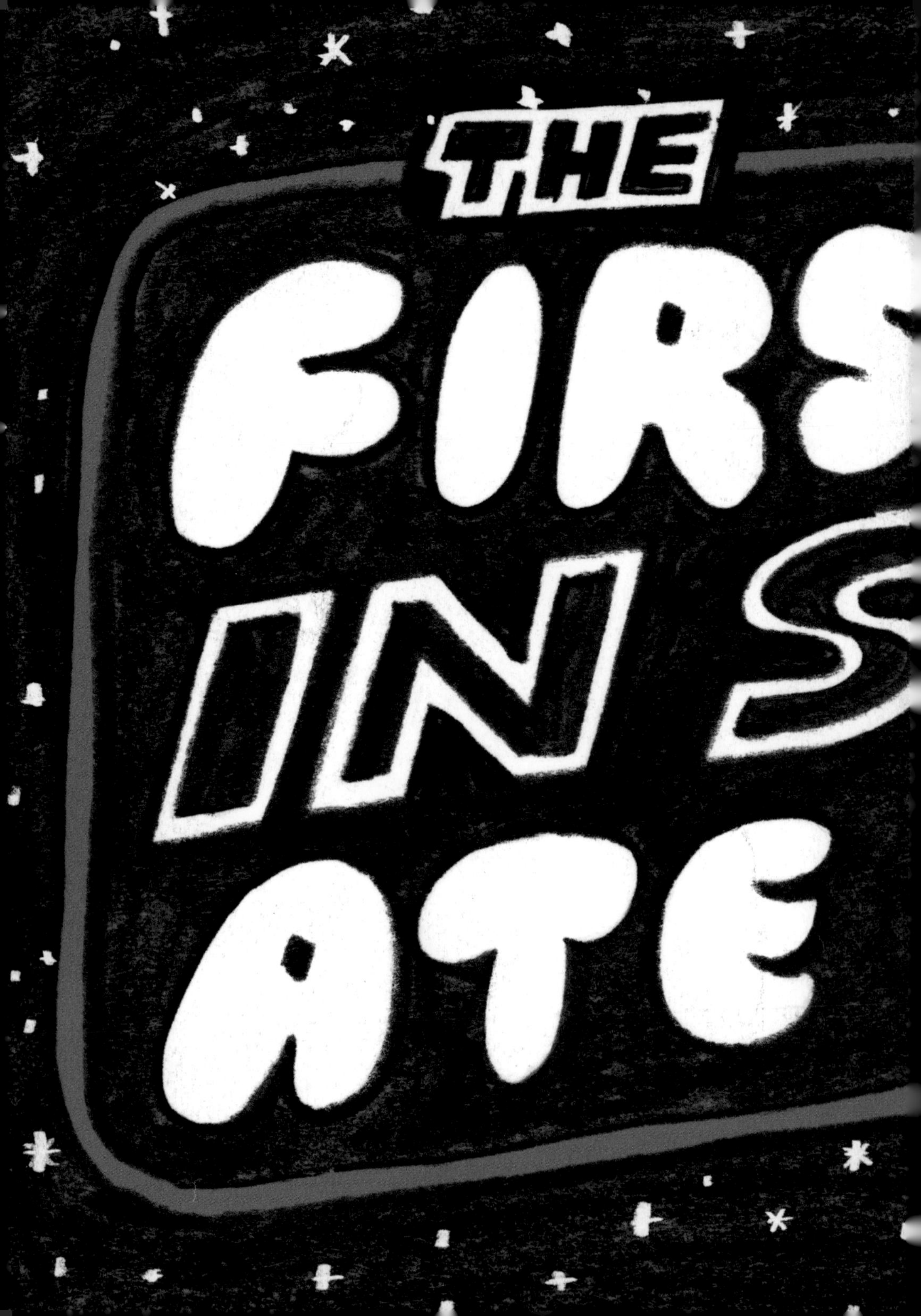
THE

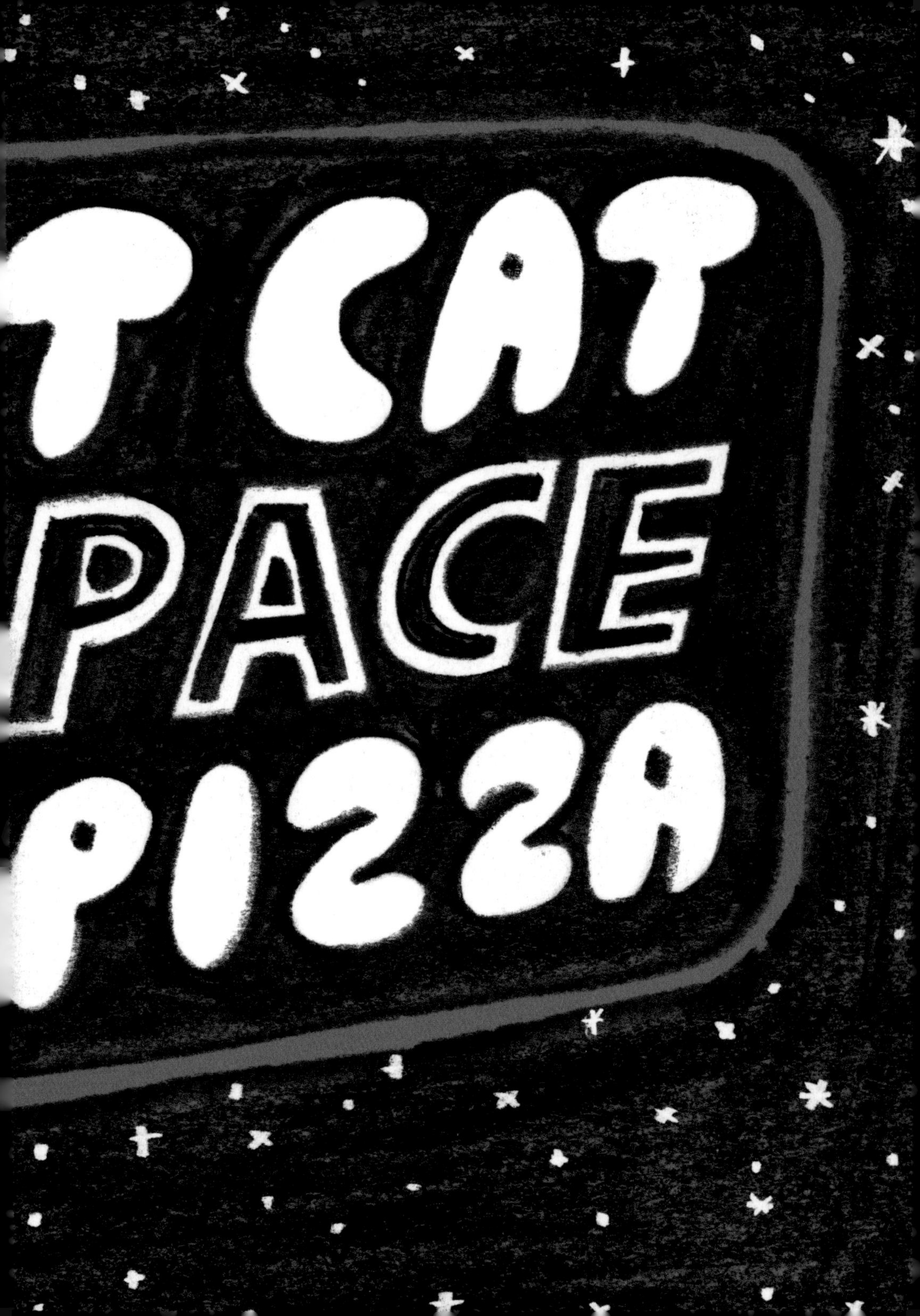
T CAT
PACE
PIZZA

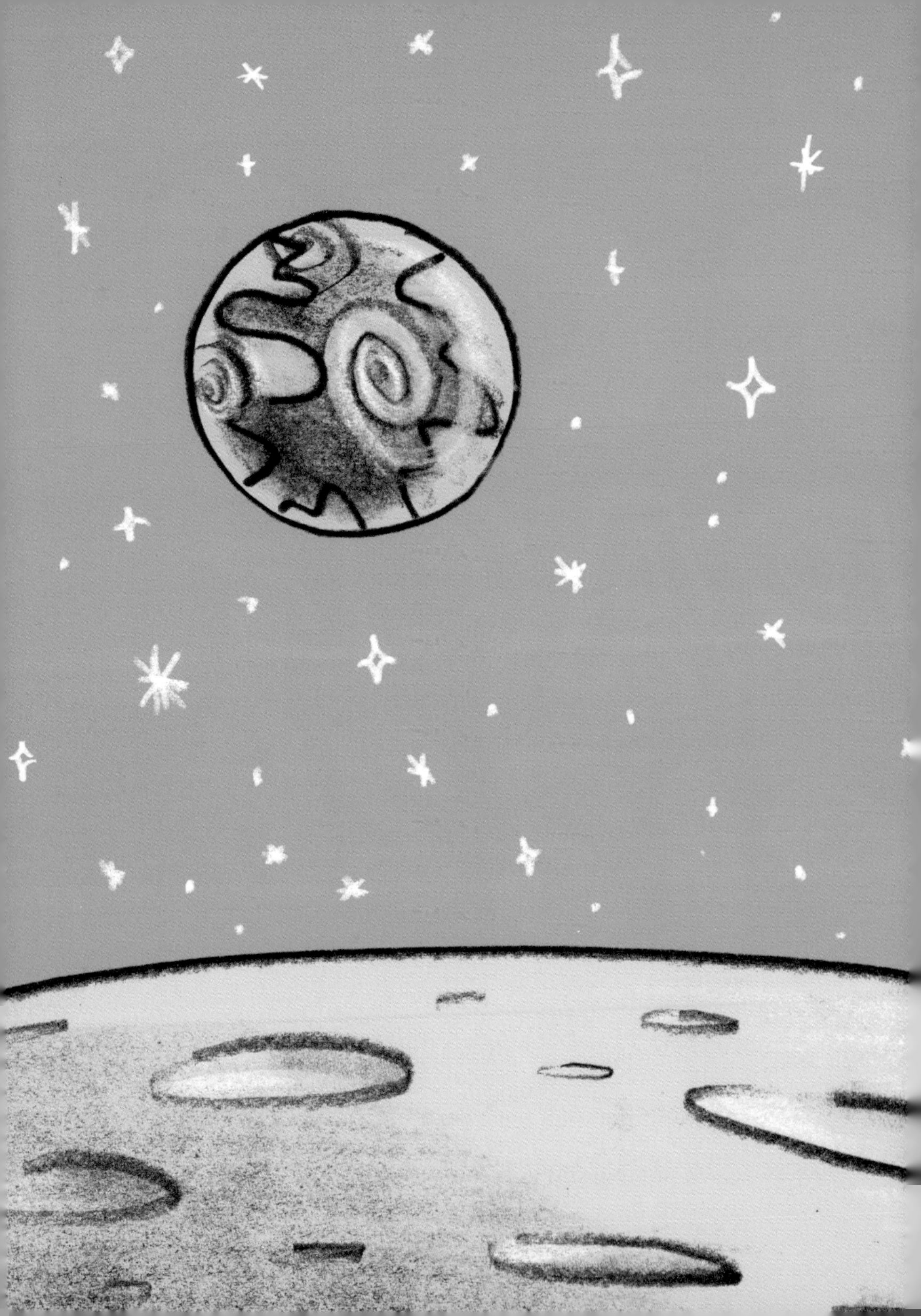

MAC BARNETT and SHAWN HARRIS

were both born in the summer of 1982 and grew up in Castro Valley, California. They were members of the youth soccer team the Thunderbolts. They graduated from Bishop O'Dowd High School in the year 2000, when they won the Senior Superlative "Best Friends." At the time they were miffed about this—they wanted different Senior Superlatives—but now they're glad. It's nice. They enjoy racquetball. Their favorite video game is *Mario Kart 64*. They live in the San Francisco Bay Area. Shawn and Mac are different in lots of ways too, but you'll have to read the bios in their other books to find out how.

The First Cat in Space Ate Pizza
is also available as an ebook.

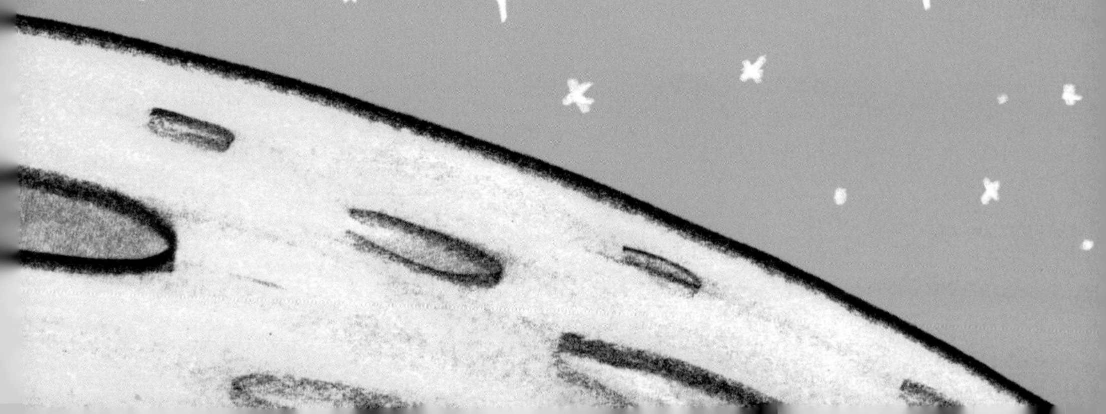

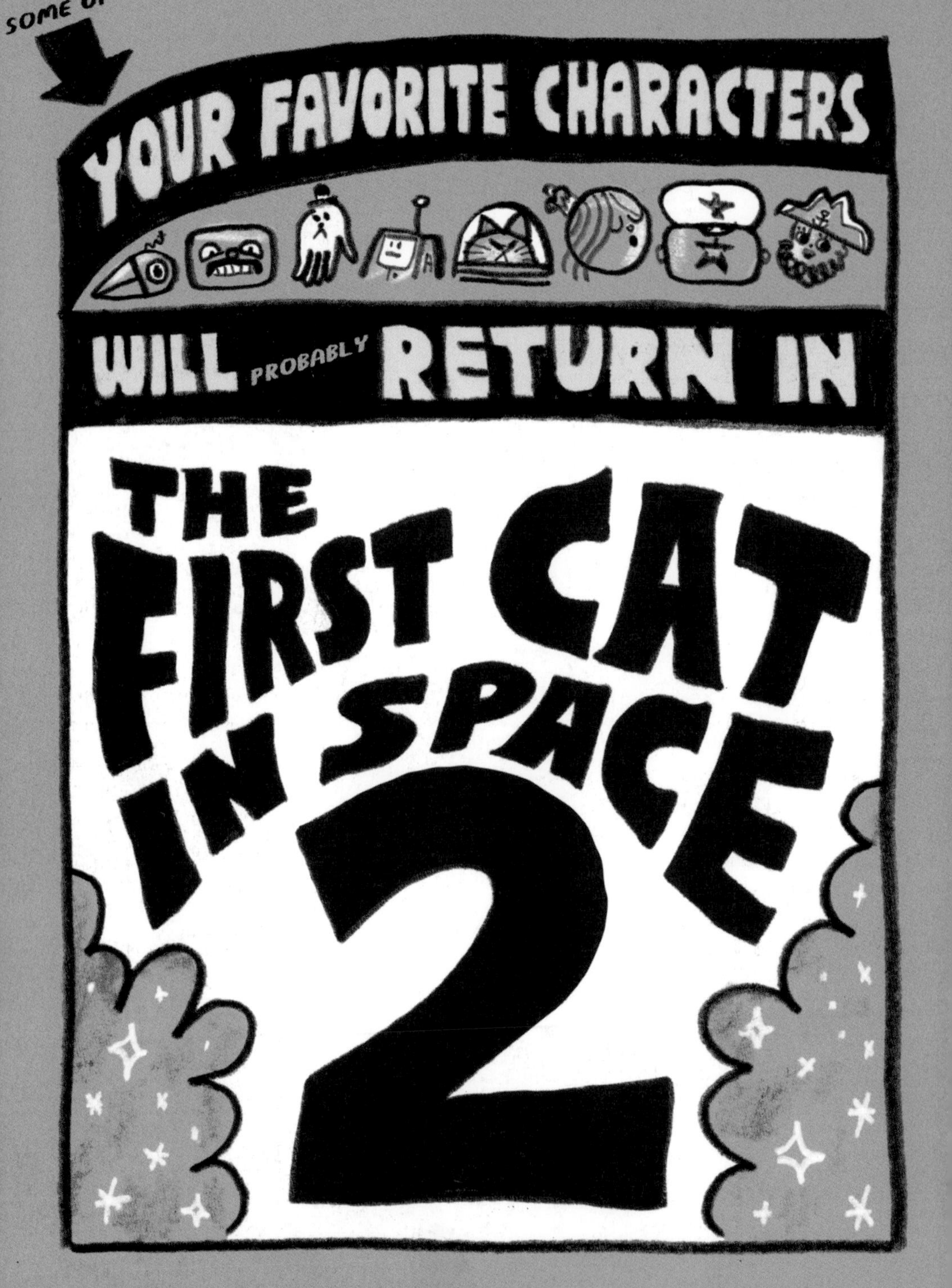
SOME OF
YOUR FAVORITE CHARACTERS
WILL PROBABLY RETURN IN
THE FIRST CAT IN SPACE 2

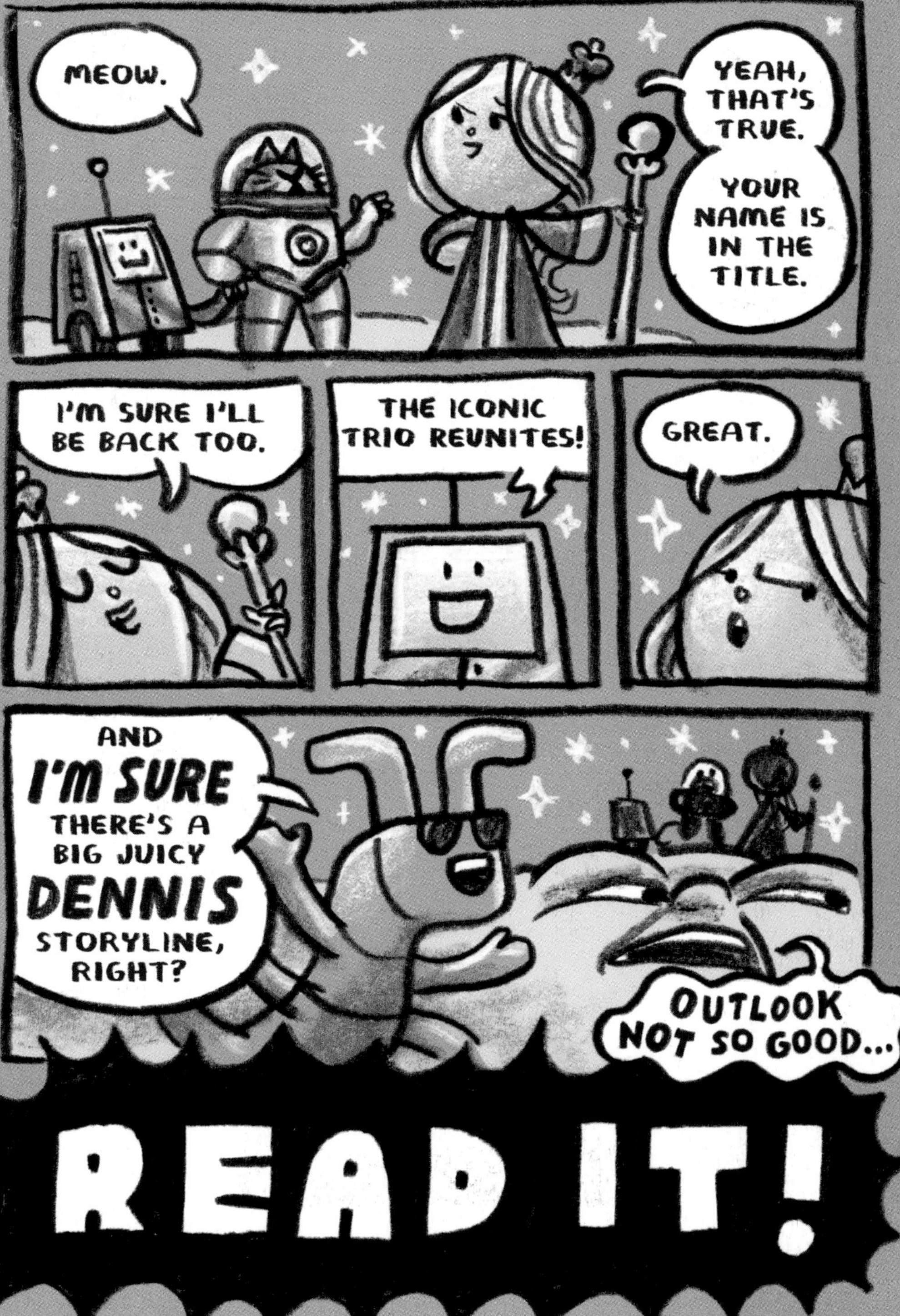
MEOW.
YEAH, THAT'S TRUE.
YOUR NAME IS IN THE TITLE.
I'M SURE I'LL BE BACK TOO.
THE ICONIC TRIO REUNITES!
GREAT.
AND I'M SURE THERE'S A BIG JUICY DENNIS STORYLINE, RIGHT?
OUTLOOK NOT SO GOOD...
READ IT!

3 1901 10014 1938